FLEET INQUISITOR

INQUISITOR

The Under Jurisdiction Series

BOOKS IN THIS SERIES

Fleet Inquisitor
Fleet Renegade (forthcoming)
Blood Enemies (forthcoming)

To purchase these and all other Baen Book titles in e-book format,
please go to www.baen.com.

FLEET INQUISITOR

The Under Jurisdiction Series

SUSAN R. MATTHEWS

FLEET INQUISITOR

This is a work of fiction. All the characters and events portrayed in this book are fictional, and any resemblance to real people or incidents is purely coincidental.

An Exchange of Hostages copyright © 1997 by Susan R. Matthews, Prisoner of Conscience copyright © 1997 by Susan R. Matthews, Angel of Destruction copyright © 2001 by Susan R. Matthews.

All rights reserved, including the right to reproduce this book or portions thereof in any form.

A Baen Books Original

Baen Publishing Enterprises
P.O. Box 1403
Riverdale, NY 10471
www.baen.com

ISBN: 978-1-4767-8194-5

Cover art by Kurt Miller

First Baen printing, October 2016

Distributed by Simon & Schuster
1230 Avenue of the Americas
New York, NY 10020

Library of Congress Cataloging-in-Publication Data: t/k

Printed in the United States of America

10 9 8 7 6 5 4 3 2 1

CONTENTS

INTRODUCTION

The Life and Hard Times of "Uncle" Andrej Koscuisko, who is Not a Nice Man

It didn't use to be a bad place to live, under Jurisdiction; the Bench coordinated trade between worlds, and Fleet enforced the regulations and collected taxes to cover the costs. Over time known Space expanded to embrace countless worlds under Jurisdiction, and the scope of the Bench's oversight expanded as well: to protect and defend civilian populations from outside threats and each other, to establish social norms, and—increasingly—to protect itself against challenges from its governed populations.

That's when things started to go wrong. In order to maintain its control the Bench felt forced to resort to increasingly harsh measures of control. It isn't working. Now terror is an instrument of State, institutionalized torture performed by trained medical professionals chartered to validate the authoritarian regime by extracting confessions that support the Bench's repressive measures.

These State-sanctioned torturers—doctors, one and all - are deployed throughout the Jurisdiction's Fleet in support of the rule of Law and the Judicial order. One such Ship's Inquisitor is my protagonist, Andrej Koscuisko. The first novel in this omnibus, *An Exchange of Hostages*, explains how a nice young man, a newly certified surgeon from a privileged background, discovers in himself a previously unsuspected aptitude—and appetite—for dominion that

1

will make him, over time, the most notorious pain-master in the Bench inventory.

He declines to surrender to his bestial appetites, even while his deeply engrained cultural values—and the Bench itself—hold him to the work. Over the next six novels he'll try, and try, and try again to find a way to affirm life—seek justice—and maintain his own sanity, even against all-but-insurmountable odds.

Some people will respect him for it: bond-involuntary Security slaves, criminals condemned to suffer the implantation of a "governor" in their brains to force them to compliance as aides and assistants to Inquisitors in the pursuit of their duty to the Bench. Others will seek to manipulate him, control him, or co-opt him to their own purposes—and, when it doesn't work, punish him for his intransigent non-compliance.

Still others will despise him for it—his rival Mergau Noycannir, determined to bring him to heel at Chilleau Judiciary, where she has the ear of the powerful First Secretary. And for others yet—Bench intelligence specialists, top-level agents with powers of extraordinary discretion, responsible only to the Bench itself—Andrej Koscuisko will be a wild card, a man with an awkward and unique ability to create chaos wherever he goes; either by doing his job his way, according to his rules, or by skating so close to outright mutiny that the line is almost impossible to detect.

In *An Exchange of Hostages*, the discovery of his hellish genius will lead Andrej to challenge the entire framework of his life, starting him on a path that will shake all of Jurisdiction before he's through with it. You'll meet two bond-involuntary Security slaves, Joslire Curran and Robert St. Clare, both destined to play major roles in the story as it develops. Unfortunately you'll meet Mergau Noycannir as well, whose malice and hatred will ultimately be responsible for some of the deepest horrors Andrej will ever experience.

Prisoner of Conscience takes place primarily in the Domitt Prison in Port Charid, destined to dominate Andrej Koscuisko's nightmares for the rest of his life. What Andrej finds—what Andrej lays bare—at the Domitt Prison will catalyze profound changes at the highest levels of the Jurisdiction's Bench; small comfort for Andrej, whose punishment for his acts will nearly destroy him.

In *Prisoner of Conscience* we'll meet two Bench intelligence specialists, Jils Ivers and Garol Vogel, who are destined to play major roles in the novels to come. Here they'll get their first taste of what kinds of trouble Andrej Koscuisko can make for the government, almost despite himself; and the repercussions of the decisions Andrej makes will link the three of them together forever after.

Lurking beneath the action of the novel the venomous echo of the terrorist Angel of Destruction can be vaguely discerned, but it's in the third novel in this volume that more of its history of ferocious atrocity is revealed. The Langsarik pirates Hilton Shires and Walton Agenis make their first appearance in *Angel of Destruction*, but the most significant partnership Garol Vogel forms is with the Malcontent Cousin Stanoczk, who will become such an important player in the story as it continues.

My debut novel was published nearly twenty years ago, but I've been pondering the central problem of the series for a lot longer than that. Over the years I've heard a lot of interesting theories about what kind of a person would come up with this story in the first place, let alone stick with it for so long—I'm sure you can imagine some of them (grin). In a sense it all goes back to the road to Damascus.

On the road to Damascus (the story goes) a man who had enthusiastically persecuted members of a religious splinter sect himself had a religious experience that convinced him utterly that what he was doing was wrong. He went forward from there to change his name, his life, and, in a sense at least, the world. And that's the first critical step in amending anybody's life, if they're doing wrong—to stop doing it.

But what if Saul's persecution of the Christians had been the most powerful emotional experience of his life, an experiential drug that was sex and power and mastery all wrapped up into a transcendently addicting passion? And what if he was forced to continue his persecution, and continued to experience both shattering pleasure and shame; and yet was determined on owning his sin, acknowledging it, standing on his own two feet?

I put Andrej Koscuisko between the grittiest rock and the hardest place I could imagine just to see what a man could do to maintain his sense of decency, his refusal to be a powerless pawn, his resistance to seeing himself as a victim under the worst possible circumstances I could imagine.

I set his story in a harsh political environment that reflected the world as I knew it growing up both "at home" and overseas, where even in the safety of a military post on U.S. soil the entire community practiced smuggling American soldiers out of imaginary countries with which we were at war; where we went on road trips on weekends because my mother was responsible for knowing the evacuation routes; where I overheard war stories that I was certainly never meant to.

What I like best about Andrej is his stubborn insistence on looking at himself in the mirror with an unblinking eye. "This is who and what I am," he says to me. "I will not deny it, least of all to myself. But I can fight to do as best I can, regardless."

These are the first three novels, each stand-alone, of the over-all story of The Life and Hard Times of "Uncle" Andrej Koscuisko, a narrative that has occupied me for most of my life. I hope you enjoy them.

AN
EXCHANGE OF
HOSTAGE

A Novel Under Jurisdiction

Under Jurisdiction torture isn't about truth. It's about terror.

The Jurisdiction's Bench has come to rely on the institutionalized atrocities of the Protocols to maintain its control of an increasingly unstable political environment. When Andrej Koscuisko, a talented young doctor, reports to orientation as a Ship's Inquisitor he will discover in himself something far worse than a talent for inflicting grotesque torments on the Bench's enemies. He will confront a passion for the exercise of the Writ to Inquire whose intensity threatens to consume him utterly.

As he struggles to find some thread of justice and compassion under the Law, as he fights to hang on to what remains to him of his sanity, he will make powerful enemies who are eager to use his knowledge, his empathy, his passion against anyone who challenges the Bench.

Dedication

An Exchange of Hostages is dedicated with profound appreciation to eluki bes shahar for making it happen. Her passionate championship of my book opened the door for me to what every writer dreams of finding someday—an audience.

Acknowledgments

During the years I've spent working on this story there were some people who just never stopped nagging me, making it their business to see that I didn't give up. There's no better time nor place than this to gratefully acknowledge the love and support of Regina Gottesman, Linda Deneroff, Sheila Willis, Security 0.5, Steve Gallacci (who coined the term "bond-involuntary"), and many others besides. This book is a product of their persistence and of the patience and forbearance of Maggie Nowakowska, who's had more to put up with than anyone else.

CHAPTER ONE

Andrej Koscuisko stood at the view-port watching with dread as the ship neared the Station. There was a signal at the talk-alert; sighing, he keyed it.

"Yes, Danitosh."

The Station came closer moment by moment, a bleak lifeless piece of galactic debris with a self-contained school for potential Ship's Surgeons sprawled over its surface. He didn't like it; but there was no sense in making things harder on the crew of this ship than they already were. It was simply their bad luck that the *Pride of Place* had been going in the same direction as the disgraced son of the head of the Koscuisko familial corporation, just at the time the ship had been ready to leave.

"Cleared through to offload, your Excellency. You're to be met. A Tutor named Chonis expects to be greeting you."

"Yes, very good," Andrej murmured halfheartedly. He was late arriving. He hadn't wanted to come. He was more frightened of what awaited him than he thought he'd ever been in his life. He couldn't take his eyes off the view-port, consumed with apprehension as the ship neared for landing.

Ugly piece of rock.

Ugly Station.

Grim cold utilitarian dock-port, the ship's tugs at least eight years old, and all alike. Fleet resources. Fleet Orientation Station Medical, where potential Ship's Surgeons all had to come to learn how to Inquire.

If he'd guessed beforehand what his father would wish, would he have completed his medical training?

He was here now, and there was no help for it. He would do what was needful. His father had said the word. That was all.

Gathering up his documents-case, Andrej quickly leafed through flimsies one final time. How to salute. How to speak to a Tutor. How to conduct oneself as a Student, soon to become a Chief Medical Officer. CMO was all very well, a position of significant influence and power on a cruiser-killer-class warship upholding the Judicial order in the space-lanes. Any young surgeon would jump at the opportunity.

It was only that he did not want to Inquire.

The wait-room on the loading docks was small, almost cramped, even with only two people sharing it; and one was Security. Curran hardly counted. There was the smell of too much waste fuel in the air, and more noise than could be comfortably borne for very long without ear-stops for protection. Tutor Chonis suppressed an impatient twitch of annoyance as he stood waiting for his Student to arrive. Just enough time for a final scan through the scroller, and he would be ready for the interview.

ANDREJ ULEXEIEVITCH KOSCUISKO, STANDARD SCAN ANDREW SON OF ILEX. PRONOUNCED *AHN*-DRAY YOU*LECHS*'VICH KOE-*SHOO*-SKOE. OLDEST SON OF RANKING KOSCUISKO PRINCE ALEXIE ILMYANITCH AND PRINCE INHERITOR TO KOSCUISKO FAMILIAL CORPORATION, DOLGORUKIJ COMBINE. EIGHT YEAR COURSE OF STUDY, MAYON SURGICAL COLLEGE, MAYON MEDICAL CENTER, MAYON, GRADUATION WITH HIGHEST HONORS IN SURGERY AND HONORS IN PSYCHO-PHARMACOLOGY. NO FAMILY MEMBERS ACTIVE IN FLEET. HOMEWORLD OF ORIGIN AZANRY, DOLGORUKIJ COMBINE, SANT-DASIDAR JUDICIARY.

Andrej Koscuisko.

Tutor Chonis shut his scroller down and marshaled his thoughts together. First contact, Student and Tutor. This could make or break the entire Term. It was important to get off on a good cycle. There was to be enough stress on Student Koscuisko as the Term progressed without the existence of conflict between him and his Tutor.

"Let's go, then," Chonis said. The telltales on the wall gave notice that the incoming craft had come to rest and was ready to offload. Curran keyed the exit, standing to one side for the Tutor to precede him out onto the apron of the loading dock.

Out on the apron, a maintenance team had taken custody of Koscuisko's personal effects; and there was the Student, standing alone, staring off toward the open end of the maintenance atmosphere.

"Attention to the Tutor," Curran called from behind him, to put Student Koscuisko on notice. Koscuisko looked over his shoulder at that; turning around, he started toward them, not quite hurrying but quickly enough. Once he was within a reasonable distance he stopped, saluting politely. "Student Koscuisko reports at the Fleet's invitation. Tutor Chonis?"

Student Koscuisko was blond and pale, and looked a little on the slightly built side of the Jurisdiction Standard; but Tutor Chonis wasn't taken in. Koscuisko was Dolgorukij. And Dolgorukij packed muscle. It was just that the way they packed muscle wasn't obvious to look at them.

"Good-greeting, Student Koscuisko. I trust you had good transit?"

There was the suspicion of a frown on Koscuisko's face at that, quickly smoothed over. "Thank you, Tutor Chonis." Tenor voice, and pale eyes. Polite enough, though, as was usually the case with aristocrats. "It was a quiet transit."

Koscuisko knew very well he was late. Koscuisko offered no excuses. On the other hand Chonis hadn't asked for any. "Student Koscuisko, as your briefing states, you are to be under my tutelage. You have only a few months in which to learn all that Fleet will require of you; no time like the present for us to begin. Joslire Curran. Present yourself."

Curran stepped forward from where he had posted himself two paces behind Tutor Chonis, to his left. "At the Tutor's direction." Curran was a little taller than Koscuisko, but not by much; and his face had more contour. Curran was as dark as Koscuisko was fair, even after his years here on Station away from solar browning. Right now Curran was as tense as Tutor Chonis had ever seen him—though Koscuisko might not realize that. Koscuisko was unlikely to have met Emandisan before. Emandisan off-world were almost always Security; and as far as Tutor Chonis knew, Joslire Curran was the only bond-involuntary Emandisan in the Inventory.

"Curran, Student Koscuisko is your officer of assignment for this Term. Student Koscuisko. I'm sure you've noticed that Curran is bond-involuntary." Watching Koscuisko's face, Tutor Chonis caught Koscuisko's quick glance at the telltale green piping on Curran's sleeves. "Curran is tasked by the Administration with seeing to your meals, your exercise, and whatever administrative matters may arise."

Koscuisko regarded Curran with a look of frank and good-natured curiosity, which Tutor Chonis found rather engaging. He hoped that Student Koscuisko and Joslire Curran would sort well with each other. The man deserved a break; last Term had been unusually rough on him. But they couldn't afford to sideline one of their best while Orientation was in session. There weren't enough bond-involuntaries assigned for that.

"The Administration anticipates that you may not have worked with bond-involuntaries before. It's important that you take this opportunity to explore their resources and their limitations."

It would be very unusual if Koscuisko had even met a bond-involuntary, outside of Fleet. There weren't that many of them to start out with.

"Curran will provide you every assistance; you should not hesitate to make any of your needs or desires known to him, howsoever personal. When you are posted to your Command, you can safely anticipate at least one Security team of bond-involuntaries will be assigned to you." In Fleet, bond-involuntaries could be assigned only to Chief Medical Officers, in fact, and to no other officer on staff.

And that about covered things for their first briefing. Nodding at Curran, Tutor Chonis gave Student Koscuisko his dismissal. "I will see you this evening in Tutor's Mess, where I will introduce you to your fellow Student. Tutor's Mess at sixteen, and be prepared to discuss your background and your interest in the field of Judicial administration. That will be all for now. Curran, you may take your Student to quarters."

Koscuisko saluted with easy grace; Curran gestured politely toward the lift-access corridor. "If Student Koscuisko would care to proceed?"

Tutor Chonis watched as they left, Curran giving directions as they went.

He hadn't known quite what to expect from Student Koscuisko.

He wasn't sure he knew any more about him now than he had before this interview.

It didn't matter.

There was no predicting how Students responded to the pressures the practical exercises put on them.

There were five levels between the loading docks and the administrative area where Koscuisko had quarters. Student Koscuisko hadn't spoken to him; nervous, perhaps. That was almost funny. Ship's Surgeons exercised absolute power over the bodies and lives of bond-involuntaries; why should Koscuisko be nervous?

Most of the Students Joslire had seen hadn't wanted to be here, though they'd volunteered. That was none of his business. When the lift-car arrived Joslire keyed the offload; as the doors slid away, Koscuisko straightened up a bit, alerted perhaps by the noise or the change in air pressure. Turning, Koscuisko caught Joslire's eye; and Joslire gazed hungrily at his new officer, anxious for something that might give him a clue as to what kind of Term this one was going to be.

Staring too long could be interpreted as insolence, and his governor would not tolerate insolence. Joslire broke eye contact, bowing hastily.

"Show me to my quarters, if you please, Curran," the officer said, moving past Joslire to gain the corridor outside. Pleasant and formal, and neither promise nor threat to be read in the Student's voice. Yet. Joslire hurried out of the car before the doors closed on him, hastening to his duty with resignation.

"To the officer's right." The senior member on a standard four-soul Security team led by direction, not example. One of the things that the officer was expected to learn was how to figure out where he was going by listening to the voice of a Security post behind him. "It will be to the officer's left at the next nexus, eight doors down."

Eight doors down the hall after the left turning. Joslire could almost hear the officer counting to himself. There was little to distinguish one door from another; so when the officer paused, Joslire confirmed the guess indirectly, disguising his reassurance as an explanation.

"The admit panel is to the officer's right. In the recess." Not where the officer was accustomed to finding it, so much was obvious. The Dolgorukij Combine Koscuisko came from was a parochial system, very rich, very insular, rather primitive in many ways by the Jurisdiction Standard. For all Joslire knew, Koscuisko was accustomed to finding rooms behind tall wooden doors, pivoting inward on old-fashioned hinges.

After a moment's fumbling at the doorjamb, the officer found the admit, and the door opened. The interior was familiar to Joslire in its functional severity: Fleet issue sleep-racks, Fleet issue floor-covering, Fleet-issue study-set, and an open closet full of Fleet-issue uniforms. Joslire already knew that there was an unpleasant surprise in quarters for the officer. He wondered how Koscuisko was going to react to it.

After a moment Koscuisko stepped across the threshold; Joslire followed on Koscuisko's heels, closing the door behind him. Posting himself near the door, Joslire watched as Koscuisko took inventory: the washroom at the left beside the closet, with the toilet's gray metal privacy barrier clearly visible through the open door and the wet-shower beyond; the sleep-rack to the right and the study-set in the middle of the room; the inner room beyond, half-visible past the partially closed slider. Koscuisko—his back stiff and his shoulders tense with understandable confusion—moved around the study-set and stood in the doorway to the inner chamber with his back still to Joslire, puzzling out the problem, looking for his luggage. It didn't matter that Joslire had only the back of the officer's head to judge his reactions by. Bond-involuntaries learned very quickly to read an officer's moods from the other side of his face.

The officer spoke, finally. "I had brought some personal effects with me," Koscuisko said mildly. "I do not see any of my house-master's packing here."

Nor would he. "As the officer states." Technically speaking Koscuisko was not an officer yet, but Joslire's governor would not fault him for using the formal title. It was safer to use the formal title, for the same reason that it was safer to keep to indirect address and avoid the first person whenever possible. "The officer's personal effects are to be forwarded directly to *Scylla*. To provide an agreeable sense of homecoming when the officer reports to his Command."

"Who—" There was predictable outrage in Koscuisko's voice, as well as a degree of frustration—which Joslire could certainly understand, and sympathize with. A note of savage humor there as well.

Humor?

It was a moment before Koscuisko seemed to master his reactions and trust himself to speak, after having bitten off his first response so sharply that the word hadn't so much as bled before it died. "Who sleeps on which of these boards?"

The boards . . . oh, the sleep-racks. Joslire stepped carefully into the middle of the room to post himself by the study-set. "The officer sleeps in the inner room, behind the slider-screen, which has been provided for his privacy. Assigned Security sleeps here, in order to be available to the officer at will."

"You and the mashounds," Koscuisko said, as if to himself.

Joslire didn't bother to mention that the privacy partition could not be secured from the inside. The officer would figure that out soon enough. And would doubtless realize that assigned Security slept between the officer and the door as much to prevent the officer from going out unaccompanied as to be available when wanted. "I do not suggest an equivalence, of course. How am I to call you, then?"

It was nice to be apologized to, howsoever obliquely; but the officer would learn better soon enough. "It is a matter up to the officer's discretion." Koscuisko would learn that, too. Here at Fleet Orientation Station Medical there were few conventions to define what an officer could do with assigned Security, as long as the forms of transgression and discipline were preserved. Fortunately Administrative staff was careful about things accordingly; it all balanced out in the end, more or less.

"As it pleases the officer to inquire, 'Joslire' would be preferable to 'Curran.'" Many of his fellows welcomed the psychic camouflage of the name the Fleet had given them; Joslire didn't. To be called Curran was a constant reminder of the place where Joslire ise'Ilet had died—or at least been shut away in legal suspension of animation for thirty years. Where the man that he had been had been enslaved for crimes against the Judicial order, and his honor and his five-knives with him.

"Very well, it shall be Joslire, then. Are you required to confiscate my clothing, as well as my travel-trunks?"

"And the officer's documents-case as well. An exception is to be made for one item of a religious nature." He was a little surprised at Koscuisko's obvious grasp of what was going on. There was no particular reason to be surprised; surely it was clear enough from the standpoint of basic psychology—the removal of anything that might be comforting in its familiarity, in order to render confused and disoriented Students the more receptive to the new rules and expectations of a whole new reality. Except that none of his other Students had grasped that meaning quite so quickly, if they ever had.

"What if the officer is irreligious? One item of a profane nature? Never mind it, Joslire, what am I supposed to wear to Tutor's Mess?"

On familiar ground with this, Joslire moved with confident assurance to the closet to cull the appropriate selections from the rack. "This is the officer's informal mess dress. It has been prepared from the information in the officer's medical profile, so the measurements may not be precise. There is time to arrange for alterations before the meal, but not very much time, and therefore the officer is respectfully requested to test these garments for size as soon as possible."

Koscuisko was a little different from the Students he'd seen through Orientation previously, perhaps.

But he could hardly be that different.

Which meant that the biggest problem facing Joslire in the immediate future—how to suggest that Koscuisko trim back the fine blond fringe of hair across his forehead to conform to the Jurisdiction Standard—didn't particularly worry Joslire now.

Anyone who could grasp the trick with his personal effects as quickly as Koscuisko had could surely be relied upon to submit himself sensibly to other Fleet requirements.

Mergau Noycannir was prompt in her appointment for dinner with Tutor Chonis, as she made a point to be in all her dealings with superiors. She'd been ready for an eighth, her glossy black hair neatly tied up, her uniform crisp and precise on her tall spare frame. She'd reviewed the schedule and tomorrow's ceremony several times, rehearsing the steps in quarters with her bond-involuntary's assistance until she was certain she knew exactly what was required. She wasn't particularly hungry, and she disliked wasting time over food; still, every opportunity to spend time with the Tutors was a valuable one, well worth the investment. The more she could learn about Tutor Chonis the better she would be prepared to manage him. And she would manage him, too, because she had no intention of going back to Chilleau Judiciary without her Writ, regardless of what it might take to obtain one.

Her Patron at least recognized superior ability when he saw it; Verlaine knew what was in his own best interest. For that, Mergau was exactly as grateful as she ought to be. Once she brought the Writ to Inquire back to Chilleau Judiciary, she could reasonably expect due compensation in consideration of the valuable resource she'd obtained. If it failed to come, she'd be prepared to ensure that a satisfactory adjustment was made.

She was always prepared.

She'd had her bond-involuntary escort her here to Tutor's Mess in good time. It wouldn't do to come too soon and be seen standing idly in the reception area, waiting for the Tutor to arrive; that would give the appearance of anxiety or that she was conscious of being in a subordinate position. She'd sent Hanbor back to quarters and then left Tutor's Mess, going down the corridor a few eighths around the nearest corner to wait.

Now she tapped her earlobe thoughtfully, checking the time. *Fifteen,* the little chrono whispered, its timer connected to a neuro-thread that lay beneath the surface of her inner ear. *Fifteen and seven eighths.* It was time to go. Arrival prior to seven-eighths would have been early. Arrival much past seven-eighths would be almost late.

She tugged at the unfamiliar uniform blouse to straighten the front creases, and made for the door.

The entry to Tutor's Mess was open four times a day, during each of the meal-breaks. Another Student was waiting in the small reception area just inside the door—a Student as tall as Tutor Chonis, with light-colored hair that wasn't groomed to the Standard for uniformed personnel. The Student acknowledged her arrival with a nod that deepened into a polite salute. Mergau didn't know enough about him to feel she could select the best response, so she merely returned the offered courtesy in precise measure, dismissing him from her mind. She couldn't afford to waste any energy on people who would have nothing to do with her. Peers and subordinates could be used to support her, but Tutors could place obstacles in her way: she only needed to pay attention to the Tutors. She tapped her ear again: *fifteen and sixty-two.* Just two until sixteen. Surely Tutor Chonis would come soon.

Tutor Chonis was coming through the open door into Tutor's Mess even now. Mergau turned her back to the other Student to greet the Tutor with the requisite salute, smiling in her most ingratiating manner. Chonis answered her salute with a pleased smile of his own; but, then, he seemed to be distracted by something that was behind her.

This was confusing.

Moving forward to take her place at her Tutor's side, Mergau realized that what had captured Chonis's attention was the other Student.

"Good, I'm glad to see you both in good time. Shall we go in?"

A modest smile and a diffident bow would be the most suitable response, Mergau decided. But the other Student was already bowing with a sycophantic grin on his face, so Mergau made sure to keep her expression utterly solemn.

She'd overheard Tutor Chonis complaining about a Student just yesterday as she waited outside his office. This was Student Koscuisko, then, the man who had so little respect for the Administration and his fellow Students that he had come at the last possible moment?

She would take precedence without hesitation. She had demonstrated her commitment to the program and the Administration by arriving in plenty of time to get settled in and complete in-processing. It was too bad she hadn't known who he was earlier, though. She could have used the few moments of wait-time to draw him out a bit, probing to discover his strengths and weaknesses.

Tutor Chonis had gone through to the mess without waiting for further response. Mergau hastened to take first place in following the Tutor, but the other Student made way for her quite naturally and carelessly, giving no sign of meaning to contest with her for precedence—as if he felt the issue was not important, which indicated that he did not take her as seriously as he should.

Tutor Chonis was waiting for them at a table set just short of the administrative equivalent of the Captain's Bar, the railing that divided the room and marked off the raised area at the back as privileged space for senior officers. She and her fellow Student would be sharing the bench, of necessity; protocol prohibited junior officers from turning their backs on Command Branch.

Mergau paused in the middle of the room, gazing at the Bar. Once she'd taken up her Writ, she would be entitled to turn her back to the Bar with impunity, as long as the Captain wasn't present. Ship's Inquisitor, Chief Medical Officer, Ship's Surgeon was subordinate only to the senior officer in the Command, and since it was the Writ that defined the Chief Medical Officer, she would be one of Ship's Primes.

Tutor Chonis knew well enough that Mergau would never be assigned to a cruiser-killer, since she could not serve as a medical officer of any sort. That had been part of the agreement that Secretary Verlaine had made with Fleet when she'd come here. Fleet's requirement that its Inquisitors be Bench-certified medical practitioners was appropriate for on-Line warships but hardly applicable to a Bench setting. Secretary Verlaine didn't need a Ship's Surgeon; Chilleau Judiciary already had Medical support. All he wanted was an Inquisitor on staff, a Writ on site at Chilleau Judiciary. A Writ that he could direct as he saw fit—without having to negotiate for a loaned Inquisitor from Fleet resources to support what was, after all, a Judicial function.

They were waiting for her, her fellow Student standing politely until she took her seat. Suddenly she was annoyed at him for making her feel awkward, even clumsy, twice already in so little time. Being here was just another step in a well-mapped career for him, and from what she'd gathered about Student Koscuisko, it wouldn't destroy his life if he failed—he was a rich man, playing at doctor, playing at Inquisitor. But she represented First Secretary Verlaine and Chilleau Judiciary, Second Judge Sem Porr Har, Presiding.

The honor of her Patron depended upon her ability to survive the tests that Fleet would put her to.

". . . Senior Security, in other words the Warrant Officers—" Tutor Chonis was saying, obviously responding to a question from Koscuisko—"the Engineer's Mates, and your own shift supervisors. You'll take your meals above the Bar, of course."

He continued to talk to Koscuisko as Mergau slid into place along the bench, Koscuisko waiting until she was settled to sit down beside her. "Then there are typically four, sometimes as many as six Fleet Lieutenants, usually one to a shift. Sometimes the noise . . . but I'm getting too technical. We'll be covering this all in session, in detail." An orderly had approached their table and was waiting for instruction. "Meal three, please. And for my Students, of course."

"You seemed to be reminiscing, just now," Student Koscuisko said as the orderly went off again. "May I ask if you were posted to such a vessel yourself?"

Student Koscuisko wasn't supposed to be controlling the conversation. She was supposed to control the conversation. And if she didn't eat her meal, the Tutor would have to ask whether something was wrong with it. She'd be able to make a point about the fact that he should have consulted her preferences beforehand, rather than being distracted by Koscuisko's obvious toadying.

Tutor Chonis seemed in an expansive mood, answering Koscuisko readily—almost eagerly. "The last was the *Oxparen,* of honored memory." He slapped the table lightly with the fingers of his left hand twice in a gesture of apparent respect that Mergau had seen him use before. "Destroyed during the reduction of Karset, but that was after my time. I was called in to help activate this facility before all of that was well begun."

Koscuisko had chosen the correct approach. She had to give him points for that; maybe Koscuisko was going to take managing. Chonis clearly seemed to be enjoying himself, rather than merely tolerating the conversation. "In my father's time," Koscuisko said, "such activity— as this facility represents, I mean to say—was considered to be a Security function." Koscuisko was working it entirely too well; she could not find her way into the conversation. He must have planned it that way. People with rank and education never spoke without such hidden purposes. He would know that no Clerk of Court had ever taken a Writ to Inquire.

Until now.

"Your father's time? I suppose that's about right." Chonis was mulling Koscuisko's statement over, obviously distracted from Mergau's very existence. "Hasn't been a Security function for, oh, fifty years. Fleet Medical only gained control of the office rather recently, compared to the history of the Fleet . . . Where was your father posted?"

"A Security assignment, the *Autocrat's Niece,* on the Desular Line. A lieutenant. When Fleet forwarded its invitation that I serve as Ship's

Surgeon—" There was an abrupt break in his response, and Koscuisko looked down at the table, very briefly. "But I am being inexcusably rude. It is a family matter, of no consequence. Please accept my apologies."

On the other hand, it might prove good policy to let Koscuisko talk. He seemed to have run into quite a sensitive subject all unawares, to judge by his abrupt silence. And Tutor Chonis also apparently shared the interest that she found in whatever could seem so delicate to Koscuisko.

"I understand it is traditional in your culture for the eldest son of a great family to go into the Fleet." Chonis's remark gave notice that the subject would not be permitted to drop quite so easily. Koscuisko seemed to swallow a sigh of resignation, and his pale profile looked a bit more melancholy than it had before.

"As you say, Tutor Chonis. Once the inheriting son went to do service to the Autocrat's Household as an officer in Service. But now in some of our old families, an oldest daughter has also come to inherit, though it is not yet so in my father's House."

What was the point of all this? Was Koscuisko saying he had an older sister? How could Koscuisko possibly expect anyone to care? Why didn't Koscuisko answer the question as bidden, and be still?

"The Home Defense Fleet has no tradition to include a woman warrior, and therefore it becomes the Jurisdiction Fleet that we serve in the Autocrat's name. There is also a matter of prestige to consider, because there are no cruiser-killer-grade ships of *Scylla*'s rating in the Home Defense Fleet. My family is old, and my father is proud to send his son to Jurisdiction Fleet rather than to a post of lesser rank."

A mild and impersonal response on the face of it. Koscuisko's points about the differences between them—he was going to Fleet as Ship's Surgeon—didn't escape her notice. One way or another, however, it gave Mergau the opening she'd been waiting for to expose the irrelevance of Koscuisko's remarks.

"It is very interesting. And this activity, it accomplishes?"

Koscuisko turned his head to look at her as if he were a little startled to hear the sound of her voice. His mild frown might seem to be simple concentration, but he didn't fool her. He didn't mean to yield the ground to her. "Two things, Student . . . Noycannir? Thank you, Tutor Chonis, Student Noycannir. One, it gives one something constructive to do while one is waiting for one's father to arrive at the year of his Retirement. And also—two—it gives one's younger brothers, of which I have four, reason to live with good hope for their futures."

Chonis snorted in amusement. Mergau hadn't heard any joke. Their meals were arriving; she could channel the fury choking in her throat into politely muted but clearly visible distaste for her food. Now she wasn't sure she could afford that bit of business, though. Koscuisko had her at a disadvantage.

"You've reminded me, young man. I've been remiss. Mergau, your companion is Andrej Koscuisko; Andrej, you have the pleasure of Mergau Noycannir's acquaintance. You are expected to use the formal title of Student with each other during class hours, in token of respect for each other's . . . rank."

She understood Chonis's momentary hesitation. Other Students would respect each other's status, each other's ability, each other's shared education and background. Chonis had been told to give her every assistance, and to make sure that she got the same training and practice that any other Student might have. Tutor Chonis was not going to let anyone forget that she was just a Clerk of Court, without Bench certifications.

"But we're not quite into Term yet, and officially this is an informal meeting. How are you liking the fish?"

Be smooth, she told herself. *Feel the pavement.* It could hardly be a conspiracy. Koscuisko had no reason to go out of his way to make her feel small. Tutor Chonis's comments were innocent, if ill-advised. Keeping her focus on the goal was one thing. Going out of her way to look for opposition was a waste of energy. Revealing that she even noticed petty slights or attempts to put her down would only work against her.

She could deal with Tutor Chonis later.

She had to obtain the Writ first.

Dinner was over, finally. Joslire stood waiting for him outside Tutor's Mess, along with another bond-involuntary who would logically be the one assigned to Noycannir. He wasn't sure what to make of Noycannir. She was attractive enough in a somewhat severe fashion, and she had certainly exercised herself to be pleasing to Tutor Chonis; but something gave him the idea she didn't like him.

Andrej wasn't sure he cared one way or the other.

His feet hurt, but luckily for him they didn't have too far to go to gain sanctuary.

Safely back in quarters, Andrej sank down into the chair at the study-set and stretched his legs out toward the middle of the room, beckoning Joslire with a wave of his hand. "Give us a hand with these boots, if you would, please. My bootjack was one of those items that you have so kindly forwarded to *Scylla* for me, to await my homecoming."

Though he couldn't be sure—having just met Joslire, and unacquainted with his expressions—Andrej thought Joslire was smiling to himself as he turned his back and straddled one leg to get the proper angle on the boot.

"The officer's footgear will be broken in within a day or two. Generally speaking, the process is completed during pre-Term Orientation."

The comment and its delivery were both aggressively neutral, even passive. But Andrej's feet hurt. He knew very well what Joslire was really saying; if he'd reported in good time his boots would have been broken in by now. The fact that Joslire was absolutely right was only annoying. He was in no mood to be nagged by anyone.

"What, are you being impertinent with me, you ruffian?" he demanded in a tone of outraged disbelief.

Joslire flinched fractionally before straightening up with Andrej's boots in hand, directing a swift sidelong glance of wary evaluation at Andrej's face.

Andrej knew almost as soon as he'd said it that he'd made a mistake. He expected to be lectured by his body-servants; and cursing at them extravagantly in affectionate response was the only protest he was allowed, whether the criticism was deserved or not.

But Joslire Curran was a bond-involuntary, not a servant in Andrej's House. He had no reason to expect this stranger to understand. How could he tell whether Joslire interpreted his joking rebuke as a serious one? And if Joslire believed he had offended an officer, Joslire's governor—responding to the specific physiological stresses created by such an apprehension—would apply corrective discipline, no matter how undeserved.

Andrej tried to clarify. "That is to say, you're right, I am quite convinced. Your point is well taken."

This was intolerable.

But souls in Joslire's category of servitude were allowed an uncharitably narrow margin for joking. There was no indication on record that primitive behavioral modifiers like the governor were capable of developing a sense of humor.

Joslire merely bowed politely and took the boots over to the sleep-rack in the corner to touch up the polish for tomorrow's events. Arms cocked up across the arm supports, stockinged feet stretched out in front of him, Andrej glared at his tender feet with a sour mind.

Unnatural, that was what it was.

The sacred bond between master and man consisted of respect and reliance, exchanged for self-subordination; to demand Joslire's obedience without granting him privilege to speak his mind was a perversion. Was Jurisdiction. And that was what this Station was all about, wasn't it? Jurisdiction perversion?

When his father had been an officer in Security, the Bench had been less strict, and interrogation less formal. The Judicial process as his father had known it had indeed involved beatings, intimidation, even torture; ugly, sordid, but human in its scale.

Now it was different.

Now interrogation had become Inquiry, formalized into Protocols and divided into Levels. Now it required a medical officer to implement the Question, because it was too easy to kill a man too soon unless a torturer knew what to do. What had started as back-alley beatings in search of required information had evolved into systematic brutalization, forcing confessions to predetermined crimes, and all "in support of the Judicial order."

It wasn't as though torment and brutality were unheard of in Andrej's home system. Far from it. Andrej himself was Aznir Dolgorukij; any Sarvaw had stories to tell of what Dolgorukij were capable of doing when they felt that it served their best interest. It was only that the Bench increased the level of atrocity year by year, as unrest within subject worlds continued to seethe and writhe and challenge the Judicial order. The public's desire to see crimes punished in proportion to their severity could serve as a rationalization for atrocity; but only as long as such measures worked as deterrent.

And there was no way the Protocols could be described as punishment in proportion to the crime's severity.

Andrej straightened up in his chair, weary with the familiar futility of it all. It did no good to worry that old dry bone. The Station was on Standard time, and Tutor Chonis had told them that they were to be on first-shift for the duration of the Term; so it was coming up on sleep-shift, which meant it was time to go to bed.

Student Koscuisko sighed and stood up. Joslire waited patiently to be noticed. It wouldn't matter if he spoke first, not so early in Term; Koscuisko wouldn't know it was a violation—but the governor would. It was best not to risk it.

"I'm sorry, Joslire," Koscuisko said. "I am brooding. There is something?"

"As it please the officer." Koscuisko's dialect seemed to include more apology than Joslire was accustomed to hearing; this was the third time, surely. It meant nothing. "The officer may wish to review the material pertaining to the Administrator's briefing?"

The information was on-screen on the study-set; Koscuisko hadn't noticed, sunk deep in thought. Now the Student leaned over the desktop, scrolling through the data, a mild frown of concentration on his broad flat face. "Presentation of the Bond, yes, Joslire. I rehearsed it in the mirror, in fact. On my way here."

Just as well. The public presentation was humiliating enough in its own right. When the Students hadn't bothered to learn their lines, Joslire felt the depth of his degradation more keenly than ever.

Student Koscuisko tagged the view off and met his eyes squarely. "There was a note in the briefing, Joslire; the option to receive the Bond now or tomorrow. Which do you prefer?"

Confused for a moment, Joslire recovered as quickly as he could. It was true. He was only required to surrender his Bond in good form. He didn't have to do it tomorrow. If Student Koscuisko would receive his Bond here in private, they'd still stand at briefing, but he'd not be forced to repeat the bitter lie of his condemnation in public this time.

"With respect. It is the officer's preference that prevails. As the Student please." He had to say it; it was his duty to try to teach Koscuisko how to use him.

"Thank you, Joslire, but I desire to consult your preference. I solicit your preference. I ask you to tell me which you would rather."

It wouldn't last.

It never did.

Koscuisko would learn soon enough to treat him as an object for use, and not as a person. But as long as Koscuisko had made the demand, he was clear to reveal it; he only hoped that his voice was professionally neutral, as it should be, and not dripping over with gratitude. It was a small thing to be asked for his preference. It was a great thing to a bond-involuntary to be asked anything, rather than told.

Koscuisko was an aristocrat; for Koscuisko asking and demanding were probably the same things. He would concentrate on that. "As it please the officer. To be permitted to present the Bond would be a privilege."

Koscuisko nodded. "We will the transfer accomplish here and now, then." Easier for Koscuisko as well, perhaps, since he need not expose himself to ridicule before the Tutor if he missed a word. "Bring me back my boots, if you would. I will just go adjust my attitude."

What did a man's boots have to do with his attitude?

Koscuisko took the boots from Joslire's hand, but he didn't want any help getting into them. Joslire had nothing to do but stand and stare at him as Koscuisko tucked in his trouser cuffs, fastening his uniform blouse smooth and straight.

Koscuisko went into the washroom with careful steps, his feet tender from wearing new footgear. He washed his hands and combed his hair—for all the world as if he were a schoolboy on his way to sit among his elders. As if he was preparing for a formal occasion. As if he felt the Bond and what it stood for was something worthy of his respect.

Then Koscuisko was ready.

"I will receive your Bond now, Joslire Curran."

Joslire opened his blouse, pulling at the fine chain around his neck to find its metal pendant. Koscuisko confused him; he was taking as many pains as it would have cost to do this tomorrow.

"This tape is the record of my trial." Not precisely true, perhaps; it had not been Joslire Curran's trial. But it was close enough. And the formula had been established by the Bench, and could not be materially amended. Requiring that he use personal language—"my trial", "I"—was all part of the ritual, personalizing his enslavement.

"Here the officer will find details of the offense for which I have been justly condemned, by the solemn adjudication of the Jurisdiction's Bench."

All of this time, and he still could hardly say "justly." He had been betrayed to Jurisdiction, condemned to this shame by the cunning and hatred of an ancestral enemy. He would survive to revenge himself. If he failed to revenge himself he would be dishonored in fact, as well as in the eyes of the Bench. He would not fail.

"According to the provisions of Fleet Penal Consideration number eighty-three, sub-heading twenty, article nine, my life belongs to the Jurisdiction's Bench, which has deeded it to the Fleet for thirty years."

Betrayed by an enemy. Bonded by the Bench, because he'd satisfied all the requirements they had for bond-involuntaries: youth, fitness, intelligence, psychological resilience . . . lucky him. He got to carry a governor for thirty years, and in return the Bench waived all charges. If he lived out his Term, they granted full retirement along with the pay that would have accrued had he been a free man; as if that could make up for it.

"The officer is respectfully requested to accept the custody of my Bond."

In two hands he offered it, the prescribed gesture of submission.

With two hands outstretched, the officer received it. With real respect, as if understanding that it was Joslire's life—and not some piece of jewelry, some dull trinket—that he was to hold for the Bench in the Fleet's name.

Koscuisko had a solemn face, a grave expression even at rest—as far as Joslire had seen of him thus far. Joslire told himself it was just weariness that made Koscuisko look so serious now. Otherwise it was too tempting to believe that Koscuisko understood; too tempting to imagine that the Bench formality could actually become the contract-of-honor that it mocked just this one time.

"I will accept your Bond, Joslire Curran. And hold it for the Day your Term is past."

It was just ritual, Joslire told himself. The words were only words, the same as those spoken by his other officers before Student Koscuisko; the same words that would be spoken by the next Student once Koscuisko was graduated and gone.

Except the promise was real this time; the hope for that distant Day was sharp and poignant, because something in Koscuisko's tone of voice utterly convinced Joslire that Koscuisko meant it.

On board a cruiser-killer, the Ship's First—the Security Officer—would husband all the Bonds for safekeeping. Here at Fleet Orientation Station Medical, the Students were required to carry the Bonds on their own person, to increase their sense of ownership and authority. Koscuisko put the chain over his neck, slipping the flat gray record-tape into his tunic.

It was over, for yet another Term.

"And now, not that it follows, Joslire, I'm tired. I should like to go to bed."

And yet he felt less enslaved—and more personally sworn—than ever he had since the terrible day that the Bench had first condemned him to the Bond.

"Attention to the Administrator," Tutor Foliate called. Chonis winced internally at the ragged shuffling sound of twenty ill-prepared Students trying their hand at Fleet drill and ceremony for the first time. Twenty bond-involuntaries and ten Tutors—the sound of their feet moving across the floor was as one sound, crisp and complete. Twenty Students, and it might as well have been two hundred from the time it took them to come to attention.

Clellelan was halfway to the Captain's Bar before the noise quieted down. Tutor Chonis could see the repressed smile of amused disgust on the Administrator's face as he passed.

Students. They ought to bring them in as cadets for the first half of Term. Really they ought.

Chonis had heard Clellelan declaim on the subject often enough. As it was, Fleet simply handed them rank and bond-involuntaries, pretending they knew how to manage both—simply because they were Bench-certified medical practitioners. But it was hard enough already to find even the marginally qualified volunteers they usually got with a Chief Medical billet and Ship's Prime status placed enticingly at the far end of the course. They couldn't afford to make recruiting more difficult than it already was.

Clellelan was posted, now, glancing briefly at the Record on the table at his left. Matching names to Students, perhaps. Trying to guess whether they'd all graduate this time.

"This is Fleet Orientation Station Medical. I am Administrator Rorin Clellelan, Directing. By the Bench instruction. The Term opens with the following Students in attendance, answer to your name when called. Molt. Angouleme. Yurgenhauen. V'ciha."

One by one he called out their names; one by one Students answered to him—nervous, diffident, confident, bored. Too much personal feeling by half, Chonis felt. They'd learn. Discipline was the best defense, as the bond-involuntaries demonstrated. Retreat into formality could help provide the insulation that these Students were going to need.

"Wyadd. Sansoper. Noycannir. Koscuisko."

Noycannir sounded bored and amused, above it all. Not obviously enough to give offense, no. But Noycannir was a Clerk of Court and a member of First Secretary Verlaine's personal staff. She clearly meant to give the impression that she was completely comfortable in this environment.

And Koscuisko?

There was no particular emotion of any kind in Koscuisko's voice, and Chonis wondered about that for a moment. Koscuisko had seemed clearly unhappy to be here during their meal last night. For Koscuisko to be suppressing emotional cues so absolutely meant he was more frightened than Tutor Chonis had guessed.

"Shiwaj. And Bilale." The Administrator came to the end of his list, and Chonis focused his attention to the fore. "Students, you are welcome. You represent a vital resource for the Fleet, as you know. And in these increasingly troubled times, you will be called upon to serve the Judicial order as never before in the history of the Bench." Because never before in the history of the Bench had civil disorder been so pervasive, so corrosive, and above all so persistent.

"Let there be no doubt in your minds, the task for which you have volunteered is a difficult one. And you will be more personally involved in the Judicial process than any of our Line officers, even those in Command Branch itself." Clellelan had to be careful with that one, Chonis knew. It was all to the good to encourage the Students to see themselves as uniquely valuable to the Bench. But if Clellelan put too much emphasis on their critical role, they might start thinking about why Line officers wouldn't have anything to do with it.

"Please be assured that I personally, as well as your assigned Tutors and all of our Staff, will render every assistance in ensuring successful completion of your Orientation. Each of the bond-involuntaries here assigned has been dedicated by the Bench to furthering your instruction in any way possible."

The Bench had created bond-involuntaries specifically to support its Inquisitors. Ordinary Security, no matter how professional, sometimes recoiled from what might be required to support Inquiry. The Bench's solution had been elegance itself: create Security whose indoctrination ensured that disobedience of lawful and received instruction would be unfailingly, immediately, strictly disciplined by a "governor" that held the pain linkages of the brain in a merciless grip. Thus Joslire Curran and others like him, condemned for crimes against the Judicial order to a thirty-year sentence with a surgically implanted jailer in their brains.

"It is prudent and proper that you take their Bonds into your hand as Orientation commences in earnest. The troops here assigned will therefore declare their Bond."

The signal was clearly flagged out in the orientation material. And still it always took them too long to realize where they were in the program, to turn around, to face their assigned bond-involuntaries and stand ready to receive the Bond. Chonis could hear the shuffling sounds behind him and see the other Tutors' Students out of the corner of his eye. He heard Noycannir pivot sharply and bring her heel down emphatically, completing the move.

But there was no sound whatever from Koscuisko.

"By the Bench instruction," Clellelan said. That was his signal to turn around and bear witness to the ceremony, in order to be sure that his Students got it right.

There was a problem, though, wasn't there?

He hadn't heard Koscuisko turn around because Koscuisko hadn't moved.

"This tape is the record of my trial."

The words were spoken in unison; no problem with Security; they knew their lines. Chonis raised his eyebrow at Koscuisko's calm, waiting face, suppressing a twitch of a gesture with difficulty. Curran didn't look concerned. Had Koscuisko taken Curran's Bond already, then?

"According to the provisions of Fleet Penal Consideration number eighty-three . . ."

Student Koscuisko met Chonis's eyes with a careful, neutral expression in his own and bowed fractionally, just enough to convey the concept of the salute.

Most of the bond-involuntary troops preferred the group ceremony, because there was a measure of defensive insulation to be had from the presence of the other troops. After Curran's last two Students, Chonis would have expected the man to stay as clear as he could from anything that might involve personalizing the relationship.

"I will accept your Bond.—And hold it for the Day your Term is past."

The Students picked up quickly. Their lines were spoken in something close to synchronicity, breaking down into a babble of incoherent noise only at the point where the individual name was given. Tutor Chonis turned back to face the Administrator, dismissing Curran's anomalous behavior from his mind.

"You have accepted the Bond from your assigned troops, to be held by you in custody for the duration of the Term. It is just and judicious that it should be so. Welcome to Fleet Orientation Station Medical, Students all. We have every confidence in you, and will do our utmost to see you successfully graduated. Tutors, dismiss."

Maybe it was a hopeful sign, and Curran's Term wouldn't be like the last ones had been for him.

With luck.

They'd all be grateful if Curran got a break that way.

CHAPTER TWO

The first few days of a class were the same no matter what the course material, Andrej mused, glancing around Tutor Chonis's office idly. There'd be introductions, though he'd already met Tutor Chonis and Student what-was-her-name Noycannir. There would be the review of the course schedule. And they would have a summary lecture, or else the first of several introductory lectures, depending upon the complexity of the coursework and the relative length of the Term.

The medical university on Mayon was a compound city the size of his family's estate at Rogubarachno, huge and ancient. Older than his father's House, in a sense. Mayon had already been a surgical college of considerable antiquity and status when the Aznir were still busily annexing worlds without the tedious interference of the Jurisdiction and its impressively efficient Fleet; that was well before their crucial first encounter with the Jurisdiction's Bench, and the subsequent substitution of armed conquest with aggressive market management. The classrooms he'd occupied during his student years had ranged from back rooms in drinking houses to the blindingly sterile theaters where infectious diseases were treated; but he didn't think he'd ever sat a class in someone's office until now.

"Good-greeting, Student Koscuisko, Student Noycannir. Thank you, please be seated."

Slept in teachers' offices, yes; quarreled with the Administration over the interpretation of some test results or clinical indications, perhaps. He'd never sat in class with only one fellow Student, either. Huge as Mayon complex was, it had always been packed to fullest capacity with students and staff even so, because it was the very best facility in known Jurisdiction Space for those who wished to learn the art of surgery and medicine. Only the strict planning codes that had controlled construction for over five hundred years, Standard, had prevented Mayon from becoming claustrophobic. Student housing varied naturally according to the needs and the resources of each Student; but there had been sky and air enough for everybody, even in the heart of the great Surgical College itself. Andrej had only been here at Fleet Orientation Station Medical for two days. He missed the night breeze already.

"You'll have reviewed the assigned material, of course. Rhyti, anyone? Please, help yourselves." The Tutor's gesture indicated the serving-set on the Tutor's squarish shining work-table, just between Andrej and Student Noycannir. She had declined to speak to him except to return his greeting. Andrej didn't care whether she liked him or not; there were too many other things to think about. He'd never had much use for overly compulsive Students. Aggression could cover for lack of skill for a time, that was true. Sooner or later, though, competitiveness failed before superior ability.

Andrej fixed himself a flask of rhyti in polite silence. Joslire had brought cavene for fast-meal this morning; Andrej didn't like cavene, and had said so. He would have had some now, though, if the Tutor suggested it. In Andrej's experience teachers expected everything they said to be taken as good advice or outright direction. But Noycannir just sat there—and did not move to take a flask for herself when Andrej nudged the serving-set closer to her elbow.

"You will have noted that the Term is to comprise six Standard months of instruction, twenty-four weeks. Student Noycannir, you'll not need to adjust your time-sense, since Chilleau Judiciary is of course on Standard time. Student Koscuisko, I expect you're still on Standard time from Mayon, unless going back to Azanry reset you to home-chrono. How long were you home?"

Azanry did not follow the Jurisdiction Standard, but he hadn't been back there for long enough to have forgotten. "Two months, Tutor Chonis. Perhaps five weeks, by local reckoning." Not long at all. There had been plenty of time to embrace his old servants, to tour his fields, to visit his land-pledges. Time enough to compromise the lady Marana and quarrel with his father. Not long enough to change his father's mind or make him understand.

"Well, you'll have leave again soon enough, I'm sure. As I was saying, the Term is twenty-four weeks. Perhaps thirty, if the Administration identifies a weakness in some aspect of your professional development."

The Remedial Levels, that was what Chonis meant. An extra cushion of time to serve as catch-up for dull Students. But if the Student should fail to fulfill some element of the teaching paradigm even at the Remedial Levels, there would be nothing left to do but to recycle her to the next Term. And Noycannir would probably be recycled to the next Term because—having reviewed the lesson schedule—Andrej could not for the life of him imagine how a woman with no medical background could hope to master such a body of information in only thirty weeks. It looked challenging enough to him; and he had nearly eight years of intensive medical training to draw on.

Perhaps he was reading more into the requirements than was really to be demanded of them.

"You'll have noted also that our time divides rather neatly into two halves: one for instruction, one for practical exercise. There is a good deal of material to cover. I cannot emphasize strongly enough the need for diligent study."

Andrej sipped his rhyti, feeling a little bored. Yes, there was a lot to get through, history, philosophy, formal structure, the legal issues, the Writ. The Levels. He wasn't sure why Tutor Chonis felt good study habits needed emphasis, however. What else was there to do here but study? Well, study, exercise, and attend lecture and laboratory, of course.

"Are there any questions?"

None that had occurred to him, at least not yet. Andrej glanced over at his partner, Student Noycannir; she sat with her eyes fixed on the Tutor, not moving. So she didn't have any questions, either. Or she simply wasn't willing to raise any.

"Your personal schedules have been carefully arranged to maximize your study time accordingly. Your assigned Security will continue to provide you with your meals in your quarters. Exercise periods are scheduled before mid-meal and before third-meal. Student Koscuisko,

Curran will be your trainer. As you know, he's Emandisan, and quite good. Student Noycannir, you'll start out with Hanbor. He'll adjust your training as required to ensure that you get the level of combat drill you're accustomed to."

Interesting. The Tutor expected her to be able to fight hand-to-hand, and clearly well enough to warrant a more advanced teacher than the one provided him. She was in good physical condition, to look at her. It seemed a little unusual to Andrej for a Clerk of Court to have any background in combat drill, but what did he know?

"Let's get started, then. Andrej, you'll remember the remark you made at dinner yesterday about the role of coercive force in the interrogation process in your father's time?"

Into the lecture, then. According to schedule they would take a week to discuss why it was reasonable to use torture as an instrument of Judicial order. They would explore the communication problem, and the unquestionable truth that the single most universal language under Jurisdiction was pain, even if its dialects—fear, hatred, and fury, terror and desperation—could not be reliably interpreted.

"Yes, Tutor Chonis. I understand from the material that the Jurisdiction Bench did not shift responsibility for such functions until the tenure of First Judge Upan Istmol?"

To a certain extent it was old material. After all, much of his early medical training had focused on reading pain and how to sort it from shame or embarrassment when the Jurisdiction Standard did not satisfy. A good general practitioner needed thorough grounding in that grammar, and he had been highly praised in his evaluations for the delicacy of his exploratory touch. Eight years from entry-level general-medical to advanced certifications in neurosurgery and psycho-pharmacology, and all of it just so that he could go to Fleet and implement the Protocols—it hardly seemed worth it.

"Quite so, Student Koscuisko. You've started the assignment, I see. Istmol's critical reading of the implementation of Fleet Procedure Five clearly demonstrates the reasoning behind the decision. Reasoning that is, of course, still current, as received."

Andrej concentrated on the Tutor's words, doing his best not to think about why it was so important to rationalize the institutionalization of torture. Deterrent terror. Swift and strict punishment for crimes against the Judicial order. The shock value of a mutilated body on display at local Judicial centers. Living, breathing examples of what a person risked when they tried to challenge the rule of Law.

It didn't matter how he felt about it.

He would keep up and do well; it was expected. It was required. For the rest—since there could hardly be any congenial drinking-places at a stand-alone Station founded on a barren piece of rock—he would simply have to find distraction where he could.

Mergau Noycannir was prompt to class, and had been prompt each of the forty-eight Standard days that class had met since the Term had opened. Forty-eight days; six weeks, Standard. They were halfway through the initial orientation phase and still just speaking in generalities. What good could all of this background do anyone?

Did they think that they were going to lecture her to death, and be rid of her that way?

She heard the signal at the Tutor's door. It would be Koscuisko, of course, since Chonis did not signal for admittance to his own office. She threw an idle taunt at him as the door opened, pretending to be providing reassurance.

"Safe you are, Student Koscuisko, our Tutor is delayed."

Six weeks. She was bored, and getting anxious. Koscuisko was a safe target. He came into the room with too much energy, like a man who'd never been forced to watch his step, moderate his gestures, or govern his expression. People who were so egocentric, so self-defined, could only disgust her. Had he never learned to be afraid of somebody? Would he ever take any of this seriously? And yet she had to be wary of him, because he had the medical education that Fleet valued so highly.

She did not.

Secretary Verlaine had seen no reason to lose one of his best Clerks of Court to years of medical training when all he wanted was someone who had custody of a Writ to Inquire.

"Thank you, Student Noycannir. I trust you had good practice."

Koscuisko answered politely, clearly not noticing her reprimand. Koscuisko didn't notice her at all, in some fundamental fashion. That was much worse than any criticism he could have turned on her; but it was not surprising.

"Thank you, I have had good practice." Of all those here, only Security gave her a measure of the respect that she had earned, that she deserved. It wasn't hard to force them to respect her in combat drill. They were not permitted to rebuke her if she hurt them or failed to observe the rules of practice. And she could fight. "Your practice also?"

Koscuisko, on the other hand, was still learning recruit-level hand-to-hand; she knew that from things Tutor Chonis said. She was better than he was in the arena. If she could have him to herself, no interference, one-on-one, she would not even ask for a weapon. She was confident that she could make him respect her then.

Koscuisko met her eyes and laughed, small and meekly. "Not up to your standards, Student Noycannir, I am quite sure. I find it much more complex a procedure than breaking brew-jugs over peoples' heads."

He knew she was better, but he didn't believe it. She could fantasize all she liked; it wasn't the same. Nor could she afford even fantasies any longer—Tutor Chonis arrived, which meant that she had to make a good show of attention.

The Tutor set his cubes down at his viewer and began to talk without looking at either of them. It was his way to try to catch them unawares. She had learned his habits, and she could best him at his own game. "Well, as I had been saying this morning. History, philosophy, a little—shall we say—political context."

The standard Judicial Structures chart was still on the projection viewer, displayed across the length and breadth of the wall behind the Tutor's chair. Nine Judiciaries; nine Judges, with Fleet shown as subordinate to the Bench in the person of the First Judge Presiding at Toh Judiciary. There was Chilleau Judiciary, Second Judge Sem Porr Har Presiding, on a line with the other eight subordinate Benches; and even at such a global scale as the Judicial Structures chart, First Secretary Verlaine was called out by name, head of Administration.

The Sixth Judge Sat at Sant-Dasidar Judiciary. Fourth or fifth on the list of circuit Courts reporting to the Sixth Judge, one could just make out the name of Koscuisko's system of origin. Secretary Verlaine's name was easy to read on the Judicial Structures chart; the Dolgorukij Combine was all but lost in the small script. It was too bad Student

Koscuisko was so clearly incapable of taking an obvious lesson from that, Mergau mused.

Tutor Chonis was still talking. "We've been through all that. The formal structure of the current organization, organizational philosophy, and so forth. I think we've worked that quite thoroughly, so unless you have any last questions? Student Koscuisko?"

She didn't have any questions, and she didn't care about Fleet's organizational structure, either. What difference did it make to her whether there were three pharmacists and a rated psycho-tech on staff rather than one psycho-pharmacist, two pharmacists, and an extra critical-care technician instead? Were the five extra staff in the complement at the Fleet Flag level ever going to matter to her? What difference did it make whether the interrogation area was within the surgical area or well removed from all other medical facilities?

Koscuisko shook his head without a word, clearly understanding he wasn't expected to raise any issues at this point. Koscuisko might well care about the pharmacists. Koscuisko might well understand what point there might be in spending two weeks and more on administrative issues like standard skill mixes on cruiser-killer-class warships. It might be important to him in the future. For Mergau herself it was a complete waste of time, which belonged to First Secretary Verlaine, and merited more respect than that accordingly.

"Very well. You're to feel free to raise any issues that come to mind at any point, of course. Later." A formality on the Tutor's part. Koscuisko gave every indication of having studied the structure carefully. More fool Koscuisko, because once he got to where he was going, none of that would matter in the slightest. Everybody knew what Ship's Surgeons were really there for.

"Let us proceed, then. You've been introduced to the philosophy behind the Levels of Inquiry, Confirmation, and Execution, which is to say the Bench endorsement of the principle of swift and certain punishment for crimes against the Judicial order. It's time for us to begin to examine these Levels in greater detail, to prepare a foundation upon which to build when we reach the practical exercise phase of Term."

And not a moment too soon for her taste, either. This was what Mergau had come here for, after all; this was what her Patron meant for her to master. The Levels. The Levels, and the Writ itself, which they were not to consider as a separate lecture subject until nearly five more weeks had passed—just before the exercises were to start.

That would not be boring, when they got to the exercises.

"Levels One through Three, the Preliminary Levels, Inquiry. The Fourth, Fifth, and Sixth Levels, the Intermediate Levels, Inquiry and Confirmation. Levels Seven, Eight, and Nine, the Advanced Levels— Inquiry, Confirmation, and Execution. The Tenth Level of Inquiry, Command Termination. Let us first consider the Judicial foundations implicit to the process of Inquiry. Student Noycannir, if you will assist us?"

She didn't mind the sly trick in Tutor Chonis's method. She was ready for him. She was almost always ready for him; not only ready but more than willing to play the Tutor's manipulative game.

"The Preliminary Levels, Tutor Chonis. The first level at which it is permissible to invoke the use of force. Security may take measures appropriate to the Preliminary Levels, but only at risk of discipline unless the Security is under the direct guidance of a fully rated Inquisitor with custody of an active Writ."

This was the beginning of the single most dangerous challenge she had ever undertaken, and she could not bear to stop and think of how complete her ruin would be should she fail to prevail in her Patron's name.

She let the joy of battle comfort her, instead, and concentrated on the fact that she was nearer day by day to victory.

"And with this discussion of the Writ we conclude our examination of the history, the philosophy, the formal structure, the Levels, and the Judicial mandate of an Inquisitor with a Writ to Inquire."

Tutor Chonis addressed himself to the summary title still displayed on the wall-screen viewer behind his desk. He knew that his Students were tense. The closer they got to the crucial break between pure lecture and the first practical exercise, the tenser they became, too. "Let's just review the block of instruction." Who should he call on first? He'd catch them both, of course, and off their guard if he could manage it. Much more than mere replay-knowledge was to be tested at Fleet Orientation Station Medical—and as often as could be maneuvered without becoming crushingly obvious.

He heard a shifting sound from the table behind his back. Student

Koscuisko. Sliding his seat away from the study-table, probably. They'd had twelve weeks together in indoctrination and review; Chonis felt confident in predicting that young Koscuisko would be scowling, his wide, high forehead scored with irritation, his mouth pursed sourly.

Koscuisko was too easy.

So he would call out Noycannir to be first.

"Student Noycannir, will you detail the Privilege of the Writ for us, please."

He could not hear a reaction, not even with the augmented hearing in his right ear—where he had all but lost the natural faculty years ago in an explosion. He knew what that no-sound looked like, well enough. She'd be stiff as stalloy in her seat, and glaring—an equal mix of aggression and insecurity.

"The Privilege of the Writ. Established by Judicial order 177-39-15228. The First Judge Caris Raber, Presiding." *Well?* her sullen, stony eyes always seemed to ask. *Is that good enough for you? I'll bet you thought I couldn't get it right. Well, it's high time you learned better.* She never seemed to be secure, even when she clearly knew the material very well.

"The Writ is granted by Judicial order, and cannot be voided except by Judicial order or expiration of contract of service. It is a failure to support the Judicial order to reject a grant of Writ prior to the expiration of Fleet contract."

She could be subtle, too, and politic; she rehearsed the abstract blandly, without the slightest hint that she even cared about that irony visible on her narrow, sharp cunning face. Once the Writ was granted, it was treason to attempt to lay it down before your eight years of service had been completed. Which reminded him . . .

"Thank you, Student Noycannir, it's quite a lot for one person to try to get through alone. Perhaps Student Koscuisko would explain the unique legal position granted by the Privilege of the Writ?"

He knew Koscuisko didn't like this part. As if Koscuisko could be said to care for any of it.

"Of the Judicial offenses punishable under Law, only one can override the Privilege of the Writ. That offense is challenging the Judicial order by act of treason, mutiny, or insurrectionary intent."

As represented, for instance, by failure to obey lawful and received instruction from one's superior commanding officer. Or in terms of

Koscuisko's birth-culture—one's oldest brother, one's father, or the oldest brother of one's father, if there was one. In other words, precisely what Koscuisko had been trying so strenuously to accomplish before he had finally submitted to the overwhelming weight of Aznir tradition and reported to Fleet Orientation Station Medical as his father directed.

"Wrongful imprisonment cannot be cried against the Writ, because the Inquisitor does not bind into confinement but only enters into the Judicial process when a suspect has been apprehended." Koscuisko was obviously of a mind to be thorough about it, since he had been asked. "Loss of function cannot be cried against the Writ, because the Inquisitor would not be free to perform his Judicial function without fear of repercussions, and one cannot be penalized for performing one's Judicial function. For the same reasons loss of life cannot be cried against the Writ. Loss of personal or real property cannot be cried against the Writ, because the Bench does not apprehend without reason . . ."

Turning around now in his seat, Tutor Chonis regarded Koscuisko with a benevolent eye. It was always gratifying to have one's mental image confirmed. Student Koscuisko was sitting with his legs crossed and one elbow on the study-table, marking off points one by one on the fingers of his left hand; precisely as Tutor Chonis had imagined him.

". . . and the integrity of the Jurisdiction is considered to be resident in the Writ. Judicial discrimination may not be questioned in Judicial process. Loss of privacy cannot be cried against the Writ—"

Tutor Chonis held up his hand and Koscuisko fell silent, folding his itemized fingers into a pensive fist. "Thank you, Student Koscuisko. Well. You have made it quite clear that you are both thoroughly familiar with the philosophy and the crucial legalities that justify, or I should say mandate, your Writ."

Not to mention keenly aware of how useful a Writ could be to an ambitious administrator like First Secretary Verlaine. What had put the idea in Verlaine's mind at the beginning was anyone's guess; all Tutor Chonis really knew for certain about it was that Verlaine had been pulling strings, trading favors, cashing in tokens with reckless abandon over the past two years in his campaign to get Student Noycannir admitted.

Verlaine didn't want an Inquisitor on loan from Fleet who would necessarily have divided loyalties. Verlaine felt Fleet could have more Inquisitors at much less expense if it waived its requirement for Bench medical certifications. Student Noycannir was here to prove that point.

If the First Secretary had his way, there'd be Inquisitors at each Bench center, for each circuit, and for each Judicial processing center— all in support of the Judicial order, of course.

And only incidentally to the detriment of the political power of the Fleet, which had up until now maintained an unchallenged monopoly over the Writ and the lawful exercise of coercive and punitive physical force.

"I have reviewed your progress with the Administrator, who has expressed very great satisfaction with your mastery of the material to date. It has therefore been decided that the scheduled week of assurance iterations will be waived. We are permitted to move directly to the next block of instruction."

Insult 101, as Tutor Jestra had been wont to call it. The Preliminary Levels of the Question started with hearing a confession out and ran through assisted inquiry—which was the maximum degree of violence that could be invoked without a Warrant. Inquisitors were seldom disciplined for violating restrictions, though, since superior officers were generally willing to overlook such lapses as long as they didn't have to look too closely at what was happening in the first place.

To Orientation Station staff, assisted inquiry seemed so benign compared to the Intermediate or Advanced Levels that as far as Tutor Chonis was concerned it did in fact amount to little more than calling a person names.

The prospect of their first practical exercise generally affected the students somewhat more dramatically. Chonis checked the reactions to his surprise: Student Noycannir froze up in her seat whenever she felt threatened, yes, just like that. Student Koscuisko straightened up in his seat, leaning over the table and staring at the carefully replicated artificial grain of Chonis's semi-veneer wall-covering as if there was a text to be read there.

"The Administrator has asked me to declare an extra half of personal time, in token of his appreciation for your accomplishments. Please prepare the material issued for first lecture, Segment Two, the Preliminary Levels. We will start first thing in the morning. Thank you, Student Noycannir, Student Koscuisko."

Fortunately by this time Students were accustomed to spending their personal time alone with only their bond-involuntary Security for company. The Administration took steps with every class to ensure that Students were isolated from each other to the maximum extent possible; training was much more efficient if Students were utterly dependent on their Tutors for approval and validation.

Now, for instance, if Students were permitted to meet and compare notes, they might conceivably recognize the schedule shift for the simple psychological trick that it was. There was no time allowance for assurance iteration.

There never had been.

Every Term it appeared on the schedule, to give the Students the false sense of temporary security that a weeklong buffer between pure theory and the first messy—clumsy—practical exercise could provide.

And every Term Students were moved straight into Preliminary, to keep them off balance and insecure and so eager for reassurance—for official approbation—that they would be willing to beat some helpless stranger with their bare hands just to get a word of praise from their Tutor.

"We start tomorrow with first-lecture, usual time. And then we'll move to theater in a few days." They needed some extra nudging to get them up and out of his office. "Your first exercise is scheduled for today week. We'll review some of the previous exercises to help you prepare prior to the practicum. Enjoy your free time. Good-shift to you, Students."

Koscuisko shook his head just a fraction, as if breaking himself out of his immobility, and started to rise. The moment Koscuisko began to shift, Noycannir was out of her chair smoothly and swiftly, unwilling—as always—to see him get one step ahead of her in anything. *Tomorrow, Students,* Chonis promised them in his mind, watching them take their confusion out of his office. *Tomorrow we will begin to test your mettle.*

And in the meantime?

In the meantime reports from the assigned Security troops usually proved amusing, as each Student sought to find some psychic balance after the unexpected shock.

The door slid together behind Koscuisko's back, and Tutor Chonis leaned back in his chair and smiled.

⊕ ⊕ ⊕

It had been a week since the Tutor's traditional trick of moving the Students straight into preparation for their first practical exercise. Joslire had taken his officer through the evening drill; now Koscuisko was relaxing with his rubdown, quite possibly thinking of nothing more than his supper to come.

Koscuisko seemed to be relaxed enough.

Lying on his belly with his arms folded under his head, Koscuisko nuzzled his chin into his fist like a blissfully happy young animal, making undefined sounds of contentment. Joslire suppressed his involuntary grin of amused recognition. Yes, that muscle had pulled tense during today's training; and yes, it did feel good, when it surrendered up its tension to an expert hand. And if he was not an expert hand, at least Joslire was good enough by this time to tend to Koscuisko's relatively minor aches and pains to his satisfaction.

He'd had Students both more and less athletic than this one in the past, but none who accepted the requirement for exercise with so good a grace. Stiff, sore, and grumbling strictly to himself, Koscuisko never hinted at avoiding practice or suggested cutting it short, except in carefully qualified jest. That made things easier for everybody. Joslire was grateful to his Student for the grace with which Koscuisko took direction; it made living with his governor much easier. He was adequately confident of his own ability to discriminate between being sworn at in the line of duty and being sworn at because he wasn't doing his duty; but the possibility of confusion arising was an unpleasant one.

The more perplexing problem remained that Koscuisko seemed to take all of Fleet Orientation—physical exercise and soon-to-be-intensified combat drill alike—as some sort of an amusement, or a joke. Koscuisko was younger than his years, there was that. The Aznir stayed children for longer than the Emandisan did, Aznir lived longer than Emandisan, and Joslire had told himself he could have expected Koscuisko's attitude to retain some of the blithe, carefree flavor of a privileged childhood even after years of medical school.

He was finished with the strained back muscle. Koscuisko let one arm drop over the edge of the rub-table, pillowing his cheek against the flattened back of his other hand—and grinning like an infant with never a care in the world. Except Joslire could feel the base tension in Koscuisko's body had yet to yield to massage. Koscuisko kept his nerves to himself. All Joslire could tell the Tutor about Koscuisko's state of mind was what little he could gain from observation and inference. The muscles in Koscuisko's sturdy shoulders could no longer be persuaded to relax as completely as they had during the first weeks, even allowing for improved muscle tone. Koscuisko was tense; but that was hardly news, not with the practical exercise scheduled for first thing next first-shift. In the morning. There was nothing new there to tell Tutor Chonis.

Working his Student's feet, Joslire pondered his problem. Bond-involuntaries who wanted to stay out of trouble kept their mouths shut, so as to avoid giving their governors or their Students cause to discipline them. Joslire desperately wanted to stay out of trouble. But part of his job was to keep Tutor Chonis up to date on what was going on in Koscuisko's head. Bond-involuntaries learned early on that their best protection was to perfect their duty, gaining a measure of immunity from their governor's strict censorship by maintaining unchallengeably correct thought and conduct. And Tutor Chonis had gone an extra pace for him before.

"With the officer's permission . . ."

Koscuisko grunted inquiringly in response, sounding half-asleep. A good start, Joslire decided, and was encouraged to go on.

"The First Level exercise is tomorrow, as the officer will remember. In the past other Students have shared comments of one sort or another. It has often seemed to help to put things in perspective."

How do you feel? What do you feel? What are you thinking? What is on your mind?

"Hmm. Well. I feel that Jurisdiction wodac is not of the best quality, which is not surprising. And that the instructional material is badly in need of a technical update, in places."

Not precisely what Joslire had in mind, but there was no way in which he could question more directly—not and keep peace with the governor that the Bench had spliced into the pain linkages in his brain. Joslire stepped back half a pace. "If the officer would care to turn onto his back."

Koscuisko didn't mind being uncovered. Aznir Dolgorukij didn't seem to have privacy taboos about masculine nudity, at least not among men of the same age; though from what Joslire had read about Koscuisko's ethnicity, relative age made all the difference. There was a

Jurisdiction Standard for personal modesty, though, as much a part of the common language as the grammar was. Koscuisko would be expected to conform to those standards once he reached *Scylla*. It was up to Joslire to instruct him by example. Joslire laid a clean towel across Koscuisko's lap and began to address the upper part of Koscuisko's right knee, where yesterday's training bruise was just beginning to mellow to a rich gold-and-purple blotch around the joint.

And after a moment Koscuisko spoke again.

"What is the manner in which an Emandisan frees himself from error, if he has sinned? Is there such a need in your birth-culture?"

It didn't seem to be related to the issue Joslire had raised, but there was no telling. Chonis had commented on Koscuisko's effective—but sometimes disconcerting—tendency to come at a question from an angle that was itself part of his answer to whatever problem.

He wasn't eager to answer all the same; such issues weren't widely discussed among free Emandisan, let alone enslaved ones. Of which latter category he was the only one he knew. He hadn't wanted to tell Student Pefisct what his crime had been, either, since it wasn't information he was required to surrender, on demand; but Student Pefisct had gotten it out of him at the last, when his enforced submission had come too late to do him any good. Joslire decided that he couldn't face the memory of his last attempt at serious reticence. It would be easier to capitulate to Koscuisko's casually phrased demand.

"If it please the officer, there is only . . . disrespect. Of steel." He wasn't sure how to say it and be faithful. It didn't translate very well; he'd never tried to put it into Standard before. Perhaps he'd been lucky that his other Students hadn't been curious about his five-knives. Joslire could imagine no worse torment than to be constrained to discuss what Emandisan steel meant to an Emandisan.

Koscuisko didn't seem to be disturbed at the vagueness of Joslire's response. Koscuisko stretched, yawning, and folded his wrists behind his head, staring up at the low gray ceiling of the cool room reflectively.

"You make it sound quite simple. Is something the matter, Joslire?"

Yes. He'd been thinking about Student Pefisct. Joslire ducked his head to obscure his confusion, following a line of muscle down the outside edge of Koscuisko's shin with the hard knuckle of his thumb. "It never is as simple as it sounds. With the officer's permission."

"There is more truth than comfort there, however." Koscuisko did not seem to suspect any hidden thought, apparently content to follow his own stream to the rock. "Where I am at home, there are three great sins, and all others relate to one or more of them in some way. But none are unforgivable except the three most grievous ones."

What three great sins were those? Joslire wondered. He had done all he could with Koscuisko's knee. Moving around to stand at the head of the rub-table, Joslire began to finish on Koscuisko's shoulders, listening to his Student talk.

"And the first, perhaps the most difficult thing, is that you must confess yourself, or never hope to be forgiven. This is very annoying, Joslire. One would think that if the whole world knew that one had spoken with disrespect about one's elder brother or one's uncle that it would be enough to have one's penance decided and made known to one, and be done with it."

This was good. This was the sort of thing that he had been hoping for when he had asked the question. There was every reason to expect that Tutor Chonis would be able to explain what Koscuisko had been getting at, when the time came to give Chonis his report.

"But one would be mistaken. There can be no reconciliation without repentance, and there can be no repentance without acknowledgment of fault, and there can be no acknowledgment of fault without individual confession. I wonder how different it can be when all is said and sung, Joslire."

Maybe it wasn't all that different at that. The Jurisdiction required punishment before setting the Record to null, and declined to apply any of the agony that could lawfully be invoked to force confession against the penalty to be assessed.

So Student Koscuisko saw a connection there, and seemed to take comfort from it.

Joslire lifted Koscuisko's head between his two hands to work the neck back to the relaxed range of supple motion that was normal for his Student.

Somehow he could not quite believe that the two parallels were really so simply aligned as that.

It'd been harder than mastering any of the technical material, Andrej remembered that very clearly. With the possible exception of some of the more arcane degenerative diseases among category-four hominids, nothing had been as difficult as learning to take a patient history; and he'd been too grateful for his teachers' praise when he finally began to demonstrate some skill to worry too much about what that struggle had said about him.

All of his life he had asked whichever question he liked, never needing to consider whether the answer would be readily forthcoming—or accurate, when it did come. All of his life, the function of language had been to communicate his desires for the understanding and instruction of others around him. There were exceptions, of course; the language of holy service was humble and petitioning enough. It was also formalized by centuries of devout practice, and no longer really signified.

But in order to take a good and useful medical history from a patient already ill and not in the most conciliatory mood because of it—that required he learn to ask. To submerge any hint of personal frustration beneath a sincere and, yes, humble desire to know. To set the patient at the very center of the Holy Mother's creation, to listen with every combined power at his disposal, to subordinate everything he was and everything he knew absolutely to whatever unsatisfactory and imperfect responses his patient would condescend to give.

There'd been times when he had despaired of ever attaining the art. There had certainly been times when his teachers had despaired of him. He'd been counseled by the Administration on more than one occasion to consider abandoning his goal in favor of a technical certification that would require no patient contact whatever, and he'd seriously considered doing just that; but he kept on trying. Graduation with full certification from Mayon Surgical College required demonstrated ability to develop a complete and accurate patient history, one-on-one—on an equal, not autocratic, footing with each patient who came under care.

Now Andrej sat in a padded armchair in the middle of the exercise theater, thinking about these things. The theater and the chair that was provided, he'd seen before; if not this precise theater, then others much like it, as Tutor Chonis reviewed paradigmatic exercises with them during their initial study. There was a door to the right through which the prisoner would enter. There was a table at his left, sturdy enough to support the body of an adult of most of the hominid categories, high enough for him to work at without tiring. Only his rhyti stood on that table now; his rhyti, and the Record. They'd add things gradually as they went along—instruments of Inquiry, then Confirmation, finally instruments of Execution, and there would be a side-table for the Recorder.

For now the table was still safe for him. He could take his rhyti from it without shuddering, even knowing as he did what role it would play in his further education as a torturer. Security was posted behind him even now, even though it was only the first of the Levels—a free offering of confession, unassisted. Andrej wondered if Security was as apprehensive as he was to be starting this. Surely even Security had feelings about the work ahead of them all, the blood and the torment of it?

Without shifting his posture from the position of relaxed attentiveness he had assumed when he sat down, Andrej concentrated on the movements of the two Security troops behind him. He used to try to guess exactly what faces his young nieces and nephews behind him were making at the kneelers during the long hours in chapel on one Saint's day or another; and now he found that the old pastime had the effect of giving him eyes in the back of his head, where the strictly subservient Security were concerned. The prisoner had not been brought in just yet, and Security seemed to permit themselves a bit more restlessness than they might have had they felt that someone was watching them—or watching them now as opposed to hours later on Record, where they would like as not be out of orb anyway, if the demonstration tapes were any indication. The image in his mind's eye amused him—a pleasant relief from the fretful night he'd spent.

"Gentlemen, a little concentration, if you please," Andrej said, sensing their surprise and stiffening posture. Quite probably they'd never been forced to kneel devoutly for hours at a time while Uncle Radu declaimed at length about the improbably perfect virtue of some probably hypothetical martyr.

Perhaps he should approach his task from a different angle after all, Andrej mused.

To take a medical history one had to connect with a patient, and he wanted as little connection with this place as possible. He wasn't interested in making any person-to-person contact with the prisoner; but he couldn't take a medical history without engaging his empathic self.

His final evaluations in that all-critical block of instruction had cited his "genuine and responsive empathy of a very respectable degree," and he was proud of himself to have won over his own limitations, proud of how completely his proctor had been surprised as she read the commendatory prose from his record.

It would be better for him if he could turn the empathy off, pretend he'd never fought through the icy bare-rock pass between his mind and heart. It would be better for him to observe clinically, without emotion. Except all that he was and all that he had won at Mayon depended upon his passionate empathy; how could he set that prize aside, and not diminish himself?

He was no further toward a solution to the problem this morning than he had been last night, talking to Joslire. What had he been talking to Joslire about? There'd been a good deal of wodac after supper. He wasn't quite sure.

The warning signal sounded at the door; Andrej remembered. Uncle Radu, the tiresome business of the confessional, and the brutal simplicity of it all. Confess or be unreconciled. Be contrite or unreconciled; accept your penance joyfully. Or be un-Reconciled.

Reaching for the glass on the table at his elbow, Andrej drank off half the rhyti in one draw, regretting his gesture immediately for the uneasiness that it betrayed.

Control, he told himself.

He had to have control.

"Step through." He could hear no tremor in his voice, no uncertainty or nervousness. He had confessed and he was contrite, but Uncle Radu—and the whole of the Blood by extension—could not accept that he was truly penitent while he still resisted his father's will. He left his home for this place un-Reconciled because he couldn't accept his father's wishes without protest. Disgraced and unblessed, and sitting here as though he'd been set by the Holy Mother to examine her children for flaw or fault . . . "State your identification. And the crime to which you wish to confess."

He looked up only as he ended the first of the listed questions. He had the series set out in text for him on the scroller at his elbow; a Bench catechism of sorts, the litany for preserving the forms of the Judicial order. Perhaps it would be better to approach it that way. As long as he was un-Reconciled, he might as well be irreverent, and be damned for it. His father had kissed him and blessed him as well as he could under the circumstances. But the Church was pitiless.

The Church and the Bench's Protocols were well matched for that.

"Abbas Hakun, Sampfel Sector, Dorl and Yenzing, your Excellency."

Familiar as the title was, it startled Andrej to hear it in this place. On his home-world his father was an Excellency, a prince not of the Autocrat's lineage. And since all of a prince's sons were princes—regardless of whether they would inherit, regardless of whether there was anything *to* inherit—Andrej had been an Excellency from his infancy. It only took him a moment to remember. Chonis had warned them that their prisoners were required to address them as if they were already commissioned.

"The crime to which I wish to confess is that of defrauding the Bench, your Excellency."

It is my shame to be un-Reconciled, and if I cannot be relieved of fault by penance I must die nameless and unwept, never to stand in the presence of my Holy Mother beneath the Canopy.

His prisoner was Mizucash, tall, broad-shouldered, and imposing for all his bound hands and meek demeanor. The language of submission and confession sounded strangely in the Mizucash's mouth, to Andrej's ear.

"In what manner have you defrauded the Bench?"

Just like the confessional. The crime had to be quantified and categorized before the appropriate penance was assessed. And if the prisoner or child under Canopy did not have answers ready, the questions themselves would elicit information to complete the Record and define the penalty.

"My employment was in a Judicial Stores contract company, your Excellency. Our contract lay in the provision of the nine flours Standard for fast-meal menus of hominid categories eight, ten, eleven, and nineteen."

Yes, my Mother's servant, I have challenged my father's will and my father's wisdom, and not submitted myself to instruction, as a filial child would not fail to do. I cannot accept my father's will, though I am to do it. He cannot know what he requires of me.

"Describe the actions that you took, or failed to take, that resulted in the crime of defrauding the Bench."

So easy, to pass from the neutral "crime to which you wish to confess" to the necessarily self-incriminating "crime of defrauding the Bench." One hardly noticed the all-important shift in emphasis. Was this how Uncle Radu felt when he heard confession beneath the Canopy?

"I operated the sweeper in the packaging area of my plant. My instructions specified that flour sweepings were to be collected and weighed for use as wastage statistics for the development of the billing rates."

What was the man talking about, anyway? "Explain how your actions vis-a-vis the floor sweepings defrauded the Bench." He had to concentrate on the task before him and set aside his brooding. What could be so important about flour sweepings that they would send a man all the way out to Fleet Orientation Station Medical to confess about them? Or was that the point, that it was an unimportant crime, and therefore it was no matter if a Student Interrogator botched the job?

"Wastage statistics reduce the billing rates by the value of the sweepings in flour by weight. My wife and I, we're in violation of the recommended reproduction levels, your Excellency, and rations only allow for two children. So instead of bringing the flour to be weighed, I took as much of the sweepings home as I could manage on each shift. In violation of my published procedure."

So he was to take the confession of a man who had cheated the Bench out of a few eighths of flour. It had to be a joke. If he were in Uncle Radu's place, he would have had so pathetic a sinner turned out of sanctuary and beaten for his presumption, or for the sin of aspiring to an excess of piety. One might as well beat the gardener for having chewed on a leaf of jessamine while cultivating the plantation. Could this be some sort of an initiation prank, like throwing the class's best student into the waddler-pond for luck before final exams commenced? Andrej decided to test it, distracted from his private conflicts by the obvious absurdity of the situation.

"Describe the value of the flour sweepings you have confessed to having misappropriated." Which would in turn define the degree to which the Bench had been defrauded, so that he could form a better idea of the severity of this crime.

"We used to have a saucer-cake for the chilties' morning meal from them. A good eighth in Standard scrip, your Excellency. Sometimes as much as four-eighths, and my Balma would eat, too."

Ridiculous.

He'd have to revise his mental comparison. To prosecute defrauding the Jurisdiction Bench at this level was like selling the gardener's children into prostitution because the gardener had inhaled too deeply of the jessamine fragrance on three consecutive warm mornings, thereby defrauding the House in concept of some minute amount and unrecoverable amount of the essential oil.

"Oh, fine," Andrej said—to the monitor as much as to the prisoner. He felt completely at ease now, his sense of the ridiculous having overpowered his self-pitying introspection. "Very good indeed. You are a very great sinner, Abbas Hakun." He couldn't tell whether Security's sudden twitchiness behind him was affront or the giggles; he didn't care. He had half a mind to walk out on this farce of a confession right now. "What impelled you to confess your crime to the authorities so that the Judicial order might be preserved?"

Or else he would continue with the questions as they were written, which had the potential for becoming really rather hilarious in the absurdity of applying them to the theft of a handful of flour.

"My wife developed an allergic reaction to one of the flours. They're not available as rations to the mill staff . . ." It was the first trace of real emotion Andrej had heard from his prisoner; and the desperation he read underneath that neutral statement was too honest to be amusing.

Perhaps it wasn't funny.

But it was no less absurd.

"She was at risk of being accused for trade on illegal markets, so I turned myself in. It's true that she ate, but it was me who stole, your Excellency. It is for this reason that I asked to be allowed to make this confession."

Torn as he was between his inability to take the crime seriously and his appreciation for the prisoner's obviously sincere desire to protect his wife, Andrej was unsure as to his next move. Azanry was too rich a world; no one lacked for a handful of flour, at Rogubarachno . . .

He decided to complete the forms.

Tutor Chonis would explain the joke—if joke there was—when he and Tutor Chonis went over the tape of this session for critique.

"Very good. There was no question in your mind at any time that your violation of procedure constituted willful fraud, then."

There just had to be a joke in here someplace.

CHAPTER THREE

Tutor Chonis was not actually angry. Perhaps a little annoyed. Koscuisko's scorn had been rather sharp, and as Koscuisko's Tutor, Chonis took that personally. Annoyed, yes, but not enraged, and that meant that he had to make a conscious effort to compose his face for the desired dismaying effect as he keyed the office's admit with unnecessary force, making noticeable show of fighting with imperfectly suppressed disgust while awaiting the tiresome membrane to slide slowly apart to allow him entry.

"Can you really imagine that we're that stupid?"

Choosing the blunt unreasonable words carefully, Tutor Chonis all but spat them into Koscuisko's face before continuing past his startled pupil to take his seat behind his desk. Noycannir was startled as well, of course—but not without a subtle under-shadowing of gratification in her flat, shining hazel eyes. Tutor Chonis wouldn't have had it any other way. It was his business to set Students at each others' throats and make them compete for his approval and respect. That was one of the reasons that Tutors handled two Students in the same Term, and on the same shift as well. Receiving a stern reprimand in the presence of a social and professional inferior could, with any luck at all, be counted on to set young Koscuisko's aristocratic teeth on edge.

"I've reviewed your practical exercise, Koscuisko. I am disgusted with the manner in which you conducted yourself. You seem to think that this is all some sort of a perverse amusement, an adolescent game."

And he could all but hear Koscuisko seething where he sat, with his spine locked rigid and his hand that lay on the table suddenly motionless; still, there was no hint of Koscuisko's fingertips whitening at the point of the stylus in his hand. Koscuisko had control.

Chonis didn't know if that was a good thing or not, yet.

"It *is* a game." Sweet and soft, Koscuisko's reply, but Chonis could hear the confusion and worry behind the response. "You explained it to us yourself, Tutor Chonis. We pretend that the crime deserves its punishment, and in return the prisoner pretends that there is hope of Judicial leniency."

It wasn't the sarcastic route Koscuisko's reasoning took that disturbed Tutor Chonis. He knew about it already, of course, from Joslire's reports; and his own experience had prepared him to expect it from a man like Koscuisko. It was not an uncommon psychological defense, especially at the beginning of the Term.

"Don't try to mock me."

He turned away from the two of them in order to emphasize his displeasure and to analyze its source at the same time. The real problem was that Koscuisko gave every evidence of possessing an unusually healthy sense of the ridiculous. He could not be permitted to leave Fleet Orientation Center Medical with that sense of the ridiculous intact.

"Capital eight-six. On the appropriate display of the accepted psychological conviction." Damn the insolent little wretch, Koscuisko was quoting his own lesson citations at him. "The Inquisitor is at all times to display clearly evident conviction that the Jurisdiction's scale of punitive measures is wise, tempered with mercy, and above all completely just. Correct moral stance on the part of the Inquisitor will greatly facilitate the creation of the appropriate attitudes of contrition and submission to the Law on the part of the prisoner."

As if he didn't know, when he had all but written the text himself. "Leaving apart for the moment the unpleasant flavor created by a Student attempting to lecture his instructor. Dare you suggest that your clownishness in the practical exercise created the appropriate sense of respect for the Judicial order in the mind of your prisoner?"

He turned slowly back to face his Students again as he spoke. Noycannir first; she seemed to be enjoying the show. If only she could learn from it. Her first exercise had been completely serious—without technical error and with every indication of utter conviction, as if her personal background—her proven skills for survival in the unspeakably sordid circumstances of her earliest years in an ungoverned Port, her demonstrated facility for carrying useful survival strategies to their logical limits—had somehow deadened her imagination. She would not make an adequate Inquisitor without an imagination. A torturer with an intensive medical background and a set of legal parameters to conform to could be considered to be a perversion of a sort, that was true. But a torturer without imagination was only a brute.

"A man," Chonis continued, "since you obviously need the reminder, who was honest enough to make a full and free confession. In order to protect his family from the consequences of his own guilty actions. Whose dignity should have been respected."

Koscuisko met his eyes squarely, and did not drop his gaze until a precise fraction of a moment before the stare would have become too insolent to be permitted to pass. Koscuisko looked rather more enraged than irritated, very much as if he was considering some internal vision of Tutor Chonis in three pieces. His glare seemed to wash the color out of his pale eyes until they almost seemed all white and no pupil—like the Nebginnis, whose vestigial eyes, no longer functional, had been replaced by sonar sensing. Chonis was gratified with the effect. It had not been easy, but it looked at last as if he had got Koscuisko's attention.

He resumed his line of discourse. "Remember well that the dignity of even the guilty must be carefully cherished. . . . And is not the painful disregard of that dignity one of the most severe marks of the Bench's regretful censure of wrong conduct?"

Except that if he didn't watch his own tone of voice he would lose all that he had gained. He sounded almost sarcastic to himself; and if he thought he sounded sarcastic—with his lifetime's worth of training in picking up linguistic subtleties—then there was the danger that Koscuisko, whose records pointed to a high level of innate empathy, might sense the same thing. Chonis pulled a weapon from Joslire Curran's daily reports to use against Koscuisko's formidable sense of center.

"You are at least nominally an adult, by the Jurisdiction Standard. I understand that in your birth-culture confessions are made only to priests, and all the rules are unwritten. It is not so here." In Koscuisko's birth-culture, no man whose father was out of cloister was an adult. The women had it easier on Azanry, in that sense at least, because women became adults with the birth of their first legitimate child—no matter how old their mothers lived to be.

Koscuisko, seemingly disinclined to be drawn out, had squared his chair to the desk and folded his hands. He appeared to be concentrating on the minuscule text printed on the index line of one of the record-sets on the library shelf, his expression one of mild, polite disinterest as Chonis lectured.

"Confession is a deadly serious legal action. And the penance voluntarily accepted by the transgressor is serious, too, Koscuisko, remember that." In order to provide the correct exemplary deterrent. "It isn't the sort of risk you ever took. That is, if you're religious."

Confession and penance. Koscuisko had nerved himself up to his ordeal by drawing the analogy himself. Koscuisko had been thoroughly scolded now, and Noycannir put on notice as to what sort of reception her first stumble would earn her. Perhaps one final pious admonition . . .

"After all, whatever penance you might have risked could hardly be said to equate with the just outrage of the Judicial Bench."

Koscuisko stared him in the face once more, and this time his gaze was frank and honest—no trace of resentment or rebellion.

"You never had to confess to Uncle Radu after an anniversary party," Koscuisko said.

Humor.

Koscuisko's ability to find humor in the current situation only indicated that there would be more problems yet down the time-stream.

"Very well. We will speak no more about it." But the Administration would watch and wait, record, and meditate.

"As you will have noted, the next practical exercise is scheduled for five days from now. We will be defining the Second Level of the Preliminary Levels. Please direct your attention to your screens."

Humor and a sense of proportion were both unpredictable traits, not subject to reliable manipulation. Koscuisko's unpredictability had to be explored, detailed, and controlled.

Because an unpredictable Inquisitor with a sense of the ridiculous and an imperfectly submerged sense of proportion was potentially more disruptive of the Judicial order than even the Writ in Noycannir's ignorant hand could be.

Standing in the lavatory, Andrej stared at himself in the reflector. He could hear Joslire in the outer room; it was a familiar set of sounds, easily ignored. His face did not much please Andrej this morning. It was too pale; and it had always seemed to him that some proportion or other had been neglected when the issue of his likeness had been controverted among his genes in utero. To be fair, his pallor was perhaps his own fault. He had taken a good deal of wodac with his third-meal, yet again, last night.

Still, a man needed more emphatic a nose if he were to go through life with such wide flat cheekbones—or at least eyebrows with dash and flair, or eyes that made some sort of an impact to draw a person's attention away from the crude materiality of his skull. Too much cheekbone and too deep a jaw; there was no help there. A plank of wood with a chip of nothing for his eyes, which were of no particular color; a splinter for a nose; and his mouth would never carry a debate against his cheek—there was too much distance there from ear to front. No color, no drama; he might as well not have a face at all. There was paint, of course, but not even the best of that had made his brother Iosev any less unpleasant to look at, so there was no help to be found in that direction.

He was only trying to put off the morning, and he knew it. Sighing to himself at his own transparent motive, Andrej dried his damp face briskly with the towel and combed his hair back from his face with the fingers of his left hand. His brother Mikhel had all the face in the family, and all of the beard as well. Mikhel, and perhaps Nikolij, too. But, then, Nikolij was such an elf-faced child. There was hope for Nikolij. And even Lo—as blond and as bland of face and feature as Andrej himself—Lo had some of Meeka's height. There was no justice in the world. Where was the benefit of being the eldest of his father's sons if all he could hope to inherit was all of the land, and all of the property, and all of the authority, and all of the estate?

Joslire would be getting nervous, and it wasn't fair of him to make Joslire wait when none of it was Joslire's fault. Andrej set his mind to silence, stubbornly determined to not think of the morning's work until he was well into it.

Successfully distracted by the simple pleasures of the fast-meal table, Andrej found himself sitting in the Student Interrogator's chair once more without a very clear idea as to how he had got there. It wasn't how he'd come back to this room that needed his attention, though. Not really. It was how he was to get out of it again that posed the more immediate problem. The Second Level of the Question—and there was every chance that Tutor Chonis would take any deviation from form as a personal insult, after his reaction to the First Level— would be more difficult.

The First Level had been Inquiry pure and simple. The Second was Supported Inquiry—a little pressure was to be brought to bear. That was what Fleet called it, Supported Inquiry. Mayon would have called it patient abuse, and summarily stripped any Student who so much as threatened a patient with physical violence of any chance for patient contact ever again in any Bench-certified facility—which also meant, realistically speaking, losing any chance of graduating with the prestigious Mayon certifications. But these weren't patients in any usual sense of the word, so what did it matter?

Except that in Andrej's home dialect, the word for the Standard "patient," someone seeking medical care, came from the same root as the verb that signified suffering, or to bear physical pain. Andrej did not care to mull over the double meaning. It was too unfortunately apt for his comfort.

He wouldn't have thought that he would mind simply hitting people so much, not really, and that was all today's exercise should entail—hitting someone. Hitting them frequently, perhaps, and the fact that they were not to be permitted to hit back was certainly distasteful, but they need suffer no permanent ill effect from the blows. He certainly hadn't come all the way through his medical training without ever hitting anybody. There was a difference, of course, when it was strictly after class hours, outside the patient environment, usually in a tavern of some sort, and never without either having been hit or being immediately hit back. He had done his share of recreational brawling, with a little thin-blade dueling thrown in. Violent physical exercise could be a great reliever of stress, and as far as Andrej could remember, he'd enjoyed it—not the residual bruises, no, but the energy surge had been a tremendous mood enhancer.

Though conservative of traditional Aznir ways, in many respects

Andrej's father was a progressive man who didn't think children or servants should ever be beaten for their misdeeds, and who refused to tolerate any such behavior within his Household. Therefore it had come to pass that Andrej had never struck anybody in his life who had not been in a position to retaliate, without hesitation or restriction. Andrej supposed it was a handicap, of sorts.

He heard the signal at the prisoner's door. Well, soonest started was soonest sung. "Step through." Still, there was something he'd wanted to remember. Something his teachers on Mayon had said about hurting people. What had it been? "State your identification, and the crime of which you have been accused."

This prisoner was a Bigelblu, his legs almost as long as Andrej was tall. He sauntered into the room insolently before sinking into cross-legged repose in front of Andrej where he sat.

"You c'n call me Cari." He had a deep voice, the prisoner had. Nearly as deep as Meeka's singing voice, which was so low that the saint's-windows shook in sympathetic vibration when he sang "Holy Mother." "I dunno, Soyan, s'a mystery to me."

Deep, and insolent. For a moment Andrej sat torn between reacting and thinking out his own approach to this problem. He knew how he was expected to react. And he didn't want to have to think about it.

Much of the medical process did involve hurting people, as a necessary part of helping them heal. Surprise was as unpleasant as pain, apprehension as noxious. When one was required to do something that would hurt—remove dried-out field dressings or palpate a sprain, or any number of contacts with wounded or painful tissue—one minimized apprehension and surprise by building up to the bad part slowly. Starting with small, impersonal contact at safe body sites, always remembering species-specific or cultural taboos. When one approached the painful thing in neutral graduated steps of that sort, patient apprehension could be significantly reduced, helping to ensure that the pain involved would be kept to its lowest level.

Now Andrej was expected to strike a man who was to be restrained from striking back, and the very idea was morally repugnant on its deepest level.

He would try to sneak up on it. That was it. That was what he could do to get through, for today.

"Stand up." Andrej rose to his feet and took the prisoner by the shoulder, giving him a little push. He was horribly reluctant to so much as touch the man; and yet he would be expected to hit him, and hard enough to at least bruise. "I said stand up, what are you waiting for?"

Security came to his rescue; Andrej imagined they had experience helping uncertain Students through the paces. They had the Bigelblu on his feet in short order, their efficient handling quite unimpaired by "Cari's" grumbled protests.

"Easy, you guys, where's your sense of humor? 'Vent I been standing all day, waiting for this . . . little . . ."

Andrej never got a chance to hear what Cari meant to call him; no, the Security were too efficient for that. One of them had the prisoner's arm behind his back, and apparently did something unpleasant to it; at least to judge from the expression it produced.

"One is expected to use his Excellency's dignity with appropriate respect," the Security troop said. With a straight face; truly, Andrej admired his control. Surely such a clumsy start as he'd made could only make him ridiculous in front of these people, and no "appropriate respect" about it.

"If he's tired of standing, let him kneel. But sitting on the floor gives one an unpleasant feeling that one is not being taken quite seriously . . ." No, he was better off staying away from that line of thought. Tutor Chonis would think that he was being insolent again.

". . . which is surely not what you meant to do. On your knees, then. No, here."

Working with his hands, pushing a bit, pulling a bit, moving the prisoner from side to side. Getting used to the warmth of the prisoner's body beneath his hand. Doing what he could to nerve himself to the shameful test, taking the edge off his reluctance to hit the man by pushing the prisoner around. He didn't like it, but it seemed to work. Andrej felt he could manage the next step, if only he could avoid being distracted by the fact that he meant to strike someone he wasn't even angry at.

He had a clear field now, even had a modest advantage of height as he stood before the kneeling prisoner. Andrej repeated the question in a sterner voice, trying to convince himself he was determined by speaking harshly.

"State your identification, and the crime of which you are accused."

"Now, Soyan, didn't I just tell you that? My name's Cari, and . . ."

The tension within him was not shame and reluctance, Andrej told himself, knowing he lied. The tension within him was irritation at being sworn at, and irritation could be relieved by directing it at its natural object. Andrej moved on his target with a smoothness born of thin-blade dueling, giving his prisoner a backhanded slap across the face which surprised all of them: Security, because they had to compensate for the force of the blow, and they had not apparently anticipated his movement; Andrej, because he was wearing his great-grandfather's ring on his left hand, and one test was all that was required to demonstrate the sense of using his right hand for the remainder of the exercise. He was going to have to remove the ring next time.

"Be so kind as to answer the question." He had done the thing, now, with never a Mayon monitor to report his lapse of professional conduct to the Administration. He had successfully raised his hand against a man restrained and defenseless. He had passed the filthy test of indecency. Now all he had to worry about was the next blow; and the one after that.

"Ah, well, Cari is short for Kerrimarghdilen. My family name is Pok." Last but not least, Cari had apparently been surprised into sensibility. At least for the moment. "I was picked up for vagrancy at Merridig, but I had some timmer on me—personal use only, really, I swear—so I'm here in front of his Excellency for illegal trafficking."

At least timmer was a little less mundane than flour. There was still a problem with this, of course. Why should he himself have unlimited access to the intoxicants traditional to his culture—every bit as destructive when abused, and without sanction as a sacrament—at the same time that an otherwise honest Bigelblu could be prosecuted by the Bench for trading in a culturally traditional and sacramentally essential hallucinogen? A problem, yes, and not the less so because the answer was so obviously a matter of whether Bigelblu or Aznir had economic clout.

But the distance between what the prisoner had done and what the Bench meant to do in reprisal was not as extreme as the first had been. That was a relief.

"You have stated your personal name, but have failed to provide your identification. Full identification is required to complete the

Record. State your identification, and the crime of which you have been accused."

Apart from the general problem of double standards—and the immediate ache of his knuckles beneath the weight of his great-grandfather's ring—Andrej was not as sickened at himself for having struck the man as he had expected to be. The Bigelblu was a prisoner, and for the striking. Andrej was required to strike him. And it wasn't as if this man had come to him for healing; he had been brought here to make confession.

Andrej had no false conviction that these rationalizations made it morally correct to strike a prisoner, or that he should feel no guilt for having done so. But just for the moment to feel little enough guilt that he could fulfill the specific requirements of a Second Level interrogation was all that Andrej asked of his life.

"What a dullump, Soyan. Nobody told me that I was going to have to put up with so much damn natter-tattering—" Andrej hit him again, with his right hand this time.

"What'd you do that for? I've got a right to—"

Andrej responded almost easily, as if there was no barrier of decency and shame between a man in power and one in chains to stay his hand and moderate his temper.

"No . . ."—it was only a short stoop to glare down at this Cari nose-to-nose, with a hand at his throat to discourage any sudden movements—"No, you've no particular right to anything, just at the moment, and you and I both will find ourselves considerably less exercised at the end of our discussion if you can persuade yourself to accept that concept now. Answer as you're bidden, I am in no mood for insolence."

The language came out of the preparatory material, with its model interrogations and its examples from the previous students' taped practica.

Andrej cultivated what irritation he could find to help him forward.

"Answer the question. Or must I repeat myself?"

If yielding to irritation would get him through this—then yield he would.

And willingly.

⊕ ⊕ ⊕

Tutor Chonis settled his shoulders back against the chair, folding his hands in front of him as he spoke.

"For the Record."

Third of three Preliminary Level exercises, third of three evaluation and observation sessions. Curran behind him, to his right—Student Koscuisko. Hanbor behind him, to his left—Student Noycannir. Third of three, last of three, and life was due to become interesting for all concerned within a matter of days. For now there was only the Record to complete, while preparations continued to be made for rougher exercises.

"Preliminary Levels, the Third Level, assisted inquiry. Tutor Adifer Chonis, for the Record. Students Noycannir and Koscuisko in the theater."

Student Noycannir had taken her place with the careful stiffness that characterized her when she was more aware than usual of being watched. Straight-backed and straight-faced she sat, her gaze apparently fixed on some point of interest midway between the prisoner's door and infinity. It was an interesting meditation to try to imagine how Noycannir would characterize infinity, when her birth and upbringing had been so sordid and so crushingly constrained. There was no hope of discussing it with her, however. From all indications, Mergau still felt that everything her Tutor did or said was first and foremost something to react against; and the conversations he had with her had been a little strained accordingly.

There was no stiff artificiality to Koscuisko this morning, however. Quite the opposite. Student Koscuisko occupied space with a sort of unthinking presence, a sense of self that was as much a part of him as Noycannir's apparently inbred defensiveness. There was no disguising the quality of Koscuisko's blood, or of his upbringing, at least. Nor any getting around the fact that Koscuisko was drunk, no matter how perfect—relaxed, confident, and apparently secure—his posture might be said to be.

Chonis sighed, and set the pause interrupt on his audio string. "Curran, he's been drinking? Again?"

Curran's grave bow managed to communicate a little of the confusion he seemed to feel. "As regularly as if scheduled, with the Tutor's permission. There does not seem to be any adverse impact on the Student's health."

Yet. Koscuisko was young; his body could still take it. What should it matter to him if Koscuisko drank? Except that Koscuisko hadn't on Mayon, not like this. Not so consistently as every night, for as long as they'd been practicing on the Preliminary Levels—every night for four weeks. Students who drank like that didn't earn Koscuisko's ratings. On the other hand, Fleet didn't expect much by way of actual medicine out of its Ship's Inquisitors once they were on Line. It was sentiment on his part, pure and simple, Chonis told himself with disgust. There was no other explanation for the fact that he could not help caring about what became of Koscuisko's medical skills if Koscuisko continued to respond to the stress by self-medicating with overproof wodac.

Chonis set the string back in braid. "Student Noycannir is calm and assured in manner." The prisoner-surrogates had made their entrance, the exercise could begin. Noycannir was on the attack from the first, raising her voice, confronting her prisoner verbally and physically. "She displays no hesitation or uncertainty in enforcing the Protocols."

Koscuisko simply sat where he was with his chin in one hand, his elbow propped up on the arm of the chair. Koscuisko liked to feel his way into things. From Curran's reports, Koscuisko was still struggling with the idea that it was appropriate to hit his prisoners. "Student Koscuisko continues to display a conservative approach. Although he has fully supported the Protocols, he provides adequate intervals in which the prisoner may offer information or other responses."

Whereas Noycannir was just a shade to the wrong side of the aggressive approach to Inquiry. Noycannir waded into her Levels like a Bladerau into a street fight, and her prisoners had to work at it to get a word in edgewise. "Student Noycannir is aggressive and confident. A point of discussion is to be made on the issue of timing. She will need to prepare herself to build more slack time into her interrogations."

Not that that really mattered, either. After all, the First Secretary would expect her to get information. That would necessarily require her to stop knocking her prisoners around long enough to listen to what they had to say.

"Student Koscuisko continues to engage his prisoner on a personal level. There is a potential cause for Administrative concern . . ." Chonis heard Curran stiffen slightly at the criticism. Students who could not learn to keep their psychic distance tended to get lost more often than other Inquisitors did. There was madness along that path, and not of a sort useful to the Fleet, either. Therefore to be discouraged.

". . . which will be addressed in the Advanced Levels if necessary. Student Noycannir maintains a commendable degree of personal separation from her subject."

An excess of empathy would not be a problem with Noycannir. She took to the habit of depersonifying her prisoners quickly and well. Chonis approved of her detachment; it was a good deal easier to kick an inanimate object than a fellow being. Far better to think of them all as mere lumps of recalcitrant matter to be worked into conformity than to spend as much time getting into their heads as Koscuisko did. While it was true that Inquisitors like Koscuisko got much better information, more consistently, it was also true that less involved Inquisitors like Noycannir tended to last a good deal longer on Line.

Koscuisko had risen to his feet, standing in front of his prisoner with his arms folded across his chest. His body language was as clear a sign as any that he didn't want to be here. But the stance was also one that presented no threat, putting the prisoner off his guard. Chonis was almost as startled as the prisoner was when Koscuisko hit him. And Chonis had seen him do it before. An ability to backhand a taller man across the face—and knock him down with the force of the blow, from that awkward angle—was no small thing; and Koscuisko made it all look quite natural.

"Student Koscuisko makes effective use of limited force. In this respect he is more apt than the average Student." Praise should be read into Record when due, and might soothe Curran a little as well. Chonis took his audio out of the string, again, to talk to Hanbor about the same issue.

"She's overdoing it again, isn't she?"

On the exercise floor, in the exercise theater, whether training or Inquiring, Noycannir did not seem to possess much of a sense of proportion. He and Hanbor had talked about the problem more than once during their daily status meetings.

"The Student did not receive the Tutor's prior comments on the issue as the Tutor would wish, with the Tutor's permission." Hanbor had his work cut out for him this Term: Noycannir was not responding well to shaping. Curran had the easier Student of the pair. "She did make a comment that may be pertinent, as the Tutor please. In reviewing the instructional paradigms, Student Noycannir called this troop's attention to the fact that when she hit people they stayed hit."

There was no hint of tension in Hanbor's voice; he was a consummate professional, like Curran. And Hanbor wouldn't bother to mention it if she did beat him, unless he felt it pertained to information that Tutor Chonis would find useful. On the other hand, if Hanbor hadn't been superlatively qualified for Security work, he wouldn't have been Bonded in the first place.

Safety for bond-involuntaries lay in exceeding the Bench requirements for professionalism. Tutor Chonis was just glad he had a good caliber of support staff to work with. Out on Line in the Lanes, only Ship's Inquisitors were privileged to receive support from bond-involuntaries.

"Makes sense," Chonis nodded his thanks, and his agreement. "We'll need to work on that, before we get much further. Thank you, Hanbor."

Back into braid. Noycannir had knocked her prisoner-surrogate into a corner, and Security were taking their time dragging him back to the middle of the room—giving him a little space to catch his breath, and not being too obvious about it, either. Koscuisko's Security had stood away from him, leaving Koscuisko alone in the middle of the theater with his prisoner. Koscuisko didn't seem to need any help managing; he had a good hold on the prisoner's arm, twisted up behind the man's back. Chonis frowned, very slightly. It would be a shame if Koscuisko broke a bone at this point; he'd be forced to call the exercise for violation of the Protocols, and Koscuisko didn't deserve that kind of embarrassment.

"Student Noycannir puts her issues forward well and strongly." He had to be careful of what he said on Record. Anyone could review these tapes; anyone with the proper levels of clearance, of course. First Secretary Verlaine, as an example. "Student Koscuisko is relatively quick to gain the advantage but continues to display a certain degree of reluctance to press the advantage once gained."

As now, for instance, when Koscuisko released the prisoner's arm with a rough push that sent the prisoner staggering to his knees. He needn't have worried about the arm, Chonis realized. Koscuisko's fault lay in reluctance to use as much force as was necessary; Noycannir's, in a consistent use of more force than was necessary.

"These issues will be discussed individually with the Students after completion of the exercise. Neither Student presents cause for any serious concern at this time."

Well, not as far as the exercises went, at least.

And that was as far as Tutor Chonis was expected to go.

". . . very commendable progress."

Tutor Chonis's voice was fat and hateful in Mergau's ears, self-satisfied and oily. She didn't mind the powerful reverberation of authority that she could hear there. It was the hint of gloating that turned her stomach.

"There is always room for improvement, of course. As an example—very quickly—Student Koscuisko, you still don't appear to be taking this quite seriously; Student Noycannir, you need to relax, the prisoner cannot strike back at you. These minor details aside, however, the Administrator is very pleased. And he's empowered me to make a tangible gesture of that appreciation."

It was a trick, she knew it; her belly was tense and cold with it. A trick like the last one had been, to push them out into unknown territory before they'd really had a chance to master the material. A cheap manipulative trick.

"There will therefore be an extra study-day in which to prepare for the beginning instruction for the Intermediate Levels. After your apt handling of the first three exercises, it is anticipated that you'll not need extensive preparation . . ."

Mergau glanced to her left across the table, surreptitiously. Koscuisko was frowning. So he was suspicious, too.

". . . therefore there's no lesson plan for this extra day. Student Koscuisko, you might enjoy a tour of the Infirmary; Curran has been instructed to obtain a copy of the pharmaceutical library for your use."

Koscuisko's scowl deepened. For herself she knew better than to display such a reaction in front of her betters—but Koscuisko didn't seem to think he had any. "We didn't do much with the Jurisdiction's Controlled List on Mayon, Tutor Chonis. Few of the drugs have positive medical applications."

The "pharmaceutical library" confused her, but "the Jurisdiction's Controlled List" made all plain. Tutor Chonis was talking about the speak-sera, the enforcers, the pain-maintenance drugs. She couldn't blame Koscuisko for disliking the idea. Where she'd come from, people feared the Controlled List even more than even the Ship's Inquisitor.

"But your skill, dare I say flair, with psychoactive applications is well documented as your subspecialty, Andrej. Perhaps the Controlled List will be made richer by your investigations."

Yes, it was gloating in Tutor Chonis's voice. Very small and very subtle, but none of his mockery and taunts escaped her. Tutor Chonis was almost too pleased with the potential he felt he had identified to conceal his pleasure. Koscuisko glared down at his left hand, which he had closed into the fist he hadn't dared clench upon the table. For no particular reason, Mergau found herself noticing that there was an odd crease in the skin at the base of his middle finger. "I will browse the library, Tutor, at your instruction. Permit me to observe that I would prefer not to add to a resource that has such potential for being misused, and which is of so little positive benefit to anybody."

Koscuisko would be damned before he had anything to do with the Controlled List, was what he meant. Noycannir shot a glance of shocked amusement at Tutor Chonis to make it clear that she disapproved of Koscuisko's near-insolence and disrespect as much as Chonis himself surely did. Tutor Chonis's face revealed no secrets, though.

"And, Student Noycannir . . ."

She blinked at Tutor Chonis's beard, demurely.

"The First Secretary has requested periodic reports from us to be forwarded every three Levels. You and I both understand how much he has invested in your training here."

She knew how to behave in front of people who outranked her, even if Koscuisko did not. Koscuisko would learn. She'd love to have the opportunity to teach him. For now she would be content to benefit from the contrast between his attitude and hers.

"Am I to be present during review, Tutor Chonis, or shall I merely assist in preparing the report?"

Making her voice meek and submissive, Noycannir projected her understanding of her subordinate position, her earnest desire to please. It wasn't easy to fawn and cringe before Tutor Chonis, though it had to be done. Tutor Chonis didn't like her. His charge to Koscuisko had been double-edged, she realized—on the one hand giving her fellow Student his orders but, on the other hand, providing yet another reminder that she had no special medical education. She was ignorant of all but the practical basics of field medicine, and her fellow Student was a neurosurgeon qualified across eighteen of the thirty-seven hominid species and the obligatory exemplar from each of the non-hominid classes of intelligent species with a secondary qualification in the biochemical applications of psychopharmacology, which she wasn't prepared to swear she could so much as spell correctly. She had no right to be here, as far as Tutor Chonis was concerned. No one would be there to intercede if she should fail, to stand between her and the humiliated wrath of her Patron.

Tutor Chonis's little smile, half-hid beneath his neatly trimmed mustache, was as hateful to her as his tone of voice had been. "That's up to you, Student Noycannir, of course." Tutor Chonis would just as soon leave her out of it. That was the principal reason she would insist on participation, just to be sure that no negative comment went unchallenged. "Report tomorrow morning, and we'll review your progress to date. All right?"

Fleet wanted her to fail because Fleet's vested interest was in retaining sole control over the Writ. Fleet was waiting for her to fail. Fleet would be happy to throw her to one of her own fellow Students for the Tenth-Level Command Termination just to express its resentment of First Secretary Verlaine's power play.

Half-sensing Koscuisko's sympathetic gaze, she stood, determined to exit with what dignity she had. Koscuisko's sympathy was intolerably patronizing. He disgusted her, him from his privileged background, money, rank, everything. She was ten times as good as Andrej Koscuisko, Bench medical certifications or no. She had worked for everything she had attained. Nobody had ever dropped an appointment in her lap.

"Very good, Tutor Chonis. Are we dismissed?"

The Tutor waved his hand, still smiling. Mergau bowed stiffly and left the room, struggling to contain the frustration, the fury, the fear that seethed within her.

She would be damned before she would give up her purpose.

Because she would unquestionably be damned if she should fail in it.

The serious concerns in life, Andrej felt, could best be pondered in one place and one place alone. One could think in one of the pathetically generic chapels that Jurisdiction Fleet provided for the spiritual welfare of its members under arms; but in chapel, one was expected to be silent, if not reverent, and Andrej had always done what he considered to be his very best thinking out loud.

Sitting on the slatted bench in the sauna that Joslire had located for him, Andrej took a deep breath of the hot, wet air and sighed with the satisfaction of it, coughing slightly as the thick heat caught in his throat. The heavy warmth was relaxing from the inside out. *Just what the doctor ordered,* he told himself dreamily. *And I am the doctor, so I know.*

Joslire had posted himself by the door, but whether it was to control access or simply to be closer to a patch of cooler air, Andrej couldn't tell. The man's posture was as correct as ever it was, regardless of the fact that he was half naked; there was something a little unusual about Joslire's state of undress, what was it?

"Joslire, will you come here for a moment, please?"

Joslire had folded his uniform for him and stowed his clothing carefully away before Joslire had even started to undress, and Andrej had been halfway into the sauna by that time. Obedient to his word, now, Joslire came to stand at attention on the wooden grating that covered the heated floor. Leather straps, that was what it was. Leather straps across Joslire's narrow slanted shoulders, binding his forearms, tight across his barrel-ribbed torso—leather straps, to anchor the sheathing Joslire wore.

Understanding came with a shock of recognition. Andrej turned his head away, waving Joslire off. He was ashamed of himself for not having considered what he was requiring when he'd decided to have a sauna. Joslire was Emandisan, and wore five-knives. And Emandisan were reputedly so private about their five-knives that you had to be married to one to even know which one went where.

"Go and dress yourself, Joslire, you look cold." He was the one who'd insisted Joslire strip to his towel; he was the one who'd assumed that Joslire would be uncomfortable in the unaccustomed heat if he tried to accompany Andrej into the sauna fully clothed. "Or will it be a violation, if I am alone for eight minutes?"

A violation. Joslire would not violate his discipline, and part of that clearly meant giving no hint as to his personal preferences one way or the other. As if personal preferences were a privilege of free men, and officers had to be discouraged from considering their bond-involuntaries' comfort as if it mattered. His insistence that Joslire take off his clothing in order to bear the sauna's heat more easily had probably generated twice as much discomfort between them as had he simply permitted Joslire to fall flat on his face of heat exhaustion in the lawful pursuit of his duty, and be done with it.

"The officer should not exercise himself." That was a joke; he hadn't voluntarily exercised anything except for his drinking arm since he'd got here. Participation in the combat drills that Joslire demonstrated for him so patiently twice a day was certainly not voluntary, or he would happily have done without. "There is no reason for the officer to be concerned on this troop's behalf."

It was disgusting. He was supposed to pay more attention than that. He was accountable for what belonged to him. "I don't believe you, Joslire. But I'll take your word for it." Because he was liable to create even more awkwardness if he didn't. Andrej settled himself against the paneled wall of the sauna, and closed his eyes. "Tell me, if you can, then. To how many Students have you been assigned, prior to this particularly thickheaded one?"

He wasn't aware of any prohibition against gossiping about former Students. If there was such a prohibition, Joslire would find some way to observe it without letting on, in which case Andrej would learn nothing, in which case he would know.

"There have been five, previous to the officer." From the sound of Joslire's voice he was back at his original post by the door. "The first of the Intermediate Levels has been a critical point for each one of them." He might as well have said "each one of you," or "all six of you."

"Am I really so obvious? You may neglect to answer that question, Joslire. I actively encourage you to neglect to answer that question."

Three levels in the Preliminary set, suitable for persons accused or suspected in regards to whom there was not yet enough evidence to make an arrest. Almost they could be said to correspond to basic physical examination, and the taking of patient histories. The invasive techniques came next, here as they had at Mayon; but the focus was all wrong. Andrej could not shake a feeling of unreality, the stubborn suspicion that there had to be something that they weren't telling him. He was certain of it. They could not—they *could* not—expect any thinking being to take such Levels seriously, and go forth to beat a shopkeeper on suspicion of having shortchanged a Jurisdiction clerk by an octe's weight of sallets on a slow day five weeks gone.

That kind of a joke was not so bad, as long as it remained a joke. His thin-blade duels had all been jokes, in the end, a recreation comprised of the hazard of lethal force against the flimsiest pretexts imaginable. It was precisely that tension that had made it so exhilarating—not that their student duels had been lethal; no one had been seriously injured in a duel in all his years of schooling. But there was always the chance. It was for that reason that he treasured the thin white scar underneath his right eye and had steadfastly refused to have it smoothed away. He had earned it fairly in contest against his friend Sourit, who had suddenly decided in the midst of their fifth-year finals that a man who sweetened his cortac brandy could not be permitted to live.

"The Administration expects a crisis. No fault is to be found with the officer on that account. The Administration simply requires that the officer continue with his orientation. Not that the officer find it agreeable."

No, of course no fault would be found, not as long as he continued to perform as expected. And it was no longer to be enough to simply hurt people; according to the exhaustively defined Protocols of the Intermediate Levels he must proceed to harm them as well.

There was no possibility of a joke of any kind in that.

"Speaking of Administrative requirements, Joslire, I am to take myself to Infirmary to meet the Resident, I understand. Have I mentioned that the Controlled List is an abomination beneath the Canopy?"

Three turnings, and he'd have to face the test and find out if he could bear to do what had to be done and stomach the passing of it. A little distraction in the meantime would not be unwelcome.

"After the officer's sauna. Laboratory facilities have also been reserved for the officer's use, during the remainder of the Term."

Had they indeed? He had no intention of doing any Controlled List research. But it would do no good to tell Joslire that. Joslire would only have to report it.

"Sing out when I am finished in the sauna, then." Since the appointment had obviously been prearranged, Joslire would obviously not let him miss it. There was something to be said for Curran's constant shepherding; he couldn't be misplaced nearly as easily as Andrej usually misplaced his other time-keepers.

"As the officer requires."

Enough thinking for the moment.

He could feel the sweat run down his face, down his ribs, along his feet.

If he really worked at it, perhaps he could convince himself that he was actually relaxing after all.

CHAPTER FOUR

Frowning to himself, Tutor Chonis put another mark down on his record, still not quite satisfied with his report. The signal at his office door was expected, if a little early; he keyed the admit without speaking, unwilling to interrupt his thought. The Administrator was satisfied with his report. He himself knew that each point he had made was solidly, independently defensible. And yet there was a problem.

He looked up.

"Student Noycannir reports, Tutor. As the Tutor instructed."

Yes, Student Noycannir. "Good-greeting, Student Noycannir. You may be seated."

She moved stiffly, as terrified of a misstep as ever. She had pride, and she was not stupid—not in the conventional sense. In ways she was clearly as intelligent, perhaps even as creative, as any of his Students had ever been, Koscuisko not excepted.

"The first thing that you should know, Noycannir, is that the channels are down. We will not be able to have our scheduled conference with Secretary Verlaine until several days from now."

Her self-control was formidable, but he had trained Inquisitors. And he could see the effect of his news—surprise, relief, joy, resentment, suspicion. Always ending up with resentment and suspicion. Tutor Chonis swallowed a sigh of resignation and continued.

"I have here the report that the Administrator has released for transmit to the First Secretary. If you like we can discuss this before it's forwarded."

What crippled her intelligence was her defensiveness and the mean-spirited narrow scope of her reason. She was too sensitive; reactionary and suspicious. Her resentment of anything that she interpreted as a personal reproach cut her off from any real support that he could offer; and her self-absorption brought her to see everything as personally directed against her.

"As the Tutor thinks best," she said tonelessly, her eyes fixed on the Record in front of her. "I know I only want to know what I can do better."

She had convinced herself that the report was negative, so much was clear. Chonis cloned the draft to her screen.

"Take a moment to scan the text, Mergau, if you please." The translator would provide a Standard version, the only language Noycannir could read. She was like the crèche-bred in that, although he doubted that she would have appreciated his pointing that out.

Tense and silent, she stared at the screen in front of her. Chonis decided to take the opportunity to read it through for one last time himself.

Student Noycannir has successfully completed the basic orientation portion of this Term. She displays a better-than-average ability to recall Judicial precedent and supports her interpretations of the discussion cases with pertinent citations. Her grasp of the theoretical basis of the Writ is above average in complexity and thoroughness.

He didn't think she was breathing. It would only make her even colder if he noticed that, though. He read the next section over to himself instead.

She has successfully completed the practical exercises at the First, Second, and Third Levels. There is no abnormality in her implementation of the Protocols. There has been no inappropriate use of force.

That was pushing it a bit, granted. She had not violated the Protocols by going further in the interrogation than was called for. She did have a tendency to hit twice, when once would have been enough; still, she was hardly unique in that. Students expressed their internal conflict over the things they found themselves doing here in different ways Noycannir hit frequently, desperate to prove that she could hit as well or better than Students with Fleet-approved qualifications. Koscuisko simply hit, and then went off to take a drink or six.

In summary, the Student is performing at or above acceptable levels and has been passed to the next stage of instruction. By order of the Administrator.

She was rereading it, he could tell, her eyes jumping from the foot to the top of the text as she scanned the lines, frowning slightly in her concentration. Chonis waited for her to look up at him before asking the customary question—a little ironic, under these particular circumstances.

"Do you have any comments to add, Student Noycannir?"

She seemed at a loss for words. And—regrettably, but predictably—resentful of that fact. "I am . . . very satisfied . . . with this evaluation." Her voice sounded curiously dead. "Is there some deficiency not mentioned that requires my attention?"

What, apart from the obvious?

"I need hardly point out that you are at somewhat of a disadvantage here, Noycannir. The practical exercises will become increasingly difficult for you." They would become increasingly difficult for Koscuisko, too, obviously. But for entirely different reasons. "As your Tutor, I feel that an in-depth review of additional records on top of those chosen for class exemplars would benefit you. This requires more of an investment of time on your part, however."

She was an apt pupil. She could learn from observation. As long as she spent sufficient energy actually observing and not seething with resentment over perceived slights, as she seemed to do in class.

"I will gratefully comply with the Tutor's suggestion," she said stiffly. Her breathing was a little ragged, as the tension she had been under when she'd come in began to wear off a bit; and Chonis couldn't tell—for once—if she was uncomfortable because her gratitude was genuine or uncomfortable because she felt compelled to use the submissive phrase. "Has the Tutor a suggestion as to an appropriate starting point?"

Indeed he had. "I took the liberty of scheduling some tapes into a reserved screen in the library." Basic exercises, carefully selected to be as similar as possible to the situation she would face during her next practical exercise. "Hanbor will escort you there. And then I'll be needing him for an hour or two, but he'll be back to wait for you before your afternoon exercise period." So she would be safely out of the way, as well as Koscuisko. "If you haven't made other plans, of course."

She stood up. "I am at the Tutor's disposal. Thank you, Tutor Chonis."

"And you, Student Noycannir. Dismissed."

Secretary Verlaine might be right, that Noycannir's lack of medical background could be surmounted.

About her attitude—the more serious obstacle, at present—he was rather less than optimistic.

The officer was in the capable hands of Station Pharmacy staff for the moment, and would remain their responsibility for the next few eights. It was the first time that Joslire had been on his own since Koscuisko had arrived—except for the class sessions, of course, and that hardly counted, since that time was usually taken up in review with the Tutor. All he had to do for the next while was listen to the same lecture he'd heard six times before; and then spend a few eighths being introduced to "Robert St. Clare," providing him with some background on the officer's habits of thought and tendencies in lines of questioning.

This was one of the worst parts of the entire Term for Joslire.

He knew where he was going, he'd been this way before. A long hallway well removed from the administrative areas where the Students lived and worked led to a featureless door among eight and sixteen others as innocuous, which led to a short corridor, which lead to an assembly room. There would be an exercise room, he remembered; a mess area, and a sleeping-bay beyond. Right now the assembly room—small as it was—was full; five Tutors at the foot of the room, ten prisoner-surrogates on the far side of the room. Day-new bond-involuntaries, just graduated from their long months of orientation, carefully selected for their superb physical health and their psychological resilience. There were only ten of them here, but there were only twenty Students on Station, and this was the briefing for the first-shift cycle. There would be another such briefing half a day from now to cover the other five Tutors, the other ten prisoner-surrogates, the other ten bond-involuntaries assigned.

Finding his place among his fellows, Joslire took comfort in the company of other Bonds, waiting for the briefing to begin.

"Stand to attention for Administrator Clellelan!"

It required no thought to shift from command-wait to salute in response by learned reflex. The Administrator returned the required courtesy with a quick gesture, coming briskly through the ranks of Staff Security to stand on the platform at the head of the room.

"Listen and attend. You all know why you are here."

Joslire remembered when it had been him on the other side of the room, only five years ago. Listening to the Administrator, curious about the Tutors and the Staff Security, and too ignorant to be fearful . . . he didn't like remembering. Which of these naive children would it be, to test his officer's hand?

Which of these fresh zombies was Robert St. Clare?

"You have each received your individual briefings, and executed the required statements of expectation and compliance. For the sake of the Record, we will review these a final time now, before the exercise begins."

Not children any more than he had been, not really. Young, so that they could absorb the shock to body and to spirit and still recover to be useful to the Fleet, but all of them adults by Jurisdiction Standard. It was only the contrast between what he'd known then and what he knew now that made him think of them as children. Blessed in their ignorance. Soon to receive instruction.

"You have been carefully selected to play a critical role in the training of senior staff officers for the Jurisdiction's Fleet. The importance of your part in the training process cannot be overemphasized."

They had to be reminded that Fleet was unforgiving. He would never have made it through on the strength of his own will; in the end it had only been his keen awareness that failure would bring suffering far in excess of what he had already endured that had carried him safely through until the exercise was over. He'd never liked knowing that about himself. But it was true.

"If you do not complete your assignment, you will have compromised the training of an extremely significant Fleet resource, a candidate for Ship's Surgeon. There has been failure to complete the course in five out of the six regrettable cases in which one of you has proved unequal to your task. A continuing resupply of qualified Ship's Surgeons is an absolutely vital Fleet requirement. We do not suffer the loss of any Student lightly."

They were likely enough to lose their Students to despair and the ultimate escape of suicide. The Writ could not be laid aside before an officer's eight years of service had expired, except as an act of treason.

"It is therefore critical that you keep the following requirements firmly in your mind. One. You are not to confess to your offense until midway through the Fifth Level."

He'd been too confused to tell when the midpoint had been reached, since there'd been no chronometer he could see. He'd forced himself to hold out till the end, because that had been the only way he could be sure he was complying with instructions. And by the end of the Fifth Level, he'd suffered from a dangerous lack of focus, so that sorting out what he was encouraged and expected to confess from what he was forbidden in the strictest terms to even hint at had taken more of an effort than he'd ever dreamed possible.

"Two. Your officer must be given no hint or intimation of your status as a prisoner-surrogate. You can expect your officer to realize you're hiding something . . ."

Not if they were lucky. If they were lucky the officer would be only too happy with the information supplied, and would gladly ignore any but the most blatant hints of anything more. He had been lucky.

". . . but you are expressly warned, on pain of a Class Two violation, against revealing any more information than you have been instructed to provide."

It was only that Koscuisko was too responsive by half to subtle clues and cues. Koscuisko had startled Joslire more than once with his odd insight; and things that Koscuisko said about jokes and playacting hinted unnervingly at some subconscious understanding on Koscuisko's part that the "prisoners" he had seen in the Preliminary Levels were not prisoners at all. St. Clare would have a harder task to hide his truth than Joslire liked to imagine.

"The Security assisting the Student will ensure that the Intermediate Levels are respected." As well as they could, when they were forbidden to intervene without direct orders from the Tutor. "Succeed in this mission, and you will have proved yourself a valuable Fleet resource in your own right."

An educated resource. A more sophisticated resource. One with firsthand knowledge of how much a man could be hurt, confused, humiliated, humbled—all within the relatively benign restrictions of the Intermediate Levels, where no major soft tissue damage could be done, where none of the senses could be seriously compromised, where only half of the body's major joints and long bones could be broken and severe burns had to be confined to a strictly limited proportion of the total surface area of the skin.

A resource that understood about fear.

"Fleet will show its gratitude and appreciation accordingly. You will receive automatic deferment from Line Fleet duty for an eight-year period of time, and four years will be stricken from your Bond. These are only tokens of the importance that we place on your successful completion of your mission."

Would it be worth the price?

Could it be worth the price?

The same event that had stricken four years off his Bond had taken six years off his life. Or so he felt.

He could only hope that for St. Clare it would be different.

He'd been born Rabin with the Ice Traverse, but Robert St. Clare was what Fleet had decided to label him. Robert St. Clare was the name to which he had learned to answer, this year and a half gone past. He wouldn't be Rabin again until the Day came.

He was Robert St. Clare, and he was as close to bored as he could remember ever being. It wasn't that he was looking forward to the exercise; no, not at all. But he was looking forward to something different; and as early as tomorrow, first-shift, it would begin.

"This man is Joslire Curran, Robert." The Tutor he had met when he'd first got here; Chonis had interviewed him briefly but thoroughly at the time. He wasn't allowed to stare at Chonis anyway, prior acquaintance aside, but he could stare at Joslire Curran all he wanted, full of wonder. Emandisan, the Tutor had told him. He hardly even knew what Emandisan meant, apart from the rumors. One thing was clear enough: Emandisan didn't look anything like any Nurail that he'd ever met.

"You're to have a few words with him, in final preparation. You may ask him anything that you feel may help you in the exercise. Joslire, I'll see you before third-meal."

A brisk salute from Curran echoed rather clumsily—he

thought—by his own, and the Tutor went away. It was only Bonded Security and prisoner-surrogates here now.

"The Day will come," the Emandisan said, laying his hand on Robert's shoulder in formal greeting. Oh, yes. Right.

"The Day, after tomorrow." Yes, that was the response, and the Emandisan—apparently satisfied—let his hand drop to St. Clare's elbow, guiding him over to sit on the bench against the wall. Joslire Curran was very dark, compared to the people St. Clare had grown up with. The Black Mackeles weave had hair as dark as that, but even so their skin was lighter, and their eyes certainly nowhere near the intense black of this Curran's. Dark, not tall, and solid as stone by the look of his shoulders. Curran had already been through the exercise. St. Clare was impressed with him already.

He let himself be sat down meekly, watching Curran for his next move. Curran had a flat face, and did not look happy. Not as if he should be surprised at that, St. Clare told himself; none of these people lacked for reason to find fault with the world, and why should they?

"Your Student—you already know this—is Andrej Koscuisko. He's Dolgorukij, and he drinks."

It was a funny way to pronounce the name. "Aandrai." *Why didn't he just say Anders and be done with it?* St. Clare wondered. Of course Anders was a Nurail name, and Koscuisko wasn't likely Nurail. That would explain it, right enough.

"What should I expect from him, friend Curran?" St. Clare felt a little awkward using the term of familiarity; it sounded almost unnatural to him in Standard. Fortunately Curran did not seem to have taken it amiss.

"Oh, there's no predicting. It's too early in Term for that." Leaning his head back up against the wall, Curran stared up at the lights. St. Clare didn't think that Curran looked particularly comfortable. "There is a consistent trend, and it may be helpful to you, I don't know. He's pretty good at putting the procedure on. The thing to remember is that no matter how much it hurts, he's only going to hurt you enough. No more than that."

What could "enough" signify? Enough to get the answers, when they both knew that wasn't at issue? "I don't understand you, friend, what are you saying?" He only had a year and a half of Standard. Well, a year and a half of intensive Standard, apart from the language he had learned for trade when he'd been much younger. There was a good chance that Curran was making very sound sense, and that he was simply too thickheaded to grasp it.

But Curran sighed, with a squinting of his eyes and a dropping of his head. "I think what I mean is that it's to be a fair test. He doesn't try to get around the Levels. You may find it useful to hang on to that while you're with him. I think that he's an honest man. Fair-minded."

Maybe he did understand what was going on in Curran's head after all. Curran had been here before. "What was of help to you, when it was your turn? Or it could be that you don't care to speak of it." Curran was uncomfortable, St. Clare was sure of that much. For all he knew, it was in as bad taste to ask about Curran's duty as prisoner-surrogate as it was to press your fellows for the details of their Bonds.

Shifting his weight a little, Curran leaned up against the wall once more. "My Student wasn't very good. It was a hard exercise, because he kept on making mistakes and had to do things over again to satisfy his need for a good demonstration."

Still, it didn't seem to be thinking about his own experience that was making Curran itchy. Something else, maybe. Maybe Curran was just an itchy sort of a man in general.

Itchy or not, Curran was still talking. "With Koscuisko you aren't going to have that problem. He pays attention to getting things right once through. That's an advantage. Just . . . try to remember . . . you can't afford to let down your guard. Not for an instant."

St. Clare thought he understood now. Curran was worried. And Curran didn't want for it to show, since he'd know that St. Clare was worried enough already, and it was bad luck.

"We've had a bit of training," he reminded the Emandisan by way of reassurance. "They try to teach us concentration. It may help out, did it you?" As long as Curran was willing to talk St. Clare was eager to enrich his flock as aggressively as possible.

"Was all I had to go on, in the end. There's a lot of emphasis on . . . focused concentration, among my homefolk." Well, and what little St. Clare had heard about Emandisan focused on fanatic devotion to martial arts. Religious veneration of their five-knives, with litanies and rites and oracles. Maybe Curran had just snagged himself on the fact that Nurail were characterized by weaves and drinkable, instead of strength of will.

Drinkable could create a state of intense concentration, that was true.

But concentration on getting more drinkable—or knocking one's neighbor's head in, or crawling into a corner to die of the body wrack—was probably not what Curran had in mind.

The room had begun to clear out a bit; it was getting to be time for Curran to leave, then. St. Clare stood up, to allow for a graceful departure. "Thanks for your help," he said, as Curran rose in turn. "I'm sure to be grateful to you for it in the morning." Such as it was. What did he know now about Andrej Koscuisko that he hadn't known before? He didn't see where honesty and fair-mindedness came into it at all.

"It'll be rough." Curran acknowledged St. Clare's thanks with a nod of acceptance. "But you'll make it through just fine. I'm confident of that."

Possibly the rumors about Emandisan self-discipline were true, and Curran was a stalloy-strong rock of unshakable will. Unfortunately he was not a very good liar.

"Until the Day, Joslire Curran."

Giving St. Clare's shoulder a reassuring shake, Curran completed the formula.

"The Day will come. Good luck." He smiled, once—it was rather alarming—and went out of the room, leaving St. Clare to sit back down and digest the whole thing.

A fair test, Curran had said. By clear inference, Curran's had not been, and that was why Curran was a little anxious. Doing a little projecting, it could be, reliving his own exercise in his mind as St. Clare prepared himself to meet the challenge.

But what if Curran was right, to be concerned?

Did Curran think there was a chance that he might fail in his duty?

Out of the question. Curran himself clearly had not wanted to make any such suggestion. And they'd know soon enough how it was going to go, either way.

He could not afford to begin to think about his sister.

Andrej Koscuisko had been up all night, and was beginning to feel the effects of the liquor that had kept him company. The easy availability of seemingly endless quantities of alcohol still surprised him, though he was grateful for the apparently limitless access to his drug of choice that was provided. As long as he was capable of asking questions and hitting people who couldn't hit back, it seemed the Administration didn't really care if he did so staggering drunk.

Staggering he was, if no longer quite incapacitated. The fragrance of the rhyti in the jug was not acceptable to his stomach just at the moment. The Security troop handed him his glass with a respectful bow, so Andrej accepted it to be polite; but he found he could only manage a deep inhalation of the steam before handing it back un-sipped. No, it simply was not a good time for rhyti.

Out of an all-night drunk came clarity of a sort. He was here; there was nothing he hadn't tried to avoid it—with the exception of a pretense at suicidal depression, and he was not inclined to be such a coward as that. As long as he was here, there was little profit in agonizing over it, because agonizing wouldn't get him out any more quickly than making up his mind to get it over with.

The instruments appropriate to the Fourth Level had been laid out for his use and consideration, and he let his eyes rest on the instrument table while he beckoned for his rhyti to come back. Surely instruments were simply instruments, and not evil in and of themselves? A thin supple stick covered with leather, something rather like the riding crops he'd carried while riding out to hunt—more for tradition's sake than anything else, the hunters in his father's stable being notoriously bloodthirsty themselves and needing no urging to the chase. A coiled whip with a weighted butt; a handful of screws and clamps; some knives as thin as needles; and a stouter stick almost like a cudgel. These were instruments of Inquiry and Confirmation, and whether or not he could imagine himself actually picking one of them up and using it, the fact remained that he would not be permitted to leave the theater until he had at least made a beginning.

The rhyti settled rather more successfully in his stomach this time. His prisoner was ready for him, he heard the signal; with a casual gesture that he expected would fool no one, Andrej waved the Security to their posts.

Very well; let it begin.

"Step through."

Tall, again, the prisoner was rather tall. That wasn't unusual from Andrej's point of view, since he himself was to the short side of the

Jurisdiction Standard. Tall and younger than the other prisoners had been—Andrej had expected as much from the Prisoner's Brief Joslire brought him last night. Joslire had seemed distracted. Andrej hadn't paid much attention at the time—he'd been concentrating on getting drunk—but now he wondered what had been on Joslire's mind.

"State your name. Your identification." He sounded decidedly cross to himself; it startled him to realize how drunk he still was. Just as well. The last thing he wanted to be right now was fully aware of his surroundings.

He did have to pay some attention to what he was doing, that went without saying. Just now, for example, he was almost certain that he'd asked a question, but as far as he could remember, he'd heard no response.

He frowned.

"State your identification, and the crime of which you have been accused. For which you have been arrested," he amended hastily. At the Preliminary Levels it was the crime of which one had been accused. At the Intermediate Levels it was the crime for which one had been arrested, and never without good and convincing reason, which was why the confession was so important. To validate the Judicial order. Because they never would have arrested this sullen young Nurail hominid if they hadn't had excellent reason—eyewitness testimony or a preponderance of circumstantial evidence.

No answer?

Andrej focused his attention on the prisoner's face. He had to look up to do it, and the lights in the ceiling seemed bright for whatever reason; so he gestured with his hand, and the Security behind his prisoner brought the man down to a more reasonable kneeling level. Where Andrej didn't have to squint at him. Where the mixture of amusement, contempt, and defiance on his clean-shaven face could be analyzed in detail. Clean-shaven: so he wasn't married. For what that was worth.

"Do you know how to speak Standard, or are you just being coy with me?" Andrej asked, watching the man's eyes for his answer. Yes, the prisoner understood well enough. "Then we have a tiresome problem to resolve, here, just as we are getting started."

If he turned his head, he could examine his instruments once again. He didn't like to brood on them; but he'd learned the use of other tools on Mayon, and there was no sense in blaming the tumor on the knife, surely. He knew precisely what each one was for. Their use and application had been demonstrated during the preparatory briefings. He just couldn't imagine himself touching any of them of his own free will.

"You know why you are here, and I know why you are here. We both know that the Bench requires a confession." Because the Bench prohibited itself from adjudging deterrent punishment unless guilt had been freely admitted, and would concede only so far as to accept a confession that had been somewhat assisted—but no further. "I could sit here and talk to myself, but that would only waste your time and make me look ridiculous in front of these amiable gentlemen. And nobody likes to be made a fool of. Be so kind as to state your identification and the crime for which you have been arrested."

To which you must confess. That was the first requirement; Tutor Chonis had been very clear. *We don't mind hearing what else the prisoner may wish to tell us, Student Koscuisko. But we never lose sight of our objective, and that is the confession as accused.*

But the prisoner only stared at him, smirking. Andrej wondered where he found the nerve; on the other hand—he reminded himself—being confronted by a half-drunk Student Inquisitor still only learning his craft was perhaps not the most intimidating experience to be imagined.

Andrej stood up.

"Have it your own way, then." He knew perfectly well what the prisoner's name was. That wasn't the point. The point was that it was in poor taste to take information as granted before the prisoner had confessed to it. And also that included among other pertinent details in the Prisoner's Brief was the identification of gene pool and subspecies ethnicity, and there was something about Nurail he'd been curious about in school. "Gentlemen, will you undress this mute for me, please? To the waist will be sufficient. For now."

The walleyed alarm on the man's face was almost funny in light of how Andrej felt about what he was expected to do. There was no sense in getting alarmed just yet, although the prisoner could not know it. For all his resolve, Andrej still did not have the first idea how he was going manage to apply one of those ugly implements forcefully enough to draw blood, and not just nervous giggles.

There was some scuffling involved in the stripping process, it seemed. But it was brief enough; and when it was done, the Security had returned his subject to the kneeling position, the only discernible differences being anger and frustration as well as contempt on the prisoner's face and rather less clothing on the prisoner's body. Andrej stood up and beckoned for more rhyti. He was beginning to get hungry. That was bad news; it meant he was sobering up.

"Let's talk about the crozer-hinge." If the prisoner didn't want to make conversation he'd have to try and interest the Security. "Peculiar to the Nurail, usually confined to the male of the race; vital to the deployment of the famous crozer-lances. Specifically, a sort of a biological fulcrum, and a little more wicked than most." Or, rather, an odd arrangement in the shoulder joint, beneath the shoulder cap. Andrej had found it a fascinating study in anatomy, but he'd not been able to convince the lone Nurail in his class at Mayon to let him do any hands-on exploration. Not surprising, really, because the crozer-hinge was vulnerable to dislocation from one specific angle, and joints when out of joint were almost always intensely painful—no matter what the class of hominid, no matter what the species of animal.

He was expected to hurt the Nurail. He was required to. If he made a test of the crozer-hinge it would hurt the Nurail badly, and still not harm him to any permanent degree. If he could persuade the prisoner to cooperate in that way, it might smooth the course of the exercise for him. Andrej took half a glass of rhyti and handed the remainder back. It was handy having the extra Security present. It was supposed to be intimidating. Andrej stepped closer to the Nurail, choosing a shoulder.

"It's one of those structural oddities that complicate our lives. You can put eight and eighty units of pressure against the joint from this angle, and it has no effect whatever." At least the prisoner had the basic decency to begin to look worried. It was about time. Andrej didn't care how drunk he seemed to be, he knew his anatomy.

"And on the other hand the wrong degree of torque from the back angle can tear the whole thing out of alignment."

It needed two fingers at the inside joint, a little help from Security to rotate the elbow in the right direction. Or the wrong direction: The crozer-hinge popped out of the protective hollow of the shoulder, a large white lump of cartilage and bone deforming the skin of the upper arm like a very large and exquisitely unpleasant bird's-egg bruise on one's head.

The Nurail's body jerked with the shock of the pain, his face gone white with it. Andrej stared at the Nurail, frowning. There was something peculiar about the unwilling contortion of the prisoner's body, his muscles tensed in pain; what was going on? "Abstract knowledge is never wasted, my friend. One has so few opportunities to examine such a complex jointure. Feel free to speak up if you should find yourself with anything to say."

No answer; only a stifled sort of gasping as the Nurail's body convulsed with pain. Skeletal pain in itself was usually a referred phenomenon, but there was no brighter or more brilliant sort of pain than that associated with the joints, especially the smaller ones. Watching his prisoner writhe against the constraining hands of the Security, Andrej found himself keenly apprehensive of the pain the Nurail suffered from his shoulder. Suffering was noxious stimulus. He had spent long years in school on Mayon learning how best suffering could be relieved. But the prisoner did have to talk to him. Any of the instruments that the Administration expected he employ would cause more gross physical damage, so this was a conservative approach— although the prisoner could not be expected to appreciate that. And he could put it right in a moment, once the prisoner had surrendered up his name.

The prisoner wasn't talking.

Andrej backed up to the chair that stood ready for him. Motioning for the Security to bring his prisoner forward to kneel close in front of him, Andrej sat down, fascinated by the struggle on the Nurail's face. The choking sound of the Nurail's breathing and the clear cold sweat of pain running down his cheeks was giving Andrej a very peculiar feeling in his stomach.

"Your name."

He was supposed to be after information, not so interested in his prisoner's evident agony. Andrej took the Nurail by the jaw to angle his face up to the bright lights in the ceiling. The Nurail's lips had gone white, and there was a stuttering sound as though his teeth were chattering; but the jaw was clenched so tightly Andrej could not imagine any teeth chattering. Intense. Yes. That was what it was. Intense.

"Tell to me your name."

No answer.

Andrej couldn't have that.

What could this miserable Nurail mean by defying him in this manner?

He was tempted to make the prisoner suffer for his stubbornness.

Loosening his grip on the Nurail's jaw, Andrej struggled with an unnamed temptation for a bitter eternity during the time it took to draw a breath and let it out once more. He felt his irritation as a physical sensation, a flush of humiliation and resentment that reddened his face and prickled his skin from head to toe.

"You, there, be so good as to take his head. How are you called, Mister . . . ?"

He wanted to be able to watch the Nurail's face carefully for his reactions, and for that he would need help. The troop at the Nurail's right bowed as best he could while holding to the shivering body of the prisoner.

"Curran, if the officer please—Sorlie Curran," the Security troop added quickly, in evident response to the confusion Andrej felt. Curran? But yes. The Curran Detention Facility was where Joslire had been condemned to the Bond. Any bond-involuntary similarly processed through the Curran Detention Facility would bear the name.

Andrej was reluctant to call him Curran, though.

"Sorlie, then. Keep his face well lifted; I want to be able to look at him." Oddly enough the flush of irritation he'd experienced had not faded away but settled on him somehow, making his extremities tingle not unpleasantly. His hands. His lips. His . . .

The Nurail's eyes were tightly shut, his body trembling. Andrej reached out to touch the taut skin across the displaced hinge, delicately. The instant his fingertips made contact, though, the prisoner cried out closemouthed with a high keening note that seemed to find a sympathetic echo of some sort in Andrej's belly. Or perhaps not his belly, perhaps it was his fish that was responding to that cry, thickening with involuntary interest . . .

Oh, what was it, what was happening to him?

He wanted more.

Laying his hand over the Nurail's shoulder with deliberate pressure,

Andrej cupped the deformation of the hinge beneath his palm. The Nurail's whimpers of reluctant pain felt like the caress of a lover's hand to Andrej, arousing him with lust for more of the same music.

He moved his fingers delicately, warming his palm on the heat of the skin, testing the boundaries of that heat with a mild disinterested pressure of his hand.

It almost seemed too soon before the Nurail found words and spoke at last.

"My—name—is—Rab. Luss—man." Rabirt Lussman, yes. Meant something like Rab-the-small-herbivore-snarer, if Andrej remembered anything of Ingles Chapnier's dialect aright. "—I—am—accused—of—"

Almost abstractedly, almost dispassionately, Andrej stroked the Nurail's shoulder as he waited for the man to finish his statement, massaging the inflamed skin over the joint between his thumb and forefinger.

"...—of—will. Of. Willful. Destruc. Tion. Jurisdict—ion prop. Erty. Pl. Pl. Please."

Then in a sickening instant of insight Andrej realized what was happening to his body.

Quite suddenly Andrej understood that the Nurail's suffering had aroused him; and the uncertain sensation in his belly twisted into a spasm of ferocious nausea. Spurning his prisoner's body to one side with a savage gesture of rejection, Andrej pushed himself out of the chair and turned his back, unable to find his balance in time to avoid falling to his knees on the hard cold decking.

Sick to his stomach.

He tasted the fluid in his mouth and knew that he was going to vomit in revulsion; but the sensation could not be denied. His fish strained eagerly against the fabric of his trousers as though the Nurail's pain were the most enticing ocean his fish had ever dreamed of in which to disport itself. Eager to get out. Passionate for more pain.

"The officer is unwell?"

Security, careful and reserved, beside him. He could not spew what little he had in his stomach out onto the floor. Such a thing would be disgraceful. Drunk. Yes. Drunk, that was it, he would pretend that he was only drunk, and not so horrified at what he thought he felt that his very vitals rose in protest against the sinful desire that had come on him so suddenly, so strongly. Drunk. Yes. That would do the trick, very well.

He had to set the Nurail's shoulder straight.

"Your pardon, gentlemen, a surfeit of wodac merely." He could hardly choke the words out, and the strained high pitch of his own voice was nothing he would have recognized as his. They would know he lied. One of them helped him up onto his feet, and for a moment Andrej stood where he was and eyed the door at the far end of the theater longingly. He could just leave . . .

Yes, and go where?

He could just leave, but if he did, he would only have to do this over again, and in the meantime the prisoner suffered from a dislocated shoulder, and for no good or necessary reason.

Reluctantly Andrej turned back to his task.

The trick with the crozer-hinge was working all too well. Rab Lussman knelt constrained and suffering, waiting for painease. Swallowing hard, Andrej approached his prisoner; it had to be done soon, or the Nurail was going to lose consciousness. Could he touch Lussman's body, and not be disgraced by his own? Two hands on Lussman's shoulder, the dislocated joint hot and swollen beneath his hands. Andrej readied himself for what was to come, half-breathless with the conflict between abject horror and frank shameless lust.

Soon; and cleanly—

With his fingers tight against the shoulder and his two thumbs pressed against the ball of the joint, Andrej forced the crozer-hinge back under the cap of the shoulder blade into the shoulder-joint, where it belonged. The Nurail shouted aloud with the ferocious shock of it, his body convulsing against the Security who restrained him, his feet kicking out from underneath him in spasms of uncoordinated protest at the pain.

Andrej fell back heavily into his chair in turn, staring hungrily at his prisoner, savoring the tense drawn lines of agony on Lussman's face.

Oh, yes, his body said to him, as clearly as if flesh could speak high Aznir.

Oh, yes, indeed.

His prisoner, living flesh, subject to his will, and all in lawful support of the Judicial order. Why—Andrej asked himself—had he been afraid that it would be difficult?

Or had he in fact been afraid that it was going to be this easy, all along?

His father had been right to send him here, and he had known from the beginning how wrong it had been for him to try to resist his father's will. He had been misguided and mistaken, and he could have had this pleasure all along, because it was all his for the taking. Lussman had to confess. It was up to him to see that Lussman confessed, and in good form, and convincingly.

He had weeks of lost time to make up for.

Saints, Saints, Saints under Canopy, what was he thinking of? How could he even imagine he was to torture an unarmed man, naked and in the presence of his enemies, and find joy in such savagery?

Andrej swallowed back the bitterness in his mouth, almost scornful of his own weakness—his pity, and his shame under the influence of the passion that overwhelmed him.

There was no need to appeal to the imagination.

As real as Lussman's pain, as real as agony, as real as blood—that was as real and sharp and quick as the delight that he felt in it.

Wasted time.

And no time like the present to claim his native right and enter into his ancestral place. The Church had tried to teach him: sin merited suffering in atonement. His teachers on Mayon had taught him differently, that suffering was to be avoided and alleviated by every possible means a man could find at his disposal; and he had believed them. He had swallowed the alien philosophy as though it could nourish him throughout all his long years in school.

He was sick to his stomach with the poison of the alien creed.

He was thirsty, hungry, starved for the sweet sound of pain in Lussman's voice, famished for the pleasure that he had in Lussman's fear of him, desperate with ferocious need for Lussman's helpless pain to feed upon and pleasure him.

All of those years.

How could he have been so blind to the simple truth?

And what could be more true than honest pain, and the brilliant scintillating sweetness of strict torment?

Rab Lussman half-lay against the Security troops behind him, with his face turned up to the light and his mouth trembling. Andrej rejoiced to see the signs of awareness returning to the man; because he had plans. And each new concept of atrocity was more beguiling than the last had been.

"Lussman," Andrej said.

The Nurail's head rolled restlessly against Sorlie Curran's steadfast grip, but he said nothing.

Rising unsteadily to his feet, Andrej took a whip up from the array that lay ready on the table for his use. A short, stout black-oiled whip with a heavy butt, the weight of it was welcome to his hand, and every fiber of his being seemed to strain to the utmost in anticipation, eager to be gratified.

"Come now, we were discussing." He was not going to vomit and flee. He was going to complete his exercise. And he was going to enjoy it. "Truly I must insist you pay attention, Lussman, answer as I bid you, or I will suspect that you are not listening to me. Yes?"

No answer.

Andrej wrapped the striking length of the whip around his fist so that the weighted butt swung free at a short drop. He took the measure of his distance and gauged the angle of approach, eager to test his grasp of the Judicial process against the shaking body of his prisoner.

"Your name. And the crime for which you were arrested. Answer to me 'yes, your Excellency,' else we will have to talk about your manners. Yes?"

Perhaps Lussman was simply a little dazed.

The best thing for that would be a sudden shock, to bring him out of it. Andrej swung the cudgel-butt of the whip in a wide, high arc and down across the Nurail's injured shoulder. He liked the sharp and stifled sound of the Nurail's cry of pain, the certain knowledge of his own absolute control over the next few measures of his prisoner's life. There was no sense in lying to himself, not now, not since he finally understood what he had been trying to hide from himself for all those wasted years.

"N-no, if it p-p-pl—"

Lussman started to speak but stopped himself, swallowing his words before Andrej could guess where he had been going with them. Andrej waited. He could afford to allow Lussman a few moments in which to collect himself.

"That is . . . I mean . . . your Excellency. Rab Lussman. Falsely accused. Your Excellency. S-sir."

Had he asked for an evaluation of the Charges? He had not. He had only asked what the Charges were.

He was all but compelled by this cogent fact to strike Lussman in order that the Nurail would gain from instruction, learning how a man would be well advised to conduct himself in the presence of an Inquiring officer.

He unwrapped the cruel thin length of the whip's lash from around his fist and took the cudgel-butt into his hand instead, striking Lussman across the face with the doubled lash so hard that the blood came in the furrow of the welt it raised in passage.

He was Andrej Koscuisko, before the Holy Mother, before all Saints under Canopy.

He was Andrej Koscuisko, Surgeon and Inquisitor, and when he left this place he would carry the Writ to Inquire, and uphold the Judicial order by its lawful exercise.

He was Andrej Ulexeievitch Koscuisko.

And he was come into his dominion now at last.

CHAPTER FIVE

Joslire Curran stood in his place behind Tutor Chonis's chair, dividing his dismayed attention between listening to the Tutor and watching Student Koscuisko. The Record was off-line; Tutor Chonis had apparently made all the official comments he felt might be appropriate. Now there was only Chonis's musing, half to himself, half for their benefit, watching the two exercises.

"I think I like that hook for the present," Student Koscuisko was saying. "Gentlemen, if you please. Yes, both arms, and perhaps you could contrive to see his left shoulder is to bear the most part of his weight."

He'd told Robert St. Clare that Koscuisko was a fair-minded man, and would only hurt him enough. Something had gone wrong from the beginning of this exercise, however. Because the pressure that Koscuisko brought to bear on his prisoner-surrogate had been more intense than any Fourth Level Student exercise Joslire had ever seen.

"Willful destruction of Bench property is a species of treason, friend Rab, we must have details in order to measure out the penalty. I cannot say that you have been very forthcoming. One would almost think you did not feel remorse for what you have done."

Koscuisko had not exceeded the Protocols, so in that specifically limited sense Koscuisko had in fact hurt Robert only "enough." But there was no trace of fair-mindedness in his Student's behavior.

Koscuisko was clearly enjoying the brutal tricks he had contrived to play on his prisoner. There was a confusing dislocation between the officer Joslire had believed Koscuisko to be and the mocking torturer that he'd been watching for these few hours past. Something was happening to Student Koscuisko, and Joslire did not quite understand what it was; but he was certain that he didn't like it.

"Once again, from the beginning. I am heartily sick of your refusal to acknowledge your whip-worthiness, there is Evidence enough to convict you a liar. You are not doing yourself any favors by withholding."

There had been Students who had liked pain, his pain, their prisoner's pain, any pain they could get, always excluding their own. There had been Students who had simply been indifferent to pain, or who had actively deplored the use of it. Koscuisko was not a man to be unmoved, from what little Joslire had learned of him. He reacted with genuine and innate compassion to the sufferings of the accused in the paradigm tapes. It made no sense for that resistance to have been superficial; Joslire had been completely convinced of the honesty of Koscuisko's empathic sympathy. But if Koscuisko's horror had been real—and this, this sharpening skill with whips and mockery was also convincing—it did not augur well for Student Koscuisko's future. For his sanity.

"Noycannir seems to have run out of options, Hanbor, wouldn't you say?"

Tutor Chonis's voice interrupted Joslire's brooding and brought him back into real time. The Tutor was being charitable, in Joslire's view; it seemed to him that Noycannir had lost control of her interrogation early on, when her "prisoner" had declined to even start to cooperate. Chonis had wanted to see how she'd handle it. Koscuisko had found a way to encourage Robert to surrender at least his false identification as a start. Noycannir had asked once or twice and then gone directly into beating her partner with the black-stick, apparently content to reproduce the paradigm tapes that she and Student Koscuisko alike had studied blow for blow.

Joslire knew which index-level tape that particular beating was on, having seen it with each of his previous Students.

It was a Fifth Level tape, preparation for the next exercise. She'd gotten her Protocols confused.

"Student Noycannir is apparently trying to pretend that her prisoner has not lost consciousness. She's unlikely to get anything more out of him today. Sir."

There was a perverse sort of professional pride on Orientation staff, a black-humored brand of "my Student is more efficiently cruel than your Student" running joke. Lop Hanbor sounded genuinely disgusted with Noycannir's overzealous approach, since she'd put her prisoner-surrogate out of the arena for a few hours. Joslire had felt that way before. Given that their Judicial function involved the methodical application of pain, bond-involuntaries tended to evaluate Students based on their ability to use enough to satisfy the requirements and accomplish the task, but no more than that. It was precisely that prejudice that gave their function what little meaning it could be said to have. They were here to support the least-wasted-pain approach to Inquiry.

"Well, we'll give her a minute to call the exercise. Wouldn't want to interrupt young Koscuisko. Speaking of whom—shall we have the sound, Curran?" Tutor Chonis asked, and it was not really a question, needless to say. Joslire didn't much care for the prospect, but perhaps Chonis only wanted to get a flavor of what Koscuisko was saying.

Lop did the honors, bringing up the sound from one exercise theater even as he muted the sound from the other.

Robert had been stretched from the ceiling, and since Student Koscuisko had specified it, Security had given his bad arm less slack so that most of Robert's weight was on it. Robert kept trying to stretch his other arm up to the anchor-bolt to grasp the hook and take some of the weight off of the injured joint. Koscuisko, however, wasn't having any of it; and Joslire suffered for the young Nurail.

"I can tell that this is going to take some practice," Koscuisko was saying. "For now I can only trust that my lack of craft does not offend you."

Robert was already off balance because of the unequal length of the chains that bound him. The impact of the whip was throwing his whole weight upon his injured shoulder, and Robert—it seemed—couldn't help but cry out against it.

"Your feedback will, of course, be critical to the success of this training exercise, although I fear I cannot promise you that it will remain confidential. Unless you would prefer to discuss some of the more interesting details of your crime. What was it, again? Willful destruction of Jurisdiction property?"

For all his disclaimers, Koscuisko had a natural talent of some sort; his eye-to-hand coordination was obviously more than adequate. Nor did he seem to be afraid to put a bit of muscle into the blows. Whether it was weals or blood there was no question but that Andrej Koscuisko was making his mark on Robert St. Clare.

Who could not catch his breath, tormented by the whip even as he was distracted by the pain in his shoulder. "I . . . won't."

They weren't picking up Robert's voice very well. Chonis frowned, gesturing for Lop to increase the directional on the plait. Even then it wasn't easy to figure out what Robert was saying. His breath came in fits and starts, his sentences chopped up into disjointed, fragmentary phrases almost devoid of meaning. "Can't. Won't. Risk. Not long enough for . . ."

Long enough? It didn't have to mean anything. But he should not have said "not long enough." Would Koscuisko pick up on the phrase?

"With respect, Tutor Chonis—"

Koscuisko had demonstrated his ability to take an appropriate tool and use it on his prisoner; and that was all that the Administration really required, at this juncture. Whatever else he might be demonstrating was beside the point.

Lop apparently had a more immediate problem. Student Noycannir had kicked her prisoner as he lay on the decking, in an apparent paroxysm of frustration at his failure to respond.

"With respect, sir, Student Noycannir has violated the restriction at the Fourth Level, request the Tutor call the exercise?"

Student Noycannir kicked her prisoner again, at the point of his jaw this time. Joslire recognized that maneuver from the index-Level tapes as well. On the index tape, the Student Inquisitor had indeed kicked a prisoner while he was down, and hard enough to bring blood to the victim's cheek.

Joslire knew that Tutor Chonis had temporarily forgotten about Noycannir, absorbed in watching Koscuisko. He'd been absorbed in watching Koscuisko, too, but he had a better excuse—not that he was going to hint that to Tutor Chonis, who took one look at the companion screen and smashed his fist against the emergency-call toggle.

"Administrative orders. All exercises to cease."

The signal went to both theaters, and Joslire watched his officer lift his head toward the talk-alert with a look of confused apprehension on his face.

"This is Tutor Chonis. I repeat. Administrative orders, all exercises to cease. Students will disengage at once." Toggling off-braid, Tutor Chonis pushed himself angrily out of his chair, swearing at himself and moving so quickly that he was halfway to the door before he'd finished his directions.

"Son of a cuckoo, useless excuse for a . . . Hanbor, come with me. Curran, shut down the monitors before you go and collect Koscuisko. Perdition take . . ."

There was a world of difference between kicking a prisoner's face and kicking him at the back of his head or up from underneath the point of his jaw. From the unnatural angle of the prisoner-surrogate's head as he lay, Student Noycannir's blow had compromised Idarec's spine—perhaps fatally so.

Alone in Observation, now, Joslire closed down the monitors and secured the tapes. Koscuisko would be expecting him.

Koscuisko was all he had to worry about.

Student Noycannir crouched down beside the prisoner where he lay, desperate to discover whether he was only trying to put a joke on her by feigned unconsciousness. The bastard couldn't be unconscious. She hadn't hit him that hard, didn't she know as well as anyone how hard you really had to hit before some thickheaded gravel-stamper finally lay down to be quiet?

The prisoner didn't move.

She could have shrieked in frustrated rage, but strangled the curses in her throat so fiercely she was sure only she had even heard the sound. He couldn't do this to her. He was pretending. She could deal with pretense, she knew how. Snatching the man's limp arm out to the farthest extent of its length on the floor she hammered the elbow joint with the heavy cudgel, once, two times, three times. Pain never failed to get a man's attention, it had never failed her before, but the prisoner did not respond. She could hit again, but she couldn't be sure that she was clear to damage the joint more severely at this Level. She didn't dare. If she should splinter bone, they would hold it against her as proof of her lack of fitness for the Writ.

Mergau stood up.

A man who lay silent and unmoving through such blows as she had given his elbow was not pretending.

If he was unconscious, how could she gain confession? Sudden mindless fury swamped her heart and mind and soul. This was unfair. They had no right. They had given her a weakling for a prisoner, a man so fragile he escaped to silence before he had so much as said his name. They would blame her for it. It wasn't her fault, it was their fault, their fault and his fault, the fault of the prisoner who mocked her where he lay in unresponsive stillness.

Be damned to all of them, she decided. *All of them be damned. Their tricks. Their superiority.*

"Get up." Snarling at the prisoner, Mergau did not bother trying to disguise her disgust, her contempt. Let them make of it what they liked. "I said get up, you pathetic coward." He didn't move, and by now she knew he wasn't going to. It made kicking him all the more satisfying, a good solid blow striking sharp against his ribs. When he woke up again, he would know she had meant to punish him. "Don't think I don't know exactly what you're trying to pull."

She kicked again, and at his head this time, to see if she could take a few of his teeth for souvenirs. She was beginning to feel better. As long as he was unconscious anyway, why shouldn't she?

There was a sharp click at the talk-alert, and suddenly Mergau wondered if she had overstepped somehow.

"All exercises to cease. Students will disengage at once."

Tutor Chonis's voice, and sounding very intent. What, there was a problem?

What had Koscuisko done?

Was it her imagination or were the prisoner's lips turning blue?

A mistake. She had made a mistake. Terror seized her bowels and bones, but Mergau dampened it sternly. She'd made a mistake, but the last thing she could afford to do was show it. Show weakness and there would be no mercy.

She knew what to do when she'd been caught doing something wrong. Her ability to project innocent nonchalance was part of her survival. Turning her back on the prisoner on the floor, Mergau set the truncheon back with the other instruments on the table, arranging them neatly. She would not have long to wait, she was sure.

Tutor Chonis's signal was almost welcome.

"Student Noycannir. You will return to quarters, instruction to be forthcoming." He was excited about something, but she—quite naturally—could have no idea what it was. Mergau schooled her face to a bland mask of mild, concerned confusion to overlay the turmoil in her heart. It didn't have to fool anybody. All it had to do was get her safely out of here.

Mergau bowed to her Tutor and left the theater, standing aside to let the medical team through as she passed.

She was glad to go to quarters.

She had to understand what had gone wrong.

But more than that, she had to decide how she was going to cover up for it.

"Administrative orders. All exercises to cease."

The sudden announcement startled Andrej. He lost his focus on the lash, stumbling clumsily to one side as he missed his prisoner entirely.

"This is Tutor Chonis. I repeat, administrative orders, all exercises to cease. Students will disengage at once."

Staring at the wall-monitor, he tried to understand Tutor Chonis. Disengage? How could they ask him to disengage when that meant he would have to leave his prisoner? Had he made an error in procedure? They'd been given instructions about command disengage, true. Under emergency circumstances the Tutor would call the exercise. No hints about what emergency it might be were forthcoming from the now silent wall-monitor; and after a moment, Andrej shook himself out of his paralysis of arrested movement.

He didn't want to disengage.

If he didn't disengage at the Tutor's instruction, they might make him wait before they gave him another prisoner, though. It wasn't worth the risk, regardless of how little he liked the idea.

What had Lussman been trying to say about risk?

"Very well, friend Rab." Folding the whip back upon itself, Andrej handed it off to one of the Security. The lash was heavy and dark with the prisoner's suffering; it had stained his hands with blood. He couldn't afford to stop and think about it. He wanted more. It would only make it more difficult for him to accept postponement of his pleasure. "Since I have failed to make myself understood thus far, perhaps we could revisit these issues in the morning." According to the Prisoner's Brief, the prisoner's offense was severe enough to warrant sequential invocation of the Fifth Level if he couldn't gain confession in the Fourth. He and Noycannir had been warned about such a possibility.

Was this an administrative trick of some sort?

Or had something gone wrong with Noycannir's exercise?

"Take him down, yes. No. One moment . . ."

The prisoner seemed scarcely conscious. Security would handle him roughly, if efficiently; and Andrej did not like the idea, somehow. He moved to stand in front of Lussman where he was bound, nodding his signal to Sorlie Curran. "If you will. Now."

Lussman cried out when his wrists were loosed from the anchor-bolt in the ceiling, falling heavily forward to his knees. Andrej braced himself against Lussman's weight with one hand at Lussman's side beneath the uninjured arm, catching the prisoner at the side of his neck with his other hand in an embrace which did the trick, howsoever awkwardly. Lussman did not fall over, and Lussman did not pass out, and Andrej stood and steadied the man for a moment so that he could regain his balance. He wasn't sure why he cared one way or the other. All Andrej could do was to hold Rab Lussman for now and hope to sort out his precise feelings about it all later.

"With respect, the officer need not concern himself, there is a requirement to return the prisoner to holding—"

"A moment," Andrej insisted, his thumb tucked across the base of the Nurail's throat. Joslire had arrived; Security would be wondering why he didn't leave. He'd been anxious enough to leave after the other exercises. "Give us a moment, he will return to himself, and he will be able to walk with you."

The pulse beneath his thumb was steadying and strengthening, but Security's evident confusion made Andrej apprehensive. They would probably be within their rights to insist on dragging Lussman off immediately. Andrej didn't want that. He wanted Lussman to find his center before they thought to suggest such a thing. If he moved his other hand to the base of the man's neck, he could perhaps find the right nerve bundle as it entered the spine.

There was an uneasiness and a shuffling of feet in the room as

Lussman stiffened suddenly. What, did they think that he was hurting the man, still? The exercise had been called. Andrej wasn't sure he even wanted to hurt Lussman now.

What had happened to him, that had fired him body and soul with pleasure in response to Lussman's pain?

It was the right nerve bundle, that was a plus; Lussman shook his head several times—as if to drain his ears of water—and started to rise clumsily to his feet.

"There, now. That is better." He continued to apply a steady pressure against the Nurail's spine as Lussman stood, dampening the noxious messages of pain from Lussman's shoulder. "If you care to go slowly with him, he can walk. Be careful with the shoulder, gentlemen, we are done for the moment."

High time he was out of here, because he had probably reached the limits of the interference he would be permitted. Since he was to be able to do nothing with or for Rab Lussman, it was best for his own peace of mind if he were to get away before something unfortunate should happen. "Thank you for your effort, gentlemen, and I will see you all in the morning, I suppose. Joslire, let's go."

All that he could do for his prisoner, he had done.

And now there was nothing left for him but to consider what he had done to Lussman, as well.

He left the exercise theater like a man walking in his sleep, responding to Joslire's polite directions without thinking about where Joslire was taking him. What had he done? How could he have enjoyed it? And, oh, how long would he be forced to wait until he could do it all again?

Quarters. That was where Joslire was taking him. That was a surprise. Swallowing hard, Andrej frowned at the time-mark on the screen of his study-set. Surely it was some eights yet to third-meal?

"What is this, Joslire, we are not to practice today? Not that I object." The idea of going to exercise was suddenly more attractive than it had ever been before. Andrej felt that he could profit from mindless and repetitive activity, something to distract his body and numb his mind with purely physical demands—something uncomplicated. Unambiguous. Safe.

"The Administration excuses the officer at the end of the practical exercises, now that the Preliminary Levels have been passed. If the officer please."

Joslire stood well away from him, eyes carefully lowered. Joslire watched his exercises—Joslire and Tutor Chonis alike. His shameful behavior was on Record.

Gradually the red haze of his passionate pleasure in Lussman's pain began to clear from the foreground of Andrej's mind to reveal the gaping chasm of horror that lay beneath it.

"Let me have a look at the next Level, then."

If he looked into the fathomless pit of his own heart, he would lose his balance and fall in. Andrej shuddered at the thought. He had to find something to hang on to, something he could use to steady himself. Review was unnecessary; they'd studied the protocol before this. But it would excuse his staring at the screen. He could take his supper early, go shut himself behind the thin barrier between his sleep-rack and Joslire before time. He was strangely exhausted, but the discomfort of his body would not permit him to wash and change into his sleep-shirt. Not just yet. Bad enough that they had watched him in exercise. That the residual signs of his flagging desire should betray him so obviously to Joslire was more than Andrej could accept.

It would take Joslire a moment to call up the correct packages. Andrej went into the washroom to clean the blood from his hands, struggling to understand. He couldn't begin to feel clean until he had changed his uniform. Catching a glimpse of his face in the reflector, Andrej stared at himself for a long measure, confused for a long moment about whose face that was, staring back at him with so much shock and distress. He would never be able to wash the stain of this away, no matter how he tried. Rab Lussman's blood had soaked clear through his flesh into his soul, and he was filthy with it. A prisoner, and he had tortured the man, and before the Canopy he had had such pleasure in it . . .

This was different in kind as well as in degree from the previous Levels. His challenge and his shame had been to simply do the distasteful thing. And today he had done the distasteful thing, and he had not minded it. He had accepted it, embraced it, submitted himself to it, and taken pleasure from pain as his reward. The message of his body was unequivocal. There was no mistaking the source of his newfound ability to strike a helpless prisoner, or the effect that it had. What had happened to him?

What door had he opened to what ancestral demon, in his desperation to find his way through this place?

Joslire had gone away from the study-set, probably seeing to some domestic chore. Andrej remembered at last to rinse his hands and shut the water-stream off. The instruction tape was loaded on-screen; Andrej found his way to his place and sat himself down heavily. The Fifth Level of the Question. A paradigmatic exercise, a prisoner naked and bloodied. A vise, a cudgel, the restraints at the wall and the pulley in the floor to stretch a man's joints from one another. The ragged sound of the Nurail's panting breath still sounded in Andrej's ear; he shivered with the memory, and knew that the source of the shudder was not horror or pity but something unacceptable. Something unthinkable, shameful, sinful.

Something powerful and passionate, basic and fundamental to his being, more intense than any explicitly sexual experiences had ever been . . .

Half-unwilling and half-greedy for renewed pleasure, Andrej watched the tape scroll forward. The image in the cube-viewer was as it had always been to him—horrible and pitiful. As long as he did not indulge in imagining trying these pleasures for himself—on the chained body of Rab Lussman, and tomorrow, a scant few hours from now—he felt no differently about those images than he had when he'd first seen them. It was an abomination under the Canopy of Heaven to do such things to sentient creatures, whether or not the Church agreed with him. Therefore, necessarily, he was an abomination, regardless of any pretensions he had cherished in his life to decency or morality. Andrej's moral conviction was unchanged by the epiphany he had experienced, as profound and absolute as anything in his life.

The rule of Law was no excuse for torture.

He could not do these things.

How could he hope to live with the shame, now that he knew he had an appetite for pain?

He would make a stand. He would refuse the duty; he would take vows and go to cloister. The Church would deny him if his father turned his back, but the Church would have to take him in if he repudiated his name and elected the Malcontent. The Church could not deny a man who chose to elect the Malcontent. He could forget that he had ever been Koscuisko, and take sanctuary. Then at least no one would ask him to strike a prisoner, or tempt him with the seductive promise of the sound of agony.

Nor would he have a chance to help, to heal; no chance at all to try to right the balance and atone for what he was to do. And prisoners would still suffer torture, and they would still die, whether or not he was there to delight in their anguish. So what good would it do him to seek sanctuary, when he took the longer view? He would be able to escape self-censure for crimes committed against feeling creatures, whether or not Church and Bench and Fleet pretended to believe that Judicial torture was no crime.

But he could never put himself behind him. Nothing he could do would ever change what had passed with him today. He had sucked the pain from Lussman's captive body and feasted greedily upon a man's torment. All that he could gain from running away, now that he knew this about himself, would be the thinnest veneer of self-respect; and in return, he would have to forswear forever any potential chance he might have in the future to do a bit of good within the work to which he was to be condemned.

He could never hope to run away from himself.

Hadn't the Holy Mother known from the beginning what she had done, when she had shaped him?

What was he to make of himself?

If he closed his eyes and summoned up the image of the Nurail, his prisoner, with an elbow locked in the vise or a hand bloodied with the fingernails split . . .

Andrej searched the confused landscape of his inner state with anxious care. He had to know. He could not afford to deceive himself, to conceal his own truth from himself. Forcing himself to dwell on details both remembered and imagined, he sought to grasp what it might be within him that had felt so differently about it all during the exercise; and he took a measure of bleak comfort from the fact that it did not delight him now to muse on what had beguiled him so keenly less than two measures gone.

There was no question that he had taken intense pleasure in the work.

But now that he was away from it, his body only remembered its pleasure with a dim, muffled echo of that same delight. He found he took no new satisfaction either from memory or in anticipation of the morning.

"What am I, to have done such a thing?"

He asked the question of the air in a hoarse despairing whisper, his eyes closed in anguished concentration and wonder. To take sexual pleasure from the pain of others had surely never been hinted at in his psychological profiles, else he would have heard of it by now. There was an urgent clinical need for people who were capable of such a response, people whose own psychology enabled them to support the treatment of those whose pain was so extreme and so intransigent that no others could so much as abide in its presence. Some of his trauma studies had left him with horrific nightmares . . . On Mayon there had been no pleasure associated with pain for him. If there had been, he would have noticed.

And had he not noticed, his teachers would have done.

"The Student has successfully completed an entirely adequate Fourth Level exercise," Joslire said.

Rapt in his own horrified thoughts as he was, it took Andrej a moment to grasp Curran's meaning, and a moment longer yet to understand why Joslire had spoken at all. He'd asked a question, yes, that was right. He simply hadn't expected any answers.

"Oh, not just that. Surely not. I was on fire with my lust to make him suffer, Joslire, and I never knew that I could take any pleasure in rank cruelty, never mind such potent pleasure as I had in him . . ."

Of course he had been cruel to the Mizucash and the Bigelblu and the Onymsho, in the Preliminary Levels. But he'd had to force himself to execute the Protocols. And he had not enjoyed any of it.

"The officer is respectfully requested to remember that the exercise was technically well performed. There was no violation."

And everything he said would be Recorded, here in quarters as in exercise theater.

"The Levels are profoundly flawed, Joslire, but that is not your fault." He didn't stop to wonder at the phrase until it was out of him and could not be called back. What did that mean, it wasn't Joslire's fault? Surely there was no reason to imply that the point could ever even be in question. It did no good to try to talk to Joslire. It was unfair of him to impose on the man. Andrej reached for something he could safely say to Joslire, something that might communicate his dread in terms that the Administration could not fault him for.

"I mean that he has already had enough pain for the Level, and a beating on top of that. By rights we should accept the man's denial, and send him off." Still, what did rights mean, for a prisoner? He knew the answer to that one well enough. He didn't like it any better for that.

"Respectfully request permission. To offer a comment, at the officer's pleasure." Joslire was standing at command-wait by his sleep-rack, looking straight ahead. He would have assumed the required position of respectful attention as soon as Andrej had spoken; but Andrej only noticed it now.

"Please. You don't speak to me often, Joslire, and I am grateful for your assistance." In fact Andrej could not remember Joslire ever asking to be allowed to make a comment. Joslire had been watching him, Joslire knew . . .

"Sir. The Student will know from his education that thinking creatures are capable of responding to a wide variety of stimuli. With all due respect, the Student is encouraged to consult his own knowledge concerning accommodations reached by the intelligent or sentient mind under high-stress conditions. Sir."

For a moment the absurdity of the situation overrode the confused welter in Andrej's mind with a sharp sense of how ridiculous it all was. "Joslire, are you trying to teach me psychology?"

No. Wrong. It was not a good thing to say to a bond-involuntary; Andrej knew it immediately from the subtle but perceptible stiffening of Joslire's body at the implicit rebuke.

"If the officer permit. The orientation of Staff Security includes exposure to a range of concepts that may be of assistance to Students of assignment during apparent crisis. Any misapplication is to be set against the troop's own failure to judge the officer's meaning correctly. If there has been a mistake, the troop in question may profit from correction."

Joslire's voice was clear and strong and utterly devoid of any emotion. Andrej pushed himself away from the study-set, burying his face in his hands in a convulsion of distress. Correction meant discipline, and discipline was punishment. Andrej tried to put Joslire in the Nurail's place in his mind's eye, bitterly fearful of the test. Joslire, with a livid whip-stroke full across his dark intense face. Joslire, breathing in great gasping sobs between clenched teeth, his body wracked beneath the impact of the whip. Joslire, screaming, that hoarse high sound that had so moved Andrej when he'd first heard it from Rab Lussman.

He could see the image clearly enough, and it did not please him.

As much as he had wanted to hear his Nurail cry, that much and more he did not want to torment Joslire Curran.

"Holy Mother. I would to all Saints you could ever be at ease with me, Joslire. Only error is to be corrected. Not a mistake. Still less the truth, no matter how ill-received it may be."

The accommodation of a sentient mind to unreasonable stress, a psychological trick played by himself on himself to make it possible for him to perform his task? No, what he remembered had been much too intense and immediate for that, and he dreaded the possibility that it might happen again next time. The body learned more quickly than the mind, and in direct proportion to the intensity of the sensation. It would be difficult not to become addicted.

Surely it would be easier for him to allow himself to become addicted, and let the perverted appetite of his mind and heart work to help him through . . .

Andrej had not bidden Joslire to stand down or released him from his position; and yet Joslire stepped up close to Andrej, kneeling down with a species of formal grace to rest with one knee flat to the floor just to one side of where Andrej was sitting on the edge of the seat. He was so close to Andrej that Andrej could feel his body's heat, and Emandisan were usually on the lower side of the Jurisdiction Standard for normal temperature. Andrej wondered at the man's intimacy.

"The officer is under a great deal of pressure," Joslire murmured, his voice low, his eyes on Andrej's boots. "There has been no exercise, no release for physical tension. Perhaps the officer would care for an alternate means of relaxation."

Sweet Saints.

Joslire was propositioning him.

Not only that, but something in his belly looked on Joslire where he knelt and saw a prisoner, and joyfully embraced the concept of abusing him.

Andrej fought with an instinct to strike Curran, to punish him for even suggesting that he was so depraved as that. There was no reason for Joslire to know that his offer presupposed two kinds of sin, two out of the three most deeply damning sins in the entire Book. This was just another one of the things that Joslire was required to do, to say, when the situation presented itself. That was all.

"Yes, Joslire, I would like somewhat by way of relaxation. You're quite right." A man was forbidden to accept such courtesies. It was an affront to the Holy Mother. And quite apart from that, the last thing he wanted to do, here and now, was misuse the man, regardless of the things the Tutors made Joslire say, regardless of the treachery of his own body. "Wodac, in fact. I think I'll have my supper early."

A man was not to take pleasure from the flesh of children, either. Children were sacred to the Mother of all Aznir; and by extension, servants were not to be exploited for personal satisfaction, since—like children—they were not in a position to refuse to grant their compliance. Andrej carried Joslire's Bond. He was responsible to the Bench for Joslire's best interest. To serve Joslire's "best interest" by gratifying the undiscriminating appetites of his own body at Joslire's expense would be betrayal of a trust that was sacred to Andrej, no matter how little protection the Bench extended to its bond-slaves.

Joslire hadn't moved. "The officer will of course be provided with the wodac, but wodac inhibits rather than releases." Joslire's voice communicated only promise, no argument. If he sat here for a single breath the more, he was going to take the implied offer greedily. He could not bear the thought of such a thing. Andrej pushed himself out of the chair with an effort and put several paces of safe distance between himself and Joslire before trusting himself to speak.

"Wodac." His voice sounded harsh and angry to Andrej, but he wasn't angry at Joslire. How could he pretend to experience moral outrage after what he had found out about himself today? "Thank you, Joslire, your offer is most charitably presented. But what I want is wodac. Nothing more. I do not wish to hear any such proposal from you again, please mark my will in this."

The passion he had learned today was his problem.

Andrej had no intention of burdening anyone else with it.

She was careful to keep her pace measured and deliberate as she returned to quarters with her slave. Nothing was wrong, after all. She had done nothing.

And she held carefully and grimly to that pretense until she was safely arrived, and the door closed behind her; then she could control her rage no longer.

"Face to the wall, slave!"

Pivoting on her heel, she shouted up into Hanbor's startled face, furious with him for being where he was, furious with him for having witnessed her lapse in Observation, furious with the entire Administration for making her feel the way she did.

Hanbor's expression of surprise iced over almost immediately into a safe and inoffensive blank. Bowing, he turned to the wall crisply, standing to attention with his nose scant fractions from the featureless surface. Fine. He could face the wall. She was sick of being watched, all the time watched, every moment under observation.

There, that was better.

"Command-wait. Until I call for you."

Hanbor was Security. Let him demonstrate his discipline. She had to think.

Mergau undressed with short, sharp irritated gestures, tearing at the Fleet's Student uniform impatiently. She despised Fleet, she despised Fleet Orientation Station Medical, she despised the uniform.

She had to swallow it and manage this somehow. Washing herself with grim determination with the water-stream turned to icy cold, Mergau began to reconstruct the events that had led up to Chonis's intervention.

What had happened?

What would they say she had done?

She had done nothing she had not seen on instructional tape.

Belting the sleep-tunic from her closet around her waist, Mergau sat down at the study-set. She knew what she'd seen. She would find proof that she had made no errors.

She would be ready for them when Tutor Chonis came to blame her for whatever pretended error they could find in her conduct of the exercise.

"I ought to be sent back to Orientation processing for this one, Ligrose," Tutor Chonis commented grimly, watching the diagnostics. "Damned if that little Aznir didn't distract me." Not as if that was any excuse. On the one hand Koscuisko was interesting to watch from a professional point of view. The usual tension and uncertainties seemed to have a way of coming out in unexpected ways that surprised Tutor Chonis, even after so many years. And on the other hand, he should have terminated Noycannir's exercise at the point at which it had become obvious that Idarec was unconscious and liable to remain so.

No excuse.

A ruined exercise, and a ruined bond-involuntary, and Fleet didn't like losing bond-involuntaries. They were more and more difficult to come by these days. Fleet was not going to be impressed by the First Secretary's protégé, or by Chonis's handling of her, either.

"You're allowed." Ligrose Chaymalt was the Chief Medical Officer on Station, and the task of running an infirmary for a constant stream of practical exercises seemed to have hardened her over the years. Most of her patients were bond-involuntaries; Fleet valued their pain at somewhat less than the price of expensive medication. Perhaps it was natural that she'd come to value their lives somewhat less than Tutor Chonis felt she should. "You haven't had a suicide for, what, four Terms now? Nobody here can match that record. Security troops are still easier to find than Ship's Surgeons, after all. No offense, Harper."

The man's name was Hanbor. But he just bowed politely, no trace of having noticed the careless error on his face. It wasn't as if her accommodation was an unusual one; there was one Tutor who never bothered to learn their names at all, addressing all Security alike by an obscure ethnic term for "slave." Chonis had never quite decided if Tutor Heson cared that everybody knew very well what the word meant.

"Gross neurological. Hmm." Chonis was too far from the medical training of his youth to be confident that his interpretation of the statistics on Idarec was correct. "Your prognosis, Ligrose?"

She shut off the imager with a gesture of profound boredom. "Not worth the upkeep. You're not going to wake him up now, not after—how many times had she kicked him? You?"

Hanbor probably did know, but Chonis felt that it was in poor taste to ask him. "Too many times," Chonis answered for Hanbor, accordingly. "We could expel her right now, for gross violation of the Levels. Except that she's too ignorant to understand exactly what she did wrong."

Koscuisko could probably braid a man's bones into his own muscles and not step one half of a pace out of Protocol. Koscuisko probably knew how to kick a man in the head a dozen times and have him wake up with no worse than a headache. But Koscuisko had education, on top of what seemed to be revealing itself as a native, if latent, talent.

"Charge the loss back to her patron," Ligrose suggested. "What's another few hundred thousand Standard, after all the money he spent getting her here in the first place?"

Andrej Koscuisko.

The presence of a Student with genuinely respectable medical qualifications was unusual at Fleet Orientation Station Medical, where most of the Students had been drawn from the ranks of the mediocre. Graduates with good qualifications got jobs in clinics, hospitals, private practice; some went into Fleet as rated practitioners. Fleet Orientation Station Medical generally got what was left once the decent jobs had been filled by decently qualified candidates.

"You've met my other Student?" And then there was Koscuisko, who had graduated at the top of his rated field from the single most competitive surgical college under Jurisdiction.

"Koscuisko. Yes, you parked him here yesterday in the lab. Too bad he's not on staff, isn't it? Bet he could fix Idarec almost as good as new."

Ligrose wasn't totally brutalized by her demanding environment; she sounded almost wistful. But she was right, though he hadn't realized it in the first flush of his wonderful idea. Koscuisko could not be asked to treat Idarec. Koscuisko would know that the man was bond-involuntary the moment he scanned the nervous system and found the governor.

Koscuisko would wonder why a bond-involuntary had been injured severely in a way that would surely remind him of the paradigm tapes he and Noycannir had studied. And the use of bond-involuntaries as prisoner-surrogates for training exercises from the First through Fifth Levels was one of the single most sensitive secrets in all of Fleet Orientation Station Medical.

Well, it had been an idea.

"Maybe next time," Chonis offered, rising from his seat in Ligrose's office. "Hang on to Idarec for now, will you? No sense in terminating until we need the bed." He'd talk to the Administrator about it. The First Secretary might want to send a medical specialist of his own, to avoid paying the replacement costs.

But it wasn't very likely.

"No sense in keeping the bed on hold, either." But Ligrose clearly didn't care one way or the other. "As you like, Adifer. Keep us informed, of course."

"Of course."

He'd talk to the Administrator tomorrow, when he would have a successful report on Koscuisko to balance it all out. And the Administrator would probably side with Doctor Chaymalt.

Then it would be out of his hands.

It was better to leave Hanbor with the impression that Tutor Chonis was at least trying to protect the interest—the life—of the comatose bond-involuntary.

Mergau Noycannir had gone to bed without her supper, unwilling to expose herself to the aggravation of speaking to the patient slave in quarters in order to get a meal. Now as she rose—refreshed and confident—from her night's rest, she was hungry—but still satisfied enough with what she had found out that she could speak to Hanbor with genial good humor as she opened the slider of her sleep-closet to come out.

"What, still staring at the wall? Release."

And had he not been, there would have been penalties assessed; she had very particularly told him to wait to be released. He was to get off easily enough for his fault. She need feel no shame for having let him stare at the wall all night.

He staggered very slightly as he turned and saluted, shifting his weight to keep his balance. Technically speaking a violation, failure to complete salute in proper form; but she could afford to let the lapse pass. This time at least.

"I'll have my fast-meal, Hanbor. But first there's something we need to get straight between us."

Hanbor knew better than to speak before spoken to, and kept his mouth shut. Just as well. She wasn't interested in anything Hanbor might have to say.

"I expect to be able to rely on you, Hanbor, to provide the correct training material, according to the Tutor's plan. There's a problem with your performance in this area, I'm afraid."

It hardly mattered if he knew that she was lying. She was glad she'd found the way out. "There are instructional tapes logged here for my Fourth Level exercise, but somehow—and I don't mean this as a personal criticism, necessarily, anyone can make a mistake—there are tapes logged for the Fifth Level exercise as well."

Of course there were. They typically studied several days ahead, and the Tutor had put them on notice that if confession could not be obtained at the Fourth Level, they would be expected to move straight to the Fifth Level the following day. That was probably where Koscuisko was right now—unless he'd got confession at the Fourth Level, of course.

"That wouldn't be a problem, Hanbor, ordinarily. But you haven't made an adequately clear distinction between these tapes. I went Fifth Level on that prisoner yesterday because of that. Tutor Chonis is going to be very angry with you."

The tapes were marked as clearly as ever, but that wasn't the point. The point was that she could claim to have been confused, could claim Hanbor was at fault for not making more of a point about it. It hadn't been her mistake. It had been Hanbor's fault. Nobody even had to believe it was true for her stratagem to work.

"If we're lucky, there will be no notice taken, Hanbor. Tutor Chonis may toggle the whole thing as my mistake. I'll take the hit for you if I have to, man, but I hope you understand the position you've placed me in."

Quarters were under surveillance. Everybody knew that. Tutor Chonis knew she knew that. They all knew exactly what she was saying. "If it comes to an issue, I'll be forced to discipline you. So let's just both hope it doesn't get that far, shall we? That'll be all. Fast-meal, Hanbor."

Her claim that she had been misled by inadequately labeled instructional tapes was fabricated, but she could insist upon it no less firmly for that.

So if they meant to speak to her about her mistake, she'd be forced to admit Hanbor had made an error; and once that happened, she'd be forced to discipline him—or else her claim would lose credibility. If Hanbor's error had resulted in her making a mistake, naturally, Hanbor would have to be punished for it. So she'd punish him, if Tutor Chonis said two words to her about it, simply in order to validate her claim.

"As the Student please," Hanbor replied, his voice flat and neutral—if a little rusty and strained from disuse. Nodding, Mergau dismissed him to go for her fast-meal, wondering whether she should overlook the wilted condition of his uniform just because he had been up all night, or whether she should rather say a word or two to him about it.

She was protected against Tutor Chonis now.

The Administration had been put on notice that if they accused her of a violation of Protocols, she'd take the next possible opportunity to beat her slave bloody for the fault he had committed.

This cheerful meditation whet her appetite.

Whistling to herself, Mergau went into the washroom to put her hair in order, waiting for her breakfast.

Andrej approached the exercise theater with a different species of dread than during previous trials, when he had doubted his ability to support the Levels and do his duty. Then he had suffered from the unnatural demands of the exercise, fearful that he would fail in the test. And now, today, this morning, he was free from the fear that he would fail the test, certain of his ability to carry the Levels forward.

His certainty itself troubled him grievously.

What if it happened again?

What if he could not do the thing unless he surrendered to the pleasure that he dreaded, and gave himself over to the passion that had made it all so easy yesterday?

They were allowed to use no drugs, in these exercises. The Administration wanted to be sure its graduates would be able to run a field-expedient Inquiry when required. No drugs; but fewer restrictions than at the Fourth Level were in force. He could break an arm or a leg, if he liked, perhaps knock out some teeth, do some real—if still restricted—damage.

None of which was particularly helpful.

His prisoner—Rab Lussman—knelt waiting on the floor, waiting for him. Lussman didn't seem to be particularly alert, and he was favoring his swollen shoulder as best he could with his arms shackled behind his back; but that was no more than expected.

Lussman's presence did give Andrej rather less time than he might have wanted to think about how he was going to go about this.

Lussman looked up at him as he came through the door, meeting his eyes briefly before he lowered his head out of evident weariness. Andrej wasn't quite sure how to read the expression—there seemed to be an element of relief there somehow.

Andrej stopped close to Lussman's side and touched his hand to a whip-welt he'd left across the man's face, testing. Wondering how he was to take command of the situation and not soil himself with the sinful sensations he had so enjoyed the last time. Considering how to approach his problem. The weal had purpled with bruising, the skin still red and angry where the lash had scraped up blood; tender, Andrej imagined. Lussman recoiled from him with a disgusted gesture, contempt and anger in his eyes; one of the Security cuffed Lussman across the back of the head with casual brutality, but Andrej wasn't affronted by Lussman's instinctive gesture. Only natural, Andrej supposed. He would very likely have done the same in Lussman's place.

"What are these things on his feet?" he asked Security, gesturing with his hand. Lussman was still half-dressed from yesterday, but he'd been shod when he'd come in here, and Andrej was beginning to have a thought. Maybe he could do it. Maybe it would not be so bad. At this point he was almost willing to give Rab Lussman pain, if only he could manage to avoid enjoying it.

"Ah, Nurail leg-wraps, if the officer please. Native footgear." Vely—Andrej thought that was his name—sounded a bit confused. It was an odd phrase to use, wasn't it? Native footgear. As if the uniform were the norm, rather than the exception.

"Have him out of them, if you please, gentlemen."

His table was here, but the complement of tools provided had increased. Andrej found what he wanted, trying not to listen. He could sense the first vague hints of an unnatural interest in the sounds the scuffling generated, stifled groans, grunts of pain. He did the best he could to concentrate on planning his procedure.

When all was settled and quiet once more, he took the shockrod in his hand and turned back to confront his problem. Yesterday he had certainly exceeded the spirit of the Levels, if not its code. Today he wanted to get the exercise over and done with, but he did not want to violate the spirit of the Levels, he wanted to be fair—as far as possible, under the requirements of practice. He would see if he could make it work without a nasty trick played with Nurail physiology. He would use the shockrod. He was only required to do so much.

"A rope, Mister Curran." Which meant that he would need to restrain Lussman somehow, and he wanted to keep Security out of it if possible. Too many hands confused the issue and muddied the waters. Nor could he imagine that the Security would enjoy the requirement they were under to participate in these exercises, as a rule. "I want twelve eighths of rope, to bind him. And a pair of gloves." Twelve eighths would be somewhat more than sufficient merely to bind a prisoner's arms, and there were shackles, after all. But Sorlie Curran wouldn't argue. And Andrej had something specific in mind for the rope. He meant to approach Lussman man-to-man and contest with him without the interference of Security. The least he owed the man after his savagery from yesterday was to engage him one-on-one in recognition of Lussman's existence was a feeling creature like himself.

Sorlie Curran was back within half a cup of rhyti's time, with the rope and the gloves and a respectfully confused expression on his face. Andrej tried on the gloves; supple and well-fitting, they would do very nicely. "I'm impressed," he told Sorlie Curran truthfully. He hadn't counted on getting a good fit, not on such short notice. "I'll take the rope now, if you please."

His idea hadn't been to unshackle the prisoner. His idea was to loop the rope through the shackles and around Rab Lussman's throat. It would have the effect of drawing his arms up behind his back at rather an awkward angle, and that would stress the vulnerable shoulder, but there was nothing to be done about that. Andrej needed to have a handle on the man.

"Very well, stand away."

"Excellency, with respect . . ." Vely was looking a little confused, a little worried. "This man, he's a dangerous . . ."

Criminal. Andrej didn't hear the last of Vely's protest, because Lussman chose the moment to kick out at him from behind. One instant in which to successfully regain his footing, or lose his balance and fall to the floor. One instant between an unexpected thin-blade-thrust and a successful parry . . .

One instant was time enough for Andrej Koscuisko. He levered himself against the rope in his hands, the rope that he had wound around Rab Lussman's throat, and it was Lussman who lost his balance and went sprawling to the floor.

Square onto the wrong shoulder.

Lussman would learn.

Andrej crouched down slowly, reluctant to look at Lussman's face. Lussman had set his teeth against the pain, his breath coming in muted sobs of agony. Andrej spoke to Security to separate himself, to shield himself from the keen temptation he felt to admire Lussman's distress. "Thank you, Mister Vely." It was wonderful, how much of an impression a little sprain could make. "A man must be involved in his work, don't you think? Else it is just an empty exercise. Instead of a contest. Now, Rab, what had we agreed on, yesterday?" He hardly dared to look at Lussman. He wouldn't look at Lussman. "Your identification?"

Twisting the rope up snugly in his fist Andrej rotated his wrist, putting an additional half-twist in the taut loop around Lussman's throat and pulling in the direction he meant Lussman to go. Half-strangled, choking on the noose, Lussman struggled to his knees painfully. Andrej knelt in turn across Lussman's lower legs to hold the man in place. He could do what he would be required to do behind Lussman's back, and be safe from himself. He could maintain control with one hand on the rope at Lussman's throat. He didn't have to look at him. He gave the rope a quick, sharp quarter turn to assure himself of Lussman's full attention.

"Well?"

"Rab Lussman. 'Your Excellency.'" The sneer was predictable, even through the man's pain. Andrej had begun to develop a great deal of respect for Rab Lussman; he was obviously no coward. On the other hand, he clearly could not be permitted to be so contemptuous in his phrasing, even out of respect for his discomfort. Andrej laid the shockrod across the naked sole of Lussman's foot, riding his prisoner's convulsion of agony as if it had been a bit of turbulence encountered while ski-kiting.

When Lussman found his voice, it bore clear witness to the strain, but was stubborn and determined all the same.

". . . Arrested on a charge of willful destruction of Jurisdiction property. Of which I am innocent. Your Excellency."

Andrej tried the shockrod against Lussman's heel, considering. Lussman snorted like a riding-ram through stubbornly clenched teeth, his back and shoulders arching involuntarily in response to the pain. "Did I ask you, Lussman?"

"No. Your Excellency."

Yesterday Lussman had his shoulder put out of joint and forced back into place without revealing more than the most innocuous information. Non-actionable information; because unless he had been condemned in absentia, there was no law against being Rab Lussman, and there was no law against being arrested by accident, either. Nor had being flogged with his weight on his injured shoulder made enough of an impression on Lussman to matter.

It was only a problem if he sought mastery. He didn't need to win. He only heeded to get through. This approach might be boring and predictable, but it had to be safer than what had betrayed him to himself yesterday, and there was no objecting to the strategy for that. Shockrods were fairly common instruments of oppression; Lussman had quite probably experienced their effects prior to this. It could not be said that the punishment was unimaginable, or even out of the ordinary. And still it was an approved and effective tool.

"Listen, I will tell to you my thought." He almost thought he could hear sharp hunger in his voice, and swallowed hard before he dared continue. "We are going to be done with this, I am very bored. I am going to ask you some very simple questions, easily understood, even for a Nurail."

He let the shockrod trail across Lussman's instep, tightening his grip on the rope at Lussman's throat as the body jerked in uncoordinated protest. He sensed the danger that lay in wait for him, but he could not decline to put the exercise forward simply because he was afraid of what might happen to him. Nor could it be said that he feared failure; when he was apprehensive of success instead—or of the thing that had helped him to succeed in their last meeting. "You are going to answer my questions. And if your answer is not satisfactory I am going to strike it from the Judicial record . . ."

Full contact, prolonged for perhaps so long as an eighth, mercilessly. Doing all he could to close his ears to the seductive music of Lussman's reluctant cries. ". . . in this manner. Well? Is that clear?"

Oh, Holy Mother.

It was going to happen to him again.

He couldn't even see the Nurail's face, and still he noted all the signs of pain with something too clearly different from compassion to be taken for reluctance to inflict the pain he had it in his power to promise Lussman.

"You are to answer me politely, Rab." His own voice sounded rough and harsh, but Andrej knew what passion roughened it, and lifted his face to the cold white ceiling in despair. *Keep talking,* he told himself. Maybe if he could only just keep talking, he could put the appetite away. If he could not curb it or control it, perhaps he could pretend that he ignored it, and get through this after all. "You are to answer me 'yes, your Excellency' and 'no, your Excellency.' Lack of good manners offends me, Lussman. Do you understand?"

Lussman didn't answer. *You have undone yourself, Andrej,* he thought. *Since you have asked, you must enforce an answer. And when you force his answer, you are going to enjoy it. You are lost. And since you have defied your father, you cannot so much as hope that your Holy Mother will raise Her divine hand to succor you.* He set the shockrod to the bottom of Lussman's foot once more, seeking the nerve that would respond best to the noxious stimulus almost despite himself. Touching the naked soles of Lussman's feet, first one, then the other, rolling the impulse end of the torture tool against the small bones, hesitatingly at first, then with increasing assurance and deliberation. The sound of Lussman's pain was more than he could find it in himself to resist. It was lovely. It was sweet. He wanted more.

"Yes. Your Excellency."

"Your name is?"

"Rab Lussman. Your Excellency."

Andrej felt his face warm with a flush of gratification, his pleasure redoubled because he took it against Lussman's will. "And you are accused of willful destruction of Jurisdiction property, yes? Have you committed this crime?"

This was the second day of Lussman's interrogation. Cumulative pain and stress should have begun to seriously cloud Lussman's judgment. Andrej could almost sense Lussman's confusion of mind as he struggled with the deliberately incriminating phrasing of Andrej's demand.

"Yes, your Excellency. No—"

He couldn't let Lussman finish, not if his plan was to work. He set the shockrod against his prisoner's foot and smiled as he heard Lussman's cry of agony.

"Very good. You have confessed to having committed the crime for which you have been arrested." Not really, no. But the Writ did not require that he play fair, as long as he got something out of it that could be considered close to a confession. Shifting his weight and rising, Andrej gave the rope a savage jerk, and Lussman struggled to his feet with his breath rattling painfully in his throat. "There remain only the details to be determined. How many of your family were involved, then? All?"

He shouldn't be asking Lussman questions like that. He wanted Lussman to submit to him, to answer his questions and make his confession. He wasn't going to get very far with the line he was taking. Wasn't such an accusation all but guaranteed to evoke the utmost resistance from his client?

He had to be clear in his own mind or he would surely only confuse the issue in the mind of the prisoner. It was reasonable to expect Lussman to become increasingly anxious to understand what Andrej wanted, increasingly eager to supply whatever was required. Lussman wasn't going to be able to do that unless Andrej gave him a clearer idea of what the requirement actually was. Andrej knew what the requirement was. He required Lussman's pain, and then Lussman's submission. But he wanted Lussman's pain more than Lussman's answers. "Talk to me, Rab. Tell me about your crime."

"Excellency, I am not guilty of . . . the crime . . ." Andrej twisted the rope savagely yet again, and Lussman's protest rattled into strangled incoherence.

It wasn't fair to Lussman to approach him in this manner; he wasn't being candid. Why should he hurry Lussman to confessing when all that meant was that punishment would follow? Because since punishment was to follow, it could not be decent, fair, nor just to seek ways in which he could prolong the punishment that Lussman was to have before confession. One way or the other, Lussman had little chance of understanding what he was expected to confess as long as Andrej continued to communicate such mixed and contradictory signals to the man.

"No, I won't have it," he warned, and let some slack out at Lussman's throat. "You are accused of willful destruction of Jurisdiction property, and I mean to have details, I tell you."

He would be master here, whether it meant he soil himself or not.

He had no choice.

"I don't believe I find that answer acceptable, Lussman." The shockrod had gotten dirty during the past hours, and there was blood on his uniform where he'd brushed it against his trouser leg in passing. "Let's try it again. I'm getting tired of your childish stubbornness."

The prisoner lay on his belly on the floor, moving one foot in little irregular spasms—as if there was some corner of Lussman's mind that thought that he could get away, if he could only manage to move. As if he couldn't stop himself from hoping that there was some place to which he would be permitted to escape. Andrej knelt at Lussman's side, quite close, and let his knee rest casually against the swollen mess that yesterday's trauma and today's punishment had made of the young man's shoulder. "You are to tell me why you chose the site—who helped you? Who was it that decided your target?"

Lussman was afraid, Andrej could hear it in his voice. "Excellency. Innocent. Of the crimes . . . accused . . ." It was only reasonable to be afraid, but Andrej wasn't going to put his weight against so obvious a target. Yet.

"You have already confessed to the crime, it is only a question of the details. What sense is there in further resistance?"

With a surprisingly determined effort Lussman moved, shifting away from Andrej where he knelt. Andrej knew how much it had to hurt Lussman to move; all in all, Lussman was clearly courageous, of strong will and determined temperament. It was really a shame that such a man should be sacrificed to the Judicial order; but—since so much was preordained—the least he could do was see that Lussman completed his confession before too much more blood was spilled. Or deeper blood was spilled, at any rate. Perhaps he would be offered a contract as bond-involuntary, a strong young man, physically fit, of such admirable strength of character. . .

"Not true. Innocent. Have not. Committed, any. Such crime . . ."

Lussman's voice dried up in his throat as Andrej leaned over him. Steadying himself with one hand pressed against Lussman's back, now, Andrej reached across his body to take a jugular pulse, wondering where that thought had come from. The Bond was only offered to Accused prior to Intermediate Level Inquiry, and then only when Judicial staff had evaluated the candidate and found him suitable. If

Lussman had been qualified for the Bond, he would have been offered one before now, and then been subjected to the implant of a governor whether he had agreed to it or not. Rab Lussman was not going to be offered any Bond.

"This has gone on quite long enough. Really, I am becoming bored." Perhaps eight hours, perhaps longer, and he had confused his prisoner and tormented him, troubled him with half-true accusations and tortured him with a rope and a shockrod and a keen sense of where it hurt—and Lussman would not surrender. Oh, the appearance of a confession had been approximated, by trickery—the doubled question that could not be answered without incrimination. It was a dirty technique, and Andrej had never forgotten his fury at the confessor who had tried it on him. But it worked—or at least it worked here, where the prisoner could not storm out of the confessional in righteous outrage. Here, where Andrej would be encouraged by his Tutor in his duplicity instead of disciplined by his ecclesiastical superiors for trying to manipulate a Koscuisko prince so crudely— instead of in the more traditional, time-honored ways.

So the forms could be completed.

But Lussman had not given in.

His throat was scraped bloody from the pressure of the coarse rope, the trauma of yesterday's beating renewed and doubled by the shockrod, his shoulder red and furious with the insult, and his face white and glistening with the sweat of his pain—but Lussman would not give in. And Andrej wanted his surrender, wanted it, quite apart from the forms and the requirements, quite apart from his respect for his prisoner's courage and strength of will.

He was Koscuisko, and he would have dominion.

He set his knee firmly against Lussman's injured shoulder and put his weight full on the crippled joint, leaning over to speak close to Lussman's ear. "Aren't you ready for a break, from this? —Because you shall have none, till you confess." He said it half in charity, half with intent to deceive. "You've managed to defy me for quite some time, but there are limits to how much you can be expected to endure." Which Lussman seemed both ready and willing to challenge, but that was beside the point. It was only a difference of degree, after all. "Be a little easier on yourself. Haven't you suffered long enough? And for what? For whom?"

"Excellency . . . Long enough?"

Lussman had begun to repeat what had been said to him in random fragments, without any indication that he understood what he was saying—as if he were drugged by shock, or by his pain. Lussman's dazed repetition of disjointed phrases could be useful in constructing a "confession." But this sounded like a real question, with real feeling behind it.

"Long enough to break for mid-meal, at the very earliest." He had indulged himself to the fullest with the halter and the shockrod. He was going to have to graduate Lussman to some sharper torment if he was to keep the man's attention focused where he wanted it. "I'll have to send out for a box, I suppose. Perhaps Mister Sorlie Curran will be kind enough to go for me."

The knot he'd set in the halter had pulled very tight over the past few hours. It took Andrej a moment to work it free. Lussman was too exhausted after half a day's struggle against the rope to need too much managing, at least until Andrej decided what new treat he should go after. It was an interesting problem, given his options, his opportunities. Unless Lussman disappointed him by capitulating too soon, of course.

"Mid-meal, halfway. Through the Fifth." Lussman sounded relieved, even through his evident suffering. Grateful. What in the name of the Holy Mother's mirror could he be talking about? "Safe, then. All right—"

Not only that, but Sorlie Curran was interrupting, and if Andrej hadn't known better he could have sworn that Sorlie Curran was anxious about something.

"His Excellency prefers for his mid-meal the bread and cheese, or perhaps the greens with protein?"

There were undercurrents here that Andrej did not understand.

Sorlie Curran had not only interrupted him but had interrupted the prisoner as well, and Sorlie Curran, as a professional Security troop, surely knew better than that.

And while Lussman clearly seemed to have something on his mind, it didn't sound to Andrej as though it was about anything that they'd shared throughout the long morning. Sorlie Curran was anxious—not obviously so, but Andrej had a lifetime's experience reading the voices and body language of Household servants in order to find out what was wrong when he had offended. Andrej realized immediately that Sorlie Curran was afraid that Lussman was going to say something— or that Andrej was going to pay attention to something that Lussman had already said.

"Perhaps not quite yet, Mister Sorlie Curran. Return to the other side of the room, if you please. Immediately." He wanted to be alone with Lussman. What had the man said? *Mid-meal. Halfway through the Fifth. Safe, then. All right.* This was almost as intriguing as Lussman's agony, and Andrej had fed long and drunk deep of Lussman's agony throughout the morning, and was not so avid for it now that he could not be distracted by this new development. Easing Lussman onto his back, Andrej carried his nerveless arms with the hands swollen from their bonds carefully to the front of Lussman's body. Granted that Lussman's back was bruised and bloodied; a little additional distraction might not be unproductive, at this point.

"That's right, Rab. It's halfway through the Fifth Level. It's all right now. You can tell me." He could only guess at what was going on, but with any luck Lussman would oblige him—

"Excellency." It was a sigh of relief, almost of gratitude. Gratitude, again. "Begs leave to confess. To you. I have committed. The crime."

And suddenly Lussman was willing to confess, was eager to confess. "Of willful destruction. Of. Jurisdiction . . ."

"Why now?" Andrej could make no sense of it. "What do you mean by telling me this now, when I've been asking you about it all day long?"

"Begs leave to confess," Lussman groaned, and his agony was clear and genuine. "Halfway—for Megh. Halfway, halfway through . . ."

Understanding came to Andrej like a basin full of icy water in his face. Suddenly Andrej knew exactly what was going on; and the horror of it banished all the delight Lussman had provided him away, body and soul, and left him cold with certainty and outrage.

He knew what was tormenting Rab Lussman, or whatever the man's name was.

He knew what was troubling Sorlie Curran.

He even realized why it had occurred to him that Lussman might be offered the Bond.

"Yes, halfway through." He lied without remorse, without compunction. They had been lying to him all along. "You're free to make confession now; it's time. It cannot have been easy for you, Lussman. Do you remember what you are supposed to say to me?"

He meant to have verification before Tutor Chonis called the exercise. And Tutor Chonis would call the exercise the moment Tutor Chonis—watching, as Andrej knew he watched, from whatever review room or vantage area—realized what he was up to. Sorlie Curran's attempted intervention had made that very clear. So he had to act quickly.

"Yes, your Excellency."

Clearly disoriented, Lussman obviously had no idea that he had revealed the secret.

"Tell to me your truth, then, what you are instructed to do. I want to hear it from you. The truth, Lussman."

Lussman had closed his eyes tightly as if he wanted to shut out the unpleasant memory of the past few hours. Andrej couldn't blame him for that. He knew exactly how unpleasant it had been for Lussman. "Halfway. Fifth Level. Not before. Class Two violation . . ."

Andrej heard the subtle shift in the background noise from the ventilators, and knew that the Tutor's intercommunication channel had finally been engaged. "Administrative orders!"

He'd heard it yesterday, he knew what it was. But they were too late. Had Noycannir found hers out, yesterday?

"All exercises to cease, repeat, all exercises to cease. Disengage at once."

And here was Sorlie Curran now, again. "Respectfully request his Excellency stand up and move away from the prisoner."

The prisoner. A bond-involuntary Security troop playing a role, forbidden to reveal the deception on pain of a Class Two violation— even at the Fifth Level of Inquiry. Even through the stern and savage punishment that "Lussman" had been suffering, forbidden to say the word that would make it stop.

Andrej rose to his feet, sickened, dazed. He had taught Chonis a lesson, then, hadn't he? They had lied to him, and he had demonstrated the futility of trying to lie to him. He had desired mastery, and he had attained mastery, but it did not feel the way he had expected. How could they play such games with men in Joslire's position—men without recourse—as pawns?

More Security were entering the theater now, and he had been expecting a medical team for the "prisoner" now that the farce was over. They were not Security that he had seen before, and he did not mind snarling at them when two of the four began to drag "Rab Lussman" off by the arms.

"You, what do you think you're doing?" He heard the horror in his own voice and suppressed it sternly. So much depended upon the correct attitude. Security might obey an irritated officer. An overemotional Student could be safely ignored. "Set that man down at once. He requires medical attention, not additional injury."

They did as they were told, right enough, even though they looked a little puzzled about why they were complying. They really didn't have any choice, did they?

Had the Administration given "Rab Lussman" any choice?

"Excellency." Sorlie Curran, once again, and it was unusual to hear the direct form of address from a bond-involuntary. Sorlie Curran sounded upset. "They are required to take him into custody. No medical intervention is permitted unless there is a life-threatening injury. By the Bench instruction."

By the Bench instruction. He should have guessed. The logic of it all was blinding in its inhuman rigidity. He should have taken one of Joslire's five-knives and slit the man's belly open, forcing "medical intervention"—except that they would only have treated the knife wound, not the welts, not the weals, not the joint. They would not treat the pain.

"Very well."

He should have hurt the man so much that they would have to treat the pain to save his life. And he had not. And therefore the man would suffer, locked up in a cell somewhere, and that was where his conservative approach to injuring his "prisoner" had got him.

"You may carry out your orders."

He had forced the issue. He was responsible.

He needed to have a word with Tutor Chonis.

CHAPTER SIX

The situation was about as bad as any Tutor Chonis had ever faced. Joslire Curran had been dispatched to bring Koscuisko to his office directly. He had an idea that Koscuisko would be coming whether bidden or not, and he had to maintain as much control of the situation as he could. If he could.

He stood up from his desk as Koscuisko entered, nodding to Curran to leave them alone and seal the entry, pulling one of the chairs at the conference table around for Koscuisko as he did so. It was no less important to maintain his momentum, his control, than if he was performing an Inquiry again, after all these years. It was more important. He guided Koscuisko to the seat by his elbow as the door sealed behind Curran's back; seating himself beside Koscuisko—like a co-conspirator, two Students together—Tutor Chonis began to try to find out how far the damage went.

"Student Koscuisko, do you know what you have done?"

Koscuisko had been still during Chonis's arranging; and it was a dangerous stillness, a waiting stillness. It was not good. Koscuisko should be too angry to think twice, not cold enough to watch and wait and see what was going to happen.

"I await your instruction, Tutor Chonis. Tell me what it is, exactly, that I have done."

For the first time in his long career Tutor Chonis wondered what his tutelage had wrought, what manner of Inquisitor he had created. How had Koscuisko caught on? He had been watching every move;

Noycannir had not yet been matched with a replacement, so there'd been nothing to distract him. St. Clare's lapse should have meant nothing to one not already in the know. How could Koscuisko be so calm now, in the face of this disgraceful secret?

"Only carefully selected Security are trusted with this portion of your training. And they volunteer for it on Safe, with a Class Two violation as the price for any failure. Do you recall what a Class Two violation means, for a bond-involuntary like St. Clare?"

Shock value. He had to shake Koscuisko's arctic calm. He had seemed emotional enough when the Security had come to take St. Clare away; he should not have been able to freeze his feelings over, not so quickly, not so well. It was unnatural.

"And that is why you were so disappointed with Student Noycannir's, ah, study partner, I imagine. After all, the Tutor had to call that exercise at the Fourth Level."

Chonis stared, genuinely confused for a moment. "What are you talking about? She lost her head, we lost the man. Our selection techniques for prisoner-surrogates have a failure rate of less than three in two eighties, Koscuisko. This isn't supposed to happen."

Wrong choice, wrong approach. Koscuisko smiled, and Chonis found that he did not like the color that Koscuisko's eyes seemed to have turned; they were too cold by half. "Then either he—St. Clare?— is very stupid, or I am very good. Is that what I am meant to conclude, from this dishonorable charade? But I don't think St. Clare is stupid at all. I've been rather admiring his backbone. I should therefore conclude that I am better at this filthy business than one hundred and fifty-seven out of every one hundred and sixty of your other Students. Did I get that right, Tutor Chonis?"

Koscuisko should not be taking that tone of voice with him. And it was up to him to convince Koscuisko to mind his manners.

"That is one conclusion to be drawn." Not that he would suggest that Koscuisko should be ashamed of a success of this nature; Koscuisko's own reluctance to be here in the first place would take care of that for him. "The other conclusion may be as important, in the long run. You said that you 'rather admired' St. Clare, I believe?"

"Indeed. Knowing what I know now, my respect for him only increases. I could never have managed so fine an effort. I am certain of it."

"Then I should like you to consider what you have done to him by expanding the scope of your Inquiry."

Koscuisko frowned. "My brief called for his confession, I obtained two, he answered as he was bidden. What is the problem?"

Finally, a line, a handle, a weapon with which to regain control of this too-successful Student. "Your brief called for a confession to willful destruction of Jurisdiction property. Had you been content with the confession you obtained—"

"With the Tutor's permission, no confession was obtained; the appearance of a confession merely."

Good, he had found a way in. "If, as I was saying, you had been content as you should have been with the confession that you had been directed to obtain, Robert St. Clare would not be condemned to the equivalent of three days of Inquiry at the Seventh Level. He would have earned the remission of four years off his Bond, and the Fleet would have rejoiced in the service of a strong and dedicated Security troop. As it is . . ."

At least he had Koscuisko's attention, and there was visible emotion on Koscuisko's face. That it was fury and hatred was beside the point. Where there was passion there was weakness. Koscuisko could not be allowed to escape Tutor Chonis's strict control; and Tutor Chonis could not obtain control without some weakness on Koscuisko's part—that much seemed suddenly all too clear.

"There will be execution of discipline for a Class Two violation, and then we'll have to decide whether St. Clare can return to service at all. There is rather a high failure rate after a Class Two violation has been adjudged, not surprisingly. We will probably have to terminate."

There was evident shock in Koscuisko's eyes now, and obvious pain. If it hadn't been for the steely front Koscuisko had presented scant eighths ago, Tutor Chonis felt he might have been fooled into feeling sorry for his Student. But Tutor Chonis had seen the temper of Koscuisko's will, and he knew better than to believe that he could afford to give a sixteenth if he was to hope to retain the upper hand.

"It makes no sense to risk the resource when failure means a loss of four hundred thousand, Standard. It is wasteful. Fleet cannot afford it."

Still Chonis was tempted, so tempted. Koscuisko's conflict was honest and clearly painful, even if he expressed it in such neutral language. All the same, Chonis knew the line he had to take for the sake of the Fleet. For the sake of Koscuisko's own survival as well, in a world where the only authority would be a hardened Command Branch officer whose word would be law and who would not take kindly to Koscuisko's autocratic defiance. For Koscuisko's own sake, Chonis had to break Koscuisko's spirit, his pride, his will.

"Fleet expects its Inquisitors to confine themselves to their stated duty. And not go off chasing hints and suspicions, that's Security's business." Of course once he got out there he would be sent hunting, from time to time, not so much to gain confession as to see what else he could uncover; but that would keep for now. For now the point was that Robert St. Clare would be disciplined then probably killed as an unrecoverable resource, and all because Andrej Koscuisko had stepped out of bounds. "Are there any questions?"

"There is one thing."

He knew he'd made his point, but Koscuisko's face held none of the conflict he'd seen there moments before. It was the face Koscuisko had come in with, all over again. Chonis knew by that token that there was hope for Koscuisko's survival after all.

"Yes?"

"If, what is his name, St. Clare is a bond-involuntary and under orders, then he cannot be convicted of a Class Two violation. The administrative instruction states that a bond-involuntary cannot be put in jeopardy by the issuance of contradictory, equally binding legal orders."

It was a weakness in the system, and Koscuisko had found it out. He had hunted it out as quickly and as surely as he had hunted St. Clare's secret out. He was too good for his own good: but as long as he could be convinced to conform, it would be all right.

"Ordinarily you would be correct."

"What is out of the ordinary about this situation? A man has been placed in artificial jeopardy through the issuance of contradictory orders. The Administrator—I presume—has ordered him to confess to one thing, but never to the other. I have ordered him to confess to me his truth, and tell me what it was that he had been directed to do."

And probably—Chonis mused—if he were to review the training record, he'd find that Koscuisko had in fact used that language, at one time or another. It was an ingenious defense. Too bad it could not be allowed to work.

"I'm afraid the Administration cannot accept your reasoning. In this instance the order you issued was not binding or lawful, inasmuch as you did not know your prisoner-surrogate to be under orders at the time that you gave your instruction. And your surrogate in turn had prior lawful clearance to disregard orders from you, for the sake of the exercise."

"And for this point of Law, the Administration would rather destroy the resource than salvage the man?"

Failure to obey lawful and received instruction was a Class Two violation either way. What difference did it make? "Explain yourself."

"My order negates the previous one. St. Clare has disobeyed me by attempting to withhold the confession I demanded of him. I have the option of disciplining him myself or referring him for the Class Two violation. And if I discipline him, Fleet need not lose the resource, since my options are restricted to the Class One level."

"You have a point, Student Koscuisko." Should he give false hope or quash any hope right now? "What reason would the Administration have for endorsing such an unorthodox resolution to the problem?"

It seemed that Koscuisko hesitated, as if searching for the right words. "I could swear very solemnly to abuse my Security whenever possible, and never forget myself so far as to let the truth get in the way of the confession that I have been instructed to obtain. Would that not conform to the Fleet requirement?"

There was the sound of genuine petition in Koscuisko's voice, regardless of the form of his offer.

But it was no good.

"Thank you, Student Koscuisko. That will be all." No, they could not afford to let Koscuisko have his way.

Koscuisko could never be permitted to doubt that he had brought an essentially guiltless man to torment and to death because he had stepped outside of his boundaries.

The door to Tutor Chonis's office opened and Koscuisko came out with a look on his face that was desperate and analytical at once. Joslire made his salute, but Koscuisko ignored it, and Koscuisko had always been careful to acknowledge, as a courtesy, that which was demanded of Joslire in respect for the officer's rank.

"I will go to Infirmary, Mister Curran," Koscuisko said. "Be so kind as to show me the way."

There was no arguing with it, of course, but he was responsible for reporting on Koscuisko's state of mind, and therefore a little probing was in order. "According to the officer's good pleasure. But the officer has not eaten, and it is well past mid-meal."

Koscuisko had turned his back, starting down the hall as if he didn't really care where he was going as long as he was going away from Tutor Chonis. Pivoting suddenly on his heel now, Koscuisko glared at Joslire, who had to step back hastily to avoid running into him.

"'The officer' does not have time. I'll eat in the lab. Let's go."

Koscuisko had to know that St. Clare was not in Infirmary. Why was he in such a hurry to get there? Joslire couldn't understand the tension that he sensed. He had to hurry to catch up with Koscuisko. The one thing he did know was that he had better stay with his officer, at all costs.

He had watched with sickened fear as Koscuisko caught the minute crack in St. Clare's discipline—"begs leave," because "this troop begs leave," rather than "I beg leave" as a man would in the first person—and forced it wide open. He thought he knew how his officer had felt when Koscuisko had realized that not only was his "prisoner" no such thing, but that the man was to be brutally disciplined for having permitted any shadow of the truth to escape him.

Why was Koscuisko going to Infirmary?

Koscuisko had full access to dedicated lab space. Tutor Chonis would not revoke it because of this incident. Was he really concerned that Koscuisko meant to take some medication to relieve himself of his guilt, and his life with it? No. He didn't read that kind of desperation in the set of Koscuisko's shoulders, or in the angle at which Koscuisko held his head. But the desperation was real and immediate.

So what was going on?

Koscuisko was silent on the way and stood mute in the security clearing area once they arrived, letting Joslire do all the talking. He wasn't looking at anything that Joslire could identify, his eyes apparently fixed on some target several eighths down the corridor on the other side of the wall.

"Student Koscuisko, with Tutor Chonis. Laboratory space to be provided ad lib at the Student's pleasure."

The Security responsible for Infirmary were Station Security rather than teaching staff. Joslire had acquaintances among the troops, but they needed a Chief Warrant to clear Koscuisko through to his laboratory space—it was procedure. It took a moment for the Security post to find the Warrant on duty and log the release in due form, but Koscuisko never stirred from where he stood. Koscuisko might have been asleep with his eyes open, for all Joslire could tell. Except that he did react immediately once Security had received the clearance they required.

"Logged and listed, very good, Curran. The officer has been assigned four-one-H-one. Travis can show the officer the way. Will the officer be requiring Curran's attendance?"

Because otherwise Joslire had no business in the Infirmary area, and good little bond-involuntaries simply didn't go where they had no business being. If Koscuisko didn't want him, he'd have to go to Tutor Chonis and let the Tutor know that Koscuisko was surrounded by every chemical substance a man could want for any purpose, and unsupervised as well; and Tutor Chonis would have to authorize surveillance inside Infirmary, and Koscuisko would notice sooner or later, and it would not sweeten his temper by much.

Koscuisko turned his head and looked over his shoulder at Joslire with cold empty eyes. Empty on the surface, because the mind was far away, working furiously to solve a problem whose identity Joslire could not begin to guess.

"I'll want to send him for my supper when the time comes," Koscuisko said. "And in the meantime, he could bring my rhyti."

It was good enough for Joslire, and good enough for the shift supervisor as well apparently. "There is no impediment. If the officer will please follow Travis."

The laboratory space assigned to Koscuisko was deep within the Infirmary complex. Joslire had to keep a sharp eye on the turnings to be sure that he was going to be able to get in here and out again for Koscuisko's meal. It turned out to be a smallish room, not much larger than Koscuisko's quarters; their guide bowed Koscuisko through, meeting Joslire's eyes with mild curiosity, and then prepared to leave Koscuisko to his work. Whatever it was.

"If the officer requires anything further, I'll send an orderly," Travis said. She had a pleasant voice, neutral and professional, that showed no hint of curiosity as to what was going on.

"I want three-eighths to think." Koscuisko's statement in response was startling after his contemplative, absorbed silence. At least Joslire was startled. "Send an orderly after three-eighths. Or show Joslire where to fetch one. From the pharmacy, of course."

And then he sat down at the documents-bench and stared at the blank screen as if the rest of the world had abruptly lapsed back into the state of nonexistence that had been its position since he had left Tutor Chonis's office.

Travis shrugged from where she stood out in the corridor, safely shielded now from Koscuisko's line of sight by the intervening wall. "I'll send the orderly," she repeated, speaking directly to Joslire now that Koscuisko had effectively dismissed her. "Are you going for rhyti, or shall I?"

"Thanks." The option was appreciated, but Travis had no way of knowing how Koscuisko liked his rhyti. Koscuisko was particular. "What if he needs you in a hurry?"

What if Joslire needed help with him, in other words. Travis grinned and answered the question he hadn't asked. "Security call, your basic black button, both sides of the door. Guaranteed response time, two skips of a 'cruit's heart. Anything else?"

"If there is he hasn't let on yet."

She winked and went away, and he retreated into the lab, closing the door.

To stand and watch, and wait Koscuisko's bidding.

After a while Koscuisko bestirred himself to activate the documents-review screen, apparently finding several entries of interest. When the orderly came, Koscuisko discussed some drugs with her, names that meant nothing to Joslire and apparently little enough to the orderly. Koscuisko sent her away to prepare an analysis cart for him, sending Joslire away at the same time; but Joslire wasn't worried any longer by then. If the chemicals, the drugs, that Koscuisko had ordered could be used against himself, surely the orderly would at least have recognized them. The memory of the exercise aside, Koscuisko did not feel like a man at risk, to Joslire's mind. He seemed too completely absorbed in an abstract issue of

some sort to be thinking about anything as messy and mundane as
suicide.

Joslire was surprised to find out how late it had gotten to be—
Koscuisko's third-meal shift already. He took a meal as well as the rhyti
back to the lab, but Koscuisko didn't react to his return—apart from
reaching for his rhyti just as Joslire got it stirred and set out for him.
Too deep in his analysis, whatever it was. Joslire sighed and once more
covered the meal tray, waiting for Koscuisko to remember that he
hadn't eaten anything since his fast-meal in the "morning."

Except that Koscuisko didn't seem to notice.

The hours wore on, and Koscuisko did not seem to be paying
attention. Joslire stood on watch, since that was what he was expected
to do, wondering how long it would be before the officer's lack of sleep
and lack of food caught up with him.

Not any time soon, obviously.

Computer analyses and reaction models, more chemical profiles,
time out to scan a long text article, then back to the imager to tweak a
holo-model of some chemical formulation or another.

Hours . . .

"Joslire."

What was Koscuisko up to, anyway?

Had he decided to lose himself in his work?

He'd had a very trying day; most Students found themselves
exhausted beyond belief by the unexpected demands of the
Intermediate Levels. A man couldn't really expect himself to work all
day on a jug of rhyti. It wasn't that effective a stimulant.

"Mister Curran, I have been remiss. Are you with me?"

What?

"I want to see Tutor Chonis, Joslire. I regret that I must insist upon
it immediately."

Joslire blinked rapidly, trying to focus. Koscuisko was standing in
front of him, eating a piece of cold egg-pie taken up from the meal
tray Joslire had brought him, how long ago?

Asleep.

He'd fallen asleep.

A fine Security troop he made.

"The officer's pardon is—"

But Koscuisko wouldn't let him finish. "I know, I know,

'respectfully solicited.' Yes? It does not import. I want to see Tutor Chonis, do you know where he sleeps?"

Well, if Koscuisko wasn't interested in being apologized to, there was nothing in particular he could do about it. "That information is not available. An emergency call can be made at the officer's discretion."

"You needn't be cross with me, Joslire, although I am at fault. I should have sent you to bed."

It wasn't that, even if he couldn't explain it very well. It was only that he was asleep, and reverting to the safety of absolute formality accordingly for his own protection. Koscuisko was still talking—

"Do please make the call, then. I don't know how much time I may have left. In fact I am afraid to ask."

Afraid to ask about what "time left"?

He'd never known an officer to break the secret. He had no idea any more what was on Koscuisko's mind. But he did have an idea of his own, something that had just occurred to him—as if it had taken an unscheduled nap to remind him of the unaccustomed freedom available here.

"Laboratory facilities are not under surveillance," he said. "Chief Belyss told me so. There is no one listening to whatever it might please the officer to say, should the officer wish to take the opportunity to swear."

In fact Infirmary and the Administrator's Staff areas were the only places in the entire facility that were not monitored, as a matter of principle. He could see understanding come up slowly into his officer's eyes; and then all the self-composure seemed to spark out of Koscuisko at once. Koscuisko reached out for him and grabbed his over-blouse— alarming; but, as Joslire realized, only for emphasis. And perhaps to keep his balance. Koscuisko didn't raise his voice, but the fiercely controlled desperation that Joslire heard was more affecting to his carefully guarded heart than howls of outrage could have been.

"How can they have done such a thing?"

Then, as if he only then noticed what he was doing, Koscuisko seemed to master himself once more. He loosened his iron grip at Joslire's collar, taking care to brush away a stray crumb from his egg-pie as he did so, and collected his energies back into himself to continue more calmly. No less desperately, however.

"The obscenity of it cannot be described. I admire that man, Joslire, that man St. Clare, and it cannot be said that he lacks discipline."

Only now, as Koscuisko fought for self-control, did Joslire realize how passionate Koscuisko actually was about this; perhaps about other things, as well. He had done such a thorough job of wearing his calm, neutral Student's mask that Joslire had not dreamed there was such passion in him, apart from the passion Student Koscuisko seemed to be developing for pain. It was like meeting a stranger in place of the man whose meals he had been preparing all this time.

"It cannot even be said that he disobeyed his orders. How could it? He revealed nothing. Oh, perhaps one little mistake was made, but no violation. And they will murder him for it."

Joslire searched for something he could say that Koscuisko could use to bring himself back under control. "Participation in the exercise is voluntary, as it please the officer. And solicited on Safe, to ensure that he was genuinely free to decline without repercussions. He knew the risks and accepted the penalty. All of us did."

"All of you . . ."

Koscuisko was pale to begin with, and now the shock had whitened his countenance until he looked almost blue with it. "Oh, Joslire. It is beyond shameful. That man is to be tortured and probably killed, for no good or necessary reason. I can make no sense of it, and yet I am to be a part of it. How can I hope to function within such a dichotomy? There is a clinical term for this conflict, Joslire . . ."

He knew what Koscuisko was getting at. "It is a useful thing to focus on—for those tasked with the officer's responsibilities."

Koscuisko was still talking, as if he hadn't heard. "But it is a false refuge, grotesque cowardice. One has need of all one's wits to survive in such an environment. One cannot afford any separation of personality."

A surprising turn, Joslire thought. His standing orders were to encourage the doubling, if possible; to support the formation of a "not-me" persona that would be able to fulfill an Inquisitor's duties, while the more morally acceptable "me" persona remained safe from taint, removed and remote, deploring the cruelty of it all. So successful had the psychological trick proven over time that the Administration was considering teaching some rudimentary techniques, to try to reduce the steady loss of functional Ship's Surgeons.

"I need not ask if you made any mistakes," Koscuisko said after a moment's silence.

The unaccustomed freedom to speak without being recorded betrayed Joslire to his own honesty, and he answered truthfully rather than in soothing words such as the Administration might have preferred he use.

"If the officer had been my Interrogator, it might easily have been different."

It was a painful idea for Koscuisko. Joslire could see that. He could not find it in him to regret his honesty in spite of it.

"Then I would have been responsible for your agony, as I am responsible for his. I must try this, Joslire; I have something that Tutor Chonis wants. Perhaps I can bargain with the man. With the system."

How could he say it? He could not but honor the officer's intention. How could he convince Koscuisko to set aside every better instinct yet un-dulled by Fleet's Orientation?

"The officer can do nothing for his prisoner-surrogate now. The Administrator will Record the assessment of penalty first-shift." And Koscuisko, in his determination to take things personally, had already done more for St. Clare than any of the other Students Joslire had served would have done. Anyone else would have written it off as a terrible conflict: *Oh, but the rules are larger than any one officer, and I cannot take on all of Jurisdiction Fleet. What must be, must be.* "Excellency, you play into the Administration's hands. The Tutor means to use the officer's pain to discipline him. Young Inquisitors must be trained to strict conformity. Do not edge the blade that rests in the hand of your opponent."

Facing the closed door, Koscuisko was apparently eager to go to confrontation. But he glanced up to meet Joslire's eyes, quickly, and he smiled.

"You are good to comfort me," Koscuisko said. "I will keep your charity in my heart. But I must try it, Joslire. I could not sleep if I did not try to stop this monstrous cruelty. This waste."

Joslire could think of nothing more to say after that.

Therefore he merely bowed and keyed the communication net to make Koscuisko's emergency appointment with Tutor Chonis.

He had been drunk the night before last. He had not been drunk last night, but he had not slept well, and it was halfway to morning now. Andrej felt his weariness like a prickle-fruit in his throat, but he could not afford to think about sleep-syrup to soothe the aching of it, not just yet.

The Administrator would Record the assessment of penalty first-shift, Joslire had said. It was already six eights into fourth-shift. He had only two eights in which to stop whatever judicial farce was customary and bind the man who had been Rab Lussman to himself, since that was the only way he could be sure of the bond-involuntary's continued safety. It was an emergency, as Joslire had explained to Tutor Chonis. Perhaps he would able to make a better case of it if he waited until after fast-meal, but he was afraid that if he put it off by so long he would be too late.

Tutor Chonis met him in his office. It was unsettling to see him out of uniform; he was waiting when Andrej got there, sitting at the table instead of behind his desk. The rhyti jug and two glasses were set out at his elbow, one of them half-filled. Like one of Uncle Radu's Counselors, Andrej thought. *Come in, make yourself comfortable, relax. What is troubling you, my nephew?*

"Come in, come in," Tutor Chonis waved him to the facing chair, rubbing one side of his face as he did so. Whatever he was wearing looked a good deal like a bed-coat to Andrej. Had the Tutor come in his bed-dress and slippers? Perhaps he wasn't out of uniform after all. Perhaps he was wearing Tutor's Rest Dress. Andrej took the proffered glass of rhyti and drank it down for concentration. He was getting punch-drunk.

"You needed to talk, Andrej?"

He couldn't think how to begin; all he could do was sit, staring stupidly at the clear vial in his hand. He'd put all of his energy into his idea—his single hope for a chance to change the Tutor's mind. He couldn't quite remember why he'd thought it was going to work.

"Maybe another glass of rhyti, then?" Tutor Chonis suggested.

Why not? He had no idea where to begin. How could he have imagined that this would work? He might as well give up, he might as well go back to quarters and accept defeat like the powerless slave that he was in this place.

Except . . .

Except that there was a chance.

And a man could not be managed without his permission—unless he was a bond-involuntary. No other could be excused for submitting to coercive management.

He was Koscuisko.

He was responsible for the work of his hand, and for the work done at his direction, and for the people who carried out his bidding.

"I want that man for my Security." The rhyti was helping; reaching out a tentative hand, he poured a third glass, remembering almost too late to top off the Tutor's glass politely—like the submissive little Student that they wanted him to be. "You know the one, St. Clare. And after our last meeting I had a thought."

Tutor Chonis's skeptical raised eyebrow was no less effective for the disorder of his hair. Granted, he looked like a sleepy scurry-hunter, but a sleepy scurry-hunter was a scurry-hunter none the less.

"I believe that if the Tutor reviewed the exercise, it would demonstrate that St. Clare did not in fact at any time give up the restricted information—until he was convinced that he was clear of the environment in which it was restricted, as indicated by the question he was asked, a question which clearly presupposed full knowledge of the entire situation." Not as if he was as confident as he would have liked to be of that, but he had to relate it as he remembered it.

"The Tutor has also expressed a concern over my inappropriate expansion of the Writ. I have meditated on the Tutor's comments . . ." —to find a way around them, a way to use them to get what he needed to have. No matter what it took—"and have determined that the Tutor is correct. There is no way in which St. Clare can be bound over to me after his unfortunate lapse. And also that the Tutor's reservations about my . . . attitude . . . must be accepted as valid criticism."

How was he going to approach this?

Tutor Chonis made no move, showed no reaction. Perhaps Tutor Chonis was asleep. He was on his own either way.

"The only uncertainty in my mind concerns whether one of these circumstances might in fact change. Because if one could change, it would be an indication that change was possible in other areas as well."

Now at last Tutor Chonis bestirred himself to drink his rhyti. "One might ask oneself if Student Koscuisko believes that the rule of Law is to be amended with no more substantial or significant a cause than one Student's vanity."

All right. They both knew what he was trying to say. It was time for his last-chance offer, the desperate gamble that had kept him at work in the lab until he'd found what he'd been looking for.

"It is the vanity of a good Student, Tutor Chonis. Whether or not I was remiss in chasing down the secret—and I will sup the sin-cake freely, if I must—the fact remains that it is not a thing often done. You told me as much yourself. With respect. Sir."

At least he thought so. He was almost certain that he remembered Tutor Chonis telling him that.

Or had it been Joslire?

He was so tired that his hand shook as he reached the clear vial that he held out across the table to where Tutor Chonis's hand rested, holding the rhyti glass. "And there is something that the Student has to offer to the Bench in consideration. Apart from any claim to skill or efficiency, at the Question."

Tutor Chonis plucked the vial away from Andrej's nerveless fingers, frowning at it as though there should be some explanatory text within. "And you are referring to?"

"The Tutor had expressed the hope that the Student would enrich the Controlled List." The Controlled List was an abomination under Heaven. So was he. He was a man who had learned to take ecstatic pleasure from torturing a bound man.

"That which you hold may well prove worthwhile from that point of view." And even with so much at stake, it was almost too difficult to promise such a thing. Andrej was surprised at how hard it was to say it.

Especially in the face of Tutor Chonis's sudden eagerness, his greedy interest too plain by half on his no-longer-sleepy face as he held the damning vial to the light and rolled it in his fingers to make the liquid sparkle. "What have you brought me, young Andrej?"

My honor. My honor and my decency, which I will give to you as sacrifice in exchange for the life of that hapless bond-involuntary. I will trade. Give me his life, and I will do as you have asked me.

"It should be a speak-serum." He was no longer quite sure what it was, in the specific sense. He was too keenly aware of what it was in the general sense, for his own peace of mind. "For Mizucash, since you gave me one of those. Or was he actually Security as well? Species-specific. But I think it can safely be deployed against a broader spectrum. Something about a handful of the protein clusters looked quite familiar, except I didn't have the time to run it all down before first-shift."

"Your duty to the Fleet requires you—"

Andrej was ready for that obvious objection. "My duty to the Fleet requires that I perform according to my Writ and according to my rated field. Which is not pharmacology. That lies outside—apart—"

"You've got it all worked out, haven't you?" Tutor Chonis sounded either sarcastic or curious, Andrej could not tell which. "Let me see if I understand you, Student Koscuisko. At the heart of the matter, you are saying that if I oblige you, then you will oblige me. The Fleet. The Bench."

No, surely not, wasn't there some problem in suggesting he "oblige" the Bench? "I think so, Tutor Chonis. I may not have expressed myself correctly, I am not thinking very well." He reached for the rhyti jug, surely near empty by now. But by the time he had it in hand, he'd forgotten why he'd wanted it, and stared at it stupidly, trying to focus his thought.

"Only give me the life of that man, I will administer discipline at the Class One level, and I will undertake to provide speak-sera . . ."

". . . And the sensory factors. And the nerve agents."

Andrej shuddered in profound horror at the thought. Or was it just fatigue? It didn't matter. All he wanted was the life of Robert St. Clare. He would do anything they wanted. "I will satisfy the Bench for it, Tutor Chonis. If only this man can be not guilty of fault, since it was none of his."

There was a silence, as Tutor Chonis mused over the vial in his hand.

"Very well." Finally Tutor Chonis tucked the vial into a pocket of his bed-dress and stood up. "I will bring this to the attention of the Administrator when the case is heard. Perhaps an exchange of hostages would not be inappropriate, when all is written and read in."

Did that mean yes?

"Thank you, Tutor."

It didn't matter any more what Tutor Chonis meant. He had done his utmost. There was nothing else he could do except wait and see whether they would take the trade or not. "May I be excused? I think it may be time. For fast-meal. And I think I may be hungry."

Tired, too tired to think straight.

"Go to your quarters, Andrej. Get some sleep."

What was Chonis talking about? He didn't have time to get any sleep. He had class in less than three eights, class with Tutor Chonis.

"You're excused from training until further notice. I have to discuss this matter with my superiors. But—in the time intervening . . ."

Between now, and what?

". . . since you already know, there is something you can do for us, quite apart from the matter of St. Clare. The man who served your fellow Student as prisoner-surrogate needs surgery within your rating. We're not rated an assigned specialist on site, so there's no one else here qualified for the job."

Between now and the decision, obviously. Andrej stood up, and nearly fell over, hanging against the back of the chair for balance. Didn't he know better than to run the time-string out like this? "Noycannir. Is he stable? I couldn't do anybody any good, not right now." Except that Tutor Chonis had told him to get some rest. So obviously the man was stable.

"I'll inform Infirmary, they'll be ready for you. Once you're rested. Curran."

He hadn't heard the door open behind him. Tutor Chonis must have signaled for Joslire, because Joslire was here, and Andrej was fairly certain that Joslire had not been privy to the entire conversation.

"The Tutor requires?"

And shame on him, too, for keeping Joslire up so late, when Joslire could hardly beg off his assigned duties—whatever they were—just because a Student had been having a long night of it.

"Curran, take Student Koscuisko back to quarters. He is to be excused from training until further notice. Once he's rested, he'll be wanted in Infirmary. We think that he may be able to salvage Student Noycannir's prisoner-surrogate Idarec."

"Heard and understood, Tutor. With respect, the officer should come to quarters now."

There was an arm at his back, steadying him. A hand at his elbow, turning him gently. It was time for him to go to bed.

Had he remembered his prayers?

"Good rest, Andrej. Try to get some sleep."

It was a voice from far away, speaking a language Andrej no longer understood.

He was asleep before he could decide whether it was important to reply.

Administrator Clellelan pushed the relish-pickle dish across the table, frowning past Tutor Chonis's head at the front end of Tutor's Mess as he did so. "No, it won't do, Adifer. It won't do at all."

Clellelan was a good man for detail, it being so important in Fleet Medical to know which details one was assiduously to ignore for the sake of one's own peace of mind. Because Clellelan was so good at minutiae, Tutor Chonis was confident that the pickles were to be taken as a sign, and not absentminded hospitality; nothing that Clellelan did was really absentminded, no matter how casual it seemed. The gesture was meant to offset a categorical rejection of Chonis's proposal with an unselfish offer of a mutually favorite—and rather scarce—breakfast salt-pickle. Chonis appreciated the balance, crunching loudly on a nice chunk of imtell to show his gratitude. Just because he was going to make the Administrator reverse his position didn't mean he wasn't happy to hog as much of the salt-pickle as he could during the process.

"Now, Rorin, you aren't paying attention. I'm offering a real benefit for us all." Intangible, perhaps, but no less valuable for that, and the Administrator had to know what he was thinking as well as Chonis himself did. "The last six Consultations all proved it. The less these officers have to get their hands dirty, the likelier they are to live out their assignments. Judicial Concern MC-double-two-sixteen, sub five, and all the rest."

The orderly came to refill the steaming-jug, and the Administrator took advantage of the moment to spear a piece of salt-pickle for himself on the end of his pronged knife. It was a positive sign. Say absolutely not, offer salt-pickles; say maybe, take some back.

Chonis gave his superior a moment to chew on his thoughts, and his pickle, before he continued. "Maximizing our resources is the thing to do these days, what with Fleet bleeding us dry out in the Lanes. Get Koscuisko's cooperation, get him busy, and we'll start seeing benefit immediately. One Inquisitor is worth any number of bond-involuntaries, as far as the Bench is concerned. You know that better than I do."

Both Inquisitors and bond-involuntaries were getting harder to come up with, that was true. But it was still significantly easier to find qualified Security material under Judicial order than it was to find Inquisitors who were capable of performing their Judicial function for even as many as eight years without letting themselves succumb to paranoia, psychosis, or other dysfunctionalities along the way.

"You really want me to do it, don't you, Adifer? Only last night you were telling me that your Koscuisko could turn into a battery with a random detonation sequence, if we weren't careful with him."

"Did I say that?" No, actually, Chonis didn't think he had. Clellelan had put in too much time in Engineering in his youth, and still tended to think of uncontrolled aggression in young Inquisitors as if it were a simple matter of reinstalling a worn-down safety circuit. "That was before he came to my office, this morning."

The conversation was beginning to get serious. Chonis paused for a moment to savor the memory of his early morning interview with that spirited little Aznir autocrat-to-be. The intensity. The desperation. The self-conscious pledge to accept being managed in return for an annulment of the consequences of what he had done, as if he had actually been at fault.

"It's usually not an issue, you know that. Most of our Students are too depressed by being here in the first place to question authority. Controlling Koscuisko could be a real problem for the Fleet. He doesn't like being told what to do—has got no practice in being told what to do—and he seems capable of putting a real sapper in the works, making a mockery of Inquisition. Remember Poneran?"

Clellelan winced. "Please, Adifer, not at the fast-meal table. Four years of deliberate obstructionism, just short of insubordination. Just short. And then she disappears, and into the Free Government, from all indications. We don't need any more like her."

"So we give Koscuisko what he wants, we leave him with a reminder of why he should behave, and out of it we get to keep the troop. And we get a rope around Koscuisko's neck, to avoid any more embarrassments like Poneran. And we extend the working life of every Inquisitor in Fleet by giving them more and more ways to do their jobs with nice clean drugs instead of the instruments of Inquiry and

Confirmation. We even make the First Secretary happy, and that makes the Second Judge happy, and that means—we might even get funded for better quarters next year."

Chonis could tell that the Administrator was tempted by the glazed look in his eyes. After a moment, however, he shook his head, reaching for a piece of brod-toast.

"It would be nice. But I can't authorize an exception, not without a Judicial hearing. You know that. And then they'd want to know how it got so far out of hand in the first place. Unacceptable."

It was as close to a criticism as the Administrator had come yet; but in the warm glow left by Koscuisko's submissive petition, Chonis felt he could easily accept so mild an implied rebuke without wincing. "That's not the least of the things that impresses me about my Andrej, you know. I still don't understand what tipped him off." Joslire Curran had said that the prisoner-surrogate had started to call Koscuisko "the officer," once, during the Fourth Level. That was true enough. But then Curran was apparently convinced that Koscuisko saw people's thoughts, and smelled what they were thinking.

"And?"

"And you can do it without having to authorize an exception. Take Koscuisko's offer of speak-sera. The regulation allows bond-involuntaries sentenced at this Level to serve as experimental subjects."

The Administrator snorted in disbelief, as Chonis had anticipated he would. "And how am I going to manage all of this? There's a Class Two violation on Record against St. Clare, we can't just lose it as if it was a Student Exception."

It was understood that Students tended to overreact to their first taste of absolute power. There was an administrative pressure valve in place to prevent the assigned bond-involuntaries from being egregiously abused. Complaints against bond-involuntaries could be set aside as "Student Exceptions," on advice from the assigned Tutor— when the bond-involuntary involved could get to a Tutor in time, that was. But that wasn't what Chonis had in mind.

"Think about the Controlled List for a moment," he urged his superior. "It is permissible for research work on the Controlled List to be carried out at this Station, isn't it? Research and testing. Valid Fleet enrichment functions."

Now Clellelan had got it; Chonis could tell by the way he chewed on his pickle. "Research and testing," he repeated slowly. "You're right, of course. Koscuisko is young, untried, we don't know for certain what he is capable of."

Just so. "There isn't any qualification on statute about what kind of Controlled List drug it has to be. Simply that the condemned can be offered the choice, at Administrative discretion."

As a matter of fact, there were only nine places in all of Jurisdiction Space where the exception could be applied. Eight research stations; and Fleet Orientation Station Medical. Naturally the provision had been made with other drugs less innocuous than mere speak-sera in mind, if even speak-sera could be called harmless when an entire community could be condemned through the action of the drug.

Most often there was very little to choose between suffering discipline for a Class Two violation and serving as a Controlled List volunteer. Since many of the drugs on the Controlled List were lethal in ultimate effect, any bond-involuntary with an eighth of self-preservation would naturally elect the purely physical—predictable, dependable—punishment.

The fact remained that on any one of nine stations a bond-involuntary who had committed a Class Two violation could be offered research duty as a substitute for discipline. And Koscuisko had developed a speak-serum. Given Koscuisko's scholastic record, it was unlikely that anything that he developed along the lines of his psychopharmacological Second Branch would turn unexpectedly terminal on Robert St. Clare.

"I like it." Clellelan took a moment longer, clearly enjoying his meditations on what Chonis's proposal could get for him. "It satisfies on a number of counts. Koscuisko gets what he seems to be so anxious for, by your report. We manage without having our embarrassing lapse show up on the replacement request." And no matter whether they had been in fact negligent, or Koscuisko was just damn good. As far as Fleet Procurement would be concerned, the request for a replacement body for St. Clare would signal a careless waste of the resource, pure and simple. "All right, Adifer, answer me two questions and I'll agree to it."

"Two questions?" He was mildly surprised; he could only think of the one, at a guess.

"Making Verlaine happy. And how do you mean to keep it all from going to Koscuisko's head, bending the regulations to get what he wants, and so forth."

Oh, well, *that*.

Chonis smiled.

"Verlaine is happy because we graduate his very own pet Inquisitor. Think about it, Rorin. She doesn't need to go through the same course as the others; she'll never be in a field environment anyway. Isn't that what the Fleet Exception specifies? We're to prepare her to assist the Bench in routine inquiry, to be exercised by direct Bench warrant instead of Fleet's Command directive?"

Clellelan was nodding, but Chonis couldn't tell if it was because he remembered or because he wanted the server who had come up to take away his hot-dish to bring him his after-sweet.

"So all she needs to know is how to press the doses through with an osmo-stylus. Koscuisko can show her that. Practically anybody could show her that, the osmos have gotten so sophisticated these days." Leaning back in his chair, Chonis paused while the server put the fruit dish down in front of him. "She'll take her Levels, all right, but just this once it's going to be drug-assisted all the way. And that's the only way to guarantee that she'll get through, with her background."

At least Clellelan was thinking about it. Chonis could practically hear the micro-gates clicking. "And, coincidentally, a neat trick on the First Secretary," the Administrator said slowly, as if tasting the idea in his mouth as he spoke. "Sending him an orderly when he thought he was going to get, well, someone like Koscuisko, for instance. Access to the Controlled List—she'll do more harm than good for him, not knowing the interaction tables. It's ingenious."

And Chonis didn't mind accepting that bit of flattery, either. It was one of his better jokes, if he said so himself. Noycannir would have access to the Controlled List without the first real notion of how to use it, which meant—even taking her native intelligence into consideration—that there simply wasn't a great deal she was going to be able to do.

There were too many intangible considerations affecting use of drugs on the Controlled List. The Administrative criteria had yet to be reduced to any expert system under Jurisdiction; use of Controlled List drugs remained a judgment call, one which Noycannir could not hope to make without killing the First Secretary's victims on too regular a basis.

The First Secretary didn't want his enemies killed.

He wanted them intimidated into submission by his proprietary access to an Inquisitor capable of plumbing their most damning secrets, who was just waiting for the word to go to work on them. Once it became obvious that their deaths were the worst they had to fear from Noycannir, Verlaine would find that all his influence and manipulation had got him precisely nowhere. Fleet would have made its point. The only truly effective Inquisitors were medical officers. That was the way it had to stay.

"Come on, man, the other thing."

He'd let his mind wander, savoring the pleasing completeness of Verlaine's future frustration. "Sorry. Yes. Koscuisko. Needs to be firmly kept down. And he was the one who proposed it . . ."

Granted, that it wasn't playing quite fair. But St. Clare still was getting off easy, no matter which way the blows fell.

"When Koscuisko came to my office yesterday mid-second, he suggested that St. Clare be considered insubordinate to him, and disciplined by him at the Class One level accordingly. I propose to keep my young Andrej in hand by requiring he administer the punishment per his suggestion. And bind St. Clare over to him for the duration, to serve as a constant reminder of what almost happened when he decided to express a little temperament. Student Koscuisko suffers his pangs of conscience very deeply, from all indications. I think it will work out very nicely."

There was a problem, of course, with suffering any pangs of conscience too deeply in this line of work. But that was not the immediate problem. The immediate problem was that the Administrator was frowning.

"You want to hazard him with the new drug, and then arrange a flogging on top of it?"

Chonis had foreseen the problem, and Chonis could answer for it. "It's only a speak-serum, Administrator." A little more formality couldn't hurt, at this crucial point. "St. Clare will lose his deferment, but you'll have the option of granting the reduction in his Bond. That's well worth a whipping, surely. And Koscuisko knows what he's doing in that lab, at least to judge from his scholastics. If the speak-serum itself is going to cause a problem, he'll let us know. We can negotiate."

Clellelan chewed on his lower lip for a long moment.

But when he spoke again Chonis knew that he had won. "Thought of everything, haven't you?"

"It's an important opportunity." There was no room for false pride. It was a judgment call, in the end; Clellelan's judgment call. "I had to be sure that it was justifiable." And neither of them were under any illusions concerning precisely what was at stake for Koscuisko's unfortunate prisoner-surrogate.

The Administrator nodded, acknowledging several layers of meaning at once. "How do you propose to execute?"

Clellelan would have to be present to adjudicate St. Clare's discipline; it was a requirement. Chonis had checked the scheduler already.

"Koscuisko is sleeping things off, and I want him in surgery once he wakes up. Idarec." No further explanation was required. The potential loss of a bond-involuntary would reflect badly on the Administrator's cost management, let alone the potential loss of two—and within a single week, at that. So he could be confident that Idarec's case had been on the Administrator's mind.

"Worth a try," Clellelan said. "This evening?"

"You've got the third quarter free, this second-shift. I don't know how long Koscuisko will take in surgery. I rather thought that making an appointment for the third quarter would be safest, if it suits the Administrator's convenience."

Clellelan nodded. "Let the scheduler know what you want blocked. You've outdone yourself this time, Adifer. Not one, but two cost savings, both at the First Judge's favorite 'tactical significance' level. Give yourself an extra commendation or two."

His words were casual as he rose to leave, his hand on Chonis's shoulder to prevent the otherwise obligatory courtesy of standing as one's superior left the table. Chonis accepted the token with a bowed head. It was a lot of money. And two lives. Three lives, if you counted bringing Koscuisko into line, and making a productive resource out of all that talent and passion.

He hadn't been certain that the Administrator would agree to go along with his plan.

And only now was it safe to see St. Clare.

CHAPTER SEVEN

Robert St. Clare was hungry and hurt, cold and despairing, but he knew enough to find his way to his feet when his guards came to sharp, heel-clicking attention. There were two of them posted on either side of his open-fronted cell—stationed there as much for their benefit as for his own—to take education from the bad example that he presented. The sudden movement alerted him: someone was there, someone with rank. He knew what to do in the presence of people with rank. It had been drilled into him to the point of reflex, and not even the hopelessness of his situation could stifle the insistent voice of his conditioning or stay the governor's inevitable response to any attempts to resist it. *Stand up:* but they're going to murder me. *Stand up:* but they're going to torture me again. *Stand up:* but there's nothing they can do to punish me if I don't, not more than what they're going to do to me already.

The Jurisdiction's Fleet had trained him all too well.

You will stand to attention in the presence of a superior officer.

Stumbling in his dizziness, he rose from the unpadded block that served as the cell's one piece of furniture—too shallow to lie flat upon, too short to lie at length upon. He stood up and straightened his spine as best he could, trying to ignore the throbbing agony in his shoulder. Perhaps it was just as well, after all. His family were dead. His mother was dead, and his father was dead; his brothers were dead; his uncles—most of his cousins—his kin-group were all gone.

Perhaps it was just as well for him to join them.

But his sister . . .

Pain that was deeper than physical seized him, writhing in his gut like a nest of adders. His sister. Because of his failure, his flaw, his betrayal, he'd never be able to find her, to buy her back from Jurisdiction, to take her away from the life that the Bench had mandated.

Because he had not been able to keep his mouth shut.

Because he had—vaingloriously—hazarded the offered chance to reduce his term, and reduce her term with his, she was condemned to a full thirty years—if she could survive that long, in shame and suffering. Never to know what had happened to him until the day when her Bond was past, and her body would be hers to call her own again.

His sister . . .

"Robert St. Clare. Do you remember me?"

It would have been better never to have tried. But those four years . . . what four years in a Jurisdiction service facility could mean to Megh—

"Sir. The officer is Tutor Chonis. Sir."

Eight years, with hers and his together. Eight years he could have won, and Security was honest service compared to what Megh was to be put to. Instead there would be nothing for her, nothing, because he had not been able to do his duty by his sister.

"Relax, man, you're not at Mast, not yet. Stand at ease. Better yet, go and sit down."

The words were meaningless. He stood numbly at attention as the guards opened the power grid, carrying a chair through for the Tutor's use. Chonis himself came right up to him, pushing him gently back until his legs struck up against the edge of the rest-block, and he sat.

"Clearly you don't need to be told what an unpleasant situation we have here."

The Tutor's words were beginning to come clear through the heavy pounding of his pulse. They might have been funny; but he wasn't sure why he thought so. "Sir."

"It may—I must emphasize that word, may—not be quite as impossible as it seems. There is no question about the offense, of course."

Of course. Despair and shame flooded his mind; but anger swamped those sapping emotions, fury at being spoken to as if his imminent torture—not to speak of poor Megh's prostitution—were inconveniences, in the greater scheme of things.

"There is no question about the offense." That Tutor Chonis gave him. That the Jurisdiction had committed. "Sir."

"Rabin, have you ever heard of the Jurisdiction's Controlled List?"

"In Orientation. Yes. Sir." And they used his name so casually, his private name, the name that none but his deprived sister had any right to speak without permission . . .

"On an experimental station a bond-involuntary who has committed a Class Two violation may elect to serve as a sentient subject for Controlled List purposes, rather than undergo other discipline. Now. Here we have . . . a problem."

Except that this was not an experimental station but a teaching station. And only a man more desperate than even he would risk the Controlled List by choice: they didn't need condemned men for the speaking drugs, after all, it was only the other sorts that would be involved. "Yes, sir. The officer states the existence of a problem."

It wasn't quite coming out the way it should. He sounded rather thick-tongued to himself, not to say disrespectful. Why should he care about disrespectful? He was going to die.

Because his governor didn't care whether or not he was going to die, and to his governor disrespect was much more serious than mere termination.

"The officer—Student Koscuisko, your Interrogator. You remember him? Of course you do."

Of course he did. Repulsive, short, pale, colorless man, his voice the only live thing about him. Oh, and his hands, his pitiless strength, his mocking eyes. "Sir."

"Koscuisko is determined that there was no Class Two violation, but that a Class One offense has been offered to him by you. For which he wishes you to be disciplined. Student Koscuisko has a gift, St. Clare."

Oh, was that what it was called, here in this place? "A gift, sir. Yes, sir."

"He has a gift for drugs. For psychoactive drugs, specifically. Student Koscuisko is willing to trade his skill for your life, Rabin. And his skill may be worth far more to us, in the end, than you could ever hope to be, alive or dead."

And, oh, but that was precisely the thing to tell him, wasn't it? This man, you see, he's a poisoner, and we need good poisoners. We don't particularly care what happens to you one way or the other. One must keep one's poisoners happy. "Sir."

"Good, I'm glad you're following me. Now. Koscuisko has presented us with a speak-serum, and we want someone to test it. Volunteer to test this speak-serum, Rabin, and the Administrator will accept it in lieu of Class Two discipline, as long as there is no question about the Class One violation."

Something was not adding up, and Robert shook his head to clear it. "Class One? Two? Experimental station? Sir—"

"Although this is not an experimental station we are permitted to carry out research for the Controlled List. Therefore the exception applies." The Tutor rose to his feet now, pacing the few measures of the cell with deliberation. As if he was not quite sure on his pronouncements and wanted to convince himself as he laid the argument out.

"You have committed a Class Two violation. Therefore you may elect to test a Controlled List candidate drug in lieu of other Class Two discipline, if you are offered the alternative by the Administrator. Koscuisko is determined that you have committed a Class One violation. Therefore we will let the Class Two pass with the token ordeal—a talking-drug . . ."

Stopped in front of where he sat, now, the Tutor fixed his eyes on Robert's face. For emphasis?

"And you will accept Class One discipline from Student Koscuisko. Your officer."

He couldn't be sure, there was too much to think about. He almost thought that he was being offered a way out, a chance, his life; but that was too dangerous to dream on. Hope had confused his mind, making him hear things that never had been implied. That had to be the explanation.

In his confusion he said the first thing that came to his mind, in response to the last thing he'd heard the Tutor say. "The greater fault overrides the lesser fault. Sir. The more severe discipline replaces all the lesser."

As if he would object on that head, if he could believe that there was any hope at all. As if that would make a difference, between a chance for life and death by torture.

The Tutor smiled. "Yes, of course you're right," he said. "At least under normal circumstances. But in this case, the greater punishment is being waived on a technicality, because Koscuisko has got stubborn about it. Do you really mean to challenge the Bench on this issue?"

Mindless panic flooded Robert's mind at the mere phrase. Challenge the Bench? Challenge the Bench? Of course he could not, dare not, challenge the Class One discipline. To challenge the Bench would be . . . it would be—

"Be at ease." Tutor Chonis was quite near to him now, speaking low and confidentially in his ear. "It's just your governor, Robert, running a little hyperactive, probably should be adjusted for stress. Of course no one suggested such a thing. I—regret—my thoughtless use of the phrase."

There was the strangest note of strained unbelief in Tutor Chonis's voice, almost as if he did not understand why he was saying the words that he heard himself speak. Believable or not, the words restored Robert's psychic equilibrium—to a degree—almost as quickly as it had been upset in the first place.

"Sir." The Tutor moved away, quickly. "No disrespect was intended, if the Tutor please. Spoken for clarification only. Sir." In fact he was unsure why he had made so ill-advised a remark; but the Tutor, nodding, merely continued in his explanation, as if he had decided to treat it as unobjectionable.

"It is already a rather extreme appeal to Administrative privilege to substitute the trial of such an innocuous drug where the other less benign ones were clearly intended. The Administrator must demonstrate that his decision was based on reason and sound Judicial practice, and the best interest of Fleet. And this has nothing to do with you, St. Clare, we aren't doing you any favors. It has everything to do with Andrej Koscuisko."

Now it began to be real, to Robert. He finally started to grasp the actual meaning of what the Tutor was saying to him. That they would offer him reprieve was not within the realm of even the wildest fantasy for a bond-involuntary with a Class Two violation. That they would reprieve him by the way, as a casual gesture designed to ingratiate them with their young torturer, made much more sense.

He remembered Koscuisko's fingers in his shoulder, the officer's cold amused tone of voice, commenting on the beating that he was administering. He couldn't suppress a shudder.

"It might be quicker," he whispered. "With the Tutor's permission. To take it all at once, and die of it. Instead of . . . what?" The conflict of emotions warring in his mind unmanned him, leaving him vulnerable to nameless imagined horrors. "What is this Koscuisko, that he wants so much to see me bleed? Again?"

Talking to himself, he did not at first realize that the Tutor was answering his question.

"If he wanted merely to see you bleed, we'd have given you to him for your Class Two violation, and see what he would make of his Advanced Levels. No, I think he's trading something he very much doesn't want to do, simply in order to get you off the charge. But it doesn't matter what either of us thinks."

The Tutor signaled at the gate, continuing to talk with his back turned as he stepped out into the corridor.

"You're to be assigned to him, as it happens. Permanently. Get used to the idea."

Assigned?

To Koscuisko?

To be responsible for the life of the man who had shamed him, to die in defense of the man who had put him to torture?

"And he's the one who wanted it that way." The Tutor stood on the other side of the gate now, with his hands clasped behind his back and an odd look of amusement and self-satisfaction on his face. "So you'll have plenty of time to decide how you feel. And twenty-six years is a long time, isn't it, Rabin? But not so long as thirty."

Then Chonis nodded—in the face of Robert's speechless stare—and was gone from his line of sight.

Twenty-six years? Instead of thirty?

Then Megh would not need to suffer the extra term, after all . . .

For the freedom to ransom his sister he could do anything.

He could even submit to Koscuisko, and wait for the Day.

Near the second quarter of second-shift, Joslire woke to the sounds of Koscuisko starting to stir. Slipping out into the corridor, he ordered the officer's meal—a little on the heavy side; Koscuisko hadn't eaten for nearly five shifts now. Koscuisko was in the wet-shower when Joslire got back, leaning up against the back wall with the water full in his face—trying to clear his head? To wake up? Under other circumstances, Joslire might have grinned, Koscuisko was so obviously struggling with his sleep. But officers were not to be smiled at, no matter how indulgently, not even in the privacy of one's own thoughts.

Joslire contented himself with setting up the meal tray instead.

Koscuisko took his time in the wet-shower. Joslire got the uniform of the day hung neatly on the rack in the inner room, without hurrying, and was just about to check the depth of steep in the rhyti brewer when the shower shut off. Koscuisko came out of the lavatory dripping and half-naked, toweling his hair; he was beginning to look a little less asleep, but only just, and Joslire stood to attention to greet him without any sort of trepidation about what sort of mood his Student might be in.

"The officer slept well?"

Which only made the shock, and his confusion, the more abrupt and disorienting. He hadn't been expecting Koscuisko to do or say anything in particular, certainly nothing like this.

"I imagine. What time is it? Good morning, Joslire, would you be so good as to remove your clothing."

It was a moment before Joslire quite understood what Koscuisko had said, the order coming directly on the heels of Koscuisko's rather disconnected response. But Koscuisko was clearly waking even as he spoke, and by the time Joslire absorbed the fact that he'd been told to undress Koscuisko had already become a little impatient with the delay. "If you please, Joslire."

In fact he sounded almost angry, angry at Joslire. Bowing quickly, Joslire moved his hand to the secures at his blouse's collar almost before he'd well completed his salute. "The officer's pardon is—"

"To be used for an improbable anatomical experiment. Did you wear your five-knives, when you were . . . when you played the game?"

The game . . . when he served as prisoner-surrogate, perhaps. There was only one probable reason for Koscuisko's order, Joslire knew; not as if it would be the first time, no. Bond-involuntaries were expected to accommodate their officers in any manner their officers might choose to specify. But what difference would his five-knives make to Koscuisko, if that was what the officer intended? Why would it matter?

"It was necessary to perform the exercise without, by the officer's leave." A bond-involuntary might be permitted his five-knives. They could be considered to fall under religious exception; and served also as a constant reminder of his shame, to have dishonored his five-knives by wearing them as an enslaved man. But a prisoner would naturally have been stripped of them immediately. For security purposes, quite apart from all the rest.

"Then you will oblige me by taking them off. Now."

Joslire dropped his head in submission, glad of the opportunity to hide his conflict. "According to the officer's good pleasure." Koscuisko's meal would be getting cold, the rhyti over-steeped. It wouldn't do to mention that, though he was just as likely to suffer for the fact. No, that wasn't so—Joslire scowled at himself, stripping off his under-blouse hurriedly. The officer hadn't seemed the type to make use of a compliant body in quite this way. What had happened to Koscuisko in the Tutor's office? The Tutor had seemed pleased about something, that was true.

Koscuisko had gone back to the washroom to leave the towel and frown at the mirror. Joslire couldn't afford to steal more than a glance; he'd been told twice now, he didn't dare keep the officer waiting. Fumbling with the catches, he loosed the sheathing that bound his five-knives to him, so close—so much a part of him—that the simple requirement to remove them had been almost as much of the torment of the game, as Koscuisko had termed it, as any of the rest. Did Koscuisko know that? Did Koscuisko care? Why should Koscuisko care, except that Joslire had imagined that Koscuisko had been serious about his Bond, except that Koscuisko had seemed genuinely distraught to think that St. Clare would have to stand discipline for a Class Two violation, and likely die of it . . .

Koscuisko stood in the washroom's doorway, watching him. Joslire laid his five-knives down on his sleep-rack as reverently as he dared, and pulled his boots off clumsily. Moving into the center of the room Koscuisko contemplated his meal tray, and for one moment Joslire cherished a forlorn hope that the officer would permit himself to be distracted. Would change his mind and decide that the satisfaction of one appetite would serve as well as that of another.

He should have known better, he told himself, and laid his trousers neatly to one side of his folded blouse and his five-knives. It was better not to indulge in such fantasies. The more quickly the officer's appetite could be satisfied, the more quickly he could get on with the rest of his job, and the Tutor would receive the report on Koscuisko's sexual activity as a positive sign of a healthy libido functioning in more or less traditional ways. Joslire reached for the drawstring of his hip-wrap, anxious—if not eager—to be on the other side of the next few eighths; but Koscuisko's cold voice stopped him a scant sixteenths short of total nudity.

"That's quite all right, Joslire, I should like you to turn to the wall, if you would. I understand that the posture is a familiar one?"

Familiar, perhaps, but not because of frequent and fond practice. Joslire turned to the wall and set his hands flat against the unforgiving steel, his arms stretched well out, turning his face to the floor. "At the officer's discretion." At least his voice was neutral, level, betraying no hint of his inner turmoil. It was a little unusual, still. He had been more frequently flogged against the wall like this than . . . than what the officer would seem to have in mind.

He could sense Koscuisko behind him, his skin prickling unpleasantly from the heat of Koscuisko's own newly showered nakedness. Koscuisko was reaching his hands out, touching his back, touching his shoulders—perhaps it would be over quickly.

Koscuisko's touch was light and clinical, considering, touching with the tips of his fingers, not his whole hand. Settling gently against Joslire's skin before stroking his back, as if he was being careful not to startle him—as if Koscuisko could startle him, Joslire thought, and knew the bitterness of the betrayal that he felt in the helplessness of that necessarily passive resentment. He should have known better than to have imagined that Koscuisko was different than any of the others. He should have known better than to have thirsted after the respect Koscuisko had seemed to show him, as grateful as a starving man for any casual gesture Koscuisko made that could be taken as an acknowledgment of Joslire's personal dignity. He was a bond-involuntary. He had no dignity. No title to his name, no title to his person, no title to his body. Nothing.

Koscuisko hadn't said anything, still touching Joslire's back, lingering for a moment from time to time over a particular spot, always moving his hands slowly enough to keep the skin from crawling in reflex trepidation. What was going on in his mind? There did seem to be a pattern, perhaps . . . Koscuisko seemed to be working his way from Joslire's spine toward his sides, from the small of his back up to the back of his neck and across his shoulders. Almost Joslire had an idea, but no, it couldn't be. It was too far-fetched. Just more wishful thinking, and why wouldn't Koscuisko have just asked?

Koscuisko put his left hand out to Joslire's hand, splayed as it was stubbornly against the wall. "I'm sorry, Joslire," Koscuisko said. "But I require a more extreme angle. Move your arms out a bit, if you would please."

What was Koscuisko after?

And why was waiting so much harder than being put to it, as brutal as that could be?

Koscuisko had both hands at the back of Joslire's shoulder, and Joslire could feel those questing fingers traveling along the line of the muscle stretched taut by Joslire's constrained posture, lingering—briefly but perceptibly—over a knot that Joslire knew was there.

No, it couldn't be . . .

Down along Joslire's flank, now, tracing the thin line of unresponsive skin—the scar tissue that shielded the insulted flesh from pain by refusing to admit all further sensation. Joslire caught his breath in a sudden sobbing gasp, startled out of all his discipline by the shock of his realization—and the paradoxical shame he felt. His scars. That was what Koscuisko wanted, his scars. Koscuisko was reading his body with his hands, feeling and finding the scars that did not show on the surface: the little dead knots where the uttermost tip of the lash had bitten deeply, the long lines down his side where the Student Interrogator had tested his silence with hot metal. The cry escaped his tightly clenched teeth in something like a cough, and Koscuisko flattened his damned hands against Joslire's back and stilled them there, waiting.

"It is very difficult?"

Koscuisko spoke gently, quietly, leaving plenty of space for Joslire to respond.

"Would it be easier for you if I consulted the record, instead? Is there a record that will tell me what I want to know?"

How could he respond? He could be honest, or he could do his duty. And his governor would not permit him to commit a violation, not if it noticed one coming.

"The officer holds the Bond." He sounded half-strangled, even to himself. "The officer is to be provided whatever the officer wishes. The information is on Record." Usually restricted, because of the secrecy of the program, but Tutor Chonis would surely release it to Koscuisko if Koscuisko asked, now that there was no further sense in trying to keep anything from him. "The instructional tape. Is on file. To be viewed at the officer's pleasure, in the Tutor's library." As if he wanted to even think about that, when it was all he could do to keep his voice from breaking . . .

"I should not have asked it of you," Koscuisko murmured, as if to himself. "You will forgive me, Joslire, please. I hope."

Joslire could sense Koscuisko turning away, stepping away, moving toward the inner room.

"On the other hand . . ."

It was forlorn, that note in Koscuisko's voice; forlorn, and utterly desolate.

"On the other hand, after all, you are obliged to."

He did not trust himself to move; nor had he been given leave to, come to that.

"Dress yourself, Joslire. I do not wish to examine your medical records, or your . . . the tapes. There is word from Tutor Chonis for me? Never mind, I will be out in a moment; tell me then."

There was the sound of the privacy barrier sliding to, and Joslire was alone in the outer room, alone and shaken all out of proportion with what little had actually happened to him.

Koscuisko had been so careful, in his touch . . .

Pushing himself away from the wall, he willed the rock-hard tension that ran through his body to subside. There had been no threat. There had been no assault, no intent to assail. And he would not have been permitted to do other than submit, had there been any.

He wiped his face and dressed himself as quickly as he could, and hoped that the officer's meal might still be judged acceptable.

It was humiliating to be so grateful to Koscuisko for the simple fact that Koscuisko hadn't used him.

But well-brewed rhyti was the only way he had to show that he was grateful, humiliating or not.

Oh, Mother of this man, Mother of us all, look upon his suffering, and may it be enough. May honor be satisfied, may you find it full punishment, and condescend to shield him from his sins in your sweet favor. Mother, so we pray, accept his suffering in atonement, and grant it be sufficient; frown no longer upon him . . .

But the Holy Mother cared only for the Aznir, her children, and Joslire was Emandisan. What could the litanies of his childhood avail him here? When he sought to do his duty, there was suffering. If he sought to relieve suffering, he made it worse. There was no getting away from it; it had been torture for Joslire to suffer his touch, and so much more torture was attested to by the mute but damning evidence of all of that subdermal scar tissue. He had no right to reach for Joslire's private heart, and expose him to his own shame. There was victim guilt to consider, Andrej reminded himself. The more one's servants were beaten, the more completely they became convinced that they deserved even stricter discipline yet—a folk truism authenticated by the common psychology of sentient species, a defensive trick played by the order-greedy mind to make sense of an arbitrary world.

Oh, he wanted a drink. Or . . . No, he corrected himself, he didn't want a drink; what he wanted was to be drunk, and not thinking about anything. Not about what he had done to that bond-involuntary, either earlier or later. Not about what he had done to Joslire's fragile sense of self-determination just now. Certainly not about how pleasant it had been to torment St. Clare, up to the moment when he'd realized that there was something that they were keeping from him. Yes, that was it, he wanted to be drunk; and still he couldn't shake a persistent feeling that there were reasons why he couldn't be, not yet.

Joslire had surely had time to dress and to regain his composure by now. Andrej stood up from his sleep-rack, sighing, pushing his hair up out of his face with the spread fingers of his right hand. He supposed he should get dressed, since he'd been staring at his uniform so intently. He couldn't hide in this tiny closet of a bedroom forever.

When he slid the partition open, feeling embarrassed and abashed, he noted to his relief that Joslire had his back to the room, standing at the door. He was spared the awkwardness of initial eye contact, at least. There was someone in the corridor beyond, and that was unusual. Andrej didn't think he'd seen anyone else in this corridor since he'd got here—part of the Administration's scheme to isolate them all and make them vulnerable to the Tutors for approval and validation, it went without saying.

Perhaps if he concentrated on what was going on, he could salvage some self-respect for himself and for Joslire alike. Standing by the study-set, Andrej poured himself a flask of rhyti and waited for Joslire to finish with whatever transaction it was that occupied his time.

"Student Koscuisko has just awakened. He'll be ready once he's had a bite to eat. I'd give it an eight or so."

Nor did Andrej believe that he'd ever heard Joslire refer to himself in the first person. His thoughtless demands had upset Joslire, breached Joslire's careful defensive formality. What must Joslire have thought he meant to do? Andrej shuddered at the enormity of it.

And still Joslire did not sound as though his nerves were on edge.

"Patient prep can start whenever." He thought he recognized the voice of whomever was in the hall. Female voice. His guide in Infirmary yesterday? Travis, her name had been. He thought. What had he been doing in Infirmary yesterday? "Just give the word."

Joslire closed the door and turned back toward the study-set, giving an almost imperceptible start at the sight of Andrej standing there beside his fast-meal. There was a documents-cube in Joslire's hand; Andrej reached his hand out to take it, realizing—now that he remembered—what they had probably been talking about. "Who was at the door, then, Joslire?"

And yet Joslire didn't surrender the cube when Andrej grasped it. Startled, Andrej looked more directly at Joslire than he really wanted to, meeting Joslire's dark, sharp, glittering eyes, trying to decipher what he thought he read there.

After a moment Joslire lowered his eyes and bowed in respectful salute, releasing the cube into Andrej's outstretched hand.

"Travis, from Infirmary, by the officer's leave." Joslire sounded a little subdued but otherwise much the same as ever. "The officer may wish to review the surgical record?"

It had been meant deliberately, as a substitute for some light quip, to show Andrej that he'd been forgiven. Andrej felt his face reddening with gratitude and relief. Wordless gestures were all a bond-involuntary had to communicate interpersonal issues to superior officers. Andrej didn't feel superior. Just now he felt—not for the first time this Term—that Joslire was very much the better man than he, governor or no governor.

Worrying the issue would only keep the memory fresh. Andrej slid the cube into the viewer, sitting down to his fast-meal as he did so. It was rather a full tray for a fast-meal, now that he had a look at it. That was a good thing, Andrej decided. He was ravenously hungry, now that he was awake.

Two keys, and the medical workup appeared on his screen. A man in early adulthood, second-class hominid, subspecies Ovallse. Traumatic injury to the central nervous system, torn fiber in the brainstem, several ugly lacunae along the spinal column, two days old—perhaps three—but not too old yet. The nerves could be persuaded to forget that they'd been bruised and frayed apart, if they could be reconnected with minimal surgical trauma before the fluid of that trauma itself—currently holding the damaged tissue static, waiting for the light—ebbed away again, and let the tenuous connections lapse.

It could be done.

What was the patient's current status?

What therapies—if any—had been engaged up until now?

How old was the Station's surgical machine?

His left hand was full of brod-toast. It was a little clumsy, keying from the right, but the information was there, right enough. Core metabolism had been submerged to the deepest level that could be sustained outside the cryogenic environment. The surgical machine was apparently two or three years old, but with luck it had not been overused during that time. He should be able to achieve primary alignment, if the apparatus had been maintained properly and not allowed to deteriorate.

He had to eat; and then he had to wait after he had eaten, to maximize the extent to which his own physical apparatus would achieve optimal recovery from the abuse it had sustained from stress and alcohol over the past few days. He could use the time to review the species-specific peculiarities of the average adult Ovallse. He had better get into it right away. It had been—what—as much as two days since the injury had occurred?

There was no time to waste.

"Did I hear Travis saying something about patient prep?" Joslire had posted himself at Andrej's shoulder instead of seeing to whatever other chores he might have had. Still trying to provide reassurance, of a sort? When it was surely Joslire who had been abused, Andrej who should provide comfort . . . Andrej appreciated the gesture, even though he was uncertain of its meaning. At the moment he felt willing to take all the supportive comfort he could get, whether or not he could feel that he deserved it.

"As the officer says. The Infirmary has a theater on standby, at the officer's disposal."

And what about St. Clare?

What about the contract he had tried to make with Tutor Chonis, the contract he still shuddered, even now, to so much as contemplate?

"What time is it? Tell them to give me an eight and four. We can be ready to start by then, I'm sure."

He couldn't afford to start thinking about St. Clare.

He was going to need all of the concentration he could muster if he was to succeed in walking through this man Idarec's brain, and leave no damage in his wake.

Doctor Ligrose Chaymalt had been curious about Koscuisko since Term had started, although her brief introduction to him had not impressed her overmuch. Alerted by Security's signal that Chonis's Student was on his way, she made it her business to be at the main entry-station when Koscuisko and his Security escort arrived. A man's life in the balance—even a bond-involuntary's life—surely called for a little formality.

Koscuisko's Security troop stepped up to the barrier at the receiving station, bowing sharply in Chaymalt's direction. "Student Koscuisko reports on Tutor Chonis's instruction to provide possible assistance within his rated field, on bed eleven. As her Excellency please."

Her usual practice was to let the Ward supervisors deal with the Students during their required referral on Wards. Signing off on her subordinates' assessments of the actual medical qualifications of the soon-to-be-Ship's Surgeons as assessed in clinical practice was as close to Ship's Surgeon as she wanted to get. This appeared to be rather a special case, however—to judge from Chonis's interest in him, at any rate. And she had to admit that his academic record was impressive.

"Stand away, Curran. Student Koscuisko and I have already been introduced." A day or three gone by, as a matter of fact. "When you came for your tour, Koscuisko, if you remember."

"It is a distinct pleasure to renew the privilege of your acquaintance." Koscuisko's response was polite, if as formal as his salute. "Am I to have the benefit of Doctor Chaymalt's consultation with the scheduled surgery?"

Almost too polite. Ligrose eyed him skeptically. He hadn't done any practicals since he'd got here. What made Chonis think that this youth—this pale and apparently under-rested child, so recently graduated—was up to pulling the complex procedure off? It wasn't for her to say, of course. None of her staff were going to be stupid enough to try it without the rated specialty. Bed eleven was a dead man any way one looked at it, unless Koscuisko managed to get through the surgery without letting the mechanical probe slip by a single fraction of a sixty-fourth in the wrong direction.

Student Koscuisko was regarding her with a look of courteously muted expectation. She shook her head. "Sorry, not my specialty. Or we'd have done it sooner, of course. But I'll be watching you." More out of boredom than anything else, and it was a useful opportunity to see what kind of surgical practitioners Mayon was turning out these days. She hadn't seen a Mayon graduate through Orientation Station Medical in all the years of her tenure here. Mayon's graduates could name their price, and students who could pay off their schooling in other environments could be relied upon to stand well clear of Inquiry, as a rule.

It was hard to stay abreast of technical innovations, isolated on this tiny station—not as if bed eleven's case called for anything new or innovative. The procedures were actually fairly basic. It was only the fact that they had to be performed perfectly that presented complications.

"In that case I would like to get started, by your leave, Doctor Chaymalt. Is there an orderly assigned?"

Not really. Shiuka had done the patient prep, but Shiuka wasn't rated for the actual procedure—he'd never been properly checked out on the monitors. Chaymalt checked the status board quickly. "Looks like Beeler is coming offshift, you can have Beeler. I'll have him meet you. You, Curran. Take your Student to theater one. Do you know where to find it? Never mind, one of the orderlies can escort you both."

For a moment she thought that Koscuisko was going to protest, to hold out for an orderly who was fresh and rested and at the beginning of his shift, instead of one who would probably not be either. Not as if it made any difference, as far as Chaymalt was concerned. Either Koscuisko had what it took or he didn't, and no orderly of hers was going to make a mistake on the monitors, no matter how tired or hungry he might be.

"Is there a problem?"

Direct challenge was a useful tool. He could hardly question her assignment to her face; it was her Infirmary, after all. Koscuisko merely bowed.

"Very well, then. I'll be observing from my office." Or sleeping, one of the two.

But maybe it would be interesting to see Koscuisko perform.

For now there was nothing in the world but the surgical machine— the operating chair—and the patient who was waiting for him.

The orderly assigned was tired and bored, obviously frustrated at being held overshift; but he did get the setup completed quickly, without incident. Andrej strapped himself into the chair to perform the calibration exercises. Each chair was different within the standardized range, because the level of detail was so specific and exact. While a deviation of the smallest imaginable fraction of a sixty-fourth in the path of the surgical beam could be easily tolerated in most cases, there was no room for error whatever where the nervous system was concerned. There was no problem with the power reserves, no focus degradation to speak of; still, the tolerances had slipped noticeably offscale. It took Andrej several attempts with the beam and the block of pseudo-flesh before he could get the instruments to respond as he liked. There was a simple test of whether or not he was in control of the apparatus, his own variation on the standard measures he'd been taught in his student surgeries. When he could sign his name precisely midway through the block of pseudo-flesh—when he could sign his name with the surgical beam, and have it all of one distance from the mark-point, and have the lines all no more than three particles in thickness—then he was ready to carve within a brain.

He was ready now.

Patient preparation had been completed, the body lay anesthetized—to ensure stability, not because there would be any pain—and selectively exposed within the sterile field. Fastening the goggles over his eyes, Andrej reviewed the operant grids one last time, to be sure that he knew what he was going to do and how he was going to come at it. Spinal first, where the nerves were fatter and the consequences of less than absolute surgical perfection were less severe. Sub-cortical function was the critical area. There was a lot of work to do, and no time like the present to be started.

He sent the machine forward into the sterile field with a quick press at a foot control, activating the enclosure. The mask was already in place. As the webbing smoothed around his body to support his weight, Andrej surrendered to the familiar comfort of the operating environment. Focusing on his first site, he saw nothing but the scanner registration, heard nothing but the subtle pinging signal that the laser made at rest. From now until he was finished with his task, he was no more than the mind of the machine, the operating chair translating his every gesture to the scale of the cellular environment. One wrong gesture could sever a nerve for good and all. One twitch at the wrong time could bisect a muscle or engrave the bone.

There could be no room in his mind for anything other than his patient—and that was relief from his other concerns. This simplification of his life, howsoever temporary, was a present that the patient had provided for him. Obviously the only polite response was to return the favor if he could.

Secure in the serene calm of pure technical expertise, Andrej began to work.

CHAPTER EIGHT

Mergau Noycannir had welcomed the call to the Tutor's office when it finally came. She knew her ground and field; she was confident. She could do nothing more until she found out how the Administration meant to respond to the incident.

"Tutor Chonis?"

He looked up from the stylus-pad on his desk as she spoke from the open doorway, diffidently. His scowl of concentration seemed to lift as if he was actually pleased to see her.

"Student Noycannir. Yes. Come in." Well, it could be that he was glad to see her, and that his smile was in anticipation of dismissing her from Term for her mistake. But somehow it didn't quite smell that way to her. This was confusing.

"I am concerned, Tutor Chonis. It has been a day and the next day, now, since I was to continue the Intermediate Levels, and I have not had the benefit of instruction."

Abstractly speaking, yes, she had made an error. Abstractly speaking, yes, she had violated the Protocols, although Hanbor was at fault—not her—for his failure to correctly emphasize the difference between the tapes that she'd been studying. It didn't take a qualified surgeon to figure that out.

But what was the Tutor going to do about it?

"Mergau, in the past two days we've come to understand that we have not been supporting your needs. In fact we feel that we may be at risk of failing you in a significant sense."

As if he was going to pretend it was the Station's problem. As if he was really concerned about her.

"I've spoken to the Administrator about it. It's not reasonable of us to put you into situations where you can't really be expected to perform. And we think we may have come up with a solution."

Something was not scanning here. There was no reason to revisit these issues yet another time. It couldn't be just that she'd made a mistake. Other Students made mistakes; that was why there were Remedial Levels. "The Tutor is suggesting?"

Rising from his desk, Tutor Chonis went to pull a jug and two cups out of his side closet. "Let me start at the beginning."

Yes, we must always start at the beginning, Mergau jeered at him in her mind. *Start at the beginning, so that you can hold the ultimate point in suspense for as long as possible.*

Setting his cups and the jug down, he poured for both of them. Warmer. Maybe the Tutor actually preferred warmer; or maybe he was trying to trick her into letting down her guard.

"You're here because the First Secretary sees a need for a qualified Writ at the Bench level, in order to pursue the Judicial function. We must stop and ask ourselves—what does the Judicial function at the Bench level entail?"

Whether he was laying a trap or not, he served good warmer. That only made her more suspicious, of course. He'd been keeping notes on her preferences.

"Our station must produce officers who can carry the Writ in the field, down to the cruiser-killer class. That's the working level; that's where the appropriate blend of authority and necessity lies. Now, there is a point to be made from all this, Student Noycannir, with your indulgence."

As if he needed her "indulgence." Oh, she hated them. Hated them all. Would she never be permitted to forget . . .

"I am at my Tutor's disposal entirely," she assured him meekly, sipping her warmer. What if there were treason to be discovered here, in the heart of Fleet Orientation Center Medical, and an Inquisitor was required to sift the sour from the sweet? An Inquisitor without a Fleet assignment, without a primary loyalty to the Fleet . . .

"At the Bench level the functions of Inquiry and Confirmation are most essential. It will always be possible to refer to a regional detention center, if a penalty is to be assessed. What I'm trying to get at, Student Noycannir, is that there's no real need for you to take the same full course of study as that for officers who must Inquire, Confirm, and Execute as well. We can best serve the First Secretary's needs by modifying the course of instruction to a slight extent."

He could not be suggesting that they compromise the Writ. Verlaine had paid so much to get her this far . . . and there was no precedent, no special category under Jurisdiction. The Writ was absolute. Either she would hold it or she would not. "I am confused." Genuinely confused, at the turn that the conversation seemed to be taking. "How can I serve Chilleau Judiciary as Inquisitor if my training is to be modified, as you say?"

The Tutor took a moment before answering her. He glanced idly at the cup of warmer in his hand with the benevolent expression of a man who had a surprise gift for a child, hidden behind his back. It made no sense.

"You know the material, Mergau." But how could he tell her that when she had violated the Protocols? Hanbor's fault, yes, but her deed; on Record, and the Record was permanent . . . "There isn't any question that you understand the theory and the rules of practice. Anyone can make a mistake. But unless we can do a little fine-tuning, as it were, you are simply going to keep on making mistakes, because your broader education is deficient."

The other Students could make mistakes without repercussions, as long as they were within medically acceptable parameters? Was that what he was saying? "I have studied the cases that the Tutor selected. There is more that I should study, Tutor Chonis?"

What was he getting at?

"The further we get, the worse the mistakes will be. The Administrator and I have been working on a way around it. And we think we have a solution. There need be no preparation in field techniques if you will never be required to perform in the field environment."

She did know the material. She did understand the Levels, and their restrictions, and the Protocols for Inquiry and Confirmation and Execution. Field techniques meant blood and striking people, and it was hard for her to restrain her hand when everything she had ever learned of hurting people was to hurt them for once and all, so that they would not trouble her again. The streets of Lathiken had not been holding cells. And from the first that she had ingratiated herself with the man who had started her in Bench Administration, she had understood that in politics as in street-fighting, prudence took no prisoners.

"The Jurisdiction's Controlled List is among the most significant resources available under the Writ. And while the employment of the appropriate drugs does not under usual circumstances satisfy the punitive scales, they are fully satisfactory as instruments of Inquiry and Confirmation."

He was talking about drugs.

This was a new thing, a novel idea, unanticipated input. It rather stunned her, but panic was not far behind.

Panic was never far enough behind.

"But, with the Tutor's indulgence—" she began, and then shut her mouth abruptly when she realized that she didn't know what to say.

"I know what you're thinking, I imagine." Tutor Chonis put up his hand to quiet her protest. "The practical exercises are required for graduation. And you will do your practical exercises, but there is something more important that we must teach you about them. You must learn the Controlled List."

How could she hope to learn the Controlled List when it relied upon more arcane knowledge of the body's function than any field-expedient physical medicine she had ever learned? Was this in the end just another step toward failing her? Had she in truth done well enough, to date, in the scheduled course of instruction, that the Administrator feared that she might successfully complete the course after all?

"Adjudicated Levels and standard interrogation techniques are not, after all, infallible instruments. Why, in a field environment, even the best Inquisitor may lose up to half the prisoners referred at the top end of the Intermediate Levels, not to speak of expected mortality rates at the Advanced. It wouldn't do for the First Secretary to have to trust such imprecise methods for information."

Yes, prisoners died. They were expected to die. It was deemed preferable that they die after they surrendered their secrets, rather than before. But Mergau was beginning to see Tutor Chonis's point.

"You are telling me that my Patron is not well served, if I am just to know the Protocols." The First Secretary wanted the Writ; the power to take the secrets. In Fleet it was not so important to get the secrets. There were always others with the same secrets available to Fleet. For Verlaine's purpose, the secrets were much more individual and private. There could be no waste of prisoners in dying before surrendering their information.

"Precisely so." Tutor Chonis agreed, sounding a little surprised. "When you are graduated and sent back to Secretary Verlaine with the Fleet's compliments, you must be able to get to the information more reliably than Fleet practice dictates." Where the whole point of Inquisition lay as much—if not more—in its use as a weapon primed with deterrent horror as in any actual need for information. "The Administrator proposes to refocus your course of instruction toward that end, and provide you with the basics regarding the Controlled List. We don't usually study the Controlled List in depth here, as you know."

They were not questioning her ability.

They were offering her additional information, and knowledge that she would need to satisfy First Secretary Verlaine's ambition.

It didn't make any sense.

"I am eager for this knowledge," she lied glibly. "How does the Tutor wish me to begin?" Would she be taking extra classwork, was that what Chonis was getting at? More individual study? How could there be any time for her to learn the Controlled List, when the length of the Term was already filled with the standard course of instruction?

"We will revisit the Fourth Level, tomorrow or the next day. Student Koscuisko will assist you in an advisory role. With his help, we mean to build a catalog for you from the Controlled List. When you return to Secretary Verlaine you will have a complete arsenal at your disposal, and—more important—you will know how to demonstrate your mastery. How to use it."

Every Student, every commissioned Ship's Inquisitor, had the Controlled List at their disposal. If she could learn how to use it, though . . . And still something was not right. She remembered Koscuisko's emphatically negative reaction to the Tutor's suggestion that he enrich the Controlled List for the Fleet. And now she was to believe that Koscuisko was going to customize the Controlled List?

For her use? When Koscuisko would just as soon walk on her as acknowledge her existence?

"For the Tutor's care, I am me grateful." The stress was too great, and her dialect was slipping. She had to maintain better control over her emotions. If Koscuisko was involved, didn't that mean it was still just a plot against her? And if it wasn't, how had they got Koscuisko to go along? "How shall I prepare for this?"

The possibilities were intriguing.

"There are some details yet to be worked out with the Administrator. We'll meet here tomorrow mid-shift; I'll send the exact time later on today. We can talk with Koscuisko, discuss the prisoner, see if he knows of something suitable on the List, and schedule your Fourth Level retrial accordingly. In the mean time, you should acquaint yourself with the architecture of the Controlled List, and how it relates to the Levels."

It was clearly the end of the interview. Mergau stood up. "I obey my Tutor gladly. Shall I go now?"

Chonis nodded, with a gesture of release or dismissal. "Hanbor has some introductory material logged to your study-set, waiting for you. You're doing good work, Mergau. With your best effort—and Student Koscuisko's help—we can turn out a really first-rate resource for Secretary Verlaine."

And where had Student Koscuisko been these past two days?

She bowed in salute and took her parting, content to let her Tutor have the last word.

She wasn't sure how she felt about this new development, or whether or not there was a trap in it somewhere.

She would study and consider. And see what came out in the days to come.

Joslire Curran stood at the authorized position of command-wait, trying not to think too much about anything. Koscuisko was in surgery. Tutor Chonis had called him to Disciplinary Mast, and there was only one real possible reason, which was—of course—Robert St. Clare. Lop Hanbor was here; he'd seen it happen from the Tutor's viewing room, even as Joslire had. Sorlie Curran was here, with the rest of his team; they'd actually been present when it had happened. The Security team that had removed Robert from the exercise theater was here, and a few of Station Security, all waiting to hear what they already knew, required by Administrative policy to witness the inexorable decree of the Jurisdiction Bench. The Administrator didn't like to publicize mistakes like the one Robert had made, but when it happened, the Administrator liked to be sure everyone who knew that there had been a problem also knew exactly what the penalty was. Certain and swift punishment was the very cornerstone of Fleet discipline.

The signal came, and Joslire stood to attention as Administrator Clellelan and Tutor Chonis made their formal entrance from the back of the room. They would occupy the raised platform at the front, above the Bar: the Administrator sitting; Chonis on his feet, in the presence of his superior officer. Robert would stand there, too. There would be no difficulty in seeing everything that went on, whether or not any of them were eager to do so.

"Attention to orders." An innocuous opening, and Tutor Chonis made it sound so routine, as if there was not a life to be savaged here. "Disciplinary hearing concerning Class Two violation, disobeying lawful and received instruction, Robert St. Clare. Administrator Clellelan, Presiding. By the Bench instruction."

Not as if he'd never been at Disciplinary Mast before. There had been one this Term already, as one of Tutor Pobo's Students cried an offense of disrespect against assigned Security. Two-and-twenty, then and there, and the Student had made an absolute botch of things. There was no two-and-twenty to be anticipated here. The Administrator had come to condemn a bond-involuntary to death by torture, and all because Andrej Koscuisko had heard the wrong thing at the wrong time, and seen through to the heart of the deception.

"Robert St. Clare, step through."

Since all the Security assembled stood at attention for the duration of the hearing there was no turning to look at the man as they brought him in through the ranks and up onto the Command platform above the Captain's Bar. Two Station Security escorted him, standing to either side as Robert turned to face the room. Medical had been at him, needless to say, dosing him with sufficient stimulants to ensure that he'd be able to walk and answer the Administrator's questions just as well as if he understood them. Joslire eyed St. Clare skeptically while the Administrator waited for Security to bring him up to the proper mark. Drugs or no drugs, the man looked half-dead already. It hadn't been two days . . . but the exercise had started three days ago, and that meant three days with an injured shoulder and a fresh whipping, and no medical support authorized. Robert was going to collapse as soon as the drugs wore off, so much was clear.

It was the Administrator's turn to speak, his responsibility to complete the Record.

"Your name is Robert St. Clare?"

"Yes, your Excellency."

It was a voice from the back end of beyond, as if Robert's brain had to travel so far past his pain to find the words that half of their meaning had got lost again on the return trip.

"You stand before the Bench for disobeying lawful and received instruction; to wit, revealing your true status to the Student Interrogator during the critically important Intermediate Level exercise. Do you understand the charge?"

Robert staggered a bit, swaying where he stood. Station Security reached out to steady him. *No,* Joslire thought. *Not that arm. That's the wrong arm.*

"Yes. Your Excellency. I understand the charge."

"The Administration has reviewed the Record." It was always a little odd hearing Clellelan referring to himself as if he were the institution, rather than the man. But it was necessary. It helped reduce a sense of personal responsibility for what had to be done. "There is no question that Student Koscuisko knew your exact status prior to the end of the exercise. Nor is there any other possible source for this information. We must necessarily conclude that Koscuisko knew because you told him. If not explicitly, then implicitly in some way."

It was wrong and it was unfair, but it was unavoidable, even if Koscuisko himself couldn't accept that fact. If Koscuisko knew, then Robert must have told him. Somehow. There were no allowances in Fleet Administrative Procedure for guessing, or for having the bad luck to draw an unusually perceptive officer, one who would catch one word—one word, out of thousands—and build a damning case out of so small a thing.

"However."

A nervous shock ran through the room, and Joslire felt himself stiffen against an involuntary twitch of surprise. However? Some consideration of degree? Some amelioration of the offense?

Some hope, where none could possibly hope?

"The Administration in review of the Record with the assistance of the assigned Tutor and neutral evaluators has been unable to determine the precise manner in which the information was transmitted. To the best of the Administration's professional judgment, there was no explicit statement on your part that could be construed as release of unauthorized information, prior to a direct question from the Student Interrogator."

The air was heavy with a sharp smell of confusion mixed with fear. There was no precedent for reading such allowances into the Record—not unless discipline was to be adjusted. And Class Two violations were never adjusted. Never.

"Since you cannot in all fairness be faulted for answering a question posed with a clear presupposition of the restricted information, it is difficult to justify the determination of the penalty. The Administration does not feel that an error was made on your part as a result of misunderstanding the question."

Fear, because Clellelan seemed to be leading up to a commutation of penalty, and that was unheard of. Fear that what seemed to be happening would turn again at the last minute to almost-certain death by torture for Robert St. Clare—who, as Joslire noted, was having a harder time of it keeping to his feet with every moment that passed.

"You understand the severity of the offense, St. Clare, and you understand what you are accused of having done. Now think for a moment, and answer on your Bond. Did you at any time—release the restricted information to the Student Interrogator?"

Biting his lip in an evident effort to concentrate, Robert closed his eyes in a spasm of pain. That had been a mistake. Joslire could tell by the way his knees buckled beneath him. It was better not to close your eyes. It deprived you of a focus that helped to keep the dizziness and the disorientation at bay.

Station Security helped him back up to his feet—leaning decidedly to one side, Joslire noted—and Robert found his voice once more. "By my Bond, as I hope for the Day. I cannot remember what I might have said. Your Excellency."

It had to be true, because his governor would not permit him to swear by his Bond otherwise. The governor could sense internal conflict, read the physiological signs of stress specific to prevarication or lying. And what the governor sensed it punished.

"It goes without saying that there was no intent on your part to compromise the exercise. But there are statements on Record that support an alternative secret to the one you were to release. We cannot set aside the fact of Student Koscuisko's realization. Student Koscuisko himself has an interest in this matter as well."

They couldn't condemn St. Clare for ambiguity, not when the exercise had terminated in the middle of the Fifth Level, whether or not the Fourth Level exercise had been prematurely called. That trick of Koscuisko's with Robert's shoulder had been as good as an augmented Fourth under any Protocol, the actual time it had taken aside. Most of the Security here had firsthand knowledge of how hard it was to concentrate with so much pain. The Administration had always been sensitive to that, overlooking sometimes major mistakes if only the Student Interrogator had not followed up on them. But this time, although the mistakes had been negligible, the Student Interrogator had pulled the horrible truth out of the concatenation of confused mis-starts, and Robert would necessarily suffer for it.

Koscuisko had gone to the Tutor to beg for remission of Robert's punishment; and the Tutor had been smiling when he had released Koscuisko to Joslire's keeping. Chonis wasn't one of the Tutors who would think enforcing a Class Two violation was anything to smile about.

The implications—even as well prepared as Joslire was, much more so than any of the others—were almost too much for him to handle.

Discipline was absolute and inevitable.

The tension held them all braced to a knife-edged sharpness of attention.

"Student Koscuisko has in fact brought a separate complaint against you. He has stated his desire to discipline your lapse by his own hand. We will be unable to comply with Student Koscuisko's lawful request if this Class Two decision goes forward." Because Robert would probably be dead, for one thing. And perhaps it was an exaggeration to describe Koscuisko's demand as a lawful request. But nobody was going to argue with Clellelan.

"Do you understand me, St. Clare?"

They were going to have to call a medical team at any moment. Robert had clearly reached the last few measures of his reserved and drug-enabled strength. "Yes, your Excellency . . . No."

"Student Koscuisko has also proposed a speak-serum for addition to the Controlled List. As a training station, we are empowered to offer a choice between the standard Class Two discipline and voluntary service for evaluation of drugs being considered for Fleet Interrogatory purposes. Are you with me?"

One of the Station Security reached out for Robert from behind him, and laid a firm hand on the injured shoulder, the swelling of which was visible even from where Joslire stood. It was a brutal trick, and Robert cried out against it, in a strangled protest against the pain. Joslire knew it had been well meant, all the same—even well done, because the sharp agony clearly helped him regain some degree of concentration. "Yes, your Excellency. The Controlled List. Student Koscuisko. Sir."

"Answer me on your Bond, then. Do you elect to serve as the experimental subject for the evaluation of Koscuisko's new speak-serum, in lieu of other Class Two discipline?"

Of all the things Joslire had imagined having gone between Koscuisko and Tutor Chonis, none of them had touched on such a potential escape. Koscuisko had gone to Chonis to bargain with him, Joslire had known that all along. But for the bargain to have been made, and in this format . . .

"Yes, your Excellency. Experimental duty, new drug for the Classified List. On my Bond, as I hope for the Day, I so elect. Sir."

This was too far beyond the realm of possibility to be happening. It made no sense. Why did Clellelan think that it made a difference? The drugs on the Controlled List were every bit as brutal as discipline administered at the Seventh Level for a Class Two violation.

"You have elected to test Student Koscuisko's new speak-serum, in order to provide additional resources for the Jurisdiction's Controlled List. There is now the issue of Student Koscuisko's Class Two claim."

Except that the Administrator consistently specified Koscuisko's new drug, and had read the complete description into the Record. Not just a new drug for the Controlled List. Student Koscuisko's new speak-serum for the Controlled List. Speak-sera were not nerve factors, were not wake-keepers, were not pain-maintenance drugs. Speak-sera were only speak-sera, even though they were on the Controlled List. And many of them weren't even fatal.

"Student Koscuisko has requested the adjudication of discipline at the aggrieved officer's level. The Administration finds his request reasonable and responsible. The Class Two violation cried against you by Student Koscuisko will therefore be struck from the Record, and Student Koscuisko will exercise the Judicial function at the Class One violation level."

What could it mean?

"Your Excellency. By my Bond. It is just and judicious that he do so. As I hope for the Day."

Robert hadn't committed any Class Two violations. And even had he done Koscuisko would not have referred it to punishment, at least not in his current state of mind. But Tutor Chonis wouldn't have made that up.

"Very well. Appropriate punishment for the Class Two violation failure to obey lawful and received instruction has been Adjudicated and accepted. Appropriate punishment for the Class One violation brought against you by Student Koscuisko will be administered by Student Koscuisko and the violation stricken from the Record. Under these circumstances your Fleet deferment is refused. The reduction of your Bond will be permitted to stand. It is prudent and proper by the Bench instruction, just and judicious in the eyes of the offending party. The Record is complete."

It was official, then.

It was done.

The Administrator had declared the Record complete; no alteration would be permitted, now that the critical point was passed.

"You will be taken to Infirmary, there to receive appropriate medical care. The Controlled List trial will be scheduled later, depending upon your recovery. The Administration will decide the timing of other discipline after the Controlled List trial has been completed. You are remanded into custody. Dismissed."

Robert St. Clare bowed in salute, a bow that betrayed him to his dizziness. He seemed to lose his balance and consciousness at one and the same time, crumpling slowly to fall forward across the Captain's Bar. Tutor Chonis stepped up smartly, coming to attention in front of the table where Clellelan had the Record.

"This session of Administrator's Disciplinary Hearing is concluded."

Clellelan rose and left the room, and there was silence for as long as it took him to step down from the Command platform and clear the doorway at the back of Tutor's Mess.

Then discipline dissolved into a chaotic mass of murmurs and moving feet, the immense unparalleled wonder of it all too much for any of them. Tutor Chonis raised his voice so that he could make himself heard over the noise, signaling with his hand for the litter to be brought forward. Joslire hadn't seen the medical team before. Clellelan must have brought them, and left them to wait outside until it was all over.

"Sorlie Curran, take the prisoner to Infirmary. Joslire Curran, stand by. I want a word with you."

Robert would test a new speak-serum, and he would not die of it— Koscuisko would see to that. That was what Koscuisko had been working on, that was what Koscuisko had offered to Tutor Chonis in exchange for Robert's life. And Tutor Chonis would force Koscuisko to administer a beating, just to be sure that Koscuisko didn't get any ideas into his head about getting his own way. St. Clare would not die of that either, and Koscuisko had done this impossible thing. Koscuisko who could read bodies with his hands and stop the grim wheel of Jurisdiction Fleet discipline and force it back on its unforgiving track. Koscuisko had done this. Robert was not to be tortured and killed.

Koscuisko was a sorcerer, and Joslire was afraid of him now, afraid as he had never been of any man on either end of a whip.

"As for the rest of you," Chonis declared, stepping out of the way of the litter bearing the unconscious body of the salvaged man. "You will return to your duty stations not later than two eighths from now. That will be all. Joslire Curran."

He needed two eighths, four eighths, six eighths to recover himself. He had to look after this Student, this sorcerer. How could he hope to conduct himself correctly in the presence of such a man?

Refuge could be taken in the forms of courtesy and discipline, regardless of the turmoil in his mind. "The Tutor requires, sir?"

Now more than ever the Tutor would need him, to report on Koscuisko's mood and attitude.

Now more than ever he had to protect himself.

⊕ ⊕ ⊕

She'd planned on keeping an eye on the theater in order to be able to update Chonis if he called. She found instead that she was interested. The screen gave her a close-up on the body: she could see the gray spidery needles walking over the semi-nude body of the unconscious man, carrying the micro-lasers to the sites beneath the skin where the fault lay. Where the damage had been done. She'd done some micro-surgery herself, although most of what they treated here was gross tissue damage; and she was fascinated by the speed, the skill, the confidence that Koscuisko—even enclosed in the operating chair—expressed with every motion of those thin gray wire-like probes. He never hesitated at the dermis level; he never seemed to reposition a probe; he never seemed to probe too deeply by accident, and have to come back out and try again. He knew the angles of approach he wanted, and he hit each and every one of them flawlessly, without a single misstep.

He hardly seemed to be working at all, it went so fast.

And when the laser fingers had traveled up the spine to nestle beneath the brain box at the base of the skull—the site of the most critical damage, where Noycannir had kicked her unconscious prisoner-surrogate in an apparent spasm of frustration—Koscuisko only slowed his pace a bit. The most delicate of all the surgical interventions, repair of critical connections at the cellular level, and Koscuisko only slowed down, as sure—as certain—as he'd been before, only more deliberate in respect to the more dangerous environment.

Then the surgical machine was moving away from the table, backing up against the wall. Chaymalt shot a startled glance at the chronometer on the wall—had it been that long? Already? She'd hardly been aware of the passage of time, Koscuisko's absolute self-confidence had mesmerized her.

But it was done.

The scanner descended from the ceiling as the operating chair retreated, and tracked slowly up the torpid body on the table. Chaymalt coded the display abruptly, suddenly anxious that she know the criterms now, when she could just as well have waited for them. The scanner report began to scroll across the desk surface: residual bruises, torn muscle fiber, edema—but the neurological damage had been masked by surgical repair.

With the astonishing speed characteristic of successful micro-surgery, the normal electrical activity of the nerves was already beginning to recover—for all the world as if the damaged tissue had not been functionally nerve-dead with shock and trauma three scant eights ago.

It was incredible.

Healing was neither instant or absolute, of course. All Koscuisko had really done had been to restore the system's integrity in the places where it had been compromised by Noycannir's assault. And he had done it with minimal surgical trauma, although the conventional standards recognized that the surgery could do as much damage as it undid, even in the most skilled of hands.

Ligrose Chaymalt knew as well as anyone how natural it was for newly graduated medical practitioners to overrate their own abilities, relative to more objective assessments.

This was the first time she could think of where the performance of a Student actually exceeded expectation.

Tracking complete, the scanner returned to its place in the ceiling, its statistical report processing into Standard language phrases as it did so. She could read the same information Koscuisko saw from within the operating chair: substantial restoration of neurological function. Baseline activity returning to normal, adjusting for effect of anesthesia. No significant operational trauma. Consciousness may safely be invoked within three days, physical therapy to be scheduled after completion of waking tests.

Prognosis excellent.

Her orderly was preparing the patient to return to the recovery room. Koscuisko had switched the surgical machine off; it unfolded from around him, the webbed restraints that had supported the weight of his body in suspension loosening gradually to ease his body to the floor. Chaymalt could not help staring at Koscuisko as the chair backed off and left him standing alone, the white of his under-blouse stark against the dark gray walls.

He looked completely centered in his life, a master of his craft, a surgeon of significant potential.

It was an obscene waste to abandon such skill to Inquisition.

Andrej stood alone in the operating theater fastening up his duty-blouse, drinking in the solitude, relishing the relative privacy of the now-empty surgery. Oh, there were monitors in place, he knew that—had this been an ordinary operating theater, there would necessarily have been monitors. It wasn't that. From the time he'd arrived at Fleet Orientation Station Medical, he'd hardly been alone for a single moment; either because Joslire was in the next room or because he was in class. And he was alone now, alone to bask in the satisfaction of a surgical procedure well completed. Alone, to cradle the comfort of having helped to heal an injured man to himself, and to cherish the blessing in his heart.

He could not hold the pleasure long.

So sensitive had he become to the expectations and regulations that being alone began to worry him. Where was Joslire? Or where was Travis, for instance, in Joslire's absence? What was going on out there, out in the working areas of the station, outside this sanctuary space?

He covered his face with his hands for a moment, then finger-combed his hair with a decisive gesture. Enough was enough. There would be sufficient with which to concern himself, he could be certain of that. It was time to return to the real world, harsh though it was. This surgery had been a brief respite of sorts, but there was still as much to be done, and as little to his liking, as there had been before.

Turning toward the sterile-lock door, Andrej saw Joslire Curran standing beyond the near-transparent membrane. At least it looked like Joslire to Andrej, and whomever it was bowed politely in salute, which rather strengthened the supposition.

Andrej went through.

"Well met, Mister Curran." There was another Security post in the corridor, but she was nothing to do with Andrej, so he ignored her, beyond using a more formal address for Joslire in token of her presence. "Is it too early for third-meal?" Because he was hungry again. A little full of himself, just now perhaps, but surely he could be permitted a little egotistic self-congratulation under the circumstances?

Joslire looked as if he'd not been fed for a few days, though. Pale and drawn, with a glazed look in his eyes that seemed to speak to Andrej of a stunning shock of some sort. Oh, what now, what now? What next?

But he knew better than to ask the question, at least in so many words.

"The officer's third-meal shift is two hours old, the officer's meal can be made available at any time. With respect, your Excellency . . ."

That was odd. He wasn't an Excellency outside of practical exercise theater, not yet, not to Fleet. Not to Joslire. "Yes?"

"Tutor Chonis has suggested that the officer may wish to provide an additional service in Infirmary, if the officer pleases. It was suggested that the officer might consent to take a moment, once the scheduled surgery was completed."

Nor did Joslire use a direct form of address when he was paying attention to himself, no matter how many extra words there were to separate "your Excellency" from "if the officer pleases." Surely he wasn't still shaken by what had passed between them earlier?

"That which my Tutor has suggested, I must me receive as instruction." It was actually a quote from Mergau Noycannir, not as if Joslire would know that. Andrej found Noycannir's dialect rather engaging. It was her bullying, manipulative personality he found objectionable. "Let's go, Mister Curran, lead on. Is this our guide?"

The Security post simply bowed, and took off, with Andrej and Joslire following up the rear. Through mazes of corridors and doors she led them, until Andrej felt a little dizzy. It wasn't as if they needed to keep the location secret from him. He didn't know where he was in the first place. How would he even know the difference, if they'd led him around the spiral steps for some obscure Security joke?

No matter.

Except that it kept him from his supper, and he wanted to go see Tutor Chonis, just to test once more whether there was to be any hope at all for his unfortunate prisoner-surrogate.

If they refused his offer, he would not be in honor bound to support the Controlled List, which was an abomination beneath the Canopy. He could hold himself stainless, in at least that one piece of his larger degradation; and it would be good to have some little thing in which he could comfort himself that he was not utterly disgraced. But if they refused his offer—an innocent man would suffer horribly, and probably die, and Andrej could not make himself believe that it was worth it that a man should die if only he could avoid the Controlled List.

Finally a long corridor with a clearly visible door at the far end—the way out. Oddly enough, the same Security team that he had had with him for that fateful exercise—two days ago? Just yesterday? — was waiting in the hallway as they came around the comer. Sorlie Curran and the rest, Andrej was sure of it. They were too busy saluting him to allow him any time to question them, however, because Sorlie Curran had apparently signaled at the door, and Joslire behind him was still moving at too brisk a pace for Andrej to feel confident of his ability to put a brake on the man's momentum before he ran Andrej down.

All right.

Into the room, then.

A minor surgery facility, clearly enough, with a body on the levels and a technician standing by with a pharmacy unit while two orderlies worked at cleaning the wounds of a man who had been beaten. It all looked quite commonplace to Andrej. What was the point behind all this?

"Attention to the officer," Sorlie Curran called sharply, from behind him. The two orderlies backed away from the levels quickly, almost as if they were timid about something. Andrej acknowledged their salutes quickly, waving them off.

He was beginning to have an idea.

"What is this man's status? . . . Best close the door." He advanced on the body that lay on the levels, unsure of how interested he really was in looking at the evidence. Swollen flesh and fiery inflammation two and three days old, bruises upon bruises, welts upon welts. A shoulder swollen and livid with insult, striped and bloodied with blows from a whip that had struck just exactly where it would hurt the most. An ugly beating all 'round, and Andrej recognized his handiwork, although he shuddered to see it. They had brought him to St. Clare. Why?

One of the orderlies, turning the record-monitor at the head of the levels so that he could see the display more clearly, gestured nervously and saluted once again. What in the name of all Saints were they so jumpy about? The medical record was clear enough. But the status block had a continuation code; frowning, Andrej keyed the scroller to see what it was that was causing such consternation.

ROBERT ST. CLARE, the status block said. BOND-INVOLUNTARY, CURRENT OFFICER OF ASSIGNMENT STUDENT ANDREJ KOSCUISKO. LAST RECORDED ACTION, ADJUDICATION OF

PUNISHMENT FOR A CLASS TWO VIOLATION, EVALUATION DUTY FOR CONTROLLED LIST SPEAK-SERUM. TO BE RETURNED TO DUTY STATUS AT ASSIGNED OFFICER'S DISCRETION TO STAND EVALUATION DUTY, OUTSTANDING CLASS ONE VIOLATION PENDING, TO BE STRICKEN FROM THE RECORD. BY THE BENCH INSTRUCTION.

St. Clare was his?

"Joslire, what does this mean?" he asked in a hushed whisper. "I cannot trust myself to understand." Or to face the bargain he had made without cringing away from what he had sworn to do. What he would do.

"With respect. Sir." Not that Joslire sounded much better, at the moment. "The Administrator has permitted St. Clare to test his Excellency's . . . the officer's new speak-serum, in lieu of other Class Two discipline. It is on Record."

And there could be no hidden trick or reversal if it was on Record. They meant to have what he had offered them, and how could he grudge it when they had delivered St. Clare from the sin that Andrej had committed against him?

He was numb with the accumulated shocks his spirit had sustained over the past two days.

He could find it in him neither to rejoice nor weep.

He checked that the sterile field was up and active instead, and started to unfasten his duty-blouse once more. "Very well. Give me the medical report, I'll want to check on this. You, there, technician, what are my clearances for practice?" As opposed to research. Obviously no decently run Infirmary would permit just anyone to gain access to proprietary stores, whether physician or no; and there was no particular reason for the Fleet to allow him to do so. Hadn't there been a nasty comment of some sort in the administrative material about different levels of treatment support for bond-involuntary troops in need of medication?

Joslire took his blouse, and the technician blushed and bowed. "The officer is cleared to order at the officer's discretion and best judgment. A credit ceiling of four hundred thousand, Standard, has been imposed to cover the cost of medication only. Doctor Chaymalt's personal instruction."

"I am deeply obliged to Doctor Chaymalt, and hope I will have the opportunity to tell her so. Joslire. Is there rhyti?" Supper would wait. Four hundred thousand, Standard, was it? The official replacement cost levied against a Fleet command whose loss of a bond-involuntary was judged to have resulted from criminal negligence. Even then it was the Command's administrative budget, and not the Commander, who paid. But if Chaymalt was willing to recompense him in this manner for the surgery that he had performed under her authority, Andrej was more than willing to accept the grant as given, crude though it was.

He could hear the door open behind him; Joslire going for rhyti, he supposed. He hoped. The orderlies looked confused; he wanted them handy, he might be needing them later on. "Who is senior of the two of you? What are your orders?"

The shorter one was senior, a Binbin woman with her head half-shaved after the fashion of her kind. "With respect. We were tasked to provide primary support in the officer's absence, and to assist the officer at his discretion. We're at the officer's disposal."

And if he didn't feel like troubling himself? There would be no secondary support. Or there would be treatment of the injuries, and it would stop well short of soothing for the pain. They would have been quite sure that he would do what was needful, though, having already paid such coin for the man. "Very good. Prepare me a double dose of hanerdoi, and I'll want a good vasodilator as well. What have you got on hand for Nurail besides extract of sandspreader?"

The shoulder first, and hit it with a deep neural block straight off, so he wouldn't have any problems if St. Clare began to wake up. Not that he expected that to happen any time soon, not with what the metabolic blood report had to tell him about protein starvation and too much jacherul for common sense and reason. They'd wanted St. Clare conscious to stand his hearing, well, that made a certain amount of sense.

Andrej wondered what St. Clare was going to think of all this.

There was a good deal to be done. The shoulder sprain, complicated as it had been by neglect and abuse and left untreated for so long, was just short of sustaining a permanent injury. It wouldn't have mattered to Fleet, since crozer-lances were not Standard issue. But St. Clare wouldn't have appreciated the chronic pain. Then there was a significant dehydration issue to be addressed, and it seemed that

St. Clare had been fasting; but whether that had been because of lack of appetite—or because Fleet didn't waste rations on dead men—Andrej neither knew nor cared to speculate.

Fluid and nourishment provided in solution, the shoulder numbed, the swelling seen to, there were still the bruises and the blood all down St. Clare's back, all down his sides, his arms, his legs, the welts across his face. Tutor Chonis would require him to scourge St. Clare all over again, and he *had* promised. He was going to have to study how it could be done, to do the least amount of damage—hopefully without anybody catching on.

By the time that Andrej was ready for the orderlies to help him turn St. Clare over onto his newly bandaged back, the man was thinking about regaining consciousness, from all indications. It was true that St. Clare was in absolutely superb physical condition, recent events aside. And also true, as Andrej had some personal reason for knowing, that the right ointment applied with a careful enough touch could really make a difference when a man was hurting from head to foot. Andrej kept an eye on St. Clare's face, watching for the movement of the eyes behind closed lids. He didn't want to use any more soporific than he had to; it could interfere with the action of the painkiller he was using. He didn't quite catch it in time even so. Cleaning fragments of rope fiber away from the torn flesh at his patient's throat, he was distracted, and when St. Clare spoke to him he started in surprise.

"What are . . . Why did . . ."

Andrej snapped his fingers for the dose he'd had the technician hold in reserve, and she pressed it through with commendable efficiency. "Shut up," he advised St. Clare, watching the muscles of his patient's face fall slack as St. Clare sank into deep unconsciousness once more. "Go to sleep. We'll talk about it later." He was certainly not going to address any of those issues now, with all this work on his hands. And he wasn't sure he had the first idea of what he was going to say when the time came.

"Is there a bed reserved?" he asked the senior orderly. They were almost done, except of course that rehydration and nourishment did have to continue, and there should be someone to see to pain reduction medication should St. Clare wake again during the night.

"Full supportive, if it please the officer." Andrej let his hand rest against the least bruised skin that he could find on St. Clare's naked chest, considering his progress on the tracks the rope had left. He'd known when he had started with the rope that it was liable to shed a myriad of irritating fragments of stiff fiber, wearing away at St. Clare's throat like spun glass ground into a wound. At the time it had struck him as an interesting concept, one that would contribute to a certain degree of erosion in the prisoner's self-control. Now he wanted to know what kind of a pervert had ideas like that, when they involved making such a mess out of a perfectly good physical machine, the body of the prisoner.

Clearly there was a conflict of some sort, here.

As if he hadn't known.

"All right, then." Beckoning to Joslire for his rhyti, Andrej wondered suddenly what time it had gotten to be, and how late he'd kept his poor Joslire up again. "There's stasis on the bed, of course? Well, one must be sure, no offense was meant. You may remove the patient to his bed. I have logged four units of amart to be delivered every two hours, and seven of storliva to be administered if his temperature should chance to rise. If there are any other developments, I should like to be notified, immediately. I trust there will be no problem with that?"

Not that he expected any unforeseen developments, because St. Clare really was rather a splendid young animal, and there was nothing wrong with him that rest and food and drink and painease could not mend. It was a good thing for them both that he was so new at his craft, Andrej decided. St. Clare would carry no scars. Joslire wore too many, even if most of the evidence had been cosmetically concealed— to render him more aesthetically pleasing in the eyes of his Students? To remove the checking influence it might be said to have if one should chance to notice that the man one was preparing to strike was already scarred, to face brutally vivid evidence of past punishment as one worked oneself up to deliver punishment? The Administration did not want young Students to think twice about beating people. The Administration did not want them to think about it at all.

And there was another problem.

Andrej knew how hard he'd struck St. Clare, and how much pain it had created, quite apart from the nasty trick he'd played with the crozer-hinge.

How much more pain had Joslire suffered, to have given him such scars? And—had it been some other physician there might have been no grant of medication, not even for worse welts—

Two-and-twenty could be decided and delivered without Charges brought, without hope for appeal or moderating influence. Two-and-twenty was Standard issue for bond-involuntaries.

He could not bear to think about it. He had been through too much today. And he had come out ahead of it all, at least in one thing, and that was an important thing—the life of the man who lay unconscious beneath his hand. St. Clare belonged to him, and he was responsible for St. Clare. It was a bit of comforting familiarity in this alien place that persisted in Andrej's mind even as the orderlies removed his patient to his bed.

Alone in the room now with only Joslire for company, Andrej drank his rhyti and remembered that he was hungry. "Joslire, am I to see Tutor Chonis, or am I to go to bed?" His rhyti was still hot, and that was odd. How many times had Joslire had to go for rhyti, to have it hot and ready for him now?

"Tutor Chonis has requested that the officer meet with him after fast-meal, in the morning. For the remainder of this duty-shift, there is no training scheduled."

No, Joslire was sitting on something, Andrej was certain that he could hear it in his voice. He glanced behind him sharply, but Joslire gave no hint of an expression on his somber, guarded face.

Maybe he didn't want to know.

"Let's have my blouse, then, if you please." Well, they'd go back to quarters and be done with the day. He did want to see Doctor Chaymalt, but a formal appointment would probably take a day or two to set up through the proper channels. He'd have to read up on his Sixth Level, and he wasn't looking forward to that any more than he had to any of the preliminary exercises, but he didn't have the energy to waste in indulging himself in conflict of that sort. "Can you call ahead for my supper, I wonder? Or perhaps a mid-meal and a third-meal at once, if it is possible, unless there are rules against permitting Students to make gluttons of themselves?"

Joslire helped him into his blouse, stone-faced and silent. Joslire keyed the door and bowed, silent and stone-faced, for Andrej to precede him from the room. Andrej could see Sorlie Curran and the rest of the security team in the corridor beyond, two on each side, standing to attention. Had they really been there all this time? If they were St. Clare's jailers, why hadn't they followed the orderlies when the orderlies had taken St. Clare off to Ward?

Andrej went out into the corridor thinking about his supper, and came to an abrupt halt.

It wasn't only Sorlie Curran, and the team who had been with him for the exercise.

There was a Bigelblu, and a Mizucash, and the Holy Mother only knew how many others besides. All bond-involuntaries. And the corridor was absolutely solid with them, standing to attention against the walls on either side to wait his passing.

Staring about him in wonder, Andrej started down the hall toward the door at the far end. How had all these people gotten in here? And he recognized the Mizucash and the Bigelblu from his Preliminary Level exercises, both saluting him with precise and respectful bows as he went past. He could hear Joslire behind him, but he could also hear the troops turning to close ranks across the corridor just behind the two of them, forming row upon row of Security troops that deepened the closer he got to the door at the end of the corridor. And when he got to the door, it was worse, because there were more of them on the other side, and most of those were Station Security and Infirmary staff, and not bond-involuntaries at all.

What was a man to do in such a circumstance?

Andrej paced the distance with grave deliberation, keenly aware of the silent formation that surrounded him. Reaching the end of the gauntlet at last, he turned to face back the way he had come, Joslire moving quickly to stand behind him.

There could be only one response truly appropriate, truly adequate to express his confused appreciation for this astonishing tribute.

He looked through the ranks for a long moment, trying to make eye contact with everyone there, trying not to wonder why they weren't at their duty stations.

And he bowed.

With every bit as much heartfelt gratitude and respect as a filial child bowing to his father, or before the Canopy.

"You do me very great honor. And I thank you for it." It was a poor return, but it was the best he had to offer. "Good night, gentles, all. I will. Never. Forget this."

Now he should leave the area quickly, so that they could disperse with all deliberate speed; but not so quickly that they would feel he was slighting their profound gesture by discarding its importance with his haste. Forcing himself to take unhurried steps, Andrej walked out of the area, with Joslire following. He could only just hear Joslire behind him, close to his shoulder, speaking soft and low, his voice pitched to Andrej's ear alone.

"Neither will we. Your Excellency."

He didn't believe that he deserved this accolade, strangely as it had been given. But there was no arguing with one's Household. When they decided that one had done well, the only thing that one could do was to accept in all humility and submit with as good grace as one could muster.

He only hoped that no one would come to grief for it.

CHAPTER NINE

There had been a disturbance of sorts in Infirmary during third-shift, and although Tutor Chonis hadn't heard many details, he considered it almost certain that Koscuisko had been involved somehow. Koscuisko was expected after fast-meal, but—Chonis realized, frowning at his time-strip—he hadn't specified a time when he'd given Curran his instructions yesterday mid-second. He'd not been quite sure how much Curran would be able to retain of what Chonis had wanted to tell him. The whole roomful of Security had been in shock, Bonded and un-Bonded alike, after witnessing the actualization of the impossible.

He need not have worried. It was the mark after the start of the normal training period, precisely as close to "after fast-meal" as a man could get; and here was Student Koscuisko, signaling at the door.

"Student Koscuisko respectfully reports at the Tutor's convenience."

And, oh, but didn't he sound polite this morning. Pale, and there were dark stains beneath his eyes, like those that signaled incomplete restfulness in some of the races of category-six hominids. He always had used polite language, that was true. It was all the more interesting how different it sounded when Koscuisko appeared to actually mean it.

"Step through. Thank you, Curran, stand by. Good-greeting, Andrej, have you slept well?"

Koscuisko took his seat a little heavily. "Thank you, Tutor, I believe so. But I have a good deal on my mind, if perhaps we could discuss it."

Yes, he'd just bet Koscuisko had a lot to talk about. "All right. Where shall we start?" That should be an interesting choice, given the range from which Koscuisko could choose.

Koscuisko lay his hand out on the table flat, palm uppermost, studying his fingers. "Well, there is St. Clare's status, and I would like to be permitted to follow up. I understand there is to be an evaluation of the speak-serum, and I wonder if I am permitted to adjust the formulation to include the Nurail lineages. Also there were some gentles to see me to my quarters last night, and I can't help but worry that the Administration might misinterpret their courtesy. I have promised to enrich the Controlled List; I would know how the Administration wishes to define my contribution, a schedule, or whatever. Also, finally, my Sixth Level. I have some anxiety on all of these points, Tutor Chonis."

He had just about hit all the marks, that was true. "I'll see if I can't set your mind at rest. You'll prompt me if I leave anything out." Because there was a good deal of ground to cover. "Let's start with the unusual occurrence last night, since I've just found out about it. The Administrator's morning report describes it as a not-unlawful assembly, not outside the range of customary and acceptable procedure. Though it seems to have pushed the limit? Hmmm?"

Koscuisko blushed and bit his lip. It was an unfair question, Chonis supposed. "No matter. There don't seem to be any problems, at least not at this time. A natural expression of concern for two fellow Security troops and bond-involuntaries, that is all."

Perhaps not all. Perhaps very much more than that, and all to do with Andrej Koscuisko, marked for the rest of his Fleet career as a man who could command personal loyalty from bond-involuntary troops.

"As to St. Clare. You will assume the responsibilities of attending physician until he can be returned to duty to stand evaluation of the speak-serum. You will administer appropriate punishment for the violation you mentioned to me . . . Do you remember?"

Koscuisko was uncomfortable with this part. Chonis intended that Koscuisko be uncomfortable with this part. That was the whole point of the exercise—or of what was left of the exercise, at any rate.

"I remember, Tutor Chonis. And I have not yet thanked you for taking my petition forward. I . . . cannot say . . ."

His knuckles tight against the tabletop, his mouth pursed white,

Koscuisko fought to contain his emotion, while Chonis watched, fascinated. Passion was not usually seen in Students, either because they had learned neutrality in their medical schooling or because they had drawn a layer of callousness over themselves for self-protection. Koscuisko was a passionate man, and it was instructive to see how he handled it in himself; though it was surely not necessary—Chonis reminded himself, a little guiltily—to let him suffer, in this manner.

"You are quite welcome, Student Koscuisko. No one on this Station but welcomed your suggestion."

There, that was better. Koscuisko took a deep breath, and his shoulders seemed to smooth out a bit as he relaxed. "Even so, I will not forget, Tutor Chonis. I understand that I must discipline St. Clare, as I have sworn to do. Naturally I would prefer to restrict myself to two-and-twenty, but that might not satisfy the requirement. I therefore must ask . . ."

Chonis already knew that Koscuisko would just as soon go two-and-twenty and forget it. He was tempted to let it rest at that. The idea had been to ensure that Koscuisko suffered for his lapse of taste in embarrassing the Administration, and that he would continue to shudder for his sins every time he laid eyes on Robert St. Clare. It was clear enough to Chonis that Koscuisko was suffering rather flamboyantly over the risked Class Two itself. There was the question of the Administrator, however; Clellelan would not understand letting it go so lightly. Given the leniency Administrator Clellelan had granted in the matter, Chonis felt it was better not to push things.

"The Administration will accept four-and-forty as a good-faith demonstration, Andrej. Yes, it is a bit stricter than you would have liked, I know." Perhaps Koscuisko had hoped three-and-thirty would do. Koscuisko had too much respect for pain, that was his problem. Bond-involuntaries were expected to stand two-and-twenty as a matter of course, six-and-sixty being considered merely adequate to get their attention.

"The choice of instruments is to be made from among those provided at the Intermediate Levels?" Koscuisko sounded a trifle choked, but obedient and submissive still. "Am I to schedule this, or is it for the Administrator to do so?"

Nodding, Chonis remembered a question he had been wanting to ask. "Yes and yes. That is, the Administrator will schedule the discipline once St. Clare is returned to duty. It goes on Record. I'd like to know, now that you've rested, if you could tell me what revealed the secret to you.—Oh, no further penalty will be assessed," he added quickly, in the face of Koscuisko's evident alarm.

It was alarm shading into a subtle sort of confusion as Koscuisko searched his mind. "I'm not . . . exactly . . . sure. I had been thinking about how stubborn he was, which meant that he had courage, moral strength. Because I could tell how much he had pain. I started to wonder whether such a man would be offered a Bond, and then I wondered why I had thought that; and what it could have been that Sorlie Curran hadn't wanted me to notice. I'm not sure. With your permission, Tutor Chonis."

No, Koscuisko had grabbed it out of thin air and St. Clare's admittedly ambiguous mutterings. But if the secret could be caught out of things of the sort St. Clare had said, then no single bond-involuntary in the program would have been safe. Koscuisko had an empathic sort of truth-sense. He would be good at his work, if only he could be persuaded to relax and enjoy it.

Figuratively speaking, of course.

Leading naturally up to the next subject, one that Student Koscuisko had asked him about—as good an opening as any, Chonis congratulated himself. "Sometimes understanding comes without understanding how it's come by. I should like you to concentrate on that aspect of Inquiry and Confirmation during your next exercise. Shall I schedule you for, say, three days from now? What do you think? Will you be rested enough?"

The Sixth Level was as bad as it got—before it got truly unreasonable. Preliminary Levels concentrated on Inquiry; the Intermediate Levels, on Inquiry and Confirmation. By the time the Advanced Levels were reached, the fine line dividing Inquiry and Confirmation was necessarily smeared over with an overriding requirement to Execute. Prisoners weren't even referred to the Advanced Levels without confession—if not theirs, then somebody else's. And the Protocols more or less ensured that if the prisoner was referred at the Advanced Levels, the prisoner would die. Then skill became an issue: die sooner? Die later?

Chonis brought himself out of his meditation abruptly. He was getting ahead of himself, and Koscuisko hadn't answered him. "Andrej?"

"In three days' time, yes, Tutor. I will be ready. And what is the Tutor's pleasure for the meantime?"

No argument, no neutral insistence on the tiresome fact that the Sixth Level had been originally scheduled for five days' distance. Not three. Chonis decided that he liked this meek demeanor: Koscuisko, as good as his word, was trying to behave.

"You're to give us half-days in the lab and spend the rest of the time preparing for your practical exercise. You're welcome to tinker with that speak-serum, if you like, but we do have a rather more specific need for your talents just at present."

"Yes, Tutor Chonis?"

"Student Koscuisko. I know how much you dislike the idea of the Controlled List. And it is not the Administrator's intent to demand disproportionate return for St. Clare. We will be content with a finite set of new drugs"—although he hadn't discussed it with the Administrator in so many words. It didn't matter. What he had decided to ask Koscuisko for would keep his Student busy enough.

"I do not regret. I will not renounce. The bargain that I made. What did you call it? The exchange, as of hostages."

Chonis smiled at how apt his Student was. "We have a special need at this time for a library of sorts. I would like you to build for me three each of the four classes of Controlled List drugs, and I must specify that the three preparations taken together cover as broad a range as possible." So that Mergau could be taught to use them for as many purposes, as many prisoners as possible, without requiring her to actually learn much of anything more than a list. "Your fellow Student will test these drugs in her practical exercises"—*that* startled him, even if he was too subdued to say anything—"and it goes without saying that all prisoners will be bona fide prisoners. Upon my word of honor, neither you nor Student Noycannir will be exposed to a prisoner-surrogate for the remainder of the Term."

It was just lucky they'd got a fresh batch in, what with the Term gearing up for the Advanced Levels. Mergau's Fourth and Fifth could be recycled for someone else's Seventh, if all went well.

"You are content to sacrifice effectiveness for applicability, then. I think that I understand."

Not the whole tape, no. Not quite yet. But soon. As soon as Noycannir's repeat on the Fourth Level, which he had better schedule for before Koscuisko's Sixth if they were not to fall too far behind. "How soon do you feel you can have something ready for me?"

Koscuisko shrugged, apparently distracted by the technical aspects of the problem. "It will not take long to update the first speak-serum for Nurail. If you have a Nurail"—for Noycannir's Fourth Level? —"we could be ready perhaps tomorrow."

There should be no problem there; the Bench was blessed with a multitude of Nurail on Charges. They'd pick one out of the manifest for Noycannir's Fourth Level. Then, of course, the formal trial of the speak-serum against St. Clare would be a redundancy; but that part of the program had never been intended as a serious test, so it made little difference either way.

Chonis nodded his approval, smiling. "Tomorrow, then. Give me your status first thing in the morning. Please don't neglect your physical exercise, Andrej; I know how easy it is to become distracted, but really we must keep you in the very best of health. And Curran is responsible to the Administrator for you."

Rising from the table, Koscuisko bowed formally—as always—but there was something different, all the same. "As you wish it, Tutor. If I am to be excused now, I will begin in the lab immediately."

Then Chonis understood.

There was no mockery in Koscuisko's salute, this time.

"Good day, Student Koscuisko." Oh, this was getting better and better by the moment.

St. Clare might be worth more to the Administration in the long run than Chonis had imagined.

Rabin was afloat in a cushiony sea of pleasant music, the air full of the sweet smell of the spring-brake that bloomed for two short weeks through the late snow in the high windy. The disconnected drowsiness that addled his brains he understood; he'd been drunk before. There was no explanation that sprung to mind for the pictures he was seeing, but they were too pretty to object to. His primary concern was whether he would be able to remember what kind of liquor it had been once he woke up.

"May I have status, please."

He heard the voice carrying through the breezy strains of the sheepshank pipes and wondered what it meant. A clear voice, a quiet voice, with a funny little accent—of course they all had accents. He'd never met anyone who could speak proper Standard, not since he'd left home. Since he'd been taken from home. But under the influence of whatever it was he was drunk on not even that nightmare of blood and screaming could move him to distress.

"His temperature is fluctuating a bit, but well within the range the officer had specified as expected. Swelling doesn't appear to be going down as well as the officer would wish, if the officer would care to examine?"

Some other voice. They were all his friends, he was certain. And because he felt so good that there wasn't any room in his limited consciousness for any other possibility. A cooling breeze had come up from somewhere, and he shifted against its soft luxurious caress, reveling in the pleasure of it. Warm and happy, and a lovely breeze. Could life possibly get any better than this?

Did he care about the multitude of ways in which it could get worse?

"I think I'd like to follow up on these with more of the bmilc ointment. You're quite right, though, this still looks ugly. I am inclined to hit it with another few sixteenths of ofdahl to get the swelling down."

Oddly enough, he could sense a sort of a pressure against his body, a pressure that made him nervous in an unfocused sort of way. There didn't seem to be any pain associated with the pressure as it shifted from place to place; nor was the pressure itself very hard or very widespread. Why was he nervous? The touch was against his shoulder, that was why he was nervous. Why it should be so, he was unsure. He cleared his throat to complain about it; he could hear some whimpering, very close by, but the pressure lifted.

"Let me have six eighths of the neural block. Immediately, if you please."

He held his breath, trying to understand who was crying. And he felt pressure, again, but only for a moment, and there was no more crying. The pressure that he felt was like a caress, now, soothing and comforting.

"There, now, that's better, isn't it? Thank you, technician, I will apply the ointment, if I may. You may be dismissed, if you like."

There was nothing to worry about, forever. Or until he was sober again, which amounted to the same thing.

He smiled and drifted off, content.

"I am not sure we should be unconcerned about this," Clellelan said, thoughtfully tapping his stylus against the stack of report-cubes. "I'm not rejecting your reasoning, Adifer. But there must have been half the Security on Station down in Infirmary last night."

"Perhaps an augmented third," Chonis demurred politely. The chairs in the Administrator's office were too comfortable for him to bother with becoming exercised over his superior's displeasure. "There've been no reports of duty stations left unattended, after all. Have there been?"

Chaymalt snorted from her position of repose at Chonis's right. "Only because there wasn't anyone left at duty stations to report anybody. What I'd like to know is how the word got out so quickly. What is it with these Bonds—do the governors lock into serial transmit when there are too many of them in one place? What? It was unnerving, is all I've got to say."

Clellelan set his stylus down, sighing in resignation. "Can't say that I blame them. 'The one is the many and the many are as one,' I've heard them say. Infirmary staff would have appreciated his surgery on Idarec, so I can understand them joining in, but I'm not sure why Station Security decided to open the clinic area to the Bonds the way they did."

Nor did Chonis, come to that. But nobody had expected anything like a mass demonstration, or they'd have taken steps, so much went without saying. Bond-involuntary troops were easily managed as long as they were surrounded by the un-Bonded, but when there were too many of them in one place and emotion started to run high—as high as it had run on this Station last night—conditioning could fail. Unpredictable things had been known to happen.

"It'll get out, of course." He was thinking out loud, since neither Clellelan nor Chaymalt seemed to have much to say. "Wrap a reputation around that boy before he so much as clears Orientation. Could be good for his old age, in the long run." Could be helpful in ensuring that Koscuisko would live to see his old age. Fleet Medical Officers could be very unpopular people under Jurisdiction. If there was going to be an attempt made on the life of any given Ship's Prime officer, it was good odds that it would be the Ship's Surgeon who would be targeted.

"Good for more than that." Chaymalt had been relatively subdued all through the late morning's informal staff review. Hadn't made a single insensitive comment about bond-involuntaries for, oh, eighths now. Chonis wondered what had set her off angle. "Good for that man Idarec's old age. Did I mention the diagnostic is calling for consciousness in three days? He was dead meat, Rorin; this time yesterday, I'd have told you to cancel his Bond and forget about it."

She more or less had told *him* that, Chonis remembered. More than a day ago. Was that what was on her mind? She certainly sounded emphatic enough.

"Compared to the talent we've seen come through here the past eight Terms, Student Koscuisko is all the way out to Gissen, all by himself. All right, we already know he's not your usual run of volunteer. I hate to think of him wasting his time with the Protocols, Rorin, I really do."

She sounded as if she meant it, which was unusual. Ligrose didn't get excited about much of anything, not that he had ever noticed. Color in her cheeks, fire in her eye—he was going to have to review the surgical record, he decided, just to see if he could figure out what had gotten through to her like this.

Clellelan was scowling at her in evident consternation. "What bit your elbow? He's a good surgeon, he's going to *Scylla*, he's got eight years to mark. Eight years isn't even all that long for Aznir. You know you can't have him."

In the general, rather than the specific sense, of course. Yes, of course. Chaymalt looked a little sulky, all the same. "I just don't like to see the waste, that's all. You wouldn't send a Tutor to teach the tweeners, would you?"

"No, and I wouldn't release restricted narcotics for a bond-involuntary on a Fifth Level, either. Let alone ad lib. And what kind of a limit is that? Four hundred thousand, Standard? Do you know what we could do with an extra four hundred thousand, Standard?"

Chaymalt actually blushed. Whether in embarrassment or vexation, however, Chonis did not care to guess. "I don't have to justify it. Any basic cost-benefit analysis would endorse the action."

Clellelan was clearly more up to date on what was happening in Ligrose's area than Chonis had realized. Chaymalt didn't seem inclined to let the issue rest, however.

"I'm having a hard time understanding why I can't have this one, while we're on the subject. It isn't as if he'd be likely to object—"

"If you declined to pass him?" Clellelan sat back in his chair. "Doctor Chaymalt. If you have any reservations to express about Student Koscuisko's medical qualifications, we should restrict them to a more formal hearing. It would seem to contradict your earlier statements, however."

This was ridiculous. Chaymalt had never seriously challenged graduation on the grounds of insufficient qualifications, no matter how sarcastic she got; and the whole point was that Koscuisko was good. There was no precedent . . . but that was what the last two days had been like, wasn't it?

"I cannot object to the Student's medical qualifications." Chaymalt sounded subdued, but still resisting. "Quite the contrary. I simply cannot understand how a qualified neurosurgeon with his ratings could be adequately utilized at the Ship's Surgeon level. There would seem to be an unusually extreme degree of difference between the two required roles."

Whereas indifferent surgeons made adequate Inquisitors, superlative surgeons made inadequate Inquisitors? Was that her point? Because if it was, all he would have to do would be to show her Koscuisko's Fourth and Fifth Levels. Koscuisko clearly had the makings of a superlative Inquisitor, whether or not Koscuisko was interested in hearing about it.

"How does the schedule look, Adifer?" Clellelan turned his attention toward Chonis, clearly determined to turn away from the potentially sticky hole that Chaymalt seemed bent on wedging herself into. Chonis put his glass down, clearing his throat. If he'd realized that Chaymalt was going to get emotionally involved, he'd have approached Clellelan privately; yet there was no help for it, he supposed, but to go forward bravely.

"It depends on Doctor Chaymalt, to an extent." He hadn't anticipated any problem, but it was always the unexpected issues that really fouled things up for one. "I've told him to take half-days in the lab, pending the speak-serum trial and his Sixth Level. I had assumed that Doctor Chaymalt would not object to waiving the clinical evaluation phase."

They usually sent Students to Infirmary for a week or so between

Intermediate and Advanced Levels. The Fleet requirement for on-site evaluation of Students' medical qualifications was a little outdated, perhaps, since their ability to perform as Ship's Inquisitor was what counted. Nobody expected leadership from Chief Medical Officers anymore, and they had staff to support them. Koscuisko might well prove a throwback of sorts; Chonis wondered how *Scylla* was going to react to the anomalous presence of a Chief Medical Officer who was clearly capable of growing into the job. For once.

Chaymalt was frowning, but Clellelan beat her to the mark. "I dare say our good Doctor has already done as much, even just this morning. What do you say, Ligrose? Any reservations signing his sheet?"

They would ignore the potential threat that she had half-made, then. Well, that was one way to handle it.

"I'll sign the sheet on instruction either way, Administrator. And no, there's no doubt in my mind about his fitness, not his technical qualifications, at any rate. I'd been looking forward to having him on Wards for a week. What's the problem?"

"We need him in his lab, Doctor." Chonis figured he'd better pick up the argument, since he hadn't filled the Administrator in quite yet. "As good as he may be on the floor, he's possibly even better in the lab. I told him he could be responsible for his St. Clare, but if we're to keep his course on schedule and make good use of his second rating at the same time, we need you to free up that referral block."

She chewed on her lip for a moment, drumming her fingers against the arm of the chair. She could insist on the week's referral; it would be within her rights to do so. They could—hypothetically—hold Koscuisko over, pretend he needed to be recycled for the next Term, use him that way. There were potential political problems with that approach, of course. Koscuisko was the Prince Inheritor of a very old, rather influential family in the Dolgorukij Combine, one that had family ties to the Autocrat's family itself—in the illegitimate female line, but they were there. The Autocrat's Proxy might well take an interest in why Koscuisko had been kept back, and no one was going to want to try to tell the Autocrat's Proxy that Andrej Ulexeievitch Koscuisko was a dunce.

Chaymalt shrugged, and Chonis knew he could relax. "To hell with Koscuisko. Who cares, anyway? I mean, really. Take all the lab time you want, Rorin. I won't bother the boy."

"Thank you, Ligrose." Chonis knew that Clellelan was genuinely relieved, from the tone of his voice. "It's a prudent decision, and I appreciate your flexibility. Adifer, what about Noycannir, where do we stand?"

Noycannir would still be a challenge.

But with Koscuisko's help they'd get her through with flying colors. Then Verlaine would find out for himself why it was a mistake to send a Clerk of Court without Bench medical certification to try to learn an Inquisitor's craft.

There were four classes of drugs comprising the Controlled List, and Mergau felt as if she had tried to read them all in the past day. Four classes, each with three basic subdivisions, and a bewildering array of suggested uses and contraindications associated with each individual preparation. How did they expect her to keep them all in mind?

How could she ever hope to keep them all in mind?

Summoned to Tutor Chonis's office toward the middle of second, Mergau paused to compose herself carefully as Hanbor signaled for admittance. Koscuisko's slave was here, she noted with interest. Perhaps she'd find out what Koscuisko's role in this new paradigm was to be, since Koscuisko was obviously also with Tutor Chonis.

"Step through."

Koscuisko sat at the far side of the Tutor's long study table, half-rising from his place to nod a polite bow in acknowledgment of her presence. There was something in his face, at the back of his pale eyes, that she found strangely familiar. What? But she had to concentrate on Tutor Chonis. Koscuisko was to be subordinate to the Tutor's course of instruction for her, according to Chonis's proposal. So Koscuisko could wait.

"I present myself in obedience to my Tutor's instruction. I hope the day has found my Tutor well." She took her place beside the beverage-set that had been arranged on her side of the table. Warmer, again, by the smell. All right, she didn't mind taking a nice drink of warmer. If Tutor Chonis felt he needed to woo her so obviously to his plan, it could only mean that she had him at a disadvantage, and she liked that.

"You'll recall the conversation we had yesterday," Chonis replied.

"For Student Koscuisko's benefit, let me just recap briefly. You are to learn a specially tailored group of Controlled List drugs with which Student Koscuisko is to provide us. This will ensure that you can successfully carry out the functions most necessary for Secretary Verlaine—those of Inquiry and Confirmation."

She waved the warmer jug in Koscuisko's direction, to catch his eye. He looked at her only briefly, then shook his head in a gesture that declined the unspoken offer. She already knew he didn't drink warmer. Chonis always set out rhyti. She would drink rhyti when she felt there was a political point to be made by doing so. The provision of warmer, however, was a very intriguing development in terms of the balance of power.

"You have been hard at work since yesterday, studying the Controlled List. What do you remember, offhand, about a primary series drug from the speak-sera class?"

She'd only skimmed the speak-sera, more anxious about drugs her Patron would be most interested in—wake-keepers, pain-maintenance drugs, psychogens. Enforcers. There were many names for them, but one transcendent reality. We can keep you from sleep, we can keep you from unconsciousness, we can keep the pain from fading off its first bright agony, we can turn the unknown horrors of your own mind against you until you tell us what we want to know. A man at Verlaine's level of responsibility wouldn't want to be bothered with speak-sera, surely. Why restrict oneself to such single purpose medications when the others were so much more terrible?

"A primary series speak-serum is authorized at the Preliminary Levels. And higher, of course." Still, the rationale behind the three subdivisions in each class was constant across the entire Controlled List. She could fake it. "To be employed at the Inquisitor's discretion as substitute for, or in addition to, the established Protocols. Therefore also restricted to disabling the internal editor somewhat, rather than depriving the prisoner of any freedom of choice in the matter of confession." It got easier as she continued, although she wasn't really certain whether she was remembering what she'd read or was making it up as she went along. "At the secondary level, speak-sera are employed that deny any conscious selection of response, although the prisoner may still decline to speak if determined enough. At the tertiary level there is an additional element of compulsion."

Koscuisko straightened in his seat. "It becomes of importance to note—with the Tutor's permission," he said, lowering his eyes politely in Chonis's direction, "—that the same drug may fall in primary, secondary, and tertiary levels, depending upon the species. Care must be taken to match the drug against the Level, else a mistake may potentially occur." A tertiary speak-sera might be "accidentally" used in the Preliminary Levels, in other words. Mergau could tell exactly what he was getting at. If she learned the species for which a primary level speak-serum was tertiary in effect, she would be clear to cheat the prisoner.

"Such errors must of course be carefully avoided." She didn't bother with whether or not she sounded as if she was making an effort to be sincere. Koscuisko simply lowered his eyes again and made an irritated expression with his mouth. She knew what it was that she recognized about Koscuisko, now. He had been whipped. His face was the face of a beaten man, in the presence of the one who had punished him. She felt a flush of pleasure, of gratitude toward Tutor Chonis for sharing the humbling of Andrej Koscuisko with her in this manner. And she thirsted to know how Chonis had done it, what Chonis had used for a belt. Whatever it was, she wanted one just like it for her own use.

"I am glad that we understand each other so well." Tutor Chonis's rather dry comment recalled her to herself; he did not sound entirely approving. She had to watch herself more carefully to avoid alienating the Tutor. But it was sweet to see her fellow Student bend his neck— his proud neck, his rich neck—to do her service in submission to the Tutor. To be below her, at her bidding, even if only in a limited sense.

Her Patron would give her people like Koscuisko, and they would kiss the ground at her feet if she bade them—and thank her for it.

"Student Koscuisko, will you brief Student Noycannir on this speak-serum, please. We've scheduled a retrial at the Fourth Level tomorrow morning after fast-meal, Student Noycannir. Proceed."

And, oh, but she was eager for the work, for the dominion.

She was beginning to have a sense of how it really felt to hold the knout.

Having slept less poorly than in recent days, Andrej Koscuisko woke a few eighths before time, feeling better than he had since he'd gotten here. Yes, there would be Noycannir's Fourth Level today, and

Tutor Chonis wanted him to observe and note the effect of the drug. Yes, he was to start work after mid-meal on developing a pain-maintenance drug benign enough in its effect to be cleared at the Intermediate Levels. He would not be asked for nerve agents, psychogens, or wake-keepers until Mergau had completed her Intermediate Levels; and the wake-keepers would present interesting problems whose application to Inquiry might not be obvious enough to be too depressing—as long as he could maintain his concentration. There was a day yet before he had to go to the Sixth Level; and he'd decided he had a positive use even for that, since he needed to learn his whip. And which whip. All in all there were to be no difficult demands today, apart from the fact that he had combat drill scheduled before his supper. Joslire was an excellent instructor, fearlessly inflexible in his demands on the exercise floor. And yet even the workout that he faced had its pleasant aspects, because Joslire would give him a rubdown after Joslire was finished demonstrating his inadequacies—in close order drill—and Joslire was quite good at massage.

Life was perhaps not good, exactly.

But he felt less morose about it than he could remember, without thinking about it too hard.

The chimer went off and Andrej reset it with a casual wave of his hand. St. Clare would be free enough from pain to wake sometime today. Andrej was not sure what their first interview would be like. He could not imagine that St. Clare would be happy to have been bound over to the man who had tortured him, let alone so clumsily. And still he took comfort from the simple fact that St. Clare healed aggressively and adequately, and was content.

"The officer is respectfully invited to rise at this time." The sound of Joslire's calm, admonitory tone from the other side of the partition made Andrej smile. It was an improvement over his old nurse, her scolding so imbedded in his mind that he could almost hear dear Gelsa even now—*Lazy little lords who aren't washed in time for prayers never come to a good end,* or *If you aren't out of bed in two Sacred-art-thous may the Holy Mother help me if your feet don't fall right off.* Yes, it was time to get up and wash, even though he hadn't said morning prayers—let alone evening ones—since he'd left home. Andrej sat up, putting the cover aside, aware of Joslire's anxious waiting presence in the room beyond.

"Thank you, Joslire. I am coming." Joslire had gotten a little shy of him in recent days—since he had shamed the man by looking at his scars. There seemed to be an extra layer of distance there somewhere, though as far as Andrej could tell, Joslire had forgiven him for his lapse. Nodding to Joslire as he passed on the way to the washroom, Andrej pondered the change, wondering whether there was a problem. As if there would be anything that he could hope to do about it if there was a problem. On the other hand, Joslire was the one who had told him that his lab space was not monitored. Should he wait until he was in his lab to try to tickle Joslire out of his reservation of spirit?

Andrej shut the shower stream off with an exasperated snap. There must have been something in his supper that had made him abnormally thickheaded about things. Of course he couldn't tickle Joslire. He'd only humiliate the man by trying. It would be asking too much of life—Andrej concluded, in his morning's meditations, rinsing out his mouth—to expect to feel content about all aspects of it.

He ate his fast-meal and read his briefings, his mood of slightly manic gaiety still on him. He was even pleased with his uniform this morning, and his boots fit with very little difficulty. A psychological pressure valve of sorts? he asked himself. Some kind of an adjustment to the stresses of the Term?

Joslire was to see him to the exercise observation area, where he would meet Tutor Chonis. As they left quarters, Joslire asked the same question he asked nearly every morning, in exactly the same tone as usual, at exactly the same moment as usual, as soon as the door had closed behind them in the corridor—but before Andrej had taken three steps forward.

"What suits the officer's preference for the mid-meal, if the officer please?"

He simply couldn't concentrate, and he was too busy enjoying his feeling of euphoria to care. "Whichever has the darkest eyes, I think." Hearing Joslire miss a pace behind him, he slowed his step so as not to lose his guide. He'd never been to the exercise observation area. He had no idea where he was going.

"If the officer would care to elaborate, at the officer's pleasure?"

"I said dark eyes, Joslire, Dark hair, dark eyes, very exotic. Twins, perhaps." Marana had dark eyes, nearly as dark as a good cup of rhyti, with the same bronzed cast to them. He hadn't thought much about

Marana since he'd been here, and it suddenly occurred to him to wonder how she was making out. Marana could take care of herself; he had always admired that about Marana. The problem being, of course, that he was not supposed to have admired anything in particular about Marana, no matter how long they had been friends, no matter that they had played together as children. Once he was married, he would be able to return to admiring Marana without fear of disapproval. Once he had bred children to his sacred wife, he could ride his favorite mare from saints to sinners; and no one would fault him except perhaps the woman he was married to, who should know better. Lise Semyonevna Ichogetrisa—the bride to whom his father had pledged him, when he'd reached the age—was no good at toleration from what Andrej had seen of her so far. He hoped she wasn't making herself unpleasant.

"Among the Emandisan, it is the officer's coloring that is exotic. If the officer permits."

Joslire sounded amused, and had clearly caught the way in which Andrej's mind was running this morning. A gratuitously offered comment. There was hope in the world.

"And tall, yes, you know? Aznir women are not tall. Nor do they tend to assert themselves, not in an obvious manner. I tell you, Joslire, there is a peculiar fascination to women as unlike those in and of my father's Household as possible."

He was telling secrets on himself, but what harm could it do? Perhaps it would even the balance out in some obscure way. He had taken Joslire's secrets, the secrets of Joslire's scarred body, and he hadn't even asked.

If the Holy Mother was gracious, Joslire would accept this confidence as a grant of intimacy, and be healed of the shame to which Andrej had put him.

Collecting his thoughts with an effort, Andrej stepped through to the exercise observation area to subordinate his attention to his Tutor.

"You had better make up your mind to it; the Bench requires your response. What is your name?"

Student Noycannir's voice was a little muted in the observation area, and Joslire knew without looking that Lop Hanbor would click the sound levels up a notch. There was only one screen to watch today, and no real reason for him to have to watch at all, since he would not be needed to relay special insight on his Student's performance.

His Student sat with the Tutor, watching Noycannir bully her prisoner. The prisoner wasn't anybody Joslire recognized. Either a new arrival—and generally there were circumstances unusual enough to call attention to themselves when new Security were assigned mid-Term—or an actual criminal. Well, an actual un-Bonded criminal.

"M-my name?" Nurail, by the accent: the flattened vowels. He'd noticed an accent of the same sort in Robert St. Clare's speech, at any rate. "A'don't understand, you know my name, it's in the detention order—"

Noycannir struck the man across the face with the ribbed stick; not because she needed to, but because that was what the paradigm tape had shown. Joslire sensed Koscuisko shifting uneasily in his seat; and Tutor Chonis must have sensed the same thing, because Tutor Chonis followed up on it.

"Something the matter?"

"She . . ." Koscuisko gestured at the screen, at an apparent loss for the words he wanted. "It would seem the drug's working, Tutor Chonis. The prisoner speaks his mind without engaging in self-censorship. She is only delaying the process if she won't let him speak."

"None of your insolence," Noycannir was saying smugly, with a knowing glance at the screen. Almost as if she'd heard Koscuisko's criticism. "You're to answer the question that I asked, no more, no less, no argument. Understood?"

Chonis pointed his finger at the screen, tilting his head toward Koscuisko conspiratorially. "That technique can be effectively used at the lower Levels especially. Consider that the usual strategy is to hit the man until he's ready to answer the question."

Koscuisko nodded. "It would seem to be the point of the exercise. By your leave, Tutor Chonis."

There were Students who simply refused to play the game; Joslire had had one. Her attitude had been that there was no sense in making any more of a mess out of a confession than strictly necessary, because there would certainly be enough of a mess as soon as confession had been Recorded. Such Students made perfectly adequate Inquisitors; but Joslire wasn't sure Koscuisko was oriented on precisely that track.

"Yes, of course, Student Koscuisko." In the exercise theater

Noycannir was continuing to play through a paradigmatic exercise, but neither the Tutor nor Koscuisko was paying very much attention to her now. "Noycannir's approach is one that has demonstrated effectiveness. Not all Students can be expected to be capable of improvising." Unlike Koscuisko, whose Fourth and Fifth Levels had been clear improvisations made up of bits of several paradigms, and at least one invention of his own.

Joslire rather wished Tutor Chonis would pay more attention to Student Noycannir. She was having a great deal of fun with her prisoner, if in a different way than Koscuisko enjoyed himself. They all knew there was a speak-serum in effect—one that certainly appeared to be functioning perfectly. Students who had too much fun with their prisoners frequently ruined them before time.

"She selects too hard a course, Tutor Chonis," Koscuisko protested. "Listen to him; he is quite willing to answer the right question. She could have her Evidence and be done by now."

Tutor Chonis turned in his chair, clicking the viewer to gray screen. "Yes, it could be better done. Do you resent the fact that it's not your prisoner? Because there are enough to go around."

As obvious as the question seemed to Joslire, it appeared to be the furthest thing from Koscuisko's mind. Half-rising in his seat, Koscuisko stared at Tutor Chonis with astonishment and horror. "Tutor Chonis. I do not know what to say. Surely I have not . . . I'm not . . ."

Tutor Chonis raised an eyebrow at the vehemence of Koscuisko's response, and Koscuisko mastered himself with a fierce effort whose stern intensity was clearly communicated in his voice. "That is to say, I ask for pardon, to have spoken unadvisedly. I have not been troubled by such a thing as that, Tutor Chonis. And still I cannot say I like to see the thing ill-done."

It bothered Joslire in some obscure fashion to see his Student so anxious to conform, when he knew how ruthlessly Fleet would use that meek submissiveness. Tutor Chonis restored the visuals on-screen. Student Noycannir was crouched over her prisoner, and appeared to be taking a statement. At last. "Your performance is all you're responsible for, Student Koscuisko."

Robert St. Clare would be sent to *Scylla* with Koscuisko, but Robert was virgin Security yet. First assignment was usually brutal for newly commissioned Inquisitors. What Koscuisko really needed was a seasoned hand to help him over the rough spots. Robert didn't have the experience to do it.

His eyes on the viewer, assessing Noycannir's performance, Tutor Chonis almost sounded as though he was talking to himself. "We'll let her run with this one; she's not violated the Protocols, and she is taking confession now—so you need have no further cause for concern on that head. I'll talk to her about it during debriefing."

As a compromise it wasn't half bad. Joslire was afraid for Koscuisko's sake that he might not recognize extraordinary Administrative flexibility when he saw it—not after having taken Robert back from the whip, the irons, the twister.

"You know best, Tutor Chonis. I don't mean to overstep my bounds."

Tutor Chonis seemed pleased with the exercise, but whether it was with Noycannir's performance or Koscuisko's, Joslire couldn't tell. Chonis laid his hand on Koscuisko's shoulder to give it a friendly avuncular shake, fond and forgiving at once.

"Oh, it's nothing to worry about, Andrej. You're very much involved in the use of your formulations, we understand that. On your way to the lab now, I gather?"

Dismissed to the lab, that was to say. Koscuisko rose to his feet, a little diffidently. "I had hoped to check on St. Clare on the way to the lab. Unless the Tutor would prefer—"

Chonis waved him off. "No, no, you know best how to deal with your time, Student Koscuisko. Let me know when you're ready to return him to duty. We can have a better look at your speak-serum then. You'll feel better."

Koscuisko bowed, his face empty of emotion.

What were they going to do with Robert after the speak-serum trial?

Robert had been assigned to Koscuisko; Joslire was assigned to Koscuisko.

Did Chonis mean to reassign him in mid-Term?

Did Chonis mean to relieve him of his duty?

Koscuisko was waiting for him in the corridor to lead the way to Infirmary. His Student quirked an eyebrow at him, but said nothing; hastily, Joslire blanked his face of his confusion.

A man would have to be crazy to be given a chance at light duty and not jump at it.

And there was no reason under Jurisdiction why he should be jealous of Robert St. Clare.

CHAPTER TEN

He had been waking from time to time for a while now, although he couldn't really judge how long the while had been. Someone would come in to reset a monitor, someone would test the transdermal patch that lay along his arm, someone would leave, and he would go back to sleep again.

This time it seemed a little different.

There was someone with him in the room. He guessed that simply because he was waking up. It seemed he couldn't set his wakefulness aside this time, not as easily as he had done before. That didn't bother him; it was probably past time to get out of bed.

He lay and waited for his body to cooperate.

There didn't seem to be a great deal of pain, which was unusual, since all he could remember—since before the start of the exercise— was pain. Not a lot of pain, not a lot of pressure; and he wasn't hungry, and he wasn't cold. It was probably a mistake to want to sit up, because the odds were good that the waking world was going to be considerably less comfortable for him than this half-dreaming one. It would feel good to stretch, though, and his mouth tasted foul with an excess of sleep and a rotten taint of old blood.

Whomever it was came nearer to him now, exposing his arm to adjust the transdermal patch. No, to remove the transdermal patch, and he guessed that there had been a drug in whatever they'd been feeding him—because his mind started to sharpen almost immediately.

A drug? That was right, a speak-serum. The Student Interrogator—Koscuisko—had taken his secret, somehow, some way, but there was to be only a speak-serum to test instead of the penalty he had incurred. The Tutor had said . . . What? Twenty-six years? And how long had he been lying in this bed to have his wounds healed to the point that he felt little discomfort from them?

Closing his eyes tightly, he nerved himself to the effort of sitting up, turning to his side to give himself some leverage. Sitting up. Yes. Sitting up, with whoever's help—and there might actually turn out to be two whoevers, from what he could gather from the count of helping hands—sitting up, and his brain fogged in immediately, and he had to give himself a moment to let his blood pressure catch up with his posture. It didn't do to try to sit up too quickly. Careful. He would be careful.

After a moment the supportive hands fell away, and he could steady himself on the bed's surface by leaning on his hands. Oddly enough, it seemed to be a stasis field, like the ones rich men slept on—or children with burns. Or people who had been whipped, he supposed, as long as they weren't bond-involuntaries. So what was he doing here?

His shoulder didn't hurt.

Setting his weight carefully over his rubbery legs he stood up very slowly, using the bed and the wall for support. His shoulder should hurt, shouldn't it? He rotated the shoulder gingerly, using his other hand for support in case he should hit a sore spot while he wasn't looking. No, it didn't hurt, and that meant that, to the very best of what little analytical ability he had, there was only one possible conclusion to be drawn.

To wit: he only thought he was Rabin with the Ice Traverse, Robert St. Clare.

There was a reflector in the room, hung above the sanitary basin in one corner. Stumbling a bit, but otherwise steady on his feet, he took himself over to look in the mirror and see whom it would turn out to be that he was. Who would have such an odd sort of delusion?

It wasn't as if being him was any fun at all. Surely it was preferable by far to be some rich man who could afford to sleep in the pressure-neutral embrace of a stasis field, who had clearly not been beaten to within an inch of his life by an up-and-coming young poisoner with a whip, who had not failed in his mission to deliver his sister from her shame.

Susan R. Matthews

Some kind of a pervert: that had to be it.

In his home valley, a pervert had generally been taken to be a man who preferred women to drinking, but allowances were to be made for the more subtle derangements of an alien species. Maybe he wasn't even a Nurail at all. It might be nice not to be Nurail; so many terrible things would not have had to have happened.

For a moment he didn't quite know his own face, staring into the reflector. He looked very white, and needed to scrape the hair off his chin. He was sorry to realize that he did recognize himself, though, once he'd had a chance to think about it. He was still unmistakably who he thought he was.

And the people in the room with him, the people he'd not been paying proper attention to, the people wearing darker colors than Infirmary staff?

Ducking his head as if to catch his wits, he stole a sidewise glance. Dark uniform, Security, no telling whether it was bond-involuntary or Station Security from the leg portion. Light-colored uniform, not light like Infirmary, light like Administrator Clellelan, like Tutor Chonis, like . . .

Best faced at once, if faced it must be, he reminded himself grimly. Straightening his back as best he could—his governor knew the color, and would not be argued against—he faced the problem head-on, to know the worst of it.

Koscuisko.

Student Interrogator, promising young poisoner, soon-to-be Inquisitor.

His officer.

He stared for a long moment, too confused to heed the yammering of the governor in his head. This was the man, then, and he looked a deal shorter than Robert had remembered, but the eyes were the same, and the pale voice—

"You should sit down, Mister St. Clare."

He was going to fall over, and that would be awkward, because he would knock into the officer if he did, and that would be a violation. He yielded himself up gratefully to the hands that guided him back to the bed, trying not to think about Koscuisko's hands. These hands felt different. Perhaps Koscuisko had extra, and traded them off, fastening them to his wrists as he had need of them for various tasks?

It was good to sit; he was dizzy. He could hear Koscuisko's voice, sending the Security—Curran, that would be—out for a seat; and all the while supported by Koscuisko's hands. As long as they were the nonviolent pair, Robert supposed that he was ahead of the game.

Still, it was passing strange that his flesh didn't crawl or his stomach turn at the very smell of the man. There was a nagging sense of familiarity tied in somehow with Koscuisko's touch, as if his body thought it was the same as the touch that had soothed his aches and comforted his hurt in his dreaming half-sleep. That was the problem with medication, a man's body took up all manner of strange notions. No wonder honest Nurail stuck to drink, although where a man could hope to find a corner to distill a bit of drinkable on a Jurisdiction base escaped him quite.

"Do you know who I am?"

Joslire Curran had left the room; they were alone. St. Clare raised his head to meet the officer's curious gaze. He was too close, it made a man uncomfortable. The last time he'd seen Koscuisko so close up . . .

"The officer."

His voice didn't seem to want to work. Koscuisko passed him a tumbler full of clear liquid from the top shelf above the bed's status bar; it was cool and sweet, and didn't *taste* like poison. Robert cleared his throat and tried again.

"The officer is Student Koscuisko. A'think. Sir."

Koscuisko smiled at his confusion, but Robert didn't take offense. He was too confused to take offense. He had thought that he had regained consciousness, but all he could remember of recent events— after his torture—were too obviously fantasies of the most unbelievable sort for any man to credit.

"Even so. Do you remember who you are, come to that?"

This question he knew. He could answer this question.

"Robert St. Clare. Sir. —As it please the officer," he added hastily, mindful of his governor. Which didn't seem to have noticed his potential lapse of military courtesy. He couldn't spare the energy to ponder on it now, however; here was Joslire with a seat for Student Koscuisko, and Koscuisko settled him gently where he sat and moved away a pace and a half to rest himself.

"Now comes the critical part, though, you will have to concentrate.

Rehearse for me if you will where we first met, and what has happened in your life since then."

Oh, he didn't want to. Really he was not at all interested. He shook his head, rejecting and resisting. "Na, the officer can't be serious." Joslire Curran—who had posted himself behind the officer, per procedure—looked shocked; and that was a hint to St. Clare that there was something wrong with what he'd said. "A'mean with respect. Boring. Little that suits a story."

Joslire started speaking almost before he'd finished. "If the officer please, there must be a malfunction. Extreme stress can disable the governor. There is surely no disrespect—"

Joslire sounded just short of frightened, as well as disapproving. Frightened? Robert consulted the silence in his mind. Oh, yes. He was supposed to remember his etiquette, and mind his manners. And never speak of "I" or "me" or "mine" in front of officers, lest he should give offense whilst not looking.

Koscuisko made a smoothing gesture with his hand. "It's all right, Joslire. I'm not about to fault him for it. But really, St. Clare, I need to know how much you remember. So that we will know where we stand with each other."

And he was also never, ever supposed to so much as hint that any suggestion an officer made was less than sweet and sensible instruction, self-evidently logical, absolutely true and correct. Never. Well, he would try to do better; he supposed it would only be prudent of him to pretend.

"Yes, sir. No offense was meant, sir. I am—that is, this troop . . . am . . . is . . ."

Casting about for the right words, the correct lie, he found himself at a loss to complete his phrase, confused about which words were safe to use. Koscuisko smiled, and finished the thought for him.

"You are only a little bit drunk, Mister St. Clare. There is a residual euphoria, I regret that it will not persist. Never mind."

He wished Koscuisko wouldn't call him Mister. He knew his place; Megh hadn't been married, after all. He'd never tried to lay claim to the authority due a mother's brother. "Not a Warrant." He shook his head, deciding to get stubborn about it—for Megh's sake, if for no other reason. "Work for my living, Robert."

He didn't see what Koscuisko found so amusing, but Koscuisko certainly seemed to be entertained. "As you like. Do tell me, Robert, I'm due in the lab, in less than four."

As long as that was settled, he supposed he would cooperate. Frowning, he set his mind to hunt back over the past few days; with luck, he would find out what he was doing here, and why he didn't hurt.

"The officer conducted a practical exercise, an interrogation exercise. The Intermediate Levels, Four and Five." There was a little uncertainty in his mind about the wisdom of reminding Koscuisko. But Koscuisko had been calling him by his name, not by his alias. So clearly he didn't have to worry that Koscuisko didn't already know he'd been a prisoner-surrogate.

"There was a failure of duty, on . . . this troop's part. I'm not sure . . . with respect . . ."

The more he thought about it, however, the more confused he became. There had to be a problem. Didn't there? He'd not been successful, he could remember that, because he'd been taken from the exercise theater to detention. Not to Infirmary. It didn't weave.

"It isn't important, Robert. What is important is that you must test my speak-serum for me, you must hold that in your mind. And also there is another unpleasant truth."

Failed in his purpose, though he did not know how. Tutor Chonis had come to see him, in his disgrace, with some bee-sweet in his mouth about substitution of penalties; and speak-sera had been mentioned. He thought, perhaps, maybe. There had been a hearing, hadn't there been?

"Something of that, if the officer pleases," he agreed, slowly, thinking hard. A hearing. His Class Two violation hearing. It rose into his mind with the brutal force of nightmare, and behind the Administrator's voice he could hear the crackling of the fires that had burned out the high-camps, and the screaming of the animals. Of his family. What had Clellelan said?

He couldn't keep his balance any more, the effort was too much. Turning to one side on the edge of the bed, he tried to keep his body more or less erect; but his arms would not support his weight, and he sank down to lie within the stasis field, awkwardly.

"Elects to test the officer's new speak-serum, instead of . . . what was promised beforetime. And the officer will discipline a matter of insubordination. But they have reduced my Bond."

How long had he had to sleep on it, to assimilate this extraordinary change in the rules of his life? Not long enough. Staring at the ceiling, now, he was vaguely aware of being set straight on the bed once more, the transdermal patch reapplied, an injection of something pressed through at his shoulder.

"There, that's quite enough for now." Koscuisko was standing beside him, from the sound of his voice, and Koscuisko sounded gentle indeed. "There will be a day or two of therapy, and when you are returned to duty, there will be the speak-serum. It will be like being more drunk, without the morning after. Sleep well."

Koscuisko, who stood beside him; Koscuisko, who had tortured the secret away from him; Koscuisko, who—as his body insisted—had salved his wounds. Koscuisko, who had a drug for him to test, but who had discipline in hand at the same time.

Koscuisko, who was to be his officer for as long as Koscuisko remained with Fleet—until the Day, perhaps, if Koscuisko should stay with Fleet for so long as that. But the Day was four years closer than it had been when they had sent him here to play at prisoner-surrogate.

What was he supposed to make of it?

He knew the answer to that one, he did, and his governor knew he knew. He was supposed to make nothing of it. He had his orders. Student Koscuisko was his officer. He was to go to sleep.

Shrugging mental shoulders at himself, at the governor in his brain, at Koscuisko's ambiguous image in his mind, Robert let himself drift away with the medication and his weariness. Sleep was a good idea. Fine. He'd go back to sleep.

With any luck he'd understand it all when next he woke.

The lab work was going well, that was a good thing. St. Clare was doing well, which was a very good thing indeed. The Sixth Level exercise wouldn't start until tomorrow morning; there was a cushion of time yet before he had to face the next trial—that was good. Life was not bad, not for this minute slice of it. It could have been residual euphoria, left over from the morning; had he really made remarks of that sort to Joslire, dark-eyed women, twins? He had to have been thinking with his fish. That was the only explanation. Sometimes a man simply woke with a brisk fish breaching from his hip-wrap, half-drunk with some unfocused and erotic dream of the ocean every woman carried with her and fish that sought their source and native place.

Hearing Joslire's signal at the door to his lab space, Andrej keyed the admit. "Step through." A moment yet to shut down on the comps and launch an analysis run, and he'd be ready to go.

"The officer is expected for physical exercise: combat training drill." Yes, yes, he knew that. Not even combat drill was actually unpleasant at the heart of it, though. And since to spar with Joslire, he had to concentrate on what he was doing—if he didn't want Joslire to bounce him off the wall—it freed him from contemplating the troubles of his life."

"Coming immediately." He could come back after third-meal to see how his analysis had run. Tutor Chonis would be able to use this drug for Noycannir's Fifth Level one way or the other, but he wanted to extend its nonlethal effect to Class Two hominids for his own professional satisfaction. Efficiency was a virtue, of a sort. "Just a moment, though, Joslire. I mean to ask you a question, if we are still off monitor."

Joslire scowled at him with his eyebrows, a restrained expression Andrej had learned to read as confusion. "The officer's communications are still privileged in lab space. If the officer please."

Rising stiffly from the bench, Andrej stretched, wondering how to phrase his question to avoid giving alarm. Or to create the least amount of anxiety. All this time together, and Joslire seemed as far from relaxed in his presence as ever he had.

"You know that the Tutor has required four-and-forty of me, in consideration of St. Clare's supposed fault. And it was part of the bargain that I would punish him with my own hand."

He felt too awkward by half to be discussing this with Joslire. Surely it was in very poor taste of him. But he had to talk to somebody about it; and he knew that Joslire had ample experience upon which to base an answer to his questions.

"So much was understood, if it please the officer."

Oh, was it, really? And by whom? No, he was not going to permit himself to be distracted. He was going to cling to his good spirits while he could. All of those Security in the corridor, the other night . . .

"I want you to tell me so if you would rather not respond. But if I am to do this, I need to know the manner in which it is best done.

Thou art scarred, I cannot help that. I need to know what you can tell me—how would a man prefer to be beaten, if he knew that there was no hope of getting 'round it?"

As embarrassed as he was to hear himself use a familiar form with Joslire, he could not regret it. Not when he saw how much it seemed to gratify the other man. Anything to make it easier on Joslire was a good thing, to Andrej's mind.

"There are requirements." Joslire chose his words with evident care. "Blood must be drawn, or the stroke repeated. So it is . . . easiest . . . when the officer lets blood with each stroke. It is over more quickly."

Thinking about the question, consulting his own difficult memories. Andrej stood silent, in respect for Joslire's pain.

"Then it is also easier when there is a regular pattern, one can prepare. Sometimes the officer is sympathetic, and the stroke is regular. Sometimes the officer has no skill or stomach for it, blood is not let, and then the stroke must be repeated. It is counted as good at the third stroke, though, and the next looked for—"

Joslire seemed to shudder, and fell silent.

Andrej decided that he didn't want to probe any more deeply into Joslire's wounded spirit.

"Thank you, Joslire. This is good information for me to have, and I thank you for it." Wanting to call Joslire back from the black moments in his past, he could afford to pass on more technical details. He could revisit the instructional material; the standard techniques addressed the issue of maximizing suffering, and surely the same information could be back-engineered in some sense to serve his purpose.

Joslire seemed to shake himself awake, and Andrej put a hand out to steady him. There was a moment, and it seemed to Andrej that it was a long one; then Joslire was recovered, taking a deep breath, bowing politely. To request the release of his arm, Andrej supposed.

"Sir. The officer would not wish to be late to his drill. It would only have to be made up for later."

A lie, a blatant lie. Joslire knew very well that Andrej would just as soon miss combat drill and makeup drill alike. Preceding Joslire out into the hall, he started down the corridor that would lead them out of Infirmary, wondering at the unnecessary comment.

They didn't go to the room he was familiar with, however. It seemed to be in rather a different area of the Station, although there was as little traffic here as Andrej was accustomed to seeing on his way to Tutor Chonis's office. He was going to need to see Tutor Chonis to describe the drug he had created for Noycannir. After his exercise, perhaps.

The exercise area itself was somewhat more spacious, at least to judge from the changing area. Was this where Joslire had brought him to the sauna before? There was a door at one end of the changing area that looked promising in that regard. Still unfamiliar, but promising.

Changing into exercise uniform was not a difficult task; the clothing was loose and comfortable, if relatively minimal, and mat-socks were much easier to get into and out of than his boots were. Joslire didn't seem to be changing, however; no, not even when he'd got Andrej's uniform folded and draped and all of the things Joslire did with his uniforms.

Andrej didn't understand.

"What is this, Joslire, are we not to dance together?"

Dance. That was what they called it at home, on Azanry. Combat drill was not unlike a young man's-dance, a challenge-dance, a test of dominance. Andrej had always liked all of the different dances, and some year he would perhaps get as good at this particular sort as Joslire was—but not without Joslire's help.

"If the officer would please step through to the exercise floor. It is considered beneficial that the officer be exposed to different combat techniques as part of the officer's instruction."

The whole thing made him rather nervous, actually, but Joslire—as usual—left him no room for protest. Well. He wouldn't know him, then, whomever his partner was to be. Perhaps Joslire was afraid that Andrej would grow complacent, having begun to learn how to dance with Joslire; and would consequently fail to generalize his knowledge and protect himself against a stranger?

"You will wait for me, I hope," he suggested. "I'm not sure I could find my way back on my own." As if he'd ever been permitted to wander about unattended. Joslire would surely see right through his transparent stratagem to the sudden case of nerves that underlaid it.

Joslire merely bowed once more, in silence. Declining—Andrej thought to himself, a trifle resentfully—to give him an opportunity to delay his exercise by responding, or pretending to respond, to Joslire's answer. There were times when he felt that he might as well be in his father's House, where at least he had some nominal clout with the servants. Joslire could be impossible.

Frustrated, Andrej pushed aside the door between the changing area and the exercise floor, and stepped through.

A much larger room than he was accustomed to, yes; large, and very dimly lit, actually. The equivalent of a docking slip, perhaps, within the maintenance atmosphere? And waiting for him—not one but four Security. Five Security, one standing a little apart from the rest—the senior man, apparently, calling the detachment to make formal notice of his arrival. "Attention to the officer!"

The senior man—was a woman.

Andrej approached her detachment, anxious to understand what this exercise might entail. Two on one, three on one, well, there was an abstract sense of a sort to that—he supposed. But five on one?

He didn't have a chance.

"Thank you, Section Leader. How are we to conduct ourselves, for this practice?"

The closer he got to the five of them the more uncomfortable he felt. Tall, yes, no problem. None of them wore green-sleeves, so they were all Station Security; that was unusual. Bodies lithe with muscle, he expected that. But there was going to be a problem, quite apart from the senior man's unexpected gender. Because not only was the senior man a woman, but so was the first of her detachment, and the second of her detachment, and the third of her detachment, and not to put too fine a point to it—they were all women, and all of them taller than he was.

Not only that.

As far as he could tell—Andrej realized, with a deepening horror that bode well to shade too quickly into utter panic to be braked—they all had dark hair. Dark hair, dark eyes, one of them with the glossy purple-black skin of a Sangreal lineage, and, oh, but he had a bad feeling about this.

"With the officer's indulgence. A series of warm-up drills, and then we would like to demonstrate the primary sequence of the basic combination throws."

It sounded innocent enough, surely. "Very well, shall we begin?"

It could be just a coincidence.

There was certainly no reason to let his masculine imagination run away with him, whether or not he was suddenly burdened with a rude fish cresting in his belly, where his self-respect ought to be.

If only he had not been so cheerfully flippant with Joslire just this morning . . .

A man could not fault so subtly planned an assault, no, not really, not even when a man was at such a disadvantage, not even when the passive role was so unfamiliar. Andrej had to concede the superior planning and execution of the exercise ungrudgingly. Combat drill continued until he had been thoroughly warmed, and no, he wasn't nearly good enough to actually compete with his opponents, but he fancied that his performance was at least good enough to spare Joslire any unnecessary mortification on his behalf. Surely he proved that he had not been a dull Student. He could almost imagine that within a year he would be able to compete on equal terms with one of the women; competition with two at once was clearly several years out of his range in his estimation, and when they teamed three on one there was nothing for him to do but to relax and submit to instruction, and hope that he was not too distracted by the unusual environment to retain at least some part of what he had been sent in there to learn.

But then the senior of his instructors called for twilight drill; Andrej had never heard of that. The lights fell to half their original dimness or more, dim as that had been. Someone switched on a ventilator, very old, very loud, and there was no hearing oneself think in such a racket—no hope to hear what the five of them might be saying to each other, at a little distance.

Twilight drill commenced with a new series of one-on-one encounters, standard positions, unusual recoveries. The first approached head-on. He could not quite find the right balance to flip her, because she seemed to have shifted her weight to her offside foot. No matter; a useful hint of what to practice next. But it did mean that he was thrown rather than she—and thrown quite emphatically, with his assailant following up with a sliding tackle of sorts, as if to ensure that, by landing on top of him, he'd stay thrown. Most unusual, Joslire had not taught him that trick yet. But the uniforms were thin and damp with sweat, and Andrej's body was immediately convinced that it knew the trick precisely, and was eager to play the game. She pushed herself up and away from him slowly, with a caressing gesture of her hand across his face and down his throat; then she was gone, and he had to concentrate on the next step.

The second approached him with a sidekick, very sharp, very precise, but he was a match for that one, and brought her down. Joslire had taught him to regain the advantage, if brought down in such an attack, by wrapping his leg around behind his opponent's knees, and trying to get a good scissor hold to compensate for having been thrown. So it made good sense to him that, once they were both down, she would throw her leg over him, around his thighs; but the manner in which it was done, and her evident intent to press close to him rather than gain the advantage of distance, were neither of them calculated to keep a man's mind on his business. Certainly nothing Joslire had ever warned him against.

By the time the third had thrown him onto his belly and pressed herself along the length of his back to give the back of his neck a sharp wet nip in parting, the piscine portion of his masculine nature was so strongly minded to seek the ocean seas of its native origin and proper place that Andrej's head was swimming. There were too many of them, and no dealing with it either, especially not when they teamed up against him so mercilessly. Professional Security, and women all the same, their bodies hard and supple with constant combat practice—except where they were soft; respectful of his rank, respectful of his modesty—except that they seemed clearly determined to ignore his rank and disregard his modesty for unknown purposes of their own . . .

He struggled virtuously with himself for long eighths, certain that he had misunderstood. Somehow. No matter what his fish might think.

But the women weren't having any of it.

Instead the women seemed intent on having him, and he could either struggle helplessly against them—and be efficiently immobilized, for his pains—or he could mind his manners and do as he was bidden. In a manner of speaking.

In the end Andrej surrendered to the unarguable logic of superior force, and gave himself over meekly to their calm deliberate hands. Their judicious, considered kisses. Their polite but unequivocal, if unspoken, demands, precise in conception and pleasant in execution. Their charitable forbearance of his fish's impertinence, which puffed itself up proudly to be so stroked and petted; and their generous permission to let his fish dive deep where it was certain it belonged, granting the greedy thing such new and delightful seas in which to disport itself that, in the end, it wilted of an excess of exercise and had to be returned with gentle hands to where fish were generally to be found.

He was surfeited with the sweet taste of the mouths of women, drunk with the explorations of his fish, utterly exhausted in the best of ways.

When they were done with him, they settled him on the floor and went away, and he could only hope that they had had good reward for the trouble they had taken with him; because for himself, he was unstrung, undone, scarce capable of moving.

He lay on his back in the dim, hushing roar of the ventilators, without thinking, without worry, until Joslire came to help him into the sauna.

There were two basic approaches to the process of Inquiry and Confirmation, Tutor Chonis knew. One followed necessarily from the other: one either depersonalized the prisoner in order to successfully ignore the common bond of vulnerability to pain; or one personalized the contest, turning it into an individual issue in which one specific person or prisoner was talking back to one specific individual Inquisitor. In this way, since the Inquisitor could take the predictable curses of the prisoner as personally directed, the Inquisitor could proceed with a comforting feeling of righteous indignation at being personally attacked for doing what did—after all—have to be done. In this way, Inquiry and Confirmation caused much less personal conflict.

Tutor Chonis hadn't yet decided which way Koscuisko would ultimately decide to go. In his practical exercises to date, Koscuisko had neither denied the validity of the prisoner's pain—with St. Clare, for instance—or let himself get personally exercised over St. Clare's insolence, no matter how intrigued he clearly was by the pain he inflicted. Perhaps the mocking humor Koscuisko displayed on the practice floor was Koscuisko's own personal distancing mechanism. Time would tell.

Sixth Level of the Question, Inquiry and Confirmation. Tutor

Chonis sat in his place to watch Koscuisko perform. His Student looked remarkably rested, all things considered; fresh and rather full of himself—as well he might be, after what had happened to him last night. Chonis knew very well why Curran had chosen the exercise area he had, and twilight drill at that. Curran was displaying an unusual degree of sensitivity on Koscuisko's behalf, as witnessed by his care in ensuring that neither sound nor sight would uncover his Student's nakedness.

Chonis wondered if he was going to have a problem with Curran.

"Step through."

It had amused Chonis to select the bond-involuntaries who had functioned as prisoner-surrogates during Koscuisko's first three Levels to form most of the team. Koscuisko stood with his back to the prisoner's gate, drinking his rhyti; already wearing those gloves he'd picked up, Chonis noted. Koscuisko was staring at the various instruments on the table with his head cocked a little to one side, as if he were making up his mind about something.

Where to start. Which to choose. Whether he could make a break for the door, perhaps. Koscuisko continued to display profound ambivalence to the concept and practice of Inquiry which seemed only to have gotten worse once Koscuisko discovered that he liked it.

"I am Andrej Koscuisko, to whom you must answer by the Bench instruction. State your name, and the crime for which you have been arrested."

Security had fallen back to the wall at Koscuisko's gesture. The prisoner stood alone in the middle of the room, defiant and apprehensive—not as if it mattered whether the prisoner were frightened or not. The course of a Sixth Level was fairly unforgiving; and whether it would take longer or less time to execute the Protocols was entirely up to Koscuisko.

"Yes?"

There was an unmistakable note of demand, of threat, sharpening Koscuisko's voice; and from Chonis's vantage point he could see Koscuisko finally make his selection. The driver. A long, thin coiled whip, black and shiny with oil, with the snapper-end tied off into an innocuous-looking butterfly knot that could tear flesh clear through to the bone, if well handled. An interesting choice.

It took practice to handle the driver, and not do oneself an injury.

Koscuisko had worked St. Clare with the handshake: less lethal a whip, less dangerous a weapon, less of a challenge.

The prisoner had still not answered, and Koscuisko seemed to grimace to himself. His voice was clear and neutral, though, showing no trace of the tension Tutor Chonis was certain that Koscuisko must be suffering.

"Gentlemen, be so good as to escort my client to the wall." Handing the driver off to the Bigelblu—Cay Federsmengdhyu, if Tutor Chonis had all the syllables right in memory—Koscuisko picked up a loosely gathered bunch of restraints in its stead.

Oh, really? Chonis thought, intrigued. *Trefold shackles?* This was interesting. A little unusual. Students were generally anxious to get right into the middle of the Protocols, get things over with. Koscuisko was making a slow start of it, but it didn't seem to be discomfort or reluctance so much as deliberation on distinct and possibly unrelated subjects.

Trefold shackles were useful, but they were considered to fall into the category of mere restraint. Koscuisko surely knew that he was expected to use far sterner measures before his exercise could be considered to be complete. Koscuisko used the restraints to bind his prisoner—a thin Chigan of middling age, barefoot, skinny—in a kneeling position facing the wall, with the loop that passed around the Chigan's throat caught tightly around ankle and wrist bonds to ensure that any deviation from correct posture would result in an unpleasantly cumulative constriction of the airway. Straightening up, now, with what might almost have been a steadying gesture of some sort on the prisoner's shoulder, Koscuisko beckoned to the Bigelblu. Chonis began to have an idea of where Koscuisko was headed with this.

"You have been referred to me on Charges to be Confirmed at the Sixth Level of Inquiry. It is yours to decline to speak. I, on the other hand, am expected to convince you to do so. Gentlemen, I require instruction, can one of you assist me in this practice?"

He was such a polite little bastard; Chonis couldn't help but smile at him. Polite, submissive, tamed—and obvious. Practicing for the discipline that he would be required to administer to St. Clare. The driver, when properly handled to avoid contact between the snapper-end and living flesh, was the fastest—most practical, even most conservative—way in which to administer two-and-twenty, three-and-thirty, four-and-forty of any of the whips from which Koscuisko would be required to chose. Had Koscuisko had words with Joslire Curran on the subject?

Chonis made a decision, keying his override. "Please stand by, the Inquiry. Assistance to be forthcoming."

Actually it was probably Vanot who was the best for the instruction Koscuisko was requesting. He could have Vanot on site within a matter of moments. "Instruction to be provided at Student Koscuisko's request. You may proceed with your Inquiry as you like."

The fact that Koscuisko might already have met the formidable Vanot would surely not interfere with his training. For one thing, Koscuisko had discipline. And for another, Curran had seen to it that the lights had been so low, the hush-noise level so high, that Chonis had been unable to identify more than one of Koscuisko's sparring partners from the night before.

Of course, he hadn't needed to recognize more than the one of them.

If the Station Provost Marshall chose to engage Student Inquisitors for her recreation, it was certainly not Tutor Chonis's place to question her about it.

Andrej wasn't quite sure whether Tutor Chonis's interruption was welcome, because it meant another few moments before he had to begin in earnest; or unwelcome, because it meant another few moments before he could begin—and he could not complete the exercise until he had begun it.

He took advantage of the temporary suspension of the exercise to recheck the trefold shackles, easing the ligature at the prisoner's throat, loosening the cord that bound the man's ankles together by as much slack as reasonably possible. He was going to practice how to use the driver; he needed a still target.

But he did not like to touch the man. The prisoner was thin and dirty and unprepossessing, and the Administration expected Andrej to do unspeakable things to that captive body. He had to separate himself from his sense of the fragility of bone and blood. If he could only manage to ignore that this Chigan felt and suffered, perhaps the thing would not come upon him again this time.

The sound of the entry-tone at secured access was a welcome distraction from his apprehensive brooding. Andrej straightened and stood away from the wall, eyeing the entrance expectantly. A Security expert sent by Tutor Chonis to provide instruction—they'd had some basic orientation, true, but it had been clear to Andrej from the moment he'd struck St. Clare the first time that there was considerably more to the successful exercise of a whip than seemed obvious.

The Security troop was Station Security, but seemed quite comfortable in theater for all that; perhaps she had been inured to her environment. "Pobbin Vanot reports at Tutor Chonis's direction," she announced to the world at large, standing in the middle of the theater. "Student Koscuisko desires coaching in the use of a . . . let me see . . . the driver, sir?"

Andrej frowned.

Wasn't there something familiar about the woman?

Hadn't he met her recently?

Of course not. That was absurd. How could he have met her, when the only contact with Station Security he'd had all Term had been that one unsanctioned formation in Infirmary?

And last night.

It was the voice of his fish in his mind, and Andrej blushed despite himself to hear it.

Of course.

He had met her last night, she was tall and dark and . . . it was better to concentrate on the problem at hand, no matter how quick his fish might be to jump to conclusions. Or jump to anything at all that reminded it of the ocean.

Andrej bowed formally to cover his confusion. "Even so, Miss Vanot. It would be a privilege to receive instruction." It had been a privilege to have received instruction from the Security team of last night's drill. Andrej put the thought away from him firmly. Fish had no sense of time or place or propriety. Fish thought only of oceans. "I have before the handshake exploited, but clumsily. This weapon seems to me much more intriguing."

The Chigan was face to the wall, and the driver had a good length to it. Separation. Andrej had good hopes that he could keep himself separate from the beast in his belly, which hungered so for agony. If only he could hold himself apart.

"Very good, sir. If the officer will permit." She took the driver from his outstretched hand and posted herself well back from the wall. *Interesting,* Andrej thought. She didn't turn to the opposite wall from the prisoner but contented herself with standing well to one side. "The officer will please attend to these basic points. The recommended beginner's stance is like so, to minimize the chances of catching the snapper at one's own back if one should fail to pull the length clear. Please note the fundamental movement, a wide arc is recommended for appropriate clearance—"

The snapper-end of the driver struck the wall of the theater with a report like that of an old-fashioned percussion-cap pistol, five spans to the right of the prisoner's head.

The Chigan's body jerked involuntarily in a spasm of startled fear. He lost his balance and fell to his side on the floor, struggling against the shackles that bound and choked him. For a moment Andrej dreaded a loss of balance on his own part; then he shut his ears to the sound of the Chigan's choked cries, and gestured Security forward. "Set this one up again, gentlemen, if you please. And see that there is a good allowance for slack around the throat." Fear could wear on a man. Perhaps it would help wear the Chigan down. He had to concentrate on learning how to manage the whip, and keep the beast at bay.

"Thank you, gentlemen, very good. Miss Vanot, if you would?" She'd moved almost too quickly, a graceful gesture swinging the long lash in a controlled arc against her target. She did it again, and the sound of the impact was like the sudden crack of a log on the fire or a flat rod striking a metal table, sharp and loud and angry. From where he stood, it almost seemed to Andrej that she had put a dimple in the wall. What would such a thing do against living flesh?

What would it not do?

The Chigan had held to his place this time, still and stiff and horribly tense where he knelt. For a moment Andrej had a thought about a blindfold. Would that not make the surprise the more unpleasant, the shock more sudden and dreadful?

He knew what was happening within him, and he could hardly bear it. But he would not let himself be beguiled by it. The Chigan was dead meat, and he had to perform a Sixth Level exercise.

He did not have to enjoy it.

"Let me try this." Yes, that was right, he was not torturing a sentient being, he was only learning an odd and not very useful physical skill. He had to concentrate on that. He was learning how to practice with the driver.

He had read up on all the whips at his disposal, handshake and rake, lictor and driver, fanneram and peony; and the driver was the best one to use for discipline of the sort that the Fleet would require of him. He was decided on that. He had watched the tapes.

If he could learn to lay the lash out horizontally, and let the snapper crack in empty air, the whip would pull a narrow bloody line across a prisoner's back. More of a scrape than an actual cut, the skin would be deeply abraded but not quite torn; and although it quite obviously hurt in many ways, it could be said to do less damage.

"From the right, Miss Vanot? Certainly I will remember to keep my elbow well in, yes. Let me see."

The snapper-end of the driver hit the far wall with a dull thud, but at least he'd gotten it there. Andrej gathered the driver up into a loose coil on the floor by his foot and tried again. Straighten the lash. Swing it. A pathetic excuse for an impact, he had to try again. Better. Again. Better yet.

Again.

It was more work than he had imagined.

But after four or five more tries, he heard the same sound when the snapper-end hit the wall as a glass candle-dish made when it was allowed to burn too long, and cracked at the base of its own heat.

"The officer approximates the basic form," Vanot noted approvingly. "Several hours of practice are recommended before progressing to more detailed control techniques. May I suggest additional training to be scheduled at the officer's convenience?"

She meant for him to practice.

Oh.

On the Chigan, for example.

Well, of course, that was his excuse, wasn't it? One had to have a victim upon whom to practice, if one wished to learn how to manage a whip.

The Chigan was his, all his; and just to think of what he had seen the snapper-end do to living flesh on tape—

Disgusted him.

Sickened him to his stomach.

Oh, no, it was not so. He could take no comfort in lying to himself—it was not disgust, it was not abhorrence, that moved within him . . .

"Thank you, Miss Vanot." He caught the coils of the driver into his hand, and bowed to his teacher. A teacher, whether subordinate Security or not, was worthy of respect; and this one was un-Bonded and would not feel discomfort at the gesture—he hoped. "I hope to prove a credit to your instruction. Till next time, then."

She returned his salute with grace and dignity. "At the officer's will and good pleasure."

He was down to it, then.

He had procrastinated; he had to begin.

"Loosen for me those shackles, gentlemen." Vanot left the theater; he was alone with his prisoner, and these Security whose sole purpose was to help him commit atrocities upon the prisoner's body. And heart, and mind, and will. "There is no profit in permitting him to strangle himself, and we have work to do."

The trefold shackles had been loosened, but the prisoner was still bound, hand and foot.

Andrej moistened his lips with the tip of his tongue in nervous anticipation, hating the eagerness that grew within him by leaps and bounds, unable to disguise his eagerness to himself even so.

He swung the whip.

It made horrific impact against the flesh of the bound man's back, splattering blood all around as it tore soft tissue and muscle alike. *Through to the bone,* Andrej thought with savage self-satisfaction, the sound of the strike—and the Chigan's cries—cutting clear through all his cherished inhibitions, clear to the core of his being.

Yes.

Through to the bone.

It was not so hard to strike the Chigan, not when he made such sounds. Andrej struck again and reveled in the music that the whip and his prisoner made for him.

It didn't matter so much after all that he was not closer to the Chigan, that he kept his distance, that he struck the prisoner with a whip and not his hand.

All that mattered was that the Chigan was his.

He could do anything he liked. Anything. Worse than anything. He could do everything he liked, and be commended for it.

He could smell blood and fear, and he was drunk with it, all his residual reservations swamped and drowned beneath the huge black tide of his obscene pleasure in what he was to do.

For now—he would practice with the driver.

There would be enough time for questions later.

If he laid the corded lash alone across the Chigan's shoulders, it would hurt the man—but not unbearably, and by no means as intriguingly as when he buried the snapper-end in living flesh . . .

The snapper-end, then.

Oh, it was fine.

Hours passed.

Andrej Koscuisko sat exhausted on the floor beside his prisoner, leaning up against the wall. Security had brought him fresh rhyti; he drank it with sated satisfaction and stroked the trembling body at his side lazily, unable to resist the temptation to pinch torn flesh between his fingers or put a little pressure on splintered bone.

"Let's hear it, then. Since you've decided that you want to talk." He had been fair to the man—in a manner of speaking. He had not hurt his prisoner to prevent him from talking, and thus ending his sport too soon. It had simply worked out well for him that the Chigan had not decided to confess until after long beguiling hours of torment. "Your name. State your name. And the crime for which you have been arrested."

It was difficult for the prisoner to speak, hoarse with screaming. Andrej fed him some rhyti to help him along. The Chigan coughed and swallowed, unable to press his bitten lips together firmly enough to keep spittle and blood and rhyti from dribbling to the floor.

"Eamish. Lintoe. Your Excellency. Please."

So far so good. If Andrej remembered the prisoner's brief, the Chigan's name was, in fact, Earnish Lintoe. Andrej gave him some more rhyti as a reward. "The crime for which you have been arrested. Yes? What?"

Lintoe closed his eyes in a sudden spasm of pain, but whether it was the memory of his arrest or the particularly painful disjoint of his elbow, Andrej wasn't sure. It didn't matter, not really. "Ah. They said, theft. Bench property. S-sir."

It was supposed to be "your Excellency," but Andrej was too well pleased with the world and himself for being a part of it to take offense. "What did you steal, then?"

"Please, no, a transport, they said a transport, it wasn't me, I don't know anything . . . about it . . ."

Something about the proximity of Andrej's hand to the gaping wound the snapper-end of the driver had torn in his shoulder seemed to make the man nervous. "You have stolen a transport?" Andrej prompted helpfully. "What manner of transport?"

"A . . . grain transport." Andrej put his hand to the floor to settle himself against the wall, and the Chigan seemed to take it as encouragement of some sort. "It was a grain transport. From Combine stores."

Andrej waited.

"Stolen in Mercatsar, they found it empty. Displacement camp. And we had food."

Which was clearly not what the local authorities had expected to be the case in a displacement camp for Chigan relocation parties. It made sense to Andrej.

"What happened then?" He didn't need to torment Lintoe. Lintoe was talking. It wasn't as though he hadn't had sufficient with which to indulge himself, these long hours gone past.

"Wanted to know why. Who." Why they had food, and who had brought it. Certainly. They seemed like reasonable questions to ask, to Andrej.

"Tell me."

Lintoe shook his head from side to side weakly in denial. "Don't know. Can't say. Didn't have anything . . . to do with . . ."

It was a little difficult to hear the Chigan where he lay beside Andrej on the floor. Andrej hooked one hand beneath Lintoe's arm to raise the man's body a bit, resting the Chigan's face across his knee. Where he could look at Lintoe. Where he could admire Lintoe's pain.

"Come, now. There must have been a reason they chose you. Why do you imagine that you are under arrest, if you didn't have a hand in it?"

It seemed to take a moment for Lintoe to catch his breath after being moved. Andrej could wait. Lintoe would not disappoint him, he was sure.

"Well . . . it seems . . . they said . . . genetic marker."

In the grain, perhaps. The Combine only sold certain classes of grain to Jurisdiction; the true grain, the holy grain, remained restricted to the Holy Mother's use, for the nourishment of her children. And her children's servants, of course: the Karshatkef, Flosayir, Sarvaw, Arakcheek, Dohan, even Kosai Dolgorukij, if one was being exclusionary about things—as Azanry Dolgorukij usually were.

"So they knew the grain you were in possession of had in fact come from a stolen transport. And your part in this was?"

No answer. It seemed clear to Andrej that his prisoner was worried about how things were going, even past his own pain. Worried about how convincingly he could plead his innocence. Displacement camps had been destroyed in retaliation for petty thievery before; or dispersed, which amounted to very much the same thing.

Andrej decided to try a modified scan. "Where is your family now?"

The Chigan groaned. "In custody. Your Excellency. Pending my trial, but . . . they are innocent . . ."

The pain in the Chigan's voice was no less persuasive for the fact that it was clearly emotional in nature. Andrej joggled Lintoe's elbow, though, just a little bit, just to have an index of physical pain against which to measure this other sort. "That isn't what I was told. I heard there was Free Government involved." He wasn't quite sure about the exact degree to which Lintoe's physical pain matched the emotional pain involved with the issue of his family; perhaps a retest was in order. Hmm. Yes. Very much more closely matched, that time.

"They said it was fair salvage, Excellency—"

"Who said?"

"There were. Two men. Infiltrated the camp. Brought it all on us . . . damn them . . . children have to eat . . ."

Clear enough. And still though Lintoe could be said to have confessed there was a puzzle here. People had no business infiltrating displacement camps—unless it was to foment insurrection.

"You were going to tell me who it was that told you the grain transport was fair salvage." Fair salvage meant up for grabs. But the

Bench didn't care; there were few allowances made for honest mistakes, under Jurisdiction.

"Family." It was a sob of anguish from the bottom of the Chigan's heart. "We sheltered them, but how could they have brought this on their own blood?"

Chigan familial relationships were nothing to Andrej. Still, if the man had been duped into breaking the law, he had suffered for the mistake he'd made in putting his trust in a Free Government agent. Family or no family.

"You aren't telling me what I want to know," he warned, taking the Chigan's chin into his hand to raise the man's head and make eye contact. He wanted to make sure the Chigan knew this was important. "Name for me the names. If they lied to you they must be punished."

"But how could young Canaby do such a thing?"

From the tone of the Chigan's voice he was beyond understanding just what he was saying. Or what it would mean to "young Canaby."

"His own kin. To lie to us. Endanger the children. You're no kin of mine, Alko. Alko isn't even a Chigan name. I don't care what he says about Free Government, Canaby. He's up to no good. Are you sure it's fair salvage? . . ."

Enough was enough.

Andrej beckoned for Security to help him to his feet.

"The prisoner has confessed to the misappropriation of grain transport from Combine stores. He states that the crime was committed under persuasion that the stolen vessel was fair salvage." So much was only fair, and he had been so unfair to Lintoe these hours gone past. "Further investigation may be focused on prisoner's relative Canaby, with specific reference to a companion named Alko, described in terms that indicate potential Free Government involvement. The Administration may wish to consider the prisoner absolved of intent to commit the crime for which he has been arrested in light of this evidence, Confirmed at the Sixth Level. The Record is complete."

And he was exhausted.

Joslire would come to take him to quarters.

He thought that he was going to want a drink.

CHAPTER ELEVEN

"Take a moment if needed. The officer has time. There's no hurry,"
Joslire soothed, holding Koscuisko by the shoulders from behind. The
corridor was empty, naturally. Student Koscuisko pushed himself away
from the wall with a species of irritation or desperation and stumbled
on.

"Are we close yet, Joslire? Before all Saints I do not wish to disgrace
myself—"

"Quite close, as the officer please. Only three turnings." Koscuisko
had far from disgraced himself in his exercise; Koscuisko had outdone
himself, rather. Joslire knew that Tutor Chonis had not expected any
real information from the Chigan, let alone the by-name identification
of the Free Government agent that the Bench suspected was involved.
That wasn't what worried Koscuisko now, though.

"This turning, as it please the officer. The door is . . ."

Koscuisko was ahead of him, having recognized where he was now.
More or less. It was hard to get one's bearings. The corridors were
deliberately designed to be as featureless and anonymous as possible.
Koscuisko hurried on ahead, and luckily enough it was actually
Koscuisko's quarters and not the stores room next door. Straight
through to the washroom.

For Student Koscuisko's sake Joslire hoped he made it to the basin
before he vomited, since that was what Koscuisko was doing now. It
didn't make much difference to Joslire; Koscuisko hadn't eaten all

day—too absorbed in the exercise to break for his mid-meal—so it wasn't as though there would be much to clean up either way. Koscuisko would be humiliated if he'd missed, though.

Koscuisko would wish to be left alone in his suffering. Joslire ordered up the officer's meal, and a good quantity of wodac as well. Starch-flats and curdles, sweethins—sweethins didn't seem to go with wodac in Joslire's mind, but Student Koscuisko had a sweet tooth. Koscuisko was going to be drinking. Joslire was still experimenting with things he could get Koscuisko to eat while he was drinking.

Koscuisko was in the wet-shower longer than perhaps he needed to be. The therapeutic effect of hot running water seemed to work some of its species-wide magic; Koscuisko looked moderately refreshed when he sat down to his third-meal. Joslire was glad, in some obscure sense.

Students were expected to suffer in reaction to what they did. As assigned Security, Joslire had always felt it only right and proper that Students suffer for what they did, in howsoever limited a fashion. Koscuisko was different. When Koscuisko suffered Joslire hurt.

"The officer is respectfully encouraged to try some of his meal prior to availing himself of his wodac."

Naturally Joslire had suffered for Students' pain before—Students who, when they were in pain, struck out. Koscuisko had yet to strike out at him. Koscuisko seemed genuinely intent on doing his best not to strike out at Joslire as a near and convenient target. That only made it worse.

"Thank you, Joslire, as you like. You have brought arpac-fowl, I see. Well done, I do like arpac-fowl." Koscuisko's voice threatened to wobble into hysteria and he shut up, reaching for a thigh portion with a trembling hand. Well, anything was better than meld-loaf, as far as Joslire was concerned. But Koscuisko's dutiful address to his meal had nothing to do with any liking Koscuisko had for the food, and everything to do with Koscuisko's habitual response to Joslire as a subordinate peer of some sort. Where Koscuisko came from, authority was absolute and focused in the person of the Autocrat; and Koscuisko was one—not the Autocrat, of course, but heir to a great House and master of all within. Well-socialized young autocrats were apparently expected to cherish a keen sense of the dignity of the people who washed their linen and provided their meals.

Koscuisko treated him as though he were a man—a full-grown and mature adult; in some ways Koscuisko's equal, and his ungrudgingly acknowledged superior in others, even while he respected the distance that the Bench had set between them. A feeling creature like himself, with a sense of honor and a right to self-respect, who only incidentally happened to be a bond-involuntary.

And Joslire felt helpless against the effect Koscuisko's respect had on him.

Bite by bite, portioning his food with careful precise gestures of the tableware in his trembling hands, Koscuisko forced himself to eat his third-meal dutifully. Joslire stood and watched and suffered for Koscuisko's anguish.

Then Koscuisko let the tableware drop to the tray, and put his head between his hands and wept.

There was nothing Joslire could do, not and respect Koscuisko's agony. He could offer no embrace. He could extend no comfort. They both knew it was only right and proper that a man suffer for having done such things to a helpless prisoner, or to any sentient being constrained and helpless.

Joslire cleared away the remnants of Koscuisko's meal, too dispirited to finish off the untouched portion of the arpac-fowl for himself. He liked arpac-fowl, too.

But Koscuisko's grief was terrible.

How could he pity Koscuisko for his grief, when he had seen Koscuisko work the Chigan?

Well, he had an appointment to see Tutor Chonis during first-shift, since Koscuisko was to be occupied in lab all day.

Maybe then he would find out the answer.

"Koscuisko's settled into workspace, then, Curran?"

Joslire Curran stood at strict attention-wait in front of Tutor Chonis's desk, reporting promptly for the meeting he'd requested. Tutor Chonis coded the secure for the office door.

"Yes, as it please the Tutor. With Sanli More assigned to see to Student Koscuisko's needs as they arise. Thank you for seeing me, sir."

It was in Chonis's best interest to see Joslire Curran, since Curran had requested command-time. Off hand, Chonis couldn't remember Curran ever doing that before. Not even with Student Pefisct. "The least I can do, and your natural right, Curran." Of course bond-involuntaries didn't really have any rights under Jurisdiction. That was one reason why the Administration—and Security generally, even in Fleet—tried to treat them carefully. To make up. "Stand down, Curran. Administrative orders in effect. What's on your mind?"

Slowly Curran's tense body relaxed into the much less formal Administrative command-wait. Taking a deep breath, Curran sighed. "Need to ask a question, sir. Respectfully hope the Tutor won't be offended, feel compelled to emphasize importance of the truth. Sir."

Even under administrative orders, Curran avoided the personal pronoun, though it was there by implication. Curran had tremendous discipline. The business with Student Pefisct had proved that clearly enough. But right now Curran looked visibly worn. "What's the question?" Tutor Chonis prompted.

If he slid the top-tray out of his desk surface, he could see the Safe. It was the only Safe on Station, and if a Tutor wanted it he had to explain to the Administrator why. Tutor Chonis had told Administrator Clellelan that Joslire Curran was coming to see him, and that Chonis thought Curran might be in distress. Clellelan had loaned him the Safe. It was as significant a mark of the respect they had for Joslire Curran as they could make.

"Sir. After last Term. Some time in Infirmary, Tutor Chonis. Peculiar emotional response to Student Koscuisko, sir. And."

The tension was all back, even if the stance was still informal. Curran chose his words with evident deliberation.

"And I. Need to know. Was my governor adjusted. Experiment on Student-Security bonding, or something. Sir."

Oh, for the aching void of limitless Space.

Tutor Chonis rose to his feet, the Safe concealed in his closed fist. "Joslire Curran." He didn't quite know what to say. "No. There was no adjustment to your governor. No such experiment is conceived or contemplated." As if the Administration wouldn't give it a go, if there were governors sophisticated enough to do the trick available. "Sit down, Mister Curran, I've got something to say to you."

It was an order; Curran was required to comply. The man was willing to listen. The governor, however, was confused, and that meant conflict. Tutor Chonis moved around behind Curran and slipped the Safe over his head, to dangle on its chain around Curran's neck.

Curran stiffened.

Safes transmitted a carefully encrypted master signal to the artificial intelligence at the heart of the governor, setting up interference within the governor itself and lulling the thing into a state of suspended function for as long as the safe was sufficiently close to the governor in question. Curran had been on Safe once, and only once, before—all volunteers for the Intermediate Level prisoner-surrogate exercise were given the opportunity to make their final decision on Safe, so that their decision could be made independent of their conditioning. As far as that went.

Chonis put his hands to Curran's shoulders to steady him. "You know how to run the call-ups, Curran. Check it out for yourself, if you need to. Clellelan said you were to have full shift on Safe. Because we are concerned about your welfare."

This was Curran's opportunity to tell Tutor Chonis exactly what he thought about the Administration and its concern for his welfare. The man was on Safe. The governor was in suspension. Still Curran kept shut, and Chonis grinned in pained recognition of Curran's core self-discipline. "You can stay here and I can leave. You can go to gather room. You can go there alone or we can call up some people for you. Take a moment, Joslire. Then tell me what you want to do."

Curran stood up from the table slowly, his back still to the Tutor. "I'm to be allowed the Safe for eight eights, sir?"

Full shift, yes. "That's right."

"Student Koscuisko has just gone to lab. Let me postpone it. Let me go on Safe at third-shift."

Whatever for?

Did Curran want to say something to Koscuisko?

Did Curran want to do something to Koscuisko?

"Curran, I don't know what you have in mind—" Chonis started to say. Curran interrupted. Chonis was shocked into silence; then he remembered. Curran was on Safe. Yes.

"I swear by holy steel that I mean neither thought nor word nor deed to the discomfort of Student Andrej Koscuisko. But if I could have the Safe and third-shift. And never imagine I don't appreciate that you've brought it for me now, Tutor Chonis."

Joslire Curran was an Emandisan fighting man, and Emandisan knifemen recognized no rank nor respect except for their own sworn associations. By that token, and the tone of Curran's voice, Tutor Chonis knew that Curran was utterly sincere about what he'd said. It was no small thing to have a grant of gratitude from an Emandisan.

"Well. If that's what you want." Curran had sworn by holy steel, and if there was anything more sacred to an Emandisan knifeman than his five-knives, nobody under Jurisdiction knew about it. The Administrator had granted eight hours; Chonis didn't think Clellelan had said when. "I'll take the Safe back for now. It's up to you to decide when to call for it. No later than sleep-shift, though, it's got to be returned before tomorrow."

Which of course implied that sleep-shift was the latest that Curran could call for the Safe and still enjoy the eight full hours that Clellelan had granted. Tutor Chonis couldn't imagine that Curran would want the Safe just to go to sleep a free man for once.

"Thank you, Tutor Chonis."

Joslire Curran bent his head and lifted the Safe off and away, slowly, but with great deliberation. Determination. The man had control.

"If the Tutor please. Mean to avail self of this very significant privilege at third-shift. Wish to express deepest appreciation for the opportunity. Sir."

Curran turned around as he spoke, but there was no reading the emotion on his face. Tutor Chonis held out his hand for the Safe, surprised and impressed that Curran had been able to bear taking it off himself.

"You're clear to go to gather room regardless, Curran. Give yourself some time to think. I'll see you at seven and fifty-six, second." Just before third-shift, that was to say.

Curran had sworn by holy steel that he meant no harm to Andrej Koscuisko.

If he'd misjudged the man—if Joslire Curran turned on Student Koscuisko to assassinate him, for whatever obscure Emandisan reason he might have . . .

With any luck Curran would assassinate Tutor Chonis first.

Because otherwise he was never going to hear the end of it.

Joslire Curran waited outside the open door to Koscuisko's lab space for the moment to arrive. He'd never dreamed of an opportunity like this; he'd never hoped so far as to pray for it. On Safe, and going to exercise drill with Student Koscuisko, after what he had learned about Student Koscuisko during the Term . . .

Time.

Tutor Chonis said the Administrator had given him eight eights on Safe, a full shift. It was an almost unimaginable privilege; freedom from his governor—for howsoever short a period of time. For a full shift he was to be permitted to think and act like a free man.

He would have to wait until the Day for another chance like this, because the token could only be passed between free men. The Administration didn't know. Would they have denied him if they had?

"With respect, Student Koscuisko. The officer is scheduled to participate in exercise at this time."

What he could say. What he could do. Was this how Koscuisko felt in theater, when the awareness of absolute license came upon him? He didn't dare. Koscuisko could be permitted to suspect nothing.

Student Koscuisko came readily enough, tense and harried though he looked. "Lead on, Joslire," Koscuisko suggested, with a visible effort to be cheerful. "And I shall follow. From in front, which is awkward, but you manage well enough. Shall we go?"

He didn't need to wonder anymore if his governor had been adjusted in some hellish experiment to bond Security to their Students of assignment. He was on Safe. And he was determined to mark Student Koscuisko as Student Koscuisko had never been marked before, as Student Koscuisko could never be marked—save by an Emandisan. A free Emandisan knifeman. He could have grinned to himself in gleeful anticipation of what he meant to do; but someone might see.

"To the officer's left at the second turning, if the officer please. There will be a lift nexus down sixteen."

"This way is not familiar," Koscuisko warned. "Is there something I should know about this exercise? Not that I mean to object in either case."

No, Koscuisko hadn't been to this exercise area before. "For this exercise period the practice of throwing knives is to be initiated, and a suitable range is required for such exercise. The officer is to see Miss Vanot on the same range at mid-shift tomorrow, as the officer please. To further his mastery of the driver."

Koscuisko received this information with an enlightened nod of his head, and went silently on for the space of sixteen paces before he spoke again.

"Do you have experience of the driver, Joslire?"

From the carefully neutral note in Koscuisko's voice, Joslire could tell that Koscuisko didn't mean its active use. Passive experience. Had he ever suffered beneath the driver.

"Here is the place. To the officer's left." He had, in fact. And it had not been used with a fraction of the skill or the restraint that Koscuisko had exhibited—and against a prisoner, at that. Joslire's Student had known that he was a bond-involuntary and helpless against him when the Student had decided on two-and-twenty, and there hadn't been any time in which to notify the Tutor and hope for Student Exception to the punishment.

Koscuisko turned through the door to the changing area and Joslire followed, thinking. In light of the deception that Joslire meant to practice upon Koscuisko, a generous gesture on his part was probably called for. Koscuisko had not repeated his question, apparently determined in Koscuisko's fashion not to press the issue where he might be said to possess an unfair advantage. Koscuisko found the open shelf where Joslire had laid out his exercise uniform and started to unfasten his duty-blouse, instead.

"If the officer would care to examine," Joslire said, and took the risk of turning his back, not wanting to meet Koscuisko's eyes. It had been so difficult to do this just a few days ago, but he had been taken by surprise then. He hadn't understood. Out of his duty-blouse, out of his under-blouse, and he would not need to take off his five-knives sheathing now that he had a better understanding of what Koscuisko had wanted. "The discipline was off Record, but the officer can see, if the officer pleases. Two-and-twenty."

In the silence of the changing room, he could sense Koscuisko coming up behind him, putting his hand out to Joslire's shoulder. He kept his hands quiet at his sides to avoid alarming Koscuisko, who was hypersensitive to his discomfort. The careful stroking of Koscuisko's hands upon his shoulders and his back was a guilty pleasure to Joslire, now that he was sure that he had nothing to fear from the officer's sexual appetite. There had not been enough unhurtful contact in his life since he had taken his Bond four years ago. Five years ago. Emandisan were less careful of personal space than the Jurisdiction Standard. He was hungry for a brotherly caress, hungry to starving for it.

"I do not wish to distress thee, Joslire."

He couldn't afford to let himself be distracted. "The officer will find the trace grouped at the top of the back, at the shoulders. The driver in that instance was not so well handled as the Student might wish." He couldn't answer Koscuisko's implied question directly, not and tell him the truth. The truth of it was that now he knew what Koscuisko was about, and the touch of Koscuisko's hand was pleasurable to him in a way that Koscuisko might not choose to find acceptable.

"The snapper did this to thee," Koscuisko murmured. "And yet I find no scar here from the whip itself, Joslire." Testing and trying, Koscuisko traced the impact vectors, seeking the track of the whip. Joslire could feel the muscles in his back give up their tension gratefully under Koscuisko's hand.

"As the officer may wish to note in particular. Other impacts drew blood, but not deeply enough to make a permanent mark." Which was the point, of course. And a natural lead-in to the thing that he had planned. "The officer is respectfully requested to examine the bracing on the back-sheath. With the officer's indulgence, this exercise period will be concentrated on familiarization with throwing knives."

The back-brace held the knife snug along his spine, the rounded pommel-end resting just where the first of his neck joints made a little round lump underneath the skin. If he bent his neck a fraction, she seemed to spring up to meet his fingers, sliding easily out and away into his hand no matter which hand used. With luck, Koscuisko would not know by looking at it that the knife Joslire was wearing was not Joslire's knife, was Standard armory issue. It was a risk; Koscuisko's background had included enough of the related art of thin-blade dueling for Koscuisko to be able to guess the balance, if Joslire were to make the mistake of letting Koscuisko handle the knife he was wearing. On the other hand, thin-blades were a different kind of knife, and the other Dolgorukij Joslire had met had worn only boot-knives if they wore knives at all. He would be sure to demonstrate with the knives Koscuisko would be wearing.

Koscuisko stroked the harness to the metal anchor-ring that centered on Joslire's back. "I've never understood how a person could breathe wearing such a thing. That, or keep it from shifting. How do you manage?"

What an opening. "If the officer will permit, the officer can test it for himself. The liberty has been taken of selecting an appropriate harness for the officer's use." And he'd brought it here during second-shift and secured it here with two of his own knives. The most important of his knives.

He'd had a good deal of anxiety, leaving his knives alone. But he hadn't been able to figure out any other way to do what he had in mind. And the opportunity was too tremendous and fleeting to let pass. "Here, if it please the officer?"

Koscuisko had been half-stripped, bare to the waist. Perfect. Joslire couldn't have arranged it better had he tried. The harness went around the chest, fastening beneath the right arm since Koscuisko favored his left hand. Two straps over the shoulders held the back-sheath in place. It took Joslire a moment to get it adjusted properly; there was more to Koscuisko's chest than he had estimated.

The smoothness of Koscuisko's skin and the innocuous slope of his shoulders gave a deceptive air of lightness and even fragility to Koscuisko's compact muscular frame. He of all people should have remembered that, Joslire admonished himself. After all, he'd had his hands on Koscuisko's naked back every third shift after evening exercise since Koscuisko'd gotten here.

"The harness is made of parbello skin, the side next to the body left unpolished. It should follow the officer's breathing; the unpolished side will catch against the officer's skin so that it does not shift. If the officer would breathe deeply, and say whether it is adequately comfortable?"

The harness would warm to Koscuisko's skin, and cling like a part of him. Joslire watched Koscuisko test the fit, taking up the arm-sheath while he waited. Left arm-sheath, to start. Right arm-sheath would come next, and the boot-sheath, and the decision to be made about where Koscuisko would carry the fifth knife. Later. The first step was by far the most important one.

"It feels a little odd, Joslire, but I suppose one could get used to it. And on my arm, as well? Not five at once, I hope?"

The innocent joke took Joslire's breath away. Joslire forced himself to breathe naturally and easily; if Koscuisko were to guess the trick,

Koscuisko might not let him play it through. He would never have another chance like this, even if he found a Student or an officer more worthy than Koscuisko. He had to brazen it through somehow.

"Two to start, if the officer pleases. With respect, if it were to be five-knives, the officer would require significantly more skill and training than the officer possesses at the present time."

Skill and training that started here and now with the heart of the steel, the soul of his honor, the blade that watched his back. Joslire held the mother-knife apart in his hand, giving his Little Sister to Koscuisko for examination to distract him. "The officer may wish to note that the knife to be carried against the arm is noticeably different from that carried between the shoulders. This knife must slide down into the officer's grasp without slicing the officer's skin open in the process."

Koscuisko handled the knife with respect, even if he didn't know yet what it was. Koscuisko seemed to understand about steel, but didn't Joslire already know that about Koscuisko? Hadn't he jumped at this chance knowing that the hunter in the man would know the hunger in the knife, no matter how widely separated their worlds of origin?

"Oh, this is a lovely thing, Joslire. Where did you find her? She is elegant. I wonder what my father's jeweler would make of this."

"Throwing-knives are Fleet-issue, as it please the officer." Not that one, of course, though an untrained eye might easily confuse the two. If Koscuisko's family jeweler recognized it, he would have a thing to say to Koscuisko that might surprise him. Moving around to Koscuisko's back, Joslire lifted up the mother-knife in both hands. He stood here in the changing room a free man, if only for a few hours, free to elect to recognize a potential knifeman, a respected fellow fighter, a man who would not shame the soul of Emandisan steel.

Joslire invoked his gods and set the knife into the sheath at Koscuisko's back with reverence and deep humility, hoping with all his heart that his petition would be accepted. Koscuisko was not Emandisan. But Koscuisko had the soul of a war-leader. A war-leader had a natural right to Emandisan steel, and the Administration had given Joslire this one chance to free his five-knives from the disgrace of his slavery by making them over, in proper if unspoken form, to a man he deemed fit to wear the soul of an Emandisan.

Koscuisko reached up over his shoulder to find the pommel with his fingertips, first with his left hand, then with his right. "One hardly feels the weight, Joslire. There is no danger of losing the blade, in practice?"

Joslire had to give himself a moment before he answered. She sat so comfortably at Koscuisko's back, springing swiftly into Koscuisko's hand. Surely she had honored his plea and gone willingly to Koscuisko to be his knife.

"The sheathing itself will hold the knife, as the officer will have an opportunity to test for himself. It will only release when the officer reaches for it. If the officer cares to sheath the other knife and finish changing, the exercise can begin."

Perhaps it was true that, as Koscuisko said, the physical weight of the mother-knife was hardly noticeable.

But in fact it was the weight of Joslire's self and Joslire's soul, the honor of his discipline that could not be diminished even by enslavement that Koscuisko carried snug against his skin to watch his back and guard him.

If Fleet and the officer permitted, perhaps Joslire would follow his knives when Koscuisko went to *Scylla*. It didn't matter as much anymore if he lived out his term to see the Day; they had given him what he needed, time on Safe to see his five-knives out of slavery. His five-knives were free.

As empty and as lost as Joslire felt without them it was worth it, more than worth it, more great a gift than he had ever hoped for to see his five-knives escaped into the hands of a man who knew instinctively how to honor them.

He could have given the knives to Koscuisko at any time, that was true enough.

But the knives were proud, and would not have listened to the voice of an enslaved man when he bid them take Koscuisko for their own.

Now he could die without shame.

And maybe some day he would be able to explain to Koscuisko exactly what it was that he'd just done to him.

She had finished her Fifth Level, she had finished her Sixth Level, and she had survived. With the help of Koscuisko's drugs, she'd surmounted the obstacles in her path; and Koscuisko was humbled before her, to be servant to her purpose. She almost could forgive

Koscuisko for his money, for his rank, for the stink of pride and privilege that he carried with him like a sensor-net. Almost.

"Tutor Chonis, I am sorry I am late." Koscuisko's signal came tardy at the door; he was behind the time, and could be sneered at for it if she chose. He was her subordinate, in a sense. She expected punctuality from subordinates. "It is my fault, I hope I have not delayed our meeting long."

Flushed in the face and sharp of eye, Koscuisko had just come from exercise. That was no excuse.

"Well, not too long." Their Tutor would not reprimand Koscuisko; their Tutor didn't need to. Koscuisko had not forgotten that he had been punished to obedience, no matter how bright the serpent-spark in his cold eyes. Mergau knew how to see the fear, regardless of how well it was covered over by the habit of Koscuisko's mind. "Curran is teaching knives, I understand? Quite a unique opportunity. Do you know, this is the first time he has ever offered?"

Pausing as he reached for the beverage jug, Koscuisko seemed a little taken aback. Chonis had set rhyti out today, but Mergau could be charitable. As long as Koscuisko continued to make such wonderful drugs, he could drink all the rhyti he could stomach, and be welcome to it.

"No? I am surprised. It seems so obvious an advantage to have Joslire to instruct. They are beautiful knives, Tutor Chonis. With respect, I think I am in love."

It was understandable that one could cherish a weapon. She had cherished weapons, when she had been in a position to be able to use them. But Koscuisko's enthusiasm seemed a bit intense, for all that Tutor Chonis took it in stride.

"Well, that's all to the good, then. Mind you don't let this new love take you away from the laboratory, however."

Chonis's tone was too mild and affectionate to carry any sting. Mergau was curious about this passion of Koscuisko's—curious almost without malice.

"And may one see these objects, Student Koscuisko? I have had knives myself, once of a time."

Almost she could feel affection for him because of his good service. He answered her without contempt, as if he were pretending not to notice all of the things that were so different between them.

"I am sorry, Joslire has confiscated them from me. So to prevent too soon an amorous surfeit, I imagine. Here is a slug he has provided, so that I may become accustomed to the weight."

He had a long blunt sliver of metal in his hand, and she couldn't see where he had drawn it from. The practice came naturally to him, it seemed; but she was surprised he didn't realize why his slave couldn't possibly permit Koscuisko to go armed between his exercises. The Administration didn't like to take chances with Students, not until they were safely out of the Administration's area of responsibility.

"Very well." Tutor Chonis's raised hand called the conversation back to order. "Let us be done for the moment with Student Koscuisko's love life. The Intermediate Levels are behind us, and it is time to consider those Advanced Levels required in preparation for the Tenth Level graduation test."

She didn't really care about the Advanced Levels, or the Tenth Level test. She didn't need to worry about violating the Protocols at the Advanced Levels. The drugs Koscuisko gave were proof against failure. It didn't matter if she let them die.

"Student Koscuisko, the Administration is very pleased with your work, both in the theater and in the lab. Incidentally, the additional trial for your original speak-sera has been scheduled for four-and-thirty-two this second-shift."

Koscuisko bowed his head. "I haven't forgotten, no, Tutor Chonis. Where is the test to be held, with the Tutor's permission?"

"Curran will show you to your usual exercise theater. Now, Student Noycannir, we must report to Secretary Verlaine. An uplink has been scheduled for tomorrow at four on second. This only gives us a few hours to review the Administrator's comments."

Of course the Advanced Levels would matter when she returned to Chilleau Judiciary. The Advanced Levels would perhaps matter most of all, and she would not have Koscuisko at her disposal then to provide her with the drugs that made it work. A problem, perhaps, because Koscuisko had quite clearly indicated that nothing he had come up with so far could be used safely against all of her Patron's enemies. Even the speak-sera had limitations. The one she had used in her Sixth Level had done perfectly well for the Sascevon prisoner, but Koscuisko said it was quick poison or any Class-One or Class-Six hominid.

"Are we to review now, Tutor Chonis?" She was a little uncomfortable asking; she knew she didn't want to be reviewed in Koscuisko's presence. But the Tutor hadn't set the study schedule for the Advanced Levels. Perhaps there would be time.

"First things first, please, Student Noycannir." And she'd left herself open to rebuke, having asked without being bidden. The Tutor knew how she felt about having her insufficiencies discussed in public. Or even in front of Koscuisko. "First it is required of me to give formal notice that you have both been passed at the Levels to date. Student Koscuisko, there is an issue with your use of the driver; not an immediate one, but one that needs to be brought before you."

And if Chonis would criticize Koscuisko in her presence, she knew he would expose her failings in front of Koscuisko. They both knew she might not have gotten this far without Koscuisko's help. What would she do when she could no longer demand Koscuisko's services?

"Yes, Tutor Chonis?"

From Koscuisko's voice there was a hidden message there that was not to be made available to her. She wondered what it might be. Koscuisko sounded a little fearful, to her ear; had it something to do with the belt, perhaps—the one Chonis had used to humble Koscuisko so completely?

"The Administrator only applauds your desire to learn the driver, and your quite obvious aptitude for it. I have been asked to clarify a minor point."

She didn't like the driver. She'd tried it, but she had been so clumsy that she had hurt herself worse than her prisoner. The driver was an ugly thing. She had known people to die from it.

Chonis was picking his words out carefully, now, as if he were speaking in some kind of code. "As you know, any of the Intermediate Level instruments may be lawfully employed for two-and-twenty as you see fit. You may wish to keep in mind that at a more advanced disciplinary level—oh, four-and-forty, for example—because of the driver's unique characteristics, the disciplinary expectation is for the snapper to be allowed to impact as well as the stock. Otherwise the discipline is not considered sufficiently serious to address the Charges."

Quite a long speech, and the bright, blissful gleam had dropped out of Koscuisko's eyes well before Tutor Chonis had finished. Had he been required to deliver discipline, perhaps? Was he to be required to deliver discipline? What could his slave have done that merited four-and-forty?

"The point is well taken, Tutor Chonis. That I may not cheat the Fleet of discipline, can the Tutor provide some ratio guidance, perhaps?"

Maybe this was the whip that had made Koscuisko so manageable, if Curran had offended. Koscuisko did not seem to be capable of maintaining good order amongst his subordinate Security. She had too often seen him fail to admonish Curran as they left the Tutor's office together.

"If you wish to be conservative in discipline, the driver is an excellent choice. But one is expected to deliver a taste of real punishment—perhaps every eight. A good hit every eight. Note this information for your use, if you will."

Whatever it was, Koscuisko didn't like it. He wasn't fit for Fleet duty, Mergau realized suddenly. Not if he shrank from discipline.

"Thank you, Tutor Chonis, I am grateful for your guidance."

But if he wasn't fit for Fleet duty, where could he be fully utilized? Where could his skill in mixing the drugs for her be effectively exploited—unless he went with her, to support her for the duration of his term of service?

"Yes, Student Koscuisko. I understand." Then Chonis brought her into the conversation once again, with an inclusive gesture. "Enough of that. Do you have any questions about the Intermediate Levels? Student Noycannir?"

In fact he would serve Chilleau Judiciary well, if First Secretary Verlaine could be made to see how useful such a talent could prove in the long run. Verlaine would find a way to hold Koscuisko back from Fleet, if Verlaine felt Koscuisko could be useful. She was certain that Verlaine could get Koscuisko on his staff, under her direction. If only she could let him know why such an arrangement was to his best interest . . .

"Very well. Your first exercise at the Advanced Levels is scheduled for eight days' time, and we have a good deal of material to cover before then. Student Koscuisko, you may be excused to your lab. Don't forget your appointment. Student Noycannir, stay as you are, and we will talk about the report we are to make to Secretary Verlaine."

They would have to report to Verlaine about the drugs. She would have a natural opportunity to raise the issue then, especially if the Tutor didn't anticipate her comments ahead of time.

Rising to his feet, Koscuisko bowed to the Tutor and left the room. If he was under her, he would have to yield to her superior position in the rank-structure; she really rather enjoyed that idea. If she could not seriously wish to have him for her prisoner, she could at least have him for her subordinate; that could be considered to be equivalent, in a sense.

"Now, Student Noycannir. Let's you and I talk about this, shall we?"

Definitely she would have to suggest to Verlaine that Koscuisko be posted to produce more drugs rather than being allowed to go free. Or to Fleet.

And definitely she would not talk to Tutor Chonis about the plan. Let him not find out until Verlaine heard what she suggested.

Let her Tutor understand that she could find a way to rule his preference, howsoever indirectly, as surely as he had found a way to rule Student Koscuisko.

He couldn't help but be a little anxious, but Andrej didn't want it to show. For one, he was the most junior officer present, and was clearly not expected to call any attention to himself. For another, it might be misinterpreted as a lack of confidence. However he felt about other issues, he knew that he was more than merely adequate in the lab.

"Your name?"

He stood behind the seated evaluators, facing St. Clare and the flanking escort behind him. Released from Infirmary to custody; to be released from custody—when?

"M'name is Rabin, from Marleborne. But my mother's people hold the Ice-Traverse weave."

Robert St. Clare, if the officer please. Tutor Chonis had gone over the first response set with Andrej before the evaluation panel had been formally seated. It was a simple set of questions; the first set of responses conformed to the Jurisdiction Standard for a bond-involuntary. Now Tutor Chonis would ask the questions again, and the panel would judge whether the speak-serum did its job.

"You will declare your Bond."

Sir. For weighty offenses committed without adequate extenuating circumstance I have been justly condemned by the solemn adjudication of the Jurisdiction's Bench. According to the provisions of Fleet Penal Consideration number eighty-three, subheading twenty, article nine, my life belongs to the Jurisdiction's Bench, which has deeded it to the Fleet for thirty years.

"I'll not, it's none of it true except the prisoning part. You know damned well it was just Simmer treachery, bastard of a Jurisdiction butcher . . ."

St. Clare looked surprised to hear himself use such language, and cut it off with an evident effort. So far, so good. Ordinarily St. Clare's clear sense of consequences would have prevented him from using such confrontational language.

There were two points to be made in this trial: one was· that the speak-serum overrode internal edits, thereby gaining access to truths a man would otherwise rather conceal. And the other was that it felt so natural and right for St. Clare to speak his incautious and uncensored truth that his governor saw nothing wrong with what almost amounted to treason.

"State your chain of Command, as here present."

Sir. The officer of assignment is Student Koscuisko. Student Koscuisko's immediate superior is Tutor Chonis. The Station Provost is Marshall Journis; Administrator Clellelan represents the Bench authority. Sir.

Doctor Chaymalt was here as well, but it was Marshall Journis that had given Andrej the worst start. Why had he assumed that Joslire's hunting party had been of Joslire's general rank? It had been ego, plain and simple, to have assumed that Joslire had somehow come up with recreation for him, instead of realizing the quite obvious fact that he'd been recreation for persons unknown. Granted, he hadn't been thinking clearly at the time, but why hadn't he realized that the senior man had worn her authority with significantly more conviction than any five given Warrants taken together? And no, he didn't need any opinions from his fish.

Still, she'd given no sign of recognition, for which Andrej was deeply grateful.

"There's the Marshall, don't know anything about her, but the name. There's the Tutor, I had a cousin once with a beard like that, died of a surfeit of rolled-meal and drinkable podge. Tutor's a decent sort from what little a dog like me would know, and Clellelan the like.

It's about yon undertall beauty that I'm not sure, Koscuisko, and what kind of an ignorant accent is it? I mean to ask."

Any sign of discomfort or reticence had passed away from St. Clare's easy—flamboyantly disrespectful—speech. Well, perhaps not too disrespectful of the senior people here, the panel members who were to pass his drug or fail it. Andrej was quite certain that for himself he didn't care to be called an undertall beauty of any sort. And it was St. Clare who had an accent, flat and nasal.

But that only meant that the speak-serum was doing its work a little too well for his personal sense of propriety, and that was all to the good. Under the influence of the speak-serum, St. Clare clearly felt so comfortable making off-the-cuff judgments about his chain of command that his governor found no actionable offense in it. Any speak-serum that could turn a bond-involuntary's conditioning off as thoroughly as that would do the same or worse to ordinary prisoners, and was a genuine find for the Controlled List—as he had promised.

The panel—the Administrator, the Provost Marshall, Doctor Chaymalt—seemed to come to much the same conclusion, if Andrej read their body-language correctly from behind. Tutor Chonis raised an amused eyebrow in Andrej's direction, but Andrej could suffer Chonis's amusement easily—as long as Marshall Journis did not turn around.

"Thank you, Robert, if we can confine ourselves to the issues before us—"

"But I can tell you that I don't care for your damned cheek, Tutor or no. You'd think a man had no right to his own name, the way you throw it about."

St. Clare was starting to sound a little drunk, a little belligerent. The internal censors were clearly eroding quickly. If St. Clare didn't like his name used casually, why had he made such a point of being called by his name when Andrej had first spoken with him in Infirmary? Had St. Clare granted the use of his personal name to him, Andrej? Or had St. Clare merely objected to being called "Mister"?

"That's fine, St. Clare." Chonis's voice was patient and soothing, even though he'd been rather rudely interrupted. "This is the last one, now. Please state your duty assignment."

Sir. My duty is to serve and to protect according to the requirements of my Bond. My honor is to die in defense of my officer of assignment. It is just and judicious that it should be so, as I hope for the Day. Sir.

Nobody expected bond-involuntaries to like what had happened to them; no one demanded that they lie about the fact that their life was a sentence of penal servitude. Their conditioning—constantly reinforced by the governor—was in place to keep them from compromising themselves, among other things. For the rest, a series of abstract impersonal formulae had been created for them to use for their protection, and those formulae had been duly rehearsed and placed on Record during Robert's first responses to the questions he'd been asked.

It was a hard test, a brutal conflict between self-preservation and the censorship of the governor on one side; the speak-serum—and deeply held, if unacknowledged, conviction—on the other. St. Clare shook his head as if to clear it of a confusion of some sort, all but physically staggering as he struggled with the question.

"It wouldn't matter but for my sweet sister, don't you see?"

The governor was disabled, silent, nonfunctional. Or at least there was no telling from his words that St. Clare even had a governor. St. Clare spoke with passion from his heart, and Andrej remembered what St. Clare had said at the end of the Fifth Level exercise. *For Megh. Halfway, halfway, halfway through.*

"It's Fleet murdered my family, and Fleet that's locked my life away, but a man can understand that, after all. Because we never looked for fair dealing, not from Jurisdiction, and I can't complain—not for myself—I've not been so mistreated, not more than any other."

Remarkable. St. Clare meant it, every word of it, as if he'd made his mind up not to rage against the bitter fate that had befallen him, taking what he found on its own terms. It was an heroic act to choose to live thus without bitterness. How had St. Clare come to such wisdom, young as he was?

"But what you've done to my poor sister, I cannot forgive it. I will not forgive it. You could have killed her just instead of that. It's as black a crime as was ever done, and the Maker requite you for it."

How could there not be bitterness in St. Clare? How could he submit himself to curses and abuse, and not grieve for himself, but only for his sister? Perhaps he set his own grief onto hers, and saved himself the extra suffering that way. Perhaps.

After a moment the Administrator spoke. "The drug certainly seems persuasive enough. Doctor Chaymalt, your evaluation?"

Tutor Chonis made a signal with his hand, and the Security escort came up to take St. Clare from the room. To a recovery area, Chonis had assured him, for long enough to be sure that the speak-serum would metabolize before St. Clare had to talk to anybody with rank.

"We'll take his report once he's recovered himself a bit, of course. But I think it's safe to say that Koscuisko's serum does what Koscuisko said it would."

Well, of course it did. Andrej thought. Hadn't he staked St. Clare's very life on it?

"Marshall Journis, your opinion, please."

The Marshall rose to her feet, stretching a bit. Andrej decided to look at something else for a moment or two, just to be safe. "Either it's a valid speak-serum or that governor needs to be returned as defective, Rorin. And his governor was working fine when he got here. I'd say you've got a solid candidate, there."

Controlled List drugs were not released on field trial alone, whether or not they were building an ad hoc list for Noycannir on that basis. The serum would have to go forward to Fleet's central research facility, where the ultimate decision as to its utility would be made. That was hardly the point.

"Thank you, Marshall, Doctor. In my professional judgment, endorsed by qualified subject area experts, the trial has been a true and successful one. Thank you for your time."

The point was that he'd promised speak-sera, and they'd given him St. Clare based on that promise—and the follow-on research he had pledged at the same time. And until the medium of exchange had been officially recognized as good coin, the contract was still potentially in question. They would not take St. Clare away from him now.

What had St. Clare called him? "Yon undertall beauty"?

Was he sure that he wanted St. Clare for his own, after that?

Andrej bowed respectfully as the panel members left the room, Doctor Chaymalt, Marshall Journis, Administrator Clellelan. There was no sense in second-guessing. And not as if St. Clare would use such language when not under the influence, whether or not he was thinking it.

"Come along, Student Koscuisko." Tutor Chonis put an end to his prickly brooding, laying his arm around Andrej's shoulders genially. "That went very well, don't you think? Let's go and have a glass of rhyti. We can talk about Noycannir's Seventh Level."

Not a promising start for a relationship, no. But better than the alternative.

And the devil take his vanity, and rejoice in it.

CHAPTER TWELVE

It was dark and quiet in the rack-room, empty but for Robert St. Clare and Joslire himself. Joslire eyed the half-drunk Nurail skeptically, listening to the steady stream of recriminations without paying much attention to his actual words.

"Oh, fine, you empty-headed bottom-dweller, you goat-stuffer, you. That's just the thing. Yes, call him names, why don't you. He's just to be your, maister for the rest of your disgusting life . . ."

Robert sat slumped on a leveled sleep-rack with his head in his hands, swearing at himself. Tutor Chonis had taken Student Koscuisko off; Joslire was free for a few hours, and Robert needed watching. The Student's speak-serum had clearly left Robert vulnerable—to himself, if to no one else. Robert was to go with Student Koscuisko when he left. Joslire was curious about what manner of man the Nurail for whom his Student had paid such coin actually was.

"Be easy, man." Pulling a rack level from the wall facing Robert, Joslire sat down. Robert knew that he was here, of course. But Robert wasn't paying any attention to him.

"Yes, there's a good start, there's a lucky beginning, it's a wonder if he has aught to do with you after all—and then where will you be, you wool-witted—"

"Be easy, I said." Joslire didn't care for the direction Robert seemed to be headed. There was no reason for him to feel so insecure. Koscuisko couldn't help but value the man in proportion to what he had paid for him. "You'll be going with Student Koscuisko when he's graduated, you don't need to worry about it. How do you feel?"

"How do I feel, he asks, as if there should be a question. I feel like a total waste of a kiss, is what I feel like, a used handful of scrape-bloom, did you hear what I said to those people? And what is the officer going to think of me after the performance I just gave, what do you think?"

He'd successfully distracted Robert, so much was obvious. Less obvious was what he could say next to get out of having to answer for Student Koscuisko, when he couldn't be as certain as he would be sure to sound.

"It doesn't matter what Student Koscuisko thinks." Well, yes, it did. If he had been in Robert's place, it would matter very much to him. "You've proved the test, that's all that matters. You haven't answered my question, Robert."

Now it was Robert's turn to lean back and rest his head against the wall. "I don't care whether I do or not; I'm not under obligation to you, am I? I feel sick to my stomach. I feel very embarrassed at myself. I feel very worried about Student Koscuisko."

They had that much in common, then, Joslire thought. Except of course that it didn't do him any good to be anxious, because Koscuisko would no longer be his business once Koscuisko graduated. "The nausea will pass, they tell me. Do you want something to eat?"

Shaking his head with his eyes closed, Robert reminded Joslire suddenly of a young fly-fetcher, still immature for all its adult size. All bright eyes and enthusiasm. Very little brain. "Na, but to drink would be nice. Except not for the likes of us. Do we ever drink, Curran?"

Joslire thought he heard a subtle alteration in Robert's words; a lightening of tone, a lessening of urgency, an increasingly careful choice of phrase. Perhaps the serum was truly beginning to wear off.

"Those who want to, yes, when leave is given." He'd never thought it helped any, himself. When the duty shift came up a man was still a slave, after all. Joslire preferred just to be left alone.

"Tell me something." An idea occurred to St. Clare now, it seemed, and Joslire didn't think it had to do with drinking. "They won't talk to me, Curran, but a man needs to know. How did it happen? Can you tell? I feel ashamed to look at you."

He hadn't been mistaken about the speak-serum wearing off; he could hear the self-control in Robert's voice. And still Robert had asked the painful question. Joslire admired the boy's courage. "It wasn't anything you did. Or didn't do. I'm sure of only so much."

There was no question in his mind about what the Nurail was asking. After all, it was the same question that Tutor Chonis had been trying to find an answer for since it had happened.

"A man feels worthless. After that," Robert admitted with terrible candor. Joslire knew exactly what Robert was saying; he'd felt the same, and his exercise had gone off without hitches. He'd never put it into words, was all. "They told me that Student Koscuisko pledged for me, else I'd have been put to it. I feel so useless, Curran. I don't understand at all."

The speak-serum could still be affecting him, yes, that was true. The questions he raised were no less pertinent for that. "He doesn't feel you failed." Joslire offered the opinion carefully. "Not from anything I've heard or seen from him. It was just bad luck that betrayed you, nothing more. I said more to my Student Interrogator than you did, Robert, but I was safe, because mine wasn't Koscuisko."

He'd said it to Koscuisko, he'd said it to himself. Only now—as he said it to Robert—did Joslire really understand how true the statement was.

"I'm afraid of him. Student Koscuisko." Careful discipline was clear in Robert's face, in his tone of voice. And still he persisted in laying himself open. Perhaps—Joslire told himself—Robert had decided that he could be trusted. He hoped that wasn't it. He didn't particularly want Robert's confidence. "You can tell me if I'm being stupid, friend. It would be a kindness of you, really."

"Well, all I can tell you is that he's never laid a hand on me." Fear was a reasonable response to Student Koscuisko, especially from Robert's point of view. "The other Students I've seen turn like that in exercise have done the same to us as to their prisoners, more or less." As if Robert should believe him, when he'd been so wrong about it before, when he'd tried to reassure the young Nurail with the claim—proved false so quickly—that Student Koscuisko was a fair-minded man. How could he expect to have any kind of credibility, when he knew so little of what really went on in Koscuisko's head? "I'd be afraid of him myself, if I was going. But not because I was afraid of what he might do to me. Not that."

The more he talked the less sense he made. Wasn't that a problem?

Robert stretched, yawning. "I'm stiff as an iced fleece." Whatever that was supposed to mean. "Are we allowed to go to exercise, Curran? I've been idle for too long. I'll be of no use to anyone unless I get some practice in soon. That, what's it called, that physical therapy, it can't have done me any good. Didn't hurt nearly enough, for that."

Six hours in isolation, Tutor Chonis had said; but there hadn't been any other restrictions, and the speak-serum hadn't been expected to create any physical impairment. Joslire didn't see why he shouldn't exercise with Robert. There was an exercise area within the quarantine block, after all. And Robert had apparently worked his way past feeling useless to feeling merely less useful in the absence of recent training, which was a trend in the right direction.

"Let's go, then," Joslire agreed, rising. "You'll be wanting to know how Koscuisko fights. He's an interesting partner because of the left-dominance, you'll see."

You'll enjoy the challenge, he wanted to say. He enjoyed the challenge, because Koscuisko was teachable, because Koscuisko had the instinct of a hunter in his body, quite apart from the behavior of his conscious self. But Robert might not ever train with Koscuisko once they got to *Scylla*. In fact once they left this station, there was no reason why Koscuisko should train at all, absent an order from his commanding officer.

Still, the more he worked with Robert, the better he'd know him, and the better he could report on Robert's recovery to Student Koscuisko. And if he could reassure himself about the Nurail's potential as a Security troop, maybe he wouldn't mind not going with them quite so much.

Mergau sat tense at the Tutor's table, trying to keep clear in her mind what she was doing. Uplink made it easier to concentrate; there were no faces, no voices. There were only the words scrolling slowly across the screen, carried on maximum power relay all the way from Chilleau Judiciary.

STAND BY FOR THE FIRST SECRETARY. IDENTIFICATION RECEIVED AND CONFIRMED. SECRETARY VERLAINE IS ON THE CHANNEL, YOU MAY GO AHEAD.

The words came clumped in awkward phrases, according to the

quanta required to carry them. Tutor Chonis spoke slowly to avoid overburdening the voice verification/transmission series.

"Tutor Chonis, for Administrator Clellelan. Fleet Orientation Station Medical. And?"

She was grateful that it had to be spoken aloud. She didn't have to worry about hidden information.

"Student Mergau Noycannir. Clerk of Court."

RIGHT TRUSTY AND WELL BELOVED, I GREET YOU WELL. Verlaine's habitual formula gave her face in front of Tutor Chonis, emphasizing her formal position at Chilleau Judiciary. I GREET ALSO THE ESTIMABLE ADIFER CHONIS, AND WOULD HAVE HIM CARRY MY GREETING TO THE ADMINISTRATOR, IF HE WOULD OBLIGE ME.

"At your request, First Secretary." Chonis would never presume to call Verlaine by name in direct discourse. "Status report on the progress of the Term, with particular reference to Noycannir, Clerk of Court, Chilleau Judiciary. The better part of the Term is completed."

Verlaine would have seen the first reports by now. He would have words of praise for her. Praise from the First Secretary meant power at Chilleau Judiciary. She wanted all she could get.

THE INTERMEDIATE LEVELS ARE MORE TECHNICALLY CHALLENGING, AS I UNDERSTAND. I TRUST YOU HAVE BEEN ABLE TO PROVIDE MY CLERK WITH ADEQUATE SUPPORT.

Else Verlaine would hold it against the Tutor's account, and not hers. That was the implication. It wasn't true, of course; he would be displeased with her if she should fail. But that was their private matter. In front of others, he would show only his trust and confidence in her, until she made a mistake.

"Indeed, First Secretary. They are more technically challenging, and the medical issues become more critical to success. We have been able to document Noycannir's mastery of the Protocols, and her successful performance at each Level so far. She has been passed to the Advanced Levels. Administrator Clellelan has every confidence in her ability."

Surely Verlaine would wonder at that, since it so clearly spoke of full surrender. And Fleet had fought him every step of the way in this matter of the Writ. Fleet would not want to lose Koscuisko to the

Bench; Fleet would want Koscuisko for themselves—Koscuisko, and his skill, and his drugs. Especially his drugs.

I'M GRATEFUL FOR ADMINISTRATOR CLELLELAN'S CONFIDENCE, BUT CAN'T HELP WONDERING HOW HE CAN BE SURE. WE ALL KNOW THAT THERE IS A FAILURE RATE OF ONE IN SIX DURING THE ADVANCED LEVELS.

Well, no, she hadn't known that. Perhaps Koscuisko would fail and be sent home in disgrace. Or else exiled to serve his duty time as the medical officer of one of the prisons, where it wouldn't matter if he had no taste or tolerance for pain. Fleet didn't care how many of the Bench's prisoners died of neglect and lack of medication in prison. Except that she had no information that hinted that Koscuisko was at risk to fail in anything.

"Based on her performance thus far, we don't anticipate any difficulty." No, she had no trouble with the Protocols. Her prisoners gratified her with their submission and their fear in the embrace of Koscuisko's drugs. It was no problem to torment them.

"And in addition. In light of the unique requirements of Noycannir's Writ, special support is being provided. Specifically, targeted instruction from the Controlled List, and a custom-built library for Noycannir's use in your service."

There seemed to be a longer pause than required for all the text of the message to parcel through. When her Patron responded at last, Mergau knew that his interest had been engaged; and rejoiced in it, to have his help to discomfit the Administration.

CLARIFICATION IS REQUESTED, CUSTOM-BUILT LIBRARY.

Yet Chonis did not seem to see the trap. "One of Noycannir's classmates has a second rating in an appropriate field, and is commendably willing to contribute his effort to his duty in more than one Lane. Student Koscuisko is creating a special set of qualified formulations especially for the support of Noycannir's Writ."

AND IT IS THIS WHICH SO ASSURES CLELLELAN THAT SHE WILL GRADUATE. KOSCUISKO. IT IS A COMBINE HOUSE, I THINK.

She could almost hear his voice, musing. Moving quickly, surely, inexorably to the same conclusion she had drawn from the same set of information.

SURELY YOU HAVE PLANS TO POST SUCH A PRODUCTIVE

RESOURCE TO AN AREA IN WHICH HE CAN BENEFIT THE JUDICIAL SYSTEM MOST EFFECTIVELY.

Oddly enough, however, Chonis was not surprised by the question. "I have discussed the option with the Administrator. Unfortunately, Fleet feels that the political risk is too great. Koscuisko is prince inheritor to his House."

What did that mean? He could not be reassigned? The prestige of serving under the First Secretary's personal instruction was not great enough for such a man? Is that what Tutor Chonis meant to say?

NOT EVEN COMBINE GRAIN CAN BUY A FLEET DEFERMENT, CHONIS.

It wasn't as if it would be asking Koscuisko to sacrifice prestige if he went to work for Chilleau Judiciary rather than Fleet. If Koscuisko worked for Chilleau Judiciary, he need have no duties beside Writ and research. Chief Medical Officers had a great deal to do quite apart from Inquiry. Surely a man would naturally prefer less complex a life to so demanding a position? It wasn't as if he could set aside his Writ before his eight years were done, one way or the other.

Koscuisko had no taste for discipline. His Security could not possibly respect that in him. So Security would not make their best effort to protect him. Koscuisko would be at significant risk in Fleet unless he reconciled himself to demanding more professionalism from his Security than he did from his bond-involuntary slave Curran.

"Koscuisko is under instruction from his father to serve Fleet specifically as a Chief Medical Officer. Fleet deferment does not recognize any talent as exceeding the requirements of a cruiser-killer's Infirmary, as the First Secretary knows."

All in all Mergau could understand no reason whatever for Chonis's attitude, except for Fleet's stubborn insistence on standing in Verlaine's path at every junction, for no better reason than that the First Secretary was a Bench officer.

"Unless he can be proven to lack competence or psychological fitness, we dare not insult the Combine by reducing him to a post suitable for a man of lesser ability. Nor dare we insult the Autocrat's Proxy by attempting to so prove."

No reason but pure spite, she was certain of it.

She knew the First Secretary better than Fleet did. Verlaine was tenacious of purpose when he felt that it was to his advantage. If he could be made to see how valuable Koscuisko could be to him, Verlaine would go up against the Combine itself, and take his prize. Had he not triumphed over the Yanjozi nations, and forced their subservience to the Blaeborn precedents?

THE SELF-DETERMINATION OF ALL UNDER JURISDICTION MUST OF COURSE BE CAREFULLY RESPECTED. She could hear the ironic humor in his voice, with poison in the sting of it. ESPECIALLY IF FLEET IS TO BENEFIT—KOSCUISKO'S FAMILIAL DUTY MUST NOT BE COMPROMISED.

"Thank you for your understanding, First Secretary." There was irony in Tutor Chonis's response in turn. Mergau wondered if it would be as clear in the text as it was in Chonis's voice. "The Administration had certain reservations concerning Student Noycannir's ability to support her Writ, which have been addressed in a very satisfactory manner, with Koscuisko's help. All can benefit."

All except Koscuisko, who had not wanted to work on the Controlled List; who did not care to discipline his slave, who did not care for the practical exercises. But the desires and inclinations of so diffident a man were not worthy of serious consideration.

MERGAU IS WITH YOU, AS I UNDERSTAND.

How was she to put her Patron on notice that the matter of Koscuisko should be pursued?

"Indeed she is." Chonis wouldn't know what she was going to say. He might expect her support, out of gratitude to him for having found a way to see her through to her Writ. "Student Noycannir, please feel free."

He was wrong if he thought that. The only loyalty that she could afford was to herself, and that meant to her Patron. At least for now.

"I greet me my Patron, and hope that all goes according to his wish." It was a thrill in its own right to be allowed to speak on uplink. It was so expensive . . . "I commend me to him. And commend also Student Koscuisko to his attention."

Chonis made neither move nor sign, but she knew that her point had been taken when Verlaine's response came scrolling across the screen.

HIS VALUE IS SO GREAT AS THAT, NOYCANNIR? YOU DO NOT PRAISE LIGHTLY, IF AT ALL.

Because she was too jealous and insecure. At least that was what he had told her before. *A word of praise is a surer trap than any vice, Mergau, remember that.*

But vice bound more securely and reliably. "So great and more, my Patron. It seems a waste to let this resource go to Fleet service rather than research, since he is so effective with the drugs."

Verlaine knew what she was saying, his response confirmed that. RESTRAIN YOUR ENTHUSIASM, THOUGH IT DOES YOU CREDIT. KOSCUISKO BELONGS TO FLEET. YOU WILL BE GRATEFUL TO YOUR TUTOR FOR BENEFIT RECEIVED. TUTOR CHONIS.

"Yes, First Secretary." Was it her imagination, or did Chonis sound a little worried?

I AM DEEPLY GRATEFUL FOR YOUR SUPPORT. I WOULD TAKE IT AS A PERSONAL FAVOR IF I COULD RECEIVE COPIES OF NOYCANNIR'S INTERMEDIATE LEVELS. IF YOU WOULD APPROACH THE ADMINISTRATOR ON MY BEHALF, I WOULD BE MOST OBLIGED TO YOU.

So that he could see for himself the action of Koscuisko's drugs? It occurred to Mergau suddenly that Verlaine would see her own fumbling inadequacies firsthand.

"I will bring the matter before the Administrator directly. First Secretary, this concludes the material we wished to lay before you at this time."

It would be worth the humiliation she'd suffer on being exposed before her Patron, if viewing the tapes convinced Verlaine to take Koscuisko for his own.

VERY GOOD, THANK YOU AGAIN. TRANSMISSION ENDS.

"Return to your quarters, Student Noycannir." The Tutor did not bother to hide his scorn, now that they were alone. He had known what she was doing all along. He'd simply felt that he was more than a match for her. "You are scheduled at the Seventh Level in five days. Hanbor will let you know when we can meet with Student Koscuisko. Dismissed."

Meekly she rose and bowed, meekly she left.

Tutor Chonis was in truth more than a match for her, perhaps.

But she had set her Patron on the scent.

Time would tell whether Tutor Chonis and Fleet Orientation Station Medical could hope to outmaneuver First Secretary Verlaine.

⊕ ⊕ ⊕

The table was laid ready with his rhyti; the driver and his other instruments were laid out neat and orderly for his delectation. Andrej set down the lefrols he had brought, stroking the smooth rolled cylinders of leaf with nervous fingers. Rhyti for now. Lefrols for later. Lefrols were good for the nerves; and he had a case of the nerves, an uneasy sort of excitement in his stomach built of equal parts of apprehension and anticipation. He was tired of watching Noycannir botch her jobs. He needed to let some blood himself, to make a point of doing it right.

His Seventh Level, the first of the last, three exercises to go after this one. He'd practiced twice a day for a week, intent on making a respectable trial of the driver. If he could manage it adequately well today, he would feel confident enough to take it to St. Clare for the punishment that was owed, whether or not the Tutor would insist on counting bloody craters as a condition of fulfillment of the contract they had made for St. Clare's life.

He heard the signal at the prisoner's door and lifted the driver from the table, enjoying the sleek cool weight of it in his gloved hand. "Step through."

He'd had a look at the prisoner's brief last night; he knew what to expect. This was a referral straight from assisted inquiry; the prisoner was accused, but had not yet been questioned herself. The fact that she was female was a little awkward. Abstractly speaking, he liked the idea of beating women even less than the idea of beating men, setting aside the fact that a contest between a prisoner and an Inquisitor could hardly be considered a fair match regardless of the prisoner's sex or age.

On the other hand, Robert St. Clare was not the only man under Jurisdiction with a sister. Andrej had three or four. It was not quite clear which, but one of them at least would mock him mercilessly should he shrink from his duty simply because his prisoner was not male.

Mayra had been Lady Abbess since the day that he'd been baptized; she was responsible for keeping order amongst all the sworn-sisters in family prayer-halls. Pain was good for the soul, Mayra had assured him. Women required much more firm a hand than men did, because the female constitution was more resilient than the male. Women were born to bear children. Pain simply didn't make as much of an impression on sworn-sisters as on brothers-dedicate, not as far as Mayra was concerned.

And this prisoner wasn't even Dolgorukij.

She was about his size, and not too clean by the look of her. Andrej eyed the woman a little skeptically: it hardly seemed likely that she would hold secrets, let alone such dangerous ones that the Bench would spike the Levels to this extent. He would find out one way or the other, but he really rather hoped she did have secrets. It would be a shame if she would have to die for nothing.

"State your name, and your identification." There was no sense in asking for the offense, not at the Advanced Levels. Generally speaking one had several from which to choose, and all of them actionable.

"I am—Davit, of the market at Cynergau. Of the People, your Excellency."

She sounded fairly beaten already, to Andrej. The People? They were all the People. Except the Aznir, of course, the beloved of the Holy Mother, and the executors of Her Sacred Will.

Well, if Davit was meek and submissive, perhaps he would just talk to her for a bit and see what he could find out about of her state of mind. He was reluctant to set the driver down, since he was eager to test himself with it; but there was no sense in rushing things—that was one of Noycannir's problems. Andrej exchanged the driver for his rhyti and seated himself at the chair that was kept for him beside the table.

"Talk to me, then, Davit. Do you know why you are here?" If she was of a Cynergau lineage, Class-Four hominid, then she would carry as much muscle as a man of her race; something to keep in mind. Skin tore differently over muscle.

She shook her head, turning her face away. One of the Security moved her head back with a hand at the nape of her neck so that she faced him politely.

"No. Your Excellency."

Surely she had some idea. "Really, you can't guess? What do you imagine that it could be?"

"Truly, your Excellency, they came and took me away from my shop in the middle of the evening, and I don't understand."

Clearly she'd not been referred due to her intransigent nature. "There was a preliminary inquiry?"

She made a gesture as though she wanted to turn her face aside again. But she did not turn her face. She was being commendably careful, Andrej thought. "There was. Your Excellency. They said I was accused of harboring, but I didn't understand. I told them so."

And they hadn't believed her, so much was obvious. Someone else must have given up information already. Andrej wondered what it was, exactly, that interested the Bench so much about this woman.

"Harboring, what did they mean by that? Did they explain it to you?"

Was he mistaken, or had she hesitated? "I . . . didn't understand what they said, your Excellency, they said . . . No, I didn't understand what they said."

"Perhaps if you were to share it with me, we could an interpretation develop, between the two of us."

The woman bit her lip and stood silent.

What she'd been asked wasn't all that difficult. The prisoner's brief contained the information: movement of suspected Free Government agents with forged papers through her shop. Andrej didn't think she hadn't understood the issue.

He did think that she was afraid to discuss it.

If there was no problem, she would not need to be reluctant. It was a simple matter, really, and easy to deny as long as one wasn't worried about being caught in an embarrassing contradiction of some sort.

"You are not being candid with me, Davit. What are you hiding?"

She could be expected to keep shut to protect those dear to her. But it seemed fair to guess from the information in the prisoner's brief that at least one of the people she was trying to protect had already given her up to Fleet to save himself. Herself. Whomever.

"Please, your Excellency, there has been a mistake. I don't understand."

He had his work cut out for him, and a driver thirsty for blood. It made him a little restless to be sitting here and talking when he could be at his exercise.

"I'm sorry. Your response is not acceptable." Now she made a liar out of him as well. He was not sorry. He was too interested in finding out more about the driver's capabilities against living flesh. He would do penance for the falsehood later. "Gentlemen, if you would do me the kindness of uncovering this woman. And then you may stand away."

Discipline was to be taken with a bare back. It was better so, since Joslire had said the stroke would have to be repeated if it failed to break the skin.

As if an abstract interest in the skill were the only reason that he wished to use the driver. . .

The woman cowered away from him, trying to cover up her nakedness with her hands. For a moment Andrej hesitated. Was it not a shameful thing to uncover an honest woman, and force her guilt from her with whips and fire?

He didn't care, not now. Not anymore. Or at least he didn't care enough to lay aside the driver and walk out.

"Come now, we will discuss." The whip snaked out, the snapper cracking in the air beside her head. She flinched away from it ungracefully; and Andrej followed up on the backstroke, marking her shoulder with an ugly stripe. "First, if you will, that crime of which you were accused, at your first interview. And so on from there. Am I understood?"

She would confess to him exactly what it had been that she claimed not to have understood. And then she would confess to him why she had wished she had not understood it; and then they would investigate the depth and the complexity of the understanding that she'd wished to disavow.

"Excellency, I don't understand, I don't know what they were talking about—"

He caught her around the ankle and pulled it out from under her, tearing a bright red bracelet around her leg.

"Harboring, you said. And how were you to have harbored, and whom?"

It was pleasant to test the whip's performance and find it so obedient to his desire.

"No, I have harbored no one, I am an honest woman. You have my documents, check my documents."

He checked her lies instead, and made her gasp with it.

Nor did he feel he would be needing to have a lefrol for his nerves.

He broke her feet with the driver; and she crawled away from him toward the wall, wishing him in Hell for his suspicious nature. He broke her hands with the driver, much more delicate work; and she lifted her voice to her goddesses and invited all of Jurisdiction to be damned as well on top of him, as long as he were to be damned most deeply and most dreadfully.

He had Security lift her to lie on her back on the table with her hands useless at her sides, giving his lefrols—not forgetting the rhyti—over into the keeping of such Security as were not required to hold her to her place. He raped her brutally with the butt end of the driver; and she begged him to consider that she had borne children, and that her womb was consequently worthy of respect, not such ill-treatment.

The Security set her back down to the floor for him, and he beat her with the doubled lash until he knew from the trouble that she had in breathing that he had compromised her ribs; and she lamented for her children, the children born to her broken body, and the trouble that they were in, the bad and dangerous things they'd gotten involved with.

And then he stepped away and let the length of the driver out of his fist, and practiced his apprentice-craft upon her until she was decently clothed in a smooth all-concealing garment of her own bright red blood. And she put out her shattered hands to him, and pleaded with him that he leave off his exercise, and asked him what it had been that he had wanted to know.

Except that by that time she'd told him more than he had thought to gain from her. Andrej didn't think there was any point to going over it all again. Without access to medication, she would be gone from him within a matter of hours, since bright pain could overrule the escape that shock provided for only so long. And she would bleed to death, drugs or no drugs, because he'd done his rape so thoroughly, and the driver had been so thirsty for her pain. No, he was the one who had been thirsty for her pain. The driver was a formidable tool, but only that. It had been his lust to hear her cry, his passion for her pain that had so damaged her. And he was sated now, and satisfied, now that she had surrendered herself to him, whether or not he had had her secrets from her earlier.

He thought about it for a moment, pondering in his mind where the monitors would be.

Then Andrej raised his head and looked to where he hoped that Tutor Chonis would be watching him.

"It would seem that the Record is complete," Andrej said. "It is to be hoped that the Protocols have been appropriately exercised to the

Tutor's satisfaction. In the absence of other topics of interest, I respectfully request the Tutor's permission to terminate the exercise."

He waited. Without a decision one way or the other, he would be expected either to continue to misuse the woman until she died, or go off on his own business and let her last hours drag out in senseless and solitary agony. Neither of which seemed entirely satisfactory to Andrej.

In a moment he heard the change in the background noise that meant that the Tutor's communication channel had been engaged. "Very well, Student Koscuisko. You may dispatch your prisoner."

She had confessed clear killing offenses as far as Jurisdiction was concerned. Once in the field, he would require no such clearance to execute; he knew the Protocols, after all. In Orientation, however, it was up to the Administration to decide officially whether termination was to come sooner or later. Here it was Tutor Chonis's responsibility to say when the prisoner was to die. Andrej appreciated the support the Tutor was apparently willing to grant to him, and received it with an appreciative salute.

"Thank you, Tutor Chonis. Mister Haspir, if I may borrow your knife."

There were needle-knives provided among the instruments, of course. But they were too narrow for his purpose. He had a clear idea in his mind about what he wanted to do, and how he wanted to do it; for that he needed Haspir's knife, since Joslire did not yet trust him with knives for his own use.

Kneeling down at the woman's back, he covered her eyes with his hand so that she could take her last few breaths in what privacy he could provide for her. First, to cut the connection between the brain and the sub-brain at the top of her spine, so that the mind need not be burdened with the body's frantic signals that it was dying. And second, to cut the connection between the bundle of nerve fibers at the base of the brain and the spine, so that the body would forget to breathe and death would come of oxygen starvation. The woman was Cynergau, her nervous system built with rather more redundancy than other hominids of her class. Breathing would continue by reflex as long as the connection between the spine and the sub-brain was left intact.

Andrej severed it.

Her body stilled, and Andrej waited. Four eighths, and the body went into spasm, the uncoordinated twitches—neural "noise"—of a machine without a governor. Twelve eighths, and she was dead, and Andrej waited until enough time had passed that he could feel certain that her mind was still before he rose and beckoned for his rhyti.

"Thank you for your assistance, gentlemen." He could read no reservation, no hesitation in any of their expressions. They had done as he had instructed them, without questions either implicit or explicit, without the slightest indication of reluctance on their parts; and for that he was grateful. It could not be easy duty for them. "Mister Haspir, is there a firepoint here someplace?"

Lefrols he'd brought; he'd issued them to himself from the range of intoxicants and inhibitors and antidepressants available to Students. Lefrols and alcohol—although he did not trust the cortac brandy, knowing too well what passed for cortac sold from Combine to Jurisdiction, and prudently confined himself to wodac. But a lefrol was no good without a firepoint, no matter how neatly the needle-knife from the table served to trim the end. Andrej felt a little foolish to be asking, but he did want a lefrol now. He was tired and he was hungry, and he didn't know what time it was, but he rather suspected that it had gotten late, because Haspir seemed a little weary. If as correct as always.

"According to the officer's good pleasure." Haspir bowed, presenting the lit firepoint as he did so. A decent firepoint it was, too, it burned clean and blue, and set a coal to his lefrol quite nicely.

"Thank you again. Your knife."

His chair was still here, although the table had been pushed back against the wall earlier. His Mizucash friend stood by with his rhyti. Andrej let himself sit, surprised at how weary he felt; and the Security did not have the option. Security were expected never to sit in the presence of an officer, even a Student. Well, it was hard, but perhaps they were better at it than he was. What time was it?

Andrej sat and smoked his lefrol and considered the corpse. He would be a little drunk in less than an eighth. Lefrols were good for that, if only one did not succumb to the temptation to take them too frequently. He wasn't drunk now, though, so why didn't he feel more affected, to have murdered the poor woman? Betrayed in her friends, betrayed in her family, betrayed in her goddesses for all that he could tell, and he had killed her. Terminated, concluded, dispatched, removed, the language of the Protocols could not disguise the basic truth of the matter; and the fact of the matter was that he had never killed a woman until now. A hare or two, a brace of game-birds, yes. A woman, never, nor a man nor child, either.

And he had had no passion for the work, aside from gratitude that Tutor Chonis would permit him to make a clean end of her, instead of condemning that close-to-finished life to bleed out slowly in pain and in confusion. It was no excuse; but he was fairly certain that he had not enjoyed her death as he had enjoyed the long slow killing of her, and therefore it was possible that his murder of her had been cleanly done, uncontaminated by the passion that he was learning how to manage and maintain. Learning to use, since he had no hope of denying its existence to himself.

The cleaning team came to take the body away, and here was Joslire coming on their heels to take him to his bed. What did Joslire think about the murders that his Students did?

Andrej rose from his place, giving his rhyti glass to one of the cleaning team, and left the exercise theater with Joslire in his wake. Stumbling only slightly, which was good. It was enough of a shame to be smoking lefrols without requiring that Joslire carry him to quarters while he was at it. Lefrols were an acquired taste. Andrej knew from experience that people who didn't smoke lefrols tended to feel rather violently about their odor.

By the time he'd reached his quarters, he was light-headed, as he had expected to be—pleasantly euphoric, lazy and blissful in a mildly drunken sort of way. He didn't want his supper, he wanted to have a wash, even if the time-keeper claimed that it was only second-shift. Andrej squinted at the time-keeper with confusion, trying to focus on its readout while the rest of the room swam slowly about him. No, not fourteen. Twenty-four. Not second-shift, but the end of third-shift. Had it really been so long? He certainly hadn't noticed it getting late, and he'd not released Security for mid-meal. He was going to have to discuss this problem with Tutor Chonis. It could hardly endear him to his Security if he was to keep them on their feet for three shifts run together without so much as a short break for mid-meal.

He gave his lefrol over into Joslire's keeping and went into the washroom, stripping as he went. His uniform was dirty, soiled through to his under-blouse with blood; and the gloves were simply disgusting.

Blood on his hands even through the gloves, blood under his fingernails—a rusty stain with a metallic smell that somehow seemed more natural than unpleasant. Blood in the waste-stream of the wet-shower, the dried smudges blooming pink as the warm moisture rinsed them from his body. He had not remembered it being quite so messy a business as this before. On the other hand, she had been his Seventh Level.

By the time that the waste-stream ran clear, by the time that he felt clean enough to face himself in the mirror once again, Joslire had taken his soiled clothing away and set his sleep-shirt out to wait for him. Padding damp and barefoot into the main room, Andrej cast about him for his lefrol, and found it in a dish on the study-set, alongside his meal. He didn't want his meal. There was a glass of wodac there as well; he'd made a practice of taking quite a bit of wodac with his suppers after exercise. He didn't want the wodac, either. He was drunk on the powerful intoxicant of the lefrol and full sated with the sweet sound of his prisoner's pain. There was no room in all his body for an appetite, the exercise had satisfied so completely. He took the lefrol and its leavings-dish into the little closet where he had his bed and lay down to finish his smoke, content to not be thinking about much of anything.

Joslire was at the door, but Joslire would not come in. Perhaps Joslire was worried about smoking in one's bed, which was of course a nasty habit, and too likely to result in fire-suppression systems going off in the middle of a dream to be indulged in with any frequency.

Well, if Joslire was worried, Andrej could afford to be done with lefrols for the evening. He was certainly drunk enough. And he had been hard at work all day; it was probable that he was tired, even if he was too euphoric to notice.

He set the lefrol down into its leavings-dish and decided to go to sleep.

Clellelan turned the record-cube over in his fingers, clearly musing over the conversation it contained—the scheduled review, First Secretary Verlaine, Mergau Noycannir. Tutor Chonis. "So, Adifer, you think that we might have a problem here?"

"Two problems. Or one problem, two lock-links." He'd spoken to the Administrator on Joslire Curran's behalf earlier, when Clellelan had surprised him by offering the Safe. So at least the Administrator was already prepared for that one. "I'd have come to you sooner, but Koscuisko ran his Seventh Level a little richer than usual."

Clellelan frowned at his time-keeper. Middle of the first-shift, the second day of Koscuisko's Seventh Level. The Administrator knew what the general schedule was—there were eighteen other Students in the Seventh Level exercises here, after all, and it would have been nineteen except for that unfortunate accident that one of Tutor Heson's Students had had with a twisted sleep-shirt. Noycannir's prisoner had died during the night, but no blame attached to her—at least no official blame. Although with Koscuisko's drugs, there had been no real reason why the prisoner should not have lived to talk for three days yet. In Chonis's professional estimation.

"Talk to me, Adifer."

What, had Clellelan developed expectations where Koscuisko was concerned? "Didn't stop for mid-meal, didn't stop for third-meal. Noycannir'd been in quarters for five eights before Koscuisko decided he was finished. Asked me for permission to terminate."

Clellelan knew as well as he did how unusual that was. "Got lost in the exercise? What? Did you let him?"

Well, yes, he supposed that Koscuisko had got lost in the exercise. In a manner of speaking. "He said that she didn't know anything more than what she'd already told us, and I believed him. Made a nice end of her, too, one cut to stop the pain, one cut to end her life. Stylish."

Nodding, Clellelan was clearly making connections. "So we didn't hear from you yesterday, what with Koscuisko so absorbed in his exercise. What about Verlaine?"

Good question. "It's a reasonable alternative to propose, one would think. But I don't think it's a good idea, even if the Bench wants in on him." Granted, he was working untried code here. Under normal circumstances, all he cared about the welfare of his Students was that they stay healthy enough to get through his course before they came to pieces, or had any embarrassing accidents with twisted sleep-shirts. Under normal circumstances that was all he could afford to care about them. He hadn't yet made up his mind about whether Andrej Koscuisko was really all that different.

"So tell me. Apart from the fact that Koscuisko's going to be able to buy as many First Secretaries as he wants, once he inherits." Blunt speech from the Administrator usually meant that he was most open to new ideas. Chonis plunged in.

"You remember Ligrose thought he'd be better off in Surgery. She likes what he's done for his man St. Clare as well, which reminds me to ask you about that Class One we've promised him."

"Don't like to keep the man hanging in suspense for longer than necessary," Clellelan noted. Which man? Koscuisko? St. Clare? Whatever. "And we'll need to allow for recovery time, before they leave the Station. Any time before Koscuisko's Ninth Level, Adifer, all right? —Say on."

"It shows up in his exercises, though, as well. When he killed that prisoner, it was like he'd hit a global reset. Absolutely no hint of how much he'd been liking it. Chaymalt says he's too good a healer to waste on Inquiry. I say he's got too much potential in Inquiry to waste him on medicine. But if Verlaine gets him he won't have any medical practice, and he'll only be answering Verlaine's questions—waste of resource. At least in Fleet he has a chance to do both. More balance, that way."

"Maybe keep him running longer, if he feels he's needed outside Special Medical." That was a good point, although Chonis hadn't thought of it in quite those terms. What burned young Inquisitors out was the exercise of their Writ, not the burden of their strictly medical responsibilities. *Trust Clellelan*—Chonis thought gratefully—*to come up with a perfectly objective reason to be concerned about Koscuisko's welfare.* "But are we going to be able to keep him out of Verlaine's understandably greedy little graspers?"

"Wants to see Noycannir's tapes, you noticed." Of course he had. "It could get to be a difficult problem. I suggest our parity-fields will be significantly stronger if Verlaine doesn't get a good look at Noycannir's tapes until Koscuisko has already reported to *Scylla*."

Clellelan nodded appreciatively. "Fleet can probably find ways to protect the investment, as long as he performs to expectation. All right, we'll do it, and if you can nudge his Tenth Level up a hair, we can release him early if we have to. The Autocrat's Proxy might even like that."

Yes, Chonis imagined that they could hurry the schedule a bit, as long as Koscuisko could take the pace. He'd see what Curran had to say about how Koscuisko was holding up, which brought him to his other problem, quite naturally.

"I'll go over the schedule with Curran, then. And Curran seems to have gotten a little intense about Student Koscuisko. No telling for certain, but he's teaching Koscuisko how to throw knives, and I suspect the knives Koscuisko's throwing aren't Fleet-issue."

Clellelan set the record-cube he'd been toying with down carefully on the desk's surface. "You think he's teaching Koscuisko five-knives?"

It couldn't be proved on the evidence at hand, no. To be absolutely certain, they would need to interrupt the practice and check Curran's knives then and there. Yet Chonis was reasonably secure in his suspicion. All Curran had done on Safe had been to take Koscuisko to a practice range and start him on throwing knives. That had to mean something.

"Just so, Rorin. His five-knives. We could pull him off now, of course. We've got St. Clare to post in replacement if we need to."

Snorting in amusement, the Administrator shook his head. "'Yon undertall beauty,' with an accent, no less. An ignorant accent. You couldn't have paid the man to make a better test of that speak-serum."

No, as a matter of fact. The demonstration had been genuinely impressive. "But if we leave Curran where he is and he asks to be reassigned when Koscuisko leaves, we lose one of our best. Good for Koscuisko. Not so good for us."

Curran could be released to Fleet if Curran wanted to go. It would be insanity to give up what was left of his deferment, but as far as Chonis was concerned all semi-mystical, ascetic warrior-cultists were already more than a little unbalanced, and the Emandisan figuring prominently to the fore of a list of dangerous loonies.

"Do you want him pulled off and sent through readjustment?" Clellelan asked, bluntly.

Bond-involuntaries sometimes formed intense attachments to Students of assignment, for one reason or another. Bond-involuntaries were psychologically vulnerable to passionate one-on-one bonding to begin with, since personal dedication could substitute for freedom to an extent. When that happened, the Administrator had the option of removing the troop from the officer assigned and arranging a respite period with plenty of food, intoxicants as required, and as much sexual contact as the troop could take. That generally set a bond-involuntary back on his or her figurative feet.

Curran and Koscuisko might be well matched for man and master, according to the peculiar cultural forms of Emandisan and Dolgorukij alike; that wasn't the issue. Whether Clellelan was willing to risk losing Curran was.

"Getting back to my basic interest, which is to give Koscuisko the best chance of long-term survival on Line. Curran has good support to offer, and Koscuisko's been raised to accept that kind of relationship. It may be too late to change Curran's mind about it anyway, what with those knives taken into account."

He didn't care about being fair to Curran, though Curran was well respected by Staff—bonded and un-Bonded alike. At least he didn't care about being fair to Curran as much as he wanted to see Koscuisko as ideally placed to perform his Judicial function as possible. "And if he's got two of them with him on *Scylla*, he might be even more reluctant to abandon them to Fleet and go off to Chilleau Judiciary."

"At least until one of them gets killed, and he decides it isn't worth the investment," Clellelan mused. "Well, give Curran the chance to get clear if he approaches you, Adifer. But if we're going to put the boy through an accelerated Advanced—and he's got to blood his St. Clare while he's at it—we don't want to be upsetting his domestic arrangements. Curran's one of the best, but he's still dead."

Bond-involuntaries were sometimes called the thirty-years-dead, their identities and rights under Jurisdiction restored only when the Day dawned at last. Which meant that technically speaking, Curran was disposable, in a sense, to be used in whatever manner the Administration saw fit to further Fleet's interests.

Fleet permitted bond-involuntaries to volunteer to place themselves at an officer's disposal, since that suited Fleet's purpose. No blame would attach to the Administration of Fleet Orientation Station Medical if Curran asked to leave. Curran might have some trouble getting Koscuisko to agree, true enough. But that was Curran's problem.

"I'll give you a revised schedule." The business of the interview was over; rising to his feet, Chonis bowed to his superior, satisfied that they were of congruent mind. "Are you going to want witnesses for St. Clare?"

"Oh, you'd better get Station Security to observe. I'll sit in if I'm free, but don't hold up on my account."

They'd see how quickly they could get Koscuisko out of there and safely to *Scylla*.

Koscuisko deserved better than to become the First Secretary's minion. Fleet could protect Koscuisko as long as Koscuisko was on Line. Once let Fleet know that the Bench wanted him, and Fleet would hold Koscuisko to its bosom like a favorite child . . .

CHAPTER THIRTEEN

He'd never had so irregular a schedule with any of his other Students. Joslire was looking forward to the break that the Administration granted them at the completion of each Term: eight days to rest, eight days to recover from any Student discipline, eight days to complete debriefing before the next Students started to arrive. Lately eight days had stretched to sixteen, once as long as twenty-four, before the Administration could collect sufficient Students for a cost-effective Term.

Koscuisko was a very tiring man.

He was going to need every single hour of that anticipated break just to catch up on his sleep.

But then he'd never had a Student who had run the Seventh Level all the way out to its logical conclusion. His other Students had preferred to leave the exercise for their mid-meal, and again for their third-meal and again for their sleep-shift, rewarded more often than not with an easy finish to the exercise—prisoners who politely and conveniently died while the Students slept.

Koscuisko hadn't seemed to notice when it had been time for mid-meal; Koscuisko had been working on his prisoner's hands. Even Tutor Chonis had been impressed at Koscuisko's skillful employment of the driver. Still less had Koscuisko apparently noted the time for his third-meal or his sleep-shift, absorbed in some abstract equation of the ratio of bruises to ribs.

There were benefits either way, of course. Going by normal practice, the prisoners died quietly by themselves during the night and the Students weren't bothered with the business in the morning. But Koscuisko's way they could both sleep until next third-meal, because the exercise was scheduled for two days, and Tutor Chonis didn't want to see Koscuisko until the next day following.

And of course the most significant benefit from Koscuisko's management style—significant from the prisoner's point of view, at any rate—was that Koscuisko had killed her, once he'd decided he was finished. None of the passive, impersonal murders of Joslire's other Students. Koscuisko had taken active responsibility; and he had taken care in killing her, mindful of her dignity even naked and abused as she had been.

Sometime during the Eighth or Ninth Levels, Students were required to make a kill at the Tutor's direction and discretion. It was a test of sorts; and most Students responded to it by ordering Security to perform the actual act. In fact by the Seventh Level, most Students were happiest to sit in their chair and direct Security rather than dirtying their own hands; perhaps understandably so. Joslire appreciated Koscuisko's apparent selfishness. It was good not to be required to beat a prisoner. It was better to be left alone to not watch, to be called upon only when an extra pair of hands were wanted for some relatively neutral task.

None of his other Students had ever asked to make the kill.

But almost all of them had bad dreams, soon after the event.

Koscuisko's cries woke Joslire sometime close to mid-shift. He rolled off the sleep-rack to his feet, halfway to Koscuisko's cubicle before his eyes were well open. The privacy barrier wasn't quite closed; Joslire had wanted the extra ventilation to clear the inner space of the stench from Koscuisko's lefrol. He was through it in a moment, to seize and still Koscuisko's restless hands as Koscuisko's sleeping body struggled with some dreamed enemy.

"Sir. The officer is dreaming. Wake up."

Small as it was, the room seemed stifling to Joslire, the air heavy with horror. Koscuisko fought against him for a moment, and Koscuisko was difficult to control in his sleep—Aznir Dolgorukij, and significantly stronger than Joslire was, even if Koscuisko did not yet know how best to use his strength. Joslire hung on, grimly embracing the dreaming man, repeating the same pale neutral phrases as soothingly as he dared.

"The officer is dreaming, your Excellency. The officer is respectfully requested to wake up now." *Come back, come back from the land of the dead and of shadows. Wake now, dear one, that thy dreams not distress thee.*

Koscuisko woke with a convulsive start and lay motionless in Joslire's arms for a long moment, holding his breath. Joslire wasn't sure whether Koscuisko was still dreaming, or what; but finally Koscuisko gave a great sigh and his body relaxed. He leaned up against Joslire, as if gratefully, letting his head back against Joslire's shoulder. Joslire didn't dare move. It was irregular, surely, and what had he thought that he was doing, coming in here in the first place?

"I have had a dream," Koscuisko said. "I did not much enjoy it, Joslire."

Surely not, Joslire was tempted to say. *One hardly would have guessed.* Instead he shifted his weight a little, preparatory to disengaging himself from the intimacy of the embrace; but Koscuisko put his hand up to Joslire's arm, and stayed him.

"The officer cried out in his sleep." He stilled himself, obedient to Koscuisko's apparent desire. "Does the officer wish to talk about it, this dream?"

"Oh, I am sick to death." Koscuisko pushed himself upright suddenly, spurning Joslire's support as decisively as he had seemed to solicit it. "Sick of being so insulated, Joslire, and I swear to all Saints that if you say 'the officer' one more time within the next eight I will— not thank you for it."

Now that Koscuisko had sat up, there was no reason why Joslire should be sitting on his bed, or sitting at all. Or even in the cubicle, come to that. Rising quietly, Joslire made for the door, and Koscuisko—with his head in his hands—took no apparent notice of him. Joslire started the rhyti brewer as quickly as he could, one ear cocked for any sound from Koscuisko. Maybe Koscuisko would just go back to sleep. There was a message posted to the study-set screen: Tutor Chonis wanted to see Koscuisko for debriefing, but they had until next first-shift before the appointed time. The rhyti was ready, but how was he to offer it to his Student if Koscuisko did not want to hear from him? If he wasn't to call Koscuisko "the officer," and it was dangerous to call Koscuisko by his name, how could he hope to help Koscuisko talk out his pain?

Joslire carried a flask of rhyti to the open doorway, Koscuisko still sitting on the edge of his sleep-rack with his face in his hands. "It is not to be helped," Joslire said. "Sir. Would . . . you . . . like to talk about . . . your dream?"

Koscuisko looked up, and his eyes were dead and empty. "I dreamed that I killed a woman, Joslire." Seeing the glass of rhyti in Joslire's hand, Koscuisko beckoned him in with a wave of his hand. "I lost a patient twice, three times, in practicals. But it isn't the same. And I didn't just dream it."

Kneeling down to be able to see Koscuisko's face, Joslire reached for something he could say. He'd been through this with Students before, but never one like this. Koscuisko was more of an effort than any of them. Koscuisko was too honest with himself for his own good.

"It was well done, all the same." And not wanting to keep his Student at arm's length by observing the safe distance of accepted forms only made things more difficult. "A man takes care of his own work, finishes what he's started. Doesn't leave the cleaning up to other people."

It wasn't coming out right. He could hear the halt and start in his own voice. He didn't know how he could honor Koscuisko's expressed wish and keep peace with his governor at the same time. Surely Koscuisko understood that?

Koscuisko sighed and drank his glass of rhyti. Right down, Joslire noted with dismay; and it had been hot. Koscuisko didn't seem any the worse for it.

"Joslire, thou art good to me. And have been good to me this while. I will miss you." Handing the empty glass back, Koscuisko laid his hand at the back of Joslire's neck and had leaned forward to kiss him before Joslire knew quite what was happening. Only his discipline kept him in his place, surprised—startled—as he was; Koscuisko touched his other hand to the side of Joslire's face, briefly, and stood up. "I think that I should have a wash. What time is it, please? Time to eat, I hope?"

Joslire found his voice, albeit with difficulty. "Even so, it's mid-shift. Tutor Chonis will see—will conduct debriefing after fast-meal tomorrow; exercise could be taken if the officer please—that is, I—"

"Quite all right, Joslire, it is not your fault. Be easy." Koscuisko had reached the washroom and turned on the wet-shower. He wouldn't be able to hear a thing; but the monitors would hear, so Joslire did not speak his thought. *Perhaps I will go with you to* Scylla, *Student Koscuisko.*

Not because Koscuisko had caressed him; he could ask that of his fellows if he needed a kind touch so much as that. Bond-involuntaries took care of each other as best as they could, and didn't ask questions, and didn't let personal preferences or inclinations keep them from comforting each other. No, not just because Koscuisko had caressed him.

But because of the respect with which Koscuisko had killed his prisoner. Because of the gentle care Koscuisko had shown while she was dying, for all that he had shown none earlier.

Or perhaps only because he was Koscuisko, and he had the blood of a war-leader.

Joslire set Koscuisko's uniform out and put in a call for the Student's fast-meal.

Maybe he needed to speak to Tutor Chonis again.

"Robert, I'd like another three-vice, please. Good man."

The Eighth Level of the Question, and the second day. Robert St. Clare had never assisted at Inquiry before; this one was brutal.

"Come, now. I am determined that you are not telling me the truth. I can fairly promise you that things will only . . . get the worse for you . . . until you do . . ."

The strangled cries of the prisoner, the self-satisfied gloating in the officer's voice were equally difficult to bear. It had been bad yesterday, even once he'd gotten past his nervousness in Koscuisko's presence. Today was worse.

"Oh. For the love of God. Leave over. I don't know."

He had to concentrate on what the prisoner was saying in order to make out the words. He didn't want to be listening at all. The rest of the Security seemed capable of closing themselves down. How long would it take him to learn how to protect himself? The officer used him neither more nor less than the others; Koscuisko had not played favorites. St. Clare was grateful for that. What little he had been called upon to do had strained his self-discipline badly, but he knew better than to let even a hint of hesitation show in his responses to his officer.

"I don't. Believe. You," Koscuisko said, punctuating his mocking words with precise movements of the knife, nestling ever more deeply beneath a fingernail. Two days, and the prisoner could still speak and be understood. Two days, and Koscuisko could still evoke such sickening sounds of agony from the man who shuddered trembling on the floor in front of Koscuisko's chair.

Koscuisko had his prisoner's hand stretched across his knee, convenient to his knife, and the three-vices kept the fingers steady and immobilized at Koscuisko's pleasure. The officer had dealt more kindly with him, although the pain was troubling to remember. Koscuisko had not made him watch his own torture so deliberately as this.

"What . . . else is there to tell you? Ah, your Excellency? Please . . ."

Koscuisko toyed idly with the knife, and the blood ran fresh. Robert could smell it.

"Please, I've told you about my buyers. My suppliers. My contracts, everything . . ."

And so he had; St. Clare had heard him. Leaning forward, Koscuisko lifted the prisoner's head by the hair on his head and purred at him. "But not enough. I don't think you've said all the truth you know, and that offends me, do you understand?"

It seemed to St. Clare that the man's eyes rolled back in his head; and Koscuisko responded to the threat of loss of consciousness by taking his prisoner by the throat and shaking him savagely. "Pay attention, when it is that I am talking to you."

"Ah . . . there's Alden for the factory, and I told you about Foratre and even Kuylige, Glenafric services the school yards . . . what? What?"

"Tell me more about Glenafric," Koscuisko suggested, and transferred his attention to another fingernail. "The school yards, is it? A relative of yours, this Glenafric, I understand?"

"My brother, and damn him for his greed. He has contacts . . . the older children . . ."

They hadn't heard anything incriminating about this Glenafric person before, not that St. Clare could call to mind. He was sure he'd have remembered if they had. It would have helped him insulate himself from the fearful pity of what Koscuisko did to his prisoner had he known all along that there were children involved.

It was a gesture too horribly like stripping bark off of a switch, like paring the rind of a cheese away at the tail end of the wheel. It was a small movement of Koscuisko's hand, merely, but the prisoner choked with it. Fortunately for St. Clare, there was too much blood for him to be able to see anything but a confused sort of mass of flesh, like the leavings after fall slaughter before the scavenger birds came chortling in to feed. "Where would one find this Glenafric Whomever, I wonder?"

There was horrified denial in the prisoner's voice, now, even past all of his pain. "No, he's my brother . . . I didn't mean . . . a mistake, your Excellency, please . . ."

Koscuisko moved the knife against the prisoned hand, and the prisoner screamed. "Tsamug! Glenafric Tsamug! He keeps his stores in his grain bin—at home, at his home, you can find the stuff there."

A man could sell addictive drugs to children, and take whatever coin he pleased in the eager self-prostitution of flesh not even sexually mature. And still try to protect his brother, at the last.

"It is a shame that we lack medication," Koscuisko said sorrowfully, turning the dagger with delicate care. "You need to suffer much before your sin is healed. Oh, and I could help you, if we had but time."

Leaning back now, Koscuisko spurned his prisoner away from him with his foot and rose to his feet slowly like a drunken man, reaching out a hand to steady himself against Vely. "But we must be content with what we have, and trust the saints to take care of the rest. And therefore, Mister Haspir, if you would for me the gel-club find, I mean to make the best start that I can."

St. Clare was not quite sure of what Koscuisko was getting at, with his vague talk of sins to be healed. The rest of it made too much sense entirely.

"I do not like your choice of relations; such brothers as you have offend me deeply . . ."

How many years was he condemned to stand and help, in this?

St. Clare stood silent at attention-rest and tried to find some sanctuary deep within himself. Where he didn't have to see. Where he didn't have to hear. Where he didn't have to think about Koscuisko, at least not while Koscuisko was wearing the wrong pair of hands.

He'd made it this far, after all, he reminded himself. He could complete the exercise.

As long as he didn't have to think about it he would be all right.

⊕ ⊕ ⊕

Andrej stood with his back to the room, smoking his lefrol, waiting for the disposal team to take the body away. He was well finished; he'd been able to keep the prisoner going for rather longer than he had expected, and that measure of success gratified him. Did they save the most offensive prisoners for the last? Did they understand that it was easier to torture a man when one could honestly feel a certain degree of personal moral outrage, even though the ferocity of the punishment still could not be said to fit the crime?

Because when it came right down to the threshing of it, Andrej didn't care about political crimes. Treason was only against Jurisdiction, and the Combine, while forced to acknowledge Bench supremacy, simply didn't take Jurisdiction as seriously as the Jurisdiction was apt to take itself.

He could hear people behind him, probably the disposal team. Another moment or two and he would be ready to leave; Joslire would take him back to quarters. He was tired. It had been two days, two long days.

"Attention to the Administrator!"

Haspir's warning call took Andrej by surprise. Pivoting on his heel, with a lefrol in one hand, he stood to attention as well as he could. What could this mean? Administrator Clellelan, Tutor Chonis, Provost Marshall Journis. Joslire Curran, behind Tutor Chonis, and Joslire was carrying a driver—and a fresh pair of gloves, perhaps? Andrej made his bow, a sudden sense of dread dispelling the euphoria that the lefrol had created in his mind. Joslire carrying a driver, and St. Clare had been posted to his Security team for this exercise. St. Clare had done well, as far as Andrej could remember. But he was tired, tired and physically weary, how could they ask that he discipline St. Clare after the end of two days of an Eighth Level exercise?

Lora and Vely had cleared away the table, setting it against the back wall. Cay had brought a basin of water for him to wash his hands. It was a supportive gesture, but now Andrej was unsure whether he could get away with the apparent hesitation that it would entail. One thing was certain: He was not the only person here who thought he knew exactly what was going on. St. Clare was as white as an Iselbiss snowfall. Had everybody known? Everybody except for himself, and Robert St. Clare?

"Carry on, Student Koscuisko." The Administrator seated himself in Andrej's chair, Chonis and the Provost posting themselves behind him at either shoulder. "Take a moment, if you need it. What was it, Chonis? Six-and-sixty?"

Andrej held his panic to himself, firmly, and Tutor Chonis hastened to his rescue. "I have instructed Student Koscuisko that four-and-forty will be acceptable, if the Administrator please. A reasonable compromise, under the circumstances."

"Indeed? Very well, then. At your convenience, Student Koscuisko."

Cay and Haspir were on either side of St. Clare now, as if he had reverted to prisoner status—no surrogacy about it. Joslire had gone to stand by the table at the back, waiting for Andrej beside the basin of water. All right, he had time, and if he was to do this, he did want to wash his hands, because his hands were filthy with the prisoner's blood that had soaked through the gloves. He had noticed that with the Chigan, with the Cynergau, and it still surprised him. Blood and the sweat of his palms together made a slippery combination. He wanted to be quite sure about his control over the driver.

He was glad that Joslire had brought another whip; the one he had been using for his practices, perhaps? The one he had been using on his prisoner was wet, and would fall with that much more brutal a stroke accordingly. As if any touch of that black braided thing could be called less than brutal . . . but he was going to concentrate. And he was going to concentrate with all deliberate speed. The longer he made St. Clare wait, the more St. Clare would suffer in the waiting.

He washed his hands and he dried his hands, but he didn't want the gloves that Joslire had brought for him. Not quite yet. Andrej went to the front of the room and beckoned for St. Clare. The two Security made no move to compel him, though he did hesitate for a moment; and Andrej was grateful for the respect that they were showing for St. Clare.

"It will be necessary for you to remove your blouse. And your under-blouse as well, Robert." He couldn't read the expression in Robert's eyes. He didn't know St. Clare's face well enough to guess whether it was hatred and resentment, loathing, disgust—or merely fear, and resignation. He had not seen St. Clare above twelve times all told, and St. Clare had been unconscious during at least six of them. But he had yet to see an expression of hatred on St. Clare's face. Fear was quite natural; but resignation—resignation, without any hostility directed at the man who was to punish him cruelly for a fault that was not his own—seemed clearly too great a charity for Andrej to hope for.

Stripped to the waist, St. Clare waited for instruction. Andrej would have liked to have assured himself that a medical team had been called up, to be ready. He did not dare to press the issue, however, for fear that the Administrator or the Provost might speak against it. Better to wait till he could speak with Tutor Chonis alone.

Andrej gestured toward the front wall. St. Clare bowed to him, formally, and turned toward the wall, posting himself precisely at arm's length from the wall and directly in front of where the Administrator sat. Andrej knew the range, he had been practicing; and yet—as determined as he'd been to be prepared—there was an important point he had forgotten. Something he hadn't ever thought to discuss with Joslire. There was no help for it now. He was going to have to simply ask, witnesses or none.

St. Clare stood at attention-wait facing the wall, his head straight and steady on his broad shoulders. Reaching up, Andrej set his hand to the back of Robert's neck in the traditional gesture of intimacy between master and man.

"Would you be bound, Mister St. Clare? Or not?"

St. Clare was surprised to be given the option; Andrej could feel it in the sudden tension of the muscles beneath his hand. But he did need to know.

"I know better than anyone how well you can stand to it, but it will be difficult for you either way. It shall be your choice." What would shame Robert least? To be chained at the wall, like an unreasoning animal? Or not to be chained, and suffer the shame of having to be restrained by his fellows if he so much as flinched away from the whip-stroke?

Robert coughed, as if to clear his throat. "Let there be no reproach brought against the officer's discipline," he replied firmly. And raised his hands, stretching his arms out to where the shackles hung against the wall waiting for him and hungry for his pain.

Truly, truly Robert was of good heart. It would make it easier for Andrej that St. Clare had consented to be constrained. It almost seemed to him that the gesture had been made for his benefit, a surrender of pride to help put the exercise forward.

"Gentlemen," Andrej suggested grimly. Haspir and Cay came

forward to close the manacles and latch them at St. Clare's wrists. It gave him an extra moment to examine the still-too-newly healed expanse of St. Clare's back one final time, to see where the skin was thinnest, to find any residual bruising or tenderness. He had already studied up on Nurail. He'd spent a good half-shift poring over the nerve map for the Nurail body, to learn to his satisfaction where it was that he could strike the hardest blows and have them hurt the least.

Taking the gloves from Joslire finally, he pulled them on, smoothing the palms carefully before he took the whip. He was as ready as ever he would be.

"Who is to count, Joslire?" he asked. Tutor Chonis answered in Joslire's stead.

"The Provost Marshall represents Station Security. The official count will be hers. You may proceed, Student Koscuisko."

Wasn't it unusual, to have so much rank at such discipline? Or was it in token of the unusual circumstances that had got them here, he and St. Clare together?

Andrej paced his ground, and flexed the uncoiled driver to work any unseen kinks out of its braiding. "Stand clear, gentlemen," he called, as much to warn St. Clare as to move the others away. Enough time to know that it would be coming, now. Not enough time to suffer the impact before it hit, in apprehension; St. Clare was to suffer enough from the whip's lash itself without being forced to fear and suffer both.

Letting the leader out, he swung a long slow stroke for the left side of Robert's upper back, and knew by sound alone that he had bruised deeply enough for blood to flow.

"One," the Provost said.

He had to find a rhythm, he had to take a regular count early and consistently. Five was too long. Two was not long enough. Three would give him time to contain the stroke, to control the stroke, ensure that it would bite deeply enough to be counted.

"Two."

Start at the upper part of the back, work down. Leave enough space to show each single welt, to make it clear that every stroke should be counted as good. He had not taken the width of the welt into account. The spacing was going to be difficult.

"Three."

And above all he had to be sure that he would hit hard enough, be sure that four-and-forty would not compound to five-and-fifty or worse just because he was desperately reluctant to hurt Robert St. Clare.

"Four."

He found his pace and held it grimly as the whip cut a series of increasingly blurred and bloody lines down one side of St. Clare's naked back. He was not going to be able to go twenty on a side; the welt was too wide for that. And he had to bring one in every eight in at the lower part of the shoulders, just to one side of Robert's spine so that the snapper-end could do its dreadful damage—what had the Tutor said? Provide its taste of "real" punishment—where there were the least number of pain receptors to register a protest.

"Seven."

He laid the eighth stroke in straight and solid, and Robert's body rocked against the impact of the pain. It would be hard. And it was only starting.

"Eight."

It was going to be important to maintain a balance if he was to deal honestly with St. Clare. Pain messages gathered from two directions at once could overload the tolerance of the spinal transmitters, so that two blows would cause Robert to suffer torment equivalent to one and one-half. If he managed really well there was a chance that he could achieve a kind of interference that would cancel out some of Robert's pain before it had quite come to Robert's attention.

"Thirteen."

He could hear St. Clare's breathing, now, shaky and strained—but only breathing, still. He set the snapper to mark the second eight, and heard a sound as Robert's body jerked against his chains with the shock of it. One in eight, Tutor Chonis had told him. One in eight, and for four-and-forty that meant that he dare not stop at five of them.

"Twenty."

At least he had not lost a single stroke, so far. Oh, almost halfway through, he had won fair count from the Provost so far.

"Twenty-two."

Half over, halfway done. It was becoming more and more difficult to find a place to strike that was not already compromised with blood. He had been very careful, he knew that he had been, but he could not see well enough at this distance to judge the interval between two strokes—not as well as he would wish. It was different when it was a prisoner; it had been different when St. Clare had been his prisoner, come to that. Then it hadn't mattered if the strokes overlapped each other. Andrej took the driver in his other hand, frowning in his concentration, trying to ignore the sweat that was running down his forehead, into his eyes.

"Thirty-one. Put your back into it, Koscuisko."

St. Clare had begun to collapse against the wall, not standing so much anymore as hanging by his wrists. Andrej could not afford to permit himself to hear that St. Clare cried when he was struck. He had been warned. He would not make St. Clare suffer a single extra stroke. He would not.

"Thirty-two." The snapper, and St. Clare caught his breath too loudly and too sharply for it to be interpreted as labored breathing. But close to finished, close, and the Provost was pleased with his effort; she had not disallowed the previous blow—

"Thirty-three. That's more like it. Don't lose your timing, now."

He was at a loss as to where he might strike next, and eleven yet to get past. He would have to do the best that he could, and never mind the placement now. At least St. Clare, adrift within a greater sea of torment, seemed no longer conscious of the blows as separate shocks.

"Forty."

A little too far toward the shoulder blade; his aim was beginning to fail him. It was difficult to see as well as he would like for the sweat in his eyes. He'd spaced the whip-strokes a little generously when he'd begun, perhaps he could fit another four in between them without the added cruelty of striking over an already-burning welt.

"Forty," Marshall Journis repeated.

Oh, this was terrible, this was the worst of what he had feared. Would she keep him to the bitter test of blood, so close now to the end? He could not protest, Tutor Chonis had warned him. Her count could not be challenged. When he was with Fleet, he would count his own stroke; but here he had no choice but to accept her count as true, and carry on. *Oh, I am trying, Robert,* he protested in his mind. *I am sorry, it is the best I can . . .*

"Forty-one. No, I misspoke myself, that last was forty-one, wasn't it? Forty-two."

He dared not feel any gratitude toward her, in case it was some kind of an obscure joke on her part. He dared not stop to think until the word was given, and the exercise complete.

"Forty-three."

One last time with the snapper, and it lit at Robert's shoulder and took an ugly bite above the other bleeding wounds on Robert's back. Too high, too high, he was not doing well, it would hurt too much—Robert would hurt, and any such hurt could only be too much—

"Four-and-forty. Student Koscuisko, you may stand away, if you wish."

Oh, it was over, it was finished. It was done. Andrej put the back of his hand up to his face with the driver still clutched firmly in his desperate grip, and tried to clear his eyes of salt and sweat. Someone made as if to take the driver from him; he thought he recognized Joslire's familiar warmth, and tried to loose his cramped fist to drop the damned thing, without success.

"Here, wipe your face," the Provost Marshall said, holding out a white-square in front of him. "Next time you'll want a towel close at hand. Anyone would think you had been crying."

Andrej reached out stupidly for the white-square, and the driver dropped to the floor as he opened his hand to grasp the linen cloth. Would they think that? What difference did it make what anyone thought? Now that he could see, he realized that Tutor Chonis and the Administrator had gone to see St. Clare where he hung chained against the wall. They seemed to be examining Andrej's handiwork, as if there was some further test to be made of him and St. Clare alike, even beyond the punishment that St. Clare had endured. Andrej pulled off his gloves and wiped his face a second time. He could not afford to fail to pay attention—not even though it ate at him to see St. Clare still prisoned on the wall. And he had set St. Clare to hang from the hook in chains during the Fourth Level, and he had thoroughly enjoyed tormenting him then. Why was this different?

Administrator Clellelan had turned from the wall, coming toward Andrej where he stood with Marshall Journis. What was he going to do with her white-square? Andrej wondered, in a sudden panic. She certainly wasn't going to want it back, not soiled as it was. He stood to polite attention and made his best salute, staggering only slightly as he straightened up.

"An . . . impressive . . . demonstration, as I'm sure we all agree." He couldn't tell from the Administrator's tone whether that was supposed to be a good thing or a bad one. He could only stand and wait, mute and desperate, for Chonis to give the word.

"Emphatically. An apt pupil, your Koscuisko," the Provost Marshall replied. "It was his speak-serum we were evaluating the other day, wasn't it?"

How could they stand and speak so casually with each other while a man was bound in agony behind their backs? Why wouldn't they just go away, and let him call for medical support?

"His speak-serum, his troop," Chonis answered for the Administrator, and Chonis's voice was affectionate and indulgent at once. Andrej blushed, but he wasn't certain why. "I take it that we can call the matter closed, with the Administrator's approval. As long as the Provost Marshall is satisfied."

She nodded. "Well and truly. And I'd go ahead and call a medical team, if it was me. Your troop stood up to that like an honest man. He's earned a few days' rest."

Yes, call a medical team, they had to call a medical team. He had used Robert as brutally as he had just so that they would permit medical support. Nobody had asked him. He could say nothing.

"Very well," the Administrator said. "We'll leave you to finish up here, Student Koscuisko. Now if you'll excuse me, Tutor Chonis, there's other business that requires my attention. Well done, all around."

Andrej kept his position as the Administrator left, the Provost following after. He still had her white-square—he'd think about it later. Tucking the crumpled cloth into his over-blouse placket, he waited as best he could for word from Tutor Chonis.

"Andrej, that was beautiful." What? The punishment? Or his pathetic attempts to minimize it? "Marshall Journis has cleared you to call for medical support, I think she was impressed. Take a day to recover, and I'll see you after mid-shift tomorrow."

A day for him to recover, surely. Surely the Tutor did not expect St. Clare to return to duty so soon as that. Marshall Journis had said "a few days." He'd heard her. "But . . . with respect, Tutor Chonis . . ."

The Tutor had turned to go out, and looked a little startled at Andrej's attempt to speak. Good little Students spoke only when spoken to . . . but there was no help for it. Andrej could not afford to let mere protocol stand in the way of painease for St. Clare's suffering.

"Yes, Andrej? There is something?"

"The medical team, please, Tutor Chonis. I do not know if I have the authority."

Understanding met with confusion in the Tutor's face. If Andrej had been any less anxious—he realized—it might have looked funny. "Ah. Well said, I'm not sure, either. Very well." The medical call was there, beside the door. Andrej knew where it was, just not whether they would listen to a Student. "Infirmary, this is Tutor Chonis, I want a medical team with a litter to Exercise Theater Second-down-five-over. And a bed for . . ."

Chonis raised his eyebrows at Andrej, and Andrej held up his fingers, not hoping that the Tutor would grant him all that he wished but unwilling to ask for less than he would want. The Tutor frowned, and went back to his communication.

"A bed for four days. The Provost Marshall has authorized full supportive medication at Student Koscuisko's discretion. Chonis, away."

It had been five days before St. Clare had been ready for therapy after the prisoner-surrogate exercise, and he had been more badly hurt, as well as worse injured. It had been fond of him to hope for so much as five days now. Four days was something to be grateful for; and Andrej bowed to his Tutor, wanting him to leave—so that he could go to St. Clare.

"Good night, Andrej."

And Chonis knew it, too, to listen to him. The door slid shut behind the Tutor's back. Andrej shook himself out of his tense formality, hurrying to the wall.

"Haspir, name of the Mother, unfasten these. Lora, Vely, help him down away from there, try not to hurt him, if you can help it."

He shouldn't be making such demands of these Security. Surely it went without saying that they didn't want to hurt St. Clare any more than he wanted St. Clare to be hurt, and it was very good of them not to show any sign of resenting his stupidity in saying such ridiculous things. They knew what they were doing far better than he could hope to. Each with one of Robert's arms around their shoulders, they backed St. Clare carefully away from the wall, and Andrej was horrified to see from the stumbling of St. Clare's feet that he was still conscious. This was terrible. He should not be awake to be suffering this pain . . .

Here was the litter at the door, and Joslire let it through to the middle of the room so that the Security could maneuver St. Clare into position to lie down on his back in the stasis field. There seemed to be good deal of blood, and white torn flesh; and blood on St. Clare's mouth as well where he had bitten into his lip. The medical team with the litter performed emergency stabilize, charging the support fields, starting a patch for fluid replacement and for pain reduction. Andrej leaned over the head of the litter, blotting the sweat of pain from St. Clare's face with the white-square; and St. Clare opened his eyes.

"Is't done, is it?"

His gaze was frank and fearless, even past his pain, without a trace of hatred or resentment. What pain and apprehension Andrej could see there did not seem to be directed at him personally.

"Yes, Robert, it's done, it's all over. We'll go to Infirmary, now."

His eyes were closing again, under the influence—Andrej guessed—of whatever painkillers the medical team had chosen to patch through. Robert blinked them open with a frown of concentration. "Again? Boring. Bad habit to get into. Really finished?"

There was a sudden note of anxiety in St. Clare's voice that filled Andrej with great trouble of spirit. "Yes, I promise you."

"Gi's kiss, then."

What?

"I'm sorry, Robert, I didn't quite catch that. What did you say?"

The medical team had finished their preparations and were standing away from the litter. Waiting for him, obviously.

St. Clare explained himself patiently, and there was a subtle undertone of pleading there as well, now. "When's over Uncle gi's tha'a kiss. Gi's kiss, Uncle, if's over."

Andrej could not bear that St. Clare should plead with him. He stooped to kiss St. Clare's bitten mouth, hastily, eager to provide what measure of psychological comfort he could.

St. Clare sighed, turning his head away with now-closed eyes, and fell silent. Surrendering his consciousness at last, Andrej supposed.

"Let's go."

The orderlies would drive the litter, and he didn't mind following since he didn't know the way. He'd see to St. Clare's new wounds and check the pain medication levels, and then he and Joslire could both go to bed—since Joslire wouldn't go to bed before him.

Was he too tired to beware of his dreams?

What did he care?

Robert's ordeal was over. Robert was safe.

That was all that was important to Andrej.

Andrej knew the spicy scent of the wood in the dark, hot room in his dream; knew the feel of the slatted bench beneath him, worn soft and smooth by the bare buttocks of generations of his family before him. He was at home, in the sauna at the hunting lodge that belonged to his Matredonat estate; so it was probably late winter, when they still set a watch to guard the early young from the wolves that came down from the mountains. If it was late winter, they'd be getting at the last of the apples—he liked them better, even winter-old, than the fresh fruit that hospitality demanded the kitchen set to table at Rogubarachno. The last of the apples, the first bitter greens, and the milk just starting to fatten with the year . . .

He stretched himself in the heat, the room so dim that he could only just discern the motto carved on the facing wall above the firebox. *Blessed St. Andrej, intercede for us, who have offended . . .* The familiar phrase irritated him. Patron saint of filial piety. But Andrej had offended, and the saint would not intercede for a man who would not repent. What difference did it make? It was only a carving on the wall. It could have nothing to do with him. The Matredonat was his own property. His father would not come here without an invitation, nor his Uncle Radu either.

Andrej heard Joslire at the door and surrendered to the distraction gladly. Joslire's five-knives . . . He beckoned to Joslire to come closer so that he could look at the five-knives. He hadn't taken adequate advantage of the opportunity he'd had earlier, as he remembered. Joslire bowed grave and submissive before him, and Andrej could not see his face; but it was the knives that beguiled him—the knives, and their sheathing. It looked so random and unbalanced to him. There didn't seem to be a single line connecting any of the straps that he could see crisscrossing his Emandisan's bare chest.

Frowning, Andrej rose to his feet to be able to look more closely.

Joslire did not stand still, though, not even when Andrej put his hand out to stay him. Joslire knelt down on the slatted bench and bent his neck, his face turned to the floor. Very peculiar. Andrej reached out to touch one of the straps to try to follow how the harness worked, but met no strap at all—only warm flesh. Bruised flesh, hot with insult and with inflammation, swollen and bloody—not straps at all, not harness. The whiplash witness, the weals and welts of a stern beating. Who had done this thing to Joslire? And yet his hand did not recoil in horror. He pressed his fingers hard against the swollen stripe instead, and when Joslire swallowed back a reluctant cry of pain he only pressed again, at the same spot, and harder.

He was the one who had done this shameful thing. He had tormented this defenseless man, and enjoyed it. He was enjoying it now. Perhaps it wasn't Joslire, now that he thought about it. Perhaps it was another, and if it was—if it was another, he had more than simply beaten him, he had more than just enjoyed it . . .

The horror came upon him from behind, catching him unawares and unprepared. No, not Joslire at all, another man. Another man, with wounded hands as shapeless and pulpy as overripe fruit shining white and red even in the dim light of the sauna. An animated corpse, too animated, its spirit crying out to be relieved of torment, trapped within a mutilated frame.

He had to kill it so that it could rest. There was nothing else he could do for the grotesque thing. He had to take it by the throat and strangle it since he had no other means to set it free; but he couldn't bear to touch it. He retreated from the horror instead, unable to stand his ground. It came after him, it followed him, begging him with its terrible hands to kill it as he had done before. There was nowhere for him to go. It was a small room, and the mangled corpse of the murdered drug dealer crawled up to him with garbled incoherent pleas and touched him with its hands—

The light went on in the outer room, and Andrej was awake at once. It was hot because he had been drinking wodac, and wodac heated the blood. He could not move because he had tangled himself too thoroughly in the rack-wrap that served under Jurisdiction for bedclothes. And it hadn't been the restless corpse of a murdered man whose unformed and insane sounds had so horrified him, it'd been his own noise, his own cries that had awakened him. Or at least awakened

Joslire, and Joslire had awakened him—on purpose, no doubt, since Joslire was quiet and stealthy enough on other occasions.

Andrej sat up, pushing the rack-wrap away from him. He needed something to drink, he was thirsty. But he was afraid to go out into the next room for fear he would discover that he'd beaten Joslire after all, as he had whipped his poor Robert St. Clare. True, there was no reason he could think of for having beaten Joslire, but there hadn't really been any reason to beat St. Clare, had there been? Except—of course—that it had been required of him.

And that was no good reason, and less consolation.

Andrej looked at the sleep-timer next to the head of the sleep-rack; hours yet till fast-meal, more hours on top of that before he was to go see Tutor Chonis. He didn't want to rob Curran of rest-time. But he did want something to drink—something without alcohol—and there was only one way to get it in this place.

"I should like some rhyti, if you will, Joslire."

His voice was stronger than he had expected it to be, steady and confident. No trace of a dream there. They would both safely pretend, the two of them, that Joslire had heard him from the other side of the room, that Joslire had not been standing just on the other side of the privacy partition, trying to decide whether he should intervene. Some rhyti, a screen or two of text, and then perhaps he would be able to go back to sleep.

But, oh, he hoped to all Saints and the Holy Mother that he had not beaten Joslire . . .

CHAPTER FOURTEEN

Tutor Chonis was reviewing the record of his interview with First Secretary Verlaine when the signal came at his office door.

"Student Koscuisko respectfully reports, at the Tutor's direction."

Cutting the cube off hastily, Chonis pulled it from the viewer. That had been several days ago. He hadn't wanted to distract Koscuisko with this business going in to the Eighth Level. It had to be discussed with the Student sooner or later, though. If the Administrator was going to ask Koscuisko to finish and leave the Station, Koscuisko deserved to be told why.

"Step through." And Koscuisko was in good time, as well. Koscuisko was punctual, when not distracted by Curran's seductive knives. He didn't look quite rested to Chonis; more dreams, then, as after his Seventh Level? He'd have Curran's report, of course. But perhaps Koscuisko had simply been exhausted, dreams or none.

"I hope the day finds you well, Tutor Chonis," Koscuisko bowed with that gratifyingly sincere politeness that had characterized his behavior since St. Clare had been released to him. Koscuisko had dealt honestly with them, and kept to his bargain with punctilious care—even though he'd had the worse end of it. The least that they could do in return was to deal honestly with Koscuisko, since his value bode fair to overbalance the value Koscuisko had received in the person of Robert St. Clare by so significant a margin.

"Yes, thank you, Andrej. Please be seated. Rhyti?"

An Eighth Level exercise drawn out for two full days, with no evasions either, and no compounding of the Protocols, and extra information—once again—that hadn't been expected when the Bench referred the prisoner. Koscuisko was welcome to do whatever he liked with the Protocols as long as he could keep on pulling information out of the aether in that unnerving manner of his. Any other Inquisitor's prisoner would have been useless and unresponsive by the middle of the second day of an Eighth Level.

Koscuisko sat in his place with his rhyti, waiting in polite silence.

"Student Koscuisko. Andrej. You did very well with your last exercise. The Administrator is very pleased." Standard phrases, and Koscuisko had heard it before and would be wondering why it mattered. "It's important that you know that, because we've got to change your schedule around a bit, and we certainly don't want to give you the idea that it's a result of some deficiency on your part." No deficiency, no. That wasn't the problem at all. "How are you doing in laboratory?"

He could tell it wasn't adding up from the confusion evident in Koscuisko's face. "I had been working on a Ninth Level instrument for Student Noycannir, Tutor Chonis. A generalized wake-keeper, since that seems to me to be her weakest area."

And he had a point, there, but Chonis wasn't interested in talking about Noycannir. Or not about her performance. "We want you to prepare for your Ninth Level exercise, Andrej, and we want you to take it in two days' time, if you feel that you can manage. Waiving your lab work if you need to."

Koscuisko's confusion was clearly only deepening as the conversation progressed. "I . . . can be ready, Tutor Chonis, if that is what you require. But surely the scheduled review itself will absorb two days. What about Noycannir?"

Time to come clean about things, perhaps. "Mentioned you to her Patron, she did. When we reviewed her Intermediate Levels with Secretary Verlaine. Verlaine wants to know why you shouldn't be placed somewhere you can be completely dedicated to Controlled List, maybe a little Inquisition on the side. Noycannir seems to have interested him in your talents in that area."

Koscuisko's first reaction was amusement, pure and uncomplicated. "What, posted to the Bench?" But realization of the implications followed swift and sobering, as Chonis had been confident they would. "But I would not have Infirmary to run, not within Courts. All the First Secretary can want is that I Inquire for him, or help Noycannir to."

That was the way Tutor Chonis saw it, and Clellelan as well. "That would seem to be the idea. To be fair to him, Verlaine hasn't had a chance to talk to you and find out what your preferences might be. Verlaine's asked for Noycannir's tapes, and we think he wants to see how well your drugs work. We rather expect him to preempt you to the Bench in support of Noycannir's Writ."

That was unquestionably what Noycannir wanted her "Patron" to do. Koscuisko was as pale as dread could make him. "I promised to Fleet, Tutor Chonis, not to the Bench, and for St. Clare. If I had a choice in the matter . . ."

No one had suggested that he had, of course. Other than indirectly, by raising the issue with him in the first place.

"Yes?"

"I would rather go to Fleet. Sir. At least I may practice my other craft on Line."

Consonant with Ligrose's prejudice, Koscuisko did not want to lose the opportunity that Fleet would provide him to function as a physician. Ligrose wanted him restricted to his healing skills; Verlaine would be interested only in Koscuisko's talent for Inquiry and the Controlled List. For Koscuisko himself, a balance was clearly desirable. If Koscuisko had to Inquire at all, Koscuisko preferred to restrict that practice to a portion of his job, not its entirety.

No matter how good he was getting at it.

"As Fleet support staff, we have an interest in preserving Fleet resources. Competent Ship's Surgeons are getting hard to come by." Koscuisko surely was aware of that, but might not have had time to apply the fact to his own situation. "Administrator Clellelan does not feel that it would be in Fleet's best interest to surrender you to a direct Bench support role."

Koscuisko was beginning to understand. "I may go to *Scylla,* as I had expected?"

"We intend that you should."

Relief was evident, on Koscuisko's face. Relief, and concern, harking back to the beginning of this conversation. "What must I do?"

"Take your Ninth Level in two days from now, Andrej. We can have your Tenth Level scheduled for a few days after completion. Transportation will be available to us within ten days, and the sooner we can get you off-Station the happier we are going to be."

Tipping his rhyti glass on its base, staring into the coppery dregs, Koscuisko thought ahead. "Once I am transferred to *Scylla* it becomes more difficult for the Bench to interfere?"

Basically speaking. "We'll take what you have for Noycannir's Ninth Level, and we'll just have to use something else for her Tenth Level. Curran will be instructed, you may cut back in your physical exercise if you need the preparation time." And the recovery time. Not even in the field were Inquisitors expected to take two Advanced Level interrogations inside of a single week and remain capable of returning to duty for a Tenth Level scant days later. For one thing it was hard work, unless one let Security do the labor—and Koscuisko did not seem inclined to pass the labor on to Security. For another, two days spent in close company with another soul in agony tended to take a certain amount of energy out of a person, regardless of any other feelings one might have in the matter. "Do you have any questions?"

It was Koscuisko's dismissal notice, and Koscuisko set the rhyti glass down and pushed himself away from the table to stand up. "I will be sorry to miss exercise," he said—and he did sound wistful, to Tutor Chonis. "I was really beginning to feel as if I could learn throwing knives, with Joslire to teach me."

Not to worry.

"Do what you must, Student Koscuisko. We have two days, to prepare you for your Ninth Level."

The odds were good that he would be able to continue his practice unmolested, once he reached *Scylla.*

But it was Curran's place to tell Koscuisko so, and Tutor Chonis was just as glad to respect Curran's right in that.

Robert St. Clare sat on the examining levels, slumping a bit. Andrej peeled the synth-skin away from St. Clare's injured back, knowing from Robert's grunt of pain how tender it still was. Healing was not as quick as Andrej would have liked; the other beating had been too recent.

"What was that you were saying to me the other day?"

He could distract St. Clare, perhaps. Changing the dressing would not take long, and he intended to send Robert back to his bed no matter how he complained of being bored. St. Clare would have excitement to distract him soon enough, after all—perhaps eight days from now, if all went according to Tutor Chonis's schedule.

"Saying to the officer? With the officer's permission—what is the officer talking about?"

Down for a day, dressings changed once, it had been two days now since his scourging. Maybe St. Clare didn't remember. He had been a little incoherent at the time.

"When the Administrator and his party had left, and you had been loaded into the litter. You called me Uncle. You don't look a bit like any of my nespans." For one thing, none of his nieces or his nephews were anything close to St. Clare's height, partly because they were all children.

"Did I say that?" St. Clare sounded a little uncomfortable. Not to mention much more direct than any other of the bond-involuntaries Andrej had had contact with. He hadn't learned to be afraid of frank language yet; either that, or something was wrong with St. Clare's governor, as Joslire had suggested. As long as it didn't get Robert into trouble, Andrej didn't care. It wasn't about to get Robert into trouble with him, after all. "It's your nuncle that's to scold you, if the officer please. Father might strike too hard, when's angry. Mother might not strike as hard as called for, when's fond. Mother's brother it is to take a switch to those as needs it. Sir. "

The fresh layer of synth-skin was all smoothed down, now. St. Clare should not be feeling further discomfort. He would scar where the snapper had bitten into his flesh, but it would not be too bad. Perhaps he'd have St. Clare into surgery and excise the scarring, once they were safely away from here. "And when you've been well and truly spoken to, there's a kiss to end the quarrel, is that it?"

In properly run Aznir households, it was the instrument of correction that was kissed rather than the administrator of discipline. Andrej's father—the Koscuisko prince—hadn't believed in corporal punishment, though.

St. Clare was blushing; Andrej could see it in his neck, even from behind. "As the officer states. Permission to ask the officer exactly how big a fool this troop made of himself. Sir."

There was no reason to be embarrassed, surely? "As well as I remember it, Robert, you explained much the same thing to me. You were not very coherent, at the time. All right, you may resume your sleep-shirt, I am finished. How do you feel?"

St. Clare stood up, carefully pulling his sleep-shirt up over his shoulders as he did so. "A little stiff, if the officer please. No offense was meant, with the officer's permission."

"Nor was any taken. Rely upon it." Tutor Chonis had granted four days' bed-rest to St. Clare; Andrej meant to make the most of it. "Go to bed, if you please, St. Clare. Your orders are to sleep and become healed, and I will see you next-shift, all right?"

"According to the officer's good pleasure." St. Clare bowed. He looked a bit ridiculous, to Andrej, to be saluting in his sleep-shirt, but he supposed Robert felt it was required.

It was good, to talk to Robert. Andrej enjoyed his company.

And he was going to miss Joslire Curran.

It was the third part of the third day of Koscuisko's Ninth Level, and Joslire didn't think his Student was going to gain the victory this time. He'd fulfilled the Protocols adequately enough—any Ninth Level that could be successfully continued to the third day would do that, and it was coming up on Koscuisko's sleep shift. Koscuisko did not seem inclined to give up on his prisoner, though the man hadn't said anything new for the past day and a half. Clearly Koscuisko felt there was something more to tell. Because when Koscuisko believed that he was finished, Koscuisko ended his exercises cleanly, with a kill.

Lop Hanbor wasn't here for this one; Student Noycannir was not scheduled to start her Ninth Level until tomorrow, as Koscuisko had originally been supposed to. Joslire was alone with the Tutor. It was a perfect opportunity to make his claim—if he could get the Tutor's attention.

Chonis wasn't saying much, watching the screen intently with his fingers templed in front of him. Security was lifting the prisoner up to lay him on his back on the table. A big man, the prisoner; he didn't quite fit on the table. But it wasn't as if the prisoner was going to move. Or at least not enough to cause a problem.

Koscuisko asked for the firepoint, and laid it gently down against the man's upper arm, as if considering. The firepoint was just that, only a fiery coal of torment, and not a heated rod; maybe Koscuisko felt it was as drastic a measure as he could afford to take at this late stage and still maintain his prisoner's consciousness.

"With respect, Tutor Chonis."

Drastic it was, however. Too much pain, after so long, and Koscuisko could lose his prisoner to heart failure, since only the most primitive resuscitation methods were permitted in Orientation exercises. Joslire knew that he might not have much time, especially not now, since they'd moved his Student's Tenth Level so close upon this one.

For a moment he wondered if the Tutor was going to make things difficult for him by pretending not to hear or declining to listen. But no, Chonis had just been distracted.

"Yes, Curran?"

Koscuisko had a light touch with the firepoint, as delicate as the knife-work he'd displayed during his Eighth Level. And Koscuisko's prisoner hadn't had quite so much to say about Koscuisko's antecedents, morality, and proper fate for hours now.

"In regards to Student Koscuisko, Tutor Chonis. St. Clare hasn't had much experience in handling officers' reactions to their work."

It wasn't to formula, no, but Chonis would understand.

The Tutor sat motionless for a moment, then reached out and turned the sound channel down. So that he wouldn't need to raise his voice to be heard above the screaming, Joslire supposed.

"What is in your mind?"

The Tutor sounded a little wary, but not surprised. Maybe he should have expected Chonis to have guessed.

"There are only three years remaining in my Fleet deferment, Tutor Chonis. Student Koscuisko seems unusually promising an officer."

As an Inquisitor as well, but that was only part of the point. It was difficult to find words that expressed how Joslire felt about seeing Koscuisko's performance in theater. The better Koscuisko got at his torturer's craft, the more difficult it got.

Chonis was not talking. Waiting for him to finish, maybe, letting him have all the time that he needed to get the whole issue out.

"In short, with the Tutor's permission. Mean to ask Student Koscuisko to permit this troop to accompany him during his tour of duty."

Chonis sighed, and stood up. "Now, Curran, let's think about this for a moment. You paid in blood for your deferment, you earned it, no one can take it away from you. Three years is three years."

And in all those years, the odds of turning up another officer like Koscuisko were not worth betting on. At least it hadn't happened within the past five. "Even so, Tutor Chonis." Other Students had been easier to see to. And other Students had almost invariably tested their newly granted authority against him. "Is there an impediment?"

If the Student for whom Joslire had performed as prisoner-surrogate was still on active status, Fleet would not release him from the Orientation Station. That was the real reason behind the grant of Fleet deferment. If the officer who had been Student Abermay encountered Joslire Curran as a bond-involuntary troop, not as a prisoner, it was just possible that Abermay would recognize him, and the secret would be out.

"Abermay is still on active status." Bad news, then. But Chonis was still talking, and hadn't said no, yet. If Chonis knew that right off, did it mean that Chonis had checked it out already? Was he really that obvious, even if only to the Tutor? "But he's recently asked for reassignment to prison duty from the Lanes. Needs a break from the stress of the Sanfort campaigns."

Joslire could certainly understand how that could be, although prison duty wasn't generally taken for recreation. Abermay was obviously desperate to get away. And if Abermay was on prison duty, he was not on Line anywhere in the Lanes; Joslire could safely be released to Koscuisko. "Then the officer can be approached, with the Tutor's permission."

Chonis nodded, his reluctance evident. "The Administrator will send you to *Scylla* if Koscuisko's willing to take you, Curran. I'm afraid you could have a problem with that part of it, though."

True. He wasn't confident at all that Koscuisko would agree, or that Koscuisko even cared one way or the other. The change in status involved a significant degree of risk, and Koscuisko might object to that; but he'd answer to Koscuisko when the time came. Right now all he had needed was the Tutor's unwilling assurance that the Administration would release him to Koscuisko, if Koscuisko was willing to accept his Bond.

"Heard and understood, Tutor Chonis. Thank you, sir."

There wasn't anything more to be discussed.

Chonis sat back down and pulled the sound levels up again; Joslire held his place, silent and steady, turning the problem over in his mind. He didn't have to ask. He could decide to let Koscuisko go alone. With only untried Security for company? He wasn't committed, not yet, not absolutely, though he had given his knives over. He wouldn't be committed absolutely until he asked Koscuisko; and he wasn't quite sure when that was going to happen. Only that it had to happen soon, because Koscuisko would be going within days.

In the exercise theater things had quieted down to a soft and understandably self-pitying whimper on the prisoner's part. Koscuisko held the upper part of the prisoner's mutilated body in his arms, stroking the raw weals and the new burns with tender care; completely absorbed in listening to his prisoner's pain by the look of him. But what was Koscuisko saying?

"Come now, my dear. You can't sell weaponry of that sort without munitions to go along. Answer me truly, what kind of a fool would think such a thing?"

Chonis raised the levels up another few eighths. The end of the third day, on an unsupported Ninth Level, no wake-keepers, no drugs—and Koscuisko could still carry on it conversation.

"N-no. Y'rex'lency. It's true."

"Then you do have a source for munitions. You've been protecting someone, haven't you?"

"No, don't ask." Slurred and indistinct as the prisoner's voice was, Joslire could still make out his words. He'd listened to too much of this. He'd gotten good at making out the words.

"You've been protecting someone, I say." Koscuisko's caress grew more cruel, touching on more grievous hurts. "Tell me."

"I won't—"

Koscuisko set the firepoint against the prisoner's chest, pressing it to the livid wounds the whip had made.

"Tell me."

"I can't—"

Koscuisko worked the firepoint delicately, and Joslire could almost feel the agony all over again. The Student Interrogator, and his prisoner-surrogate exercise. But Student Abermay hadn't had a fraction of Koscuisko's instinct, of Koscuisko's art.

"Please don't ask me that. Don't ask me. I can't tell you. I can't."

Koscuisko worked bruise and burn between the thumb and forefinger of his left hand.

"Oh, but I am certain that you can."

There were no words for several long moments. Koscuisko took his pleasure with his prisoner, and Joslire—watching him—could understand if the Tutor were confused about why he would want to go. Tutor Chonis hadn't challenged him on it, though. That had been a mark of respect on Tutor Chonis's part, which Joslire appreciated deeply.

"Please. Please don't ask. They don't know. I lied to them, don't ask."

This was as close to absolute surrender as Joslire had ever seen. There was no indication from the prisoner that he would not answer whatever question it might beguile Koscuisko to raise; only an honest, final plea that Koscuisko would graciously refrain from asking.

Koscuisko declined to refrain from asking.

"Then surely they are in jeopardy, if you lied to them. They will appeal to the local Judiciary for their funds, and be prosecuted for making a fraudulent claim. Tell me who the people are, and the Bench will satisfy itself as to their innocence."

"Torture them until they say what's wanted—what you mean . . ."

Joslire couldn't see what Koscuisko did, but the strained, anguished rail in the prisoner's throat was clear enough. Too clear. "Well, then, they're for it one way or the other, aren't they? And it will go easier with them if you have already confessed to the deception. Tell me."

Whatever it was that Koscuisko was doing, it was finally too much for his prisoner.

"Stop. Stop. Please stop. Please. I'll tell—I'll tell you, tell his Ex'lency, stop—"

Koscuisko passed the firepoint to Cay and took the prisoner's head between his hands with his thumbs at the base of his prisoner's skull, rolling his fingers until he found the place he wanted. "There. Better, yes? Now talk to me."

No drugs, and still Koscuisko could shut a portion of the pain away with pressure upon nerves. Koscuisko was a sorcerer: Joslire had known that from the moment Administrator Clellelan had declared the Record closed on St. Clare's punishment. The prisoner's voice was stronger now, but his dead hopelessness was all the more difficult to ignore, that way.

"Yes, Y'rex'lency. I get munitions; four, there are four manufactures, all small. None local. One in the Gystor prefecture, a collective, Irmol city, Irmanol commune. One in Silam, owned by a family, Fourrail."

Koscuisko made an adjustment in his grip at the prisoner's neck; and the man continued, swallowing hard between his phrases. "One near Baram, in a place called Hafel, owned by a woman named Magestir Kees. And one at Getta, in Nannan—"

Silence, as if it had become too difficult for the prisoner to speak. Koscuisko waited for a moment, but took the question up again, relentless.

"There are many manufactures in Getta. Probably several in Nannan. Which did you have in mind? Specifically?"

Koscuisko had loosened his grip from its warding place, and the prisoner turned his head restlessly, as if seeking the comfort of that touch—the relief of pain that it seemed to have provided.

"No, surely there will be enough, how can I give them over . . . to the torture . . . no one should have to suffer, as I have—"

"Come, now, they will." Oddly enough—in Joslire's understanding, at least—Koscuisko had settled his hands back in their place, blocking the rise of pain messages to the brain. Maybe Koscuisko wanted to be sure that the man was listening to him, and had the strength to understand. "You've told me Getta, in Nannan, you must tell me more. Or they will all suffer, every manufactury in Nannan, you know that it is true."

"It's monstrous, there are six or eight in Nannan, no—not even Jurisdiction butchery—"

"I have not lied to you, not in all of this time. Is it not so?"

Something was driving Koscuisko forward now, something quite different from his lust for torture or the twisted pleasure that he too clearly took from pain and used to further his Inquiry. Koscuisko sounded focused, keenly aware, no longer distracted either by the sounds of his client's torment or the prisoner's submission to his hand.

"Excellency, please, just one of four, just one."

"It will be six or eight instead of one unless you say the word. You have given the evidence, and the Bench will be satisfied."

"The Bench can rot and burn for all I care—"

"Only one of six or eight is even involved, but you have condemned them all, unless you tell me which one. You must tell me which one. We do not have much more time."

"And once I'm dead I can't be made to tell, so that's just fine."

"Tell me which one," Koscuisko said. And Joslire believed Koscuisko's desperate determination; believed that he understood Koscuisko's change of mood. Koscuisko was telling the absolute truth. Now that the Record showed that a manufactury in Nannan was supplying munitions for the illegal sale of weaponry to Free Government terrorists, the Bench would not be satisfied until every facility in Nannan with capacity for such production had been intensively audited. And that meant Inquiry, which of course assumed Confirmation, which would almost inevitably require Execution.

"No, no, I'll not . . . I'll not—"

"Which one," Koscuisko said. "Or they are all for it."

Taking his hands away, he let the prisoner's head drop back to rest against the tabletop, deprived of even the small protection Koscuisko had been providing against the pain. Joslire was surprised that Koscuisko risked so much, so late. Certainly it seemed the most that Koscuisko dared, if he wished to get the word he wanted before the prisoner died and condemned who knew how many honest souls by his stubborn silence. "Which one?"

"My. Mother's people. Excellency. Damn you."

It was enough.

Koscuisko did not need to know what "my mother's people" meant exactly. The local Judiciary would be responsible for that. But it was enough to isolate one manufactury from any other. Koscuisko would know that much.

"It is well done of you," Koscuisko said. "For every soul the Bench will make to suffer, you have saved as many as you could. And for this may all Saints remit your punishment. Tutor Chonis?"

Joslire was humbled, in his heart. He had not believed that Koscuisko would have mastery this time. He should have understood that Koscuisko would have mastery in all things, he told himself. Because it was the temper of Koscuisko's will.

Chonis leaned forward, keyed his communication channel. "As you like, Student Koscuisko," Chonis said.

Koscuisko set his hands at the back of the prisoner's neck again, and the body's tension seemed to ebb away. Then there was a crack as of a sodden stick underfoot in heavy leaf-fall, clearly audible over the sound channel; and the prisoner's head fell to one side in Koscuisko's grasp, fell to one side at the wrong angle. Dead. Koscuisko had taken the man's resistance and his secrets. But then Koscuisko had taken the man's pain, and finally his life.

"You'd best go and collect your Student," Chonis said, switching the monitor off. "Keep me informed about your status. Any changes. And be certain that we'd hate to lose you, Curran, even to Student Koscuisko. All right?"

Joslire bowed in respectful silence and left the room.

Koscuisko would want a shower, a lefrol, wodac, maybe even his third-meal.

And he had to study how he was going to ask.

Andrej was too tired to think. It had gone on for so long. He had indulged himself so shamelessly. He went back to his quarters with Joslire and stood naked in the shower with his face between his hands until the stream startled him by cycling off of its own accord. Had he been standing there that long? Giving the control an impatient, unbelieving push, he set the stream for as hot as he could bear it, hoping to lose some of his tension in the waste-stream.

It didn't work.

Drying himself in a desultory fashion, he left his wet hair only half-combed and went out again into the main room. There was his supper; there was his wodac; there was Joslire, with his face professionally empty of expression and his uniform as perfect as it ever was. Andrej sat down at the study-set heavily, suppressing an irrational and uncharitable urge to scuff Joslire's boots. There was no sense in being offended at Joslire simply because Joslire was safely collected within himself while Andrej felt frayed at every seam of his being.

There was no sense in grieving for his innocence.

It had been bad enough when he had lost a patient for the first time—an infectious disease case, referred too late for certain intervention. He'd tried the recommended course, and he'd got permission to try an additional intervention; but when neither had stemmed the course of the disease, he had been forced by the absolute logic of Mayon's medical creed to transfer all of his energy to supportive care to ease the dying. He had hated it, hated to give up, hated to be beaten even by one of the most virulent of plagues under Jurisdiction. And he could not argue about it. He was expected to concentrate on his patient, and ignore the outraged protests of his ego. He had to bend his neck and submit himself to the service of mortality, and ensure that the passage he so fiercely wished to bar would be accomplished smoothly, with as little fear or pain as possible.

His proctor had sent a priest to see him a few days after that. One of his brother Mikhel's priests, not Uncle Radu's, Andrej had been grateful to note. Unfortunately the message could not have been more offensive had it come from Andrej's supercilious uncle in person; he was not to feel depressed, the priest had counseled him, because it was not his fault that the patient had died. He was not responsible.

And that had made him angry, as well as depressed, because a Koscuisko prince's life was defined by responsibility. To suggest that he was not responsible—simply because he had not been at fault—was a profound violation of Andrej's basic sense of self-definition.

After he'd thrown the priest out into the street, however, he'd begun to understand what the man had actually been saying. He couldn't practice medicine at its highest level without accepting the fact that disease was no respecter of Dolgorukij autocrats. He had to separate his absolute responsibility for his Household from the more limited responsibility of a professional physician. The rules were different. He had thought that he had understood that fact; but after his first patient death, he had found himself evaluating his understanding all over again.

Now he was a murderer three times over, and he had no more tolerance within himself to entertain the polite fiction that he was not responsible. Yes, he was only one of many Students, to be one of many Inquisitors. True, that the prisoners accused at the Advanced Levels were as good as dead from the moment Charges were Recorded against them—because even if they declined to confess, the implementation of the Protocols would kill them. There was no question that had he not killed whomever it was—no, Verteric Spaling, it was a man he had murdered, not an anonymous abstraction—had he not murdered the man Spaling, someone else would have, or someone else would have left him to die of worse wounds than Andrej had given him.

None of the rationalizations proper to the practice of medicine could be applied appropriately to murder.

He was Koscuisko, and he was responsible for the work of his hand, the more so because he had enjoyed it. Or much of it.

Joslire wanted to take his now-cold food away to be replaced with a hot meal, but Andrej waved him off. He wasn't very hungry, and the food had little savor in his mouth. He made a point of drinking the tepid rhyti in his flask; he had been working hard all day. Or he had been exercising himself all day, if it was not proper to try to call it "work" when one derived such obscene satisfaction from it. He needed fluid, one way or the other, especially if he was to end up drinking yet again. There was his wodac, right enough, still cold in its icer tray, sitting promisingly next to the glass with its saucer and its bit of sharbite-peel as if it really thought it was an aperitif and not an end in and of itself.

He was too tired to drink wodac. How long had he been sitting here, brooding about the sin that stained his honor? How could he grieve for his innocence, when the Fleet and the Church and his father all three refused to acknowledge that it was a sin against the Holy Mother's Creation to put a soul that could suffer to such torture for any purpose?

Emptying the rhyti flask of its last swallows, Andrej stood up and turned toward his bed.

He was so tired.

If only sleep could bring him rest, this time . . .

He could not close his eyes, because the stubborn habit of his weary mind was to review what he had done, and each time he closed his eyes, he saw his work once more—and shrank from it. He lay on the sleep-rack, trying to let go of his conflict, promising himself accommodation after accommodation to try to soothe his guilt-wracked spirit to sleep.

He would buy prayers for their souls.

None of them were Aznir, and why should their gods listen to his coin, when the Holy Mother herself almost never listened to anyone who was not Dolgorukij?

He would find their families, lie to them about their next of kin and about the manner of their dying.

Their families were probably either dead or compromised, or had sold the victims of his lust to Jurisdiction in order to save themselves.

Whatever it was that he was doing—Andrej told himself finally, with disgust—resting was not it. There was little sense in wasting energy struggling with himself. He needed all the energy he had to keep him through the ordeal of this place.

"Very well." He said it aloud to himself, pushing himself up off the sleep-rack with an effort. He was not too tired to drink after all, as he had thought. He would go out to his supper and try again.

The wodac would not have gotten very far, surely?

"There, if the officer would consent to rest for a moment, it'll get better now, just rest. Shallow breaths, if the officer please . . . Yes, that's right . . ."

Andrej Koscuisko lay sprawled ungracefully across the washroom floor. Joslire supported Koscuisko's shoulders against his knees as best he could while struggling to keep Koscuisko's head from falling too heavily against the basin set in the cold gray tiling. The lights in the washroom were harsh and unforgiving, and Joslire couldn't help but think Koscuisko was as ashen as a corpse—considering what Joslire could see of Koscuisko's face, clay-colored, beaded with sweat, his forehead an anxious agonized cording of care, his eyes shut tight against the brutal glare. Koscuisko was sick to his stomach with the drink, and Joslire was only surprised it hadn't happened any sooner in light of all the drinking that Koscuisko had done throughout the Term.

Koscuisko tried to move, evidently wishing to push himself up into a more normal seated position. Koscuisko didn't have the strength for it, and Joslire caught him around the chest from behind to stop him from falling over backward. "Just breathe, if the officer please, don't try to get up just yet. Just rest, yes. Like that, that's good."

It did seem that the drink was minded to be revenged upon Koscuisko; for now—having gotten sick to his stomach with the drink finally—Koscuisko was not only sick, but unstrung, shaken to the floor with the violence of the action of the poison, wrung too weak to so much as keep himself levered adequately over the basin. *A thorough man, Koscuisko,* Joslire told himself, putting the damp hair out of Koscuisko's eyes absentmindedly. When he studied his lessons, he studied the references as well as the text. When he was to administer discipline, he spent his spare hours practicing the whip and studying the physiology of Nurail so that he could do the thing to his best satisfaction. And when he poisoned himself with alcohol, he did so with characteristic care and concentration, if the violence with which he vomited the wodac could be taken as any indication.

Dozing again, now, Koscuisko was a dead weight in Joslire's arms. Joslire didn't want to wake him, not at any cost—no matter how awkward it was to be half-lying on the washroom floor, embracing his drunken charge. Drunken was not the word any longer, Joslire decided, shifting one arm forward carefully to make a pillow of sorts between Koscuisko's head and the basin. Koscuisko had been drunk hours ago. What Koscuisko was now was a perfect paradigmatic picture for a cautionary tale about people who put their faith in wodac to redeem them.

Koscuisko woke with a spasm of retching, sudden and fierce. They didn't need the basin any longer, not really—there wasn't anything left in Koscuisko's belly to vomit up. Still, Koscuisko clung to the basin's rim with a trembling hand as he struggled for breath against the convulsions that wracked him; as if, in the middle of his exhaustion and his pain, the thing that really worried him was the danger that he might disgrace himself by heaving onto the floor.

"You're fine, you're fine. your Excellency. No, just lie still, try to think. Is there something I can get for you?"

It didn't matter what he actually said to the officer, at this point. He could probably call him Andrej and ask him for a loan of Jurisdiction specie, and Koscuisko would remember none of it in the morning, and the Administration wouldn't care. Although if Koscuisko were capable of thinking for long enough to tell him, he could go and request whatever antispasmodics or painkillers might ease the suffering of a bad case of ethanol toxicity in Aznir Dolgorukij.

Koscuisko was out again, asleep, limp and defenseless and utterly trusting—or too tired to care. He couldn't really leave Koscuisko, not just yet. A man as sick as Koscuisko was could lapse into hypothermia lying on a cool tiled floor, without the protection of Joslire's body heat. And there was no sense in even beginning to gamble that there wasn't enough fluid, enough matter, enough anything left in Koscuisko's stomach to choke him if he turned wrong in his sleep—without somebody there to ensure the airway remained clear. A man could choke on his own blood as easily as on wodac, and if Koscuisko wasn't bleeding yet, he would be soon unless the dry heaves eased up more quickly than Joslire judged they would. He could be wrong, of course, he knew that well enough. Koscuisko could sit up and rub his face and demand his fast-meal, for instance. There was no telling with Dolgorukij.

He just couldn't afford to take that risk.

He settled himself as best he could to wait the liquor out.

Usually—Ligrose knew—only she and the Tutors attended the Administrator's morning report; there was no need for the Provost's attendance. What was going on? Clellelan looked grim. And only Chonis was here of all ten Tutors on Station, this time.

"Doctor Chaymalt." Not only that, but Clellelan was being formal with her. "This concerns your favorite Student, or at least your favorite this Term. Come in, sit down, close the door. There's a problem."

Koscuisko, was it? His man St. Clare had spent some more time in Infirmary lately, she'd noticed that. She'd made it her business to find out why; she'd even gone so far as to review the tapes of Koscuisko' s Eighth Level, and what had happened after. She should have known better than to look at Koscuisko's tapes. His control and his precision were just as impressive when he was beating his Security as she had found them when he'd been performing surgery; and she'd already decided that she didn't want to get involved.

"What's the problem, Rorin?" The Provost Marshall was nearest to the Administrator in rank. She was correspondingly most informal with him in private. "I hadn't expected an executive consult."

Oh, was that what they were doing? This wasn't adding up. Executive consults were called to evaluate dismissing a Student to civilian status because they were incompetent, or because they simply could not implement the Protocols. It happened rarely, not because the quality of the candidates was so high but because Fleet was so desperate for the bodies.

What could any of that have to do with Koscuisko?

"We've heard from the Bench offices at Pikanime," Clellelan replied indirectly. Pikanime was the nearest nexus-point between Fleet Orientation Station Medical and civilized space; less than three days, Standard, there and back. The comment seemed to mean something specific to Chonis, but she was still in the dark. She shrugged, and ventured to ask the obvious.

"Anything in particular, Administrator?"

He nodded grimly in response. "Let me provide a little background, here. Student Koscuisko is supporting our efforts to graduate First Secretary Verlaine's creature. We—Adifer and I—had made the decision to let her take it on drug-assist; Koscuisko's been supplying the drugs."

Well, of course; she knew that. But Journis might not have.

"Now, some days ago, Adifer had an uplink with Verlaine, with Noycannir present. She seems to have interested Verlaine in Koscuisko. And he's a little too interested, for my peace of mind."

This she hadn't known. "Seems logical," she commented. "If he's good enough. We don't have many who are good at all." Particularly not good at more than one thing at a time, medicine, Inquiry, Fleet discipline. She was in a position to know exactly what the driver usually did in the hands of lesser Students. Koscuisko's achievement was all the more impressive, accordingly.

"If it's any good, the Bench will annex it," the Provost said with a snort of disgust. "You're not going to void him out of Orientation just to spite Verlaine, though."

Clellelan shook his head. "No, but it gets more complicated. During the uplink, Verlaine asked for Noycannir's tapes—so that he could evaluate Koscuisko's potential, we suspect. It isn't too difficult to separate Noycannir's performance from the effectiveness of Koscuisko's drugs, if you know what you're looking for. But it could take up to nine days for tapes to reach Chilleau Judiciary from here. Now we've received a formal request from Pikanime. If they're relaying to Verlaine, we don't have nine days to work around."

"So Verlaine has some Clerks review the tapes, uplink to him, give him a good report. Verlaine issues a Bench warrant through Pikanime. Koscuisko is frozen on-site." Journis sounded thoughtful, putting it all together. "Anyone talked to Koscuisko about this? Adifer?"

As if a Student had anything to say about the disposition of his Writ. On the other hand they were talking about Andrej Koscuisko, which meant that Combine politics complicated things even more than his own respectable potential.

Chonis was nodding. "The Administrator and I had decided to accelerate the program, try to get him out and off-Station before Verlaine had a chance to look at those tapes. I talked to Student

Koscuisko, and suggested that his Writ might—potentially—be annexed to the Bench."

She'd wanted to see him taken off the Line for pure medical practice. She didn't see how releasing him to Verlaine would do any good, either for him or for any of the patients in need of his abilities. "What did he say?"

Shaking his head, now, Chonis sounded a little amused. At the First Secretary's implied discomfiture, perhaps. "He said that if he had a choice, he preferred Fleet. For some reason he didn't seem to feel that he would have much opportunity to practice the medical skills he values, if he were to be assigned to the Bench at Chilleau Judiciary."

Indeed not. Journis put the question that was still only half-formulated in Ligrose's mind to Clellelan directly.

"What are you going to do, then?"

"Well." Clellelan made a palms-up gesture as if appealing to reason. "If we're going to protect him from Verlaine, we've got to get him off-Station as soon as possible. We can't afford to wait for Verlaine to get a report on Noycannir's tapes, and the tapes go out on the next run. Forty-eight hours from now."

Ligrose was beginning to get the idea. "You can't be serious." It had never been done in all her years at this Station—but then she'd told herself that more than once this Term, and each time with specific reference to Student Koscuisko.

"I don't see why not." Journis was looking a little out of the loop, so Clellelan made it explicit for her sake. "We have the option to grant the Writ without it, as long as we are sure he can perform. And Koscuisko can perform. He's consistently pushed the Levels on each exercise—and not the Protocols, either. Is there any doubt that Student Koscuisko is capable of executing a better Tenth Level Command Termination than anyone on Station?"

Journis made a face of amused realization, apparently understanding at last. Clellelan spoke on.

"Waive the Tenth Level exercise on the strength of his Advanced, and he can leave with those damned tapes. He'll be halfway to Hollifess before Verlaine knows he's gone."

And therefore Clellelan had called for executive consultation, so that they could graduate Koscuisko without the usually required final test and send him out to his ship of assignment before the Bench could lay hands on the boy. Because without explicit evaluation from all of them, the Tenth Level could not be waived: but Clellelan was absolutely right, in perhaps the single most important respect: there was no doubt that Koscuisko could perform.

The only question was whether he could continue to do so without destroying himself in the process. There had to be conflict within a man capable of such sensible and sadistic cruelty as his Levels recorded, when the same man was capable as well of the surgery that had saved Idarec, the empathic compassion that had seen St. Clare healed of his various hurts so well and quickly, the precision and control with which he'd scourged a man bloody with so little actual harm done.

"Let it be done," Marshall Journis said. "Just tell me what you want from me, to support the Record."

Nor would she object, Ligrose decided. The odds were not in favor of Koscuisko's functional survival on Line, in the Lanes. But his chances had to be better on board ship than under First Secretary Verlaine. His concern for his man St. Clare in itself would almost have decided her; Koscuisko would not be permitted to take any bond-involuntaries with him if he went to the Bench, since they belonged to Fleet. And his bond-involuntaries seemed to be important to Koscuisko.

There was only one problem left to resolve in her mind. "What does the inside man say, Adifer?"

Koscuisko's assigned Security had a vital part to play in the Administration's formal decision to pass or fail. Curran was closer to Koscuisko than anyone else, and had the best vantage point from which to judge strengths and weaknesses. If Curran thought Koscuisko would be better off with Verlaine . . .

"Curran wants to go to *Scylla* with him," Chonis said. Journis grinned and didn't look surprised; nor did Clellelan seem completely shocked. Perhaps she should have expected it. People who could be bothered to engage themselves about the welfare of bond-involuntaries on a human level were rarely met with. She supposed that it was only natural for Curran to want to keep Koscuisko once he'd found him.

"Well, you'll get no argument from me." Arguing was never worth the energy. It would take less time and trouble to document the waiver than to argue. And she didn't think she minded being asked to document the waiver.

"Adifer, you'd better let your Student know," Clellelan suggested. "He'll have to finish up whatever he can in a hurry, if he's to be ready to leave in a day and a half. Provost Marshall. Do we have his Command briefing? We'll have to send it with him, he can review it in transit."

Journis rose to her feet briskly. "On my way, Rorin. Adifer, I'll have the material ready for you soonest."

They would send Koscuisko off to *Scylla* on a freight run. He'd need to be met at Pikanime by a Fleet escort, but the Administrator could easily arrange that over secure channels. Noycannir would be starting her Tenth Level exercise at about the time Koscuisko would be leaving Pikanime. By the time the First Secretary made his move—if he was going to make the move at all—the only things left of Koscuisko on Station would be his tapes, and Idarec.

She liked it.

"I'll have the documents you need to you by mid-shift, Administrator. No time like the present to be started."

It would even be fun to tweak the Bench a bit.

In a small way she'd be getting her own back on the Bench for sending her here in the first place.

CHAPTER FIFTEEN

"Thank you, Curran," Tutor Chonis said from his place at the desk inside the office. "You may stand in on this. Step through, the pair of you."

It had been two days, Standard, since he'd spoken to Tutor Chonis, and Joslire hadn't found a suitable opportunity to talk to Koscuisko. Koscuisko had come off the exercise too tired to drink, and had gone straight to bed; had been unable to sleep for dreaming, and had started to drink. Had fallen asleep or had passed out, which Joslire supposed was a species of sleep—if one without any of the restorative nature of normal sleep—but had been unable to rest, for the emetic effects of alcohol poisoning.

"Student Koscuisko respectfully reports, at Tutor Chonis's direction."

After an hour or three spent together on the washroom floor while Koscuisko retched his bile out, Koscuisko slept; but not because he was tired, because he was utterly exhausted. Then after a while Koscuisko woke up and made an effort to review his Tenth Level material—but came down with the dry heaves again. Had slept, and wept, and slept, and dreamed again, and when finally at last Koscuisko had gotten a good start on some decent rest, Tutor Chonis had called for their immediate attendance.

"Yes, Student Koscuisko, sit down."

Joslire hadn't found time during any of it to tell Koscuisko that he wanted to go with him. He wanted to be sure Koscuisko understood that it was his choice, even a selfish choice, to request the reassignment. The last thing he wanted was for Koscuisko to imagine that he was making the offer just to comfort him, for pity's sake.

"This will be quick, but not because it's any less important than it would be if you were graduating with the rest of our Students this Term. Curran, secure the door. Privacy barrier in effect."

He suspected he knew what Chonis had in mind. He thought he recognized the Orders documents on Chonis's desk, even if Koscuisko would not. Had he missed his chance already? Joslire set the secrecy level on the sound dampers inside the room. The interview would be Recorded, like so much else that happened at Fleet Orientation Station Medical, but the Tutor must have wanted to be very sure that no one outside could eavesdrop. Someone like Student Noycannir?

Chonis waited for Joslire's bow, in token of having completed the task. "Now then. Student Koscuisko. The Administrator believes it to be important that you leave the Station within a day's time. Secretary Verlaine is possibly more interested in you than we had imagined, and we do not wish to risk losing you."

Joslire listened with dread. He wasn't going to get his chance, not unless he could find it within a day. He couldn't possibly get Koscuisko to agree with only a day to work in. His knives would leave the Station without him. Not his knives any more; they were Koscuisko's knives, and they felt different to him when he carried them for safekeeping between sessions. It comforted him to be near them, although he was a slave and they were free. He had to let them go away from him. He'd lost his chance.

"With respect, Tutor Chonis . . ." Koscuisko sounded confused, as well he might. "There is a Tenth Level exercise yet to accomplish, and three days minimum—"

Chonis held up his hand for silence. "The Administrator has decided that in this instance the final exercise is to be waived. Your previous exercises are accepted as sufficient proof of competency. You will, of course, continue to work on the Controlled List, once you are safely to *Scylla*."

The Ninth Level had gone three days. Joslire was certain that it could easily have stretched to four, had Koscuisko intended that from the beginning. There was some sense in that. And Chonis wasn't finished; he didn't pause long enough to let Koscuisko get a word in, had Koscuisko been eager to respond. Which he wasn't, by the look of him; he looked too startled to have anything to say.

"These Orders do not in themselves comprise your Writ, Student Koscuisko. Your Writ is granted by the Administrator as Bench proxy and forwarded to Fleet Judiciary by special transmission. Secured transmission, I hardly need point out." Transmission that no one could intercept, in other words. The Administrator certainly seemed intent on taking no chances.

"There are two copies here. One you will present to Captain Irshah Parmin upon your arrival on board *Scylla*. One is for your personal archive. You are required to take these Orders into your hand, Student Koscuisko, to signify your acceptance of commission; and once you have taken these Orders in your hand, not even the Bench can deny your Writ. Nor can you set your Writ aside before the expiration of your Term without explicit authority from the Jurisdiction Bench over the First Judge's attested seal. The Record requires that you state your understanding of these requirements and restrictions prior to your taking your Writ into your hand."

Koscuisko stood up now, pale but apparently resolute. "I am obliged to the Jurisdiction's Bench by my sworn oath and in consideration of multiple benefits received," Koscuisko recited firmly. "Therefore I claim this as my Writ, and I will execute the same at the Fleet's discretion until such time as the Bench may consider my duty to have been amply and honorably discharged."

A formula, like so many other formulae provided for Fleet's use in binding sentient souls into servitude. Koscuisko spoke it well for all of that, clear and correct, with no hint in his voice or in his manner of the horrors that came to him in his sleep.

"It is prudent and proper that you should do so, just and judicious that the Bench grant privilege along with responsibility. No Charges less than mutiny shall be Recorded against you while you hold the Writ. Take up your Orders, your Excellency."

It was always a shock to hear the Tutors use the formal rank-title with their Students at the end of Term. But Koscuisko took up his rank and his Writ together when he took his Orders into his hand. And therefore, consequently, Koscuisko ranked over everyone on Station now, with the exception of the Administrator's Staff and his assigned Tutor. If only technically so, at this point.

Koscuisko took the Orders from the Tutor's desk and tilted them against the light from overhead, examining them curiously. There was nothing to see. Orders were not eye-readable. Koscuisko wouldn't need to know exactly what they said to know exactly what they meant to him.

"Leaving tomorrow, Tutor Chonis? So soon; it seems precipitous."

"Perhaps a little awkward for you, but you'll have an escort team to ensure that your passage to *Scylla* is a smooth one. Come and embrace me, Andrej, let me say good-bye to you now."

Joslire stepped forward to take Koscuisko's Orders now that the formalities were done. Koscuisko was not his Student any longer, and would never be his officer, unless he could find the time in one short day to ask. Tutor Chonis caught his eye for a brief moment of evaluation; Joslire hoped that his despair was not as obvious to Koscuisko as the Tutor seemed to find it.

"I will not see you again, Tutor Chonis?"

"I'll see you off in the morning. But there will be more people there." Chonis put his arms around Koscuisko, and Joslire had never seen him so apparently reluctant to let a Student go. "You've been an interesting problem, Andrej. And you have great potential, in more than one way. Remember your duty, and be a credit to Fleet."

Unusual as it was, it seemed to Joslire that Chonis had become actually fond of Koscuisko. Who stepped back a pace and bowed, simply and respectfully.

"Thank you, Tutor Chonis. You have dealt honestly with me, and I am grateful to you for it. And for your help as well."

Student Koscuisko was not fond of Tutor Chonis, no. But he was not so mean-spirited as to deny him respect or reject his sense of obligation, on such petty grounds.

Chonis nodded, apparently content. "Go and get packed, 'your Excellency.' You're to go to exit briefings; they should be on your scheduler by this time. Curran, you and St. Clare will get . . ."

But Chonis couldn't say "your officer" because Koscuisko was St. Clare's officer, not his. ". . . his Excellency to embarkation area five-up four-in, mid-shift tomorrow. The transport will be final loading at nine and sixteen."

Nine and sixteen was nearly a full thirty-two eights from now, one full day. There was hope left. He'd thought that he would have more time, but if he could only find the opportunity he might still be able to win Koscuisko's consent.

He bowed in the face of Chonis's understanding gaze and followed Koscuisko out of the office, back to quarters.

Andrej sat at his study-set, staring at his scheduler, trying to come to terms with the speed with which things were happening. Surely it hadn't been two days since he'd murdered his prisoner, his third prisoner, his third murder. Two days, his Tenth Level to begin in two more, and now this—brusquely summoned to Tutor Chonis's office, given his personal copies of the documents attesting to his Writ, and told to pack. To have Joslire and St. Clare pack for him, at least.

His brain was still too full of sleep and alcohol. He could make little sense of it; but here he sat, at the study-set in his quarters, and Joslire and St. Clare were in fact packing. Most of his uniforms weren't even coming; there was only his personal linen, his boots, and the few uniforms that were common to both Student and Chief Medical Officer. New travel dress, in token of his new status. Exercise uniforms. The knife-harness for the throwing knives, and the knives themselves sheathed and packed as well. What was the use of sending the knives with him, if he was not to have Joslire to instruct?

Joslire and St. Clare were busy at the closet with the blouses of his travel dress, setting and checking the Section markers and the ship's identification he was now authorized to wear. St. Clare was in new uniform already, darker than Andrej had seen on Station; the bright green piping at St. Clare's sleeves was all the more difficult to ignore set against dull gray. The ship's identification was the same, but St. Clare wore no other rank than his slavery. Andrej supposed that it lent a certain amount of uniformity to one's escort if they were all marked alike. He would wear no rank, either, come to that. The color of his uniform signaling his status, the piping on the sleeves sufficient to identify him as a Medical officer. Black was the color of age and ease on Azanry. He was too young to be wearing the raven's wing, it was unnatural.

He couldn't afford to lose himself in meditations on the color of his uniform. The rest of the day would be too full for that. Exit briefing with Doctor Ligrose Chaymalt within the hour. Exit briefing with Provost Marshall Journis somewhat later, and he was a little uneasy about that one, but he did have to clear the Station. She would have material for his review—his itinerary and his Command briefings. He would need to go over the travel plans before he went to bed if he was to know what to expect in the morning. There would not be time to take exercise with Joslire. If he meant to speak to Joslire, he had better get it done and over with before they had to leave for Chaymalt's office.

"St. Clare, would you excuse us for a moment." There was no reason to discuss it in front of Robert, whether or not his quarters were under surveillance. From the very first Joslire had made it clear that he preferred to be humiliated in private. Andrej meant to do what could be done to set the pain at its least personal level.

The door closed behind St. Clare's silent exit. Rising from the study-set, Andrej took himself over to where Joslire stood waiting—and confused—beside the open and near-empty closet where his uniforms had been.

"The Tutor has delivered my Orders and my Writ, Joslire, but he did not demand your Bond. What are we to do?"

According to the briefings they had been required to study, the Bonds held by Students were to be surrendered to the Administrator at the same time that Orders were accepted and the Writ taken up. He hadn't given it a thought, earlier today in Tutor Chonis's office; things had been happening too quickly. But obviously he needed to return the Bond before he left the Station. Going by the manner in which Joslire had chosen to deliver it to him in the first place, Joslire would surely prefer he surrender it in the relative privacy of quarters.

Joslire looked paled to yellow—and pained, almost angry. To be reminded? Andrej felt at his neck for the chain to pull the pendant out from beneath his blouse; and Joslire startled him by seizing his hand at the wrist as suddenly and fiercely as if it had been a weapon that Andrej had been reaching for.

"Permission to speak to the officer," Joslire said. For all the world as if Joslire hadn't been up all night holding Andrej's head while he'd vomited up the overdose of wodac he had taken. As if there'd never been any contact heart-to-heart between them.

"Joslire, please—what is it?" Joslire loosed his grip at Andrej's wrist the moment Andrej spoke, as if Andrej's wrist had suddenly burned his hand. "Tell me, directly, I request of you." There wasn't much hope of that, though, not really. Joslire didn't trust him enough to speak to him directly. Nor could Andrej hold that against Joslire in fairness; he was only a departing Student now to Joslire, with a new one coming in as soon as he had left.

"Tutor Chonis did not require his Excellency to surrender my Bond because Tutor Chonis knows . . ." Joslire seemed under an unusual amount of stress, even for him. He ran out of words abruptly, screwing his narrow slanted eyes into thin black slits of concentration in his dark Emandisan face. ". . . knows that I meant to ask the officer, his Excellency. to retain my Bond. But have been unable to find a good time . . . in which to do so."

Andrej reached slowly out to take Joslire by the shoulder, in wonder. Joslire's shoulder was as hard as stalloy under Andrej's hand. What could Joslire be talking about that created so much anxiety?

"I'm afraid I find myself in the dark, Joslire. I am leaving, I can't keep your Bond. Unless you were to come with me, and that would mean . . . Don't you have some years of safety left? Here on this Station?"

"Hadn't made up my mind for certain." It was almost a gasp, from Joslire. "Until the officer's Ninth Level. Just could not be sure. And now it's too late to make you understand. Sir."

Whether he understood or not, it was clear enough to Andrej that Joslire was in torment. "Come, Joslire, stand down a bit. Explain. You worry me." He'd caused Joslire torment more than once during the Term, in his ignorance and clumsiness. And nothing he had tried to do to provide comfort had ever seemed to have its intended effect, either; but he had to keep on trying. "What is this thing that it is too late for me to comprehend?"

Joslire dropped his head, rolling his underlip against his upper teeth. "My Bond belongs to Fleet. But. If the officer please. I may request assignment. To the officer."

Wait, there had been something, a few lines of text merely—glossed over with the briefest of mentions, and it had seemed so unlikely to him at the time that he had taken no notice.

"That is to say, with the officer's permission. Active Line duty assignment to Student Koscuisko. To go with his Excellency," Joslire concluded. And fell silent.

Shaking his head in horrified denial now, Andrej backed away from Joslire where he stood. "This is some test they put you to, Joslire, you cannot mean to come with me to *Scylla*." And an evil test, to make a man ask to be even more cruelly bound than he had been already, to force Joslire to pretend to want to go. After what Joslire had seen of him. His exercises. His excesses.

But the accusation seemed to strike at Joslire's pride as if it had been a slap across his face. "Indeed it is not, and I do. His Excellency is respectfully requested to consider my petition as made in earnest. There are so few decisions about my life that I am still permitted to make."

Joslire's reproach shamed Andrej to his heart; but he could not accept the idea, even so. Surely the last thing anyone would want— after watching him, throughout his training—would be to seek a dedicated assignment.

"You have been good to me, Joslire, and I have had great comfort from you. If I were to let you come with me, it would be selfishness, your deferment—"

"If the officer is serious let the officer prove it; let his Excellency respect my request and honor it. We are slaves, except in this one thing. His Excellency should not seek to deny me what piece of freedom even Fleet permits."

He had asked Joslire to speak directly, and this was blunt speech indeed. Almost, almost Andrej could believe that Joslire meant precisely what he said. Was he tempted to believe Joslire because Joslire was serious—or because he welcomed the prospect of Joslire's support in the trying days to come? "But I could be other than you may think me to be. And if I held your Bond, you could not appeal if I were to abuse you. You cannot be sure of what you do. No, I won't let you."

Joslire seemed to have lost his fear and cleared his mind of conflict. He stood rock-solid on his feet and looked up at Andrej from the bottom of the very pit of hopelessness.

"The first Student to whom I was assigned did not desire to punish my unsatisfactory performance above four times in Term. The Tutor was unable to obtain Student Exception, it was my first such assignment and I was ignorant. Discipline the second time was three-and-thirty. The Student signed my return-to-duty documents on the following day, and was praised by Tutor Mannes for being conservative with expensive medication."

There was no petition in Joslire's voice now, only cold recitation, merciless and inexorable.

"The second Student liked to use the driver. His Excellency has examined his handiwork. The third Student took very little notice of my existence and her sexual requirements were not in themselves difficult to fulfill to her satisfaction, so that was not a bad Term all in all. But the fourth Student to whom I was assigned demanded more particular attention to specific personal needs, and found his gratification much enhanced if he was free to inflict pain while he enjoyed pleasure. The most recent Student, prior to his Excellency—"

"No, Joslire, please, be still."

"—preferred to discipline in ways not specifically referenced among the techniques of Inquiry and Confirmation, which methods therefore lay outside of the range of adjudication or exception. The Tutor encouraged his experimentation, and he was held back for the Remedial Levels, so there was adequate time for him to explore areas that interested him."

Andrej could not listen; he could hardly breathe. He turned away from Joslire, overcome. Oh, he deserved to have such things said to him. It was discipline for his selfishness, just and judicious retribution for the wrong he had done Joslire by challenging his request. It was proper punishment, and it tore at his stomach sharp and keenly.

"None of them would have cared about St. Clare. None of them would have practiced with the driver to protect him rather than torture him. None of them cared to minimize the number of souls at risk as a result of confessions. If his Excellency remains unconvinced, I stand ready to supply as many additional details as would amuse his Excellency to entertain."

There was no arguing with such cogent proofs. Joslire already knew the full horror of being trapped without recourse, at the mercy of a brutal officer and a system no less brutal. Andrej knew he had no further right to question or deny him. He had wanted to reject Joslire's request, because Joslire had years yet of deferment that he could spend safely here on Station. Joslire had disillusioned him of that. Joslire was not safe.

"No, no more, Joslire, I will not deny you. It is what you want, that I should hold your Bond?"

He couldn't face Joslire, not just yet. It was not good for a man's pride to see how deeply he was pitied.

"For as long as Fleet and his Excellency permit. Yes. Permission to accompany his Excellency on dedicated duty assignment."

Andrej took a deep breath, trying to clear his mind of the objections that he still wanted to raise—of the doubts he was in honor bound to swallow. Joslire had made his claim. "It shall be so, then. Come with me to *Scylla,* Joslire. I will take you to me, and I will hold you to me while I can."

He would submit and be humbled before Joslire. It was the least that he could do in the face of Joslire's courage.

"Thank you, your Excellency."

Joslire sounded grateful to him, in Joslire's subdued style—his usually subdued style, that was to say. As if it was Joslire who was to receive benefit, Andrej who was making the sacrifice.

"If you are to be my man, and I your master . . ."

Joslire meant to make contract with him, and accompany him on dedicated duty assignment. Such an honor could not be accepted lightly. Turning back to the study-set, Andrej sat down and motioned Joslire to come stand in front of him. He didn't even care anymore about the monitors. Fleet protocols were all very well and good, but this could not be said to be between a new officer and a Security troop merely. This contract could only be made man to man.

"Thou must come to thy knees, Joslire, and cut thy mouth. Give me to drink, of thee."

Confused and apprehensive, trusting all the same, Joslire sank to his knees gracefully in front of Andrej where he sat. "His Excellency requires?"

"Thy mouth, Joslire. At the inside." He had been too young to manage; his father had helped him to draw blood. He was the prince inheritor, and his father had marked him publicly as of his blood and substance by incorporating Andrej's life into his own. His younger brothers and his sisters had never gone through such a ceremony; when Andrej inherited, they would all make their submission to him in the traditional manner, and through him to the Blood of ages.

Joslire had pulled his back-sheath knife, but looked a little puzzled yet. Laying his hand over Joslire's hand, Andrej guided the sharp point of the blade to cut against Joslire's cheek from the inside. The mouth bled easily and freely, and healed most quickly. It was better, done so, than the older ways.

He let Joslire take away the knife, and set his left hand against the back of Joslire's strong stout neck. He'd never thought to make contract in the old fashion, or at least not until his father died—let alone with a man who was no kind of Dolgorukij. But he knew what had to be done.

"Give me to drink of thee," he repeated—reassuringly, he hoped. He put his mouth to Joslire's mouth, and closed his eyes, and waited.

After a moment Joslire made submission, opening his mouth and surrendering himself to Andrej's greedy—if symbolic—thirst. The taste of Joslire's blood was different from his own, but that was the whole point. The Holy Mother understood of blood. And once Joslire had given of his blood—once he had given up his substance for Andrej's nourishment—the Holy Mother would look upon him as blood and bone of her own children.

That was the way it had been explained to Andrej, at any rate.

Long moments, and the blood ceased to flow from the shallow cut in Joslire's cheek. Andrej lifted his head and leaned back, his mind reeling with the unexpected emotional impact of the ritual act. "There, it is done." Joslire was quiet and calm, with him, but Joslire had only been Aznir for a few short moments now. It was not to be expected that he would understand it all at once. "Now it is bonded, and cannot be broken. Thou art to me, Joslire, and may our Lady's Grace be satisfied."

Be of Koscuisko, forever.

But he did not say it.

There was a limit to how much arcane Aznir superstition he could reasonably expect Joslire to tolerate at any given time. And they would not let him take Joslire with him when he left Fleet.

"According to his Excellency's good pleasure."

As pleases my master, most pleases myself. It seemed so close, it sent a shiver down Andrej's spine. Surely the Holy Mother had set her seal upon the contract. If he had been a religious man—as Andrej did not feel himself to be—he would be forced to take Joslire's choice of response as nothing less than a patent sign from the Canopy itself, instead of simply being something that Joslire said from time to time that only happened to echo ancient fealty formulae of the Blood.

"Go and let St. Clare back in, if you would, Joslire. You need to see the Tutor, I expect. And I'm expected in Doctor Chaymalt's office."

It was easier in a way to be grateful to a Mother that he only half-believed in than to contemplate by how slim a margin he had gained what he had won from the Administration. The life of Robert St. Clare, although he had traded his honor for the boon. This unexpected grant of companionship from Joslire, so that he might yet find a way to return good for the good Joslire had done him—and continue to learn how to throw those lovely, lovely knives, as well.

It would give him something to think about on his way to *Scylla*. The better to avoid thinking about his apprehensions, facing his first assignment on the Line.

"Even so, your Excellency. St. Clare can take his Excellency there. He knows the way."

His first assignment had just gotten significantly easier to face.

CHAPTER SIXTEEN

There had been a flurry of some sort, St. Clare was almost certain of it. Not that anyone was saying anything to him about it, but what could Curran have in mind to go racing off on his own like that? A flurry, or his name wasn't Robert St. Clare.

Wait a moment, he admonished himself.

His name *wasn't* Robert St. Clare.

All right, perhaps his name was not exactly St. Clare, but he would be expected to answer to it for twenty-six years, so what was the functional difference?

The officer had appointments with the Medical Officer, and the Provost Marshall after. Fortunately he had had plenty of time to study the physical mapping of the place.

"To the officer's right. And again, at the next turning, if the officer please." He'd be glad to get to *Scylla,* even so, where he would necessarily be junior man on whichever Security Five-point team he ended up on. It would be up to the senior man in Koscuisko's escort to walk behind the officer and direct him at the same time. All he'd have to do, then, was to pay attention and follow instructions. That couldn't be said to be a hard life, now, could it?

"Past the lift-nexus, to the officer's right once more." He expected he could even get used to Koscuisko in time. Up in the high windy, people who looked like Koscuisko—short and pale, pale hair, pale eyes—were suspect; it wasn't honest herding blood, at all, it was farmers who had been sea-raiders beforetime. A long time before, but memory ran long in the high windy, because there was nothing to do for entertainment but sit and tell stories, and argue about the weaves. Koscuisko could be a throwback to the sea-raiders, from his face, but what weave would a man wear who was for Inquisition?

There was a troop waiting for them at the receiving area, someone Robert thought he recognized: Omie Idarec, from the same group he'd come in with, but wearing Station Security. That was right, there'd been gossip. He wondered if Koscuisko knew who Omie was.

"If his Excellency would follow me?"

There was no sign on Omie's face, so Robert guessed not. The subject made for interesting speculation, as he trotted along after Idarec on Koscuisko's heels. If Koscuisko had only ever seen Omie as an anonymous body in surgery or as a set of statistics in the medical reports on Line, there was no reason to imagine that Koscuisko had more than a general idea of what he actually looked like. He could ask Omie, of course, once the officer went through to see Chaymalt. But he was still learning the hand-language. There was probably a limit to how much he was going to be able to find out.

Here was the place; no guard posted, but this was a training facility, not like *Scylla* would be. Omie signaled smartly at the door, pivoting into a perfect attention-rest just beyond the threshold as Koscuisko came up to announce himself. Robert tried to match the smoothness of his counterpart's move, taking his place at the near side of the door. Well, not bad.

But plenty of room for improvement.

"Student Koscuisko to see Doctor Chaymalt, as Tutor Chonis has instructed."

The door slid open; Koscuisko stepped through, and then he and Omie were alone in the corridor together. Only the two of them, which made conversation rather more difficult, because there was no mirror man to reflect the messages, and greater care was required not to break the discipline of attention-rest. They'd practiced together, though; that was a plus.

St. Clare glanced quickly down and over, to find Omie's hand; the thumb was already canted at a subtle angle, *wanna talk.* He couldn't distinguish statement from question at this point, though he knew it could be done, since they'd both seen more experienced bond-involuntaries demonstrate.

He knows you?

There was a pacing issue to keep in mind; if a word was held too long, it wasted precious time; but if it wasn't held long enough, there was a risk of losing the word. They were expected to be looking straight ahead, after all. Generally speaking.

No. Don't think so. Leaving?

This time the question was fairly obvious, so Robert answered more directly. *At nine and sixteen. Scylla. Nice ship-mark, I like it.*

Omie made an amused knuckle, coupled with a finger twitch denoting a superior admonitory tone. *Not alone, though. Joslire Curran.*

Spelling out the name made interpretation more difficult, since St. Clare had to sound it in his mind before he realized who it was that Omie meant. He knew how to spell his new name in Standard script, but he was still getting used to reading it; and for a moment he thought he'd misunderstood.

What, my uncle's man? Dark broody sort, muscles all over?

Koscuisko's man, yes, Curran. Just now. Almost sure of it.

Well, that would be interesting. Had that been why he'd been invited to leave, then? Curran, to be coming with them; and Curran had been on Station for years, now, but not eight years, which implied that Curran had given up the balance of his deferment to go with them. That was startling, but it was comforting, too. If a man of Curran's experience had decided that Koscuisko was a man to take on dedicated duty assignment, St. Clare could consider himself lucky by implication. He hadn't been offered the choice. But maybe he'd gotten a good one anyway—even if the man did have better hands and worse ones. At least he knew which pair he preferred Koscuisko to wear.

That'll be nice. Company. You?

No response; St. Clare wondered if he'd gotten it right. There was only the fraction of a cuticle's difference between "you" and an improbable form of recreation. After a moment, though, he could see the answer taking shape, and realized that Omie had only been trying to figure out how best to phrase himself, within the limited vocabulary the two of them had in common.

Held over. Popular demand. Try again, next Term.

Try again? Face the prisoner-surrogate exercise all over again, next Term? He didn't like the sound of that.

Choice?

Maybe he shouldn't ask so personal a question. He put a fingernail's worth of apology behind the question mark. Omie didn't seem to have taken offense.

Beats work. Just think, I'll be ahead of the next bunch. Extra months of deferment, too.

True, Omie would be ahead of the rest of the prisoner-surrogates, he'd already gone through the test. Or started the test, at any rate. He hadn't answered the question, one way or the other; St. Clare decided that was an answer of its own.

The Day will come.

He didn't expect Koscuisko's interview to be a long one; there was no telling when they'd be interrupted. It was best to signal close of conversation now, in good time, rather than leave the exchange unfinished. It was bad luck to leave things unfinished, when there was no way to guess whether he would ever see Omie again.

The Day, after tomorrow.

Omie was apparently content to let it rest there, having passed on his news. Curran was coming? Well, that was good. He thought.

He quieted his mind, and stood in wait for his officer.

Andrej bowed to the Provost Marshall politely. "Student Koscuisko presents himself for the Marshall's Command briefing, at Tutor Chonis's instruction." Unlike Doctor Chaymalt, the Marshall had called St. Clare in with him. To guard against an appearance that his fish might misinterpret, so that it need not fall prey to the impertinence that was the common burden of all fish? He didn't know.

"Thank you, 'your Excellency.' Watch out for 'Student Koscuisko,' from now on. You'll report to Parmin as 'Chief Medical Officer,' remember."

So he would. Marshall Journis had risen from her desk as he saluted, and invited him to be seated with a gesture of her hand. She had not put St. Clare at his ease; was it expected of him, that he should? But he had not yet left the Station; she was still a step up from him on his chain of command. Therefore if she hadn't put St. Clare at his ease, it was because she felt that he should stand at attention, for reasons of her own.

"Yes, Marshall Journis. With your permission, I understand you have information about *Scylla* for me?"

She came around to the front of the desk to take the other chair, facing him. She had a stack of cubes in her hand and dropped them one at a time on the edge of the desk nearest him, counting them off as she went.

"Tactical history of the Jurisdiction Fleet Ship *Scylla,* from shipyard to current mission status. Fleet biographies on the Captain, the Primes, and other assigned Command Branch officers. Latest readiness assessment on Medical, and files on the assigned staff." She paused for a moment, tapping her fingers against the third cube. "I've taken the liberty of including the Bench-specific issues—historical performance of Ship's Inquisition both on *Scylla* and under Irshah Parmin, incidents per eight, required Levels. Things like that. If you're interested."

So that he'd have a better idea of what to expect, or what would be expected of him. Significant information indeed; but she continued her itemization, without waiting to give him a chance to make an appropriate remark.

"Finally, because of the peculiar nature of your Security, the files on the troops assigned to the Security Five-point teams, and the Chief Warrant Officer who is responsible to the First Officer for them. Chief Warrant Caleigh Samons, that is, at present. You'll find her very professional, but I'd advise you to let her know up front that you don't want people interfering with your green-sleeves."

If Samons was a Chief Warrant Officer, she couldn't possibly be a bond-involuntary. What was the Provost getting at? "I am not sure I understand your point, Marshall Journis."

"You've got delicate sensibilities where bond-involuntaries are concerned. She needs to know if you're going to take it personally every time someone's up for two-and-twenty. Or just have her strip St. Clare down, and tell her it was four-and-forty, with a driver. She's intelligent. She'll get the point. By the way, do you mind if I have a look? I didn't get the chance to admire your work close up before."

It was still a little confusing, but Andrej was beginning to think he grasped her meaning. He was to be sure that Samons knew he did not feel six-and-sixty should be handed out with a liberal hand; and St. Clare—whose back, newly healed, still showed by evident if fading bruises that he had been beaten recently—was to serve as a demonstration model of his personal reluctance to mutilate his assigned Security. Andrej expected that he could probably communicate as much adequately well to his new Chief Warrant in plain language, now that he comprehended the problem. Why did Journis want to "admire" his work, though? To see how St. Clare had mended? To critique his handling of the whip? What?

"With respect, Marshall Journis, I would prefer not. He is a man, not an ornament." Reluctant as Andrej was to deny the Marshall—especially after having received benefit from her, professionally and personally—he could not see taking St. Clare's clothes off to gratify her curiosity. There were limits. And he had to set them; because St. Clare was not permitted to.

She looked a little surprised, to have him talk back to her. He was surprised at himself, come to that. Fortunately she did not seem to be offended.

"Very well. As you like." He was leaving here; it probably didn't matter one way or the other, if he had offended her. But gratuitous insult was almost always a bad investment. And she had counted the stroke when Robert had been beaten, and she had not made him repeat a single blow.

"Be advised, then, that discipline for bond-involuntaries is usually liberally assessed and applied. It's only fair that you let her know first thing that you don't want to see any general-purpose assessments. She'll take it from there. You might want to talk to your First Officer about it, as well, and tell him I sent you when you see him."

If that was what it took to hold the hand of Fleet discipline back from meaningless punishment, then he would gladly do as much, and more.

"Thank you, Marshall Journis. Will that be all?"

He thought that he had sensed his dismissal in her last phrase. But apparently he had been mistaken; or, rather, his timing had been off. He was not to be dismissed quite so immediately.

"No, one more thing, Andrej. An important one. You know St. Clare, here. You know Curran." And she knew that Curran was coming with him, why should he be surprised? "Do what you can to let the others know that they count, too. It means a lot to anybody. More to these, because they have so little else."

A warning against jealousy, perhaps? What had he ever done to St. Clare that anyone would envy St. Clare for it? What had he ever done to Joslire Curran, other than to make his life miserable?

"A man deserves the respect due any sentient creature, Marshall Journis." On the other hand he hadn't beaten Joslire, or tormented his body, or required sexual services of him. Maybe for bond-involuntaries that was enough. "Thank you for the reminder. I will keep your advice carefully in my mind."

It was a good point, an important point.

But he had been raised to keep peace in his Household.

He was confident that he knew what to do.

"Then take your briefings, and back to quarters with you. Exercise. Sauna. Wherever." This was unequivocal; the interview was over. Andrej took the four-stack in his hand and stood up.

"Thank you again, Marshall Journis. Your remarks are very much appreciated." Except the one about wanting to have a look at Robert, perhaps. There didn't seem to be any sense in quibbling over that, however, especially since she'd not slapped him down for his rather acerbic rejection of what had apparently seemed to her to be an entirely reasonable request.

"That's as may be, and you're welcome. Good day, 'Student' Koscuisko."

She'd risen to her feet in a parting gesture. Andrej tried to make his salute as polite and respectful as he knew how.

There was nothing left to do but mark time until tomorrow. The knowledge made him anxious to be away, and on with things.

Andrej sat at one of the windows of the passenger compartment, watching Fleet Orientation Station Medical shrink slowly against an expanding background of black featureless space. Better for him had he never come here, better for him had he never known . . . he could have lived his life out in blessed ignorance, and been happy. But it was too late for that now. Even if he never made a single Inquiry within the next eight years, he would still know. He was a monster; and he had always been a monster. The passion to which St. Clare had introduced him was not an alien thing, but a part of him, as surely as was his passion to comfort and to heal.

And since it was part of him, he would not deny its existence. He would not repudiate the beast, as dreadful as it was. He would have to live with himself forever, whether he went home tomorrow or never went home until his father declared the year of his Retirement.

He thought he'd known what he was to face, when he came here. He had been wrong. And it had been far worse than he had imagined. How could he have guessed the horrors that St. Clare and Curran were expected to bear uncomplaining, as part of their duty? The worst part of it was that they accepted it, they all accepted it, and looked at him with confusion when he protested. Joslire, who expected to be abused. Chonis, who expected him to discard St. Clare like so much soiled toweling. Tutor Chonis had praised him for engaging in his training exercises on such a personal level. It was true that it made things much easier during the exercise itself to be able to enjoy it, and so keenly. But it was still wrong to take pleasure from the pain of helpless prisoners. Intrinsically wrong, absolutely wrong, no matter what crimes they might have committed.

And still there had been benefit for him from Orientation. Because they had permitted him to sell himself for St. Clare's life, so he did not have that blood-guilt on his hands. There had been ways to approach his Inquiry that provided opportunities, scant though they were, to affirm the dignity of the dying and protect the innocent. He had not compromised the safety of the unaccused for his pleasure, at least not yet. That was a hopeful thing.

But more important, most important, there was Curran, with his private torment and his guarded self. Brutally misused body and soul by the system that had enslaved him, Curran had still reached out to him to give him comfort in his pain, without holding the sins of the previous officers against him. Joslire had been charitable and generous with him even while Joslire fully expected Andrej to use him as the others had. It had been an act of significant courage on Joslire's part, the gesture of a great heart to offer what could not be demanded of him, freely, when it could have cost so dear.

And St. Clare did not seem to hate, not even when Andrej stood before him with the whip that was to bring him agony.

If such as these could hold fast to their human dignity beneath the crushing weight of inhuman discipline—then so could he.

If St. Clare could take the beating from his hand and fire back so mild a bolt as "yon undertall beauty," then perhaps he could deal as mildly with himself, and try not to despise himself beyond all hope because he was a monster.

If Joslire Curran could find courage to demand a piece of his self-determination back, then perhaps he could find the courage to perform his assigned task. Because as dreadful as he found it, as obscene as he felt his pleasure in it to be, still what he was called upon to do could not be weighed on the same scale as Curran's task had been, nor St. Clare's, either.

He would be guided by their approach to their lives, as he was humbled by their courage.

With Joslire and St. Clare to help him through, Andrej knew that he could survive, no matter what awaited him on *Scylla*.

EPILOGUE

Mergau Noycannir paused for a moment before signaling for admittance to Tutor Chonis's office. Almost there. Almost. The Ninth Level—distasteful as that had been—was behind her; only the Tenth Level remained, and with Koscuisko's drugs she had no fear of failing in the final test. It was time she went back to her Patron. The contemptuous scorn of the Security troops assisting her exercises was becoming impossible to ignore, if impossible to prosecute. And she had found it expedient to decline the offered increase in her personal training sessions from two on one to three on one, because she realized that the Administration would not intervene should three become too many for her to handle. It didn't matter. One more exercise and she would be clear of all of these—clear, and free to return triumphant to Chilleau Judiciary, to secure herself in Verlaine's favor, once and for all, with the Writ to Inquire.

Signaling at the Tutor's door, Mergau went in.

Tutor Chonis was alone; she'd not seen Student Koscuisko for days—not since her Seventh Level, Mergau realized with a start. He'd not been present for her Ninth Level orientation, when Tutor Chonis had explained the action of the drug. There had been questions in her mind during her Ninth Level; the prisoner's behavior had not seemed entirely consistent with the action of the drug as Tutor Chonis had described it. She had intended to bring the anomalies to Student Koscuisko's attention, as a reminder of her now-dominant role in their relationship. She did not mean to be cheated of her treat.

"I greet me my Tutor, and hope that the morning finds him well. Student Koscuisko, is he not to meet with us, Tutor Chonis?"

So close to the end, so close to finished, she did not need to be as careful as she otherwise might have been. She didn't have much time left in which to submit herself meek and humble to the Administration. Only one more exercise and she could safely leave the entire Station and everyone on it, discarded as worse than useless. One more exercise.

"Student Koscuisko will not be joining us, Mergau. Be seated."

Tutor Chonis barely looked up at her when she came in, apparently concentrating on sorting a set of cubes that lay before him on his desk. The beverage service that had been an invariable feature of the classroom table was different than it had been; only one glass had been set out. Pulling the serving-set closer to her, Mergau poured herself a cup: rhyti. It was close to a slap in the face to serve her rhyti, if only she was expected.

"I hope that all is well with my fellow Student? I am anxious for his sake."

She didn't expect the blatant lie to fool Tutor Chonis, although the situation could be honestly interpreted in such a way as to hint at a problem. A suicide, for example. Chonis would be more distracted in his behavior had Koscuisko tried to escape in that way, though. There would be political repercussions, complications, a scandal, if the oldest son of the Koscuisko prince had killed himself after his family had entrusted him to Fleet.

"And I'm certain that Student Koscuisko cherishes the same fondness for you. Now. First Secretary Verlaine has asked us to send copies of your Intermediate Levels to him through the Administrative center at Pikanime. Administrator Clellelan has released your records on the freight run that went out yesterday, and he released the complete record, so Secretary Verlaine will have a chance to evaluate your Advanced Levels as well."

That was a strange thing to have done, wasn't it? They both knew that Verlaine had asked for the record so that he could judge Koscuisko's potential for himself, if indirectly. Koscuisko's talent would only be more obvious in her Advanced Levels than they were at the Intermediate. "I am unsure about the drug Student Koscuisko selected for the Ninth Level. I had wished to make a private question of it, Tutor Chonis."

Tutor Chonis almost smiled. "No doubt, Student Noycannir, no doubt. But the best drugs in the world won't help unless you pay enough attention to working with, and not against, them. Let us consider your Tenth Level exercise. The final test is crucial to your graduation, as you know."

This was getting frustrating. "I hope to profit from instruction, if I may speak to Student Koscuisko in this matter . . ."

Meeting her eyes squarely, blunt and candid, Tutor Chonis declined to take the bait; offering her instead a sop of teasing information clearly intended to be deliberately provoking. "That will not be possible, Mergau. I suggest you concentrate your energies on your Tenth Level. You must pay more attention to what you're doing, if you mean to graduate at the end of this Term."

Why would it "not be possible" for her to talk to Koscuisko? All Chonis had to do was issue the summons, and Koscuisko would of necessity come promptly, no matter what he might have been doing. Such a pretense on Tutor Chonis's part made no sense.

Nor did the Administration's willingness to release her Advanced Levels to Verlaine, unless . . .

"The drug was not correct for my last exercise, Tutor Chonis. You told my Patron that I would receive support."

Verlaine had asked for her records so that he could judge Koscuisko's worth and decide whether to preempt Fleet's posting to take Koscuisko for his own. The Administration had sent the records Verlaine had requested, those and more. Tutor Chonis knew very well what she had been trying to get Verlaine to do—Mergau was certain of that. The conclusion was easy to derive but impossible to credit.

"This Administration has done everything in its lawful power to accommodate First Secretary Verlaine, Mergau. But nothing will do the job for you if you cannot remember the most basic restrictions of the Levels. Rehearse for me if you will the requirements for satisfaction of the Tenth Level exercise, Command Termination."

If they had sent the records directly to Chilleau Judiciary, she would be graduated and gone before Verlaine would have the time to prepare a requisition override for Koscuisko's posting. Tutor Chonis had said Pikanime, though. That meant that Verlaine had asked for more immediate access. A requisition override could be prepared and delivered to Fleet within a matter of days from Pikanime. Tutor Chonis had also said that it would "not be possible" for her to speak to Student Koscuisko. Therefore and necessarily, Tutor Chonis had released her records to Verlaine because he felt that Koscuisko was secure from any intervention from Pikanime Judiciary; and Koscuisko would only be secure from such last-minute revisions to his orders if his orders had already been issued.

"Mergau? I'm waiting. If you would be so kind."

They had sent Koscuisko away to Fleet, so that the Bench could not have him. It was an outrage, so blatant an insult that it took her breath away. It was also a mistake, because her Patron knew how to deal with intriguers of this sort.

"The Tenth Level of the Question, Tutor Chonis, Inquiry, Confirmation, and Execution. Command Termination. The required elements include the cumulative execution of the Fourth through Ninth Levels, over a period of not less than three and ideally lasting five days."

Would they defy the Bench and deny Verlaine access to their prize Student?

Would they indeed?

She would be out of here in less than three weeks' time; she would bring the Writ to the First Secretary. She would bring words and knowledge to him as well.

Let Koscuisko hide in Fleet, and pinch his nose in mockery toward Chilleau Judiciary.

Her Patron would know well enough how to repay Andrej Koscuisko for this insult.

PRISONER OF CONSCIENCE
A Novel Under Jurisdiction

He wanted to be a doctor, but his family sent him to be a Ship's Inquisitor. Only his fierce determination to hold to justice wherever he can find it has preserved his sanity—his own force of will, and a peculiar partnership with a man condemned by the Bench to serve on pain of agonizing punishment inflicted by the "governor" in his brain.

In Port Rudistal, a defeated people have been consigned to the authority of their ancestral enemies to suffer and work and die like cattle.

Bereft of his friend, drunk on absolute license to work his will on prisoner after prisoner, will Andrej realize what horrors are contained within the walls of the Domitt Prison, and can he bring the truth to light before his enemies silence him forever?

Acknowledgments

My protagonist was raised according to a strict standard of filial piety that includes reverence for his ancestors. I'm not Dolgorukij, but it rubs off. Therefore, taking up a bundle of lighted incense sticks, I clasp my hands before me and face north to bow to my ancestors, who will always have guest-place in my house.

Devra Langsam was my great-grandmother. Joanna Cantor and Lori Chapek-Carleton were my great-aunts. Ellen Blair and Bev Clark were my earliest confidants. I had too many godmothers to count: I can only bow.

To Maggie Nowakowska: for all the extra loads of laundry, sinks full of dishes, plumbers and electricians intercepted, bills written, cars washed, and errands run while I was holed up in a dark room writing, I dedicate this book; with my gratitude for her support in years past, and my hope for her continued companionship in many years yet to come.

CHAPTER ONE

Fanner Rigs hugged the visioner at his station, fascinated and horrified at once at the sight of the enemy fleet that faced them. The enormity of the task was overwhelming: how could they hope to challenge the Doxtap Fleet, in all the pride of the Jurisdiction's might?

The Bench had left no choice for them.

They had to try.

Eild was their home-world, and the orbiting artillery platforms that defended it had to be protected from destruction by those mighty warships if Eild was to have any hope of remaining free.

"Our target." It was his brother's voice on inter-ship, Marder's voice. On this little courier they almost didn't need the inter-ship to hear each other—the ship was tiny, built for speed and maneuverability, both of which were crucial to its intended task. They had to get past their target's own defenses, its Wolnadis, after all.

And the Wolnadi fighters were visible even now, clearing the maintenance atmosphere and coming toward them at frightening speed.

"Jurisdiction Fleet Ship *Scylla*," Sonnu's clear calm voice confirmed. It was useful to remember that Sonnu was there. Fanner had often fantasized about marrying with Sonnu, if he could catch her eye for long enough to make his case with her. This was his chance to show her his true mettle.

And still it was a desperate enterprise.

They all knew that.

His party had the most desperate part of it, for while the others in the attack on *Scylla* were to draw the Wolnadis off toward the carapace hull—the topmost shell of the warship—his party was to feint for the carapace, and slip at the last minute through the atmosphere barrier into *Scylla's* maintenance atmosphere, beneath the ship.

They had the schematic firmly fixed in mind.

If they could only be quick and nimble enough about it, agile and canny enough about it, slip through the startled defenses of the maintenance atmosphere—*Scylla* could not fire upon itself, for fear of damage to the ship—

To fail meant death.

To succeed meant death as well, because if they won through to the main battle guns they could destroy *Scylla*, and everybody on it. Including them.

He would never marry with Sonnu now, but if he could be part of the freedom of port Eild it would not even matter.

"Initiate tactical plan," Marder said; and Fanner engaged the overthrust boosters on the courier, and sent it leaping forward.

Toward *Scylla*, and their death.

If they could only take *Scylla* with them it was worth it.

Snatching a breath as best he could in the close quarters of *Scylla's* maintenance corridors, Joslire Curran steeled himself for the next desperate sprint. He couldn't stop for long enough to catch his breath. He couldn't afford to. There were Nurail sappers in the corridors, they'd breached the maintenance hull and gotten in through the maintenance atmosphere and if Joslire and his team couldn't stop them in time—

Kaydence Psimas came up on Joslire's left and nudged Joslire's shoulder with his elbow, wordlessly. Joslire nodded toward the access to the recirculation systems, and Kaydence grinned and went, dropping to a roll halfway across the corridor as he was fired on. Joslire checked the crossfire zone with a swift movement of his head: no blood on the deck. So maybe Kaydence was unharmed.

The Nurail would know where to watch for them now, though, and there was nothing they could do but get across as quickly as they could. The Nurail sappers had only left one man to try to slow them down. The rest of the party would be three corridors away by now.

The only thing that stood between *Scylla* and destruction was the fact that men who knew the ship's architecture from living there could navigate more quickly than anyone else.

Kaydence fired back down the corridor at the Nurail who had pinned them there, as much to remind his fellows that he was waiting as to encourage the Nurail to go away. Erish Muat went across, stumbling on the decking and sliding to safety, Kaydence covering him with a shot. They couldn't afford to use full charge on board ship for fear of starting a fire. The enemy didn't care.

Toska Bederico brought up the rear, but there was no fire at all from the Nurail, so maybe Kaydence had shot him down. It didn't really matter. All that mattered was getting through to the main battle guns before the Nurail sappers could get there.

The main battle guns—lateral cannons forward, in this case—could not be turned back toward *Scylla*'s interior. But they could be spiked. And the resulting explosion would destroy everything within a standard orbital.

Down the cross-corridors now to food-stores three. The sappers were taking the main access corridor, but the back wall of food-stores forward abutted a waste-chute that could be vented into armory two levels above. The sappers wouldn't be able to use the lifts. The lifts had been shut down by Engineering as soon as they'd realized that the crew of the small Nurail scout ship that had cleared the maintenance atmosphere had shot its way in to the maintenance corridors.

It would take the Nurail time to break into the access hatch beside the lift nexus and squeeze through the narrow laddered way. Maybe it would take the sappers enough time for Joslire's team to get through to the cannons before the Nurail did.

Shoot out the secures on food-stores forward door four, struggle through the half-opened door into the room. Joslire took refuge with Erish and Kaydence behind a shelf full of soup concentrate cartons. Toska piled up a hasty barricade of flour boxes to crouch behind and fired pointblank at the back wall.

There'd been no time to clear the shelves. Shattered bits of storage containers flew like a sandstorm in the little room as Toska fired. Joslire grabbed a chip of something that imbedded itself firmly in the storage shelves behind them: dried sindal, for the mess's approximation of meat roast. Too bad. He had been hoping for a bite of dried fruit.

Toska was through the wall. Joslire joined Kaydence in clearing away the rubble till they could get at the smoking gap and through. If the Engineer fired the conversion furnaces to hasten the ship's progress, they were done for. The vacuum that the huge furnace would create would pull them into the engines, and they would become propulsion—not protection—for *Scylla*.

Joslire put the thought out of his mind. If they didn't stop these Nurail sappers, *Scylla* wouldn't go anywhere, ever again, except perhaps out in a three-sixty orb in fragments not exceeding seven eighties in size and five eighties in weight.

The waste-chute hadn't been cleaned for a while. The handholds were full of debris and particulate matter. There were three sets of handholds spaced out around the tubular waste-chute, and Joslire scooped and swept out each of them as he went, mindful of Kaydence waiting beneath him to follow him up the waste-chute.

It was easier going here than the mech-access at the lift nexus would be for the Nurail sappers, and they could only get one person up the mech-access at a time, while three could fit at once in the waste-chute.

The time it took to move up eighth by eighth was still maddening.

What would they find when they got there?

Toska popped the chute while Erish climbed up to hang opposite the opening, nursing his injured arm. When had Erish been injured? It didn't matter. They couldn't stop to think about it. They had to go on.

They were in corridor five, Kaydence running for the end of the corridor while Joslire was still helping Erish through from the waste-chute. Sprinting after Kaydence and Toska, Joslire heard the voices, but Kaydence's voice was closer—

"We're behind. They're in third forward!"

They'd come too late. The enemy had already cleared the lift nexus. The voices they heard were Nurail sappers on the way to Cannon Three.

They ran.

Corridor three wasn't a straight shot through; none of the corridors ran more than a few eighths without turning. There was a Nurail at the first turn waiting for them, and the round she fired stopped Erish in his tracks before Joslire's return shot separated the top half of her body from her legs.

The shower of gore and bits of flesh made it hard to keep their footing. But they had to catch up with the sappers before the sappers could get to the guns. There had only been eight Nurail to begin with, and they were down to three now—two once Kaydence killed the one waiting behind the next turn, taking him by surprise.

Two.

They didn't have time to take the turn carefully, whether or not waiting Death should stand behind the next wall. They had to stop the sappers. There were only two turnings left.

One turning.

No turnings.

They could see the sappers ahead of them in the corridor now, and the still-open door into Cannon Three's loading chamber further on. Joslire checked his weapon's charge one last time at a full run, steadied it as best he could—and fired. He didn't have much hope of aim, not running all out as he was.

He didn't need much aim.

It was a lucky shot, he got the furthest Nurail, and he fell against the wall to clear the field of fire for Kaydence and Toska behind him. Kaydence bolted past like a man in pursuit of his destiny, screaming, firing as he went—one shot, two shots going wild against the bulkhead at the far end of the corridor. The Nurail wasn't looking back, and from what Joslire could see the Nurail was gaining on the open door—

At last the door started to close, the engineers beyond overriding the system safes that prevented the load-doors from closing when the cannon was active. Closing the door wouldn't stop the sapper. But it would slow the sapper down.

Kaydence threw himself to his knees in a smooth skid and fired as the last of the Nurail sappers, turning, started to slide his body through the fast-closing door.

Joslire couldn't see at first what had happened. The Nurail he'd shot was beginning to stir, raising a weapon, which was trained on the back of Kaydence's head. Joslire had to shoot the man, and make sure he stayed shot this time, before he had any business trying to see through the mess of dust and smoke at the far end of the corridor.

It was quiet in the corridor now, no sound but for the subtle rain of pulverized metallic debris settling out of the air to the decking.

Picking himself up carefully, Joslire staggered over to where Kaydence sat slumped on his heels in the middle of the corridor. It was critically stupid to sit there like that. They'd be too easy a target to miss if there were any sappers left to shoot at them.

"Make the hit, Kay?"

His throat was rough and strained from running too hard, too fast, for too long. Manning the Wolnadi fighters was nothing like this. On the Wolnadis at least you sat down while you either chased down or ran from your enemy. Just their luck to have been on Ship's Security duty when the *Scylla* joined the Doxtap Fleet to help reduce the artillery platforms at Eild.

"Hard to say," Kaydence replied, hopelessly, staring at the ceiling with his head well back on his broad solid shoulders. "But we'll know in a bit. The ship will blow up. Or it won't. Then we'll know."

There was no help for it but to go and see, then.

Joslire limped forward—funny, he was bleeding, when had that happened?—toward the door at the end of the corridor, half-open, dimly visible now through the clearing dust. There was the door. There was the body on its belly facing toward the door, limp and ungraceful in abandonment—but what about beyond?

Stepping over the prone body of his enemy, Joslire Curran leaned into the doorway to find out.

The cannon.

He couldn't see the cannon for the face or Erling Miroah, standing in the doorway with a clearing-lever in his hand. As if you could stop a Nurail sapper with a clearing-lever. As if anything could stop a Nurail sapper within sight of his goal; these people were demented. And their insanity made them all but superhuman in what they had proved capable of doing . . .

"The cannon?" Joslire rasped.

Erling wasn't moving, calling back over his shoulder into the room beyond.

"No, it's Curran from Security. Send damage control. Send a med-team."

Why?

"The cannon," Joslire insisted, beginning to get annoyed. Why wouldn't they answer his question?

Erling moved to one side, working at the controls for the door. Joslire saw the cannon at the same instant that he realized why Erling hadn't bothered to answer his question. If the cannon had been hit, they wouldn't be here for him to ask. That was why. It must have seemed too obvious to Erling.

Joslire sat down between the bulkhead and the body of the Nurail sapper. It had been a fine effort. First Officer was going to have things to say about the fact that sappers had breached the maintenance hull in the first place. Kaydence came reeling drunkenly across the littered decking to sit down heavily at Joslire's side; together they watched Toska help Erish come up to join them. Erish's face was wet with tears of pain—or perhaps simply rage, and sheer frustration. Erish hated to be left out of the shooting. It was just Erish's bad luck to have been shot, but since he was walking it hadn't been too bad.

Joslire closed his eyes, exhausted.

Too much excitement.

At least things were quiet now.

He could hear ship's braid as if at a considerable remove, the Engineer dispatching damage control teams, First Officer reporting status to the Captain. He could hear ship's ventilators struggling to process all the chipped bulkhead and metal dust they'd just blown into suspension.

He could hear Kaydence's shaky breathing beside him, Toska catching his breath, Erish grunting softly with reluctant pain. He didn't hear the med-team coming up, even though they had probably been running. Well. Maybe he had had a short nap, then.

"Joslire, what's your status, here?"

"Sitting by, team leader." He couldn't rightly say "standing" by, could he? "It's Erish to go first. He's had the worst of it, I think."

"Right, move this one out to triage. Gala, Marms, on Erish. Joslire. You're hit. Robert, see what you can do about this, we'll have the next team up as soon as we can."

Joslire met Robert's level gaze and grinned. It was Robert's fifth-week in Infirmary, and he was working harder than any of them. They were all sitting down resting, after all.

"Oh, you're going to be in trouble," Robert warned. Joslire knew the joke. The officer didn't like them to let themselves be injured. The officer took it personally. "Extra duty for at least a month, Jos."

Right.

He'd worry about it when he faced the officer.

For now he thought that he'd just close his eyes.

Robert St. Clare wheeled the mover with Joslire on it into the next slot in the triage line. Infirmary was strange to look at on battle status; the clinic walls, the office dividers, the treatment room partitions were all pulled up into the ceiling or dropped down into the decking underfoot to clear as much space as possible.

The triage officer had already sent Erish on to Station Four. Their officer was at Station Four, though Robert couldn't see him, Infirmary being crowded, and the officer short.

One of the techs at the triage station cut open the fabric across Joslire's thigh, and the triage officer—Doctor Bokomoro, Degenerative Bone and Muscle—raised her eyebrows at the wound. "Five eighths' span of bulkhead, Joslire," she said, sounding impressed. "How did that happen?"

Like the rest of Infirmary staff, she called Joslire by his personal name. Joslire didn't care to be reminded of the Curran Detention Facility, where Joslire had been Bonded and given his Fleet name. Robert didn't care. He'd been assigned a name at random, like other Nurail bond-involuntaries, to destroy even so small a bit of information that they might have had about one another.

"It must have been in food-stores three, as the doctor please. Because this troop can't quite remember. With respect."

Still Joslire was formal with her. Formality was safety, for bond-involuntaries. It was all a part of their conditioning. Doctor Bokomoro palpated the ragged edges of the wound in Joslire's thigh with delicate care, frowning a bit. "Well. You'll do for Station Four when it clears. You're the last of it, are you?"

Her question was directed at Robert, who looked back over his shoulder down the length of the corridor, checking the triage line. They seemed to have hit a slack period.

"There aren't many in queue just now, Doctor, no, ma'am." So she could afford to set them aside, and let the officer perform what triage he liked. There would be time.

Doctor Bokomoro nodded. "Right. Take Joslire across, Robert, take these with you. Next?"

"These" were Toska and Kaydence and Code, the rest of Security 5.4. All of them weary. None apparently injured. When Station Four cleared, Robert took the lead to their assigned slot, pushing Joslire on the mover before him.

The officer was leaning on the treatment table with both arms braced stiff-elbowed to the surface, frowning in evident anxiety.

"I am becoming bored with bleeding people," his Excellency was saying, his frustration clear in his tenor voice. "When is the Captain going to get to it, and take this ship out of harm's way?"

Shaking off wordless offers of assistance, Joslire slid awkwardly from the end of the mover to sit on the edge of the treatment table, facing the officer. Koscuisko scowled thunderously when he saw the exposed gash in Joslire's leg.

Sarse Duro, the senior medical technician teamed with Chief Medical, took one look and broke open a fresh gross-lacerations pack. "Shouldn't be too much longer now, sir. They said three eights to close." Noticing Robert, Sarse shut up to concentrate on Joslire's wound. It was out of respect for his feelings, Robert knew. He appreciated Sarse's delicacy.

Eild was Nurail.

He was Nurail, though he was from Marleborne.

"Erish is to be uncomfortable, but has not too seriously been injured. Joslire, you are bleeding, you had noticed." His Excellency changed the subject without comment, putting a dose through at Joslire's thigh. Joslire steadied himself against the surface of the table, and Koscuisko put one hand out to Joslire's shoulder to help stop him from falling over. Muscle relaxant, maybe. Powerful pain medication, almost certainly.

"Kaydence. You are not moving as beautifully as usually you do." Their officer talked as he worked, Sarse Duro content to keep supplies coming. "I should make you all sit down, but then I would not be able to see you. Metal coming out, Joslire."

Along with a freshet of blood damped off almost immediately with a stop-cloth. "Talk to me, gentles all, how do you go? I have seen none of the others, at least so far."

Well, he didn't have to answer this question, Robert told himself.

He could just stand here and listen. That way he would find out before the almost-inevitable embroideries began. That could be useful for later.

"Kaydence did it," Joslire said, his head bent to watch Koscuisko clear the wound. "We were only there to wa—ouch." Something seemed to twinge unpleasantly; Joslire raised his head to meet Koscuisko's mirror-silver pale eyes, and Koscuisko smiled. Robert had always considered that Andrej Koscuisko had a very pretty smile, all those white teeth, and all of them in such an even line.

"You are a very great liar, Joslire, if I may hope to be forgiven for saying it. And you should be ashamed."

Grin answered grin, now. Joslire had known the officer for even longer than Robert had, and they had known him longer than anyone else—since Fleet Orientation Station Medical, before they'd been assigned to *Scylla*. But that had been three years ago.

And almost the first thing they had learned about Koscuisko was that they were clear to make jokes with him. Not that the others had been easy to convince that it was really safe; and that had depressed Robert at the time, because of what it indicated about the usual treatment bond-involuntaries expected to receive in Fleet.

"But it's true, your Excellency, I swear it by the officer's chin-beard," Joslire protested. There was no response from their officer to this impertinence; Andrej Koscuisko didn't have a chin-beard, smooth-skinned as any unmarried man. Koscuisko concentrated on smoothing the edges of the wound in Joslire's thigh flush with the layer of anaerobe that would protect the raw flesh while it healed.

After a moment Joslire spoke on. "Kaydence's shot was the only one that really mattered, when it comes to that. All the other ones do us no good if the last one doesn't go in." Serious now, Joslire was giving his report, which meant that the others were free to contribute.

"But it was Jos's idea to get through the waste-chute behind food-stores forward. Or we wouldn't have gotten there in time." Toska Bederico, apparently no more than bruised and tired, was leaning against the stores table that would normally back against a wall that was now braced up in the bulkhead. "Can you get Jos to admit it, though? There's the question."

As a joke it was not a very fortunate one, in Robert's mind. Andrej Koscuisko could make anybody admit to anything, once he but got them down into Secured Medical and got started. Toska was tired, or he wouldn't have made so potentially ambiguous a remark. The officer didn't seem to have noticed anything; Koscuisko was tired, too.

Of course Koscuisko had been hard at work since the first casualties had started to trickle in. For Robert's own self he considered that he had the better part of the contract, since he only had to fetch and carry. That wasn't really work.

"Was that my idea?" Joslire sounded genuinely startled. "I don't remember it being my idea. I thought it was Erish. Are you sure? I'll take full credit, of course; Robert, write that down."

Joslire would do no such thing, needless to say. Joslire was scrupulous about credit where credit was due, sometimes too much so.

"Don't think so," Kaydence frowned. "I thought it was Toska. Whose idea was it? Because someone's got to go clean that up."

"Light duty, ten days." Their officer tagged Joslire's trouser-leg closed with a few strips of closing-tape to spare his blushes till he could change his trousers. Joslire blushed differently from people Robert had grown up with; he didn't pink from pale, he toasted from tan.

Of course there was the fact that Joslire was simply the color of meal-cake to begin with. The officer put his hand to Joslire's shoulder for emphasis. "And keep your weight off your leg, you may walk if you must but no further than two turnings at a time. Now you must go to rest."

Joslire was subdued enough to let himself be moved by Robert and Code in tandem. Off of the treatment table. Back onto the mover. Koscuisko raised his voice and called for Kaydence, who was doing what he could to disappear; but there weren't any walls to hide behind just now.

"Kaydence, you are next. The shins of your boots look as though you had been using scour-skin for bootblack." Koscuisko's desire to lighten the atmosphere a bit was clearly evident in his bantering tone; and it worked, too. Quite apart from the fact that Koscuisko was their officer, he was a personable man, whose determined cheerfulness communicated itself to his Bonds almost immediately. "Tell me about it."

Koscuisko was right, the front of Kaydence's boots were scratched and abraded across the shins. Kaydence actually did blush, and since

Kaydence was the same generally clay-colored sort as the rest of them, it made him go all feverish in the cheeks. Well, clay-colored like Robert, at least. Their officer was so pale he was nearly blue in the face. And Toska was a little butter-colored, but Salom hominids were supposed to be that shade of sun.

"Sat down to make my shot, sir. Didn't stop moving. Probably just bruised, though, your Excellency—don't make me take off my boots, sir, please, there's a hole in my boot-sock—"

As if Kay thought pleading would do him the least bit of good.

Andrej Koscuisko merely tilted his head fractionally to one side with one of his most killing "Oh, but you know better than that" looks, and snapped his fingers.

Toska and Robert knew what was expected, and moved in to implement their officer's will and good pleasure.

There was no standing between Koscuisko and the welfare of his Security assigned, and whether or not said Security would rather not have an unmended undergarment exposed before all Infirmary had nothing to do with it whatever.

It could be worse.

Security Chief Warrant Officer Caleigh Samons could be here.

Their officer was only interested in the well-being of the skin beneath the stocking, not the condition of the boot-stocking itself, but let Caleigh Samons once find out that the officer had seen one of her troops out of uniform and there would be the very Devil to pay.

Command and Ship's Primes, Jurisdiction Fleet Ship *Scylla*, never met more informally than this—and in the Captain's office, rather than in meal-hall. There were allowances to be made for the state of exhaustion the officers shared with the rest of ship's assigned resources, but Andrej Koscuisko was too tired to make them, and he wished that his fellow Primes—and Ship's Command Branch officers, as well—would just go away and let him sleep.

"—carapace hull," Ship's Engineer was saying in between sips of hot shurla. "We lost most of the fiber-loads. Secured Medical as well. Significant damage to the maintenance hull, but the atmosphere hasn't been compromised, we were lucky."

Wait, wasn't that good news, about Secured Medical being stove in? Andrej almost thought that meant something. Surely it would be significant once his brain started to function again, after he had slept perhaps five shifts. No, that was only forty hours. Perhaps six shifts, then.

Ship's Intelligence paused on his way to his lounger to offer Andrej a flask of rhyti, talking as he went. "Prelims from the rest of the Doxtap Fleet indicate that we actually did comparatively well. We only lost three flyers in action, Fleet's quite pleased. Goes without saying Eild is a little depressed about the whole thing."

Andrej accepted the flask of rhyti with a nod of thanks. Of course Eild was unhappy. The planetary population of Eild had lost its final bid to retain autonomy; and if recent history was anything to go by, they had only want, repression, and relocation to look forward to now. Relocation for selected portions of the population, at least, scattered, dispersed among sixty-four eights of Bench-integral worlds.

Not as though there was much left of the population of Eild by this time, and it had been an outpost world to start out with—like most Nurail worlds, with typically a hundred and twenty-eight grazing animals to every Nurail soul.

It was still a lot of people.

Even after starvation, plague, and war, there were surely sixteens of eighties of Eild Nurail to be moved. To be removed. To be raped from their native soil and abandoned in alien worlds where nobody would even speak their language.

"That's as may be." Captain Irshah Parmin's voice was dry and uninflected, clear indication of how he felt about the use to which his Command had been put. Irshah Parmin was a professional Fleet Captain whom Andrej had grown to respect deeply over these three years of assignment to *Scylla*. Irshah Parmin never let feelings interfere with his duty.

He didn't make too great a secret about the fact that he had feelings, all the same. "There's a relocation fleet standing off at Formiffer to take over. We'll go to admin refit, ourselves. Chief Medical, your report?"

The rhyti was very reviving; he was very tired. It didn't usually have so strong a stimulating effect on him. "Apart from First Officer's losses we have a mortality count of seventeen on wards, mostly due to the hit the carapace hull took at channel two. Of my other patients I list five as being in very uncertain condition, but upwards of ninety lacerations or wounds requiring bed-rest or light duty, while the number of bumps and scrapes cannot be calculated."

There were seven hundred and thirty-five souls assigned to *Scylla*, and total fatalities rested at a mere twenty-nine so far. Even should they lose the five on close watch, they had gotten through this one with little scathe: though naturally enough the dead might think differently.

"Triage run the way you like it?"

That was delicately done. That was the Captain's way of asking whether Fleet had failed any of *Scylla*'s crew by failing to have the resources on site that would have saved their lives. Strictly speaking, triage was Medical's business; but Andrej could best honor his Captain's concern by answering the question.

"By our Lady's grace. Which is, I mean to say, yes, your Excellency, we have been fortunate. We have not lacked for the beds we needed when we needed them."

He was more tired than he'd realized, but his lapse into idiom had amused—and not offended—his peers. Not as though he really was their peer, except for the formality of his rank. Irshah Parmin had in the past honored him by asserting that he might develop into a really top-class battle surgeon, some year. In Andrej Koscuisko's considered opinion he had quite a distance yet to go.

"Good to hear, Doctor. Thank you. First Officer. About that Security five-point-four. Precedent?"

What about Security 5.4? Andrej frowned. Security 5.4 were his people, bond-involuntaries, though 5.4 had been on Ship's Security during the engagement, rather than flying a Wolnadi. Precedent for what?

"I believe so, your Excellency. Bassin—" the Intelligence Officer's name was Bassin Emer—"has pulled the index cases. They call for evidence of innovative thinking in crisis making possible some success crucial to the survival of significant Fleet resources. Case is stronger the more significant the Fleet resources, and I think *Scylla* counts. I know Jik's angry about the wall—"

Now the Ship's Engineer, Jik Polis, grinned and nodded her long perfect oval head in confirmation; Andrej was more lost by the moment.

"—but I think we can document. That was clearheaded thinking under fire. It probably made the difference. And there's no question about the performance under extreme circumstances. I will file the request for Revocation next shift."

"Does the officer of assignment know what we're talking about?" Irshah Parmin asked with evident amusement in his voice, clearly having noticed what Andrej could only assume was the transparent befuddlement on his face. "Never mind for now. We all need a rest-shift. Engineer, cut to minimum, administrative status in effect. We'll tell you all about it at staff first-shift, gentles, the usual time and place."

They were dismissed.

But Andrej didn't move.

"Captain, with respect." They were saying something about his people. He wanted to know what it was. "You were saying something about Security five-point-four."

First Officer Saligrep Linelly, rising to her feet, stretched to the full height of her sinewy body and yawned before she saluted to leave. The other officers followed as Sali left; they were alone. Captain Irshah Parmin stood from behind his desk-table in turn, grinning as he twitched his left shoulder. The captain had never been quite right in his left shoulder. Something to do with an implosion round and some shelving, Andrej understood.

"What your people had to do to stop that sapper, Andrej. Those Nurail were so close to taking this entire ship out. First Officer thinks we have a case for revocation of Bond, if we can just get it through channels before they all die of old age."

Revocation of Bond?

Freedom?

Bond-involuntaries were slaves to Jurisdiction, condemned for crimes against the Judicial order to thirty years of dangerous duty in Security with a semi-organic artificial intelligence implanted in their brains to help guarantee their good behavior. Revocation of Bond would mean freedom here and now, retirement with honors and pension and accumulated pay as though they had somehow managed to live out the term of their servitude and seen "the Day" dawn at last.

"Revocation of Bond can only be granted by the First Judge at Fontailloe Judiciary." Andrej spoke slowly, thinking aloud. Trying to remember. "And endorsed by the majority of Judges Presiding on the Bench. That's five. Getting five Judges to agree on anything—"

Still, it was an administrative matter when all was written and read in. Not a point of Law or Judicial precedent. There was a chance. Captain Irshah Parmin nodded solemnly, then spoiled the effect by yawning in his own turn.

"Even so. That's what we mean to try for. Needless to say, no word outside this room, premature release too painful if eventually refused, and all that."

He should get up, Andrej knew. He should leave. He was going to fall asleep in the chair. And it wasn't even so comfortable a chair. "Of course, Captain. Anything I can do, naturally. It would be a great thing, if."

No, it was no good. He was hardly making sense even to himself. Captain Irshah Parmin waved off the incomprehensible jumble of words with an understanding gesture of his short square hand.

"Of course. We'll talk again. Now get out of here. Go to sleep, Andrej."

Of course.

Turning the wonderful possibility of a Revocation of Bond over in his mind, Andrej went only semiconscious to find his quarters, and fall into bed, and sleep the still unmoving sleep of the exhausted.

There was someone coming through the open door to his office, and Andrej Koscuisko let his stylus sag to one side in a loosened left-handed grip as he glanced up to see who it was. One of the staff physicians, almost certainly. Nobody else would walk into a senior officer's workspace without pausing to announce himself—not unless it was an officer even more senior, and the only officer senior to one of Ship's Primes was the Captain himself.

Oh.

It was the Captain, himself.

Andrej was almost too startled to remember to stand up. Three years on board of *Scylla*, and the number of times the Captain had come to Andrej's office—rather than calling Andrej to come to his— could be knotted on a short string. There was an uncommonly serious look to Irshah Parmin's otherwise quite pleasant round face; waving Andrej to sit back down, the Captain palmed the interlock on the desk surface to seal the office door before he sat down himself.

"As you were, Doctor. Only take an eighth. I've got good news, bad news, and news."

Being behind closed doors with the Captain was a very

uncomfortable sort of thing; it only happened when Irshah Parmin had things to say he didn't mean to share, and in the past that had meant points on which Andrej's own behavior had failed to conform to expectation.

"Rhyti, your Excellency? Cavene?"

Andrej thought he sounded too serious by half, even to himself. What could this visit signify? He hadn't done anything he shouldn't have done, not recently.

"Neither, thanks, not staying. Which news do you want first? Never mind, I'll tell you. Good news, Secured Medical is out of order indefinitely, it won't be operational again until after we refit."

"Yes, Captain, good news. Bad news to follow?"

Something to do with the orders-packet that the Captain drew from the front of his uniform blouse, with a sigh of resignation. "This just in on courier. Since you're surplus, in a sense, with Secured Medical off line. Chilleau Judiciary's requisitioned you for the Domitt Prison until such time as we can demand you back to support the tactical mission as *Scylla*'s battle surgeon."

The Domitt Prison? Had he heard of that? The orders the Captain carried would tell him all about it, Andrej knew from experience. He had been detailed on temporary assignment before: always over the Captain's explicit objection.

"Prison duty, your Excellency. I don't believe I've done a prison tour yet." Prison duty didn't have to be too bad, as long as it was a standard Judicial correctional center, and not a processing center. The only thing the Bench needed Inquisitors for at correctional centers was to provide legal sanction for the exercise of prison discipline, and handle the occasional Accused. Not like processing centers at all.

Captain Irshah Parmin frowned. "It'll be weeks at best before we can call for you, Andrej. I haven't spoken to First Officer, but we're going to want to keep that Nurail of yours here on board, the Domitt Prison being in the middle of a Nurail displacement camp. Well, in a sense."

Oh, this was worse.

It was a processing center.

So what they wanted an Inquisitor for was to conduct Inquiry, exercise the Protocols, and perform his Judicial function exclusive of any other duties he might have had elsewhere; and for how long?

"I quite understand." Andrej could hear the strain in his own voice.

"Quite impossible. Who is to accompany me, then?" Bond-involuntaries, that went without saying. The Bench's primary purpose for creating bond-involuntaries in the first place had been to provide Inquisitors with helping hands. The bond-involuntaries' governors ensured that they couldn't decline to inflict whatever tortures their officer required of them simply because it was grotesquely indecent to do so.

He had eleven bond-involuntaries assigned to him here on *Scylla*, but that only made up two five-teams, with Vance as the only Bonded member on Security 5.1. So it had to be either 5.3 or 5.4. With Robert—and 5.3, by extension—held back, 5.4 would be assigned: well, why not? If it was to be hard duty for them, there was at least the hope in Andrej's heart that it would be their last assignment before the Bench revoked their Bonds.

"You'll probably end up with 5.4. And Miss Samons hasn't been told, First Officer wants to keep things to herself to avoid rumors. It could take months to get the petition through."

Andrej could understand that. The possibility in itself was almost too much to keep to himself; it could only be worse for Chief Samons, who worked with Andrej's people much more intimately. "That's good news and bad news, then, your Excellency. What about news?"

"Ah. In quarters, actually, I didn't hold it, none of my business." Irshah Parmin's raised eyebrows gave him the look of a man suddenly realizing that he'd misplaced something or another. "Came in with the courier, letters for you from home. There's a packet of some sort. We're to turn you over to the Dramissoi Relocation Fleet when it arrives, Andrej, that's just three or four days out."

The Captain stood up as he spoke, and rubbed his face with his hands as though just waking up. "All I can do is promise to try to get you back as soon as possible. My hands are tied. I'd rather have you here."

Because his Captain felt that the Ship's Surgeon should be with the ship, regardless of how young and inexperienced he might be. And would have spared Andrej the ordeal that awaited him, if he could have; and yet Andrej had learned years ago that once he got started with the Protocols he had no difficulty at all implementing them.

"Thank you, your Excellency." The respect he owed his superior officer was offered freely, out of genuine appreciation. "I'll tell someone to pack."

Three or four days, well, he'd have plenty of prep time with as many as three days to reckon with. But what had the Captain said?

Letters from home?

From whom, at home?

From Marana, with pictures of his child, and news of how the son he'd yet to meet was growing?

Or from his father, grim and formal and imbued with decorous grief over the fact that Andrej—in violation of the very filial piety after whose Saint he had been named—refused to be reconciled to the duty his father had set him to, and still declined to beg forgiveness for having challenged his father's desire that he go to Fleet to be Inquisitor?

His father had no more idea of what Andrej's life was like in Secured Medical than Andrej himself had once had, before his training. Andrej had never tried to more than hint at the horrors that comprised Inquisition. His father would only take it as cowardice on his part, evidence of shameful reluctance to do his duty to the Bench and Jurisdiction.

"Security Chief Warrant Officer Caleigh Samons. For his Excellency, Chief Medical."

The calm clear voice that sounded from the talk-alert provided a very welcome distraction for Andrej. Chief Samons. That was right. It was exercise period. She would be wondering where he was; or if not where he was, what excuse he might be thinking of to offer this time in his half-hearted but perpetual efforts to get out of the extra laps she would require of him.

"Coming directly, Chief. Koscuisko away, here."

Nothing was going to change his father's mind. Nothing was going to change the test to come, however many months at the Domitt Prison. Nothing could change the horror that he had of the hunger in his blood, but while he ran his laps he did not think about any of the things he could not change. He only thought of laps, while he was running.

That relief from mindfulness alone would have compelled him to seek exercise, were it not for the fact that Chief Samons put limits on his laps, to prevent injury.

Andrej went to join his Security and run his laps, and tried not to think too hard about the Domitt Prison.

CHAPTER TWO

It was five days after her early return from Worlibeg before Mergau Noycannir could get in to see First Secretary Sindha Verlaine, Chilleau Judiciary. She'd come back early on purpose to be sure that she was on site when the decision was made, only to discover that the decision had been made without her, the assignment she coveted given away to the last person in the world to whom she would wish it to go.

She'd waited five days for an explanation.

Admitted to the First Secretary's office, punctual to the eighth, Mergau stared at him as he sat behind his desk and did what she could to disguise her hunger. He was a thin reedy man, red-haired and pale-skinned, with watery eyes and a thin high-boned nose that made him look like a prey-animal flaring its nostrils anxiously into the wind to scent for hunters.

He looked small and rather insignificant, behind the great glaring expanse of his desk-table. And yet he held the power she desired above all things.

"You have sent Andrej Koscuisko to the Domitt Prison instead of me." She had been Clerk of Court under Sindha Verlaine for only five years, but she was the one who had earned the Writ for him. She was entitled to speak to him directly. She was different from the others. "Why? I thought it was my assignment. Especially after what I did for you at Worlibeg, First Secretary."

He didn't look particularly receptive, his expression blank. Perhaps she should have been more formal with him: but no, she was expressing her natural sense of outrage at being denied a privilege well-earned and well-deserved. To be mistress of the Domitt Prison . . .

Reaching for a stack of report-cubes, the First Secretary toppled them toward him, walking his fingers over the edges one by one. "Yes. Worlibeg. We're getting reports from Worlibeg, Mergau." He had a deep voice somewhat surprising to hear from a thin man. "They'll be talking about you for years. It's not exactly the kind of talk I'd hoped for, though."

He was avoiding the issue, and she wasn't about to let him. "I did as you instructed. I investigated and obtained confession, with collaterals. I executed the Protocols under my Writ, all as you desired."

Verlaine sighed, and kicked the stack of documents-cubes back with a decisive flick of his index finger. "Rather too much so. Mergau, I question your judgment sometimes: how likely was it that all of the Provost's family were plotting against the Bench? Five of them less than sixteen years of age, Standard."

"Confessed under speak-sera and were remanded to the Bench, with a neutral observer on site at all times." She was surprised at his expressed discomfort. She knew how to handle children under the Protocols. Hadn't she been especially gentle with the youngest? "And there was no question that a message had to be sent. You said so yourself. To send a Fleet Inquisitor to the Domitt Prison sends a message too, and I believe I have a right to understand why I am being publicly disgraced in this manner."

She'd thought carefully beforehand about whether she should use the word "disgraced." The First Secretary didn't take well to manipulation; it was necessary to be subtler with him than with previous Patrons. But she had held his Writ for three years, the only person in the history of the Fleet to be admitted to Orientation Station Medical without a medical degree.

It was in his best interest to save her face. She was the visible symbol of his power and his influence.

Still, from his reaction she realized she should not have used so strong a word. "'Disgraced.'" He spoke it as though it were not plain Standard, as though it were a word in a language unknown to him. "How are you disgraced because Koscuisko is to go to the Domitt Prison?"

Andrej Koscuisko to be master of the place, Andrej Koscuisko to enjoy the absolute power, but he would not. He didn't have the temperament to understand how to be master of the Domitt Prison. This was a man who would not discipline his slaves. The Domitt Prison would have as little respect for him as she did.

"It is a very significant. Highly visible. Politically critical job that needs to be done there. And you have chosen to send a borrowed Fleet resource rather than me. The message is clear enough."

Verlaine nodded. "Yes, indeed it is. Chilleau Judiciary elects an independent Inquisitor at the Domitt Prison because it is vital to our credibility that the evidence be perceived as sound. Andrej Koscuisko has acquired a bit of a reputation in Fleet circles over the years, Mergau. I've been keeping an eye on him."

She knew. And she needed to fix his attention on her, and not her hated rival. "I don't think it's unfair to say I earned that posting, First Secretary, and I had a right to expect it. Or at least to be privy to your decision before it became clear to all that I hadn't been so much as informed beforehand."

Verlaine reached for a dossier, looking bored. "You were in Worlibeg, Mergau. Or at least I thought you were in Worlibeg. I have an assignment for you of particular sensitivity, you may as well have this to begin review."

Mergau took a long slow breath, concentrating. All right. There was to be no discussion. It would only expose her to his irritation to press any further. She had to do what she could to salvage something from this interview: people were watching, listening, talking behind her back. She knew. She had informants.

So did he. He had more of them, and in more places. She was one of them, after all.

"Very good, First Secretary. The nature of the assignment, sir?"

He accepted her retreat into formality without any visible sign of having noticed it. "The Langsarik pirates. Bench specialists Ivers and Vogel have been working the problem. There are prisoners in transit to Chilleau Judiciary with what may amount to very pertinent information."

Langsariks!

The Langsarik pirates had been the mercenary fleet employed by the world-family of Palaam against its neighbors until those neighbors had cried to Jurisdiction for admittance and protection. Since then the Langsariks had persisted as pirates, never quite stamped out, and of late their depredations had become increasingly savage and frequent.

The severity of the problem could be judged by the assignment of not one, but actually two, Bench intelligence specialists to find the Langsariks and their backers and put an end to them once and for all. Under most circumstances, one Bench intelligence specialist was considered more than adequate for any three given wars: one Judicial Irregularity, one Bench intelligence specialist.

If she was to have Langsariks to question . . .

"Are there any preliminaries?" Mergau asked eagerly, reaching for the dossier. She could use Langsariks. With careful handling, the interrogation of some Langsariks could easily overbalance the snub the First Secretary had handed her over the Domitt Prison. "And am I to work with the Bench specialists involved?"

Verlaine held on to the dossier for just long enough to cause her to lift her eyes to his face, startled, to see what was the matter. "The usual statements." His expression was unusually severe. "I want you to take every precaution with these people, Mergau. Full cooperation with Medical staff. I'll have someone detailed to cull the Controlled List for you. We must have information, not just confessions. This could mean the end of the Langsariks, if Ivers and Vogel are right about what these people should know."

"Of course, First Secretary." Only now did Verlaine release the dossier into Mergau's anxious grasp. "I'll get right on it. When do they arrive?"

If she could get the confessions, that would enable Fleet to put paid to the Langsarik pirates at last: she would be the crucial element in the Second Judge's triumph, a stunning achievement that would easily silence the critics who continued to question Chilleau Judiciary's handling of the Nurail problem.

"Twenty days out yet, Mergau. Plenty of time to start your preparations. And I want you to put everything else aside and concentrate on this. Information. Not just confessions. Information."

Twenty days.

Twenty days, and then she'd get what she needed to more than make up for the fact that Andrej Koscuisko, and not she, was to vindicate the Second Judge at the Domitt Prison.

⊕ ⊕ ⊕

Working their way through the displacement camp, row by dreary row . . . this was one of the most depressing places Joslire Curran had ever been in his life, the Curran Detention Center where he'd lost his name and taken his Bond not excepted. Most of the population of Port Eild was here. The city itself hadn't been badly damaged, but the Bench had determined that the population would be easier to handle if they were removed from their homes.

How many souls had there been in Port Eild?

How many souls were here in these shacks, huddled together in misery and distress?

Their Captain had seconded them on order to the Dramissoi Relocation Fleet, to serve with Bench Captain Sinjosi Vopalar's other medical resources and travel with the relocation fleet from Eild to Port Rudistal in the Sardish system, weeks away from this world. Where the officer would place his Writ at the disposal of the Domitt Prison.

The sky had been overcast since they'd got here, six Standard days of unrelieved mist and fog. Dirty yellow clouds, and the cloud cover no relief from the oppressive atmosphere, though it wasn't as cold as it could have been—and a good thing, too. The local stores were grievously inadequate to supply a population with sufficient clothing and bedding for cold weather.

He'd heard it said—by displaced Nurail, and more than once—that it had been deliberate, an artificial shortage to increase their suffering; but Joslire knew better. To imagine that the Bench spared a second thought for their suffering was to be misguided. The Bench simply didn't care.

It was Koscuisko's responsibility to work through the holding areas, the ad-hoc cells set aside to hold the Nurail identified as prisoners as well as deportees. There was a difference, and it could be a critically important difference—deportees were subject to privation and dehumanization, but they could not be put to the torture merely because they were no longer to be permitted to die on their own land.

All of the people his Excellency had examined in the past three days were prisoners detained for Inquiry, though no Charges had been filed absent a Writ—until now. When they got to the Domitt Prison, his Excellency would himself record Charges where appropriate, but for now the Relocation Fleet Captain wasn't pressing him. There was no question but that he had as much as he could manage, just working his way through these eights of sixteens of people, trying to decide whether they were fit for the trip and free from communicable diseases.

Finished in yet another overcrowded eight of cells, his Excellency came out of the dark low-ceilinged shed into the chill light again. Koscuisko had been working hard, he was tired; and if Joslire knew his officer, the prospect of having all these souls to be subject to his will at the Domitt Prison was beginning to eat away at him inside.

"I will for a moment in the air sit," his Excellency said to whoever was listening. "I would not mind a cup of rhyti. Very much would I like to smoke. But it would be more cruel than decent to those around, if I did that."

Lefrols stank, but they had their place. His Excellency was not an habitual smoker of lefrols; instead of being mildly addicted to them, for the stimulus they provided, he had recourse to the herb when he needed distraction and could not get drunk. The relief from his cares the lefrols provided was moderate, to be sure; but at least afterwards he was not hung over.

Kay snapped the camp-stool he was carrying smartly into shape and set it down in the middle of the barren graveled patch that led between the long lines of temporary cells. Toska had the jug across his back, and broke the thermal seal to pour a steaming cup of rhyti as Koscuisko sat down wearily. Koscuisko took his cup of hot rhyti but didn't take a sip, not right away, resting the cup on his left knee, staring at the drink with an anxious frown on his usually tranquil face.

It wasn't easy for any of them to be here.

It was going to get a good deal worse before it got any better.

"How much further do we go today, gentlemen?" Koscuisko asked, squinting up into the sun with slumped shoulders. Code Pyatte flipped the status-leaves and squinted in turn, gazing down toward the end of the line.

"Says two more cellblocks in this section, sir. Eighty souls—no, sorry, hundred thirty. Doubling up a bit. It'll be just sundown, sir."

As difficult as it was to be here during the day, it only got worse at night. The whole camp was like one large, dark, cramped and overcrowded room at night. And then it started to get cold. It was a sharp depressing thing to know that he was warm and well-clothed, if a bond-involuntary Security slave, while there were children shivering in their parents' arms unable to sleep for the chill in the air.

Koscuisko drained his cup of rhyti and handed it back to Toska for safekeeping. "Better pick up, then. Thank you, Kaydence, I'll go on. Code?"

Koscuisko wanted the roster for the next cell-building; Code found it for him and passed it over. Koscuisko scanned the ticket and seemed to set his mouth against something unpleasant.

"All right. Joslire, if you would go ask for the key-man, please."

The key-man had been waiting, and propped the door wide open so that the officer would have as much natural light as possible. It was dark in the cells. Nobody in the cells had any grounds to insist on light—except that it wore upon the spirit to be kept in the dark like a chained animal.

These were Nurail, not animals.

But leave them alone in the dark for long enough and there would be no difference.

The first few cells were opened for the officer's inspection and closed again without incident, their occupants distressed and dispirited—hungry, cold, and thirsty, rations being adequate but on the frugal side—but hale and whole beyond that. It was only at the fourth cell at the back of the cell-building that the prisoner refused to move when spoken to, and Koscuisko tested the air as though he smelled something that he did not like. What was there to like in the smell of a temporary prison? None of these people had been permitted to wash for days. They weren't going to be here long enough to justify construction of facilities.

"Open here," Koscuisko suggested to the key-man. "Erish, if you would bring up the spare light. What can you tell me about your prisoner, key-man?"

The key-man looked anxious and weary himself. It couldn't be easy, Joslire decided, to have eight souls in care, with so little to do about basic problems of light and warmth. "I've had custody these four days past, your Excellency." The key-man was local, Joslire realized, with a bit of a start. Maybe he'd been a collaborator. Maybe he was thinking he'd backed the wrong side. "I can't get much out of him, he just lays there. He wasn't brought as sick, though, sir. I've let him be."

The key-man knew something was wrong, and was afraid he'd be blamed for it. So it seemed to Joslire. Koscuisko stood in front of the now-open cell as the portable beacon Erish had brought in lightened gradually to full illumination; it had to be brought up slowly, or else the sudden brilliance could be very painful to people who'd spent a week in a dim room.

"Has he eaten? Taken fluid? Voided body waste?" Thoughtful and considering as the officer's voice was, Joslire could hear contempt and reproach there. The key-man as well, to judge from his response.

"I don't want anyone neglected under my care, your Excellency." Stiff, and offended, but more than that convinced that despite his best efforts he was going to be held responsible for something he hadn't done. "I've had the man in the next cell see to feeding him. And the rest. You could ask him."

If the prisoner was ill, the key-man would have known to report it right away, or risk an epidemic in camp. So what was going on?

"Thank you. Perhaps in a moment. Joslire."

The prisoner lay on one side with his back to the room, with a standard-issue blanket wrapped around his huddled body and his knees drawn up a little as if to try to conserve warmth. Still wearing Nurail foot-wraps, Joslire saw, but at least one of them was torn, or had been rewrapped by third parties who weren't familiar with native footgear. It was beginning to look ugly.

The cell was almost too small for both of them at once, but the closer he got to the prisoner the more convinced Joslire was that he knew what the officer smelled. The prisoner's tag said he was a young man, somewhere between twenty and twenty-five years of age Standard. Nurail could run short and slight for their age. Taken as a whole they tended to be underfed and undergrown, which only made a man wonder what they could have done against the Bench if they'd had adequate nutrition.

The Nurail in his blanket looked unnervingly like a child to Joslire, pale skin and clean-shaven cheeks and all. Nurail shaved till they were married. This one's beard clearly didn't grow quickly, if it grew at all, because there wasn't the usual several days' growth of stubble on that sweat-clammy face.

Koscuisko touched the backs of his fingers to the Nurail's forehead and waited, counting breaths. The prisoner was hot, Joslire could feel

392 Susan R. Matthews

the radiation of body warmth clear through the blanket. Feverish. And there were other reasons a man would lose body heat at the back.

"I don't suppose you've got any transmit docs?" Koscuisko called over his shoulder, to the key-man. To Joslire in a quieter tone, he said, "Let's see about unwrapping him, carefully. Tell Toska I'm going to want my kit."

"No documentation," the key-man replied, sounding relieved. To be shown an out? That he couldn't be made to say where the prisoner had come from or who had brought him? "Some Fleet Security, I think, sir. Brought him, took the first available cell, left."

Oh, yes. Of course. Right.

Fleet Security.

And it could be. That was the hell of it.

Koscuisko worried the blanket free from the prisoner's nerveless fingers gently, and the man—or boy—opened his eyes suddenly, staring up at Koscuisko without moving his head. Terror, wild and anguished, and the white of the eye gleaming in the light reflecting off the back wall; terror and a good deal of pain, and Joslire beckoned for the officer's kit, where he kept his drugs—his anodynes.

"Shh," Koscuisko said. Not as if the prisoner had said anything. "We just need to have a look. We'll try not to hurt you." And drew the blanket back in careful folds, hissing through his teeth at the sight of the prisoner's exposed shoulders.

Raw meat.

And there was more of it, most of the prisoner's back had been laid bare, as though his back were all half-masticated flesh abandoned mid-meal by a predator.

"Your Excellency—" Joslire started to say.

"It looks like a peony to me, Joslire. Open for me my kit, I want a strong dose of asinjetorix. Kaydence? No, don't come in, name of the Mother." The horror Koscuisko felt at the suffering those wounds represented resonated in his voice, muted though it was to avoid giving alarm to the tortured man. "Go order me a litter for emergency care. And tell them I want it now. And I will need a surgery, as soon as one can be opened for me."

Joslire found the dose and passed it to Koscuisko, who took it in his hand to show the prisoner.

"A pain relief drug," his Excellency explained, as quietly and soothingly as Joslire could imagine. Their officer had a gentle touch with patients. "Not any other kind. I'm not going to ask you what happened. The Bench has forfeited its right to ask you any questions, any more, ever, about anything."

No comprehension on the prisoner's face, but why would there be? Joslire wasn't quite sure he caught his officer's meaning himself.

The key-man's anxiety would not let him keep still and speak when spoken to, apparently. "Your Excellency, what is it?"

Pressing the dose home, Koscuisko waited for a moment, then stood up. "Fleet Security, you say? We will want a statement. It is abuse of prisoner outside of Protocol. He has been put to torture without authority of Writ, because there was no Writ at Eild until I got here, and if I had taken the peony to any man I would remember it."

The peony was the ugliest whip in the inventory, its multiple thongs heavy and barbed. Koscuisko never used the peony except to Execute. It could kill quickly; there was a species of mercy in a quick death— even when it had to be by torture.

Otherwise the peony was good for very little but to chew up flesh like warmed spreadable, and it was accordingly a proscribed weapon outside the custody of an Inquisitor. It was illegal for anyone but an Inquisitor to carry a peony, unless it was the bond-involuntary under orders.

"I don't understand, your Excellency. Peony?"

Maybe the key-man didn't know what it was. Maybe whoever it was who'd been responsible had been counting on just that; or didn't care whether they left clear evidence. Populations were subject to multiple abuses in the aftermath of a final defeat, and this was one of them. And no, Joslire was not in the least interested in what the prisoner's feet would look like once they got this anonymous victim to Infirmary.

"Take a message," Koscuisko suggested. "I am logging this prisoner as released without prejudice due to Judicial irregularity. I will not tolerate abuse of prisoners outside of Protocol. And I don't care who knows it."

And at the moment, here and now, it was because Koscuisko's better nature shuddered at the damning witness of the wounds on the prisoner's back. And not because Koscuisko was jealous of interference.

"If you say so, sir." The key-man sounded dubious. "I had no way of knowing."

Like hell he didn't.

How could any man keep a torture victim for four days and not know?

Still, the key-man got credit for letting one of the others nurse the prisoner, Joslire supposed.

He'd better get a word in to Chief Samons as soon as he could manage.

Something told him this was going to cause trouble for his Excellency. The funny thing was that it was precisely the better part of the officer that was constantly creating problems. The worse part— the appetite Koscuisko had for pain—won him praise and commendation, though not from Fleet Captain Irshah Parmin.

And Fleet Captain Irshah Parmin—the Bench Captain by extension as well—would certainly have expected Koscuisko to raise this issue privately before taking the irrevocable step of logging release without prejudice.

Chief Warrant Officer Caleigh Samons, Chief of Security for Andrej Koscuisko, found her officer of assignment in a surgery within the temporary hospital that served the displacement camp. Having no brief to interrupt, she stood and watched him work through the sterile barrier that set the surgery apart.

The patient would logically be the Nurail who was responsible for Captain Vopalar's summons, the one Koscuisko had so summarily removed from the jealous grasp of the Dramissoi Relocation Fleet. Koscuisko worked with a look of absolute concentration on his face, salving the man's feet with exquisite care. From where Caleigh stood it looked like nasty burns on the soles of the apparently unconscious man's naked feet, a firepoint most likely; from Koscuisko's distressed expression he thought he knew exactly.

And he probably did.

What difference did it make?

People were tortured without benefit of Writ all the time. The fact that it wasn't supposed to happen was not material. There could have been information wanted, and no time to put in through formal channels for an Inquisitor's services. Things got out of hand when people were stressed, and being shot at tended to aggravate people.

Or maybe it had been something much simpler, someone taking advantage of the uncontrolled environment to express long-standing hatred for a personal enemy. Koscuisko could still be astonishingly naive, from time to time, for all the authority of his position.

He knew very well that such things were done. And still he let it surprise him.

"With you in just a moment, Miss Samons," Koscuisko said, finally noticing her waiting on the other side of the sterile barrier. "Very nearly finished here. Sweet Saints, it is ugly."

Laying one final gauze wrap carefully across the raw skin of his patient's foot, Koscuisko stepped back from the treatment table at last, nodding for the orderlies to come remove the patient. Pressing through the sterile barrier to join him now that the work was done, Caleigh handed him soap to lather up his bloodied hands, and stood by with the towel. This whole thing was off to an inauspicious start, but there was nothing to be done but make the best of it now.

"Bench Captain Vopalar would like to see you, sir. First Officer and Chief Medical as well. In the Captain's office."

It was well past sundown, cold and clammy with the fog. They'd been waiting for Koscuisko for more than two hours now. Her orders had been to find him and bring him when he was finished with whatever he was doing; that was a good sign, they weren't simply arresting the officer. But senior officers waiting on junior officers in Command offices well past third-meal never made for good hope of a forgiving mood.

Koscuisko had no comment as she helped him into his duty-blouse, finger-combing his hair and setting his cuffs to rights in silence. When he was ready to leave, though, he asked the obvious question.

"Am I in a very great deal of trouble, Miss Samons?"

It was funny of him to be so formal with her, when she knew very well that he found her physically attractive. Koscuisko was all the more formal and reserved with her for the fact that he would like to go fishing, to use the Dolgorukij metaphor, in her ocean. No. That wasn't right. It wasn't going fishing. It was that his masculine gender was a fish, and her ocean shores the place where it would very much have liked to frolic.

"I think it may be bad, sir." It could be all right. Irshah Parmin had been white-hot furious with Koscuisko on more than one occasion, and Koscuisko had come through without scathe. "Let's get it over with, one way or the other. Because your people are worried."

The Security that escorted them to the Captain's office were Dramissoi resources. Vopalar had Koscuisko's bond-involuntaries with her, a fact that could be construed as ominous. Caleigh didn't particularly care to mention that. Koscuisko would find out soon enough.

Command had administrative offices near the launch-field, in temporary buildings not much better furnished than the camp itself. Koscuisko was lodged in one of these, with his Security housed all five in a room of equal size adjacent, and a closet for his chief of Security between the two rooms. The Captain's office was the size of Koscuisko's quarters and Caleigh's put together, but that didn't mean very large. There was no room for the bond-involuntaries, for instance, so they were all lined up at command-wait in the hall, and Koscuisko was so surprised to see them that he missed a step and nearly fell on his face before he recovered his footing.

Caleigh didn't want to give him time to wonder what they were doing here. She hurried him through to where Captain Vopalar was waiting, instead.

The orderly knocked at the door and opened it, and there they were, Captain Vopalar, the First Officer, and the Chief Medical Officer for the Dramissoi Relocation Fleet—Doctor Clontosh.

"All we know for sure is that we've still got the right number of bodies in Limited Secure, Captain," the First Officer was saying. Caleigh knew what he was talking about, and listened with keen curiosity.

Nurail displacement parties arrived day by day to swell the ranks of prisoners and detainees in camp. There had been some confusion a few days past surrounding one particular group of detainees and prisoners; a near riot, in fact, only barely contained—with commendable restraint, Caleigh thought—by Dramissoi Fleet Security.

She hadn't realized that a question still remained about whether or not the bodies had all got sorted into the correct categories when it was over. That seemed to be what was on First Officer's mind, though. "The numbers seem to add up. And if anyone ended up in the wrong part of camp, nobody's saying."

It stretched the imagination a little past its point of maximum flexibility to imagine anyone substituting themselves for a prisoner from Limited Secure. Those were political prisoners, and destined to stand the Question from the start. One way or another, though, Caleigh reminded herself, it was First Officer's problem, and not hers.

Captain Vopalar nodded to First Officer as Koscuisko entered, rising to her feet as the First Officer spoke. Once it was clear that First Officer had finished his thought, Koscuisko bowed, making his salute.

"Bench Captain Vopalar. I report, according to her Excellency's good pleasure."

Captain Vopalar received his salute with a curt inclination of her head, gesturing to Caleigh to follow Koscuisko in and shut the door behind her. Not a good sign, all in all.

"Yes, Koscuisko, I want to check with you about something, some misunderstanding, I'm sure. There's a rumor of some sort going around to the effect that you found a prisoner you felt to have been abused outside of Protocols, and that you summarily excused him without prejudice."

Koscuisko would probably have protested that there was no such rumor as such, that it was fact; but Vopalar didn't give him the opening.

"But that would be inconsistent. It's hard to imagine a ranking officer taking such a high-handed approach without at least thinking about how it was going to look. There could easily be an interpretation made that you felt our First Officer was a party to Judicial violations, at least passively. I can't imagine why you'd want to do any such thing without letting us know. I'd like an explanation of this rumor, Koscuisko."

So far, so good. Vopalar put her case strong and fairly, setting the issues out where even a very naive and thickheaded young officer would be able to see them all too clearly. On the other hand, there was absolutely nothing Koscuisko could say for himself unless he was going to prevaricate. Koscuisko would on occasion interpret the truth in a creative manner to get someone off the hook for some minor lapse or another, but Caleigh Samons had never known him to lie.

"I am. Surprised. That such an interpretation might be put on it, your Excellency," Koscuisko said. He sounded surprised, too. "But I must first confess myself, and then hope my actions may be leniently judged. There was a prisoner who had been abused outside of Protocol. The key-man had no information that would indicate any Dramissoi Fleet resource had anything to do with the matter. And I have logged release without prejudice for this prisoner, and spent these hours past addressing his wounds. Had I known you wished to see me, Captain, I would have come sooner."

She waved this off with casual goodwill, which Samons hoped would not disarm the officer. "No, no, Samons was told to find you and bring you when you were finished with whatever. But tell me, Doctor. What do you think having done what you did says to the world about the honor of the Dramissoi Relocation Fleet? You've accused us of abuse of prisoners, we're convicted without even a chance to make an investigation. I think I take that personally. You son of a bitch."

Captain Vopalar sat down. For all the venom in her language her face was relatively clear; she seemed calm enough. She was willing to give Koscuisko a chance to recognize his mistake, and her officers—seated against the wall—would take their cue from her. Caleigh hoped that Koscuisko would make the right choice when he opened his mouth.

"To the contrary, Captain, with your permission. To have hesitated one moment would have been to suspect that the Dramissoi Fleet was corrupt in some way. To take immediate action was only possible because there was no danger of compromising any of the First Officer's people, your Excellency. The Dramissoi Fleet would not for a moment tolerate such abuse. Surely that is the message to be taken by its disposition of a prisoner found to have been improperly handled."

Captain Vopalar stared at Koscuisko for a long moment, as if wondering whether he was being honest or insolent.

The moment stretched.

"And of a truth," Koscuisko added, slowly, reluctant to expose himself to rebuke but clearly aware that he'd better come clean. "Of a truth I did not for a moment consider the potential for the interpretation that you have suggested, Captain Vopalar. The man had been savaged. He had earned a full clearance. I thought no further."

Vopalar glanced over to her officers, clearly soliciting reaction; the First Officer spoke. To Caleigh he sounded almost more exasperated than angry. Of course Koscuisko's action was more potentially compromising to Captain Vopalar than to the First Officer.

"So someone got knocked around a bit, Koscuisko. You know better than anyone that he was only going to get more of the same in Inquiry, what was the critical issue? Prisoners are abused outside of Protocol all the time, and no harm done to the Judicial order."

Not where Andrej Koscuisko could do anything about it, they weren't. But Koscuisko prudently bit back the rejoinder Caleigh knew to have been on the tip of his tongue and answered the reproach mildly and reasonably.

"He was much more than merely knocked around, with respect, First Officer. Someone had laid him open from neck to thigh with a peony or something very like it, and burned his hands and feet and genitals as well. We are not talking any spontaneous roughhousing here, and it far exceeded what the Protocols prescribe for the Preliminary Levels."

Koscuisko turned his attention back to Captain Vopalar, who had sat back in her chair to listen as Koscuisko continued. This was new information, it seemed. Caleigh felt hopeful. "If my professional judgment were to be solicited, I would have no hesitation in calling it a solid start on a Ninth Level. Except that there were no Charges recorded. There is no excuse for it."

Koscuisko was getting a little emotional there, toward the end. A little too absolute. Caleigh frowned, willing her officer in her mind to be sensitive to the currents around him.

"Prisoners are the First Officer's responsibility, Koscuisko." All the same, Captain Vopalar seemed to have made up her mind in Koscuisko's favor. "I'm sorry it didn't occur to you to let the First Officer be the one to log your discovery. Makes us look bad, no matter how you choose to interpret it. I don't expect you to take things into your own hands this way. I require you to observe your chain of command, and if you just didn't think about the consequences, maybe you should be sure you think things through in the future. You understand?"

It was a fairly mild reprimand, considering. Koscuisko would have a hard time swallowing the idea of going through channels where a clear injustice was concerned; but Captain Vopalar had a right to demand he behave like a subordinate officer, since he was one. He'd know that. Caleigh hoped.

"As Command instruction I receive and comply with this direction, your Excellency." Stiff and stubborn. They'd know he was angry, but that wouldn't hurt. They would expect at least that much. "First Officer, that I exceeded my authority, I must to you apologize. There was no intent to create an unfortunate appearance. But I should perhaps have guessed that such might happen still."

"Shouldn't happen again, Koscuisko," First Officer agreed, without rancor. "I'll detail an officer to accompany you on rounds from now on, just to be sure you can reach me at a moment's notice. I'm satisfied, your Excellency. No harm done."

They'd put a watch on Koscuisko, to be sure he didn't take it into his head to exercise his Bench authority without prior clearance again. But that was all right. In point of fact she liked Koscuisko, she respected his ability and his instinct, but his judgment was subject to occasional lapses. It wouldn't hurt to have someone there whose presence would remind him to stop and think things through a bit more thoroughly.

"Dismiss, then, First Officer. Doctor Clontosh, make sure that Koscuisko has no cause to complain of the treatment his patient gets in hospital, goodnight. Koscuisko, stand by."

The First Officer and Doctor Clontosh left the room in silence, and Caleigh thought that both of them looked a little relieved. Koscuisko had not relaxed, however. Koscuisko knew better than that.

Once the door was closed again behind them, Captain Vopalar spoke.

"Koscuisko. There are five bond-involuntary Security troops in the corridor outside. You may have noticed them when you came in."

It would have been difficult not to. Koscuisko waited, without replying to this obvious statement.

"You're outside the scope of most forms of discipline, which is too bad, because you need discipline. Tell you what. You ever. Forget your place like that, again. And I'll find discipline that is within my scope, except it won't be your back, which needs it, but one of those Bonds outside. Because I can't have your hide, but I can have theirs. This is the way it's got to be, Koscuisko. Get used to it."

Captain Vopalar was right, too. She could invoke sanctions against Koscuisko's bond-involuntaries that would be unthinkable in the context of disciplining an officer. Koscuisko seemed to rock back on his heels, fractionally, in obvious shock at what she was suggesting.

"Captain Vopalar, they have no recourse, how can you think to punish them—"

"Not them, Koscuisko," the Captain interrupted. "You. Make no mistake, if I invoke six-and-sixty against any of those people it will be only because I think you need discipline. From your behavior today that's the only way I can be sure of getting your attention." She held his gaze for a long breath, as if to be sure that her statement received the appropriate emphasis.

And then she looked past Koscuisko to where Caleigh Samons stood at command-wait. "Miss Samons, why hasn't Fleet Captain Irshah Parmin killed this young officer yet?"

This was a clear attempt to lighten the atmosphere once the point had been made. It was also an interesting question. "It's not for me to say, your Excellency." Which was perfectly true. "With respect, he's never found it necessary to invoke sanctions. I'm sure you'll find no further fault with the officer's behavior, Captain Vopalar."

She didn't think Sinjosi Vopalar would take that approach with Koscuisko unless really pressed to it. Captain Vopalar sighed, and seemed to relax a little. "There's the problem with pretending people like you have any business exercising authority, Koscuisko. Fleet's given you the rank. But you don't have the authority. Because you clearly aren't competent to exercise it at this level, but we're stuck with you. Don't take any drastic actions. I don't want to flay your Security any more than you want them flayed. But I won't tolerate insubordination. And that includes taking actions without keeping your chain of command informed."

As deeply offended as Andrej Koscuisko was likely to be by this, Caleigh Samons thought Captain Vopalar had a point. Koscuisko had rank without having been promoted to it; he hadn't spent years in Fleet learning to watch out for pits of the sort he'd just fallen into. Maybe that was why Irshah Parmin hadn't killed him.

"Even as you say, Bench Captain." Yes, Koscuisko was offended and angry. But Koscuisko was capable of demonstrating sense and discretion. "If we may be excused."

Koscuisko didn't understand how much he *was* excused by Fleet, in respect for his difficult position. On the other hand, Koscuisko earned those indulgences every time he went to implement the Protocols.

"Get out," the Captain agreed, with no further anger in her voice.

"And take those miserable Bonds of yours with you. I hope not to have to speak to you again, either of you."

For a moment Caleigh could hear Koscuisko's acid "The feeling is entirely mutual" so clearly that she was afraid he'd actually said it.

But the moment passed.

Koscuisko had got through this better than Caleigh had expected.

Now all she wanted to do was to get him and his bond-involuntaries back to quarters and lock them all safely behind doors till morning came.

CHAPTER THREE

The Domitt Prison stood on the rising ground above Port Rudistal, looking down on what had recently been a quiet port city distinguished only by its relative squalor and its Nurail population—which was redundant, in a way. Sentish had traded profitably with Nurail and Pyana alike for generations, true. Still, tolerating a Nurail population could only contribute to a progressive failure of civic hygiene.

The Domitt Prison stood apart.

Almost a year had passed since Administrator Geltoi had received his commission and arrived here in Port Rudistal with a Pyana construction crew and a line of credit against Chilleau Judiciary for the construction of a processing facility to serve the relocation camp that the Second Judge intended to establish on the other side of the river. There had been few Nurail available to him in Rudistal at that time; it had been before the refugee parties had begun to pick up, to be intercepted and shunted into his keeping.

Now that the last of the morning fog had finally burned off, Port Rudistal shone beneath the crisp cold rays of the autumnal sun, its peaked black rooftops glittering with dew. Administrator Geltoi— supreme authority under Jurisdiction at the Domitt Prison—looked out of his office windows over the city, toward the relocation camp across the river; and sang a bit of a traditional tune over to himself, absent-mindedly.

"*Your grazing animals are my meat, your children are my cattle, you I spare to dung my fields, the Pyana triumphs over you.*"

403

It was an old song. Administrator Geltoi paid little attention to the actual words, lost in pleasant meditation on the general gist of it. Nurail and Pyana had clashed for generations, because Nurail did not know their place and would not learn it. The scorn of the Nurail had been directed against defeated Pyana in song after song, insolent tunes and contemptuous melodies; that was all over now.

A signal at the door to his office reminded Geltoi that he was expecting Merig Belan for a tour of the penthouse, to make sure for himself that everything was in order to receive the Writ. Turning from the windows, Geltoi touched the admit, not bothering to raise his voice for so inconsequential a person as Belan.

"Good-greeting, Administrator." The assistant administrator was Nurail, and grinned a good deal to demonstrate his approval and acceptance of the new situation in which he found himself. Geltoi bore no grudge against Belan for his blood, though it was true that Belan was a Sarci name, and the Sarci Nurail had been with the Wai during the successful defense of Port Mardisk—in which Geltoi's own family had met an undeserved and ignominious defeat.

That had been a long time ago, though the songs were still popular amongst the Nurail. Belan was a good Nurail, one of the decent Nurail. Belan knew how to behave in the presence of his betters.

"Good-greeting indeed, Merig. Is the car ready? Let's go."

He already knew the car was ready. He'd seen it approaching on the track between the containment wall and the administration building. It was a standard administrative official's touring car; passenger cabin, retractable roof, the driver's well separated by a privacy barrier, six Security posts alongside on the running boards. It had been an acceptable vehicle for his use for these past months.

His status had changed, though.

The prison was to be fully operational at last, with legal authority to produce admissible evidence—authority that resided in the Writ to Inquire, and the person who held it.

He wanted something new that would reflect his more exalted position. Something to inspire the respect that he deserved: a senior officer's touring car, fully rated against assault with incendiary and impact projectiles to three thousand impact units and the melting point of stalloy.

He'd had no unrest that slaughter or starvation had not served to easily contain to date: but Geltoi took no chances. His life was a valuable asset to Chilleau Judiciary and to the Bench. His duty clearly called for him to protect that life as best he could.

"Ready and waiting, Administrator," Belan said, but Geltoi was already halfway across the room. Belan hurried to catch up; the sound of his heavy breathing amused Geltoi. "There's a delivery coming, sir, seventeen ships cleared by the Port Authority to your custody. Two hundred and thirty-four souls."

Once the Dramissoi Fleet arrived his supply of replacement workers would logically start to diminish; the Port Authority would be forced to process them through the displacement camp, rather than the Domitt Prison. He would have to shepherd his resources wisely. Two hundred and thirty-four souls? Excellent. He had plenty for them to do.

The lift at the far end of the corridor was waiting, properly attended by the day-watchman, who bowed respectfully to the Administrator as he stepped into the lift. The day-watchman was Sentish, not Pyana, but he knew his place. It was gratifying to receive such marks of submission from Sentish now that the Pyana had triumphed at last—even if they'd had to cry to Jurisdiction in order to do so.

Administrator Geltoi paused once he stepped out of the building, taking a moment to savor the air and the beautiful bright morning. The breeze from the river came up through the town with news of the wealth of the water and the kinds of things people ate for fast-meal here in Port Rudistal, and swept any lingering unpleasantness that might still have shadowed beneath his fortress walls safely away from any conscious perception.

It had been nearly two months, now.

Within a few more weeks the accelerant would have done its work, and there would be no hint of rotting flesh in the air to disturb the senses; nor any distinguishing the bones from those of Nurail who had died of quite natural causes years and years and years gone by, Standard.

"Administrator?" Belan prompted, sounding confused and a little uncomfortable. It amused Geltoi to note how nervous Belan still was of the filled-in pit where the construction crane had anchored, where they'd buried their mutineers. Belan had weak nerves.

Descending the steps without bothering to reply, Geltoi stepped into the passenger compartment of his touring car, settling himself against the deep blue cushions. Belan followed him meekly and pulled the door to; and the touring car swung away from the apron in front of the administration building for the prison proper.

It took long minutes to travel the distance.

The stark black walls of the Domitt Prison rose six stories high, and behind those walls—

Coming around the southeast corner for the main gate, the touring car turned in to the great central courtyard. To the left, the mess building, with the kitchen at the back with the laundry. To the right, administrative in-processing for new arrivals, and the prison's internal security detachment. There were only a few work-crews present, busy at sanding the pavement smooth.

The dispatch building that faced the great gate was quiet this time of day; the work-crews had already been dispatched to their day's labor. Only the replacement carts stood ready at the front, waiting for the word to carry fresh workers out to the land reclamation project as prisoners failed under the requirements of their task.

Geltoi took particular pride in maintaining strict accountability. The same number of workers that had left on work detail in the morning could be counted reliably to the soul returning in the evening. The fact that they were not the same workers was hardly material. What was important was that the numbers added up.

Pulling up at the back of the great square, the car halted to let Geltoi descend. This was prison internal administration, where the prison staff took their meals and guests could receive orientation before taking a tour. The day-warden was waiting.

"Good-greeting, Administrator Geltoi." It was his third cousin at five removes, Delat Surcase; a poor relation, but a solid Pyana nonetheless. "To what do we owe this unexpected pleasure, sir?"

Surcase was a little nervous; Geltoi knew how to read his kinsman's resentful glance at Belan in the touring car beside him. It didn't hurt for Belan to know that he was resented on all sides. It helped to keep him honest, a difficult task with Nurail.

"Don't stir yourself, Warden, I'm just going to have a look at guest quarters. How are things going, by the way?"

Visibly relieved, Surcase nodded as if in agreement. "Nice quarters they are, too, Administrator. Quiet today, all work details hired out. Eight, maybe eleven replacements so far. No loss."

Quite so. Their hire more than covered their keep, true enough, but Nurail were vermin. The fewer of the malingering scum left in his prison by nightfall, the more room he'd have for the fresh shipment of Nurail livestock Belan had promised him.

When the Inquisitor arrived he would be brought in through here, and would use the main lift to travel up to the roof level. Administrator Geltoi kept a critical eye on his surroundings as the lift rose, thinking.

There was no reason for the Inquisitor to realize that this lift was normally locked off on the fifth level. The officer would have no reason to leave his penthouse at all—except to go to the Interrogations section that had been built beneath the penthouse, with its own lift for the Inquisitor's convenience.

Access was quite properly restricted between Interrogations and the rest of the prison. There were ways in and out of Interrogations apart from the penthouse lift, of course; there had to be communication between Interrogations and the rest of the prison for shift change, and prisoner transfer and feeding, and everything else. It was only reasonable for Geltoi to make sure that traffic was carefully controlled.

The lift rose to the roof and stopped there, locking into place on the receiving dock of the penthouse Geltoi had built for his Inquisitor's keep. Geltoi quit the lift, but not to go directly into the main portion of the penthouse; he went out the back of the receiving dock into the garden instead, to savor the full effect of the artificial reality that he had created.

They were on the roof of the Domitt Prison, six stories high; but with a climate-brake in place and warmth vented from the furnaces, it was as tranquil and quiet as any garden. Six stories high, but shielded from the weather so that a man could look out over the fields toward the river on one side and the land reclamation project on the other, and yet feel no urgent and ungentle wind in his face.

And on the roof, a garden, with a gracious penthouse to be their Inquisitor's quarters for the duration of his stay, and everything a man could need provided in abundance.

A kitchen, the cook already on station; bowing nervously as the Administrator passed through to check the pantry. The pantry well-stocked with liquor and delicacies.

Quarters provided for the Security an Inquisitor would bring with him to help him in his work, two domestics—decent Pyana, not Nurail, unlike the cook—to make sure that the officer's effects were properly maintained. Exercise facilities. A laundry.

Belan had done a good job. Associating with Pyana was improving him, so much was obvious. The living quarters were well-appointed, bathing facilities very inviting, the sleeping room itself positioned so that the penthouse's panoramic view of the town of Port Rudistal could be enjoyed at its very best; and yet there was something missing.

"Very well done, Merig." Geltoi's praise was sincere; Belan had truly exercised himself. It had to be that much harder for a Nurail scant years from savagery to comprehend what a civilized man required for his comfort, and Belan's achievement was all the more impressive for that. "My congratulations, in appreciation for a job well done. One last thing, though, minor perhaps, but important. He might want women. We should have someone from the service house to start him off, at least until we find out what he likes."

Something seemed to shadow Belan's face for just one instant; or perhaps it was just a wisp of cloud crossing the face of the sun. There was no shadow in Belan's voice as he answered, that was certain.

"Administrator. Absolutely correct. So obvious now that you mention it, and I hadn't even thought. I'll see to someone suitable myself, sir, that is—unless you'd like to make an inspection visit—"

Geltoi waved the idea off. "No, Belan, you've done so well here, I want it to be all your accomplishment." And most of the women at the service house were Nurail, which meant one might as well have carnal relations with a beast of burden. Geltoi had rather too much respect for himself to do any such thing, though an Inquisitor's standards might be rather more flexible. "I'm very pleased. Everything a man could reasonably want for his comfort and recreation. It's all right here."

Once there were women on site this would truly be a self-sufficient installation.

Once Belan took care of that detail, Andrej Koscuisko would have no reason to leave his little piece of the Domitt Prison at all, until his Captain called him back to Fleet and *Scylla.*

The local planetary police fleet that had intercepted their fleeing ship—just off the Gelp shoals, so close to the Ninies vector and escape to Gonebeyond—had brought them here, to Port Rudistal. They were bound over as a group to the Domitt Prison, and the Domitt Prison held them at the landing site until night fell. They could see where the relocation camp was being built, across the river, the lights gradually brightening as the sun went down; but when the Domitt Prison came to move them, they were not urged in the direction of the river and the bridge to the relocation camp, no, they were marched through to the town instead.

First in one orderly group, at an easy pace, across the launch-field and into the dark streets beyond. It was the landing area, the warehouse section, no one there but night security, and that likely all automated; and the Domitt Prison began to move them a little more briskly as they went out until they were all crowded into a fast trot through the side streets.

Herded like cattle through the town, they were run all the way into the courtyard of the prison by men in transports with shockrods and other weapons. Some of the people stumbled in the streets; they were pulled into the transports by the Pyana, and once they were out of the town dropped out of the back of the moving cars once more, but on a rope this time. Dragged, if they couldn't find their footing.

Robis Darmon was one of the lucky ones; he could run as well as the next man, even older as he was. He did not lose his footing. They tried to help the ones being dragged up to get their footing and run, to avoid injury, but the Pyana would just as soon drag a Nurail in the dust as spit on them, and drove them away from the backs of the cars with the shockrods turned as high as they would go.

One of Darmon's companions, trying to get a young boy back on his feet, was struck by a shockrod, and he went down as well. They were out of the town by then. The Pyana didn't bother to tie his hands, they tied his feet, and dragged him headlong in the dirt all the way up to the Domitt Prison before they stopped to cut his body free.

He was not dead; Darmon saw him breathe. They threw him on a cart full of limp bodies, and the cart went away into the corner of the courtyard, and rising high above the wall in that corner were the steam-vents of a furnace.

They couldn't burn the body.

The man wasn't dead yet.

Darmon raised his voice to protest, but was only clubbed for his pains; and began to understand.

They didn't care that the man wasn't dead.

They were more than willing to burn him alive.

They were Pyana; and Darmon and his fellow prisoners were in their power.

As beaten down as Darmon was by everything they had suffered, this final shock was too much to comprehend. He let himself be gathered with the rest and pushed into the darkness of the cellars beneath the wall, packed into store-room spaces almost too many to a room to turn around. The bolts were shot, the locks engaged, the lights turned off; the jailers left.

It was as silent as a tomb.

He heard somebody start to shout or scream, as though one or two cells removed from this. He understood. They were hungry. They were thirsty. And they did not believe the Bench would treat them like animals, not even though the Bench was their enemy.

He heard the shouting, and the lights came back on in the hall. He could see the thin edge of light shining in underneath the bottom of the cell door. The sound of heavy booted feet, Pyana jailers. Voices raised in angry obscenities, going away, as if into a room, coming out as though from a room, the sound of blows. And screams. And cries for help, and finally no cries, but only blows out in the corridor on the other side of the cell door.

Then the lights went off again.

And it was quiet.

Young Farnim beside Darmon began to weep, and Darmon put his arms around him to comfort him. And keep him quiet.

This was too horribly unreal.

As terrible as it was to have been taken, as terrible as it was to lose their freedom, they had thought that they were to be bound over to a Bench relocation camp. Not to Pyana.

Robis Darmon was a war-leader, though defeated; there was no dishonor in defeat against superior numbers with superior force of arms. If he had known that refugees were given to Pyana, he would have fought to the death. An honorable death in battle was to be preferred to a Pyana prison; but there had been no talk of the Domitt. They hadn't known.

He was too stunned to think.

He held to young Farnim beside him and stared into the darkness, trying to make sense of what was happening.

They stood there in the dark for untold eons before the lights came on and the door was flung open on its hinges. After so long in silence, the sound itself was almost like a blow. There were armed men outside, and some with shockrods, and they were prodded with shockrods and threatened with blows until they filed meekly from the cell and down the hall. It was hard to see. The lights were blinding, after having been held so long in the dark.

There were toilets there, and a trestle-table, with food set out. They hadn't so much as smelled food since the Fleet had signed them over to the Domitt Prison and gone away; they found their places eagerly and fell upon the food, and it wasn't till Darmon had consumed the portion on his plate that he noticed that there were more prisoners than portions.

Limited space, well, he could understand that. He should be sure to drink all that he could, thirst could be a worse enemy than hunger, but once he had drained his cup—and the one the man across from him had already abandoned, in his hurry to get to the toilet—Darmon stood up from his place so that the next man could sit down and have his portion.

They didn't put out any more portions.

The men who hadn't found a place were left to stand and stare, and were not fed, not even when the tables had been cleared of any food, not even when they had been pushed at the toilets one by one, not even when they were gathered up at the door to be taken back to the cell once again.

Not even then.

The rage among the prisoners was palpable, and there was a movement, a surge toward the Pyana who surrounded them. But there were too many Pyana. And they had the weapons; and one round served to stop more than one Nurail, fired at close range. Some were shot and some were clubbed, and one who seemed to have gained their attention was pinned to the floor by Pyana standing on his arms and legs and head and punished with shockrods until he stopped responding to the stimulus, bleeding at the mouth. And nose. And ears.

Then they were all run back into the cell.

There were fewer of them.

Would that mean more would be fed next time?

Or would the Pyana take away the food as their numbers dwindled, in order to maintain their suffering?

Darmon sought Farnim in the dark, whispering his name.

There was no answer.

Things couldn't go on this way, Darmon promised himself, fiercely. The Bench would demand an accounting. Surely.

He could not silence the dread in his heart.

And what about his family?

His son?

The survivors had all dispersed under assumed names, knowing the Bench was eager for blood and would destroy all of the fighting men that they could find. It was all the more important that his child escape. They had lost this war, here and now. There would be other wars. The Bench's cause was unjust. It would not prevail.

The verdict of history was on their side, but history would be silent unless the weaves survived to bring their story to the world. He had been the war-leader. His name was a rallying cry and a watchword to his people. To destroy the Darmon would be to destroy a piece of the Nurail identity forever.

Where was his son?

He had to survive this prison, if he could.

It was his duty to live and cry the crimes of the Pyana to the Bench.

It was a long time before anyone came for them again. They heard movement in the corridors as the other rooms full of Nurail were moved in and out for whatever reason; but once it was quiet it stayed quiet. It seemed to be forever.

It was only a matter of hours, Darmon knew that by the fact that he was hungry and not thirsty.

They took them to the feeding room again, and everybody ran to the tables as quickly as they could. Darmon held back until he could see that there were to be enough portions before he found a place, but his restraint was rewarded, because the place he found was by an empty place and he could share the extra ration with the others if they all ate quickly enough. There was only barely enough time to eat, and they were gathered up into a herd again, but not back to the cell this time—no, up the stairs, prodded by shockrods as they went. Up to the surface.

It was morning, but which morning? How long had they been here?

Morning, and the fog lay heavy in the courtyard. They were formed up into a company, four rows, with eight people in each, staring at the wall of a building in the courtyard. They could smell food. There were people all around, rows of people dimly glimpsed passing between buildings, shouts and curses and cries of pain and rage.

Things quieted down.

The sun cleared the wall of the Domitt Prison and burned off the fog.

They were in a great open central courtyard with the prison all around. One great building faced to the gate, three stories tall; and two other buildings faced each other from opposite sides of the courtyard, at right angles to the gate. They had their backs to the corner where the furnace's stacks were. Far above it all at the opposite wall Darmon could just barely see what seemed to be a roof-house of some sort, perched atop a flattened place on the roof of the Domitt Prison, six levels high.

The day grew warmer, and the light and the warmth of the sun was welcome to Darmon after so long a period in the dark.

They stood there.

One of them fainted as they stood, and the Pyana guard dragged him out of formation and hit him with an oiled whip until he revived and struggled to his place.

It started to get hot.

A transport came around the corner of the building, headed for them, passing them. Darmon was on the end of the formation; he could see into the back of the transport as it slowed toward the back wall. There were limp bodies there. The transport went around behind them, and Darmon knew as certainly as though he had been told that they were taking the bodies to be burned. Nurail bodies. He prayed that they were dead.

The transport came around the other side of the formation, as though it had barely paused to offload its cargo. Dump the trash. A Pyana prison-guard hopped down from the tail-gate and started to move Nurail from the formation into the back, where the bodies had been; two, three, five Nurail.

Then they left.

Their guards formed their company up into new rows. Darmon didn't see; maybe they brought replacements from the other cellar rooms.

They stood all day.

The transport came up two more times, and twice or three times one of the prison guards came down their rows with a pail of water and let them have two dippers-full each. It wasn't enough. But it was better than nothing.

The sun fell below the back wall of the Domitt Prison and work-crews began to return, Nurail work-crews, some on foot and some in transports. The people who had been taken out of formation during the day were not returned to formation. Where had they gone?

When they were taken back down to the cellar, Darmon concentrated on getting as much to drink as he could. There was enough food. Their jailers didn't seem to be too bothered by the existence of extra portions, but they got restless before there was time to eat all that there was, so Darmon and the others stuffed what they could into their clothing surreptitiously.

Back into the cell.

There was room to lie down, now, and Darmon even slept. When he woke up, the extra portion of bread he had hidden away was gone; but he didn't mind so much. Someone had been hungrier than he was. That was all.

He was to blame for all of this.

He had been the war-leader.

If he hadn't failed his people they would still be free to herd the grazing animals on home slopes, and argue about weaves. Free to kill each other over squabbles that ran uncounted generations back, without the interference of Pyana. It was his fault, and their right to demand whatever surplus he might have to offer any of them here.

But next time he would eat the food himself, before he slept.

On the second or third day, they came to him as he stood in formation and made him get into the transport with two others. So

now at least he'd find out what had happened to the rest of the people
who had been taken away.

He wasn't entirely certain that he wanted to know, but he was too
tired to really care about what might be about to happen to him.

The transport took him out to a great earthwork; he was prodded
into a line, to pick up a tool that lay where it had been dropped. By
one of the bodies in the back of the transport?

They were packing dirt into buckets to be carried up the slope, and
further along the earthwork he could see the foundation of a dike
taking form in the ditch below them. The dirt was heavy with
moisture, at the bottom of the ditch, and he could smell the river from
time to time. Land reclamation. Some Pyana would profit from slave
labor, clearly enough; but he couldn't spare the energy to think about
it.

It took all the strength he could command to fill his bucket before
it was jerked up and away by the conveyer and an empty one moved
up to fill its place. People were beaten for not filling their buckets, he
could see examples enough. But the overseers brought water.

No food, no, but water, and Darmon was grateful enough for the
water after however many days of being kept dry that he was almost
eager to work for a water reward. Survival meant doing whatever it
took to conserve strength, to avoid punishment, to get as much to eat
and drink as possible.

He filled bucket upon bucket with damp heavy earth as the sun
crossed the sky and his hands blistered.

But when they were driven back to the prison, he didn't go back
into the cellar. He stood in work formation instead, and the overseer
called off names one by one, and people went forward into the mess
building as their names were called.

Shelps. Finnie. Allo. Burice. Ettuck. Ban.

One by one the people to his right turned away and hurried to the
mess building. When Darmon was next in line the overseer called a
name, and Darmon went; and the overseer nodded at him with what
might have been approval of the cleverness of an otherwise dumb
animal.

From that time forward, Darmon was Marne Cittrops to the
Domitt Prison.

And he understood.

He would be Marne Cittrops till it was his turn to drop his shovel in exhaustion and be hauled back to the furnaces, dead or alive.

Then the next in line from the cellar would become Marne Cittrops.

How many Marne Cittropses had there been?

Whoever Cittrops was, he had a sleep-rack in a cell with his workmates assigned, and better rations, and enough to drink.

He would be Marne Cittrops.

Maybe he'd survive.

He could be grateful to Marne Cittrops for dying, for failing at his work, because this was a better chance at life than he had had shut up in the cellar, constantly short of food and sleeping with one eye open on the floor.

He slept better that night than he had since he'd been brought to the Domitt Prison.

In the morning they were roused well before dawn, but they were fed and watered, and a guard went down the line as they waited for transport with ointment that seemed to numb yesterday's blisters— toughening gel, perhaps. When the overseer called Marne Cittrops, Darmon ran meekly to his place in transport; and it was a long day, but he lived through it. He could do hard labor. He could beat this prison. He could survive this.

If he could only have word of his child, he could hope.

Now that he had finally gotten through all of the prisoners that the Dramissoi Relocation Fleet held in its displacement camp, Andrej Koscuisko walked standard rounds like any of the Fleet's assigned physicians. It had been three weeks since the Doxtap Fleet had destroyed the artillery platforms above Eild, and taken the world for the Jurisdiction. Some of these people were only now being seen.

Doctor Clontosh's staff had been double-shifting, triple-shifting, robbing themselves of rest and sleep to see that the minimum standards of patient care at least could be upheld; the Dramissoi took its responsibilities to its deportees with admirable seriousness.

Tent after tent-full of tense and resentful, desperate, or resigned and always suspicious people—was it because it had been this long before they'd had access to a physician? Or was it because they knew him by his uniform and his bond-involuntaries for an Inquisitor, and would as soon spit on as speak to him?

"Joslire, bring the satchel, please." The Bench Lieutenant, young Goslin Plugrath, had excused himself to see to an administrative problem that had surfaced in Andrej's tour of the last tent. Plugrath would be back: but not in a hurry. Andrej couldn't blame Plugrath for finding this tedious, still less for resenting being leashed to the heels of a senior officer like a watchdog.

"Gentles, stand by. And someone go for rhyti?" Toska would go; but the point was that he and Joslire would go into the next tent alone.

There were five people in the next tent, all adult males, oddly enough. Or four adult males and one adolescent, but that was by the way. All of them very suspicious to see him. Oh, very tedious. With any luck, their mutual understanding of the fact that he was outnumbered would settle their nerves. It did nothing for his, but life was imperfect.

Two men seated, three on their feet, watching him warily. One with a soiled wound-dressing on his face, clearly more than a few days old; the best place to begin, clearly. Andrej beckoned for Joslire to bring his travel-kit.

"You, friend. If you would sit down here, where the light is better. I would like to change your dressing." There was no sense in asking what wound it was, where he had gotten it, how old it was. The fewer questions he asked, the more chance he had of gaining grudging cooperation. And it seemed clear enough to Andrej; something had sliced the man across the face possibly as long ago as would be consistent with Eild's last desperate struggle to retain its freedom. Carefully but crudely dressed, as though by persons with time but no resources—like persons in a displacement camp, sensibly reluctant to draw any attention to themselves if it could be avoided.

Working in silence, Andrej dressed the wound. It had been kept clean. There would be scarring, but there were no obvious signs of infection; and though it was quite obviously very painful, the Nurail bore his ministrations with quiet patience, unflinchingly. Clear across his face from above his right temple across the space between his eyes at the top of his nose, traveling the full distance of his cheek to terminate at the jawline—almost too precise to be accidental or inflicted in the heat of battle.

But that was none of Andrej's business.

"It's healing well." Two of the other Nurail had come to stand to one side where they could watch, being commendably careful not to alarm the Security outside by stepping between Andrej and the open door. "I do not envy you the sting of it. Are you able to sleep? No matter, here. Accept these, to be taken if the wound should begin to trouble you, three at a time but only twice a day. You have access to drinking water? Good. And if your temperature should start to rise, present yourself on emergency report. Any infection in tissue so close to your brain must be treated with absolute seriousness."

If Robert were here there would be an unspoken joke on this issue, communicated in its entirety with one quick glance—how could it be that there should be an issue, when he had been so many times instructed that there was not enough Nurail brain to begin with for damage to be detectable? It would be a joke, if it were Robert, but Robert was not here. Andrej missed him.

It had been Robert St. Clare at Fleet Orientation Station Medical, all that time gone, who had shown him how he was to carry himself to survive the use to which Fleet meant to put him; Robert, and Joslire, of course. And Robert had been sent with him to *Scylla* as part of the bargain that he had made with the Station Administration for Robert's life. But Joslire had elected to follow him of his own free will.

Joslire—

As Andrej's thought traveled from Nurail to Robert to Joslire he glanced around to find Joslire, just to see him there. Joslire stood at the ready with the travel-kit; but something was a little peculiar, almost wrong.

Joslire was upset about—what?

"Thank you, sir." The wounded Nurail's voice startled Andrej back into focus. "It has been a little wearing. But all's well here aside."

It had to be painful to speak, with his face cut in that manner. Andrej appreciated the courtesy all the more; thanks were something he almost never got to hear, any more, not since he'd been seconded to Dramissoi. Andrej nodded, smiling in appreciation but unable to quite take one man's word for it even so. "That is good to learn. All is well with you, then?" he asked the nearest Nurail, a short and stocky bearded man who seemed to be frowning, by the lines of his forehead.

"As well as can be hoped for, in such a state as you find us—"

Then he bit the phrase off short, leaving Andrej to wonder if it had been all he'd meant to say. But it wasn't up to him to press it. If the Nurail said he was all right, he was all right. Andrej had no brief to force examination upon these people without good and evident reason to do so.

Therefore he merely took the statement as complete, and did a quick scan of the other faces in the tent. The second Nurail beside the bearded one, also bearded, but tall and well built like Robert rather than being short and more or less square in shape. Two others sitting on a sleep-rack together, the younger wearing a blanket across his shoulders as if he were cold, meeting his eyes gravely as Andrej looked at him.

Something . . .

The younger man had unusual eyes. Andrej couldn't decide what it was he noticed, from where he stood, but if he went over to look— to satisfy his curiosity—he would probably give the wrong idea. Something peculiar. The blanket across the young man's shoulders was lapped over his knees, falling in concealing folds over arms clearly folded across his chest—

Joslire.

Joslire had noticed something.

And suddenly Andrej knew exactly what it had been.

His mind racing, Andrej stared at the young Nurail on the sleep-rack, trying to consider—judge—evaluate—balance, and decide as many of the questions in his mind as he could manage in an instant. Joslire had noticed, but Joslire had said nothing. Joslire said nothing now, only bowing in acknowledgment when Andrej looked back over his shoulder at Joslire standing by the door.

Lieutenant Plugrath was off with the quartermaster and did not care to pay too much attention one way or the other. But he had his clear duty, how could he not cry this to the First Officer at once?

Because the blanket folded so carefully across that young Nurail's shoulders and across his knees did not conceal arms that were folded across his chest.

The angle of the curve of the upper arm was wrong; it was a little thing, and he never would have snagged on it but for his unusually rich experience—especially recently—of dealing with people whose arms had been shackled behind their backs.

He had been quiet for too long. The Nurail had all noticed; and although Andrej was careful not to notice in turn, there was a savagely repressed sense of desperation in the eyes of the Nurail in the tent, all fixed on him. All except the youngest, who had turned his face away with a fine air of casual unconcern. It was very well done. It was valiantly done. It was a splendid effort.

It didn't work.

"That is a nasty scrape, across your throat," Andrej said to the young man. "If you don't mind, I mean to have a look at it." And there truly was a scrape, visible now that the Nurail had turned his head. Had there not been one Andrej would have been forced to invent it.

"It's nothing to trouble the officer's self over, really, no need—"

"There is no use in arguing with physicians." The tension levels within the tent were mounting moment by moment; and he had to have control of the situation, for Joslire's sake as well as for his own. Uncomfortably aware that the odds of being jumped out of sheer helpless rage and frustration were increasing to a dangerous degree, Andrej forged ahead.

He couldn't walk out on this now. One way or the other he had to resolve it. "Especially not physicians with rank, we expect to be allowed to make up our own minds about things, regardless of appearances. Howsoever obvious they might seem." Maybe that would be a hint. Maybe.

Andrej crossed the small space in the tent past the seated Nurail with the wounded face, willing himself to display in his posture and his pace a confidence that he did not feel.

A rope burn, that was what Andrej had seen on the young man's neck, and it only convinced Andrej that he did in fact know what was going on. What had happened.

"If you would shift," he suggested to the Nurail who sat on the sleep-rack next to the younger man, glaring up at him with affront and savage hatred. "I'd like to sit down and look at this welt."

What should he do?

Clearly the young man had been somebody's prisoner.

Clearly it was his duty to report it.

Yet he had heard First Officer say that there were no prisoners unaccounted for, and that Nurail who had been half-flayed with the peony had also been somebody's prisoner—and unlawfully misused by them. What did he care if somebody had meant to send the young man to the torture, so long as the Dramissoi Relocation Fleet had overlooked him?

There were so many prisoners already.

He was tired and angry, tired of tent after tent full of frightened people held in straitened circumstances, angry at the casual abuse so many of them had suffered prior to their arrival here.

Could he rationalize taking the Law into his own hands, to aid and abet a fugitive from justice?

That was the point exactly, though, at least in a sense.

This young man was not a fugitive from justice.

He was a fugitive from a vengeful Bench, and that was something else entirely.

Slowly, as if almost despite himself, the Nurail shifted to one side, making room for Andrej to sit down. The young Nurail himself was watching Andrej carefully, and the expression on his face looked to Andrej to be at least as much challenge and curiosity as fear.

Andrej sat down beside him and lifted the blanket carefully from behind the young man's back, draping it to the front over the young man's shoulders to preserve the illusion. Yes, chained at the wrists behind his back, and the hands themselves swollen—it had been days, perhaps, with no way to get to a tool intelligent enough to decipher the Bench-standard manacles or sturdy enough to hammer the bonds through by main force.

Just as well.

Hammering through the bonds would have damaged the wrists badly. The Bench was very careful about its security encoders; the likelihood of finding a key sophisticated enough to do the job was not good. Keys for manacles were restricted issue, much more tightly controlled all in all than the manacles themselves.

These Nurail probably would not be able to find a key at all, still less before the damning fact of the matter would be revealed—as it would surely be during in-processing at Rudistal, if not before.

Few Judicial officers were assigned master keys.

But he had one in his travel-kit.

He was Andrej Ulexeievitch Koscuisko, Ship's Inquisitor, Jurisdiction Fleet Ship *Scylla*.

He was expected to have lawful need to loose a prisoner's manacles, even if it was only to be in order to bind them over into some other form of restraint.

"I'll want a salve, Joslire." It was dim at the side of the tent where he sat, but Andrej didn't need more light to know what he was looking at. The skin would have suffered the effect of those manacles, especially over a period of days. But that wasn't so much the point as that his salves were in his travel-kit. "Bring me my bag, if you would, it's the shorris ointment, I'm not certain how to tell you exactly where to find it."

Shorris ointment would go for the welt at the young man's throat as well. Someone had dragged the young man by a halter, perhaps. There were marks from a beating, blood soaked through clothing and dried, but that would wait. First things first. The Nurail were confused, and anxiety could make a man irrational.

He had to keep talking. "Have you other hurts, that I should be told of?" Joslire brought his kit, but had not handed it to him; Joslire knelt down in front of where Andrej sat, instead, searching through the contents of the kit he opened on the floor. Andrej noted that Joslire had his back to the door. No one standing in the brighter light of day outside the tent would be able to see quite what Joslire was doing.

"Shorris ointment," Joslire said, pulling something out of the bag at last to pass it to Andrej in both hands. "I think that this was what his Excellency wanted?"

The right ointment, too, all of these years of fifth-week duty in Infirmary had served Joslire well. He knew what he was doing.

There was more.

There was something underneath the ointment pot as Joslire passed it to him, something familiar to his touch.

His master key.

"Precisely so." Over the years Andrej had learned that he could do sometimes quite irregular things in Inquiry without causing his Security distress. The governor that ruled a bond-involuntary's life apparently recognized that by the Bench instruction only mutiny and treason were forbidden to Inquisitors.

This was significantly different.

This was active commission of a near-criminal act, could the fact that Joslire knew what Andrej meant to do truly keep Joslire's governor at bay?

It had to wait. Whatever the explanation, it was clear that Joslire was at peace with his governor here and now; Joslire suffered no pain. Unlike this young Nurail, who was due for a sharp discomfort as the manacles came off—

"Thank you, Joslire." He kept his voice casual, business-like. "You, there. This may sting a bit. You might want to come and hold your friend still in one place, for me."

One of the men came to stand in front of the young Nurail, taking him by the front part of his shoulders carefully. The expression on the man's face almost gave Andrej pause; this seemed more intense even than the care a man had of a young relation, and if this boy had escaped from Limited Secure, he could be of political importance.

Almost Andrej wanted to think twice, but no; any man with a cousin or nephew or son would be desperate to see his kinsman safe from torture, free from threat. Andrej saw all of the confusion and wild hope that the young man declined to share with him in his expression, gazing up at his older companion.

Three small adjustments. Feeling with his fingers in the dim light, Andrej fit the master key to the secure that locked the wrist-pieces of the manacles. The mechanism unlatched, and the shackle's locks cleared; but as Andrej had feared, they'd been in place for too long. The flesh had swollen around the wrist-pieces and held them in place.

"This will not be pleasant," Andrej warned whoever was listening. A quick dose of something generally soothing was what he wanted, but to call for such a dose or to be seen to press one through would be inconsistent with the handling of any given welt, and might raise an unwelcome question in somebody's mind. If not now, perhaps later. "Joslire, topical anesthetic. Please."

He had to expose skin before he could anesthetize it. He peeled one wrist-piece open carefully, first one half-ring, then the other, and the greedy manacles carried bits of torn skin with them as they came away.

"Not too much longer, now. Try to breathe." *That's one*, he'd almost said. He couldn't say that. One what?

Daubing the topical anesthetic around the livid bracelet of scored skin, Andrej waited for the numbing to take effect before he tried the wrist-piece on the other hand. The other wrist was worse, because it had been uppermost of the crossed arms, and had more trauma accordingly. Andrej did what he could to make the prying bearable, but it was hard on the young man to suffer the pulling apart of the manacle's wrist-piece.

Andrej salved the wound in silence while the Nurail muffled his cries against the jacket of the older man, who stood and held him, stroking his hair with grim tenderness. Circulation would increase almost immediately, and that could be even more difficult for the young Nurail than the removal of the manacles had been.

With help from the men who were clustered now around him, Andrej shifted his patient's arms gently to the front to lay forearm across thigh, careful to keep the blanket folded to conceal the wounded wrists. The wrists would heal. The livid welts would stay hidden by the cuffs of his shirt until they healed. It would be all right.

"Well, there need be no permanent damage." Now that that was taken care of, Andrej laid ointment on a sterile pad, which he applied to the rope weal across his patient's neck with a delicate touch. That had been his excuse, after all. "Sometimes massage can be helpful, improved circulation speeds the healing. Carefully done to avoid breaking the skin open, of course."

He couldn't be too obvious. He didn't know whether Lieutenant Plugrath had returned yet, and might be waiting outside, listening to what he had to say. "Are there other hurts that I should know about? This is the time to speak, to tell me them."

The older Nurail who had been holding Andrej's patient stepped back a fraction now, unfastening the young man's shirt to open the garment and uncover his back. Andrej revised his assessment of the young man's age, studying the bruised shoulders and the muscles that showed beneath the skin. Not yet a man. Not a boy either, but in the borderland between them. Perhaps so many as seventeen years old, Standard, but that was stretching it.

It had not been a bad beating, Andrej could see that as the fabric fell down from the patient's shoulders to his waist. The beating was not the problem. The problem was the burns beneath the young man's arm, long stripes, precisely spaced, in the tender skin at the underside of the upper arm and on the side of the torso beneath the armpit.

Torture.

Torture, again, abuse of prisoners outside of Protocol, and Andrej was glad to see it, because it removed any nagging questions in his mind over whether he should not really report this to First Officer.

"Let me have a burn-dressing, Joslire." If he spoke quietly enough, no one would hear from outside, or at least not enough to make them think twice. "And some sampers cream."

If this ever came out, it would be Joslire to suffer for it, Joslire or another of his Bonds. He was hazarding their pain against his whim. He had no right. Yet Joslire clearly seemed intent on putting the gamble forward.

Andrej stood up.

"Shorris ointment, five days, three times a day applied to broken skin with clean hands, carefully." Holding the salve-pot out to the older Nurail standing beside the sleep-rack, Andrej counted off instructions and indications one by one.

"Sampers cream for burns, lift the dressing and apply the cream, then lay the dressing back down. I'll bring a fresh dressing the next time I see you." If he ever saw them again; and he didn't expect to. Regardless of whether he was going to reveal their secret, they knew that he knew the secret, now. They would do whatever it took to disappear into the metaphorical woodwork—changing places with other Nurail who would pass during meals or sanitation breaks, perhaps.

"That's it, then?" One last chance for any further requirements. He could feel the weight of the manacles in his pocket; he'd transfer them to his case in the next tent. Chief Samons didn't go into his case, and Security wouldn't ask questions. If he put them in one of the back-slits, he could always pretend they had been there all the time.

"If his Excellency would care to give his name," the man with the scarred face said. "It may be possible to exclude you, from the general curse the Bench has earned."

As thanks it was more than gracious, really. "My name is Andrej Koscuisko, and I have earned my share of the blame well and truly." They would know why. They could read his rank as well as any of the others. "But I am grateful for the thought regardless. Good-greeting to you all."

Nodding his head in general salute to the room at large, Andrej quit the tent with Joslire at his back, and paused just outside the doorway. Down one long graveled lane he could see Bench Lieutenant Plugrath, on his way back from his errand to rejoin them and resume his nursemaid duty. Closer to them, but coming from the opposite direction, Toska with rhyti; Andrej moved down to the front of the next tent to wait, just to make it clear the last tent was finished. Nothing interesting there.

"Joslire. You amaze me."

Quietly spoken. And tried to express his confusion, concern, appreciation, anxious inquiry in four short words that would send no message to any casual eavesdropper.

"I know your mind," Joslire answered, as quietly. Clearly convinced that they weren't in danger of being overheard or the conversation remarked upon, for the next few breaths; because Joslire spoke as a free man, not as a bond-slave. "The officer is the rule of Law to me. My trust in thee is absolute."

Now Toska was here with the rhyti-jug. Andrej sat down on the campstool that one of the others brought up for him, finally, covering his confusion with attention to his rhyti. He'd learned that trust could give a bond-involuntary back a measure of freedom; he'd learned that from Joslire, in fact, early on. Joslire's utter conviction frightened Andrej a bit: what if Andrej should fail, and betray him?

He could not fail a man who knew him so well—and who trusted him anyway.

The realization steadied Andrej, and comforted him.

Handing his empty rhyti flask back to Toska, Andrej nodded to the newly returned Plugrath as though nothing had happened; and turned in serene self-confidence to go into the next tent full of Nurail.

There was work to do.

No time like the present to be back at it.

CHAPTER FOUR

The days passed one like that before and after, and day by day Robis Darmon began to lose hope of ever leaving the Domitt Prison.

There was no alteration of the schedule, and no lack of bodies to replace those who failed beneath the task. Many failed. It wasn't that which disheartened Darmon, or Cittrops. He was not losing strength, not too quickly; he was holding his own.

He saw too much.

Day after day, as people fell, to be dragged off still twitching to the furnaces.

People who slipped into the deep trenches being dug for the foundation of the dike, and who were left there, screaming in pain or calling out half-delirious for help, until they stopped crying. To be buried in gravel, whether still or not, as the work of the foundation went forward.

Gradually day by day he realized that men who saw such things would never be released to speak of them, because it was a crime by Bench precedent to murder men in such an offhand fashion. Even if they were only Nurail. Slave labor could be levied by a prison, there were rules, but work-crews had to be treated like laborers and not like cattle, and when they left the prison they had to be paid off for their work.

Not killed and replaced, killed and replaced, killed and replaced again day after day.

The prison administration had no intention of permitting them to live.

There was no hope, no future, and no sense of time or purpose. He had almost forgotten that he was not Marne Cittrops. He didn't know who Marne Cittrops was. It didn't matter.

All he really remembered was a son.

He hadn't seen his child here, not yet; he hadn't heard the overseers gloat that the only surviving child of the Darmon had been taken or killed. They didn't know they had the Darmon himself, yet; he had been taken prisoner under an assumed name for self-defense. Now it was even better. There was no connection between Marne Cittrops and Robis Darmon: and no word that would indicate that his child was a prisoner.

He could keep breathing as long as his child was free.

He would not leave the Domitt, not alive.

But Chonniskot was free.

And there was hope.

He labored next to the second man he'd come to know as Shopes Ban. The sun was coming later, leaving sooner; he had no way to tell the time as such, but anyone could see that the sun rose less completely opposed to where it set day by day. Tracking south, by Standard convention, which meant winter, which meant shorter days; but it was still brutally hot and dry work at the bottom of the great ditch, and he was still as grateful for water when it came.

Five days after the new face had come to be named Shopes Ban, the overseer came with troops in the middle of the day, searching the line, looking for someone. Robis kept his head down, kept his eyes down, looked as stupid as he could. Shopes looked at him out of the corner of his eye, but Robis forced himself to look ahead, sending his warning low-voiced through half-parted lips so that the sound would not betray them.

"Keep working. You're nobody. Concentrate."

He knew who Shopes had been in a previous life; he thought Shopes had recognized him, though it had been a day or two before he'd noticed that the searching confused gaze Shopes would turn on him had been replaced by despair and fathomless sorrow. Shopes had been a junior officer. His name was Shopes for now, though, and Robis fixed that firmly in his mind.

He had forgotten everybody's name.

He had made it his business to bury all the names he used to know beneath the gravel that came down the slope to line the bottom of the foundation ditch. He buried a name every time a Nurail fell and was kicked beneath the huge stalloy rollers of the loader to be ground into dust with the refuse from the work. The fewer names he could remember, the fewer names he could be made to say if they found him; but they hadn't found him. They seized Shapes Ban instead, and carried him away to special transport. Up the slope.

When the overseer came with dippers-full of water, Robis begged the extra from him and was allowed to gain the gift by groveling. He didn't mind. It was nothing to do with him, and everything to do with just survival. He had to do whatever he could do to get enough to eat, to drink, to survive. No matter how it burned within him to beg of a Pyana what would be granted any dog in simple good husbandry. It was too late to die with honor and go to glory. His duty was to survive as long as possible, because the longer he survived the greater were his chances of somehow getting through. Some way. No matter how hopeless it might seem to be.

Twenty-plus days in vector transit from Eild to Rudistal with the Dramissoi Relocation Fleet, with little to do but play cards and accompany Koscuisko and his young shadow Plugrath as he did his rounds through the transports. Koscuisko would much rather be with the rest of the fleet's medical staff even now.

Caleigh knew the thought that was in Koscuisko's mind as he stood at the top of the steps in front of the dock-master's Administration building, gazing over the river to the relocation camp beyond. But he hadn't been sent here to help keep the relocation camp healthy. And soon he would no longer be the Dramissoi Relocation Fleet's concern at all.

Bench Lieutenant Goslin Plugrath stood one or two steps lower than the more senior officer, with his hands clasped loosely behind his back, looking bored. Taller than Koscuisko, bigger than Koscuisko, dancing attendance on Koscuisko had all too clearly not been Plugrath's idea of a good time. Caleigh gave him good marks for professionalism all the same: he'd been polite and respectful throughout.

"That's done the last of it, Chief," Toska said, wiping the dust from his hands with his white-square. "Loaded and ready."

The Dramissoi Relocation Fleet had put a car at their disposal, and a Security escort under Plugrath's command. There wasn't all that much luggage to stow; bond-involuntaries traveled light, partially because they had no personal possessions to account for. Caleigh nodded.

"Be at ease, then, Toska. Stand by, we should be getting out of here."

The sun was setting over the hills west of Port Rudistal, the brilliant glare of its long rays throwing the low tents of the relocation camp into high relief against the lowering clouds to the east. It was cool and damp on the loading field already. Once the sun went down it was going to get cold.

Lieutenant Plugrath shifted his weight where he stood, turning his head on his short neck to the officer. "I'll just go send a reconfirm, your Excellency." Plugrath didn't believe senior officers should be kept waiting any more than Caleigh did. Koscuisko was willing to wait, in this instance, but unwilling to make a fuss about it; he just nodded gravely.

As Plugrath turned to go up into the building, however, Caleigh saw something coming from between the towering hulks of the launch-field loaders, weaving its way toward them through the canyons between the close-packed warehouses.

"Bench Lieutenant." Calling him down to the loading level with her, Caleigh gestured, pointing with her chin. "Our escort, sir?"

As the car cleared the maze of warehouses and picked up speed along the launch-field perimeter, Caleigh could see that it was a touring car, luxurious and expensive, with a carload of what was probably Security behind it.

"So it would seem, Chief. And about time."

Once Koscuisko set foot in that transport he would be halfway between the Dramissoi Fleet and the Domitt Prison, properly assigned to neither. Caleigh wondered whether Koscuisko had fantasies of hijacking the transport, and making for—for where?

There was nowhere for him to go.

He couldn't go back to *Scylla* without clearance from Vopalar and the Domitt.

She was being silly.

The touring car and its escort pulled up in front of the landing with a fine flourish of kicked-up gravel; and the Security troops, hurrying out of their transport, formed up to receive the officer. Caleigh was not impressed but they were merely Bench resources, not Fleet, and only prison security at that. She was privileged to work with bond-involuntaries. The standards could not be compared.

Now the touring car's passenger cabin door opened, and a man stepped forth from the open-roofed interior. Looked vaguely familiar, in some way. He shifted his gaze uncertainly between Caleigh and Lieutenant Plugrath, as if not quite sure who he should address; and settled on Plugrath at last. Very properly.

"His Excellency?"

He didn't take Plugrath for Andrej Koscuisko, no, clearly not. He wanted to verify Koscuisko's identity.

"Waiting," Plugrath affirmed, not very helpfully. "And you, sir?"

"Assistant Administrator Merig Belan, from the Domitt Prison. Come to carry his Excellency's party to quarters on site. If you'd present me, Bench Lieutenant."

So he'd studied the rank-markings, even if he'd had to concentrate on the rank Plugrath wore for a moment before deciding on the appropriate mode of address. Plugrath gestured for Belan to precede him up the stairs to where Koscuisko stood patiently, secure in his knowledge that they'd come for him when he was wanted.

"The Domitt Prison's assistant administrator, your Excellency. Merig Belan. Administrator Belan, his Excellency, Andrej Koscuisko."

On the one hand, technically speaking, the assistant administrator might rank equally with Koscuisko in the prison chain of command; or perhaps higher. On the other hand, Belan had asked to be presented, which clearly indicated his expectation of assuming the subordinate role.

There was the fact of the Writ to consider. When his Excellency was not in the presence of his administrative superior, he was a functionally autonomous power in Port.

"Administrator Belan. Are we to go to quarters, now?"

Belan bowed. "The Administrator's profound respects, your Excellency, and I'm to tell you that he's indulged himself so far as to prepare a small reception in your honor on site. It's not too long a drive, if your people would care to load?"

Koscuisko was looking to Lieutenant Plugrath instead of responding directly; Plugrath answered in Koscuisko's stead.

"Administrator Belan, with your permission, I'll see his Excellency to greet Administrator Geltoi personally. Because if I failed to escort the officer to the threshold of the Domitt Prison, Captain Vopalar would have some very unpleasant things to say to me about lack of respect and neglect of military courtesy."

Well, they'd be a little bit of a traveling-party, then. Because Belan had brought Security, and Plugrath had quite naturally had Security, even if Belan's Security seemed a little on the ceremonial side of an officer's escort and Plugrath's Security looked a little to the assault-ready side of an honor-guard.

For a moment Caleigh hesitated, looking down at the open roof of the touring car at the foot of the stairs; surely Koscuisko's blond head would make too good a target against the dark plush fabric of the interior?

It wasn't for her to say.

Nor was Rudistal a hostile Port. It was a Bench protectorate, and there hadn't been any trouble at Rudistal, or Vopalar's First Officer would have let her know. Surely.

"Follow us, then, by all means." Administrator Belan's hearty agreement was a little forced, but not insincere. Caleigh decided it was just that Plugrath's presence hadn't been anticipated. "And now. Sir. The light will be going."

Was it her imagination, or did Lieutenant Plugrath frown as he caught sight of the touring car?

The officer was beside her, at her elbow. "Miss Samons. We don't want to keep these gentles from their third-meal." He sounded a little amused about something; the careful dance taking place between Plugrath and Belan, perhaps. "A reception, perhaps there will be dancing girls. I beg your pardon, Miss Samons, that would be of limited interest to you, please excuse me."

If she was tense enough for the officer to feel a need to tease her in so formal a fashion—she was too tense by half; and for what?

Caleigh Samons knew the answer to that one.

"Life is full of surprises, your Excellency. Who knows. Maybe dancing boys provided specially for Chief Warrant Officers."

It was up to Plugrath and Belan to be tense just now. Especially Belan; it was his Port, after all. Oh, perhaps not his Port, but certainly his prison.

Caleigh squelched her errant thoughts firmly into decent self-respecting silence, following Koscuisko down the stairs.

The touring car that the Domitt Prison had sent for him had positions for three Security to stand on the running boards on each side, which meant that Chief Samons insisted on her place at the leftmost, rearmost post, and very tiresome of her, too. But there he was.

There Miss Samons was, more to the point, with Code and Toska on his left, Kaydence and Joslire and Erish on his right, and no one for him to talk to except Lieutenant Plugrath and his assistant administrator, neither of whom were anything close to as stunningly seductive as Caleigh Samons even on a bad day.

Perhaps it was just as well she was on the running boards behind him. Well out of arm's reach. He was tired and he was very depressed, and in the mood he was in just at present he might very likely have suggested some activity to take his mind off his troubles that would be inappropriate. As well as just as likely to be politely rebuffed, which would only make his mood even more black and hopeless than it was already.

"His Excellency had a good transit, one hopes?"

Their cargo was loaded and the three-car convoy was under way, and Belan was trying to make conversation. Andrej had not had a good transit, unhappy about the souls entrusted to the Dramissoi Relocation Fleet and apprehensive about what awaited him at the Domitt Prison. But there was no sense in being gratuitously unpleasant to Administrator Belan even so.

"Thank you, Administrator. Twenty-one, twenty-two days, almost restful, really. Rounds, of course."

The car traveled on through the dark streets, one long block of narrow buildings after another to either side and rather too close for Andrej's comfort. A man could get claustrophobic in streets such as this, which was more than ridiculous on the face of it—that a man should have grown accustomed to live in *Scylla*'s narrow corridors and yet feel closed in upon and prisoned in the open air just because the warehouses in Port Rudistal had been built close and high. There had been an open area between Rudistal and the Domitt Prison, if Andrej remembered aright of what he'd seen from the launch-field. That would be a welcome break; but then they would be at the prison. That was not to be welcome.

"Quarters are actually on site, then, Administrator?" He'd gathered as much, but he might as well have it confirmed, Andrej decided. That way he could get started on a truly world-class case of self-pity now, rather than wait a moment longer.

Of course he had been preparing to immerse himself in self-pity ever since Captain Irshah Parmin had first told him that he was to be sent on this assignment. Still, truly professional results depended on thorough groundwork and advance preparation. There was no time like the present to finish off the foundations, and lay the first course of a monumental attitude problem.

"There's a penthouse suite prepared for his Excellency and his party," the Administrator confirmed. "Every convenience. We hope you'll be very comfortable, sir. And if there should be anything lacking you have only to let us know."

The car was slowing, but they were nowhere near the Domitt Prison; no, they were still deep within the cavernous bowels of the warehouse district, for all Andrej could tell. The car was slowing to avoid running into the car in front of it, the lead car with Belan's Security from the Domitt Prison.

Lieutenant Plugrath seemed to become a little agitated, all of a sudden.

"Administrator, why are they slowing down, tell them to drive on. It's not a good idea to idle in the streets with rank like this on board."

Behind him Andrej could hear the canopy rising to meet over his head and form a roof for the car. Who had decided to close the car he didn't know. Maybe Chief Samons thought it would make the Bench Lieutenant feel better.

"Of course, Lieutenant," the Administrator agreed, his eagerness to please as evident as his confidence in the innocuous nature of the slowdown. "Bad in principle, though no cause for alarm, I assure you."

The car had almost stopped. Through the now-enclosed windows Andrej could see Plugrath's Security detachment pass at the double, six men to the front car to see what the slowdown might be. His own Security would stay with him, naturally.

The Administrator, frowning unhappily, keyed the car's com-braid for transmit. "Sami, this is Belan. What seems to be—"

Then Andrej saw the car in front of them explode into a black fury of dust and scrap, with a huge furious roar that struck him like a blow and deafened him.

An explosion, yes, he knew it had to have been an explosion, he knew what an explosion looked like, but still he only sat and stared without comprehension at the ruin of shards and fragments against the windows at the front of the car while the Administrator struggled frantically with the handle of the car door. Trying to get out. Yes, that was right, they should get out of the car, a car stopped in the street was a sitting target, but who in the name of all Saints could they be shooting at?

Lieutenant Plugrath was shouting something, but Andrej couldn't hear a word, deafened by the blast. He'd better get out of the car before the Lieutenant was hit by accident. Not that he was interested in being shot at. He'd been shot at before; it had made him angry, the first time it had happened, it still made him angry. Were they shooting at him?

Were they, indeed?

Administrator Belan got the door open at last; the door was pulled open from outside, and frantic hands seized him on his way through the door to hurry him out. Security. Andrej started out of the car in turn, but they wouldn't let him step foot to pavement.

They grabbed him and threw him headlong to the street, and themselves down on top of him to half-drag his body bruisingly away from the car—toward the nearest wall, Andrej supposed, stupid with the shock of it. People were being shot at, Andrej could hear the impact of rounds against the pavement and the sharp report of Security's weapons returning fire. Carbines. Mortars. Flame-throwers. Thorough of them, Andrej had to admit it.

The ground lifted beneath him and struck him in the face with a bone-shattering blow that flattened his entire body and took his breath away.

Shocked body and soul by the force of the blow, Andrej lay for long moments open-eyed, open-mouthed, before he could think to try and catch a breath.

And then it hurt so much to breathe that he didn't want to, and he stilled himself out of fear of the pain to come until his body made him gasp for air—which only hurt even worse.

Years passed.

Andrej fought for breath, and fought with the unwillingness of his own body to breathe, and tried not to notice the pain that came in to fill up the empty spaces as shock ebbed away and left him vulnerable.

His heart began to beat again.

He was lying on his belly on the pavement, the stink of rock-dust and overheated metal was in his nose, his cheek scraped raw against the rough pavement. There was something heavy and hot on top of him, covering him, pressing down on him—was he buried under an avalanche?

Something told him no.

Something told him he knew what had happened.

If only he could put his finger on what that was —

Then the weight shifted. Kaydence Psimas and Caleigh Samons alike rolled away from him carefully, and Andrej could turn over onto his back.

"Excellency." It was Toska, who should know better. "Excellency, are you all right, sir?"

When it should be Kaydence and Chief Samons who should be asked, they had been more at risk than he had been. He had been protected by their bodies. If anybody was not all right, it would be them.

The sudden shock of stunning pain ebbed rapidly, now. He was sore, yes, but not more than bruised from what little he could tell. He had to get up. He had people to see to. Kaydence, how was he? Toska? Chief Samons? The others?

"Miss Samons," Andrej croaked. His voice had got jarred loose in the explosion, as it seemed. He cleared his throat and tried again as Toska and Kaydence lifted him carefully to a seated position. Oh, holy Mother, he hurt. He was going to truly regret this, in the morning. "Miss Samons. Kaydence. Are you all right? What has happened? Where is everybody?"

Now that he was sitting up, Andrej's mind cleared moment by moment. He could see Kaydence, crouched down at his side. He could see Toska, whose face looked to be somewhat blackened with blown ash, but not burnt. Testing himself, arms and legs and knees and joints, Andrej took inventory, listening to Kaydence's report.

"No harm, your Excellency. Chief Samons and I had something to cushion the fall." Andrej himself, that was to say, and if Andrej considered that his body was not near so pleasant a pillow as Chief Samons's might be, the point remained that he was somewhat more yielding than the pavement to land upon. "Two explosions, your Excellency, probably mines. Buried in the street. Casualties mainly the prison Security in the lead car, and some of the Lieutenant's people. Some shots fired, but none after the second explosion, and they seem to have run off the ambush pretty well."

"Where is Chief Samons? Toska, your face is dirty, have you been burned?" A man couldn't help asking. A person got anxious.

Toska pulled his white-square out of the front plaquet of his duty blouse and moistened a corner with his tongue before scrubbing at his cheek with experimental fervor. The white-square came away black; Toska's skin was the color it was supposed to be, beneath—a little reddened from the chafing, but otherwise unburned. "Seems to be just soot, sir. Are you sure you want to stand up? Already?"

Yes. He was sure. He knew he was alive; Kaydence and Toska appeared to be all right. Chief Samons had left his side as he'd sat up, and had not yet reappeared to make her report. There were Code and Erish and Joslire yet unaccounted for.

Supported by Kaydence and Toska to either side, Andrej found his footing in the rubble and stood for a moment, grateful for the steadying hands of his Security. Looking around.

To his right, the rearmost car, emptied now but apparently undamaged. That was the way they'd come, then.

To his left, the wreck of the lead car, and the pavement torn up in chunks and heaps of rubble. Bodies, some half-buried in the debris, some apparently caught up in the twisted carcass of the lead car itself. Lieutenant Plugrath and the Administrator, talking to one of Plugrath's people; hurrying over, once Plugrath noticed Andrej on his feet, making what haste they could over the chewed-up pavement.

"Field-expedient ambush, sir, probably recognized the touring car on its way in. Two mines, apparently laid in maintenance traps beneath the pavement. Expected two cars, with the Administrator in the lead rather than second place. Lucky for us."

Not so lucky for the lead car. That went without saying. Andrej eyed the wreck of the touring car in front of them with grim distaste. If he had been in the car when the second mine had gone off . . . and the driver probably had been.

"Casualties?"

"Rough count, fourteen, sir. Six out of eight in the lead car. Five of mine who'd come up to investigate. Driver in the touring car, one of mine shot in firefight. Your man's not quite dead yet, help's on the way."

His man?

Caleigh Samons stood up from her place of concealment on the other side of the wreck of the touring car. She didn't do anything as rude as beckon, as vulgar as whistling. She didn't need to. The expression of grief and distress on her face spoke more clearly than words, and carried its meaning with persuasive force.

Andrej started for her, carrying Kaydence and Toska along with him in his wake.

Erish Muat was seated on a curved wheel-housing blown clear of the touring car, his face clean and white, blood soaking his trouser-leg from thigh to calf. Code was cutting the fabric away from Erish's knee as Andrej made his way toward them; oh, lovely, a furious laceration across the top of Erish's knee, and splintered bone glistening with sickening brilliance under the emergency flares that Plugrath's people had set up. And it was the same leg that Erish had injured chasing those Nurail sappers down the corridors of *Scylla*, in a race for the main guns.

It was a nasty injury, but it was well short of threatening Erish's life; and that left only—

Andrej put his two hands to either side of Erish's neck and kissed his forehead, briefly. "You are hurt, my dear." Which Erish had doubtless noticed. "Kaydence. Have we any hope. Of finding my travel-kit, in all of this."

But in the turmoil of his mind, beneath his immediate focus on Erish's pain, the calculation raced toward its grim conclusion. Here were Erish and Code. Here were Kaydence and Toska. He had seen Chief Samons. And that left only . . .

"Sir. Joslire's down, sir. You've got to see to Joslire. Your Excellency."

Erish knew the fear in Andrej's heart as well as he did. Andrej didn't want to slight Erish's pain, just because of the terror that he felt—but as long as Erish understood, perhaps it would be all right, the Lieutenant had said that help would be arriving—

Stumbling over the uneven surface in the street, Andrej struggled to where he had seen Chief Samons last.

There was blood everywhere.

As Andrej neared, Chief Samons rose to her feet from where she knelt beside Joslire, and almost despite himself Andrej took note of the way Joslire's body lay upon the ground. He didn't want to see. He knew what it meant. He couldn't not see, couldn't not understand; he was a doctor.

It was Joslire.

But he was still a doctor. He couldn't turn the analysis off in his mind. He knew almost before he saw that there would be concussive injury to the body cavity. Trouble in breathing. Slow drowning in his own blood, as the lungs filled with fluid.

Joslire.

Kneeling down in the rubble at Joslire's side, Andrej took Joslire's right hand, rubbing the knuckles with his thumb as though to work some feeling back into a hand numbed with cold.

"Joslire."

Oh, it was frightful, it was bad. Joslire lay facing up in the debris in the street with his head cradled back into a hollow of some sort, blood pooling at the hollow of his shoulder, his uniform black with it. Pooling, not overflowing, so there had been some traumatic cauterization; Joslire was not bleeding to death quickly. Slowly, yes, that, but it was the fluid in his lungs that would do for him. He had to be raised, no matter how it hurt because the pain in his lungs would only get worse until they did.

"S-sir." Joslire stuttered in his pain, but as he spoke his voice got stronger. Shock was good. Shock was useful. Shock could help to insulate Joslire from his agony; if only help would come before shock killed him. "Sir. Is it. Morning. Yet. I pray it may be."

Morning?

It wouldn't be morning for nearly two shifts. They had come out at sundown, and it was the time of year when nights began to run long in Rudistal. It would be getting cold. What could Joslire mean by "morning"?

"Come and help me, Chief. Have Kay and Toska found my travel-kit? Yes, we need to lift, now, Joslire. This is going to hurt—"

Did hurt.

Joslire cried out short and sharp, a sudden shout of pain that seemed to echo against the far wall and shake Andrej to the pit of his stomach. Joslire cried out, but then fell silent; and there was no telling they were hurting him but for the shaky shattered sound of his rough breathing. Andrej held Joslire in his arms, and Chief Samons searched for material to make a support of some kind. Joslire settled his head against Andrej's shoulder, breathing hard.

"Please. Your Excellency. Is it morning, come. I've waited for it. For so long."

Chief Samons found some cushions from the passenger cabin of the touring car, some all but destroyed and good for padding, one or two almost intact to make a back support. Kaydence and Code helped them settle Joslire in Andrej's arms so that he could breathe. Toska was helping Erish across the short stretch of street between where Andrej had left them and where Joslire lay; that was good. They would all be together.

"What is he saying?" Andrej half-whispered, to Chief Samons. "About it being morning?"

Kaydence heard the question, and Kaydence paled, seven degrees whiter than he had been before.

Then Andrej understood.

The morning of the Day.

The text scrolled through his mind unwelcome and unbidden, but he could not make it stop.

A bond-involuntary with sufficiently serious an injury sustained in the line of duty may elect to terminate his Bond under honorable circumstances rather than incur the expense to the Bench required to return him to duty status. Termination of Bond under such circumstances is equivalent to successful completion of the full Term for purposes of nullification of Bench issues outstanding.

Joslire meant to claim the Day.

He meant to die.

The Bench was willing to forgive the balance of Joslire's debt as a matter of economic practicality. If it would cost more to heal than to replace him, the Bench was willing to let Joslire die and that was the question that Joslire was asking him.

Furious denial rose up into Andrej's throat; he swallowed back angry words of rebuke with difficulty. Claim the Day? Whoever heard of such a thing? What could Joslire mean by trying to do this to him?

"Oh, no," Andrej murmured, almost to himself, horror-stricken. "Oh, please, Joslire, thou can'st not—"

He heard himself speaking, and choked his words back down into his heart, where they burned horribly. It wasn't fair for him to try to keep Joslire, not if Joslire wanted to go. He had no right to so much as ask it.

Joslire was waiting for him to continue, watching him, as though all of Joslire's soul were focused in his eyes on Andrej's face. Joslire was in pain. But Joslire was not worried. Shouldn't he be worried? It was a bond-involuntary's right to claim the Day, but Andrej held the Writ. He could do anything to his bond-involuntaries he wanted. He could deny Joslire the Day; it was for him to decide whether Joslire was to be permitted to go.

Joslire could be healed, with time.

But to live on as a bond-slave would be torture.

And after all that Joslire had given him, and done for him, and taught him, to betray Joslire would be worse than simple ingratitude; because for Joslire to live enslaved—and betrayed as well, by a man in whom he had placed his trust—would be ceaseless anguish upon torment.

As much as Andrej wished, he could not do it.

"It is true." It was Joslire's right; Joslire had earned his freedom too many times to count, and could not be challenged on the manner in which he chose to elect it. There was nothing left. Andrej looked around, Erish, Kaydence, Code, Toska, Chief Samons. Cradling Joslire in his arms, Andrej laid his cheek against Joslire's forehead, speaking the words in dread and misery.

"It is true, Joslire, the Day is yours, to claim as you wish it." The faith, the trust that Joslire had in him, how could he grudge it to Joslire to find his freedom here and now—when Andrej would leave Fleet at the end of eight years, while Joslire would be bound for twice as long yet?

"Oh." Joslire had closed his eyes, apparently overcome with emotion or with pain, there was no telling. "It is well come. You'll give me my pass, then, your Excellency."

He should not hold Joslire so close to him. It could not make breathing easier. And breathing was hard already, and would only get more and more difficult, where was his kit, where were the drugs that would ease Joslire's dying?

Joslire didn't want any painease.

Joslire only wanted to die, and embraced his pain as the glad proof that he was to be free.

"Stand all apart." If this was Joslire's will, it would be so. But Andrej couldn't help but try one last thing; Joslire had a right to the information, so he could make his decision in full knowledge of all of the facts that Andrej had at his command. "Joslire. Our Captain has petitioned to revoke thy bond. It may be that thou art to be free, and yet alive. Oh, reconsider."

Reconsider, Joslire. For my sake, if for no other reason.

But Andrej knew he had no right to say it.

He knew Joslire had heard him; he could tell that Joslire understood. It made no difference. "No better way for me to die than here and now. And by thy hand." Shock was steadying Joslire's words; there was to be no chance of pretending that Joslire was not in full command of all his faculties. "Even if. I've waited for this. Whether or not."

No mercy.

No yielding; and no hope.

"Come, then." Andrej raised his voice and beckoned to Code, who stood nearest to him at a few paces remove. "We must all say good-bye to Joslire whom we love, because he is to leave our company very soon. It is your moment, gentlemen, only someone must kiss Joslire for Robert, who will be sure to fault me that he was not here to cheer Joslire's parting."

Pain made a man selfish. Andrej could hardly stand the thought of Joslire dead, but there were others here, and who was to say they did not love Joslire as much or more than he did? They had been closer to Joslire, in a sense. They had lived together, trained together, worked together, fought together—and even taken comfort in one another, when comfort was needed.

Stumbling awkwardly to his feet, Andrej struggled over the chunks of street and pavement to find a place where he could be alone, to try to gain some mastery over himself. He knew what Joslire meant for him to do. He could think of no token that would show more love and gratitude.

And at the same time Andrej could not believe that he could do it, that he would be able to do it, that he would not falter and fail at the last.

Standing in a daze like a man about to crumple, Andrej stared out into the street without comprehending the scene he saw there. Support had arrived; the street was full of people, ambulance crews, Security. Wreckers. The Port Authority. Lieutenant Plugrath came up behind Andrej where he stood and spoke to him, but it was a moment before Andrej began to understand what Plugrath was saying.

"They'll take Curran to hospital, sir. There's the life-litter just now coming up, had to clear the wreckage on the other side. If we're not too late, sir. It'll only be—"

Once he could grasp Plugrath's meaning Andrej started to shake his head, struggling to keep his voice steady while he wept in desperate sorrow. "No. Lieutenant. Joslire is not to go to hospital. Erish, but in a moment or so, not before."

He hadn't said the important words. Plugrath was confused, and Andrej didn't blame him. "Sir, surely it's Curran worse wounded; we'll get him to hospital. There's time for your other man once the emergency is safely in transit."

No.

The emergency was safely in transit now, to a refuge more secure than any hospital. Plugrath could not know that.

"Joslire will not be with us much longer, Lieutenant, he has claimed the Day, as is his right. I would have you keep these people clear of us. It is bad enough that he elects to die in the street in this manner without there being arguments in his last breaths over whether he is to be allowed to go."

Yes, Andrej told himself, sternly.

No arguments.

No matter how bitterly Andrej wished to dispute Joslire's decision.

"Sir." Plugrath had been startled into silence, more or less; but at least Andrej had made his point. "I beg your pardon, sir. No idea. Excuse me. I'll see to it directly."

Plugrath went away; and the noise and bustle seemed to abate, somewhat, but whether it was because the cordon of Security that formed between them and the world shut out the noise—or whether he was in shock, and could no longer quite hear—Andrej didn't know.

Too soon, too soon, here was Code at his back, tear-streaked of face but resolute of voice. "Sir. We're ready for you, sir. We're all ready. Joslire most of all."

He couldn't face it. He needed more time. But every moment more was another anguished breath in Joslire's ruined lungs, another gross insult to Joslire's shattered body. Andrej went back, and knelt down at Joslire's side once more, taking Joslire's hand into his own.

Joslire was smiling, and it wasn't a grimace of pain, it wasn't a rictus of agony, it wasn't the hysteria of shock. Joslire was smiling because Joslire was free, or as good as, and the pain Joslire was in was as nothing to Joslire compared to his honor, and the reclamation of his name.

The sound of Joslire's breathing hurt to listen to, because Andrej knew how much each ragged breath hurt Joslire, and the smell of raw flesh and drying blood was heavy and oppressive in the chill air.

"Joslire." He knew what Joslire meant to have, of him. He wanted it to be soon for Joslire's sake, even while he wanted it never for his own. Desperate to deny Joslire his freedom in order to have the comfort of his company, Andrej only asked one final question, knowing that he would not betray his man. His friend. The support of long black hours, and his unfailing bulwark in the adversity that was his life. "Joslire. Thy knives. What is to become of them, when thou art dead."

Emandisan five-knives had profound religious meaning to Emandisan, though the knives themselves looked almost exactly like Fleet-issue to Andrej. Once Joslire was dead, there would be no one to drill him in his technique in throwing-knives, technique Joslire had taught him; and yet the knives Joslire had taught him were a part of him, now, how could he put a part of him aside?

Joslire's smile widened, even as his hand tightened in Andrej's grasp. The pain. Joslire reached up his free hand to the back of Andrej's neck; what did Joslire want? A kiss to speed his parting? That was the Dolgorukij way of it, when taking leave. Andrej bent his neck to Joslire's purpose, but Joslire did not want a caress, Joslire wanted the knife sheathed at the back of Andrej's neck between his shoulder blades, the mother-knife that had been the very first Joslire had taught him to wear.

"They have been here all along," Joslire said. It became difficult to understand him; it was harder work for Joslire to catch his breath moment by moment, and the fluid in his lungs followed his breath up into his throat to garble his voice horribly. Joslire spoke slowly. "Since the first. That I came. To understand your nature."

Joslire could not hold the knife at eye level, his hand sinking slowly to his chest. Twitching his hand impatiently for pain, Joslire settled the knife that he held loosely in his grasp so that the point of it pricked at the back of Andrej's hand as he held to Joslire. Joslire's hand in Andrej's grip tightened yet again, with a sharp spasm of pain crossing Joslire's face. *Who was holding whom?* Andrej wondered.

"Thy knives," Joslire said, and his body convulsed in ferocious agony, his grip like iron. The knife Joslire held bit deep into the back of Andrej's hand, and with an effort almost superhuman in its terrific concentration, Joslire drove the knife clear through between the bones, pinning his hand and Andrej's hand together.

The pain was very sharp, very surprising.

But Andrej was too startled to cry out.

"Thy knives and my knives. One and the same. Give those on my body back to Fleet, they're nothing to do with me. My knives are thy knives, now and forever. To the end with thee, my master. And beyond."

Pinned together, palm to palm, blood flowed and mingled. Joslire was staring at him with uttermost intensity, as if to will him to understand something Joslire had no words to communicate.

Oh, had it indeed been so, for all this time?

How could he have been so blind, as not to see?

"Give me my life. And let me go, Andrej."

But whether Joslire actually spoke the words—or Andrej only imagined that he had—Andrej could not begin to say.

Joslire lost his grip on the hilt of the mother-knife, his hand falling like a dead weight to one side.

"Chief." He could not move. He was tied to Joslire, pinned to Joslire, sewn into Joslire's life. "If you would, please. I require some assistance."

She hardly knew quite how to approach it; Andrej could imagine she felt awkward. She pulled the knife out through the back of Andrej's hand, and the blood ran hot down his forearm. Andrej cherished his pain to himself to fix his last moments with Joslire in memory.

"Thank you." He held his bleeding hand out for the return of the blade, and she reversed the knife to pass it to him hilt-first, out of habit. It was time. It was almost too late. Joslire meant to die by his own blade. It would be cheating him, to let him die of loss of blood or dry-land drowning. No matter how much it hurt, both physically and emotionally. In a way, the physical pain was bracing to him; it helped to deaden the agony in his heart, and see him through to do right by Joslire.

Andrej put the point to Joslire's throat.

"It is the Day." Joslire's gaze was unwavering; and grateful. "Thou hast been good to me, Joslire, and I have loved thee. Go now, and may the Holy Mother grant thy spirit easy passage to thy place."

He knew how hard to push, and at what angle, and to what exact depth.

One final breath, as Joslire gasped, as if in surprise or in ecstatic pleasure.

Andrej kissed Joslire's staring eyes for love, and Joslire's mouth for parting.

But even as Andrej kissed him, Joslire died.

Vanished from his body; dissolved into the air.

Even as Andrej kissed him, Joslire's spirit fled; and it was only a dead body, now, only an abandoned piece of damaged flesh, only something inanimate and unimportant that had once housed a man that he had loved.

Andrej rocked the empty shell in his arms and cried aloud to the uncaring night, blind with grief and deaf to any sound in the reverberation of the emptiness in his heart. Alone. Joslire had gone away. He was alone.

Never to have the comfort of Joslire's companionship, ever again—

CHAPTER FIVE

He was alone, abandoned, and bereft; but he was still Andrej Koscuisko. He had responsibilities that he had to see to.

It was cold in the street. The icy air caught in his throat, rough as it was with weeping. Every bone in Andrej's body seemed to ache, but whether it was because he had been kneeling for too long on rocks and gravel holding to a corpse as though there was some trace of Joslire there, Andrej didn't know.

It was only a corpse.

There was no one there.

But other Bonds were with him still, and though he took no comfort in their presence he could not in fairness overlook them. He was still responsible for them. He had been selfish in his grief for Joslire. They had loved Joslire, too.

And—what was more to the point—not only would they grieve, but they might fear that he would be resentful of them for being here when Joslire was dead. Erish had to go to hospital. Someone should probably see to the new wound in his hand. There was a body to be disposed of. The Domitt Prison was still waiting for his Writ.

He had to get a hold over himself, and be an officer, not some ordinary bereft soul who had the freedom and the luxury to grieve for his dead without a thought for what effect his behavior had on those around him.

"Miss Samons. If I could see you for a moment. Please."

There was a good deal of activity around him, as it seemed. The sounds of movement and of people talking seemed to increase gradually in volume, as though the information they contained was coming into focus, in some way.

Chief Samons knelt opposite him, wiping her face. "Sir."

"Erish and our others, how do they go?"

He had got stiff, holding the stiffening corpse. Frowning, Chief Samons reached out for his hand to help him to his feet. "They've given Erish good drugs. Code's in pieces. Kaydence is with him. So far, so good."

"Call Plugrath to me, then." He must have been holding Joslire very tightly, from how his muscles ached. "What's happening?"

"Plugrath's got the street locked down. The Port Authority would like to murder that administrator, Belan." Raising her voice, Chief Samons called back over her shoulder. "Bench Lieutenant. His Excellency is asking for you, sir."

He wanted to go see his Security, but he had to get this out of the way first. Lieutenant Plugrath had brought Belan with him; Belan was very pale. Plugrath hardly less so.

Lieutenant Plugrath spoke. "What's to be done, sir?"

Yes, with the body. People who died on duty were cremated, the remains returned to point of origin by special courier. That was the common fate for anyone who died in service; Fleet could not afford to handle bodies, still less concern itself with the myriad different rituals and rites required by all the souls under Jurisdiction. They would need facilities to burn the body. Hospitals would have them. Erish had to go to hospital, because even if Andrej had not taken a cut through his palm he was not an orthopedic specialist. Erish needed to be seen by bones-and-joints, not neurosurgery. It all fell into place.

"We'll go to hospital, Lieutenant." There could well be a wake-room at the hospital. It was Standard procedure to provide one. "There is a rated facility in Rudistal? There must be. Administrator, I am sure you can for us your senior's pardon obtain, and say that we will be a little late."

They were already late. How late were they? He had no idea what time it was. He didn't care.

"Yes, sir. Of course, sir." Belan almost stuttered in his nervousness. Andrej could empathize; it was a hard thing to be shot at in the first place, and a senior officer's being ambushed while in one's company was probably the stuff of nightmare from an Administrative point of view. "There is Infirmary at the prison, sir. Shouldn't your party rather proceed now to your station, rather than make a side trip to the civil facility?"

"No, we should not." Prison infirmaries were not hospitals. Erish needed a hospital. He deserved a specialist. And more than that, the body was to burn, but it was not to be considered for a moment that Joslire's corpse should be put to the fire in a prison—as though still the Bench's prisoner, a slave, a bond-involuntary. Joslire was free. He would be decently cremated with all due respect. And at a hospital, since as far as Andrej knew there were no Emandisan churches.

It was too much to hope that Belan would understand, and so Andrej didn't try to explain it at all. "Take us to emergency receiving, if you please. At hospital. We will once the sun has risen see to the body. Lieutenant, you must arrange for handling after that." They had not been at the Domitt Prison when the attack had taken place; formally they were still the Dramissoi Fleet's concern. Perhaps. One thing was for certain; they were bound to go to the Domitt Prison, but what remained in the world of Joslire Curran should not.

"As you say, sir. I'll tell the Administrator." Belan was confused and a little resentful; he hadn't given Belan any good reasons for his apparently high-handed behavior, Andrej realized. His insistence must seem arbitrary to Belan. He didn't care. He didn't have the energy.

"Tell also your service house. I will want a suite. And sufficient professional assistance, for my gentlemen. For tomorrow morning. I am sure the Domitt Prison will not grudge us a day for mourning. We have lost somebody that we loved."

As had some of Plugrath's Security, but it was different. None of them were Bonds. Or perhaps it was the same, but his own people were all Andrej could be expected to keep in his mind, surely.

Belan nodded, unhappily, but went away.

Andrej hoped he wasn't in trouble with the prison administration even before he'd gotten to the prison. But if he was there was no help for it.

"They're ready to load you for the hospital, sir. You can all ride together, if you'd like."

All ride together?

Did Plugrath mean with Joslire in the car?

The street had been swept clean, debris cleared away. Far above in the black sky Andrej could see the brightest of the stars over Port Rudistal shining in the night. This was the street that had taken Joslire away; Andrej took one final look at it, convinced that he would remember every detail for as long as he should live.

But Erish had to go to hospital.

Turning away, Andrej climbed into the transport-cabin to go to hospital, and put the street behind him.

Their baggage had been packed in the rearmost car, recovered more or less undamaged after the firefight. Once they got to the hospital's wake-room, the first thing that the officer did was wash and change his uniform. The one he had been wearing was soaked with Joslire's life's-blood, clear through to the skin; and while they'd dealt with such issues with their officer before—on other assignments, mostly—it had always been the blood of someone else, someone they didn't know.

Code almost thought Koscuisko didn't want to wash the blood away, because it was Joslire's blood, and rinsing himself clean of it was letting go of some small piece of Joslire. But it couldn't be helped. Joslire was dead. The officer had to change, because he couldn't go into treatment rooms with his uniform so heavily contaminated with blood and dust.

Once he had changed, it seemed to Code that the attitudes of the hospital staff changed, as well. As if they only just realized that Andrej Koscuisko was a ranking officer, rather than just one step up from Bench Lieutenant Plugrath.

They'd all trooped up to check on Erish, and by that time the bone man was just finishing glazing the last chips of patella back into place preparatory to closing up Erish's knee. Koscuisko lectured Erish about the brace he had to wear, too, which was a joke on their officer, because the bone man noticed the field bandage wrapped around the officer's hand while he was gesturing to make his point, and called a soft-tissue specialist.

Having just made so strong a point to Erish about obeying medical instruction, their officer had no choice at all but to sit and let them do things to his hand. It was funny. Almost it was funny. If it hadn't been for what had happened to them it would have been funny.

Then it was two hours before sunrise, and they had all gone back down to the wake-room adjacent to the body-mill. Joslire's body was there, and Joslire's kit. The officer claimed it was important that the body be dressed in clean clothing when it was burned, and Code didn't see where that made any sense at all, but as long as it made the officer feel better they would all go along with it.

It wasn't as if they'd never lost a member of a team before, though this was the first time it had happened to Code since Koscuisko had been assigned to *Scylla*. With Joslire and Robert St. Clare, who was bound to be hard hit by this event; Robert was sentimental.

So they all took off their duty-blouses and rolled back the sleeves of their under-blouses and undressed the body that had been Joslire, and washed the wound that had once been his chest as best they could, and dressed him once again in clean undamaged clothing. Code wondered whether Koscuisko wasn't right in some sense about it being important.

Handling the body helped to separate his sense of sorrow from his here-and-now, in some way. There was so clearly nothing left of Joslire there, not even when he knew it was Joslire's body, and Joslire's clothing.

One thing was more than obvious: Joslire was gone from there. There was no sense in grieving for Joslire. Joslire was feeling no pain. For himself, yes. But later.

The officer took away the knives and gave them to Chief Samons. The knife that had killed Joslire had been cleaned, and Koscuisko was wearing it once more in its harness between his shoulder blades. To think that Koscuisko's knives had been Emandisan, and all this time they'd all assumed that they were so much better than Fleet-issue because Fleet issued better to officers. To think. All of this time. Emandisan steel. Joslire's own five-knives.

Erish could not do much, because he was drunk on the drugs they'd given him; but Erish cut the braid away from Joslire's sleeves once he was dressed in his clean uniform. Joslire was free. He should not wear a slave-uniform, not even to be burned in.

Code could envy Joslire, being dead, because though he was dead Joslire was free.

It was almost time.

The sun would rise within the eighth.

It was important to the officer that the body not go into the fire before the sun came up. It made no sense to Code, and there was a question in his mind about whether the officer had a reason or was simply carrying a childhood pattern forward because he was in shock.

Scant moments before sunrise. Koscuisko had called for the precise time from the Port Authority and marked it by the clock in local reckoning. The furnace was ready: square and white and featureless, the door standing open, the interior gleaming in reflected light.

The corpse for burning on a narrow gurney, ready to wheel up to the mouth of the furnace, when the body would be slipped onto the high gridded floor of the furnace on a plank.

The officer, waiting, and the rest of them with him, exhausted and addle-headed with grief and the medication that they had all been made to take, and waiting for the next part to be done.

Now the time had come.

The sun cleared Port Rudistal's horizon, though there was no telling from inside this room. It would be sending its first long feelers across the relocation camp, across the black cold sullen river, into the Port, up to the foot of the Domitt Prison that had caused them all so much grief already—and before they'd so much as even arrived there yet.

Koscuisko spoke.

"Oh, Holy Mother," the officer said, and just for once it wasn't an oath or a profanity. Code realized that the officer was praying; and it sent a shudder through him to hear it.

"This is Joslire, your child, the child of your body, who you love. Whom we have loved. Now it has pleased you to take him back, and we bitterly regret it, though I am grateful that you took only one of their lives."

Koscuisko was not religious, though he kept the icon with its ever-burning lamp tucked into the corner of his sleeping-room. So much was merely habit; Koscuisko had never paid the slightest bit of attention to his patron saint—of Filial Piety, as he'd once told Code—in all this time.

"Send therefore guides and adequate equipage, and see your child safety home to shelter beneath the Canopy. And extend your hand over me and mine, Chief Samons not excluded, for you have bereft us all to your own purpose, which we are not empowered to understand. Holy

Mother. So prays to you with all his heart your child Andrej, unfilial and unreconciled, but your child yet."

A gesture of his hand for them to move the body into the furnace let them know that he had said what he felt needful.

Koscuisko stood and watched while they put Joslire in the furnace. Chief Samons secured the door.

She touched the switch, and the safeties engaged, and then the telltales on the wall began to move as the temperature within the furnace started rising.

Long moments, and Koscuisko watched the telltales, and Koscuisko wept, but to himself this time—not like before.

Code wept as well. He didn't notice what the others were doing. He and Joslire had had a rocky start in the beginning, because of some forgotten issue with Robert, and Joslire trying to keep Code out of trouble with Koscuisko while Code had thought Joslire was trying to cover for Robert. Who had annoyed him.

The index on unreduced organic matter within the furnace started to fall off, first bit by bit, then in a smooth slow curve. Flesh did not long remain in such temperatures. Bone was more resistant: but the furnace had been built to serve the dead.

When the index fell below its breakpoint, the officer straightened his shoulders and wiped his face with his white-square.

"It's done," Koscuisko said. "As done as done." Though it would be a while before the furnace could be opened. It took time, to vent such heat. "And we have nothing left. Oh, Holy Mother. Gentles, let us go away from here."

Nothing except each other.

Kaydence in the lead, and Erish limping, they left the room.

Left Joslire behind.

Joslire was gone.

Koscuisko had cleared it with Plugrath and with the Domitt Prison—Administrator Geltoi, if Caleigh remembered the name correctly. The prison was treating the issue very carefully. Bond-involuntaries were much more exotic than ordinary mortals, and common report embroidered upon a special relationship between them and the Inquisitors in token of the unusually absolute power a Ship's Inquisitor had over their lives.

No one who had witnessed the death of Joslire Curran—howsoever indirectly—could doubt that the relationship between Koscuisko and his dead Emandisan bond-involuntary had been intense and highly personal. At this point Koscuisko could probably have told the Domitt that he was going into retreat for two weeks, and taking his people with him; and no questions would have been asked. At least not right away.

As it was, he was simply going to Rudistal's service house, and for a day. More than reasonable. Really.

They left the hospital in the bright morning; it amused Caleigh to see how many more Security posts there seemed to be, suddenly. Ship's Inquisitors were even more rare a commodity than bond-involuntaries. To have hazarded the life of one created a huge embarrassment for Dramissoi and the Domitt alike, even if it had most likely been the Domitt that the ambushers thought they were striking at. Well, they had. Indirectly, maybe. But no less effectively for that.

An uneventful transit to the service house, uniformed troops at every turn. It wasn't the most luxurious facility Caleigh had ever been to in Koscuisko's company, but it would do. Koscuisko made a point of visiting service houses at every opportunity; it was for the benefit of his bond-involuntaries assigned as much as anything else, from what little Caleigh could tell.

Koscuisko's bond-involuntaries had few opportunities to develop social bonds for recreation on board *Scylla*, though Robert St. Clare was a great favorite amongst the ladies in both Security and Medical. For what that was worth. So Koscuisko went to service houses so that his people could enjoy what transient pleasure could be lawfully obtained in the embrace of the professional partner of their choice.

Caleigh hoped there were free women at this service house. As far as she knew, St. Clare was the only one of Koscuisko's people with a sister that had taken a Service Bond, but the other bond-involuntaries were sensitive about the issue as well.

When it came down to it, though, it wasn't an issue of recreation as such that brought them to the service house this morning. Nobody had slept. And they were all in shock. And the officer was in no condition to stand an in-briefing with prison administration.

Koscuisko went up to the senior officer's suite while Caleigh made arrangements for his people. A suite of rooms beneath the one

Koscuisko would be using, with direct access in case of emergencies, per standard operating procedure. Food and drink and sexual contact ad lib: but these were all just comfort items.

It was as important for the bond-involuntaries to be left to themselves to share their common grief and observe what forms of mourning they might choose. There were ad-hoc rituals that bond-involuntaries shared, ways of coping that they had developed over the years; and that was strictly their own business.

Once she had assured herself that her people were to be properly seen to, Caleigh went up to the senior officer's suite to give the officer a status report, wondering whether she should bother.

The senior officer's suite was as large as the troops' gather-room taken all together. Caleigh identified herself to the doorkeeper and sought out the suite's exercise area, where she expected to find her officer.

She had to cross the front room to get there. They were laying the table for his meal; and she could see through to the bedroom with the bed made up and waiting, the bed-clothes arranged invitingly. It made her want to cry. And she hadn't cried since she could remember. Wept, perhaps.

She was perhaps a little bit hysterical. She'd valued Joslire Curran as much as the next man; he'd been as genuine an asset as a Chief Warrant could wish. She'd learned early on to rely on him and St. Clare to manage the officer on those occasions when Koscuisko—for whatever good and sufficient reason of his own—had had too much to drink, and got the terrors.

Being in Security meant that people that you knew and relied upon were frequently killed, and usually traumatically so. It wasn't that. She'd never seen a Bond claim the Day. She'd never dreamed of seeing Koscuisko so naked in his grief, on his knees in the street in front of everyone, the deepest—most private—secrets of his heart on display for anyone who cared to notice.

There was no reason for the sight of a waiting bed to make her want to cry.

She went through to the exercise area, where she could count on finding Koscuisko having a massage.

Right first time, Caleigh congratulated herself, stepping into the warm dark room. Koscuisko lay face-down on the padded bench-table with the house masseur frowning over his upper back and a towel draped discreetly across the middle part of his body. He wouldn't be surprised to hear from her; she cleared her throat, to put him on notice that she was here. All right, she was intruding, but Koscuisko liked to know. Sometimes the masseur took it a little personally, however.

"H'm. Sir. I've seen to arrangements made for your people, sir. As you would wish it."

Her interruption earned her a glare from the masseur. Koscuisko intervened to head off a confrontation.

"Thank you, Fishweir. I am very much obliged to you."

Fishweir sounded Chigan to Caleigh. Impressive. The best masseurs in known Space were Chigan. A group of fellow Security had taken up a collection to buy her a massage for a promotion gift, years gone, when she'd made her first rating. She could remember it as though it had been yesterday. Wheatfields. The masseur had been of Wheatfields, not of Fishweir. Chigan was Chigan. Caleigh wondered, suddenly, whether she had just worked her way out of any chance of a massage herself by offending the man.

"I don't like to prescribe, your Excellency." Fishweir, whomever of Fishweir, shrugged it off, wiping excess oil from his hands on a clean towel. "But your whole body's in knots. I think the only thing for it is a glass of caraminson wine. I'll send up a flask."

Yes, Chigan by the accent. Koscuisko made as if to rise; Fishweir placed a hand firmly in the middle of Koscuisko's back and pushed. Koscuisko subsided, capitulating.

"You are very kind. It is generous of you to offer." Koscuisko had the authority to prescribe whatever he liked for himself to ease his pain; many Ship's Inquisitors took that way out, and became addicted to mood-altering substances. Koscuisko's mood-altering substance of choice remained alcohol.

That didn't change the fact that for most people a flask of caraminson wine was a once-in-a-lifetime experience, worth every bit of the cost. And only licensed professionals could provide it. "Here is my Chief of Security, Fishweir, her name is Samons. She knows that I am worried about my bond-involuntaries. One wonders whether massage might be made available for her benefit as well."

Of course it might. That wasn't what Koscuisko was asking. Professionals at a Chigan's level were to be approached as carefully as if they were—well, Ship's Surgeons, for example. Koscuisko was asking whether Fishweir would condescend to favor Caleigh herself with the skillful medication of his educated hands.

Fishweir shook his head with polite regret. "Sir, I'm Unreform, I'm sorry. No offense, Chief." And while most Chigan off-world simply treated women as though they were female men and dealt with Chigan cultural taboos in that manner, "unreformed" Chigan were prohibited by their creed from any form of physical contact with the sex of hominid that carried young in utero. Caleigh didn't mind Unreform Chigan. It was nothing personal. Fishweir was clearly well intentioned as he spoke on.

"I'll tell you both something, though, and you can take it for what you feel it may be worth. The nature of grief is heavy, wet, and cold. It settles in your stomach. You need fire to drive it off or it'll make you sick."

Fishweir had been stroking Koscuisko's body as he spoke, as if restlessly. Now he stilled his hands, one at the small of Koscuisko's back, one at the back of Koscuisko's neck, and rested himself there. Caleigh wondered that Koscuisko would submit to being touched at the back of his neck, when he was so selective about who he would touch in that manner, and when. Perhaps it was to do with surrendering himself into the capable hands of a professional.

The thought ambushed Caleigh Samons, and took her breath away.

Surrender herself.

Into the hands of someone who could take care of her.

She shook herself to clear her mind. She was a senior Security warrant officer. She could take care of herself. She had been taking care of herself—and her officer, and her troops assigned—for years.

But the shaking didn't work to clear her mind and rid her of the alien thought. Someone who could take care of her, even if only for a few hours, even if only in a sense.

Someone like her officer.

She knew the strength of his body from combat drill, she knew the strength of his will. She knew the strength of his passion from these few hours past, watching him grieve for Joslire Curran. She knew the quality of his mind from what she had heard of gossip from Infirmary, surprise at his skill level, appreciation for his ability, finally gratitude for the healing in his hands.

Oh, someone to be responsible for the next few hours, someone to see to her needs—

The very idea was so foreign that it turned her stomach.

At least there was a sudden strange sensation there, in her belly. And surely it was revulsion at the very idea.

Unless it was desire for comfort, after what they had suffered last night?

"There, now." Fishweir stroked up the length of Koscuisko's body one last time and turned away, his voice low and calm and caressing. "You're to lie still for at least four eighths. Miss Samons, time him. I'll have the kitchen send up some warming, drying food. Good-greeting, your Excellency."

Professional courtesy was all very well.

But Fishweir was Chigan.

And Koscuisko was beautiful, in a masculine sense; his body maybe a little white but smooth and sleek with the lithe lines of his Dolgorukij musculature. It wasn't the bulk of the muscle but how the muscle tied in to the bone that made the difference with Dolgorukij. Koscuisko was much stronger than he looked, and if he took her into his embrace—

She shouldn't be having these thoughts. He was her officer. Granted that Koscuisko desired her; most men did. She didn't want him.

She only wanted comfort.

And that desperately.

All of her life spent taking care of things, seeing to the well-being of her troops—

"Slow count, Chief," Fishweir reminded her, on his way out.

Was it her imagination?

Or did that damned Chigan know exactly what was going on in her clearly stress-addled mind?

"Have you made plans, Miss Samons?" Koscuisko asked, casually, after a moment had passed. "They could lay two places. Unless you've found something of interest here."

Did he mean that he hadn't?

"Haven't had a chance to check, sir. Settling the others." Hadn't been particularly interested. She was tired, and she just wanted to sleep. She'd thought. And hiring a man wasn't the same as surrendering an hour to someone she could trust, and there she went again, and she was going to have to concentrate. And take a nice cold shower. Which would not be relaxing.

"It is said that grief likes company. But only aggrieved company. I would be glad of your companionship, I do not feel like talking with a stranger."

"That would be nice. Thank you." It was an effort to keep her voice calm and casual; when she was hungry. "I should probably get a wash in before we eat, though."

"Plenty of time." Koscuisko's voice was muffled against the pillow on the bench-table. "Perhaps so much as an eight, but I hope not. I'm hungry. We didn't get our third-meals in, last night, and fast-meal gone begging as well. Tell the kitchen, Miss Samons, and we will sit down together. That will be comforting. I will enjoy that."

Leaving her officer to lie quietly in the serene calm of the exercise room, Caleigh called the kitchen to arrange for doubled portions. And had them send up a second wrap-robe as well. If Koscuisko thought it was just too odd of her, she could cover for it somehow. But it didn't need to mean anything. Fatigue could explain it. And she didn't care. She was reckless with weariness and hunger to be the one taken care of, just this once.

She went through the officer's bedroom into the washroom beyond, and stripped, and lay in a tub full of hot water until she knew by the quiet sounds outside the bath-enclosure itself that the house staff had carried away her clothing to be cleaned, and left her a wrap-robe.

Clean white toweling, sweet with a fragrance of sun. It was probably a perfume. Caleigh didn't care. The warmth of the robe was comforting, and the silk slippers for her feet were very caressing as well. They had put out a sleep-shift for her, much like the sleep-shirt that had been waiting for Koscuisko in the exercise room, hanging on a hook. Koscuisko had already had his wash. It was the first thing Koscuisko always did when he came to a service house, regardless of whether or not he anticipated seeking entertainment.

She was as dressed as he was, and had seen him naked, what was there to think twice about? Caleigh tied her long blond hair up in a loose damp knot and went out to find the meal-table.

Koscuisko would have known she had gone into the washroom; he would have heard her. He seemed a little surprised at it, but took her reappearance in stride. Maybe he wasn't taking it in stride. Maybe he was too beaten down by everything they had been through to be surprised at anything.

Their meal was ready for them, one way or the other, and that took care of having to talk about much of anything for a while. Dinner? Supper? Fast-meal? She'd lost track. It was mid-meal by local reckoning, and she didn't usually take much of a mid-meal, but she found herself to her surprise accounting for her fair share of the meat-dish.

Some of the bread.

Quite a bit of the side-vegetable.

And one of the two glasses of caraminson wine, no more than two mouthfuls of fluid really, but a powerful soother and muscle relaxant that would ensure they both slept well and deeply, to the effective healing of their bodies—when they slept.

She couldn't talk to the officer.

She kept getting distracted.

It was not precisely comfortable, but it wasn't awkward, either; she couldn't say quite how she felt about it.

The servers took away the dirty dishes and laid out fruit and cheese and sweets, and went away. Koscuisko crossed his forearms on the table's edge and leaned forward, regarding her with a very inquiring look in his mirror-silver eyes.

"Tell me what is in your mind, Chief," he suggested. "It may be that I should know, and if I have offended I can only ask for consideration. But I am very stupid just at the moment. And I am not accustomed to the sight of your shoulders—"

The sleep-shift was a little loose, and the wrap-robe was not snug. The collar lay open across her shoulders; it might even have slipped to one side or another during the course of the meal without her taking much note of it.

"—and it becomes very difficult to remember that you are Chief Warrant Officer Caleigh Samons. Rather than a woman whose body I desire very much."

Well, that was nothing new. Was it? He'd never told her, not in so many words. She'd never needed to be told. It had always been obvious enough.

She was making a mistake.

She shouldn't be considering it, only—only she couldn't shake the thought. One eight, two eights, that was all she would ever ask. Two eights to lie in the arms of a man who could take care of her. She was more than Koscuisko's match in combat drill; it wasn't that.

Joslire had trusted him.

Joslire was dead.

"That's two of us tired, your Excellency." To gloss things over and go away would be best. It would be safer. Koscuisko did not have to do with subordinate troops; and had apparently set that between them in his mind from the beginning. She had always appreciated his respect for her professional skill. She didn't want to lose that. "I should go see about a room. I'm glad to have had company, though. After what's happened."

Stupid Koscuisko might be, and she might be in shock. He looked at her directly, no defenses, no pretense. He was not the Chief Medical Officer, nor the Ship's Inquisitor. He was Andrej Koscuisko. Just at this moment that was all he was.

"It is not strictly speaking necessary for you to go out to an empty bed. There is in the next room one which is very suitable, and already made up to welcome you. We will be Caleigh and Andrej just this once, perhaps. I could take comfort from your body, Caleigh. And it could be that you would have some comfort from mine."

Oh, yes, precisely. The idea exactly. Yes.

She didn't know exactly how to say it, so she didn't say anything. She only stood up slowly, debating moment by moment about the wisdom of this course of action.

She walked uncertainly in slippered feet toward the bedroom and stopped in the doorway.

Now or never. Point of decision. Make or break.

Koscuisko took her carefully around the waist from behind, and kissed the side of her neck with contemplative deliberation; and she knew that at that moment she was the center of Koscuisko's universe.

He had the power of complete absorption, absolute concentration on whatever had caught his interest at the moment.

Right now he was centered on her; and raised his bandaged hand to stroke the opposite side of her throat as he kissed her.

She was drunk with arousal, but whether it was the pleasure his caress gave her or her enjoyment of the intensity of his attention—or even the caraminson wine—Caleigh didn't know.

She didn't think it mattered.

He had said that he admired her shoulders, of all things?

She shrugged the wrap-robe down around her elbows, and leaned back against Koscuisko's welcome strength.

To affirm life honored life, and to honor life was to respect the dead.

Koscuisko kissed her throat, and Caleigh shivered with the pure pleasure of it, and ceased to think about anything at all in the world except Koscuisko's touch and Koscuisko's kisses.

Andrej awoke to a restrained bustle of activity in the other room and blinked his eyes at the ceiling, trying to make sense of the confused memories that jumbled in his mind in the disorder of an uncompleted dream. It was not a familiar bed. There was a warmth to it that was more than of his body, and a fragrance that was familiar, but out of place. What was going on?

Someone was speaking low-voiced in the outer room. Kaydence. "Packed and ready, Chief. There's word with the housemaster from Lieutenant Plugrath. Wants to inspect the officer's escort before we're to leave. Something like that."

"I'm not going to ask you how you know, Kay."

There, that was Chief Samons's voice, quiet and serene and even affectionate. Kaydence had an insatiable appetite for information that he was not supposed to have, and was always fraying braids in which he had no business just to see whether it could be done. Within limits. Kaydence's governor kept him from too much meddling.

It had been meddling with Bench systems that had gotten Kaydence his Bond in the first place, after all. "Chief." Kaydence sounded aggrieved. "I came by the information honestly. Courier delivery, voice confirm. You slander me."

It was like an addiction of sorts with Kaydence, and in the years Andrej had known him he had fallen foul of his governor more than once when enthusiasm outran prudence. There was something else, though. Andrej frowned, thinking hard.

"I don't know if that's possible, Kay. You'd be twice as offended if I implied you couldn't find out."

Chief Samons.

It was the fragrance of her body, in the bed.

Sitting up suddenly, Andrej stared at the still-dimpled pillow to his right.

Chief Samons?

It had been Caleigh, and there was one of her long blond hairs on the pillow.

Caleigh, and she had called him by his name, and he had numbered all the secrets in his mind that he had ever wanted to know about her body and solved them one by one with self-indulgent thoroughness.

His fish rose up amidst the bedclothes and crested at the very thought of it, but Andrej could not be bothered with the importunities of his masculine gender. Let his fish breach. There were people in the next room. He had to get dressed. It was morning. The clock-panel in the headboard of the bed made that quite clear.

"How's the officer?" Kaydence asked.

Andrej had turned to get up and find his under-linen, but the question froze him in mid-pivot with a handful of bedclothes half-raised in the air.

"He slept well, I think. There's a Chigan masseur. And he prescribed caraminson, I'd tip him twice if I could."

Nothing.

No hint of hesitation, no vague suspicion of a concealed truth, no stutter. Nothing. Freed from his paralysis, Andrej set foot to carpeted floor to find his clothing. It was to be their secret, then.

"I don't know how well Code slept, Chief, not even with all the help he had." Kaydence's voice sounded thoughtful. "What about our Chief, how is she doing?"

It wasn't the sort of question a bond-involuntary would normally ask a superior. It was a little too personal; and that could mean impertinent. But Kaydence asked it quite naturally and calmly, taking care of Chief Samons as though she were one of them—one of the Bonds. In a strictly limited sense.

Kaydence's artless question brought home the full enormity of Andrej's loss with renewed force. They had all taken care of each other. Now one of them was dead; and if they weren't careful, Code might follow where Joslire had gone. A bond-involuntary who couldn't work his way through survivor's guilt could force his governor into overload. It was one of the ways in which a bond-involuntary could commit suicide: a particularly self-punitive way, to brood on one's own failings until one's governor took over the task of self-flagellation and carried it to its ultimate extreme. Very horrible.

But not as horrible as what he meant to do to the people who had stolen Joslire away from them. A governor on overload meant death in agony, but without the proper drugs that death could take mere hours to conclude. He would execute a masterpiece, a Tenth Level Command Termination that would last eight days and more before it was concluded. Joslire would be avenged.

He had to get to the Domitt Prison, because he had experiments to perform before the Port Authority found his prey.

That meant getting dressed.

His uniform was waiting in the bedroom for him, but his boots were not; Andrej went out in slippered feet to see how he was to speak to Chief Samons, and get his boots at the same time. Kaydence had gone. Chief Samons sat at the meal-table having some cavene; and stood up as he entered the room, bowing her salute.

"His Excellency slept well?"

Only a very subtle hint of the joke, there. And no mockery. But no trace of the woman who had welcomed his embrace, either. Just as well that his fish had got tired of being ignored, and tucked its head back sullenly into his hip-wrap, where it belonged.

"Thank you, Miss Samons. Excellently well. And you?"

"Just what the doctor ordered. With respect."

No awkwardness, and no denial. This was not so difficult as Andrej had feared. It was not to be necessary to pretend that nothing had happened; it was not to be expected that it would happen again.

Fair was fair.

"I'm glad to hear it. Did I hear Kaydence telling you about a word from Plugrath?"

He was better off without the distraction she would represent, had she hinted that he might again embrace her.

He wanted nothing to interfere with his vengeance for Joslire.

Administrator Geltoi watched the small convoy approach, frowning into the early morning sun. To have waited so long for a Writ, only to be delayed at the last moment by this unfortunate accident— really, he had suffered reversals before, but this was a bitter one.

That wasn't even all.

Koscuisko had injured his hand during the attack, and would doubtless need some days yet of recovery time.

Couldn't he just direct his Bonds to the work, wasn't that what they were for? Yet a wounded man had a right to expect light duty in respect for an injury. Try as he did, Geltoi couldn't make out the execution of the Writ to be "light duty" no matter how he approached the problem in his mind.

The little convoy was closer by the moment, and would soon be hidden behind the compound wall that circled the administration building and the prison alike. Geltoi got out his conning-glasses; he could tell which one was Koscuisko from Belan's description—seated in the senior officer's place, wearing duty black in token of his station as one of *Scylla*'s Ship's Primes, short and fair-headed, no beard.

Geltoi frowned.

From where he stood, Koscuisko almost looked Nurail.

A trick of the light, surely, and there was no cause to suspect any such thing. The officer's brief said his system of origin was the Dolgorukij Combine. There were no Nurail in the Dolgorukij Combine that Geltoi had ever heard of, still less any Nurail contaminating the blood of one of the Combine's oldest and most influential—if not richest—noble houses. It was an accident of nature, a freak of genetics. Yes.

The convoy didn't swing wide at the crossroads to make for the gate outside the prison's entrance, though. Instead the convoy took the branch that led toward the administration building.

This was interesting. For Koscuisko to come to him straightaway— and it would be Koscuisko's own idea, Belan had his instructions—was the behavior appropriate to a subordinate officer; and very gracious of Koscuisko to have made the public gesture. Geltoi smiled.

Yes.

Not Nurail at all.

The convoy cleared the perimeter gate and pulled up in front of the administration building, out of Geltoi's line of sight beneath the second-story overhang. Geltoi sat down behind his desk-table to wait.

After a moment's time Belan signaled. "Administrator. Your pardon, sir. The Judicial officer has asked for a short meeting."

Yes, very nice. It was an interesting sensation, to receive such public tokens of respect from a ranking Fleet officer. Making up his mind to forgive Koscuisko in advance for the days he would surely be less than productive, Geltoi keyed his respond.

"A surprise. Of course. Immediately, Belan." If he'd been able to foresee this, he might have laid a small welcome out in his office, some pastry, something to drink. But that might indicate that he'd expected Koscuisko's courtesy as his right, rather than being pleasantly surprised, not at all intending on asserting his technically superior rank as Koscuisko's administrative commander, and so forth. So perhaps it was just as well this way after all.

When the door to Geltoi's office opened it was both wings of the double doors at once, two people opening the door, two people coming through it—and behind them, Andrej Koscuisko. With his surviving Bonds, yes, the green piping on the sleeves of their uniform set them apart as bond-involuntary. The woman behind Koscuisko in turn would logically be the Chief of Security who would accompany a senior officer, and a stunning Chief of Security she was, too.

Koscuisko stopped four paces in front of Geltoi's desk-table and bowed with formal and unforced respect. "Administrator." Well, he could still be taken for Nurail, Geltoi supposed; tear his clothing, soil his face, let his hair grow unkempt and greasy, and perhaps some confusion might exist. But for the rest of it Koscuisko was clearly too intelligent and too well-educated to be taken for Nurail. He had manners.

"I am Andrej Koscuisko, I present myself with apologies for the delay. We are obliged to you for your kind understanding." In the matter of a day for mourning, clearly. "That the Domitt Prison has also some loss suffered, our condolences. I have brought the Writ to Inquire to support the Judicial function at the Domitt Prison, Administrator, and to that end I am at your disposal and command."

Very prettily done. And sensitive, too, to remark on the loss of the personnel assigned to the Domitt Prison. Two of the dead Security had been Pyana.

Geltoi raised his hands in a gesture of acceptance and dismissal. "Not at all." Was he to call Koscuisko by his name? Was he to call him "your Excellency"? He was senior. Perhaps he should use Koscuisko's professional title, that would do the trick. "We're off to a rocky start with you, I'm afraid, Doctor. You're injured. I expect you'll need—how long? Before you're fit to work?"

Koscuisko looked a little confused, frowning slightly, turning his head fractionally to one side as if avoiding an unexpected draft of some sort. "I had not anticipated delaying further, Administrator. I had expected to make the orientation inspection today. And review cases waiting through tomorrow, to be started the day following."

This was a surprise. But not an unpleasant one. They were as ready as he could have wanted to be for an inspection; Geltoi had directed that the replacement bodies on standby be moved back into the cellars, just for today, in order to spare Koscuisko the sight of them.

It was a little odd, though. Everything that he had heard about Koscuisko from Chilleau Judiciary had prepared him for a man who would be taking advantage of any opportunity to put off his duty. Not that anyone could fault an Inquisitor for the quite natural impulse to delay unpleasantness.

"Excuse me, Doctor. Of course. I had misunderstood. Has the Port Authority any news for us on those who attacked you?"

The one issue resolved, Geltoi turned his attention to testing Koscuisko's attitude on the only other issue of concern before them. There was probably some way for Koscuisko to make the assault the Domitt Prison's fault. The Port Authority was certainly taking a critical approach, and the Port Authority should know better, too, than to scorn the source of good patronage.

Administrator Geltoi himself would not have gone into Port Rudistal without more Security than they had sent for Koscuisko, but that was exactly the reason fewer Security had seemed called for to escort the officer's party. Administrator Geltoi needed protection: the locals knew who he was, and didn't care for his no-nonsense approach to prison management. Koscuisko looked nothing like him. Koscuisko had not been at risk of being mistaken for Administrator Geltoi. It had been sheer vandalism, really.

"I have this morning spoken with Lieutenant Plugrath from the Dramissoi Relocation Fleet." Who had made an unflattering report to his superiors about the manner in which Koscuisko had been escorted; but that was by the way. Plugrath was a very junior Lieutenant. And the only reason there was any to-do at all was that a Fleet officer had been inconvenienced by-the-by. Koscuisko was unhurt, for all the fuss the Port Authority was making.

"He tells me there is not yet anything definite. I have asked him to come and see me from time to time to make report. I hope that he can be cleared to do so, Administrator."

Geltoi rather liked the idea of the Lieutenant dancing attendance on Koscuisko until they came up with satisfactory results. Perhaps it would teach Plugrath to amend his attitude and his behavior. Perhaps.

"And gladly. Doctor. I won't keep you, you'll want to get settled in to quarters. I've scheduled a small welcome for dinner, how would it be said in Fleet, third-meal. I will anticipate with pleasure making your acquaintance then. In the meantime please pace yourself, Doctor; you are willing to work I see, but you have been wounded. You must not strain yourself."

Inquisitors as a class were vulnerable to stress. That was one of the reasons it was important to provide a secure place for Koscuisko, a safe haven, insulated from the sordid environment in which he was required to work.

"With respect, Administrator, you mistake the situation, to an extent." Koscuisko bowed with formal grace; it was clear he only wished to clarify an issue. "It is very good of you. But I have no desire to put anything off, quite the contrary. When Lieutenant Plugrath for me finds those who have murdered Joslire I have promised myself a suitable execution. I shall be needing the practice, while I wait."

More and more interesting.

"Commendable, Doctor. And very understandable. Belan will see you settled, and we will meet again for dinner."

Hadn't the report said that Koscuisko himself had actually killed his bond-involuntary?

But the Nurail who had ambushed them would still be responsible. Yes. Geltoi had no problem with that.

He had plenty of Nurail for Koscuisko to practice on.

CHAPTER SIX

Bored for two days, and now right terrified: Ailynn had heard that to be characteristic of the life that Security bond-involuntaries led, but up till now she'd never had the experience herself.

Bored for two days. She'd been ordered for the day before yesterday, mid-shift, to have her briefing and meet her betters in the place they meant to keep their Inquisitor. Terrified right now: because finally the Inquisitor had arrived. And she to be available to him for his use, whatever that might suit his fancy to be.

She'd never met an officer with so much rank. She'd never met one of Fleet's torturers, though she had known her share of Pyana ones. And even the Pyana in this place spoke with respect and fear of an Inquisitor.

They would enjoy her suffering.

Or perhaps not enjoy it; the housekeepers had not been aggressively cruel to her these two days past so there was no particular reason to expect they would delight in her bruises. But they were Pyana. Pyana didn't think Nurail even had souls, not really, though they used the common phrase. "Nurail souls" was just as much to say "Nurail beasts" or "Nurail chattels."

Ailynn stood waiting in the front room beside the officer's bedroom doorway in the gracious roof-house that enslaved Nurail hands had built for him, listening to voices as they approached. The housekeepers had greeted the officer at the loading dock where the main lift came to rest. Cook had waited to be introduced in the kitchen, his proper place. Ailynn had been hired for the officer's use for relaxation and had been placed next to the bedroom accordingly, to meet the officer.

"Belan, this is astonishing."

It was a clear voice, a cold voice, and it spoke without much inflection, even though the language was emphatic. Ailynn suppressed a shiver.

"On the roof. One might as well be in the country. And so extensive a plant, as well, it will be difficult to return to *Scylla* after such luxury as this."

The officer. Ailynn told the data over in her mind, counting the beads in her fretting-cord one by one as she went with her hands decently concealed beneath her apron. Aznir Dolgorukij. An aristocrat, at least in his home system. Surgeon, and Inquisitor, Jurisdiction Fleet Ship *Scylla*. Five bond-involuntary troops, except that there were only four to come here now, and nobody had bothered with the names. A Chief of Security, a Warrant Officer. Miss Samons.

Andrej Koscuisko.

"His Excellency is very kind. We hope you'll be comfortable here, sir. Your personal quarters are in through the sitting-room, this way."

Belan. More Pyana than Nurail, and fed at the enemy's table rather than be penned with his family. She didn't think she blamed him for the choices he had made, because it was only common sense to elect to be safe and respectable if such was offered. But he forgot his family and his kind. That was more difficult to decline from blaming.

Here they were.

Coming into the beautiful front room, with its great windows and its well-padded furnishings, its polished wooden tables and its bright clear lights. Its Service bond-involuntary.

She knew the officer by his uniform, the Bonds by the piping on their sleeves, Belan by sight, Chief Samons by her sex.

Ailynn bowed as the officer scanned the room. He might not even see her. He might not notice her. She was only part of the furniture, as one with the toweling or the linen that had been provided for him to soil as he liked.

Only when she had made her bow and straightened up she found that the officer was looking right at her. Not tall. Very elegant, in his black uniform; and his black uniform made her afraid, because only senior officers wore that color, and senior officers frightened her. Frowning. And no color in his eyes. Like ice. Like the cold moonlight glittering on the water.

"And this?" the officer asked Belan.

Belan seemed to hesitate, almost to blush. He was the one who had come to hire her. The house-master knew that she was scarred, and would suffer less damage if the officer used force. Belan had wanted a Service bond-involuntary rather than another woman, because no one knew what an Inquisitor might like for recreation, and it was not to be considered that he should be answered back. Belan had wanted her particularly, a slave, who could not raise her voice regardless of what Koscuisko might put her to.

"This woman is from the service house, your Excellency. For your convenience. Though if you'd prefer some other accommodation— you've only to state your preference, sir, the Administration means to spare no expense."

Koscuisko crossed the floor toward her, and Ailynn watched him come in an agony of humiliation. Would he reject her as below his standard? Or would he accept her, inferior though she was, because the less worth she had in his eyes the more easily he could use her?

She'd thought that she'd become inured to the degrading treatment to which the Bench had condemned her.

She was wrong.

He stopped too close to her. He had no right. She had no right to step away from him. Looking her up and down. Leaning more close yet, to speak into her ear.

"You would perhaps tell me, if you are from Marleborne?"

What had he said? She couldn't grasp his meaning, so different was the question from the suggestive sneer she'd more than half-expected. He waited for her answer for a moment, but she could not answer; he explained.

"Because I could not bear to keep you, if you were from Marleborne. My Robert St. Clare was Bonded there. He once said that his mother's people held the slippery slope, no, I misspeak myself, he said the Ice Traverse."

It still made no sense at all to her. "I have no threads in that weave. Sir. Your Excellency." She answered to him as low-voiced as he'd spoken, out of involuntary response to his tone. "As it please the officer."

"His" Robert St. Clare. As though the man were his possession. None of the Bonds he had brought with him looked Nurail: just as well. This was a fearful place to be Nurail, the Domitt Prison, built on Nurail bones by Pyana slave-masters, a prison for her people with the enemy of their kind to hold the key.

"We will not dispute with the Administration that they have brought you here like a commodity, in that case. Be at ease. We will try not to make things difficult for you."

Koscuisko was still speaking very close to her, but stepped away, raising his voice as though he were just finishing his thought. "And we shall sort well enough together. Very well. Now. Administrator Belan. There must be office space, where I can the briefs of prisoners review. Jurisdiction procedure requires I perform an inspection tour, I understand, and this we could accomplish here and now?"

They would all assume he had been laying down his law to her. Ailynn felt the heat rush into her face; but it was only what they would expect. Why had he concealed his question, in that way?

"Office space on the next level down, your Excellency, and the work area as well. A separate lift, though. Shall we get started?"

There were ways up onto the roof, but few ways down. Did Koscuisko understand yet that he was to be a prisoner, here? Administrator Geltoi controlled traffic within his prison very carefully. It was the only thing that had saved him from the hatred of the prisoners who toiled beneath his damned Pyana oversight. But the less she knew about what had gone on here, she reminded herself, the more easily she would be able to rest.

If rest at all, in the presence of a torturer.

A torturer for whose personal satisfaction she had been procured, she, scarred and damaged goods, and Nurail, no loss if she should take an injury, and no one to intervene for her in this man's sleeping-room.

"Perhaps Miss Samons will see to settling in. Code, come with me, we will with the Administrator go exploring."

The officer drew one of his Security with him and left the room with Administrator Belan.

Ailynn stood as still as the others. Waiting.

Once the officer had left, the Chief Warrant Officer broke from her polite position of attention, starting toward Ailynn, beckoning for the Bonds.

"Right. My name is Caleigh Samons, I'm Chief of Security. These are Kaydence Psimas, Erish Muat—" the one who limped stiffly, one leg bound straight in a walking-brace—"and Toska Bederico. The officer has taken Code Pyatte with him, we can introduce you later. And your name?"

They were strange to her. But they were all bond-involuntaries, the same as she was. Ailynn felt oddly comfortable, surrounded by their friendly curiosity.

"Called Ailynn." She all but croaked it, her voice so stiff in her own throat. "Ailynn Stoup, Chief, sorry."

"You would prefer to be called which? The officer generally uses first names. By and large."

"Ailynn, then, Chief." The Chief Warrant Officer was as tall as she was, but seemed a little thinner, if more muscular, and the Chief Warrant Officer had rank. They didn't see too many women with rank in the service house, for one reason or another. Ailynn found the Chief intimidating; it made her a little annoyed, to be so awed. She was only afraid of the officer, and projecting. Yes.

"Ailynn, we'll talk. After we're settled in. You should know some things about the officer. I wish I could tell you not to worry."

They were on her side.

The unspoken message was communicated clearly in the Chief's reluctant candor. On her side, and with an issue in common, the officer. That wasn't an issue. That was a man. Ailynn felt a little better all the same.

"Kay will bring you the officer's personal luggage, and you and he can get things put away. Come on, Toska, let's go make sure nothing else gets lost, those boots took me a month to break in. Erish. Sit down. Critique Kaydence's folding of his Excellency's boot-stockings."

She had been isolated and afraid for two days in this prison place. Now suddenly she was part of a group, accepted without question, gracefully included, one of them. If only in a sense.

The relief she felt was almost as unnerving as the tension itself had been.

There would still be the officer to face.

But she would not be as alone as she had feared.

"Folding socks is an issue?" she asked the one called Kaydence, timidly. Kaydence was big and broad-shouldered, with a huge grin full of white teeth and dark black glossy curls that fell a little long on the back of his collar. They were all big. Only the officer himself was sized for her.

"We'll make it one before we're through, Cousin Ailynn. Come on, Erish, you can't critique from here, come through to the bedroom with us."

Cousin Ailynn.

Bond-involuntary code.

You are not my sister, but you could be my sister, and I mean to treat you as though you were.

It was Kaydence's statement that he would not be taking advantage of her availability in the officer's absence.

Much encouraged, Ailynn followed the bond-involuntary Security with the officer's luggage into the bedroom to get things put properly in their place.

Andrej Koscuisko walked with Administrator Belan across the garden with Code at his back. At the far end of the garden there was a lift let into the peaked black slate roof of the Domitt Prison, which would provide them access to office and working levels.

Belan didn't seem to have much to say, so Andrej amused himself with his own thoughts. Belan looked more Nurail than Pyana. Administrator Geltoi was emphatically Pyana by his ruddy complexion and the characteristically haughty expression that typically resulted from the notoriously bad teeth of the Pyana as a race.

The woman from the service house was Nurail, both by the astonishing beauty of her complexion and by the color of her auburn hair. Maybe Belan suspected that it was in poor taste to have called for a woman on site, but would not say so. Naturally.

It was a very pleasant garden, warmer than Andrej would have guessed a roof-garden could be in a place as near the cooler extreme of this world's temperate zone as Port Rudistal was. Fruit trees, and bearing ripening fruit at that. Fountains, and graveled paths on which Chief Samons would doubtless insist he run his laps.

Which he and Code and the rest of them would run alone, without Joslire, for as familiar as Chief Samons had become to him—as sincerely as Andrej cherished his surviving gentlemen—it could not be denied that Joslire had been much closer to him.

Joslire's unspoken sympathy and unwavering support had seen Andrej safely through his orientation; he had hoped to see Joslire go free, his Bond revoked. And now some Nurail terrorist had murdered a man who was better than any sixteen of them could possibly be, with their families figured in—

Oh, he had to concentrate, there would be time. He would have his revenge.

The lift opened to a signal of the hand, and tracked so smoothly down to the next floor that Andrej was only vaguely aware of being moved at all. He almost expected to see the garden again, when the lift door slid apart.

"We'll stop on this floor first, your Excellency." Belan sounded as though he were apologizing; but for what? "Your office, sir, if you'd care to have a look. To your left."

Apologizing for being a Nurail in a prison run by Pyana, perhaps. The office conformed to the penthouse for luxury, the furnishings rich and well-appointed. There was a beverager beside the door and a meal-area, but what caught Andrej's attention first and foremost were the windows that stretched the length of the office.

The view was spectacular.

He could look down from here at the roof of the Administration building to his left, if he liked; but it was the view out over the city to the river that held the most interest. The city, and the camp beyond, stretching twice as far as the city itself to either side of the pontoon bridges that crossed the river from the landing site.

"Secured com-access." Belan's remark rather startled Andrej; turning around, he saw that Belan was standing at one side of the desk, where the holo-cube stood. "From here his Excellency has access to the visuals from the next floor, or the Record, or the prison administrative offices or Security, as the officer please. This bank pertains to the penthouse suite."

So he could let people know if he was going to be late without the tedious necessity of sending Security all the way up one floor and across the garden to tell them so. Well, of course.

"I'm sure I shall find everything perfectly satisfactory. What about the next floor?"

Nodding, Belan started for the lift as Code stepped hastily out of his way. "Yes, sir. This way."

The Interrogations area.

Sixteen cells, eight to a side; from the lift he could either walk through the restricted cell block or bypass it if he cared to go around. Andrej went through; sixteen cells occupied. He'd seen these people before. Their faces were unfamiliar; but their expressions were not— suspicion, fear, hatred. He knew these people very well indeed. And before their acquaintance was concluded they would come to know him; nor were they likely to take any benefit from that.

Through the restricted cellblock to another area of closed doors, with a pair of prison guards who jumped to surprised attention as Andrej opened the communicating door. His work-rooms. Belan hurried past to open one, a middle room to Andrej's right. Code posted himself to one side of the door in obedience to Andrej's gesture, to wait while Andrej and Belan went in.

The room was clean and sweet-smelling; it had never been used— nor could it have been, in the absence of a Writ assigned. Standing in the middle of the room, looking around him, Andrej could not tell if he was more apprehensive or eager to be back here when the time came. He hated what he did, and he hated himself for doing it, but there was no denying the soul-shattering fact that while he was at it he could hardly get enough.

And, oh, Joslire was dead . . .

He was to be master in this place, the undisputed and absolute authority from working-floor to penthouse, with no check or requirement but that he gain confession from those criminals referred for his Interrogation.

He would gain confession.

He was good at this.

There was no question in Andrej's mind but that he could perform his Inquisitorial function in such wise as to uphold his Writ in an exemplary manner. And someone had taken Joslire away; and would suffer for it. He couldn't bring Joslire back, not even as the autocrat of the Domitt Prison with the Writ on site. No skill in surgery, no degree of rank, no amount of money could bring Joslire back into the world.

Since he couldn't change the fact, it was clearly the idea to concentrate on changing how he felt about it. He knew that he would derive pleasure from the exercise of his lawful authority, pleasure more intense and addictive than that to be taken in the embrace of a woman.

Perhaps it wouldn't make him feel any better, but he'd feel good, and that would be a welcome change from the state of anxious stress he'd been in since Captain Irshah Parmin had first told him that he was to come to the Domitt Prison and be Inquisitor here.

"Quite as it should be," Andrej assured Belan. "Let's go on."

He would be back here soon enough, to practice his revenge.

The officer's briefing had stated that the Domitt Prison had been built on time, under budget, and its Administrator recognized by an impressed Bench for his good management accordingly. Code knew what to make of that: slave labor, and plenty of it.

The prison didn't have to pay prisoners more than a token amount for the labor it could lawfully demand that they perform while they were awaiting trial. It was supposed to offset the charges to the Bench for lodging, clothing, food. And if prisoners were convicted—whether executed or not—the prison didn't have to pay them at all.

"You have many work details, it seems, Administrator. One wonders what work there might be for so many, that they don't run out of jobs."

Code could read the question in the officer's voice. They were sitting on a tracked-mover, touring cellblocks from the middle of the long side of the prison, where the lift through the far doors of the Interrogations section had placed them, three floors down, to the corner, where they would take another lift to the ground level.

And there weren't more than four in eight of the cells occupied at all, let alone fully occupied.

Four-soul cells, and how many of them on a side, how many floors, how many sides, how many souls?

"No worry about that, your Excellency," Belan replied. Code's place was at the back of the mover; looking down the length of the corridor, he tried to calculate the numbers. The officer's briefing had said maximum occupancy was three times eight hundred souls. "We have enough to keep us busy for quite some time. There's to be a new industrial complex built up on reclaimed land, the Domitt has title to the acreage."

Almost too great a temptation to exploit prison labor to its fullest, then. But the Bench would just as soon recycle Nurail into something useful, like public works, as stand the expense of relocating them. Code didn't like the idea.

"How long have you been receiving prisoners?"

Yes.

The prison had been a collection site until the displacement camp had started up; and not all of the souls it had collected had been prisoners per se, but refugees of one sort or another. Bodies the prison could put to good use on construction.

"We've been authorized to process only for six months, your Excellency." And did the Assistant Administrator sound a little uncomfortable? "Unfortunately we had a bad outbreak of parlic fever. Just two months ago. We lost nearly half of the prison population."

As an explanation it was a reasonable one, Code supposed. Being condemned to the Bond carried with it some benefits, after all; Code knew more about epidemiology than he'd ever thought to learn.

Associating with medical staff for the fifteen years he'd been a bond-involuntary, Code knew that there were any number of prison illnesses that could create a problem if they once got out of control. And they could spread particularly rapidly on work-crews because of the contact and redistribution of souls between exposed and unexposed work-crews from day to day.

Two months ago?

The relocation camp had been established two months ago.

Was it just that fraction too convenient that there'd been an epidemic, mass death, mass burial, just at the point at which the Domitt Prison was faced with accounting for the people that it held?

But if he didn't like it, that meant the officer was four laps ahead of him already. Code knew he could rely upon the officer's judgment.

Down a lift at the elbow of the building to a ground-floor corridor, mover and all. Thence to the exit, halfway down the length of that corridor, administrative offices by the looks of them; and out into the courtyard. Across to the nearest building, and the mover carried them to the entrance on the short side nearest to the dispatch building that faced the gate.

Mess hall.

The serving lines were empty now, sterile and featureless between meals; there were five in all, and once Code had followed his officer through one of them, he could see row upon row of ledges set at elbow-height that stretched nearly to the back of the building. People didn't sit down to take their meals, then, but stood with their dishes on a serving-ledge and ate as best they could. Efficient, Code supposed.

Downstairs to the kitchen to admire the lifts that carried food up to the serving lines in series.

It was warm in the kitchen. It hadn't been very warm outside. But the furnaces were running, they'd all seen the thick plumes of smoke from the smokestacks, both on the roof and from the ground level. So the kitchen was harvesting some of the heat from the incinerators to use to cook the prisoners' daily rations.

That made sense. There were a lot of prisoners. Every day was baking day at the Domitt Prison, obviously, too obviously to have to comment on it, except that Code didn't smell any baking. Not that he was hungry. He'd had enough to eat at fast-meal just this morning to last him well into the week to follow, if need should be.

Baking day or no, the officer was satisfied with the preparations under way for the evening meal, the long rows of cold loaves set out, the ranks of soup-vats with their broths simmering. Code shrugged it off, following his officer and Belan through the kitchen to the back of the building where the wash-house was.

The officer wandered through the great cavernous vault of the communal showers, turning every ninth or fifteenth spigot on to test the temperature of the water. Not scalding, no, and it was not supposed to be. But adequately warm, to judge by the temperature of the mist and steam that the officer kicked up in passing.

The furnaces must be heating water for the communal showers as well, Code decided. He was glad that there was at least plenty of good hot water in the showers. Prisoners on work detail deserved a little comfort at the end of their day.

Pausing at the far end of the showers, the officer took a bit of toweling from the nearest stack of linen on the shelves to dab at his boots. Code appreciated the gesture on Koscuisko's part, even though it wasn't his week to see to that detail of the officer's uniform. Water spots on boot-leather were to be avoided.

Looking around for the soiled linen hamper, Koscuisko caught Code's eye, and smiled, a quick grin that demonstrated Koscuisko's appreciation of just that fact. Code bowed, the only response expected or allowed in so public an environment. Which was to say, in the presence of another soul, beside Koscuisko and bond-involuntaries assigned.

Yet all the while he knew that there would be worse things to clean from Koscuisko's uniform than mere water-spotting, in the days to come.

By the time they were finished touring the mess building there was a formation drawn up and waiting in the empty space behind the dispatch building, between the mess building to one side and the prison's internal Security building on the other.

Approaching on foot, Andrej suffered himself to be led through the ranks and have shift and section leaders introduced to him. Standard procedure, of a sort; and very proper, too. It was in everyone's best interest that prison staff know what ranking officers looked like.

Once through the formation, Belan, joined by the prison's senior Security officers, escorted him to the Security building for a tour of the prison's receiving area. This was where statements were taken and decisions made about release to the general prison population or referral to the Inquisitor for questioning.

There was a smell here that Andrej knew, the familiar stink of blood and terror, agony and abuse. But it was no longer fresh. If there had been violations committed it had been days since the last of them, and now that the prison had a Writ on site there would be no need for prison security to overstep their bounds. No sense in making any fuss about something that was no longer an issue.

At the back of the building Andrej found the holding area, where breaches of internal discipline could be evaluated and corrected.

Punishment block.

When people were in prison it was difficult to get their attention, because simply locking them up wasn't much different from not disciplining them at all. Cells were shared, though, and the need for companionship was powerful; isolation could be an effective form of punishment. That was why there were blind confinement cells in punishment block.

Andrej looked into an empty cell, because it seemed to be expected of him. There were as many cells occupied as unoccupied; and at the end of the row of isolation cells he could see three or four square latched hatches cut at floor level, not very high, and a screened opening above each one near to the ceiling.

"Whatever are these for?" he asked Belan, who stood with the shift supervisor in charge of conducting this portion of the tour. They might be storage hoppers of some sort, he supposed. But what would storage hoppers be doing in punishment block?

"Er. Ahem. Lockboxes, your Excellency." The shift supervisor sounded a little diffident. Perhaps a little uncomfortable. "For prisoners with self-discipline problems, sir. They go in through there."

Lockboxes?

People crawled in, through those latched hatches in the wall?

"I'd like to see one." Something in the idea tickled Andrej's fancy. Crawling, through a confined space. "They don't seem to open, or am I mistaken?" If a man had a fear of enclosed spaces, it would be difficult to do.

Part of him liked it to be difficult.

"Indeed not, your Excellency," the shift supervisor—Thamis—confirmed, readily. "If you'd care to have a look, though. We'll fetch a stool. Only one occupied at present, sir."

Someone was in one of those?

Oh, better and better.

One short moment, and someone came running with a stool to place it in front of a particular grate on Thamis's direction. Andrej stepped up onto the stool to peer through the grate, realizing after a moment that he had to open a blinder-shutter in order to do so. The moment that he did, however, someone inside screamed; and did not stop.

"Please, please, don't. I won't. Not ever, not again. Ever. Please. I can't bear it, oh, oh, please."

Andrej stepped down.

It was hard to get a good look into the box with someone in it taking up space, soaking up the light. He could move the stool and look in another room, an empty room.

Or he could gratify a growing curiosity.

"Shall I?" he asked Belan, with a nod toward the trap near the floor. "I must admit. I would like to see how it is done, to get in and out of such a place."

Belan and Thamis exchanged glances; then Thamis shrugged,

good-naturedly. "I'm sure our Lerriback has learned his lesson, Administrator," Thamis said. "We'll let him out for your inspection, sir. Just don't expect the prisoner to show due respect. This is the third time this week he's been confined, he won't learn manners on work-detail."

Thamis came forward as he spoke to unbar the catch securing the little hatch at floor level, and pull it open with the toe of his boot. "Come along, you dirty little Nurail beggar," Thamis called; his voice was more genial than his words, perhaps out of respect for Andrej's presence. "Out."

Wriggling with convulsive spasms that might have been funny, the man named Lerriback scrambled out, sliding on his rump into the corridor to huddle against the far wall and lie there trembling.

Andrej stepped up on the stool once more to look in; and Thamis crouched down to shine a torch up from below obligingly. The lockbox seemed impossibly shallow to Andrej, too shallow for a man to so much as put his arm out to the opposite wall without being forced to bend it at the elbow. Square. He had just seen how difficult it was for Lerriback to get out; it would be as difficult to get in, and once one had stood up there would surely be no way in which a man could hope to lie down and rest himself.

To be faced to the wall for hours on end was a petty torment, common enough because it was not sanctioned under Protocols and therefore not forbidden as an ad-hoc exercise in bullying. It was difficult to condone such insidious torment.

But at the same time it could not be condemned out of hand; there were no rules against it. He, himself, had used the trefold shackles—officially recognized only as restraint, and not as punishment—to wear down the resistance and erode the spirit of a stubborn prisoner; and that was not much different.

Gesturing for Code to come to him, Andrej leaned one hand against Code's shoulder to steady himself as he got down off the stool again. He knew why he was trembling, within himself. Joslire had loved him despite it all; and Joslire was dead.

"You, what is your name?" Andrej asked. "Lerriback?"

The Nurail had been trying to make himself as small as possible. He reached out, clutching blindly for Andrej's ankle as Andrej spoke to him. There was no threat; he clearly only wanted to show his submission.

But Andrej had already made work for Toska by letting his boots get water-spotted. He was not inclined to suffer smudging hands, and moved away from the Nurail, who stared at Andrej's feet as he stepped back with an expression in which desperate hope was replaced by helpless fear.

Andrej could follow the progress of the emotions in Lerriback's face. That he was not allowed to show abject self-abasement could only mean that there would be more punishment. Lerriback gathered himself up into a fetal curl of misery and wept, covering his face with shaking fingers.

"Lerriback, I have spoken to you," Andrej warned. He shouldn't be doing this. He knew it. The anguished fear the Nurail had of the lockbox ate away at the better part of Andrej's nature and exposed the beastly passion that lay at the foundation of his being. His interest had already been aroused by the idea of such close confinement. And now arousal began to touch his appetite as well.

"Sir. Beg pardon. Yes, sir, as you please, sir."

It was shameful to see a grown man so reduced. More shameful still to enjoy the sight of it. "You do not like your lockbox, Lerriback?"

"No, sir—or—yes—"

It was a cruel question, taunting and unfair. If Lerriback was afraid of the lockbox, he would not want to go back. He would not want to do anything that would get him sent back. He would not want to be disagreeable. He would not be able to guess whether he was supposed to tell the truth; or pretend that he had enjoyed his own punishment, so as to avoid an implicit criticism of those who had punished him by characterizing the punishment as disagreeable.

What would it be like, if he said that Lerriback was to be shut up again?

Lerriback raised his eyes to Andrej's face; but could not seem to quite make eye contact, glancing away to one side in repeated twitches as though it was painful for him to look at his tormentor. And he'd never even seen Andrej before. Andrej was impressed; Lerriback was very much afraid of the lockbox.

His knowledge only made Andrej desire the test more passionately; and he knew that he was wrong. Wrong to desire that Lerriback be afraid. Wrong to anticipate the pleasure he would have in it.

"Mister Thamis. I cannot deny the obvious effectiveness of this for discipline."

He had to raise his voice, and speak out against what was in his own mind. Or he would shame himself in front of all these people; when usually it was only a prisoner, and his Security, who were witness to his moral degradation. And prisoners were almost always as good as dead.

"And still, though I am not the one who should say this, we should not rely upon such methods for good discipline. This Lerriback, is he under Charges?"

"Prisoner awaiting disposition, your Excellency." Thamis betrayed no sign of confusion in his voice. Polite. Never hint to an officer that you think his behavior may be contradictory. "Disciplined for disruption in work-crew. Attempted assault on crew supervision. A chronic offender."

"The Domitt is a new installation, we should guard against the appearance of irregularity. Prisoners should be punished after evaluation of offense, and according to the Protocols." Thus-and-such a range of punishments for thus-and-such a range of offenses. The Levels for investigation of the offense, and the restrictions.

If the suspected offense is misappropriation of Judicial stores to a value not in excess of two million Standard and confession cannot be obtained at the Sixth Level you must find that no cause can be proven and release your prisoner . . .

"It would be prudent if we were to restrict ourselves to the Standard range of adjudicated punishments. Forgive for me this Lerriback the balance of his offense, Mister Thamis. If he offends again he must be punished under Protocol."

"He has been a very persistent offender," Thamis warned. "With his Excellency's permission. If his Excellency is certain that it is the right thing to do."

No, he wanted to stay away from "right"; he didn't want to begin his association with the Domitt Prison by implying criticism of its Administration. Captain Vopalar's reaction to his release of that one prisoner was too fresh in his mind, even at some weeks' remove.

The thought distracted him.

Joslire had been with him when they had discovered that savaged Nurail prisoner. Joslire had handed him the key when they had found the escaped prisoner. Joslire had trusted him. Joslire was dead: Nurail had murdered him.

Did Andrej really care whether some Nurail suffered in excess of what was decent or deserved, when a Nurail had taken Joslire away from him?

"Only that it would present a better appearance to be seen to observe the letter of the Law, Mister Thamis. And it might cause embarrassment for honest prison Security if there should be tales told in some manner."

Maybe Thamis thought Andrej only wanted to have six-and-sixty from Lerriback sometime. It didn't matter what Thamis thought. And he'd have as many six-and-sixties as he wanted, starting soon.

"We yield to your professional judgment, your Excellency. Styper. Take Lerriback back to the cells. Oh, he can have a day off work-detail, just because, in honor of the officer. And full rations besides."

Whether Thamis was merely indulging him didn't matter either. Lerriback would be excused the balance of the torment he was to have suffered; and he—Andrej told himself, firmly—had better get on with his orientation. There was doubtless a great deal more of the prison to cover. "Mister Thamis, I deeply appreciate your flexibility in this matter. Administrator Belan. Shall we continue our tour?"

"Infirmary next, your Excellency." Belan sounded as though he were just as glad to be away from here. He'd made Belan uncomfortable, then. That was too bad. Belan could have no idea what Andrej's Security went through.

What he would begin to put them through, and all too soon.

All too soon? Or not quite soon enough?

Code was waiting. Code's presence steadied him.

Andrej nodded, and followed Belan out of the punishment block, to complete his tour of the Domitt Prison.

"We've never been in a situation quite like this, Ailynn," Caleigh said. "We don't know exactly what to expect from it. But there are some things we may be able to predict."

Unpacking completed. Facility secured; the penthouse, servant's quarters, gardens. Supplies delivered twice daily or as needed via the same route they'd come up on. No need to worry about unexpected visitors; there appeared to be only the two ways up onto the roof, not counting the fire-stairs.

The Service bond-involuntary Ailynn sat calmly waiting opposite

Caleigh at the common table in the dining room. She seemed a sensible woman; one of the auburn-headed run of Nurail, deep red-brown hair, blue eyes with the matte-gray sheen of stalloy to them just at present. Like any sensible bond-involuntary she had the self-discipline to speak when she was spoken to, but not otherwise.

Koscuisko's people got spoiled.

Would it recoil on them, when Koscuisko was gone?

"Now. We've been assigned to the officer for more than three years gone past. We think we know a little bit about him. Such as, he's a good doctor." It was a little hard to approach the issue that was on her mind; but it needed to be done. With Joslire dead, their need for allies to help deal with Koscuisko was even more pressing than it would have been otherwise. She had to level with Ailynn. No matter how reluctant she might be to say things that could be sensationalized to the detriment of Koscuisko's dignity.

"He's also a very effective Inquisitor. Something to do with empathy. Hands-on practitioner. He can't do the work unless he does it personally. When he tries to get by with just using drugs he can't get into it and follow through."

This was the most delicate part, and Caleigh chose her words as carefully as possible. "Although the officer is under normal circumstances a compassionate man, he suffers an alteration of behavior when he's asked to implement the Protocols. He doesn't like to hurt people until he starts hurting them. But once he starts hurting them he enjoys it a great deal; can you understand what I'm saying?"

Now Ailynn bestirred herself, having been asked the question direct. "I'd guess your point is that he's to be savage, Miss Samons."

A little sharp for a bond-involuntary, but Caleigh had been speaking as frankly as she knew how, and had asked for a response in as blunt language.

"Well, yes. More or less. He tries not to take it out on us, though. Tries. It's very hard on him, sometimes, he'll be so involved with what he has been doing. And then has to interrupt for a night's sleep."

Involved was not the right word. Or it was, but not applied in quite that sense. Impassioned. Absorbed. All right, aroused, and if the source of his arousal was not directly sexual in nature, its expression quite naturally was.

"What is it to do with me, Miss Samons?"

Caleigh sighed. Oh, what, indeed. What it came down to was that this could be hard on Ailynn, because Koscuisko at loose ends—with days spent at Inquiry behind him and days yet to come—was going to be very much in his own world. It wasn't the world in which Koscuisko usually lived, which was full of other people that Koscuisko cared for. It was much more exclusive than that, and comprised almost solely of Koscuisko himself and prisoners who existed to give him pleasure. And incidentally information.

Caleigh took a deep breath. "We don't know how he's going to react to being here, Ailynn. But I want you to be ready for whatever. I mean muscle relaxants. Lubricants. He might not stop to think, not with his head full of his day's work."

What it came down to was rape, even if that was not the word the prison administration would use to describe it. Ailynn was here for Koscuisko's use, and whatever use he made of her would be considered lawful and unremarkable.

Whether Koscuisko would take advantage of her presence was something they wouldn't know until it happened, but if it happened it was likely to be sudden, quick, and brutal. Not because he meant to be cruel to her. Simply because all that was in Koscuisko's world at such times were people who existed for his gratification.

"It wouldn't be the first time. Even the third, or fifth." Caleigh thought Ailynn's response pertained more to what she'd thought than to what she'd actually said. "But I'll be guided by what you can tell me, Miss Samons. I'll do what I can to preserve the Bench resource."

Did she mean Koscuisko?

Or that she had no more value for her own body than to avoid damage, if she could, because she was to "preserve the Bench resource"?

"And if he frightens you. Or if you're hurt. Don't keep it to yourself. We're all in this together. All of us. You can help us. We'd like to be able to help you. I am asking for your trust, Ailynn. It's your decision whether or not to extend it."

She couldn't put too much emphasis on that word, "asking." Too much weight and it would come out a demand, and a bond-involuntary was required to submit to a demand. That wasn't what she wanted. Not at all.

Ailynn simply nodded, and stood up, apparently comfortable

enough that the interview was over. Or willing to trust that she would not be reprimanded if she was mistaken.

Was that an answer?

"Thank you, Miss Samons. It's kind of you."

The woman was not giving anything away. On the other hand, to have survived she had to have learned to protect herself. Caleigh rose to her feet in turn.

"Let's check on the others, then. The officer should be back from his inspection shortly. You haven't met Code yet."

Time would tell.

She'd done what she could.

When she had been to bed with Koscuisko, he'd been careful. He'd engaged her with a female-superior position, minimizing the impact of the strength in his body. And still she'd known that she'd been to bed with a Dolgorukij, even after hours of sleep and a glass of caraminson wine to speed the recovery.

She didn't like to think of how it would feel for a woman if the officer was distracted, absorbed in the urgency of his need, not paying attention. If Koscuisko injured the woman, it would only add to his burden of cares.

They all had cares enough already.

Ailynn stood aside for her to pass, yielding precedence to rank.

Having her here could make things much easier on the officer.

But if Koscuisko hurt her, it would be worse.

CHAPTER SEVEN

His third day at the Domitt Prison, the first day of his first Inquiry here. Andrej Koscuisko had set his documentation in order yesterday; and had made his choice.

He knew what was about to happen. He would have some soul into work-room. He would hurt some soul who was to be helpless against him. He would gain evidence and put a confession on Record, for the use of the Second Judge at Chilleau Judiciary; and he would enjoy it.

"Cell Twelve, gentlemen." Standing at the entrance to the restricted block, Andrej made his announcement in a clear voice. Cell Twelve would know that he was to go to torture. But the other prisoners would know that their doom was to be delayed, at least for a day. "Through to work area, if you please."

Cell Twelve hadn't been here as long as some of the others, might be a little more resilient than people who'd been shut up in the dark for too long. Well, not in the dark, but in holding cell, where the food and the exercise both made available were not calculated to sustain good health.

The prisoner didn't struggle much against Code and Toska—what would be the point?—but suffered himself to be bound and taken out from his cell, staring at Andrej white-faced with a sort of keen hunger. Curiosity. Dread, mixed with challenge. The experience of the prison had not worn him down yet. There was to be some friction there. That would make it easier, in a sense.

They took the prisoner through to the work area. Andrej stayed behind in company of two of Geltoi's turnkeys, standing in the holding block, looking around. Some of the prisoners would meet his eyes. Some of them would not come to the front of the cells, not even when bidden; why should they?

There was no question about who he was, or why they were there. He would be getting to each one in time. They would give satisfaction, and then they would die, and the sooner he got a good start on Cell Twelve, the sooner his people would come for the next he would select.

The door to the work-room that his gentlemen had prepared for him was standing open, Toska and Code waiting on either side of the open doorway. The prisoner, within, waiting for him. Andrej paused on the threshold to assess the situation.

His chair and his lamp, on a bit of carpeting with the table convenient to his hand.

A rhyti-service waiting for him, a thin wisp of steam curling off the surface of the cup that had been poured out to be ready. Sintermayer leaf, by the smell of it, a good enough grade of rhyti, if not top quality. Not that the prison administration could be expected to know. For most rhyti drinkers, a brew from sintermayer would be more than satisfactory.

The prisoner, half-stripped and faced to the wall, his wrists bound behind his head with a stalloy bar threaded between neck and elbow to keep his arms well back and prevent his folding them around his face to protect it from the blows that would come.

Starting his prisoners only half-stripped was conservative, though it meant calling Security in later on to finish the job. Sometimes he found other hands that were willing to do the work—

Unbidden in his mind's eye, the image rose up white and red in all of its pitiful horror, the shock of total nakedness, and the brutal surprise of an assault . . .

He shook himself clear of it, bidding his beast to heel. "Quite in order, gentlemen." Code and Toska bowed from their posts, their faces clear of any trace of what they might be feeling. His praise was carefully couched in neutral terms, and intended to address their professionalism pure and simple. This was the job to which the Bench had condemned them for crimes against the Judicial order. It was not necessary to require them to pretend that they enjoyed it.

Stepping through into the room, Andrej closed the door. It seemed his prisoner winced or recoiled as the latching mechanism engaged; but there wasn't much the prisoner could do about it.

Crossing the room to sit down in his chair, Andrej took up the controller. The tether that leashed the prisoner began to move, tracking up and across the ceiling, dragging the prisoner with it into the middle of the room. The length of the leash from anchor-point to the prisoner was a little short once in that position.

The prisoner arched his body as if in pain and rose up on the balls of his feet, trying to relieve the pressure on his throat from the leash, turning about slowly to face Andrej where he sat. Andrej adjusted the controller to let some slack into the tether. There was no sense in rushing things.

He drank a cup of rhyti, thinking about how hard it had been for him—once upon a time—to start an Interrogation. A long time ago; three years, nearly four years, at Fleet Orientation Station Medical.

The prisoner was watching him, his whole body stiff with apprehension. There was a part of Andrej's spirit that shared that apprehension; he knew what was going to happen to him—had already begun to happen—and what it would mean for both of them.

Andrej let some more slack out at the tether, and the prisoner lost his balance, falling down heavily to his knees. Yes, precisely. Andrej took up a length of chain and fastened it around the prisoner's knees, hooking it to the anchor in the floor. He didn't want to have to deal with watching out for stray kicks. The prisoner had been decently hobbled, right enough, but a man could not be faulted for striking out on an instinct when he was being tortured. It was best to deal with such potential problems up front.

"My name is Andrej Koscuisko." Finally he spoke to his prisoner, who stared tight-lipped and resolute at him. White in the face. "I hold the Writ to which you must answer, by the Bench instruction. And the information I must have from you requires that you betray your friends, and cause, and family."

His blunt speech startled the prisoner, a little. Andrej spoke on. "You know you are accused at the Intermediate Levels, and this means that you may win your liberty by resisting all temptation to betray your secrets to me, because the Bench will not accept use of speak-sera under these conditions."

Not to coerce confession, no, and it was not quite honest of him to make such an assertion when he was clear to use another drug—by accident, of course—which would betray the prisoner to himself, without Bench invalidation of the evidence. Without reproach or reprimand, even though the Bench would surely know that he had cheated, and condemned the man out of his own mouth by means of a dirty and underhanded trick.

Bright pain and glittering blood were clean and wholesome, when compared to such despicable ruses—

"Here we are about to begin, and I can almost promise you that you will submit to me in time. It is nothing to do with you, and everything to do with pain. If you are willing to confess to me right here, right now, I have it in my authority to accept your confession and verify it with a truth-teller, and the Bench will grant you simple execution in consideration of your cooperation."

Was he making sense? He was speaking to a prisoner, a Nurail taken captive and locked up in prison waiting for torture. How could he know whether the prisoner understood what he was saying? "Speak now, and die a swift and easy death. Or defy me and be tortured till you speak, because you will not die until you speak, if I can help it."

There, that was much better. That made sense. Andrej could see it in the prisoner's face.

"I'll not."

The prisoner's voice was strained and hoarse, but determined. "It may be as you say, torturer. But not if I can help it. And I hope to God and free space to defeat your purpose, you and your Bench with you."

It was well said, and honestly. No vainglorious boast of endurance or resistance. The prisoner would know better than to think that endurance and resistance had anything to do with Protocols. If he could, Andrej would deal honestly with his prisoner, and give him a fair chance to go to death without betraying his secrets. There was little indeed that could be called honest or fair about torture. But he would do his best.

Not even in the black depths of his passion was he so depraved as to cheat on the Protocols.

He'd never needed to.

The Protocols themselves provided everything a man could ever want, and more—

Andrej put his two hands to either side of the prisoner's face, for emphasis. "I know a great deal more about this than you do." It was fair warning. "Please be sure of what you choose."

No answer.

No sense wasting energy repeating oneself, Andrej supposed. A prudent choice. He went to the instruments-rack against the wall, and chose a whip. He would need one that he could control in his right hand, his left hand was still healing. The prisoner had made his choice. Somebody had to suffer for the fact that Joslire was gone; and though it couldn't be said to be the prisoner's fault, this prisoner was all he had right here, right now.

He unloosed the bar that clipped the prisoner's arms behind his neck and drew the chain up to stretch the man's wrists overhead. Stepped back a pace, and struck from behind, watching the welt start to ooze blood as he gathered the whip back into his hand. The prisoner cried out, when he was struck, but as much startled as hurt; it was all right. There would be time. It would develop.

Again.

He was just warming up.

The prisoner flinched away from the blows; but there was nowhere to flinch to, he was alone in the middle of the room, pinned knee and wrist to floor and ceiling. Nowhere to go. No way out. No escape, except confession.

It did feel better to be hitting someone.

Or at least it felt good, and any good was better than the icy agony in Andrej's heart where his friend Joslire had been.

The officer was late to supper, as he had been these two days past since he had started processing his prisoners. That was what the housekeeper said, processing, as though that could cover the fact that people were being put to torture. But they were only Nurail to the housekeeper: not really people.

The officer did not try to pretend differently.

He sat slumped on the edge of the bed unfastening his under-blouse while Erish Muat pulled his boots off one by one to take them away. A freshly polished pair of boots was already waiting for the officer's use in the morning; there were three pairs, they rotated. And carried the Emandisan knives from pair to pair as need should be, because the officer would not be parted from his knives except in bed.

Erish went out with the boots, and the officer sat in the dim warmth of his bedroom with his clothing half-undone, silent. Ailynn stood at the open door to his washroom and waited. There was clean linen laid out, and warmed toweling, but she dared not speak to urge him to his bathing. She was afraid of him. She couldn't help it.

His people were afraid of him, and trusted him at the same time; she didn't understand it. She didn't need to understand to know that she was frightened of him, coming up from torture-room with the blood of his work staining his uniform and a serene expression on his face that made her shudder to look at it.

After a moment the officer ran his fingers through his fine blond hair, and stood up wearily. He had been working all day. It was physical labor. She was sure he would accept a massage; but was it permitted to her to suggest one?

Or had she not better just keep her mouth shut and mind her own business? Physical labor; yes; but it still meant torture. Perhaps it was more appropriate if his body ached from it.

"I am not sure that it is good for you to be here, Ailynn," he said. "Would it not be better for you to sleep in your own place?"

She didn't have a place. They hadn't provided one. She had a pallet behind the screen to go to when the officer was done with her, if he declined to suffer a whore to sleep with him in his bed. Koscuisko had not scorned her from his bed. But he had made no use of her, either.

"According to his Excellency's good pleasure." As in all things. "Would the officer prefer one of the men to help him wash?"

Raising his head slowly, he looked back over his shoulder at her, eyebrows raised. "I am not sure that I myself express well, Ailynn. I mean that I begin to fear for you. I am so much beguiled, by this work, and it may be that I forget myself. Should you not go?"

Well, one thing was certain, she could agree. He didn't express himself well, at least not so she could understand him. She could hardly guess at his meaning.

But there was nowhere for her to go.

"I have been procured for your comfort, sir. The rate schedule puts no limitation on what form of recreation the patron may wish to elect." He knew that, surely. "You are the officer. I am under Bond. If I am unacceptable, more suitable entertainment can be provided, as the officer please."

Koscuisko put his hand to the back of his neck, arching his spine as though a pulled muscle troubled him. "No, it is not that. And I do not wish it. There would be fault found, and then a beating."

He moved as he spoke, so that he stood beside her when he asked, leaning against the doorjamb. Very close. Facing into the washroom. Looking at her. She didn't know quite how to respond; and he continued.

"It is only this, Ailynn. I am a man like any other, which means that my fish desires thy ocean." Whatever that was supposed to mean. "It is in my work-force and violence, all through the day. And I do not want to hurt you, should I forget how to respect the privilege of your body."

It was hard for her to tell the threads in his weave, but Ailynn thought she began to grasp his pattern. "His Excellency should not concern himself. I have no feeling, sir." Nor was it "fish" which had damaged her, and left her so badly scarred that they could send her to any given rapist without concern that she would lose her economic value at his hands.

Koscuisko stared, and she couldn't read his face, his eyes too pale in the uncertain light for her to even know for certain if he was looking at her. "Oh, is it so indeed, Ailynn?" She couldn't interpret his tone of voice, whether sorrowful or relieved. "And still the thing is that if you were not here neither of us would have cause for concern. Surely you could share with Kaydence or with Code, Erish is a little stiff yet, or there's the divan in the front room. Out there."

"If his Excellency is pleased to direct me to entertain his Security—"

They had called her "cousin." But that wouldn't make any difference. They would all do what the officer wanted. If the officer wanted that.

"No, not at all. Oh, this is going nowhere." Whatever it was that was on Koscuisko's mind, she clearly wasn't catching at his meaning. He wasn't angry at her for her stupidity, and that helped. She wasn't stupid. She didn't understand him. "We will forget I ever raised the thought, Ailynn, I can find no solution to this trap, and you are in it."

Chief Samons had said he could be violent, but why would he try to shield her from that? She had been leased to service his desires. She couldn't imagine that he didn't understand that.

"Does his Excellency bathe tonight or shower?"

If it wouldn't come together then it wouldn't, and she was safer to retreat into routine either way.

"Run the bath, please, Ailynn. I'll have a soak." He started to strip slowly, and she slipped past him to run the bath before collecting his soiled clothing for the housekeeper to see to in the morning.

"Beg for me Cook's indulgence, and ask for some of his good casserole. I will want cortac and some cards, have you to play the game of relki ever learned?"

It was his custom in the evenings, so far. He bathed before he ate, and played card games with his Security, drinking quantities of cortac brandy that staggered her—without setting him to staggering. And interfered with her as little as though he had been stinking drunk, which was to say not at all.

She could deal easily enough with this, if Koscuisko were to turn out to be a mere drunkard; drunk men posed few threats, unless it was a beating.

All of this concern for her, lest she should suffer violence at his hands—did they think she didn't know what it was like already?

But as long as she could avoid it, she would take their care for her and be grateful to be treated like a human being.

Instead of a Nurail.

Bench Lieutenant Plugrath came escorted by Chief Samons, and did not look to be in a happy state of mind. Toska could appreciate that. It had been five days, here at the Domitt Prison, and nobody in a happy state of mind except the Administration, who were coming to understand what the officer could do with captive souls when time and inclination both permitted.

"Lieutenant Plugrath reports to wait upon his Excellency's pleasure," Chief Samons said to him. Chief was bearing up all right. Koscuisko did what he could to insulate them.

Toska bowed to signal his receipt of her instruction. "Yes, Chief, I'll just go tell the officer. The Lieutenant may wish to wait here—"

No, the door to the torture-cell opened, and here was the officer himself. "Toska, I want—" Two hours into his morning's work, lost to the appetite within him, Koscuisko was flushed of cheek and glittering of eye. Smoking a lefrol.

Toska cringed in his heart from the sight and smell of the officer's lefrol, and not because he objected to the stink of it so much as that he knew Koscuisko's mind. A smoldering lefrol was an honest stink. The officer was as likely to find a dual use for it, inside.

"Your Excellency," Lieutenant Plugrath saluted. Very formally. "You've asked for a report. Shall we go to your office, sir?"

Because Lieutenant Plugrath had never been in torture cell before, so much was clear, Koscuisko only smiled.

"Not necessary, Lieutenant, come on in. Toska. Come with me, I've a small task for you. Lieutenant?"

There was no graceful way for a junior officer to refuse a senior officer's instruction. Toska had even less choice in the matter. Reluctantly, as if making up his mind only as he went whether he was going to object or not, Plugrath followed the officer into the torture-room. Toska stepped across the threshold and secured the door.

"Your Excellency." Plugrath's formality was one way of insulating, himself; Toska knew that. Formality was one of his own best defenses. "You've asked for a report on our investigation. There's been a concerted effort on the part of the Port Authority—"

But Koscuisko held up his hand. "One moment." Gloved hands. The officer wore his gloves when he was working to save the tearing of the skin over his knuckles when he struck someone. Toska supposed it protected the bandage on the officer's left hand as well. "Toska, you are to strip the rest of this clothing, leave the hip-wrap for the present. Then I will have you to set up the wheel. Go to it."

Their officer was sensitive to the constraints imposed upon them by the governor. Koscuisko was usually careful to suggest, advise, request, rather than put his orders in so short a form. It helped them preserve some dignity, howsoever artificial, to comply with instruction because they had been asked politely; rather than because the requests were actually orders which they had no choice but to obey.

In the middle of a torture-room Koscuisko took the opposite approach, but it had its source in the same consideration. Koscuisko gave orders to his Bonds in torture-room, short, blunt, unambiguous. In order to keep clear the understanding that they had between them: None of the Bonds would do any such thing of their own free will, if given the choice. Koscuisko took pains to emphasize the fact that for a Bond there was no choice.

Toska had wondered why Koscuisko had taken the Writ to Inquire, when the officer had first been assigned; bond-involuntaries had no choice, but Koscuisko was not under Bond. Since then Toska had learned that not all such coercive "bonds" relied upon a governor. Koscuisko was under Bond to his father's will, and for Koscuisko at least that was enough to hold him to the work he feared and hated.

Koscuisko had started on this one yesterday at about mid-meal, and there was little difficulty managing the prisoner accordingly. Difficult to handle, yes, because the body had been cruelly marked already, and it hurt the man to move him even as little as was required to strip what was left of the prisoner's trousers and footgear from off that misused flesh. Toska cut fabric away with a utility knife swiftly, with practiced skill. The officer did not like to be kept waiting. And the sooner he was done, the sooner the officer would let him leave the room.

"You will give me just a moment, Lieutenant, I should not like to lose momentum. Momentum is very important in maintaining interest in a conversation, don't you think? H'mm?"

Standing at his prisoner's head while Toska worked, Koscuisko nudged the man's cheek with the toe of his boot. The prisoner groaned, but with more fear than pain. Koscuisko smiled.

"Yes, I think so, too. Continuity. You are only one part finished with your story, and it is interesting, I am eager for more details."

Toska bundled the rags of clothing into a wad and set it aside, hastily. The wheel, the officer had said. Slipping the catch, Toska raised the framework from its storage space in the floor-slot, locking the axle into the lifts. The officer preferred the wheel to the more traditional stretcher because the wheel was only chest-high, and could be adjusted. The officer liked to be close to his work. He liked to be able to concentrate on the expression on a prisoner's face without straining his neck.

Toska couldn't spare a moment to look at Lieutenant Plugrath, but the subtle desperation in Plugrath's voice as he protested was as expressive as anyone could have wished. "Excellency, really, it will take just a moment to update you, shouldn't we step outside while these— preparations are going forward?"

The prisoner couldn't move himself to help or to hinder them. Toska took the man by the naked ankles to move him to the wheel; Koscuisko had clamped his lefrol between his teeth and taken the prisoner by the bleeding shoulders. Helping out.

It was another of the things Koscuisko was careful about, he didn't call them in unless he needed them, and when he did Koscuisko did his best to minimize the extent to which they had to do things that would actually hurt.

So Toska got the ankles, which had been bruised through the foot-wraps by the occasional blow but which were otherwise undamaged. The officer himself handled the raw skin of the prisoner's shoulders, lifting with Toska to arrange the body on the narrow stalloy rim of the wheel.

Chest-high.

Just as his Excellency liked it.

Toska fastened the prisoner's newly bared ankles to the anchor in the floor. While the officer chained the prisoner's wrists at the other end, Toska leaned down to fetch the cross-braces up from the storage well. Cross-bracing fixed behind the prisoner's knees and elbows along the curve of the wheel was called for in order to provide the required stretching effect.

"Quite impossible," Koscuisko insisted. "Toska needs my help. My client needs to be decently settled here before we can go on, isn't that right?"

Talking to his prisoner, talking to Lieutenant Plugrath. The prisoner's head hung down against the wheel's rim, the sweat of his pain shining in the bright lights overhead. Koscuisko gave the floor-pedal a few experimental taps, and the wheel rose by a few eighths. Toska got the elbows fixed just in time.

"You were telling me, Lieutenant?"

Toska stood away and waited. Koscuisko would send him out when Koscuisko noticed him. But Koscuisko would have to notice him first. And it could be that Koscuisko wanted him for something else; there was no telling what the officer would come up with next, during his exercises.

Toska hoped it wouldn't be very long before Koscuisko noticed him.

None of what Koscuisko had in hand to deploy against a prisoner could be said to be pleasant: but the wheel was terrible. Koscuisko had no idea. If Koscuisko had known how frightened Toska was of the wheel, he would have had Kaydence in to help instead. Toska was as certain of that as he was sure that the sun would rise over Port Rudistal in the morning.

"You asked for a status report."

Now Plugrath was furious; he knew that he was being manipulated, now, and as deliberately as the officer tipped hot ash from his lefrol into his prisoner's eyes to make him cry out.

"Concerted effort on the part of the Port Authority has failed to disclose significant information to date. Investigation is ongoing. Findings include confirmation that the Domitt Prison— Administrators Geltoi or Belan, preferably both—were the intended targets of plotted ambush activity in Port Rudistal. We're on to a few strands, but the braid is fraying fast, the trail's running cold already. Captain Vopalar has authorized resources not needed to secure the relocation camp to assist in the legwork. That is all I have to report at this time. Your Excellency."

Koscuisko had leaned his elbows up on his prisoner's naked chest, and smoked his lefrol thoughtfully with his forearms crossed in front of him. Nudging the wheel's level fractions higher from time to time, to make the prisoner whimper. Toska knew that Lieutenant Plugrath couldn't want out of this any more badly than he did: yet was constrained by Koscuisko's superior rank almost as effectively as a bond-involuntary under orders was constrained by a governor.

Neither one of them could flee until the officer was graciously pleased to let them go.

"It is not good enough, Bench Lieutenant," Koscuisko said. Touching the fat coal end of his lefrol to a bloody welt across the prisoner's belly. Making him choke back a shout of protest and of pain. "I don't care who they thought they were attacking. I don't care why. Someone has bereft me of one of my Security. It is bad practice to permit one's Security to be shot down around one. I want better news than this the next time I see you, Lieutenant. Would it inspire the search to greater effort if I asked your subordinates to me also, to express my sense of urgency in person?"

Burnt flesh stank, and the knowledge that it was living flesh seemed to make it even more nauseating. Plugrath was as white in the face as

Toska imagined he could ever get. "Sir. With respect. This is beneath you. And to bring hardworking troops in here—I resist that notion, sir, as strenuously as I possibly can, and will do so to my Captain if necessary."

"Lieutenant." Koscuisko only sounded entertained. The Lieutenant didn't know how Koscuisko was, during times like this. The Lieutenant had only seen the better part of the officer up till now. "Your threats amuse me. It will be even more amusing to receive you at my workplace should you try to avoid the reports you have promised. I want results, and if I need your squad leaders' attention I will have it, and if I want reports every day I will have them too. Do we understand each other?"

He stepped on the floor-pedal, and the wheel moved, and the prisoner shrieked out loud. "Oh, please, oh, please, I can't tell you, I don't know—"

Plugrath ignored the prisoner as best he could, but Toska couldn't help but understand. There was no defiance there, at least not up front. Koscuisko was tormenting the man for Plugrath's benefit. Of course it was up to the officer who he tormented, and how; how long, and to what end. But it was a bad sign.

This was only going to get worse, as time wore on.

"His Excellency makes himself transparently clear." Plugrath was at least as much angry as disgusted. Toska granted the Bench Lieutenant good marks for a strong stomach: it wasn't that he lacked grit. "I will wait upon his Excellency in two days' time to make report. It will not be necessary to invite the shift supervisors. Sir."

Koscuisko eased off the wheel by a few marks, and the prisoner caught his breath in surprised gratitude. Terrified and surprised gratitude. Toska could empathize. He didn't want to.

"I will to myself reserve the pleasure of being judge of that, Lieutenant. But am content to wait for the decision. That is all there is for you, Toska, show the Lieutenant out, and don't come back. Oh, except to bring some rhyti, have Kaydence do it."

Toska hoped his own gratitude was not too obvious; it would be a breach of etiquette to imply that he wanted out of there, howsoever indirectly. Their officer valued their professionalism. They valued his selfishness in Inquiry.

"According to his Excellency's good pleasure. Your mid-meal, sir?"

Koscuisko waved him off; Plugrath was already at the door.
Koscuisko wouldn't talk to them with the door open. "I will call for
mid-meal when I feel the want of it, Toska, rhyti for now. And leave
me."

Koscuisko would be anxious to be on with it.

Toska made his salute and opened the celldoor for the Bench
Lieutenant, following him out quickly and closing it up once more.

What Plugrath might have to say to Chief Samons, if anything, was
nothing of his business.

"Officer wants rhyti, Kaydence, says to send you."

If he stilled himself at post and blanked his mind, the image of the
tortured Nurail would not torment him for long.

Ceelie Porlich could no longer see, and breathing was so difficult
that he longed to be done with it. It had been so long. It had been so
hard. And as much as he tried, he could neither make it stop nor make
an end of himself, out of what they did to him—

"You're holding out on me. Nurail scum. When will you learn?"

Sneering words, and brutal blows. Ceelie tried to shield his body;
but he was bound. He didn't understand it. When they had taken him
from the work-crew they had told him he was to stand Inquiry, under
Charges.

"Please."

He could barely speak, his mouth too badly torn by blows.
Someone squeezed a spongeful of cold water out close to his face, quite
close, he could feel the moisture on his cheek; but he could not get
more than a drop or two of the water. And he was so thirsty. "Told you.
Everything."

There had been no Charges. There had been no Inquiry. There had
only been this fearful room in the detention block, forever. If he was
to be tortured, why was there no Record? Why was there no
Inquisitor?

"But not everything you know. You're holding out. Tell, you filthy
piece of—"

Frantically, convulsively, Ceelie tried to flee away from the pain that
possessed him. It was no use. It held him, white-hot and ferocious, for
three thousand years. And when it finally stopped, Ceelie could hear
the voice speak on as though only a moment had passed.

" . . . until you tell me what you're hiding. Well?"

Hiding. Oh, for someplace to hide, someplace to get away from here. Why wasn't he dead by now?

Or—great God—was he dead already?

"What about 'the war-leader'?" the voice demanded, suddenly much closer. And the beating had stopped. War-leader? The war-leader was safe. He had not betrayed the war-leader. No, he had kept silent, all of this time; he had not so much as spoken the Darmon's name.

He wanted to die.

Once he was dead the torture would have to cease.

There was a new pain, now, and it was as sharp as acid, as heavy in his chest as monuments. He couldn't breathe. He couldn't hear. Oh, was this it at last, was he to die?

It faded.

It faded, and there was something in his mouth. Real water. Cool and sweet. He drank it gratefully, not minding how hard it was to swallow for the slaking of the worst part of his thirst.

"War-leader Darmon, on your work-crew." The voice; but this time it had to be his imagination. Because he hadn't said it. "Which one of your work-crew is the war-leader?"

Right beside him, to his left. And he hadn't even recognized him at first, although he'd been one of the Darmon's lieutenants for the raid on Moltipat. That had been a wonder, that raid. They had given the Bench something to think about.

"Pay attention," the voice said, and there was pressure that Ceelie didn't like against the pulpy shattered mess that they had made out of his foot. Oh. Centuries ago. "Never mind Moltipat. What was his name?"

Someone was crying, very close. Some other man put to the torture, that was it, and Ceelie hoped he'd die soon, whoever he was. Ceelie hoped for his death breath by breath, because that was his only way out of this. But the war-leader was safe. Nobody even knew he was the war-leader. Cittrops had no thread in the Darmon's weave, whoever Marne Cittrops had been. No, the war-leader was safe from these men with their cudgels and whips and irons and—and—

"Good little bootlicker, yes," someone said, approvingly. "Extra water, for that. And how would you like a little—extra—current, to go with it?"

Agony in waves, torment in gusts that felled his spirit lower than it had ever been. Ceelie lay in his suffering and trembled, waiting for his death.

Unless he was already dead.

Unless he was dead, and being punished, what could he have done in his life that would have earned him such monstrous torture to balance it out?

"Pick him up," the voice said. "Another for the furnaces, but whack him good first, he's earned out. Going by the name of Marne Cittrops, same work-detail. There should be a bounty, for that one."

He could have betrayed the war-leader—

No.

He could never have betrayed the Darmon. Never.

It was the last thing in Ceelie's mind as someone hit him across the back of his battered head with a stout cudgel, and set him free from torment.

The things they'd done to him, the torture he'd endured, it had been more than Ceelie's mind could grasp.

But he had not betrayed War-leader Darmon.

It was cold in the mornings, now, and a man looked forward to being set to work. Not for the work itself, though that work seemed to have a good enough goal. But for the warming of it. The cells were cold, and the blankets thin.

There was misery in the cells, misery in the work-crew, misery going in, misery going out. The only things that made a bit of relief in the hard cold relentless grind of his life were the few moments they were given in a week to have a hot wash, and the time it took to stand at the high tables in the warm mess building for the evening meal, and the moments on the work-crew when the mindless routine of the body took over from the ever-anxious working of the mind to suspend time and transcend reality with the simple physical act of work.

Marne hammered at his bit of hardened ground and lifted his shovels full of heavy earth and did what could be done to cover for those around him when they began to fail. The foundation ditch for the dike got deeper, wider, longer day by day. But every morning it was full of water, to be pumped out by Nurail on the most primitive of manned pumps Marne had ever thought to see being used for work—rather than a museum—in his life.

He wondered, from time to time, what they would do when the weather started to freeze overnight; none of the Nurail on the work-crew had winter clothing, and it didn't seem to be something to expect the prison administration to make up. He supposed they would find out when it got colder whether they would be given clothing—because they were needed for work—or not, because the Pyana had too many Nurail prisoners at their disposal to be bothered over preserving their health. Their lives.

There had been no protective clothing up till now. When a Nurail injured a foot with a pickax, the overseers simply rolled him down the slope into the ditch, to either drown or die beneath the next avalanche of gravel. When a Nurail was struck in the head by a beam or a bucket being hoisted it was the same story.

Marne worked in his place on the line, knowing he could not afford to admit the horror of their situation into his mind if he hoped to survive. Concentrating on making it from one round of water carried down the line to the next round. From water to the end of day. From end of day to the mess building. From the mess building to his cell. From his cell to the morning call.

He was getting so good at concentrating that he didn't notice the guards arriving on site, paid no attention to whatever was happening upslope. The guards had come for Shopes Ban days ago, Marne couldn't remember. They had come for one other in the work-crew since then. It was better not to think too hard about it, since there was nothing he could do.

They were for him, this time.

The guards came down the slope with the overseer, but they didn't pass him to go down the line.

They stopped.

Marne kept working. Showing that he could. Demonstrating the only skills the Pyana valued in this place, ability to shovel heavy earth and keep shoveling.

"This one," the overseer said, and it could no longer be ignored, they were looking at him. "Marne Cittrops. Who did you say?"

The guards came up around him. "War-leader Darmon," the squad leader said. "He doesn't look like a war-leader to me."

Marne kept working. Maybe it was the next man. But they surrounded him, and they were staring.

"He looks more like a Nurail mule, to me. But the order tag says war-leader. No roughness, now, friends, he's for the Inquisitor, and the Inquisitor doesn't hold to 'abuse of prisoners outside of Protocol.'"

That was good for a laugh. Marne took his chance, swinging with the shovel at the nearest guard, jumping at the man who stood down-slope from him. He could make them angry. Any defiance was brutally dealt with on the work-crew, with shockrods and with clubs. If he could make them angry enough, they would not be able to take him back to the Domitt Prison, they would be forced to let his body roll into the ditch and cry an accident.

It didn't work.

The one guard dodged the shovel, and though he went down in the gravel he didn't seem to take much hurt.

The second put his fist to Marne's stomach, as Marne charged, and Marne went headlong into the dust himself, with two Pyana dragging at his heels before he'd even landed.

"Careful," the squad leader reminded them. "Like I said. No unnecessary roughness. We wouldn't want to interfere with the exercise of the Writ. No punishment he might earn here and now can compare with what the Inquisitor is going to do to him."

All too true.

All right.

He was for it.

Marne kicked out at the hands at his ankles and stood up, climbing the steep slope with Pyana all around him to where the car was waiting. He would have liked to get a drink of water before they left, but there was no hope of that.

Poor Ceelie.

What he must have suffered, before he died.

But at least that meant that Robis Darmon was free to confess whatever he liked of Ceelie's role in their struggle; Ceelie was dead, and could no longer be made to suffer for what the Bench had decided were his crimes against the Judicial order.

"At Kosova. Your Excellency. Yes, I was there, and—oh—I threw a bottle-rocket through the window of the Bench Administrative building there, yes, that was me, I confess it—"

Andrej shut off the firepoint with a disgusted snap, turning his back on the prisoner. Young Nurail. Quite young, actually, but a man by his beard still, unless he'd been in prison longer than possible had he truly been part of the street-fighting in Kosova. Which Andrej did not for one moment believe.

"Be still. I am in no mood to be played with. You were nowhere near the Ailleran system when it happened. You are making it up."

Inventing it. Confabulating. Spinning a story. Faking a weave.

Lying to him.

Perhaps lying was too strong a word, it had been two days. There had been a confession to a lesser offense early on, and then confession in form to the Recorded offense just after mid-meal today; but nothing since then except for garbage. Could he blame this prisoner, this Kerag Darveck, for making things up to try to satisfy the Bench requirement?

Andrej was expected to develop leads, pursue issues, obtain proof of collateral involvement and cross-accusation where he could. He had no need to reproach himself on that subject: what he had done to Darveck, these long hours past, had been squarely within the Bench requirement, and all well within the Protocols.

But there was nothing there.

He'd thought that there might be, at first, and that Darveck was grasping at clearly implausible straws in order to put him off the scent of some true thread. He'd tested for it, and ingenious cruelty had never failed him yet; nor had failed now.

Andrej knew.

Darveck was guilty of a crime to which he'd been brought to confess in due form: but no more than that. He had been part of the defense of Meritz. He had quite probably been taken there, or not long afterward. And that was all the Bench could in justice lay against Darveck's account.

It was a problem.

How could Darveck have been referred on the much more serious charges that were on Record, when he'd been nowhere near the system—and all too possibly even in custody, already—before the troubles at Kosova were well started?

Darveck lay shaking on the floor, in fierce torment from the vise and clamps. He clearly could in honor have no more of young Darveck. No more at all. True enough that "honor" was not the word to speak in torture cell; it was also true that in order to be able to put the Protocols forward it was absolutely necessary for Andrej to be able to pretend that he was bound by them.

To be bound by the Protocols meant sending this one away.

"Please, sir." Weeping in pain, and in fear of more pain. It was lovely. It was perfect. He wanted more: and he could not have it. Or rather, he could have all he wanted, but he should not take it, because Darveck had done only so much wrong as he had already suffered for in overabundant measure. "Please, sir, it's true, it's true, oh. I'll tell you what you want, take it away, my foot . . . "

Had told Andrej everything he knew; and a very great deal more besides. There was simply nothing there. And no help for it. The sound of the Nurail's weeping was a constant stimulation to Andrej's nerves, the fear Darveck had of him as exciting as the weight of a woman's braided hair sliding undone between his fingers. More so. Differently. But to the same effect; and still he could not countenance making Darveck suffer any longer.

He had to relieve and remand.

There was no help for it.

"I don't want to hear it." Calculating doses, Andrej loaded an osmo, then another. Something quite strong to start off with, because as keen and sharp and merciless as the pressure of the vise was against the bone, it was only going to get worse as the vise came off. "I do not in fact believe a word that you are saying."

There was no use pretending to practice here for vengeance upon Joslire's murderers when Andrej knew quite well what Joslire himself would have trusted him to do. All the more reason why he had to do the right thing for Darveck: who stared in wide-eyed terror at the dose in Andrej's hand, the white of his eyes brilliant and grotesque in the light from the overheads. "Please not the List, oh, please, your Excellency. I can't—"

Trying to reassure Darveck would do no good; Andrej knew that. The best thing was to simply go ahead, and let the action of the drug speak its own truth. "There is nothing here to be afraid of," he promised, pressing the dose through at the prisoner's throat.

After a breath or two young Darveck blinked once or twice, in clear astonishment. "Yr'Excellency?"

"This is going to hurt. I'm sorry. Here we go." Loosening the vice, pulling the needle-pins whose job it was to find the nerves within the joint and wear on them. Pain receptors within a joint produced a signal that did not decay in the same way as those nearer the skin. For fierce white-hot bright pain that would not abate there was nothing like prying a joint apart fiber by fiber; and certainly nothing like that now. He had finished with this one interrogation. That was all.

Finished, but had had no resolution for the thirst within him—

Not an issue. The vice came away from the ankle joint, the skin beneath livid with bruises and insult. There would be a matter of days before Darveck would be able to put weight on that leg without danger of an injury. The drug did good work, Darveck did not scream.

By the look on Darveck's face—the relaxed muscle of the cheek and jaw, the eyes traveling with slow deliberation from object to object in the room—the drug had taken hold, now. Andrej pressed the second dose through, just to be sure, because he wanted to assure himself that Darveck would not succumb to shock and die.

It was late.

Too late to start with a fresh prisoner.

The gentlemen had been on their feet for hours and hours on end, on either side of the door outside.

Andrej went to the door, toggling the switch. "Kaydence." Security could sleep standing up with their eyes open, that was true. That was no excuse for keeping them on watch without a break simply because his body ached with the pleasure of the torment he'd put Darveck to and the fierce consuming desire to have more.

"Kaydence. Yes. Call to Infirmary. This one is to be dismissed to the civil authority, but he'll need a few days in hospital, Infirmary must stabilize before we can in decency refer."

It wasn't the best idea to send torture victims to civilian hospitals. The infirmary at the Domitt Prison would logically be both equipped to address the injury and more inured to the sight of it. Kaydence bowed low with a calm serene face and stepped away from the doorway to the common call; Andrej leaned up against the doorjamb and rubbed his eyes. Oh. He should remember. It was prudent to remove one's work-gloves before one rubbed one's eyes.

Infirmary was perhaps not much occupied, this time of day—this time of night. There was a litter and a team with a physician before too much time had passed. Andrej waited to let the staff physician make preliminary examination; then the doctor came to him and saluted.

"His Excellency intends us to release this prisoner, sir?"

Sounding a little dubious. Well, it was a prison, and one of the reasons Andrej had particularly wanted to be here when the doctor came was in order to be very clear about his intention.

"Precisely so, Doctor—Forlop, yes, thank you. You have the documentation with you brought? You will need this."

The Infirmary staff would be responsible for developing the medical record, but Andrej was the only one who could sign disposition of prisoner. He, and Administrator Geltoi.

He had not satisfied himself—

Doctor Forlop bowed in polite acceptance. "As his Excellency says, sir. Thank you. I'll send a report to your office. Shall we be going?"

A hint. Straightening up—he had been slumped against the wall, trying not to think about tension—Andrej gave the nod.

The party left.

He was alone with his Security.

They needed to be sent to bed; and he needed to wash.

The penthouse was warm and quiet. Andrej sent his gentlemen through to the kitchen. He couldn't remember if they'd eaten.

He couldn't remember if he'd eaten; but he didn't want to eat, his hunger was for screaming, not for food. The sooner morning came the sooner he could satisfy his need. He had to go to sleep, so that it would be morning when he woke.

His bedroom was quiet and dark, familiar with the smell of his favorite soap and comforting with the fragrance of a woman's hair. Ailynn. There was a thought. Perhaps he could lull the beast to sleep in Ailynn's arms.

She only slept beside him in the bed because he liked the companionable warmth; waiting for him, she was not in the bed now, but napping on a low cot behind the screen in the corner. He knew she had a pallet there, and he didn't like it; but that seemed to be the only allowance for her privacy in this place. He hadn't told her to put it away. He could hear her breathing, calm and regular. Soothing.

Could he not take comfort in her embrace, and be at peace, even if only for a few hours?

He had to wash.

She had been ready for him, there was his nightshirt on the warmer with the bath-towel, and the other things that he might want for grooming laid out ready in a tidy array. A comb. A nail-brush. A jar of fragrant lotion to take the stink of sweat and blood and terror from the forefront of his senses.

He started the shower to run, to get the temperature of the water right. Ailynn usually took care of that small chore, she'd learned the precise mix he liked almost immediately—people learned quickly, when their safety depended upon avoiding aggravating some slave-master. And he was one. At the very least he was to Ailynn a slave-master, and if there was to be no help for it why should he not at least make use of her body?

Scarred, she had said.

Stripping, he left his clothing on the floor and unfastened the sheathing of Joslire's five-knives with fatigue-clumsy fingers. He wondered whether he should be wearing Joslire's knives in torture-room; wasn't it a little like making Joslire come in there, with him? There was something unusual about the back-sheath knife, as well, though he didn't think he could tell anybody and have them take him seriously.

The knife had gotten heavier, since Joslire's death.

Andrej set the knives and the sheathing up on a shelf apart and stepped into the shower. There was a little draft that lasted for a moment; that would logically be Ailynn, Andrej knew, awakened by the sound of water running, creeping into the washroom carefully to carry away his soiled clothing.

Lathering up the soap, Andrej started washing, rubbing hard at the dried blood that had soaked through his clothing to his skin. His fish was half-tumescent, irritable in his hand, half-ready to raise its head and rage against the world: at such times his fish was no friend to him, but a quarrelsome member of his household for whom he was responsible but whose behavior he was powerless to amend for the better.

His fish had been stroked by the anguish of tortured souls all day. Now it resented being rubbed down with soap and warm water and bidden to sleep, and grumbled at him while his belly ached with unresolved tension.

His body was as clean as he could wash it. More or less.

Andrej dried himself, grateful for the small luxuries of warm clean toweling and a quiet room. Slipping his sleep-shirt over his head, he went back out into his bedroom, knotting half the ties absentmindedly and ignoring the rest.

He liked Ailynn; he didn't want to distress her.

But he was on fire with the remembered sound of that Nurail's weeping. If he could not find some way to ground the tension, he would not be able to sleep.

Ailynn was sitting very straight-backed on the edge of the bed with her hands resting on either side of her, flat against the coverlet.

Waiting for him.

The bedclothes turned back, and she herself in her bed-dress, which meant that the contour of her shoulders was clearly visible beneath the thin white fabric even in the dim light of the night-glows. Her hair was drawn back in a thick heavy braid, tied neatly in a knot for sleeping. Andrej sat down beside her, taking her braid into his hands to undo the ribbon-loop that kept it from coming undone in the night.

Her braid came loose and lay against his palms, heavy and silky. He laced his fingers in between the plaits, remembering Marana. The joy he'd had in taking down her hair, knowing she would welcome his fish within her ocean.

Ailynn didn't speak.

That was fine, too.

He unraveled her braid twist by twist until he'd worked his hands up to the base of her skull, and paused, cupping the heat of her skull against his palms, feeling the seductive caress of her hair against his fingers.

Oh, he wanted.

And he couldn't have.

But he could have Ailynn, and maybe that would do the trick.

She put her hand out to the back of his neck, very sweetly indeed, and drew him down to lie with her across the bed. There was no reason she should know what a Dolgorukij would have meant by such a gesture. Andrej took no offense; and teased her little tongue out of her mouth with kisses, so that he could suckle at her while he reveled in the sensation of her unbound hair against his arms wrapped around her back.

It was a very pretty little tongue, a cunning tongue, a sweet and tempting tongue, and would it be very wrong—Andrej asked himself, half-drunk once more with passion and with need—if he pretended to himself that she was willing?

Her body was soft beneath his hands as a woman's body properly was, as he had learned to define and appreciate what was desirable about women's bodies when he had been young. He had learned to appreciate the desirability of other sorts of women's bodies since, and that of Chief Warrant Officer Caleigh Samons—as an example—exemplified one of those other sorts neatly indeed.

But there was no arguing with one's fish.

And his fish felt that the woman in his arms was just exactly what a woman ought to be; and wished to crest the breakers of her surf and gain her ocean now, right now, immediately.

And still there was the thing that she had said to him, days ago, what had it been?

Scarred.

Andrej kissed her parted lips a few more times for friendship's sake and went exploring down the lines of her throat. Her shoulders . . . but he was not going to be distracted, because there was a natural limit to how long he could demand that his fish wait before it disgraced him by breaching the dikes and expiring of exhaustion on dry land.

Soft and fragrant, and open to sensation, too, as far as that went, willing to admit pleasure when it came—Andrej mapped out the soft woman-flesh of Ailynn's breast and shoulders, and all the while set his right hand to find out about her scars.

She stiffened, when his fingers slid gently between her thighs; stiffened in fear, and opened to him in duty. Which was not of course the best reason, but it would suit his purpose here and now.

Whether the warm moisture he sought out was arousal or simply the sensible precaution of a professional woman made while he was in the shower, Andrej didn't know. There was an easy way to find out, but he didn't care to know. It would be awkward. He stroked her carefully instead, making up his mind as to where it was that she was scarred and whether she could be enticed to take any delight at all from his caress. Imposed on her or no.

The fish that complicated the lives of men was a stout and very self-respecting thing that did not hesitate to breach and put its head up to see what might be going on around it. That which was private to women was a more modest and reticent little minnow, though sweet to the taste; unlike other fish, which were stronger in flavor and indelicate in their appreciation of an affectionate salute.

Ailynn's little minnow was of brave heart, willing to be coaxed out of its safe place beneath the shelf by the seashore to permit itself to be admired and stroked. She had been scarred by rape, then, and not otherwise mutilated by design. That was something.

But his fish was urgent with him to let it seek the ocean.

She would have been within her rights to suffer his embrace in stoic silence, or return only what caress or endearment he might instruct her to employ. That was the privilege of paid women. One could purchase the hire of their bodies, but it was in poor taste to demand that they pretend that they enjoyed it.

Ailynn was more generous and charitable with him than that.

The shaking of her breath was unfeigned, the flush of sweat that made her sweet breast taste salt was not cosmetically created, the eager stiffening of her nipples did not result from surreptitious pinching or a light touch of astringent. She consented without words, without being asked, to trust her body into his hands to be gently used by him, and the frank honesty of her arousal served to keep him focused on what a man was to do with a woman in bed.

Seek the ocean, yes, that was what it was all about. But carefully. Mindful that too great a splash at once could lay bare rock. Ensuring that the wake of his fish's passing washed well over her minnow in the shallows, to rock it to its ultimate delight as his fish pleasured itself in the salt deeps of her secret ocean.

He tried.

But there had been too much.

He'd spent long hours keyed up to a keen-edged anticipation, only to have denied himself gratification at the last. The flesh was intent on being recompensed for being made to wait so long, with such persuasive provocation to his lust.

His fish went all the more furiously to work because it was half-mad with being denied, determined to have its pleasure before its opportunity was withdrawn.

He worked the angry tension of his body out within hers, caught up and consumed by the day's pent-up frustration, desperate to find physical release.

He didn't want to hurt her.

But he had to have an end to the thirst that tormented him.

And when the crisis of his body's need resolved itself at last, he was too grateful for the grant of two breaths of time spent without thought to want to drop back into conscious awareness before he absolutely had to.

Gathering Ailynn up into his arms, Andrej laid her properly in the bed and pulled the covers up over them both.

Oh, for just one hour, to exist without awareness—

His mind was stilled and emptied in the aftermath of all-conquering sensation.

Andrej slept.

CHAPTER EIGHT

Be still, Ailynn admonished herself, fiercely. Be still, be quiet, breathe as evenly as possible. Don't hold your breath. Slow. Shallow. Even breaths. The officer will go to sleep, but not if he knows. Be very quiet. Relax. Pretend.

The physical effects of fear diminished in her body, her breathing slowed, her heart began to beat more regularly. Clipped close in the arms of the sleeping officer, Ailynn focused on being in her body, deep inside her body, making her body an insulation to shield and protect her against panic. She was far, far away, inside her head. No one could touch her here. And what they did to her body, if they hurt her body, it was so far away it would be centuries before she realized that she was in pain.

Yes.

Better.

The officer stirred in his sleep and stroked her back, settling his cheek against her forehead. Calm. Her body was calm. Her breathing was regular. Her body was asleep; the officer would not wake.

Her mind raced, circling a familiar track and accelerating on every curve. Her little kitchen in her apartment in Ogis. The Bench order to evacuate for relocation; the men who came to hurry her along. Or leave her there, so long as she was dead, but since she wasn't dead—after two hours, three hours of sport—rape her from her home and natal place to bend her neck to Jurisdiction bitterly against her will.

The ambush of the relocation party, her escape, those bitter cold and fear-filled months of underground resistance, the wounds so slow to heal. Her capture. No trial; the rules of Evidence were satisfied in the facts of where and how she had been taken. No trial, and no execution by torture or otherwise; something far worse instead.

The Bond.

The Bench had made the Bonds to serve Inquisitors, because free men could not be forced to implement torture. Service Bonds were a quite different category, it was pure punishment with no excuse of Bench utility except to serve as deterrent.

We will take you and those of yours who are fit enough, and we will make them bond-involuntary, and if we will not torture them in obvious ways we will make sure they suffer—we will require them to assist in the torment of others like themselves. And if they are fit for Service and not Security, we will harvest the use of their bodies in a more traditional fashion.

Service Bonds.

To be put to the rapists, night after night, and the fees collected by the Bench that owned her—by its own enactment, that had by superior force of brutal arms taken her for a chattel slave for crimes committed against the Judicial order . . .

It had only been four years.

How was she to hope to last thirty?

The officer had treated her with unusual courtesy, not—as far as she could tell—because she was a woman so much as because that was the way he treated all his Bonds. And the officer had not come to her in anger or in mockery to confront her with her helplessness or demand the forms of self-abasement frequently invoked by other rapists.

She had not minded opening to him, though she would have rather been left to herself. And still he had reminded her that she was a slave, not intentionally, but only in the fact that she was not permitted to grant or withhold her consent.

And she was afraid of Andrej Koscuisko.

He had come to her as gently as he could, she was sure of it. And still he had lost himself in the act. The pitiless strength of his arms still around her was terrifying.

If he should use her as strictly as he had just now when he

approached her with good will, how was it to come with her when he should be annoyed?

She was trapped and prisoned in Koscuisko's sleeping embrace.

She had no hope of escape or of protection.

Service Bonds had to get used to that, but could she ever?

Ailynn had little pain from the passage, having been put on notice more than once that he might be abrupt with her. Little physical pain, and even a small echoing reverberation of the pleasure he had given her with his touch; but in her heart Ailynn was desolate.

She wept.

She couldn't bite her grief back down into her heart, betrayed to grief, ambushed by it here in the warm quiet dreaming dark with the officer asleep beside her. Ailynn wept to be reminded that she was a slave, and though Koscuisko might be a good "maister"—to use the Nurail of it—it was still as a man who owned her that he came to bed.

She grieved; and the worst possible thing happened, the officer woke up, stilling her cries gently with his hand put to her mouth as he rose up in the bed to lean upon his elbow.

"Ailynn. Oh, hush, please, Ailynn, my gentlemen will be distressed for you, do you have pain?"

Folding her close, as though that could make it better. Rather than worse. She put her face against the crumpled warmth of his half-laced sleep-shirt and wailed in desperate anguish as quietly as possible.

He pet her and rocked her, and she wept because she could not know from day to day whether the next five men to whom the Bench sold her would be decent men or brutes, and whether Koscuisko kissed or clouted her was up to him entirely. Nothing for her to choose.

She cried herself out and clung to him, exhausted. He had a cool damp cloth in his hand, now, and patted at her flushed cheeks and swollen eyes with a delicate concern; she had waked one of her cousins, then, because she knew Koscuisko hadn't gotten out of bed.

Ailynn caught her breath.

"One trembles to ask whether it is something in particular one has done," Koscuisko said. "Because of two problems. And one is that politeness interferes, and people under Bond are not permitted to accuse or upbraid officers without suffering the reproach of their governor. And the other problem is that it must be, and therefore there's no sense in even asking. Ailynn, I have grieved you, I am sorry."

It wasn't exactly that.

It was.

She had no words to explain herself to him and yet he did not deserve to suffer because the Bench had put her beneath him. It wasn't Koscuisko's fault. And he had tried to be careful, even as caught up as he'd been in his own body's need; and her body was grateful for the small pleasure that it had of him, because there was so little pleasure else for her body in her life.

She was embarrassed to caress him in the presence of some possible other, since she did not know who else might be in the room. But she should try to explain. Trembling in fear of her own temerity, Ailynn put her face up to the officer's, and kissed his mouth with hesitant care.

"It's not what you might think, sir." And it wasn't. "I'm heartily sorry to have wakened you. Nothing of what the officer has done. Or almost nothing."

That was true, and her governor didn't bridle at her candor, even though it came a little close to a reproach of sorts. That was the trick of living with a governor, to learn to speak truth in such a way as to avoid conflicts in her mind.

"I will want to make examination, later." Whether or not Koscuisko believed her was difficult to say; she couldn't tell one way or the other, from the sound of his voice. The officer was accustomed to living with bond-involuntaries. He might suspect that what she said was at least as much what she was trained to say as how she felt. "But now I want you to lie quiet and rest, Ailynn. Erish, comfort your cousin as you like, or as she likes rather. I am going downstairs to my office."

And since Koscuisko was familiar with dealing with Bonds, Koscuisko would know that what she said to him in unsolicited physical contact was from her heart, unedited and unforced. It had been a risk to offer a kiss; some men did not want intimacies with whores beyond those that they themselves demanded. But perhaps he would think about the statement that she had tried to make to him with the gesture.

She had instruction and direction from Koscuisko, to lie quietly and rest.

Tucking the covers close against her back, he rose to dress, giving the damp cloth to Erish to continue the work of patting the hectic flush of desperate sorrow gently from the skin of cheek and forehead.

Ailynn knew how to do as she was told, she was a slave under Jurisdiction. And it was very nice, Erish's tending of her. So she closed her eyes and invoked her memory, not of before or after, but only the time during that Koscuisko had brought joy to her body; and went to sleep.

Andrej pulled on his rest-dress rather than wake anybody. He was only going to his office. Rest-dress meant very full trousers that belted around the waist, with a soft wrap-tunic to cover; it looked almost like skirts, to Andrej, and it had taken him a little while to get used to that, but it was only part of an officer's wardrobe. Not a calculated affront to the holy Mother, an attempt to claim the superior status of femininity by dressing as a woman. There was no apron, after all.

He could wear padding-socks with rest-dress, he didn't have to put on his boots, and that was another significant thing about rest-dress. Collecting Code on his way out toward the office access lift, Andrej stepped carefully from flagstone to flagstone in his padding-socks; the night was cool, the ground damp with dew, and padding-socks were not moisture-impervious.

The lift was waiting, of course, and his office was dark in the night. Andrej could see the lights from Port Rudistal and from the displacement camp beyond from the corridor as he approached. Would they be able to see him, he wondered?

Code started the rhyti while Andrej sat down to stare at the surface of his desk-table, brooding. He had frightened Ailynn, or hurt her. Perhaps both. He could send her back to the service house, and she would be in no further danger from him; but the problem with that was twofold.

He had forgotten who and where he was, in her embrace; and it seemed to Andrej that he had to have that avenue of escape, or else he would not survive until he was called back to *Scylla*. The distraction was short-lived, perhaps, but it had been genuine. He wanted to know that it would be available again.

Two, of course, was that if he sent her back they'd think that she had displeased in some way, and things would be made unpleasant for her. And also she would simply be put back to work accommodating multiple patrons instead of one, howsoever moody and difficult that one might be.

Poor Ailynn.

What was a woman's hire, for a night?

Senior officers weren't charged at service houses, though Andrej always made a point to tip well. The expenses they incurred were all charged back to Fleet as preventive medicine. He didn't know how much Ailynn's time cost.

He could find out.

Pulling a piece of notepaper toward himself, Andrej picked up a stylus to start calculating.

When he had been in school at Mayon Surgical College, the charges for recreation had been standardized by the school administration. Students paid out twenty Standard for two hours of company, eighty to be accompanied all night. Mayon's Service professionals had been an elite of sorts, because the standards set by the school administration had been aggressively strict in terms of the benefits packages enjoyed by the staff.

If he figured eighty a night for Ailynn's company, and the prison was providing lodging, linen, and her meals—it had been four weeks, that was thirty-two days.

Nearly a month.

Had it really been a month?

Had it been so long since Joslire claimed the Day?

He'd dressed by himself in the dark, and not retrieved his knives from the washroom. He hadn't thought about it. But once he realized that he was without Joslire's knives, the place between his shoulders where the mother-knife should have been started to ache.

A month.

A month, bereft of Joslire, and trying to soothe the hurt with poultices made up of the atrocious torment of his prisoners . . .

It could not have been a month.

Eighty a night for Ailynn's company, unless there were allowances made for livery and maintenance; that was thirty-three thousand—and some—for a year, and the term of the Bond was thirty years, so that was something in the neighborhood of one million. Standard.

If he were to rent her from the Bench until the Day came for Ailynn, because the Bench would not accept a forfeit for her crime.

Still, what were salary monies for, if not to buy things that he wanted? It wasn't as though his living expenses were burdensome. And more than enough money for his needs in rents and other income from his holdings in the Koscuisko familial corporation. He was its prince inheritor, after all. By any Standard measure he was rich.

Nor had the Koscuisko familial corporation gotten rich by throwing away money on self-indulgences that could profit them nothing —

Joslire was dead.

Joslire had been his man, and had died in his service.

It was the right of household retainers who gave up their lives to defend their masters to be remembered in the family chapels as house benefactors, with prayers and litanies, and inclusion in the family's Catalog for pious observance.

Could he not justify it to himself if he hired Ailynn to be Joslire's nun? Religious professionals came more dear than those who provided personal services of a sexual nature. Ailynn would even be cost-effective, considered in that light.

It was an absolutely idiotic idea, and the more Andrej thought about it, the better he liked it. There were funds set aside for the maintenance of religious professionals and the support of religious establishments. Joslire had died in Port Rudistal, he should be remembered here. He would hire Ailynn to be Joslire's nun, and buy a house to be a nunnery.

Uncle Radu might question Andrej's choice of abbess, but it was in Andrej's right to build and maintain chapels from dedicated funds so long as a rule of devotion was established and maintained. Ailynn was not Dolgorukij, but neither had Joslire been; why should he not?

He would have to think about it seriously.

Once he was awake.

Setting the sheet aside, Andrej pulled the nearest stack of documents toward him. He hadn't spent much time in his office over the past few days. Technically speaking he was the senior medical officer at the Domitt Prison, though nothing to do with Infirmary; it was up to him to review and countersign mortality and incident reports.

There were a lot of administrative reports; he was backlogged to a significant extent. Had it really been so long since he'd reviewed the mortality roster?

The newest one was dated just yesterday, that explained it. But the one from three weeks ago was still sitting open, waiting for disposition.

This was odd.

He had four weeks' worth of mortality reports before him. He could track the numbers from week to week.

When he'd got here, the Domitt Prison had been losing more than one in sixteen a month to preexisting injury or illness, and Andrej had been suspicious about trailing mortality due to the epidemic Administrator Belan had mentioned to him.

To be losing one in sixteen was high mortality. But Andrej could think of many reasonable explanations. It made sense that prisoners taken in the aftermath of one Bench campaign or another might not have had enough to eat in the days before their capture and imprisonment.

The Nurail that the Dramissoi Relocation Fleet had taken in had been badly stressed, and not all collectors of refugees could be counted on to treat their wards with as scrupulous care as Captain Sinjosi Vopalar. Andrej had expected the mortality rate to decline, though, as the prison population stabilized.

Mortality rates had gone down.

But not by enough.

He'd been here nearly one month, Standard, since this was one of the short six-week months. Any prisoners referred by the Dramissoi Relocation Fleet had been here for as long. But there were more admissions on the mortality report than there had been prisoners with the Dramissoi Fleet: Andrej was in a position to be confident of that.

Where were the new admissions coming from?

Were they some exhausted and half-dead survivors of yet another Bench campaign against the Nurail?

Hadn't Eild been supposed to be the last?

There were disquieting indications that something was wrong, here. Too many dead. Prisoners referred on accusation of things they could have had no part in, and more and more of the prisoners seemed to have been physically stressed as he worked through the cells and they filled the cells back up behind him. Physically stressed as though they had been overworked and underfed, and for how long?

He could request a kitchen audit, ensure that the kitchen served decent rations on a decent schedule. Work-details were entitled to increased rations to support the physical labor they were asked to perform. Maybe the Administration didn't know.

He saw Bench Lieutenant Plugrath twice a week, in his office, in the morning. There had been no real news for this past while and in his heart Andrej knew that they would never find the people who had bereft him of his friend. Not now. Too much time had passed. A kitchen audit, and he'd ask Plugrath for an admissions report, just to set his mind at rest about who all those Nurail on mortality report were and where they were coming from. It would be a simple enough task.

In light of the high mortality rates at the Domitt Prison, he would take steps to assure himself that there was an explanation beyond the Administration's control. That would protect them all from possible reproach. Once he had but reviewed the kitchen audit and gotten an admissions reconciliation from Lieutenant Plugrath, he could sign off on these documents with a good conscience.

He was hungry himself, now, thinking of those stressed starved prisoners. He was going to wake his poor Code yet again.

Maybe if Cook could be persuaded to make Code's favorite fast-meal, Andrej could be forgiven for the unsettled night-walking of the sleep-shift now all but past.

Administrator Geltoi signed off on the daily transmit to Chilleau Judiciary with a very satisfied flourish as Belan watched. "Another sound day's work from our Inquisitor," Geltoi announced. Unnecessarily; but Belan enjoyed hearing it regardless.

Countersealing the secures, Geltoi tossed the completed documents-cube into his transmit stack as he continued. "The First Secretary will be pleased, there should be no further questions about our prisoner handling. This will have shut the mouths of any critics, by now. Were it not for our effort, the Second Judge would still be exposed to reproach in the public eye from others on the Bench."

As long as Geltoi was content Belan was happy. Geltoi was Pyana, and if there was anything Pyana were good at, it was administration. Geltoi knew how to take care of things.

"It needed only that you be provided with appropriate resources, Administrator," Belan assured his superior. "Once you but had what tools were needed. That was all. They'll know better than to make you wait next time, sir."

So much was only understood. Geltoi wasn't really listening, picking up a piece of documentation with a frown. "At the same time, however. And only his job, true, I grant you that ungrudgingly, Belan."

Grant what? Belan had no idea what that document contained. He waited, humbly, for the Administrator to explain, knowing all would be made clear to him. And that if he didn't understand, it was because he was mere Nurail, not Pyana.

Geltoi spoke on. "But at the same time one wonders if a more— shall we say—mature officer would have made quite this same choice. There is a time and a place for everything."

Something Koscuisko had asked for, Belan grasped that much. Something Koscuisko wanted to do, or to have done. He'd had his inspection tour his first day on site, and he'd been satisfied—at least he hadn't said anything to the contrary. So it couldn't be that.

"What is it, Administrator?" Belan asked, waiting to hear something quite obvious and innocuous. Something he could laugh at himself for being concerned about. Something Geltoi would certainly laugh at him for being concerned about, though the Administrator seemed to be setting up the joke to be on him. It was Pyana humor, at the expense of a dumb Nurail. Belan supposed he was lucky Geltoi didn't indulge in more of it in public.

"Our young Inquisitor. A question about 'mortality rates,'" Geltoi said dismissively, flourishing the document. This wasn't what Belan wanted to hear. He was concerned about the mortality rates. He knew Geltoi had everything under control, Geltoi was smart, Geltoi had told him so. He hadn't been able to quite cure himself of worry, though. He didn't understand Geltoi's brilliant management plan, whatever it was. "And requests the preparation of a kitchen audit, to be used to validate his endorsement. It's awkward, that's all. A waste of time, complying with a mere formality."

Belan wasn't sure what that even meant. "A kitchen audit, sir?" He was free to ask questions, though, when he didn't understand something. Geltoi was always willing to explain. Sometimes the explanation didn't make any sense.

"Number of measures, Standard, of flours number this and that ordered daily to be used in the preparation of thus and such a number of baked goods of whatever sort and fed to so many at what times with thus much wastage and that much returned. A kitchen audit. Easy enough to prepare, Belan, don't get me wrong. But a bother."

Belan wanted to frown, concerned. He didn't want to give Geltoi any cause to wonder about his loyalty, though. And Geltoi would figure out a way to make it right. "I'm surprised, Administrator. The requirement almost presents the appearance of questioning administrative practices. Have you spoken to the Writ, sir? Perhaps he'd like to withdraw the request."

How could Geltoi allow a kitchen audit? The kitchen staff was Pyana, and there were no records kept as a Nurail understood them. Geltoi had assured him that none were necessary, and Belan knew better than to question Geltoi's judgment. It was probably true that Pyana didn't need to keep records to know exactly how much of what had been fed to whom and when.

That the kitchen had been selling food back to the local markets surreptitiously—through Pyana contacts—Belan knew; Geltoi had been up front with him from the start, and he had his cut. Geltoi had promised him it couldn't be traced back.

Belan had sometimes wondered.

Geltoi was looking at him, considering; as though he thought Belan had actually had a good idea and was wondering whether to endorse it or not. As a Nurail idea it was obviously crude and unformed, probably flawed in several important senses that Belan could not hope to begin to guess at. Maybe with some adjustment Geltoi could find it useful, but after a moment Geltoi seemed to make up his mind, shaking his head.

"I agree, Belan, thank you for your delicacy. I'm sure he would have done it differently if he'd stopped to think how it might look. But now that he's made a request, it's best just to respond in good form. I'll make your point with him when we discuss his findings."

The Administrator would rather Koscuisko had not asked.

The realization chilled Belan to the bottom of his stomach.

"How can I best support you, Administrator?" he asked, just a hint of the anxiety he felt showing in his voice. It wouldn't do to show too much anxiety. That might call his confidence in Geltoi into question.

Geltoi set the document down, pushing it away from him, turning in his chair to look out of the window. "Oh, nothing for you in this one, Merig." Geltoi was clearly dismissing him; and Belan was just as glad. "Just put in a word to the kitchen-master, ask him to get on my scheduler. Sometime soon. Today. Tomorrow. It wouldn't do to make our Inquisitor wait. And on the other hand we mustn't act precipitously."

This Belan understood almost too well.

"Thank you, Administrator, I'll see to it directly. Myself."

Geltoi wanted to be careful about this audit.

In all the time Belan had worked for Geltoi, all of the long months it had taken to build the Domitt Prison, he had never known Geltoi to hesitate. The Administrator's fearless decisiveness in the face of unknown factors had first impressed, then won Belan over to the Administrator's service; he had come to realize that Geltoi knew what he was doing with such assurance, such a grasp of cause and effect and time and place, that Belan could only watch in awed wonder.

All of this time he had supported Geltoi, certain that Geltoi was in complete control.

This kitchen audit, though it worried him, was going to come out all right. It had to.

If Geltoi had been wrong, and all of the things that Belan had done in his service should come to light after all—

It was unthinkable.

Belan shut the idea off.

The sooner he saw the kitchen-master, the sooner all of this would be resolved.

The officer came up for his supper in good time, today, perhaps because of his early morning. Ailynn helped him into the bath as she had done all of these days gone past, and the officer would not look at her. She thought she knew what was in his mind. She thought she understood.

She didn't know if she had the nerve to make her stand, after last night —

She carried his soiled uniform away, careful as she always was to clear his pockets and set his hand-manuscript aside on the bed-table. She was an honest woman, though she was a slave, Ailynn reminded herself. She had a right to speak to him.

She'd been thinking about it all day.

The officer came out of the washroom with his rest-dress trousers on, but she had his upper garment. He was not in uniform. He could not go out of his bedroom like that.

"Ailynn, I cannot find my, have you seen—"

She held the garment up in both hands, before her; seeing what she held, he started for her quite naturally and easily to receive it from her.

She put her hands behind her back, and his wrap-tunic with them. The skin of his uncovered body was very white, in the dim calm of the bedroom. Fair-haired men were frequently very pale, Koscuisko almost unnervingly so.

"If I could have a word, sir."

Koscuisko stopped in his tracks and stared, and Ailynn struggled on.

"I. Want to talk to you. There are things that we should be clear on, you and I. Your Excellency."

She had a chance.

She hadn't understood, until last night.

It was too wonderful a chance to let pass just because she was afraid of him.

"Give me my clothing, Ailynn, I am cold. Please. We will abide and talk."

Oh, yes, her heart said to her, and she all but lost her balance in relief. And with the sudden tears of fear relieved that burned in her eyes, but she kept her voice calm as she answered, handing him his wrap-tunic. "You hurt me, last night. But—"

He had stopped in putting on his wrap-tunic almost before he'd started; she knew she had to speak quickly if she was to hope to avoid misunderstanding.

"But not so much that it should stand between us. How can I do my job, if you won't have me, until you need so badly that you. Well."

His Security were Bonded, as she was. He let them take care of him, and he took care of them in turn as best he could. In a month she had seen enough to understand that what was between Koscuisko and his Bonds was more than duty. They were more free than Ailynn could imagine, and she wanted some of that liberty for herself, even if it could only be for a little while.

Koscuisko belted his wrap-tunic thoughtfully. Thinking. It took him a moment to answer her; because he was listening. Paying attention. Taking her seriously.

Showing respect, for all that she was a slave.

"It is an offense to make you whore for Jurisdiction, Ailynn. I say it, and I do not expect to hear any denial." Because she would assert that she was repaying her debt to the Bench that had spared her life, if he asked her. That was the formula she'd been taught. She also knew that what he said was true. "It is also a sin to have to do with people who are not permitted to decline. It is in a sense as much as to exploit children, oh, holy Mother."

How careful he was in what he said. And how he said it. It only made her more determined.

"The officer would not wish to deny me my dignity." The word was almost ridiculously incongruous, applied to herself; but Koscuisko gave his other Bonds their dignity. She saw no reason why she should not have at least equal respect from him. "I have a purpose and a function, though it is defined by Jurisdiction. I have come to envy your Security, you let them do their job, and you respect them for it. Let me then do mine, and have your respect also."

It was hard, so hard. She was afraid. She knew Koscuisko didn't want to hurt her, but she couldn't help the fear. She had to go on through it because knowing Koscuisko didn't want to hurt her was no longer enough.

Gazing at her in something like horror, Koscuisko shook his head. "There is nothing to envy my gentlemen, Ailynn, Joslire dead and Erish still limping, and all of them to be called into the torture-rooms with me—"

Closing the small distance between them, Ailynn put her fingers to his lips to stop his speech. Hardly believing that she found the nerve. Sensing the uncertainty of her governor. "Their job to protect and support you. You let them. You give them respect. You permit them their own judgment."

Not in torture-room, no, she didn't know about that. But here in quarters, where they shared in partnership to cope with where they were and what they had to do. All six of them. The trust they had in him, and he in them, was astonishing. She wanted in. "I only ask so much as that, your Excellency. It is my job to ease you with my body. Let me help."

She could watch and wait in passive silence, do as she was told, hope for the best and fear for the worst. Or she could pretend that she had a job as real and as important, in its way, as the job Security performed, if Koscuisko would permit her that privilege. "I don't want to be pitied for my Bond. I want to be granted self-respect. Pretend you value what I have to offer. Condescend to let me comfort you."

She wanted to belong.

And it was her job.

The Bench had condemned her to the Bond for punishment and deterrent example, but the Bench had done so equally to his Security. It was worse for them. All she had to do was suffer abuse. They could be required to inflict it.

"I will be frank," Koscuisko said, at last. "This is the problem. The problem is that it is not you I want, Ailynn. It is nothing to do with your desirability. It is because of that which is monstrous and unholy in my nature."

As if she didn't know that already.

"I will trust you, as my cousins outside this room trust you. And say what is on my mind." It got easier as she went along. "His Excellency found relief for the lack he felt, last night. Was it not so, sir?"

He only nodded, his eyes fixed on her face. She couldn't tell whether he was getting angry at her or not; in the dim light there was no separating rage in his face from concentration, for Ailynn. She didn't know him well enough. She'd been sleeping in his bed for a month; and still she hardly knew him, but that was only the way of her life.

"Take comfort then in a way which is not monstrous or unholy, and it may make it easier for you." And would let her be truly one with the others, part of the group, someone who belonged. "I will not pretend that I don't desire comfort as well, sir. And have had little pleasure of the sort you shared with me last night, for a long time."

She was sure he would know what she meant.

But would he accept her argument, weak though it was?

Whores were never to solicit pleasure for themselves, not unless it was the patron's pleasure to assign them that role in advance and pretend to be subordinate.

And still Koscuisko did not let his people lack for food, or rest, or medicine, or anything at all that could be got to comfort them. She would be grateful to have a caress, even purchased with the use of her body. It would be profit the Bench could not keep from her . . . if Koscuisko consented.

"You do not mean to ask to be misused," the officer insisted. The tone of his voice was still unbelieving, but he had not rejected her offer. Or not yet.

"If only the officer did not let frustration build within for overlong." She put her two hands flat against his chest, feeling the warmth of his body through the wrap-tunic. "It will go easier with me if you come more often to embrace me, sir."

He would admit the sense of this.

He almost had to.

"I have heard you," Koscuisko said. "Is this what there was to discuss, Ailynn?"

Her heart turned to stone and sank within her bosom. He would be cold to her. He would not accept. He would not let her in.

"You have not answered me, your Excellency."

What had she asked him?

"It could be said to be owing," Koscuisko murmured, as if to himself. "One does not know if one dares risk it, Ailynn. Kaydence will be very severe with me should there be tears. He is your champion, did you know that?"

"Either that or simply has a weakness." She had heard the good-natured teasing. "And a question apparently exists over the exact location of it."

Koscuisko had a beautiful smile, when he was caught off-guard and smiled with all his teeth. They were small, even, and regular, but it wasn't that, it was that being surprised into a smile took layers of weight of care from off his face and made him look much younger.

"Listening to Code, and should'st not, has weaknesses of his own, Code does."

She had been standing very close to him. Now he put his hand around her waist to turn her toward the door, in perfect friendship and amity. But spoke to her quite seriously, for all that. "It is your right to claim consideration from me, Ailynn, according to the rules that I was raised to."

Ailynn couldn't tell if that meant he was agreeing.

It demonstrated well enough that he was listening to her.

She wondered if Koscuisko understood how strange and rare that was.

Just short of the still-closed door he stopped. "You wanted to talk, Ailynn. Have you for now had satisfaction from me?"

His meal would be getting cold; his liquor warm. "I will tell you in the morning," she teased, daringly.

Koscuisko laughed, and gave her a quick kiss that had none of the torturer about it.

It might work.

One way or the other she would work in partnership with his people; and belong, belong by choice, for the first time since she had been sentenced to her Bond.

Taken from work-crew as War-leader Darmon, locked into a place to wait for torture. He wondered at the luxury of these cells; the sleep-rack was almost a bed, the bedding itself warm and clean and comfortable, water for washing that was sweet enough that a man could drink it at his will. Perhaps this torturer was of dainty sensibilities and only wanted fresh clean healthy prisoners. He hadn't eaten so well since he'd come to the Domitt Prison.

And it looked as though he was to have his chance to find out about the torturer himself, little interest though he had in the question.

The holding cells were open all along one wall so that there could be no hiding at the blind angle of a room while a door opened. That was probably why it was warm in here; it wouldn't do for prison staff to take a chill. Darmon was amused by the insight.

There was a trade-off of sorts between closing people off and holding them in solitude to fret and fume until their nerves were raw; or letting them watch their fellows go away one after another and never come back. The Domitt had clearly opted for the latter means of increasing the torment of the condemned.

It was an advantage, to Robis Darmon.

The more he could learn of who and what he faced, the better prepared he could be for his turn when it came.

And it would come.

He watched this young Inquisitor come through the holding area, twice a day, sometimes more often. Bond-involuntary Security troops at the officer's back, and Pyana turnkeys to open and close doors. A slim but solidly built young officer, an alien name, Anders Koscuisko—no, Aanderi, he had heard. Aanderi Koscuisko. The Writ in residence at the Domitt Prison, and had his mother guessed at the look on Koscuisko's face when he came out from torture in the evening she would have drowned herself rather than deliver a son who could take such pleasure in the pain of suffering captives. Darmon was sure of it. And Koscuisko not even Pyana.

Morning of the fifth day since he'd been taken from the work-crew, and probably two eights after fast-meal. They were fed three times a day, in holding cell. The torturer wanted them strong and able to answer all of his questions. *What would the torturer do with answers that would compromise the Domitt Prison?* Darmon wondered. Because as satisfying as Koscuisko clearly found his work in and of itself, he was as clearly unhappy with the Administration.

"See you this man, Administrator." Koscuisko had brought Belan with him this morning. Belan. Fat and well-fed, sleek and stout and fattening on the flesh of his own kind. There was a special place in Hell for such as Belan. He would look much more than merely just uncomfortable there. "As I have warned you. You can read as well as I, this Brief says Lerriback, and says that this is the man we saw in punishment block. Has it been seven weeks? Or eight, now?"

There were only sixteen holding cells; though Darmon couldn't see everything, the sound carried as clearly as anyone could wish. Koscuisko stood in front of the cell two souls down, with his back to Darmon. And Belan beside him, and the Security, green-sleeved bond-involuntary Security slaves. Darmon wondered what it must be for them to be put to such work as Koscuisko could demand. Bond-involuntaries were not the enemy. The enemy was Koscuisko; and Belan.

"His Excellency has been eight weeks in Port Rudistal." Belan's answer had a sound of grasping for a wisp of reed in a current that was sweeping him to destruction too fast for recognition of the danger. "Not quite so long here. You were tired, and I can't say I remember, sir. It looks like the same man to me, and of course the documentation—"

"My point exactly." Koscuisko sounded upset, even angry. "The documentation gives the name, and even could be made to describe the man we saw during my tour. But not this man. You cannot have neglected to notice, this man has no gray, and the Lerriback we met looked nothing like so young. I would expect experience of a prison to age a man. Rather than the reverse."

Oh, if Koscuisko was confused at seeing two men named Lerriback, how would it be if he should start to count up how many Lerribacks there were. How many Cittropses. Maybe he'd suggest it to the man, when it was his turn to go to die by torture.

"With respect, sir." Belan was polite, but not beyond standing on his dignity as the Assistant Administrator of the Domitt Prison. A true Pyana under the skin, no doubt, Darmon told himself. No, he did not believe that, Belan was Nurail, no matter how depraved. "I wonder you don't note the obvious. Almost everyone of your Interrogations to date has proved to yield some assumed name. This prisoner was masquerading as Lerriback, or as someone else named Lerriback. That's all. I'm sure."

This was too good to want to miss a word. Didn't Belan watch where he was going?

"Prisoners coming in under assumed names one expects," Koscuisko agreed, easily and freely. "And identified by the face, and their also-called. The war-leader you have brought for me, for instance. Taken for us not as Marne Cittrops, though, but as War-leader Robis Darmon, lately so called. And this is different."

"Sir?"

Darmon couldn't decide if Belan sounded confused and resentful because he didn't follow Koscuisko's reasoning, or was simply not playing along. Pretending it wasn't perfectly obvious where the argument was headed.

"So here is described a prisoner on Charges, and very pertinent Charges they are too. Named Lerriback. It is the man we saw, this description sorts with what I remember, see you here? There are notes in the file. Confined in lockbox for fractiousness. I was looking forward to Lerriback, Administrator Belan, and this is not the man, nor is he the same man under the name of another. Who can this be, and how can the Protocols be lawfully exercised against whomever Lerriback, when this is not the man?"

Just as well he was a prisoner here, Darmon told himself, and confined behind security grid in cell. Elsewise he might have kissed the Domitt's torturer; and the gesture would almost certainly have been misinterpreted.

"Maybe the other wasn't really Lerriback—"

"The documentation describes the man I wished to make go back into the lockbox," Koscuisko insisted. "And prisoners are referred on documentation. Take me away this not-Lerriback, Administrator Belan. And either bring me Charges against him—whoever he is, but him, charges I can match to the man by more than name—or find for me my Lerriback. Wherever he is. I will have nothing to do with prisoners referred on insufficient documentation. And to do otherwise would be dangerously close to a failure of Writ."

So either Koscuisko was a raging hypocrite, or the prison administration had made an error. Perhaps both. Darmon knew it wasn't likely that the last, or next, or original Marne Cittrops had looked anything like him, except by accident.

Would they waste valuable Inquisitorial time on prisoners with no secrets, just because a man could be made to say anything?

No, it had to be that when they referred it was for who the prisoner actually was. Not who the prison administration called them on work-crew. War-leader Darmon, and not Marne Cittrops at all. Someone had something on the prisoner in the cell. The Administration had used that prisoner to fill a place on work-crew vacated by somebody named Lerriback. They hadn't got the details all updated. The bodies didn't match.

"Doctor Koscuisko. I protest, in the strongest possible terms. Throwing around language like that."

That had got Belan's attention. Failure of Writ. It meant that there were too many procedural or other faults within the system to lawfully support the Judicial function; and therefore the exercise of the Judicial function was not lawful. And therefore the people who had exercised the Judicial function were guilty of violations of Law and Judicial procedure to the extent that they had executed functions lawful only in support of the Judicial Order in the absence of true justification.

It was worth dreaming about.

If the Writ failed at the Domitt Prison, all of the murders would be recorded as such. All of the murderers treated as murderers, not good Bench officers upholding the Judicial order.

It was a lovely fantasy.

And it would never happen, because the only person who could invoke failure of Writ was the torturer who held the Writ to Inquire; and that meant Andrej Koscuisko here and now. The last thing Darmon could imagine Koscuisko doing was putting an end to his own recreation.

Not having seen him come from his daily work, these five days past, with that drunk drugged look of utter satiation on his face, and still always ever eager for some more.

"I beg your pardon if I have offended you." Koscuisko was doing nothing of the sort. He didn't care. "It is only out of respect for your Administration. We must tolerate no such discrepancies. I want this one remanded to Dramissoi today, Administrator, if there are no charges against *him*."

And, oh, wasn't Koscuisko rubbing Belan's face in the dirty little problem he'd uncovered. A torturer through and through. If it hadn't been Belan, Darmon almost might have wanted to feel sorry for him.

"Of course, your Excellency." Belan wasn't happy, but there was next to nothing that Belan could do about it. "I'll launch an investigation into how this might have happened, and report back to you. Was that to be all for today, Doctor Koscuisko?"

Darmon didn't envy Belan his position; it had to be uncomfortable, Pyana on one side of him, Koscuisko on the other, family ties and friends cut off from behind him by the choices he had made for his life and nothing to look forward to. It couldn't be enjoyable. And Belan deserved every bit of it.

"Thank you, Administrator Belan. I know that you could not but be as shocked as I that such a thing could happen. We're just lucky in this case that we caught it before things went too much further."

How many people had this torturer murdered asking questions that they couldn't answer about crimes that they had not committed?

Koscuisko walked down the row of holding cells, and stopped in front of him. Darmon stepped back from the security grid. He had no desire to be struck with a shockrod for the crime of standing too close to the front of his cell in the presence of an officer.

"I will with this war-leader start while we are waiting," Koscuisko said to his green-sleeves, looking at Darmon with a measuring eye. "War-leader Robis Darmon, I understand. Or are you to claim to be Marne Cittrops, instead? It will delay the progress of the exercise. I will not disguise that fact, from you."

Now the torturer was talking to him. Darmon knew that he was afraid, because he had no illusions about the sort of pain that he was going to suffer. The more he could control the interchange, the better off he'd be. Even the illusion of control could help a man cope—

Darmon filled his face with as stupid a look as he could muster. "Excellency, there must be some mistake." If he looked at the Pyana standing with Koscuisko's Bonds it was easy enough. "My name is Lerriback."

The Pyana guards started forward to pull him out of his cell and beat him for his insolence. Darmon wondered whether it might not be worth it even so, for the look on Koscuisko's face.

Koscuisko held up his hand, and the guards came to attention.

"Oh, indeed you must be," Koscuisko said. "I can see the family resemblance. How you have managed to grow back your hair in such short order is a wonder to me, Lerriback. And taller as well? There must be some unusual healthful effect in the water here."

Darmon knew a moment's grim panic. Family resemblance—there was a family resemblance, for people who knew how to look. His son was beardless yet, but Chonniskot was his son. He had his father's green-gold eyes, and that not usual among Nurail.

Was the torturer playing with him?

"Take for me this prisoner to work-room, gentles, if you please. You know what to do."

No, the torturer was just playing.

Why not?

The Domitt Prison was his own resort, in a sense. A private recreation field for those that could find recreation in such work as a torturer performed.

Koscuisko might not know that the war-leader of Darmon had even had a son, or that Chonniskot had escaped with Farlan and Sender. If Koscuisko knew and Chonni had been taken—taken or killed, identified, one way or the other—Koscuisko would surely let him know about it, to increase his despair, to impress upon him that he had nothing further to lose.

There were worse ways to be taken to torture than with good hope for his child's freedom, by an Inquisitor who seemed at least as interested in scoring off the Domitt Prison's Administration as paying attention to his work.

And still Darmon was afraid, because he knew that he was being taken to torture.

This was a torture cell, then, and would be his final battleground.

Darmon looked around him as the torturer's green-sleeves stripped off his shirt and shoon and everything that had been in between, cutting away his boots, binding his wrists with chains.

It didn't look like much.

But it smelled.

He'd always thought of torture cells as dark, and this one wasn't, every corner was clearly illuminated. He didn't understand most of what he saw, though: a large square block in the middle of the room, coming waist-high. Some sort of a raised pan set against the wall, but not the obvious, because there were no coals, no smoking irons.

The grid on the wall and the hooks in the ceiling he could understand altogether too well.

The torturer said nothing, looking at the beverage-server on the table next to the armchair that waited there for the officer's comfort. Darmon suppressed a shudder: it was cold, and he was afraid. Naked he could urinate on his torturer in contempt, though that would probably not be worth the pleasure he would derive from it. He wasn't sure he had the water to urinate with. He was that frightened.

Fear was shame to nobody.

No war-leader worthy to send other souls to death could have illusions, though it was important sometimes to pretend. People had fear. It was a natural response. Courage lay in going forward with fear, not in the absence of fear.

Once they had finished stripping him, they uncoupled the chain between his wrists and hooked the manacles to tethers in the ceiling, drawing his arms well out in two different directions. Shackled his ankles, he was disappointed to note, and anchored them to the floor. No kicking, then. He would have had to get in a lucky hit to do the torturer any damage, barefoot as he was, but it was still a shame to have the fantasy taken from him.

"That will suffice for now," the torturer said. Oh, good. Then he could go back to his cell. No, of course not, it was the Security that the torturer addressed, and Darmon knew better than that. It was a lame joke, if a private one. Jokes helped. "I will call you when I want you. Go away."

Now they were alone together.

Darmon considered blowing a kiss, but restrained himself.

There was no sense in being provoking.

At least not yet.

He would save his provoking till later, when things were far enough along that if the torturer lost his temper for one moment he might make the critical mistake that would let Darmon out of this.

Seating himself in the armchair, the torturer looked Darmon up and down; then spoke.

"I am Andrej Ulexeievitch Koscuisko, and I hold the Writ to which you must answer. State for me your name, and your identification."

"My name is Marne Cittrops. But my mother's people—"

Wait.

He didn't know what Cittrops's weaves had been.

The torturer had taken a little book from out of the front plaquet of his uniform, and opened it, sitting there with a stylus in his left hand, waiting. Smirking. Darmon thought hard and fast.

"—would not share so much as the name of their weave with any damned Pyana. Or their pet torturer."

The torturer would know very well what was going on; or he would guess. Koscuisko smiled more broadly.

"I am a Judicial officer, War-leader, and the Bench transcends all of your petty ethnic differences. I am particularly anxious to hear your weave, Darmon. I am collecting. See?"

Koscuisko said "petty ethnic differences," but without much pretense at conviction. It occurred to Darmon that Koscuisko was an odd sort of a torturer, but the book that he held up, what could that be?

"I can't see from here. Sir. Why don't we trade places, and you can swing on these ropes for a while, and I'll sit down and admire your work close up."

Koscuisko was collecting weaves?

"It would mean nothing to you unless you read church music. It is an Aznir script. You are evading. I have asked you for your weave, for posterity's sake. If you are Marne Cittrops, you will give me—one. If you are not, well, all to the good, I will obtain another."

Nurail had been murdered here by this man, but if the weaves were passed—the tune and the telling, or even the telling alone—the knowledge they contained would not be lost. The people that had been killed on the work-crews, crushed to death or in some other manner, had not been given time to pass their weaves before they died. How many had they lost?

"If I was not Marne Cittrops I would have the same answer."

No. Perhaps not.

It was true that some of the weave-lore was outdated. The hill-people had started to sing the weaves as a way to preserve technical knowledge about land navigation; and their importance as maps had gradually become outdated as the Nurail had spread throughout their worlds.

By then the weaves had collected much more than just land-lore. Words and music, the telling and the tune of it, there was history in them, genealogy, contractual and family relationships centuries deep and as much a part of a Nurail as his very skin. Nurail were passionate for a start, and the emotion that invested the war-weaves could inspire fighting men to awesome feats.

They were defeated and dispersed in this generation, but there would be Nurail in the next, and the weaves their only inheritance now. The music. The knowledge of the Nurail collective unconsciousness preserved in old lyrics and older tunes, the voices of the dead speaking to the living yet with words of advice and of admonishment. The power.

He was the war-leader of Darmon, and his mother's people had held the most powerful war-weave of them all; but his daughters—to whom he would normally pass his mother's weave—were dead. If Koscuisko wrote down weaves it would be there, and if someone should find it later—if Koscuisko were telling him the truth, and not making a joke at his expense, and the document did not simply get lost—

Koscuisko closed his book and put it away. "I'm sorry to hear that. I was looking forward to it. Well, then, which is it to be? Marne Cittrops? Or War-leader Darmon?"

This was too obvious to be allowed to pass, even if he was bound naked in chains while the other man sat at his ease in an armchair. "Why don't you tell me? What possible profit could there be in being a war-leader, of all things? Rather than the harmless innocuous little slave-laborer that I am—"

The torturer looked him up and down with insolent amusement in his eyes. "I would not have said 'little.' And it is of course your choice to remain Cittrops as long as you can support the pretense. You are here on good suspicion of being the war-leader, though, and therefore

I have it at command to put you to the Question until you confess to being the war-leader, whether you are or not. It is only a question of time."

"Oh, well, in that case, yes. I'm the war-leader. The one that rogered your mother at her mam's knee. If you kept your mouth shut and looked stupid you could pass for Nurail, did you know that?"

The chains that stretched his wrists out to the ceiling rubbed uncomfortably. Darmon tried to resist the temptation to worry at them. He wasn't going to get any more comfortable than he was right now. That was a given. "Then you could be the war-leader. We'll trade places."

Now Koscuisko was on his feet, plucking a record up from his side table. He carried the document over to where Darmon stood half-stretched to the ceiling, turning so that Darmon could read the text on the clear assumption that Darmon could read plain Standard; or was it part of the trick to get him to admit to his identity?

"War-leader Robis Darmon. Your family is dead, it says here, you have no one to protect any longer. If you will not provide the Bench with a confession you know what will come of it. The exiles will cherish your memory and those left on site will romanticize you until the whole thing starts over in the next generation but one. Confess, and it will help in the integration of the Nurail into Jurisdiction, with a better life for what hypothetical grandchildren you might have."

He could read plain Standard, come to that. His family was dead, the record listed them out—and well it should be so, because if the record said his daughters were killed no Nurail could be tortured to death for the crime of being heir to the war-leader.

But there was no mention there of Chonniskot.

"You already said that you can make me confess to being whomever. And I believe you. What's the point?"

"Collaterals," the torturer said, and he sounded a little surprised. "In order to restore the Judicial order, the Bench needs to assure itself of war-leaders, generals, lieutenants. I want your evidence, and what you know of other persons of authority hiding under assumed names, as you were."

Poor Ceelie. Darmon kept his face as blank as he could. He'd known as soon as they'd come for him that Ceelie had been pressed beyond the limit of his endurance. He could not afford to exhibit any grief for someone he could not admit to having known; and still it burned. It was his fault Ceelie had suffered, and Ceelie had died, because he had failed against Jurisdiction. Ceelie and so many others . . .

"So you torture a man till he names a name, and then you torture the next. That's not good evidence. That whoever you took away from work-crew, that Shopes Ban, he may have called me out as the First Judge for all I know, why should you believe him?" The shackles cut against his wrists. Already his elbows began to ache; but then he was not a young man, any more.

The torturer frowned. "I have had no Shopes Ban, I'm sorry. You're unraveling the wrong plait."

All that Ceelie must have endured before his death, and the torturer would not so much as admit to knowing of him. Robis's voice was a little sharper than he'd expected, when he spoke. "No doubt you've had too many of us, torturer. I wonder you can keep any apart." Sharper than was prudent for use by a chained man, for a fact. Koscuisko just stared.

"I would that you were right, Darmon or Cittrops." It was a peculiar tone of voice; and a peculiar expression on the torturer's face, as well. "But when they visit me at night I know each one of them, and all too well. But never a Shopes Ban among them. Believe me. I would know."

People were taken from work-crew all the time; and always it was assumed that they'd been taken to the torture. If Koscuisko was telling the truth, it was someone else who had tortured Ceelie Porlich. Darmon had been a good judge of character, in his time. He believed that Koscuisko was telling him the truth.

"They took Shopes Ban away," he insisted. There was something gone wrong here, and he hadn't quite caught it by the mane. "Eleven, twelve days ago. Who took him away? Where did he go?"

"And why does it matter?" Koscuisko mocked at him; but there was a serious question beneath Koscuisko's belittling jeer. "Because he was the only one who could have identified you as War-leader Darmon?"

For a moment sheer outrage and disgust possessed Darmon entirely. "Listen, someone took Ban. If he was killed it was by you or by prison security. If he wasn't killed he'd be back on work-crew till he died. And you're the Writ here, don't tell me you don't know what's going on. You killed him. Or he was murdered—"

Wait, that was almost funny. To be tortured to death by Koscuisko was different from being murdered? Well, in the eyes of the Bench it was, for a fact.

But Koscuisko had gone to an instruments-case that he let down from the wall to reveal an array of whips, with a flail, and a knout, and divers other lashes. Thinking about what Darmon was saying, perhaps. But more likely just deciding which of his toys he wanted to play with, just now.

"Take care before you make such accusations," Koscuisko warned, turning toward him with a whip in his hand. Darmon knew the sort of whip it was; it was the same sort that had killed his uncle Lijon, years ago. "I will not suffer my Writ to be dishonored. Not more than in its exercise itself. You are the war-leader of Darmon, and you have information that I require. Let us begin to controvert together."

Controvert.

That was a funny word for torture.

Darmon felt the first burning caress of the whip, and closed his eyes, and wondered.

Who had murdered Ceelie?

Could he convince Koscuisko someone had?

If Koscuisko knew that referrals were being obtained unlawfully, by prison guards and torture outside Koscuisko's Writ—would Koscuisko take steps to avenge that poor young man?

The impact of the whip was a steady insult, and the fiery lines of aching torment it laid down with every stroke were maddening.

Darmon fixed his mind on Ceelie Porlich as a touchstone.

Shopes Ban.

He had to remember Ceelie was Shopes Ban.

And if he could concentrate on something extraneous to him, perhaps he would keep the torturer from the victory, this time.

CHAPTER NINE

Administrator Geltoi was interviewing the Pyana housekeeper Eps Murey when Belan arrived with the kitchen-master. Letting himself in quietly, he gestured for the kitchen-master to step through before he closed the door again behind them.

"What's changed up there recently, Murey? Anything?" Geltoi asked. He sounded angry; but it was just his way of interacting with subordinates. Belan had long since stopped feeling that it was personally directed.

"Well. There's the woman. The bed-linen to change more often. Seems to have taken an interest in her, with the Administrator's permission."

Belan winced. What a thing to say, a crude reference to Koscuisko's personal relations with the woman from the service house. It could have been worse, of course. Murey could have been Nurail, then the Administrator would have been disgusted at his forwardness, as well as his crudeness of speech.

As it was, Geltoi splayed his fingers wide with a gesture as if deflecting a noisome insect. "Oh, very good indeed, Murey. I need different information from you. Has Koscuisko said anything in your hearing? Any gossip amongst his Security? Anything you've heard from that Chief Warrant?"

They'd considered putting in snoop-sensors when they'd built the penthouse, and only refrained at the end because it would be difficult to justify should the Inquisitor find out they were there. Geltoi was obviously feeling the lack, now.

"I'm sorry, sir, there's nothing. The officer complains of the documentation he has to process. The Chief Warrant Officer ensures that Muat completes his physical therapy, Muat protests that the officer is not completing his. They play relki. The officer would rather not put in his laps and the Warrant Officer sees to it that he does. I've heard nothing to report to you, Administrator."

So either Koscuisko didn't have a hidden agenda, or he was keeping it to himself. Why should he share his concerns with his Security? One might as well ask a Pyana to unburden himself to a Nurail. It wasn't done.

"Complains of documentation, you say." Administrator Geltoi did not seem to have come to the same conclusion. "Anything specific? Think, Murey. I'm half-convinced Koscuisko is out to cause trouble for all of us."

"Only about having a backlog on his desk, sir. I'd have spoken to Administrator Belan direct if I had heard anything that might point to a problem."

Koscuisko's documentation was backlogged because Koscuisko didn't spend much time in his office. He got up, got his laps in, had his fast-meal, went to work; then up to bed late, usually after having his mid-meal at least and sometimes his third-meal as well in the cells with his clients. Prisoners.

Victims; but that was a Nurail thought. The Pyana word was better, clients. It helped disguise the precise nature of the services Koscuisko provided. And glossed over the helpless suffering of the prisoners entirely.

Geltoi drew a dish of vellme closer to him across the surface of the desk-table, glaring irritably at the light reflected in the milky liquid. "Very well, Murey, but I rather hoped for a more complete report. See if you can't get something out of the woman. And maybe you'll report to Belan every day or so whether there's news or not. I don't want any surprises like the kitchen audit."

Murey hadn't known about the kitchen audit, from his reaction. And would have loved to have had the details, exactly what Koscuisko wanted; but had been dismissed in a fairly obvious manner. Murey bowed with reluctance and went out of the room, eyeing Belan with a mixture of curious greed and hostile resentment as he passed.

Belan was used to it. There wasn't a single Pyana in all of the Domitt Prison who wasn't convinced that they had more right than he did to stand next to Administrator Geltoi in the order of things.

"The kitchen audit, Administrator. We have an appointment to review it with you before we submit it to the Writ."

It was hard to tell if Geltoi was listening. Dabbing a forefinger into the dish of vellme in a contemplative manner, now, Geltoi sucked the drops of fluid from the wet fingertip thoroughly before he spoke.

"Absolutely, Merig. I'm not taking any chances. Koscuisko hasn't shared any concerns with me, if he has any, and that would have been the normal thing to do. Still, I may be overreacting. Let's have a look at the audit, then."

Belan agreed, if only within his own private thoughts. Geltoi was overreacting. Belan had read up on the formal relationship between a Writ on site and the prison administration. The Writ was responsible to the Bench for reasonable and prudent measures to ensure that prisoners were housed and fed, and the Protocols respected. The kitchen audit was just another item on the list of things an Inquisitor might do to fulfill his formal responsibilities.

Also Geltoi was not overreacting a bit. If Koscuisko realized that prisoners were not being fed full rations even when they were on work-crew, Koscuisko could cry failure of Writ at the Domitt Prison.

The kitchen-master laid the six required reports out on the Administrator's desk-table in careful array. "Stores and disbursements, showing rations received, Administrator. The audit standard says on average an under-run of two in eighty up to a cumulative overrun of eleven in eighty is acceptable variation. It was hard to decide how to determine what population figure to use, though."

The Domitt Prison was at its full lawful capacity with the new arrivals from Eild's collections and the aftermath of that siege. Belan knew that it had been at more than full legal capacity for longer than that. It hadn't been an issue earlier, when the prison was being built; they'd received prisoners without manifest, and that meant nobody really knew how many of them there were.

That one riot had taken a lot of the pressure off, as well, one hundred and seventy-four killed trying to reach the gate, surely as many again wounded, and the offending parties gathered—living and dead—and buried all at once in the pit that had anchored one of the materials-cranes that they'd been using to hoist heavy items up to the upper floors of the prison.

Dead and alive together.

Belan kept his eyes focused on the audit report by an act of will. Outside the Administration Building, beside the outer wall of the Domitt Prison, safely shielded from any curious eye in Port Rudistal by the containment wall, and the pit already there and ready to be filled in. He could still hear the screaming as the accelerant was broadcast onto living flesh, screaming that muted only gradually as earthmovers pushed the excavated dirt back into the pit.

It didn't matter.

They were dead.

He was Assistant Administrator Belan. He had a position of privilege and influence, even amongst these Pyana.

Pyana had done so well as they had over the years in just such a manner, why should he have nightmares? It was the Pyana way. Feeling guilty only indulged his own inferior Nurail nature.

"You've gotten the traffic reports from the landing field, Belan?" Geltoi asked. His tone of voice hinted to Belan that his inattention had been remarked upon, and he hastened to reclaim his fault by providing reassurance that all had been done as Administrator Geltoi would wish it.

"Together with best estimates from the relocation camp, and tied in with reports on blockade intercepts, Administrator." He was proud of how thorough he'd been. None of his figures stood out by itself. He had support for everything, and convincing reasons why the Domitt claimed so many fewer souls on its admissions than the remanding parties might have thought they were transferring.

Geltoi had been completely correct on that issue. Nobody could ever tell the difference. There had been too much confusion, and records not well kept, and sometimes lost for a very small fee.

The population statistics were valid.

"As long as you're satisfied, Merig." Administrator Geltoi leaned back in his chair with the dish of vellme in one hand. "All right. Go ahead and sign for me. And get it delivered right away, and be sure that if Koscuisko has any questions he knows to ask us first."

For a moment Belan stared, confused. Him to sign? It was for the Administrator to sign the audit . . . but when understanding came it was complete and comprehensive. Of course. The Administrator was delegating. That way if there should be a problem further on . . .

Wait.

If there was a problem further on, it would be Belan, not Geltoi, to answer for any discrepancies in the kitchen audit.

What was there to worry about?

Geltoi was Pyana. Pyana were sharp. Administrator Geltoi was smarter than anyone Belan had ever met. There weren't going to be any problems.

And if there were . . .

Geltoi was watching him closely, clearly searching for signs of disloyalty or rebellion. Belan swallowed his reservations and stepped up to the desk-table, pulling out his idiostamp to sign the documents.

If there was a problem he was damned.

He had no hope of outwitting a Pyana.

His only chance was to keep being useful, and hope that Geltoi would protect him.

He had been forever at the Domitt Prison, now. Not even Ailynn's graciously extended efforts to help him through the night were quite effective; which meant Andrej became more and more irritable day by day. There were so many screaming trembling bodies in this place. And he was so careful with each one of them.

The body that half-lay across the block was neither trembling nor screaming; Andrej knew what was required, but there was a problem, he had no more of the drug that he desired in the set of doses that he carried with him. No more within the cell. He would have to requisition wake-keepers from Infirmary, but for the present he would just borrow from stores in the next cell.

"Kaydence."

Going to the door, Andrej keyed the admit, blocking the interior of the room from view by standing well within the doorway. Kaydence saluted, bowing toward the center of the room without turning to face Andrej, knowing that Andrej didn't want him to look. "Kaydence, into the second cell to the dose-rack go, and for me the dose-unit store of midipar bring out. You are to come through with it, when you come back."

He needed the wake-keeper in a hurry, or he was going to lose this prisoner. And there were still just one or two more questions before this particular prisoner could die, and leave Andrej to concentrate on the other projects he had going in other cells even now.

So many.

And so hard, to keep himself to the rule of conscience every time. He had not abused a prisoner outside of Protocol. He'd never needed to violate the Protocols in order to gain dominion.

The prisoner who was accused of being War-leader Darmon, with whom he had spent the morning, was an unusual experience for Andrej in that respect; and by now—four days into that exercise— Andrej really rather hoped that he would lose, that Darmon would go to his death unconfessed. Andrej admired him.

But it was more difficult all the time to do the decent thing and let them go, when he was finished. There was so much. He'd thought the surfeit of suffering would slake his appetite; it didn't, it only seemed to sharpen it. The war-leader's resistance, admirable though it was, made Andrej the more savage with other prisoners—Tarcey, here, for instance. And day by day the unholy accumulation of the suffering of helpless captives scraped away new layers of raw nerve like a flensing-knife, until his resolve was frayed to the snapping point.

Kaydence came into the cell with the drug Andrej wanted and stood waiting, patiently, to see if the dose was right. Andrej put the dose through at the throat of his prisoner, fresh meat to the bestial hunger in his soul; the prisoner stirred, with a grinding groaning sound of fathomless despair, and Andrej forgot all about Kaydence being present.

So many, and so much, and not enough. Never enough. His sharp keen agonizing knowledge of how wrong it was to embrace such a thirst only heightened his thirst, and he had kept himself from the slaking of it with a stern effort time and again, determined not to take advantage beyond what measures served the Judicial purpose.

Fetching a glass of water from the potable-water spigot at the back of the cell, Andrej touched his prisoner's face to get his attention, offering the glass. For a moment he wondered if the prisoner had escaped after all, there was madness in the look of that dark eye, glittering feverishly under the lights from the ceiling. The moment passed. The prisoner closed his eyes, exhausted and submissive to Andrej's will, and drank from the glass of water gratefully.

"Now let us talk," Andrej suggested.

He had a camp-stool that he could pull close, to sit upon and be at a good level to watch his prisoner's face. The man tried to flinch away from him on instinct, but his wrists were chained to the side of the block on which he half-lay, sprawling. There was no "away" for him to flinch to.

"Yes. Your-ex. Len. Sie."

Wrists pegged to the sides of the cube, arms stretched to either side of the near corner, and the prisoner's body across the block so that most of his torso lay atop it on his belly while his legs fell unsupported off the opposite comer. A very awkward position to be in, really. One in which it would be almost impossible to rest.

"The Tanner's raid on Port Preyling, who planned it?" Andrej asked gently. At this point a man needed very little by way of persuasion to speak out. It was deciding if he was telling the truth—

"Don't know." It was a protest from the heart, one pregnant with fear and horror. "Told you. Please. Don't know. Please."

Yet it was in Andrej's power to hold this man and torture him until he accused someone, anyone, just to make it stop, just to win his death. Then there would be another soul to torment, and good cause and justification to invoke the Advanced Levels, and as little chance that whomever was accused had real guilt to confess as that this man was lying. It was a seductive concept.

"All right. I'm sorry. Just making certain. Can you tell me why Haren Morguiss went over to the Darmon, at Fidenbanks?"

Four days of torture, and this the fifth. The prisoner swallowed hard. Andrej gave him another drink of water.

"Not sure. Heard. Assault on family. Bench in Pyana pockets."

The prisoner's face was dirty, under the bright lights; dirty, and pale. Bruised, and altogether disreputable to look at. Why would anyone think twice about spurning a piece of such human trash under his foot, and taking what pleasure there was to be had in the death-throes of human vermin?

Why should he torture himself, day in, day out, precise to Protocol and strictly to the Judicial standard, when any of these prisoners confessed could be lawfully tortured until they died for crimes against the Judicial order?

"What came of it?" The defection of Haren Morguiss had been a matter of much debate in recent months, debate about whether Nurail were inherently treacherous because of their savage animal nature or were simply incapable of understanding more complex concepts of loyalty and fidelity. Andrej knew better than to imagine that Nurail were incapable of loyalty. He had firsthand experience: much of it here.

"Family was compromised, children sold. Disrespect of Bench. Pyana treachery."

The Domitt Prison had been built by Pyana with imprisoned Nurail slave labor, was staffed almost exclusively by Pyana as far as Andrej had seen—

"It's illegal to sell children under Jurisdiction, Tarcey. Watch what you say," Andrej warned. But not because he meant it. He wanted more information; and also Tarcey was fearfully sensitive, by now, to any criticism from his torturer.

"No disrespect—sir—please—no disrespect—"

So sensitive that his fear of punishment was almost as strict and terrible to him as the punishment itself. Almost. Andrej knew that he should reassure Tarcey, and pose the question in a form that Tarcey could understand; and yet why should he?

Why shouldn't he take one, just one, of all these souls, and instead of keeping constant guard over himself to prevent the commission of some cruelty in excess of the gross cruelties that the Bench required of him, put his conscience aside, misgivings away, shut up the voice of decency and pity, and revel in the rich wide field of horror that the Bench had granted him?

So many souls in torment, why should he not take one, just one, and see if he could satisfy his lust once and for all by indulging it to its fullest extent?

"Sent to prison for civil offenses by Pyana torturers, one of the daughters indentured—I—I think, oh, please. Your Excellency. No disrespect."

"It's all right." His voice was soothing and reassuring. The prisoner lapsed into silence with his eyes shut tight against the bright lights and remembered horrors, weeping. Andrej rose unsteadily to his feet, half-sick with conflict, desire, and self-loathing; and went to put the extra doses Kaydence had brought away in the shelf-rack.

Wake-keepers.

Pain-maintenance drugs.

Put them together and a man went to Hell, and lived there, abiding in ferocious torment for eternities before the body finally failed or the dose wore off. Or the torturer took pity. Whichever came first.

And Tarcey was so frightened, of the mask.

Just next to the dose-rack, cleaned and returned to storage. Waiting. Promising.

Andrej slipped the catch, and opened the equipment-rack, reaching out a waiting hand to touch the cold heavy surface of the thing.

It had worked for him in Tarcey's case, right enough; but Tarcey had confessed, and had no more to say that Andrej was interested in hearing. And would be put to death. Lethal injection.

What if . . .

He was the rule of Law at the Domitt Prison. He could do anything he liked.

Staring at the equipment-rack, one hand to the cheek-piece of the mask, Andrej stared at the wall unseeing for long moments. Struggling.

Realizing only gradually that someone was speaking to him.

" . . . for third-meal."

What?

"If you would care to take it in your office, sir. Or perhaps go up to quarters now?"

Kaydence. That was right. He'd had Kaydence run an errand for him. He'd forgotten to send him away.

What had gotten into Kaydence, though? Bond-involuntaries were not to speak unless they had been spoken to first. Andrej didn't want third-meal. He wanted to take the mask to show Tarcey, just to show him. Tarcey was so afraid of the mask. Andrej wanted to enjoy that helpless terror.

"Oh, go away, Kaydence." Kaydence wasn't being insubordinate, not really. Kaydence was trying to help out. It was so hard to close an equipment rack up and walk away, sometimes. It got harder and harder as he went along. "I don't want my supper. Go and wait outside. I will come when I am ready."

Kaydence's intervention was grounded in genuine care and enabled by trust; was it best in the long run—Andrej asked himself—to have given his people the idea that they could trust any officer?

Because Kaydence was not doing as he was told.

"Yes, sir. Going immediately, sir, except that the officer should come away as well. If the officer please."

Or, in plain language, *you are not in command of yourself and should be removed from this environment before you do something you'll regret later*. Andrej wondered at Kaydence finding the nerve to speak to him like that, issues of trust aside. This was far from the strict standard of careful respect and formality that bond-involuntaries were expected to exemplify—for their own protection.

He stroked the mask, distracted, his fingers feeling their way from the cheek-piece to the eyepiece almost without conscious volition. The eyepiece. The earpiece. The—

Kaydence was nearer to Andrej, now, standing very close behind him. Moving slowly, moving deliberately, Kaydence reached around from behind Andrej to take his hand at the wrist, plucking it away from the seductive surface of the mask with careful but unapologetic firmness.

"There's a nice bit of savory for the officer's third-meal," Kaydence said. Coming around from behind Andrej now to close up the equipment-rack and lock it into place, putting his back to it, placing himself between Andrej and the temptation that tormented him. "Baked apple for after-sweet. The officer will wish to wash. Please. Sir. Come away from here."

Kaydence's voice had begun to tremble, just a bit. As though he were beginning to realize how flagrantly he was violating all that he'd been taught. Backing up toward his chair, staring in astonishment, Andrej sat down, trying to understand how he felt about this.

Insubordination.

Clear and repeated failure to comply with lawful and received instruction, utterly contrary to conditioning.

His Security had learned to take liberties, over the years. As long as Andrej himself was careful to take no notice, Security weren't forced to evaluate their actions against their codes of conduct. Without the internal stress state resulting from having done something one knew one should not have done—or having not done something that one should have—the governor did not engage.

The governor.

Hardwired into pain centers in the brain, and calibrated to respond to specific internal stress states by providing a corrective noxious stimulus direct—

Like the most merciless torturer imaginable, literal-minded and absolute, and one that was immune to appeals to conscience or affection, one that Kaydence himself had invoked and surrendered to . . . one that would continue to execute a fearful penalty, defined on a predetermined scale and measured against the extremity of Kaydence's distress, for as long as Kaydence believed that he had earned punishment—

Oh.

It was an astonishing idea.

And Kaydence knew that he had been insubordinate. No, worse than insubordinate, he had actively interfered, Kaydence had committed an intervention. Bond-involuntaries were never to handle instruments of torture without explicit instructions, though of course they were expected to tidy up from time to time in due course. Still less were they to use coercive force against their officers, preventing or compelling in any way—

Kaydence knew, because Kaydence was white in the face and breathing a little shakily, standing at attention now but with his eyes fixed desperately on Andrej's face.

Andrej smiled.

It was too perfect; he couldn't help it.

Kaydence knew that he'd earned punishment.

And Andrej didn't even have to touch him to make him suffer.

"I am surprised at you," Andrej observed, and kept his voice careful and level. To give no hint. To provide no hope of indulgence or forgiveness. "How do you mean to explain yourself to me, Mister Psimas?"

Kaydence was tall and powerfully built, broad-shouldered and as steady as an oak.

Now Kaydence staggered under the ferocious force of Andrej's cold rebuke, and crashed down to his knees as though he had been struck by lightning.

"You'd only. Hate yourself." Kaydence's words were heavy with a burden of fathomless grief and dreadful fear. "Even more. And there's so little we can do."

Kaydence couldn't keep to his knees. He fell onto his face on the floor, crawling forward awkwardly to crouch trembling at Andrej's feet. The governor. It didn't know Kaydence had acted from love. It didn't care. It only knew that Kaydence had taken a chance, and was to be disciplined for insubordination strictly enough to put teeth into the mildest of rebukes from his officer.

Leaning his forehead against the edge of the chair just to one side of Andrej's knee, Kaydence clutched at Andrej's wrist, seeking reassurance, forgiveness. His voice staggered and halted like a drunken man, so brokenly that Andrej could hardly make sense of his words.

"Only. Touch me, if you're going to. Punish me. I could still pretend—I mattered to you, then—"

Time stopped, and the instant shimmered in Andrej's mind too full of conflict and promise for comprehension.

Kaydence.

Suffering.

Loved him and trusted him, how much more would Kaydence suffer to be punished—

Andrej blinked once, and time was, once again. Oh, no. Not Kaydence. Holy Mother, in the name of all Saints. Not Kaydence.

Paralyzed with horror, Andrej could not move.

Kaydence had reached up for Andrej's hand, petitioning for some small comfort in his pain. But Andrej could not move to clasp Kaydence's trembling fingers. Kaydence's hand slipped slowly down to cover his face, instead; curling his other hand around Andrej's ankle, Kaydence started to shake, shuddering with pain and weeping with desolate grief.

Andrej knew how to translate that language in Kaydence's body. Kaydence's governor had not stopped, when time had stopped. Kaydence believed that Andrej was angry with him, and meant for him to suffer. Kaydence's governor was equal to the task of punishment.

Not Kaydence.

Oh, holy Mother, in the name of all Saints, not Kaydence.

Out of his chair in a spasm of ferocious anxiety, Andrej cradled Kaydence to lie on the floor, desperately trying to get through. "Please, Kaydence, you've done nothing wrong, you were quite right to mention my supper, Kaydence, don't—"

It was too late.

Kaydence was lost, his governor hell-bent on performing its function. Punishing Kaydence. Putting him to torture for his crime of trying to take care of his officer, trying to protect his officer, trying to do right.

Kaydence's eyes were open and staring, fixed on some point in space that had to be more horrifying than anything Andrej had ever seen. To judge from Kaydence's expression.

The governor had engaged. And the governor punished out of all proportion with the severity of the offense, because bond-involuntaries were criminals after all; and had to be strictly disciplined, to ensure they took their lessons to heart. There was nothing that could be done but put Kaydence out, interrupt the pain response with induced unconsciousness so that the governor could complete its punishment sequence without Kaydence quite feeling it.

No time to kiss Kaydence's staring eyes and beg forgiveness.

Andrej put his thumbs to either side of Kaydence's neck and pressed until the body relaxed, limp and unconscious.

It wouldn't last.

Kaydence would wake again to agony within too short a time. But Andrej could get him to Infirmary by then, and get the drug he needed. He didn't have it with him. Kaydence wasn't Nurail, Kaydence was Class One, an entirely different category of hominid. The drugs Andrej had brought for Nurail patients and Nurail prisoners would do no good for Kaydence.

He had to get to Infirmary.

And what punishment a man might merit who had been for even that one instant willing to consider torturing an enslaved soul who trusted and believed in him—

Later.

Andrej sprinted for the door to fetch Toska, leaving his prisoner to fall asleep and die.

His overriding need to shut off Kaydence's pain canceled all others.

The Domitt Prison's Infirmary was as bleak and depressing as everything else about a prison was. Erish envied Code his familiarity with the place: Code had been here before. He'd been the officer's escort on his tour of the prison.

Nine weeks ago, now? Ten?

Maybe as long as that. Erish didn't remember, exactly, and he didn't want to think about it. He had been Bonded in a prison. The operation had been done in a prison surgery, although one considerably more sophisticated than this. He could remember the terror as he woke as clearly as though it had been yesterday, rather than seven years ago.

The operation. The implantation of his governor. And how vulnerable it had made him feel, how difficult it had been for the Infirmary staff not to take advantage, just that little bit, of the fact that he was helpless and terrified, and could only comply with whatever instruction as quickly as he could and hope to avoid punishment.

Kaydence's governor—

Erish didn't know what was going on; nobody did. Chief Samons had got the call from Toska, they'd arrived just in time to hear the officer tell the guards to take them to Infirmary. Right away. Immediately.

Kaydence laid out on a carry-plank, guards as guides. Koscuisko had hurried them all through to Infirmary to transfer Kaydence to a treatment table, calling for sixteen units of one of the most powerful anodynes in the entire Inventory.

Chief Samons waited until Koscuisko had put the dose through before she asked the question.

"Your Excellency. If you'd care to say what happened, sir."

Joslire dead, Kaydence in agony . . .

"He said only three words to me," Koscuisko replied, in a voice full of anguished self-reproach. "And I let him believe that I had taken offense. Oh, Kaydence."

Erish thought he understood.

It was hard on them all being here, but no question existed in Erish's mind that it was hardest on Koscuisko himself. Koscuisko got lost. Joslire had been able to call Koscuisko back when he was in danger of wandering; Kay had misjudged his moment.

Kaydence trembled on the treatment table as though he heard Koscuisko's voice; Koscuisko frowned at him, in horror. "No, it is not to be imagined. Kaydence must be unconscious, there was enough vixit in that dose—"

Setting his fingers to the pulse of Kaydence's throat, Koscuisko shook his head, clearly unwilling to accept the evidence he read. "Where is the staff physician. This is wrong."

And took Kaydence's head between his hands at the back of Kaydence's neck to shut Kay's mind down with the pressure of his thumbs. "I cannot afford to repeat the simple approach too many times, it is reduction of blood flow, there can be no chances taken. The staff surgeon!" Koscuisko snarled at the Infirmary aide standing nervously at the door to the treatment room. "The staff surgeon at once, the need is critical, why are you standing there?"

The Infirmary aide bolted. Koscuisko drew a dose from the same vial he'd drawn on for Kaydence's medication and discharged it over the palm of his hand, sniffing at it, tasting it, finally breathing the fluid in three short sharp sniffs. Then Koscuisko swore, and went to the stores shelf in a furious and furiously controlled rage.

Searching the shelves.

Striking through the secures with a savage blow of the heavy bowl of a powder-crusher. Scattering medication as he went, talking to himself while Erish stood with Code and Toska and wondered. Chief Samons opened Kaydence's cuffs and collar, beckoning for Toska to take off Kaydence's boots as Koscuisko muttered.

"Exhausted the dose, maybe the lot was old, shouldn't be old, and someone had used some of it. Where's another. Should have more dissiter, here, prison full of Nurail. Yes, I need some vondilong, running short. Pink-tinged, bad sign. Chief."

Koscuisko tossed a vial over his shoulder in Samons's direction, not pausing in his search, not looking around. Chief Samons caught it: vondilong, a standard stimulant for Nurail, but what had Koscuisko meant by its pink tinge being a bad sign?

Chief Samons tucked it away and opened Kay's over-blouse. Erish was glad to see that Kaydence's boot-stockings were beyond reproach, for once.

The officer blamed himself for Kaydence's suffering, and might well have good reason. But they were all in this together and the officer blamed himself for entirely too much already.

Should they risk a grouping? Erish wondered. The officer needed balance. It had gone better with him once he and Cousin Ailynn had come to an agreement. A grouping . . . it had never been done.

And had it been anyone other than Andrej Koscuisko, Erish couldn't imagine even entertaining the idea for a moment.

There was activity outside the room: a senior medical man came hurrying in. With a vial of something in his hand. The staff surgeon? Or as good as, Erish guessed, not envying the man his position in light of the ferocious face the officer turned on him.

"Your Excellency. Your pardon, sir, no word, what seems—"

The officer wouldn't listen, not for a moment. "Your stores are outdated and your vixit doesn't work, when was the last time you ran an assay on these drugs? I require narcotics, and I require them now. My man Kaydence. Is in pain. And the dose I got from emergency stores, it may as well have been sterile solution, bring me vixit. Now."

The staff surgeon offered the vial he carried, in a hesitant sort of way. "I took the liberty, Cabrello said . . ."

Koscuisko snatched the vial out of the staff surgeon's hand. "And pray to the holy Mother that your stores are merely outdated, and not adulterated, if I should lose my Kaydence after all that we have been through I will not rest till I have taken reparations. In coin of my own choosing."

The officer knew what he was doing. The officer had never made a mistake in his medical practice, not in the years he had been on *Scylla*—not one that had cost life or suffering, that was to say.

No man was perfect.

That wasn't the point.

The point was that the officer was absolutely confident that what he'd given Kaydence had not been any sort of medication. The last thing Koscuisko was going to do just at this moment was hazard Kaydence's life against an overdose.

So Koscuisko was convinced.

The Domitt Prison had lost control over its pharmacy stores.

Did Koscuisko think that the staff was in on it?

Some of the staff almost had to be, by definition, but how far did the corruption extend?

The officer put the dose through.

Kaydence's body lost some of its tension.

Koscuisko stood with his head bent close over Kaydence's face, listening to Kaydence breathe as he rested his fingertips lightly against Kaydence's throat.

Finally Koscuisko straightened up, and fixed the staff surgeon—who did not look like he knew whether he was more anxious or annoyed—with a sharp querying gaze that Erish would have found very uncomfortable, had it been directed against him.

"And it was truly vixit, this time, I trust," Koscuisko stated flatly. "I am concerned about the state of this emergency stores area, Doctor."

The staff surgeon blushed. "Ah, only a senior technician, sir. Our senior physician hasn't quite reported on shift yet. If we'd only known you were coming. Sir."

But that was too clearly compromising a statement. If they'd only known Koscuisko was coming, they would have shown him into the treatment room reserved for prison staff, instead of prisoners. Where the real narcotics were. Instead of outdated or adulterated ones. Erish could decode that well enough; and if he could do it, the officer could obviously do it that much more quickly.

"We'll take a monitor back up to quarters. You do have monitors?"

The officer had clearly elected not to follow up—not now. There was Kaydence to consider. Still, the question was a little pointed, and the staff surgeon—or senior technician—scowled briefly before he smoothed his expression out.

"Yes, sir. Medical monitors available for issue at his Excellency's pleasure."

Because once Kaydence had been drugged deeply enough to deal with his pain, he was drugged deeply enough to need to be on monitor. Just in case. That meant a grouping was right out for now, Erish realized. Someone would need to sit with Kaydence. Two someones, if one of them was the officer, because the officer would be drinking.

Also Kaydence had to be a part of any grouping. It wouldn't be a true grouping without him.

So much for that idea.

"Thank you, senior technician. And I'll take the rest of this vixit with me for if I need it."

Removing restricted drugs from Infirmary?

His Excellency was a Chief Medical Officer. He knew better.

His Excellency held the Writ at the Domitt Prison, and could do anything he liked.

"According to his Excellency's good pleasure," the senior technician agreed, a little sourly.

Kaydence had the best of this, Erish decided. Kaydence was unconscious.

It would be up to the rest of them to deal with Koscuisko for the next few hours, and Erish for one was not looking forward to it.

CHAPTER TEN

Andrej Koscuisko lay on the tiled floor of the washroom singing quietly to himself and thinking about alcohol. Wodac. There had been cortac brandy, at one point; but cortac wasn't strong enough to answer to his need. It didn't matter. As long as there was enough of it, Andrej didn't really care what kind of alcohol it was.

Singing in the washroom had several advantages when a person was drunk. One of them was the classic acoustics of the tiled room, something he'd only discovered as a student at Mayon. At home, washrooms were wood and stone like the rest of the house. Wood rather dampened the reverberation of one's voice.

There were stacks of toweling and a carpet in this washroom, which had the same dampening effect, but the carpet had been rolled up and taken away. Andrej suspected that it might have become soiled, in some way, but he could not be sure.

He took a drink.

Someone had wrapped him in a blanket, because the tiling was cold and he was only half-dressed. It had been a gesture of concern, Andrej was sure; but one with an unexpected side effect. He'd rolled over onto his side facing the wall. Now he couldn't seem to get himself unrolled.

His drinking arm was free, and the bottle was half-full, so that did not present an immediate problem. It could create difficulties further down the line. Andrej could only hope that someone was keeping an eye on his wodac bottle. It would never do to run low on wodac, he could not stay as drunk as he was without a fairly steady infusion of fresh wodac, and the last thing Andrej wanted to be was not-drunk.

There were reasons.

He was certain that they were very good reasons.

He didn't even want to know what those reasons were. That was the whole point of getting drunk, after all. He couldn't have called those reasons into his mind if he'd wanted to, except that he had an idea it was something to do with—

Almost a glimmer of a thought. Andrej swallowed several mouthfuls of wodac hastily. That had been close. He had to pay attention.

Lying on his side facing the tiled washroom wall, drinking wodac and singing to himself. The odds were good that these washroom tiles had never been exposed to the saga of Dasidar and Dyraine, so it was a public service he was providing, really, cultural enrichment of naive tiles.

Dyraine was the mistress of meadowlands, she had six spinners for each weaver and four weavers for every loom in her long weaving-house by the flax-fields.

The tiles echoed pleasantly, so close to his face that he could hear the vibration in sympathy with the catalog of Dyraine's wealth. It was an interesting effect. There was a word for it, vibrato, Andrej thought, but the whole point of drinking was not to think.

He sang instead.

Six flax-fields for every spinner, six fat ewes and six times sixteen pretty lambs, and all for the looms of dark-eyed Dyraine.

Settling his head in a softer place on the floor—he'd got a corner of the blanket beneath his head at the temple, it wasn't comfortable, it annoyed him—Andrej closed his eyes and concentrated on the words to the old song. It was good to sing about Dasidar and Dyraine. It was safe. They had had misunderstandings too, but it had all come out right in the end. Well, eventually.

Each of her looms twelve spans high, and each of her looms three spans wide, no skill of any on the Lake's broad shore could be compared to the weaving-women of dark-eyed Dyraine.

H'mm.

Something was wrong.

He didn't hear the buzz of the vibration.

Maybe he'd forgotten to open his mouth?

She dyed her fine wool with the sapin-flower on the white shores of the Lake, and took the tiny currit-shell to make her lustrous purple.

No, he could hear his voice, but no vibration. What was wrong? Andrej moved his head a little to stretch his throat. Maybe he wasn't singing loudly enough. He didn't want to sing loudly, there were people he didn't want to disturb. But he was focused now on finding out. The song sounded so much more poignant, somehow, with the buzz of the vibration of his voice in the tiling. Like the background drone of the lap-lute that traditionally accompanied the singer.

Perfumed with rare Myelosin and patterned with swallows in flight, the tapestries of wide renown came from the looms in the weave-house of the dark-eyed Dyraine.

Well, there was the vibration, right enough. Andrej sang on, but twisted his body a little as he went. He was lying on his side, and one elbow lay beneath him. It was beginning to go to sleep.

Needlewomen of astounding skill put linen thread to woolen weave and woolen thread to fine spun flax to glorify the house-mistress and praise the pride and management of the dark-eyed Dyraine—

Halfway through the phrase, though, the vibration stopped. Andrej stopped and opened his eyes, scowling. What was happening, here?

He'd moved.

Were there faulty tiles here in the washroom?

That would be a discrepancy. Everything else in this fine house was perfect. The tiles in the washroom could not be allowed to destroy the overall perfection of the house.

Which one was it?

Now, he had to keep his eyes open for this, Andrej admonished himself. It was difficult, because he was having trouble focusing. He took a drink. Well. Better.

Flax shining like the stars, like the sun on summer waters, flax that shone like milk or cream, such was the flax spun for the linen that was cut and sewn into the apron with long strings that tied around the linden waist of dark-eyed Dyraine, of the weavers . . .

Four tiles up. Four tiles down. The tiles were as square as his hand was broad. And they all sang back to him as he chanted out the old story, giving him their approval by providing background music. All of them but one.

Dyraine's wicked brother-in-law, clearly.

Or maybe Dasidar's pledged sacred-wife?

Snowy flax as pure as light, shining flax like running water, flax as fair as morning bells was cut and hemmed and trimmed in braid to overlay the bird-wing arms, the fir-branch shoulders, the sweet-apple bosom of dark-eyed Dyraine.

Second tile from the floor. Just by his nose. Defective.

It would have to be replaced.

It seemed a little out of true, as well, not quite as much in line with the others. Perhaps it could be set right, and then it would not be the brother-in-law or the pledged sacred-wife at all, but could represent Sarce of the mountains instead.

That was a much more sympathetic role.

The tile would thank him for setting it right, for saving it from the eternity of hatred and contempt that was the self-elected destiny of Dyraine's spiteful brother-in-law and Dasidar's uncharitable pledged sacred-wife. No tile in its right mind would prefer to be Kotsuda or Hoyfragen when it could be Sarce of the mountains.

Andrej tapped at the corner of the tile that was out of true with the mouth of the bottle of wodac, pausing thoughtfully to refresh himself as he did so. It was a thick bottle. He tended to break bottles, when he was drunk. His people did their best to give him his drink in a stout flask.

He wasn't doing this right.

The corner wouldn't be tapped down to true.

The tapping only jarred the other corners out of true as well, cracking a thin outline in the tiled wall.

Oh, how aggravating.

All right, if that was the way of it, the tile would simply have to go, and make way for some more worthy tile. A tile that would appreciate its place and understand its role in the greater scheme of the washroom wall. The wife of the wicked brother-in-law, who refused to sleep in the bed furnished with unseamed linen for as long as Dyraine was in exile . . .

Scratching at the tile with impatient fingers, Andrej concentrated on prying the wretched villain out of the wall. He had never liked the wicked brother-in-law, not even at the wedding when he'd brought the golden skeps with their heavy hives of pure black honey from the blooms of each of the four mountain berries. Never. The brother-in-law had only gotten what he deserved, and not enough of it.

The tile came away from the wall and clattered softly to the floor.

Andrej saw what the problem had been immediately.

It hadn't been the tile's fault at all.

There was a scrap of cloth there, between the tile-bed and the wall, dampening the vibration, muffling the sound.

Seized with a sudden spasm of keen remorse, Andrej picked up the poor scorned tile from the floor and kissed it for an apology. Poor Elko. It hadn't been Elko's fault.

He'd had no choice but to take the lambs, since that wretched Simar was his mother's brother's daughter. Oh, how remorseful he had been, and how sweetly Dyraine had forgiven him, and how nobly Dasidar had requited the tender impulse that had led him to hide the one rimeno yowe. It was too poignant.

Andrej wept, and pulled the bit of cloth away so that the tile could be restored to its proper place. Oh, only one, only one little rimeno yowe, but all that Dyraine had been left with to comfort her—no, it was too much.

Pieces of the wall came with the cloth tag.

Pulling something behind it.

Someone had come in to comfort him in his grief; or had they been there all along? Someone was here now, one way or the other. Maybe they didn't know about Elko. There was more than one of them; they moved him over onto his back, away from the wall, but Andrej kept a firm grip on the bit of cloth.

Lying on his back was a mistake.

The pain in his stomach was astonishing.

Someone offered him the bottle of wodac, but just for once Andrej wasn't interested.

Rolling onto his side again away from the wall, Andrej curled his knees to his belly in a ferocious spasm of retching, clutching the cloth tag and the packet that had come out of the wall with it in his hand.

Oh, he was drunk, and it would be hours before he could see straight, and hours longer still before he would want to.

But that was what happened when a man got drunk.

Oddly enough it never seemed to stop him.

⊕ ⊕ ⊕

Now it was morning come.

Ailynn went as softly as she could with a chilled cloth for the officer's head, wondering how he managed to sit up at table. She'd tended her share of drunks at the service house; she'd even been drunk herself, once of a time.

And what she remembered most particularly was that she hadn't been able to tolerate so much as the smell of food for at least three days after. What the officer had been last night had not been drunk: he had been right stupefied. And still wanted his rhyti, in the morning; or if he didn't want it, he still asked for it, and drank it when it came.

Chief Samons had brought medication from the officer's kit that seemed to help. Koscuisko's people knew how to manage Koscuisko drunk and then hung over; it was a hint, to her, that it had happened before upon occasion. It was perfectly true that the officer drank every night. But nothing like this. She could not have come to know his body as well as she had, otherwise. Koscuisko drank, but he didn't come to her drunk; or not in any way that she could recognize as interfering with his concentration or impairing bodily function. She was in a position to know.

"I woke up with a wad of cloth in my hand," the officer said to Chief Samons, with a grateful glance at Ailynn in return for the chilled compress. "What on earth was I up to? I am afraid to ask."

A good question. Chief Samons smiled not so much in mockery as in chagrined recognition of the situation Koscuisko found himself in. "Singing in the bathroom, sir. One of the tiles seems to have offended you. You pulled this out of the wall with it."

The wad of cloth. Or something wrapped in cloth. What had it been doing in the wall? Chief Samons set it down in front of the officer, and Cook came in with a glass and a tray. Flat unseasoned crackers. What was in the glass was anyone's guess.

Koscuisko nodded his thanks politely, sniffing at the contents with an expression of hesitation and doubt. Seeming to take his courage into his hands, Koscuisko drank from the glass; hesitantly at first, then with renewed confidence.

"What. Is this?" Koscuisko asked the cook, who had hung back waiting for a response. And grinned.

"As it please the officer. I'm Nurail. If anyone knows about body-wrack, it's Nurail, sir. Or so they tell me."

Hangover remedy. Nurail folklore held that cooks were magicians second only to weavers in their occult powers. Koscuisko was staring at the empty glass in awe.

"Go to the school at Mayon when you can, and your future is made," Koscuisko said. "From the pockets of grateful students, if not from medical research. You are a phenomenon. And I am in your debt for this exceedingly."

The cook made a small bow of gracious acceptance, still grinning, and went back to the kitchen while the officer tipped the glass back to get at the last drops of the potion.

"I am a new man," the officer said. "I am reborn. I am renewed. I am—going to eat a cracker. Ailynn, if you would, open, here. But Chief. Kaydence, how does he go?"

It was that short a moment between the opening of a window out of the house of Koscuisko's pain and the flying wide of the great doors to re-admit the anguish that had set the officer on his drunk in the first place.

"He's been up to have a drink of water and wash his hands. He made it back to his bed just in time. Sleeping off the meds, sir, no apparent complications."

Not in pain, that was to say. Ailynn pricked open the knot of cloth that secured the outer layer of the wad, concentrating on her task as Koscuisko mused aloud.

"The hell of it is. I cannot swear. That I didn't mean. To hurt him."

It was difficult for the officer to come out with the damning self-accusation. Ailynn smoothed the cover layer of fabric flat on the table's surface. It was none of her business.

"That's to work out with Kaydence, sir." Chief Samons wasn't offering much reassurance. But she wasn't blaming. She was right, after all; whatever had happened, it was between Koscuisko and his man. That was the tally of it.

"Ailynn, what have you got?" the officer asked in wonder. Distracted from his private pain. There was to be nothing he could do about that until he could speak to Kaydence.

Ailynn folded back the protective layers of cloth to reveal the secret that had been hidden behind the tile in the washroom. A book. Sixteen, twenty-four leaves of paper, not much more than the size of her hand, and rolled back upon itself twice to make a compact cylinder. A book.

Ailynn stared at it, in horror of what it might reveal.

The officer laid tableware down on either side to hold the edges flat. It hadn't been in the wall for all that very long. It couldn't have been. The Domitt Prison was less than a year old, Standard. The paper was as crisp and square-edged as it had probably been when the book went into the wall. But it hadn't been very good quality paper to start out with.

"Standard script," Chief Samons noted, looking over the officer's shoulder. "But I'm not sure I can make any sense of it."

Ailynn could.

Standard script, but it was a Nurail dialect.

The words spoke all too clearly to her Nurail heart.

"Ailynn?"

The officer had noticed a change in her expression; or the officer had guessed.

"'My name is Morse Wab, from the port at Cluse. My mother's people hold the Time-smoothed Stones.'" Ailynn read the cramped script off in dread of each next sentence, translating as she went. "'In order that the weave of our suffering should not be lost. This record I have made. Look for others, we are all dead men.'"

She didn't want to read any more.

But she was the only person here who could read it.

"This prison was built by Nurail work-crews." The officer's tone of voice was neutral. Careful. "I remember Belan told me so—"

"Slave labor," Ailynn interrupted, in terror of her own temerity. Dread of the document's secrets outweighed her natural sense of self-preservation. "Sir, it should be kept close. At least until you know what it says."

Nobody was surprised at the suggestion. Ailynn blushed, suddenly, and sat down.

"There are, how many pages here? Ailynn. Let me to know what the document says. I need for you to translate it, and write it down for me, but do not under any circumstances set the document down and go away. I will set Toska to watch at your back, to see that what you do keeps secret still."

She'd been afraid of that.

There were stories, fragments of stories, rumors, pieces of horrible suggestions whispered in the night . . . some of them probably real. Some just imagined.

Yet if the officer had not had questions of his own already about what had happened here, would he be as anxious as he seemed to know what this dead Morse Wab had to tell him?

"According to his Excellency's good pleasure."

Of course.

Koscuisko put his hand out to her shoulder, in apparent sympathy with her feelings for the task that he had set her to.

Took up a handful of the crackers, and rose to go complete his morning grooming and set out to work.

So then would she.

She didn't want to know what Wab had seen, but the dead had a right to be heard out.

Kaydence's sleep-shift wasn't scheduled to end before first-shift, and here it was only a few eights into fourth; but he was awake and rested, looking for something to do.

He was excused from exercise period because the officer had said he was to rest for at least three days.

He was excused from having to spend much time on his uniform, as they all were. The housekeepers that the Domitt Prison administration had installed here did laundry, linen, pressing, and a very tidy job they did, too—every pleat perfect, razor sharp, crisp as anything. He tried not to wonder whether prison labor was responsible.

Being excused from exercise period, and not having boot-stockings to mend or boot-leather to dress, Kaydence Psimas was at loose ends; but he knew what to do about that. If he was at loose ends, there were plenty of other people here strung taut as a reverb string. The best thing to do with his extra time was go and donate it to someone with use for it: so Kaydence went to find who had the night-watch duty with the officer, to send him to supper and early to bed.

The officer was below in his office.

Erish stood in the dim corridor outside the door to Koscuisko's office. Erish was weary; they all were, because the longer they stayed here in the Domitt Prison, the less sleep anyone got for dreaming. Erish was tired.

And Kaydence hadn't had a chance to speak to the officer since he'd disgraced himself, two days gone by now, trying to step into Joslire's place—and failing to do what Joslire could have done.

He hadn't quite understood how deep their loss was.

Part of him was terrified of Koscuisko, as well.

Frightened of the officer all of them were, at least in a sense; it couldn't be helped. A man who was capable of what Koscuisko could do was a force to be feared, quite apart from the pain that he had at command. Frightened of the officer: but trusting him, as well.

One of the things that happened to bond-involuntaries was that the power their officer had over their lives made them unusually vulnerable to their officers. Now Kaydence realized how much of his self-worth he'd placed in Koscuisko's hands, serene and confident that Koscuisko would handle his sense of self-definition as gently as possible.

He wished more than anything he hadn't said what he thought he remembered saying. He wasn't going to ask. He could remember the words in his mind all too clearly: *if you want to hurt me, it's up to you, but at least let me know you take pleasure from it. That way I know that it means something to you.*

Passion was extreme, and extremes were dangerous, but he couldn't stay out of Koscuisko's way forever. And he didn't want to.

Coming up on Erish in the corridor, Kaydence gestured with his head for Erish to leave. Erish looked a little skeptical; Kaydence nodded, to reassure Erish that he meant to relieve him. Once Erish was sure that it was what Kaydence wanted, he didn't hesitate longer. Sensible man, Erish. It was one of the many reasons Kaydence liked him.

The officer was at his desk within, concentrating on the document he'd pulled from the wall together with the prose-scan Ailynn had prepared. Kaydence slid smoothly into his post and let his mind blank, standing content on watch.

There was no sound except for the hushed murmur of the ventilators, the subtle sounds of the beverager on the other side of the door talking to itself, the rustling of papers, the turning of pages. For a long time.

Then the officer raised his voice and called for his Security.

"Erish. I want you to go and fetch Kaydence for me."

From the sound of it, Koscuisko was speaking as he moved, rising from his desk—to fetch a flask of rhyti from the beverager, perhaps. Kaydence stepped into the doorway, making his salute, glad of the moment to steel himself before he was to look upon the face of his officer.

"Here, sir." He heard only a little of his own discomfort in his voice. He wondered how much more Koscuisko was reading; the officer could do that. Joslire had said that Andrej Koscuisko smelled what you were thinking. "In what way. Can I render assistance. Sir."

No, he was still calling Koscuisko "sir" rather than the more oblique "the officer," and he had clearly heard himself refer to one Kaydence Psimas in the first person. As "I," not as "this troop." Frightened of Koscuisko he might be; humiliated over what he might have said to Koscuisko in the torture-room. But in some basic way nothing had changed. He still trusted the officer.

So could he get Koscuisko to believe that?

Koscuisko blushed, staring at Kaydence with an expression of surprise.

"Oh, Kaydence." It was a cry full of grief and guilt, and yet it was muted. Koscuisko had already convinced himself that there was nothing he could say to make things right between them: that was so like the officer. "I cannot say how ashamed I am, to have caused you to suffer. And at the same time I need information. I want you to try to find some of these Nurail for me."

Kaydence couldn't think about it; his mind shied away from the memory every time. He knew what his governor could be like. He started forward with a confidence he did not feel; pausing at the beverager to draw a flask of rhyti for Koscuisko, as sweet and milky as Koscuisko liked.

"No man as full of such good drugs as I got could possibly complain, sir. On a buzz for three days still. Can't be had for money." The cheerful cover-up sounded almost natural to Kaydence. Almost like normal. "With respect, your Excellency. Which Nurail?"

Koscuisko looked at him for a moment longer yet, as though suspicious that his blithe demeanor masked residual pain—which in a sense it did. But that was Kaydence's business. And as long as Koscuisko believed that Kaydence suffered no physical distress, Koscuisko would leave it that way, out of respect for Kaydence's privacy.

"There is first a person called Shopes Ban whom I wish to see in the morning, if he can be located. But then the man who has written this narrative, this Morse Wab. I want to know what happened to him, and to the people he calls out by name. Something is not right here, Kaydence, we all know it, and yet I cannot yet grasp how wrong it may be."

The narrative would certainly so indicate. Kaydence had helped Ailynn with parsing her translation out, so he had read the translation—in a sense.

Allegations of murder by overwork and underfeeding and neglect were serious even by the Judicial standard. Prisoners could expect to suffer privation, without people like the officer to insist on their welfare. But prisoners were not supposed to be put to death prior to the processing of specific charges; let alone by torture.

Offering the rhyti to his officer with a bow, Kaydence went past Koscuisko where he stood to sit at the com-access on the officer's desk-table. It felt very odd to be sitting in the officer's chair. But the sense of being out of place faded fast as Kaydence concentrated on his task.

Shopes Ban was first; no difficulty. Kaydence tagged the officer's referral for the morning and went on.

Morse Wab was a Nurail name, and Ailynn had given it translated flat without any hints about its Standard spelling. He didn't need to have worried, though; he found his man within moments.

Morse Wab was in the system, on remand.

According to the prison records, Morse Wab had arrived at the prison six months ago; and was still here, prisoner pending development of Charges. Assigned to a work-crew on the land reclamation project.

"Not dead?" the officer asked, surprised, looking over Kaydence's shoulder. Kaydence surfaced out of his concentration.

"Not according to this, sir." Kaydence pointed out the status blocks confidently. "In pretty good health, actually. On the work-detail."

"Because a person has to be fit to do heavy labor, yes, of course," Koscuisko agreed, thoughtfully.

Koscuisko standing at his shoulder; Koscuisko at his back. There was a token Kaydence wanted; suddenly he wanted it more than anything. And he could not ask. "The other names, sir?"

"Here, I have a list for myself made. What status can you find for them?"

It was a simple thing with ties as deeply braided into the fabric of Koscuisko's being and ancestry as the rest of his genetic structure was. Time-honored. Traditional. Something that belonged to a quite different sort of relationship than that in which the Fleet had bound them over to Andrej Koscuisko. The words were not very different in plain Standard: Fleet saw officer and bond-slave; Koscuisko thought of it as master and man, in a context in which both terms meant something quite particular to him.

"Skein in braid, sir. There's Mannie Bellose. Also alive. Also on work-crew."

Kaydence read the names off from Koscuisko's list, keying as he went. Several names. The spelling betrayed them on some, the prison would yield no record. But they got good hits on more than half of them, and all of the hits they got were listed as on the prison rolls and working.

"What is a man to make of it?" Koscuisko mused, leaning forward over Kaydence's shoulder. Kaydence tried hard not to tense.

"Four possibilities, sir. On the off chance that the officer was asking."

"H'mm." Koscuisko was focused on the stats Kaydence had called up for him, his attention apparently absorbed by the problem. "I will speculate, and you will correct me in my recitation, Kay."

Koscuisko would only touch people at all if he liked them. Bond-involuntaries only if he trusted them to interpret the intimacy as affection, not as any of the other things it could be to a bond-involuntary—starting with casual violation of personal space, and ending all too often in physical bullying or demands for sexual services.

Did Koscuisko trust him still?

"One, that the name is wrong, simply like enough to another. But you have checked twice eight names, Kaydence, and here are ten replies. And no prisoner so named is found here dead."

Kaydence nodded. Happy to be working on developing this problem with the officer, one on one, and on an equal footing. Miserable with longing for a sign.

"Two, that these living prisoners simply share the name by coincidence. They're different people. But we should see multiple hits on single names if that happened. One dead, one living."

"Three," Koscuisko said eagerly, as though enjoying their shared understanding of the problem. "They are the named prisoners. Morse Wab, or someone representing himself as Morse Wab, simply lied, to cause embarrassment to the prison. There are speak-sera. A man could ask."

Especially his Excellency could ask. Only his Excellency could lawfully ask, with a speak-serum. Koscuisko held the Writ.

"Or there have been prisoners who have died without a record made, and the question of how they died and why it was not recorded is something the officer will want to investigate."

Those were the four ideas Kaydence had in mind, at any rate.

After a moment Koscuisko decided. "Order me up these people, Kaydence, we need not tell anyone why we wish to speak to them. Let the Administration believe they were named in Inquiry as collaterals. We cannot ignore the narrative. But it will be prudent to keep quiet about it."

Because there were only two out of those four ideas that seemed likely to be true; and if Morse Wab had not been lying, it meant that the Administration was committing systematic murder in full knowledge that its conduct was criminal. And under a Bench authorization, at that.

"Directly. Your Excellency."

He knew what to do.

But as he moved to invoke the prisoner calls, Koscuisko leaned over Kaydence's shoulder to peer at the com-access, putting his hand to the back of Kaydence's neck so that his thumb lay at the base of Kaydence's skull and his fingers rested naturally and comfortably around the side of Kaydence's throat.

"How could such a thing be managed?" Koscuisko seemed to be talking to himself, puzzling out a problem. "But there is money to be made, and the staff is Pyana. I do not know what to think of it. I tremble, that it could go further than this prison alone."

The muscles of Kaydence's neck, the muscles of his shoulders, the muscles of his upper back surrendered up their tension gratefully at the touch of Koscuisko's hand. The officer was not going to stand off from him. He was still Andrej Koscuisko's man, though he was a bond-involuntary.

Relief and gratitude betrayed Kaydence to himself. He had always suffered the embarrassment of having a sentimental nature. Kaydence caught his breath and bowed his head; Koscuisko, startled, started to move, started to take his hand away. Kaydence didn't want Koscuisko to take his hand away. He couldn't ask. He couldn't explain. Had he been able to explain, he wasn't sure but that misplaced pride might have prevented him from speaking anyway.

Kaydence raised his right hand to cover Koscuisko's hand instead and hold it to him, claiming his status without words in terms Koscuisko himself had taught him meaning to.

Turning the chair on its seat-pivot, Koscuisko folded his arms around Kaydence where he sat, and held him close. Kaydence wept. There was no way in which to make Koscuisko understand. The thing about Andrej Koscuisko was that it had never been necessary for him to understand in order to be able to understand, nonsensical as that was.

After a while Koscuisko offered Kaydence his white-square.

Kaydence grinned, though his eyes ached. It was a joke of sorts. Chief Samons had put him on extra duty for being out of uniform more often than any of Koscuisko's other Bonds. Boot-stockings not mended. A bit of seam come undone and not sewn back. A frayed under-collar not made right. Failure to carry a clean white-square at all times.

He had a perfectly good white-square in his blouse-plaquet.

He'd use Koscuisko's.

Tradition.

"Pyana, sir?" Kaydence asked, just to show that he'd been listening.

Koscuisko seemed to shrug, fractionally, uncomfortably. "Nurail are to Pyana as Sarvaw have been to Dolgorukij, which is to say cattle. Also, like Dolgorukij and Sarvaw, Pyana and Nurail are more alike than not so, deny it though they will."

Ethnicity and prejudice, then. Of course. Koscuisko spoke on. "In the history of the Dolgorukij Combine the most savage atrocities have been most constantly committed against precisely those people who are most like Aznir Dolgorukij. I do not mention Chuvishka Kospodar, Kaydence. But he was my great-great-grandfather."

Well, if the officer said so. "His Excellency would be interested in a staff profile, then." In order to be able to judge with more precision the extent to which Pyana held the majority of the influential positions in the prison. Affecting their potential willingness to commit murder in the full expectation of getting away with it, accordingly.

"Forgive me, Kaydence."

Kaydence froze, electrified. He had never thought to hear—he had never wanted to hear—but Koscuisko continued speaking in a quiet but utterly determined tone of voice, not waiting for an answer. Not expecting one.

"I never thought to sink to such a thing, not even with everything else that I have done. And I am so ashamed, but my shame cannot answer to your suffering."

He couldn't let Koscuisko talk like this.

He couldn't handle it.

"The officer is who the officer is." *You are what you are, your Excellency. There is no getting around it for anybody.* "It's just something we all have to deal with. Together. Sir."

This was too true to allow for argument or exploration.

The officer knew better.

Had the officer forgiven him for being alive, while Joslire was dead? He hadn't realized he'd even been worried about it.

Now he could put the whole thing out of his mind and concentrate on pulling a report on prison staff for Koscuisko's use and analysis.

Robis Darmon's world coalesced gradually around him from a dark stifling mist of aching agony into a small cold stinking torture-cell in the Domitt Prison, and he groaned aloud to realize that he was not dead yet. Not though he longed to be. Not though he waited for it. Not though his death was the salvation of those whose names he might have been able to remember once upon a time, lost now to pain and dread.

He was terrified of the sight and sound and smell of the torturer, who brought new pain with every breath.

His torturer, who tipped the cold sharp rim of a glass of water against his lower lip, lightly enough that Darmon did not recoil from the pressure against the broken skin but drank instead. His torturer was good to him, careful to see that he lacked for nothing that would preserve his life for more pain.

Still something seemed a little unusual.

He didn't seem to hurt.

His body ached, yes, and his flesh was sore, but where was the huge sharp transcendent all-consuming agony that had been his constant companion now forever?

He remembered this.

He could remember a life without pain, without physical pain, a world in which agony of spirit had been his only burden, grief for his dead, fear for the living, rage against the wrong that sought to grind them all into the mud and make good citizens of them. Yes. He could remember.

There was that glass again, and Darmon drank. The fluid caught a bit going down; his throat was rough. Screaming would do that.

"Talk to me," the torturer said, softly. "Your Shopes Ban, the one whose fate so troubles you. Describe to me this man, if you would, please."

Drugged.

That was what it was.

Drugged to put away his pain, but if the torturer was using drugs against him he was for it.

The desperation was swathed in cotton-wool, muffled in a resistance field; only dimly reverberating through his mind.

They had to have been powerful drugs.

"Thinking."

Because the torturer would know that he could hear, and speak. Shopes, poor Ceelie, what had been done to him? Of all the atrocities he'd seen since he had come to the Domitt Prison, it was this unknown horror that preyed most upon his mind. There was a point to be made. Somewhere.

"Middling tall for a Nurail, about your height, about. Dark in his features. Scar on his arm, from the fire, don't know how old he was. Couldn't have been above the age of twenty-five years, Standard."

"No, that won't do." Darmon felt a moment's panic; but the tone of the torturer's voice was light and humorous. And he was drugged. "That won't do at all. I have Shopes Ban outside this room right now, and he looks nothing like the man you have described. You simply must do better than that, for me."

This was a joke. It had to be. Yet if it wasn't . . . "Ask him about me, then. You will find. The man he knows is different. Let's bet."

"What do you say?" The torturer sounded genuinely startled. Darmon wanted to laugh.

"There are more than one of us. Shopes Bans. Marne Cittropses. None of us either Ban or Cittrops. Couldn't be. Not for months now."

There was a warmth at the wall beside him, and it made him uneasy. A sound of shifting fabric; the torturer sitting down on the floor beside him. Why?

"Explain," the torturer suggested. And tipped the tumbler to let Darmon drink, once more. Darmon hated himself for being so grateful for a swallow of cool water: but hating himself did not change the fact of his gratitude, or its shocking depth. "What is your experience of this place, that you should say such a thing?"

It had been so long.

He had suffered, since.

And still the anguished outrage that he'd felt when he had realized that Nurail were to be burned before they were so much as dead rose up into his throat and nearly choked him.

If Koscuisko wanted to hear, he could tell things that would make Koscuisko heartily sorry that he had asked.

"There were people in the cart. Fallen on the way. Young Haps, dragged. By heels. Not dead. They took him to the furnace—"

He started at the beginning, and went through the middle to the end, when he had been taken out of work-crew to the torture. It took a long time. Every so often the pain began to build within his shattered body, from his savaged joints, his lacerated skin, his broken hands and feet. Every so often the torturer pressed him in his recitation and fed him a drink of water. And more drugs, he suspected, because the pain would fade away till he could almost forget he even had a body.

Years.

Centuries.

Centuries upon centuries, but Darmon kept at it, trying to remember, trying to make sure each man who had been drowned screaming in the water at the bottom of the ditch would be numbered, every man who had been beaten with shockrods until he bled from the eyes and ears and nose would be remembered, every man who had been worked and worked and worked—and tossed into the grillwork of the gravel-crusher, or taken living or dead to the furnaces, when he could no longer work—was named and tallied up.

The names of the dead. The names of the overseers. The names of the guards. The names of the dogs that had been set on exhausted prisoners to provide some amusement for their captors once they could no longer shovel earth.

And ever and always, the soft clear voice of his torturer, asking questions, probing for details, calling out the threads that formed the braid that was the Domitt Prison. Ever and always, the furnaces, smoking in the background of his mind.

Why did Koscuisko want to know?

Why should he care?

Finally he was finished, Koscuisko was done with questions at last, giving him to drink of cool sweet water in grave silence. And there was no pain. Nothing like the pain that there had been. Nothing like the pain that there would be, once the torturer tired of this game, whatever it was, whyever he was playing it.

Darmon drank the water and thought hard.

"You understand, such evidence must be tested before it can be freely relied upon," the torturer said. "I have in mind a speak-serum, because you are very close to dead here and now, did you but know it. I will a dose of wake-keeper administer, excuse me for one moment to fetch it."

To confirm evidence was all very well, though Koscuisko had not confirmed any previously offered evidence that way. If Koscuisko had obtained evidence. Perhaps he hadn't. Darmon really didn't know, any more, what he might have said; and what managed to conceal.

One thing he had decided, though, during the long day's telling of his story. It was not the painease that decided him. It was because Koscuisko had heard the long list of the dead, and taken it into Evidence. Darmon had lived to the end of the Domitt Prison in at least that sense, howsoever small. He had survived for long enough to bear witness.

Longer than this he had no wish to live. So long as he could only get one final thing out of the way, before he died—

He remembered the first day, it had been two hundred years ago. Koscuisko had a book. Koscuisko was collecting weaves.

Darmon heard the torturer put the glass down, shifting to get up. And had sat beside him on the floor all of this time, leaning up against the wall, comforting him with the warmth of the proximity of another human body. Or a torturer's body. It had still been a comfort, in the cold of the cell.

"One thing the more, torturer," Darmon said.

Koscuisko stilled beside him. "You have something else to say about my parents, and how closely it was that they were related?" Koscuisko replied, gently, so that Darmon knew that he was listening. Darmon thought about smiling. But it would take too much energy to smile.

"If thy mother had but known. How much she could have saved us all, by hanging herself." But Koscuisko already knew that. "It's something I only imagined. I think I may have heard a weaver, once. Take out your book and write it down. If I can remember the weaver said it was the Shallow Draft."

The torturer had dealt honestly with him, through all the obscenity of his craft. Had not forced the weave from him in all this time, that Darmon could remember. Had not asked him any questions about—

"Are you sure of what you do?" Koscuisko asked, quietly.

"There's no telling. The weaver may have gotten the threads mismatched. But it was a persuasive weave. I can remember it almost as well as if it were my own."

Blame it on a weaver. That would do nicely. Scum of the earth; with power that transcended it. It was a weaver who had first coded the song in the pattern of a piece of cloth, a way of writing before there was writing among the Nurail.

All a man could properly sing was his mother's weave, unless he was a weaver. A weaver could sing any weave; and make new weaves when the occasion warranted. Stricken with the calling from on high, destroyed and exalted at once; with the power to communicate any passion they felt to any Nurail within hearing distance, but powerless to control that communication—

Oh, had there been weavers here, to die in the Domitt Prison?

Koscuisko's book was like a weaver, then, if it held a store of weaves. That made the torturer a weave-keeper, and the thought was as good a joke as Darmon could imagine. Weavers were depraved, though it was not their fault; it resulted from the divine disaster that marked them as separate and apart, outside the secure ward of decency.

And weave-keepers, having weavers in their charge, participated only in the degradation; and had no share of the respect a man could not but grant the force within a weaver. Oh, sympathy, yes, that. Koscuisko a weave-keeper . . .

"Listen as the weaver sang it. It was about the clinker-built hull and the high curved prow of the ship that carried the daughter of the house over the chain and across the harbor, up the stream in summer muddy, past the shallows bottom-scraping to bring the wrath of the hill-people to take vengeance on Pyana for the burning of the houses down around her family as they slept."

The Shallow Draft.

There was something of the weaver to Koscuisko, in a sense. He too was struck down, destroyed, and even in an obscene way exalted in the conduct of his craft. There was no accounting for all of the ways in which men walked in the world. Nor any understanding of what reason there might be for such a thing.

Waking and sleeping, dreaming and dozing, Robis Darmon sang his mother's weave, hearing from time to time the scratch of a stylus in Koscuisko's hand, the turning of a leaf of paper.

Now he had discharged his duty to the living, as well as to the dead.

Now he could die at peace with himself.

"Let the Record show twelve units of resinglas in solution for the purposes of confirming evidence received."

The torturer's voice was far, far away, and receding further moment by moment. "Three units of vondilong per body weight used for the purposes of wake-keeping for the duration. Adjusted downward in order to take the conservative approach, in allowing for dehydration."

It was only a whisper, now, drowned beneath the rising sound of the water cascading over Branner's Falls. And his wife dimly glimpsed just on the threshold of the family meeting-hall, with the child on her hip, his son, his Chonniskot. His daughters chasing around the corner of the building, the voice of the youngest brisk as a meadow-bird.

The sound of the falls was soothing in his ears.

He rested; and the trial of his life ended at last.

CHAPTER ELEVEN

"How can you tell me that War-leader Robis Darmon is dead?"

Belan had seen Administrator Geltoi angry, but seldom so angry as this. He cringed in his heart for Koscuisko's sake, but the officer did not seem to feel the force of Geltoi's wrath.

Koscuisko stood politely in a relaxed position of attention-wait in front of the Administrator's desk. Somewhat closer than he had stood the first time he'd come into this office, Belan noted. As though there was more intimacy between them now . . . or less strict a gradient of rank to separate them.

"I am heartily sorry to have to report so distressing a reflection on my ability," Koscuisko replied smoothly. Too smoothly. "At the same time, Administrator. And I must point this out, at risk of seeming to excuse myself. It would not have come so soon had the drug not failed me."

Geltoi had hoped for great things from the testimony of War-leader Robis Darmon. Koscuisko had done such wonders with other, less promising prisoners. And for Koscuisko to come to report that the war-leader had revealed so little actionable information before he died was a blow. Belan didn't see what the failure of a drug could possibly have to do with it.

Geltoi sat back down, having half-risen from his chair in shock at Koscuisko's news. "Doctor. You are responsible for knowing your business. If the drug failed isn't that the same as to say you failed? To exercise professional judgment in the selection of application of specialized tools."

All in all, Geltoi was more visibly upset than Belan could remember seeing him. It was a bad sign. Evidence from the war-leader was to have been of special value to Geltoi, since it would emphasize how deeply Chilleau Judiciary was obliged to the Domitt Prison for the resource. But it wasn't as though Geltoi had needed the additional leverage. Surely.

"Precisely so, Administrator Geltoi," Koscuisko agreed easily, with no hint of resentment. "The exercise of my professional judgment. The drug should have served as a wake-keeper, critical to that stage of the interrogation. It did not have the requisite effect, not even at a doubled dose. This is a troubling indication of potential adulteration of pharmacy stores, Administrator."

Geltoi had been so angry when Belan told him of Koscuisko's words over the Lerriback confusion that Belan had half-expected him to call for an immediate reassignment. Belan was a little sorry for Koscuisko. He was probably accustomed to having his own way in everything— like a Pyana. When in the presence of a Pyana, however, Koscuisko was obviously outclassed.

"How so?"

Those two words were loaded with all the imperfectly suppressed outrage that Geltoi could bring to bear on a man. And yet Koscuisko did not stagger back from the force of Geltoi's contempt.

"These were stores I brought from the Domitt Prison's Infirmary, Administrator. When I brought my man Kaydence in. Based on the effect it had on my prisoner—lack of effect, perhaps, I should say rather—I can only conclude that the drug had been adulterated, but who would expect to have to do an assay on restricted stores here in the very heart of your Administration?"

They'd gotten off easy at the time, Belan remembered. Koscuisko hadn't said anything about stores. Belan had just assumed that the shift supervisor had been on top of things. Now it seemed that Koscuisko had not been as carefully watched in Infirmary as would have been prudent.

"Really, Doctor. Grasping at straws. As though a man of your caliber relies on drugs to effect his persuasion."

Geltoi was trying to deflect the force of Koscuisko's point back onto the original problem, that of the war-leader's death.

It wasn't working.

"A man should be able to rely upon his tools. And it is my responsibility, after all. Given the circumstances I must either report myself as incompetent or conduct an Infirmary audit immediately. And I am not incompetent. I know my job."

Well, Belan told himself, Geltoi had walked into that one. He'd as much as told Koscuisko that he was incompetent. That had more or less forced Koscuisko to make the claim of adulterated drugs in order to defend himself against a bad report. Geltoi should rather have left the point alone.

"I hardly think that now is the appropriate time for such an audit, Koscuisko—"

Geltoi had seen the trap he'd laid for himself, but it was too late. Koscuisko merely insisted, with polite deference, on what it was Koscuisko's lawful right to demand on whim.

"Forgive me for saying so, Administrator Geltoi, but I cannot agree. I must know whether the stores in Infirmary are reliable. Only in this way can I protect myself from a recurrence of this shocking incident. To have lost so important a prisoner to death by systemic shock, because the wake-keeper was adulterated—it cannot be tolerated."

Koscuisko had a right to defend himself against accusations of incompetence, too.

Why hadn't Geltoi seen this coming?

"Very well." The Administrator had no real choice but to concede. And they all knew it. "You may conduct your audit two days after tomorrow. I'll send an escort for you."

Kitchen audit. And now an Infirmary audit. As far as Belan knew, Geltoi hadn't heard anything back from Koscuisko on the kitchen audit yet. On the other hand, Koscuisko had been busy.

"Thank you, sir. And good-greeting, Administrator Geltoi, Assistant Administrator Belan."

Day after tomorrow . . . so that Geltoi would have time to ensure that stores were rotated and replaced. A day in which to cover for themselves. If Koscuisko had meant to make trouble, he would surely have insisted on going now, and there would have been a scandal. Why had Koscuisko agreed to the delay?

In order to give Geltoi time to make the shortfalls good?

What sense did that make?

Koscuisko would find no serious irregularity in his Infirmary audit. Geltoi would see to that. Or, rather, Belan would see to that, on Geltoi's instruction. That meant Koscuisko's story about losing the prisoner to an adulterated drug would seem the flimsiest of excuses: Geltoi would probably enjoy making that point with him, too.

"As you say, Doctor Koscuisko. Good-greeting."

Of course Koscuisko could always claim convincingly that the medication he had taken was one bad lot in an otherwise unremarkable stores inventory, and cover up his error that way.

It hadn't been an error.

They all knew that very well—he, Administrator Geltoi, Koscuisko, all of them.

Koscuisko would come out of this looking incompetent, surely.

Except nobody could take Koscuisko as incompetent on the strength of his previous performance.

Was this some sort of a signal that Koscuisko meant to transmit thus indirectly to Chilleau Judiciary?

And if it was—could he really trust Administrator Geltoi to see what was going on, in light of how easily Koscuisko had maneuvered him into the trap just now?

Administrator Geltoi watched grimly as Koscuisko left the room, glaring at the Inquisitor's back as though to plunge daggers into it. Large ones. Long blades. Sharp points.

The glare made no perceptible impact on Andrej Koscuisko.

The door closed behind the Inquisitor, and Geltoi turned his cold furious gaze to Belan's face, as though he were to blame for the scene, having witnessed it.

"You know what must be done," Administrator Geltoi snarled. "Get cracking. There isn't much time. Spare no expense. And be sure the documentation is in order, this time."

Still smarting over what Koscuisko had had to say about the Lerriback confusion, clearly.

Not to speak of the amount of money it was going to cost to make Infirmary stores whole, after all of these months of harvesting prison stores for the black market. The drugs were there for prisoners, of course. But prisoners couldn't complain about their treatment.

Belan bowed in respectful silence and left.

He wasn't happy.

Administrator Geltoi had not come off the better in this interview. Koscuisko had handled the Administrator as easily as—as easily as if Geltoi had been Nurail, and Koscuisko Pyana.

What if he'd been wrong?

What if Koscuisko found out the things the Administrator had assured him would stay buried forever—

No.

Belan shuddered, and had to stop in the corridor, leaning up against the wall to steady himself.

They had been buried alive, he could still hear the screaming, and on late nights as the mist rose from the damp ground it was hard to avoid seeing faces in the night-fog. Nurail faces. Dead and half-rotted. Screaming in disbelief and terror forever, as they had died.

He had put his trust in Administrator Geltoi, and Administrator Geltoi knew what he was doing.

No other possibility could even be entertained.

Infirmary audit.

Yes.

If he went to see the senior staff physician now, right now, he could be well clear of the containment wall before the sun went down, and he would have nothing to fear from the tortured dead.

Mergau Noycannir could have shrieked in rage and frustration, but she had more control than that. It was just that the provocation was extreme.

Two of the prisoners were dead.

One of them useless for days to come, having bitten her own tongue clear through to avoid speaking. The First Secretary's censor might well claim it had been in response to an excess of pain, but if people bit their tongues through every time they were put to the stretcher there would be no evidence obtained from seven out of eight of the wretches.

Three prisoners, and no information.

Mergau slammed her fist down atop the open tray of doses from the Controlled List that were arrayed in the work-room, ready for her use. It wasn't fair. She was being watched too closely; this wasn't an off-site. She didn't dare spike the Levels with the First Secretary so interested in what results she might be getting, day by day. And she had lost three out of seven, two for good, and had got no useful information. Oh, information, yes, that. But nothing the Bench could use against the Langsariks.

She mastered her emotion with an effort. Her fourth prisoner was in the room with her, behind her on the work-table; and she had to maintain her superiority before him. Granted that he was probably not paying attention: there was never any telling when a prisoner might notice what, to the detriment of the exercise.

The whole difficulty lay in the fact that these people were accused on circumstantial evidence alone. The Protocols were clear. People could not be forced to incriminate themselves on the basis of circumstantial evidence; they could only be pressed to do so. If they were determined enough to withstand the maximum lawful degree of pressure, the Bench would grant them not guilty by default; and release them.

She was not allowed the efficient out, the obvious out, the one best technique for obtaining confession. The coercive classes of speak-sera were only authorized at the Advanced Levels, and she wasn't authorized to invoke the Advanced Levels against these people. Yet.

The Bench required more evidence than circumstantial before it would allow the Advanced Levels prior to receipt of a confession. She was to be expected to obtain the high-quality evidence that only a speak-serum could reliably deliver without the use of the only tools she had to obtain it reliably.

If she'd been offsite she could have cheated, gone off-Record and invoked the Eighth Level. Then she could have her confession, and after that whatever speak-sera she wanted. There were ways to invoke the Eighth Level that left no obvious visible physical evidence on Record; it had worked for her before.

She didn't dare.

There would be too many questions about the chronological gap, if she went off-Record in the middle of one of these interrogations.

Taking a deep breath, forcing herself to be calm and in control, Mergau started to sort the doses back into array on the dose-tray. They had been jarred ajumble when she'd struck it with her fist. The Controlled List, but what good did it do her? Wake-keepers were authorized, yes, but only at a very low level. Pain-maintenance drugs not at all. Nerve agents, so moderate as to be functionally useless to her need, and speak-sera restricted to the guarantee of candid speech, with no coercive aspect to them.

The doses had got mixed up.

It took some thought to get them sorted out again.

And when she had finished sorting the doses, she noticed that she'd inadvertently included an Advanced Level instrument in amongst the Intermediate Level drugs that the psycho-pharmacologist from Gatzie had selected for her use.

Nor was it just any Advanced Level instrument, it was her favorite, Andrej Koscuisko's finest contribution to the Controlled List, the one she used more than anything else. It worked on almost all classes of hominid, and in much the same way.

And if it frequently hastened the prisoner's death, what difference did that make, as long as she got the information? It was an Advanced Level instrument. Referral at the Advanced Level meant a death sentence one way or another, either execution for crimes confessed or death under torture to obtain confession in order to put the prisoner to death for crimes confessed.

And here it was, neatly replaced, in with her row of authorized and appropriate medications.

Did she dare pretend?

Advanced Level for most classes of hominid, yes; that was doubtless why it had been held out from her work-set this time. But Intermediate Level for some classes of hominid, and very effective in the Intermediate Levels at obtaining satisfactory results if a person chanced to make a small error and use it on the wrong people. Its inclusion in her work-set would not surprise her. She could easily have overlooked its sudden appearance in her work-set, in her concentration on her task.

She could make it work.

Even if the First Secretary reviewed the Record—and there was no reason to expect he would—no one need ever even notice. She had expected to use one drug. She would announce the drug she intended to use, on-Record. It would take a psycho-pharmacologist or an autopsy to surface any small mistake on her part. Mergau anticipated neither; and once she had the information . . .

She picked out the stylus with the dose and turned back to her waiting prisoner.

She would prevail.

She was not Koscuisko; but she was as good as, and all that she was doing was exactly what he must have done, to have built up such an inflated name for himself.

"Let the Record show administration of six units of tincture of quillock per body weight."

Six units would do it, all right.

Yes, that would take care of the problem once and for all.

"So we'll get an Infirmary audit out of the way, all to the good," Administrator Geltoi sneered bitterly. "And we haven't had any complaints on the kitchen audit. Still our young Koscuisko makes demands, then calls for prisoners off of work-crew, and not so much as three words in courtesy to explain why he needs thus-and-such a soul."

Well, because the prisoners currently under interrogation had named the names, Belan thought to himself. Standing quietly beside Geltoi's desk, waiting for his instructions. Geltoi was annoyed about the prisoners as much because they had to be pulled from work-crew as anything else; and the work-crews were starting to thin out a bit. The Domitt hadn't gotten a good shipment of replacements in since Koscuisko's arrival.

"What are you going to do, Administrator?"

That wasn't exactly Koscuisko's fault. Or was it? They couldn't afford any irregularities, not right under Koscuisko's nose. Captain Sinjosi Vopalar seemed as little inclined to leave administrative details to locals as Koscuisko had proved himself to be. Their Port Authority contacts were worried about questions one of Vopalar's junior officers was asking, and it was rumored that Koscuisko had put him up to it.

Maybe that was actually Koscuisko's fault, come to that. Rising from his chair, Administrator Geltoi turned his back to gaze out of the window toward Port Rudistal. "Losing money on work-detail, we can't supply the labor, not between Koscuisko and that Captain Vopalar. Losing money on victuals, the kitchen's gotten nervous and timid, insists on serving what we're issued for the duration. Losing a great bloody chunk of money just so Koscuisko can't find anything wrong in Infirmary. And he killed Robis Darmon, Merig, make no mistake about it. We could have had more evidence from him."

Which would have strengthened their hand at Chilleau Judiciary in case of any awkwardness; that was the unspoken subtext to

Administrator Geltoi's argument. Belan didn't like it. Why did Geltoi feel the need for insurance?

The Port Authority and the kitchen might be excused for suffering a failure of nerve. But Geltoi was the mastermind. Belan believed in him. If other Pyana started to feel concern, did that mean that they weren't smart for Pyana?

Or that Geltoi wasn't smart for a Pyana?

If Geltoi wasn't really in control of this—

The idea was unthinkable.

"Perhaps if you were to make complaint to Chilleau Judiciary," Belan suggested, a little diffidently.

"And why the people he wants for the work-rooms?" Geltoi ignored the question, clearly more concerned about his own issues than what Belan had to suggest. "There isn't any logic to it. What's he up to?"

They could just ask.

Belan was tempted to propose they do just that. Koscuisko had been blunt enough about whether or not Darmon's death had been attributable to a blunder on his part. Maybe all they had to do was ask—and Koscuisko would tell them.

Maybe it was important that they know.

There were voices in the fog between the wall of the Domitt Prison and its containment wall, when the fog rose. It could be clear in front of the building. It could be clear at the north of the building. The fog would still creep out of the ground on the south side of the building, at a little remove.

Right where the massive crane had been anchored in the ground to lift materials onto the fast-rising floors of the Domitt Prison.

Right where the bodies of those dead were buried, but they hadn't all been dead when they'd been buried, and the chemical accelerant the Pyana had dumped into the pit to speed decomposition ate into living flesh and burned like fire.

Belan had been there.

He had heard the screaming.

The voices didn't scream, they only hinted, teased, warned, proposing riddles that drove him half-mad. He hadn't gotten out of the building in time, last night. He'd been forced to spend the night in his office, pretending to be working diligently.

Now Geltoi turned back to the desk-table and sat down once again.

Sighing deeply. "He's really left me with no other choice, Belan." Geltoi's tone of voice was aggrieved, as though forced into some action against his better judgment. "I'd rather we had been able to work things out, but he's chosen not to bring his concerns to me before taking official action. This isn't the sort of conduct one expects from a ranking officer."

The words and phrases flowed in majestic measure. Rehearsed, almost. Maybe Geltoi *had* rehearsed. Artificial, one way or the other— all except Geltoi's undoubted frustration with how things had worked out for them.

"I can't accept a working relationship that's all take and no give, the Administration does deserve some consideration, after all. I'm asking Chilleau Judiciary to recall Andrej Koscuisko to *Scylla*. No Writ at all would be better than this one."

One hand flat to the table's surface, Geltoi waited for a response, staring at Belan. Oh. It was time for the chorus, then.

"Such an undeserved disappointment." Yes, that had been his cue; the look of irritation that had started to build in Geltoi's eyes faded into bland self-satisfied self-pity. "After you took every measure to see him comfortable and provided for. Treated him with every evidence of respect."

Shut him up on the roof, and that so effectively that as far as Belan knew Koscuisko hadn't noticed yet. Koscuisko had taken guards from the torture-block to show him the way to Infirmary. Not their fault if Koscuisko had refused to wait even as short a time as it would have taken to call down to Infirmary and let them know Koscuisko was coming.

"Thank you. Good friend. You're a great help to me, Belan." And an accomplice, in this up to his neck. That was the way to translate Pyana. Praise was only given to point out the threat. "We should be through with Koscuisko's stunts soon enough. I can be gracious. He won't get the satisfaction of provoking me into undignified reprisals."

No, Belan thought, in sudden silent rebellion. *You'll get me to make them.*

"You're a true leader, Administrator." Aloud he only recited the lines he knew were expected of him. "It's too bad Koscuisko couldn't have learned from your example."

Else Koscuisko would be butchering his prisoners and demanding adulation for his hackwork. Rather than taking a slow and methodical approach, which yielded results for almost every death on Koscuisko's hands since he'd arrived at the Domitt Prison.

Administrator Geltoi waved Belan away in dismissal, a look of pained and patient noble suffering on his face. Belan bowed and went away.

Just in time.

He had had all of Administrator Geltoi he could take for now.

What if Geltoi wasn't smart?

What if the truth about the Domitt Prison should come out, somehow, some way, despite all the Pyana cleverness that had surrounded it from the very start?

It wasn't going to happen.

Pyana were smart, and Geltoi was Pyana. Also Koscuisko was leaving. Things would be back to normal in no time.

But he'd brought a nice length of good rope to the office, just in case he was mistaken after all.

"'Multiple and egregious instances of behavior betraying a regrettable lack of delicacy and sensitivity to his position of responsibility within the structure of Judicial Inquiry,'" First Secretary Verlaine read aloud, his voice remarkably light for such a deep bass and his tone emphatically less than serious. "'—Which would be in themselves unimportant if support for the Inquisitorial function was being exercised at an acceptable level of skill and professionalism.' Oh, my. He *has* annoyed somebody."

Morning-meeting, and Verlaine was sharing the new items on his desk. Mergau was resigned. Her disgrace was temporary; and could be best managed if she showed herself to be quite unconcerned about it. Not dismissing the gravity of the situation, no. Simply serene and confident that anyone could make a mistake.

Inquisition was an imperfect science at best, and it would all be behind her soon enough. The language the Domitt Prison's Administrator had used to complain about Andrej Koscuisko was unquestionably strong; if even Koscuisko could fail, that would strengthen her point. On the other hand, Verlaine was unquestionably not very upset: that would have rather the opposite influence on the question.

"Koscuisko's Captain wants him back," Bench Specialist Vogel observed. "There's a request in. To support his medical function, not his Judicial one, since *Scylla's* duty status is still suspended. Maybe it would be just as well, but there's something that should be bothering us about all this."

The timing couldn't have been better had she planned it, Mergau congratulated herself. She could see the record-cubes in Bench Intelligence Specialist Vogel's loose-fingered grasp; autopsy or Record or both, it hardly mattered. If Andrej Koscuisko, for whose reputed skills and talent the First Secretary had such evident if undeserved admiration, could lose a prisoner before time to a bad dose—why, any failing on her part was more than adequately covered.

"Bothering us?" The First Secretary leaned back in his chair, relaxed and receptive. "Please, Bench Specialist."

"Young officer, historical behavior pattern of doing first and asking later. Only look at what he's doing. The kitchen audit was mentioned in the First Secretary's morning report."

As part of the usual summary of daily activities at the Domitt Prison. Yes. Mergau remembered it, because otherwise very little had changed in the Domitt Prison's morning report for weeks.

Vogel spoke on. "Kitchen audit is standard operating procedure. I was reading the Fleet staffing reports for Rudistal, though, they've got an officer working on admissions reconciliation. Vopalar's got a lot on her hands and no reason to detail anyone to make-work projects. I haven't asked, but I'm willing to speculate that Koscuisko's asked for a population movement analysis."

Bench intelligence specialists got into everything. Gluttons for information, no matter how inconsequential. Clearly Vogel felt called upon to come up with a story to justify the fact that he spent all of his time with his feet up on the furniture, reading laundry lists.

"Now this." Ivers picked up the thread as though she and Vogel were in the same braid. Maybe they'd rehearsed, to see if they could impress Verlaine's staff with their superior knowledge. "Koscuisko invokes an Infirmary audit, but he's given the Domitt Prison time. So he's not out to find something wrong. Gave them—what? Three days? To make any shortfall right."

Which was proof of Koscuisko's clumsiness if any was needed. He could have had the Administration of the Domitt Prison in the palm of his hand, if rather than tipping them off so far in advance he'd made a surprise raid.

Unless he knew very well that there was nothing wrong with the drug upon whose adulteration Koscuisko blamed the premature death of War-leader Darmon. That way when he found no discrepancies, he could claim that the Domitt Prison had cleaned itself up during its three-day grace period: his failure was covered.

Maybe she'd have to reconsider, reluctant though she was to do so.

Maybe Koscuisko was a little less useless at political survival than she'd thought.

"All in all, First Secretary, it looks like a signal. It's possible that Koscuisko is trying to get our attention. Learning from past mistakes, perhaps."

That went a bit far, Mergau thought. But the First Secretary sat up, leaning over the desk surface with his forearms propped against the edge of the desk.

"Something's wrong at the Domitt Prison?" Verlaine asked. "Or at least Koscuisko thinks there is. And is trying to get us to think about what he's doing, so we can get an audit team in there without embarrassing the Second Judge?"

No, Koscuisko was nowhere near so deep as that. And for once it seemed that even the Bench intelligence specialists realized it. Ivers knit her dark straight eyebrows and qualified, carefully.

"Possible, First Secretary. There's no way to tell for sure without either talking to Koscuisko or sending an audit team. The Domitt Prison hasn't stood an operational audit yet. It's due."

Verlaine frowned. "If we asked him . . . but there's no way to do it. Not informally. If he's trying to get us to send in an audit team on the whisper-run it's because there's something he knows we don't want on Record." The First Secretary should learn from the Bench intelligence specialists, Mergau thought. He'd been too impressed with Koscuisko from the start. "And it is due, you're absolutely right about that."

Shifting in his seat, restlessly, Verlaine took thought for the problem before him while Ivers and Vogel kept shut. As she did as well, naturally. She was in disgrace. She'd failed him.

"Mergau."

First Secretary Verlaine caught her eye, and stilled himself where he sat. She braced herself, but she wasn't too concerned, not right now.

The conversation had yet to begin to touch on any delicate questions about how a drug that was lethal for a certain class of hominids had ended up in her rack. It was just bad luck, really. How was she to know?

"Yes, First Secretary?" She kept her voice bland and neutral; not blaming, but not accepting blame, either. If the doctor had excluded the speak-serum because it was poison, rather than merely not authorized, the doctor should have told her. Accidents happened. And it wasn't as if more than one of the prisoners had died of it; that left four to be forwarded to the Fleet Inquisitor Verlaine had called for. One of whom should be able to speak again soon enough.

"We send in an audit team here and now, just as we're pulling a Writ on reassign, it'll raise a question or two," Verlaine mused aloud, looking at her. "I have an idea that could serve instead."

Vogel and Ivers were looking at her as well, now. It was difficult not to blush, just out of frustration. Vogel and Ivers blamed her: she knew they did. Too bad for the Bench specialists. Their Fleet resources would get them no further than she had done already. She had gotten very little information, but at least it had been timely.

Their decision to hold the remaining prisoners for the *Ragnarok*'s Inquisitor rather than suffer her to do her job only meant that what information they got in the end would be so old it would be functionally useless. If in fact they even got any more information, at all.

"Could control it that way," Ivers conceded, with evident reluctance. Mergau wasn't quite sure she believed what she thought they were going to propose to her, but if the First Secretary meant to entrust her with this—well, the Bench specialists could divert Fleet Inquisitors all they liked.

She was safe from challenges to her position, if the First Secretary was willing to put this into her hands, but Ivers hadn't finished with her thought. "One of us might accompany Dame Noycannir, in that case. Speak to Koscuisko in confidence, let him know that you heard what he had to say, First Secretary."

Verlaine nodded. There was relief in his voice, underlying the undoubted seriousness of the situation. "Very well. Mergau. We'll send orders to relieve Koscuisko, you take his place. Give us an on-site evaluation once Koscuisko's got out of there. We'll take a few weeks to get it cleaned up—whatever it is—and then we'll have an audit. We probably need one. But we don't need it public."

Keeping her face grave—she'd made a mistake with the speak-serum, she felt badly, because even though it had not been her fault she was too professional not to take it personally—Mergau made explicit the job Verlaine seemed to intend her for. "I'm to go to the Domitt Prison, First Secretary?"

To be mistress of that place, after all. To hold the dominion. Even better now than it would have been before, because Verlaine needed her to manage a problem that he couldn't afford to let become public. Up to her to protect the Second Judge from Bench criticisms over the irregularities that Andrej Koscuisko apparently thought existed.

She would have more influence than ever before.

"And right away, Mergau. Miss Ivers, if you'd do the errand for me I'd take it very kindly of you. Carry Koscuisko's orders by hand. No inadvertent miscommunication."

And wouldn't Koscuisko like that, to be turned out of the Domitt to make room for her?

"Four days, by courier," Ivers reminded him. "Do you want to send word ahead?"

Verlaine thought about it, but shook his head. "Can't risk it, Miss Ivers, or rather I don't want to risk it. He has a right to know it'll get fixed, whatever it is. It's just not reasonable to expect a man with his history to go home to *Scylla* without saying something, if we don't reassure him."

Reassure Koscuisko all you like, Mergau thought. *You and your Bench specialist. Coddle the darling dandy all you want.*

I will be mistress of the Domitt Prison.

Security escorted Shopes Ban from cells into the work-room, following Andrej. Once the door to the torture-cell closed, they seated the prisoner on the block; and then came forward, standing to either side of Andrej where he sat in turn.

"Shopes Ban. My name is Andrej Koscuisko, and I hold the Writ to Inquire here at the Domitt Prison. There are some questions which I wish to ask."

No answer. Well, why should there be? He knew the crucial difference between simply stating that he held the Writ, and affirming that he held the Writ to which the prisoner was to be required to answer; but there was no reason to expect Shopes Ban to know.

Turning to his drugs-rack against the wall, Andrej checked his secures, out of habit; good. No one had tampered with these medications. If the Domitt Prison was as corrupt as he had begun to fear it was, it could well be that someone would take it into mind to thwart him of his purpose by silencing his sources before time.

Taking up an anti-anxiety agent to couple with the speak-serum, Andrej turned back to the prisoner, who was looking confused. Still very worried. Sensible man, Shopes Ban. An older man, older by perhaps eight years or more than War-leader Darmon had been. Andrej put the dose through, and explained.

"This is a Fifth Level speak-serum; it will not compel your speech, but will assure me that what you say is true. This is required for the Record to stand in Evidence, let the Record show administration of twenty-five units of eralics in sterile solution, five of dition to accompany."

The Record was secured. Only a Judicial officer could read it, since the Record was the basic legal document upon which all legal actions under Jurisdiction were founded. Administrator Geltoi was not a Judicial officer for the purposes of access to the Record. And the only Bench officer in Port Rudistal with a Judicial function was Captain Sinjosi Vopalar, serving in the dual role in token of her command.

Andrej was counting on that.

"Dition is a soother, Ban. It should help you relax, because although you are in prison and have been called here to me you are not here to answer to Charges, but to satisfy my curiosity."

Not as if that would mean anything either. Questions were questions. That was the real reason Andrej needed Erish and Code here with him: their unspoken—but unwavering—support was his best help against temptation to put his questions more forcefully than necessary, just because he could.

It would take a few eighths for the drug to take effect. Andrej sat down. He would use the time to establish the ground rules for this interview.

"I have of late with a prisoner named Marne Cittrops spoken. He has claims against the Domitt Prison, and they are damning. And also he was afraid that a man named Shopes Ban had been murdered, and yet the Shopes Ban he described to me is nothing like you."

Was it his imagination, or did the prisoner flash him a look of scornful mockery at that?

"His accusations were specific, and of a very serious nature indeed. For this reason I mean to question you about these allegations. The speak-serum will guarantee the veracity of your responses. Also for the same reason—" the seriousness of the allegations, he meant, was he even communicating, at all?—"you are not to be returned to the work-crew, but sequestered here in holding till I have concluded my investigation."

He couldn't possibly keep them in here, in torture-rooms. And the Administration had filled the sixteen holding cells full of prisoners for the torture as quickly as he could empty them. There were eight cells up on the next level, however, where his office was, being used for storage.

There was obviously no way in which he could risk returning these people, once called out, to the general prison population. If he had been in Administrator Geltoi's shoes, he would have found ways to justify putting pressure on them outside of Protocol or in violation of Protocol in order to discover exactly what Andrej was doing with them.

"Can't help you," the prisoner said, suddenly. His voice sounded a little strained. Code drew a tumbler full of water and gave it to Shopes Ban to drink. Ban emptied it greedily and held the tumbler up, soliciting another go—testing the boundaries of this environment. Astute. Andrej nodded, and Code refilled the tumbler from the drinking-tap. This time the prisoner only drank half of it off, but he kept a good grip on it, declining to return it to Code. Still thirsty.

"I can't help you. I'm not Shopes Ban. Whoever Shopes Ban is, he's dead. It just happened to be my turn when the name was called."

"Even so." It was a disappointment; but one that he had half-expected, based on Darmon's testimony. "What is there to tell me of Marne Cittrops?"

"Now, there's an interesting question." The prisoner sounded bitterly amused. "When I came on to work-crew Marne Cittrops was this one man, big and square-like, eyes green-gold. Changed mid-shift into some half-starved child, beardless, eyes as black as the lake-deeps."

As he spoke the bitterness seemed to lift a bit, replaced by simple enjoyment of his joke. Maybe the drugs were taking effect. "And more

than that. Ten days ago, or thirteen. They called him out as Marne
Cittrops to the work, and by sundown they'd changed his name, he
was a different man. Imagine that."

Very much as Darmon had said. They'd arrested Darmon as Marne
Cittrops on evidence that Darmon had believed could only have come
from Shopes Ban—who was almost certainly not Shopes Ban to begin
with. They'd filled behind Cittrops with another man, but they hadn't
bothered to change the name until they'd realized that Andrej was
becoming concerned about accountability.

Thirteen days ago?

Had it been so long since he'd called Belan to account over that
supposed Lerriback?

"Then if you would tell me what you know of Shopes Ban, if you are
not he." If someone had gotten evidence out of Shopes Ban, it had been
obtained outside of Protocol. Any special authorizations at the Domitt
Prison had to come across Andrej's desk, and there'd been none.

The prisoner shook his head. "I've no threads in that weave, your
Excellency. Is that what to call you?—Only that he went out on work-
crew on one morning and was killed. Or died. Most likely murdered.
And I called out to the work-crew in the afternoon, to take his place
so that the count would be correct when we returned to prison in the
evening."

Exactly as War-leader Darmon had said.

There was no help for it, then. He had to take testimony. The
Domitt Prison had to be brought to account. And to do that he needed
evidence.

He had the prisoners named in Wab's narrative to ask. He could
ask the sixteen miserable souls who sat in cells waiting to be tortured.
They wouldn't understand why he was asking. But he would still find
out.

"Tell to me how you came to the Domitt Prison. How it has gone
with you since. What you have seen. What you have heard. Tell me
what you know about this place."

It would need as persuasive a set of interrogatories as he had ever
prepared to bring him and his Security safely through the storm that
would break over them if he declared failure of Writ at the Domitt
Prison.

⊕ ⊕ ⊕

Three days, and Infirmary was ready to stand audit.

Merig Belan had checked the stores himself prior to calling on Koscuisko in the penthouse to escort him. Koscuisko brought his Security with him, his Security and his Chief of Security all together. There were procedures for Infirmary audit: among them, the requirement to team in threes, one to count, one to record, one to watch and attest by countersigning. Koscuisko had to bring all of his people with him. It was the only way he could make two teams.

Down the main lift, where Koscuisko hadn't been since the day he'd arrived here. Out on the first level. When Koscuisko had come down to Infirmary before with his stricken bond-involuntary, it had been a different way. But that had been because he'd come through the work area. Unexpected. Unlooked for. And very unfortunately, in the end.

But why hadn't Geltoi expected this?

A medical officer, a pharmacy, what was more natural than that Koscuisko would feel himself called upon to certify stores?

Here was Infirmary, neater and brighter than Belan thought it had ever been. All the duty staff present and waiting. All of the uniforms clean. But Koscuisko wasn't interested in meeting staff; he let Belan introduce him, he was polite, but once that was over Koscuisko excused them all.

Threw them out.

Secured Infirmary stores against them, locking the pharmacy up. Belan didn't like it. It made him uneasy. And he was part of it; Geltoi would not for one moment tolerate such an audit of his stores without an observer.

Part of it, yet, but with nothing to do but sit or stand around and watch the procedure as Koscuisko and his people took dose by dose, store by store, exhaustive inventory of everything there. Belan wished they'd thought about the linen; there wasn't enough on the shelves, not really. But the staff didn't worry too much about linen for Nurail patients.

And why should they? Any patient referred to Infirmary came in dirty from work and left dirty for work, so what sense did it make to invest in clean linen?

Then one of Koscuisko's teams went on to keep counting while Koscuisko himself turned to assay-work. The lab setup at least could not be faulted; the lab facilities had scarcely been used since the Domitt had opened its gates to its first inmates. Geltoi needn't worry about the sufficiency of lab facilities.

Was that a problem?

Was there some point that Koscuisko could make about the fact that the lab was so little used, with a prison population of more than four thousand souls?

Not four thousand. No. He had to remember. Two thousand and four hundred, and no more. And maybe it was so few as that; it had been a while since there had been any new bodies.

Time wore on.

Shift changed, at third-meal.

Belan knew the work-crews were returning to the prison, being fed in the mess hall and hurried into cells. He was beginning to feel a little hungry himself. A good eight into third-shift, the prison would be quiet, the guards would have eaten, the Administrative offices closed up for the night—

If Koscuisko didn't hurry, Belan told himself, he'd be stuck here till morning. Of course he could go out of the main prison gate, and avoid the Administration building and the fog beside it. Maybe that would work.

"Very well, Administrator Belan."

Koscuisko's people were finishing up, putting things away. Belan stood up stiffly from where he'd been sitting, bored and irritated.

"It's all in order. If you've got the report, please."

He could have told Koscuisko that hours ago. He knew it was all right. And how much it had cost to make it so. "Very good, your Excellency," he echoed, stupidly, then wished he hadn't used those exact words. Koscuisko might think he was making fun of him, and nothing could be further from his intent than that. "If you'd care to sign, sir. His Excellency doubtless knows where the validations are required?"

Setting the documents out on the countertop in the lab, Koscuisko bent over them. "There's for you as well, Administrator. Here. And here. Also on this back page, see the place, here."

Yes, attesting to the fact that he'd watched the audit. Affirming, alongside Koscuisko's statement, that a physical inventory had been made, and in proper form. The assay slips were all stacked to one side. Once Belan had signed, Koscuisko took the assay slips and sealed them in the documents-case with the rest of it.

Good, Belan thought to himself, wearily. *We can go home now.* Of course for Koscuisko "home" just meant upstairs, back to the penthouse, and no problem for him if it was after the third-meal, there was a cook to feed him whenever—

"All quite correct." Koscuisko passed the entire package over to him; Belan took it in two hands. Koscuisko's Security had gathered around him, waiting for their officer. But it was a little odd; and suddenly Belan felt insecure. "Now, one thing else, and we won't trouble you further. I need to make an unannounced inspection."

"Of course." Belan's response was immediate and automatic. Unannounced inspection? Of what? Where? "His Excellency has only to direct. The Domitt Prison is open to you, sir."

There was some sort of an unspoken message passed between Koscuisko and his people, from him to his Chief of Security and to his Bonds. "You are very obliging," Koscuisko assured him, courteously indeed. "Take us then to the furnace-room. And I must insist that no one anticipate our arrival, Administrator."

The where?

The furnace-room?

The sound of the screaming grew louder and louder in Belan's memory till he believed that he actually heard it. Koscuisko must hear it, too. Why else would Koscuisko want to go to the furnace-room, if it was not that the dead Nurail cried out to him for vengeance?

"Quite impossible. Sir." He had to protest: he couldn't allow it. To take Koscuisko unannounced to the furnace-room would amount to betrayal of Geltoi's trust. He couldn't do it.

"But I insist." Cordially, politely, Koscuisko took his arm, and turned Belan toward the door. "Just the seven of us. Show us the way. There's nothing to hide, surely, Belan?"

Of course there was nothing to hide. There couldn't be. Administrator Geltoi ran an efficient prison. There was no answer for Koscuisko's question, none that would not compromise them one way or the other.

Koscuisko took Belan's silence for an answer in itself, or pretended to.

"Well, then. You see. Take us to the furnaces, Administrator Belan. Take us now."

There was nothing that he could think to do but comply.

CHAPTER TWELVE

Andrej Koscuisko had been dreading this since the moment he had begun to understand that it had to be done. There was no way around it. He had to see the furnaces, himself; and he had to see them as they were, at the end of the day's work, when the garbage was to be dumped into the incinerators. Before anybody had a chance to hide something that might be compromising. He hated doing it to his Security, but it had to be done.

He didn't want to see the furnaces.

Joslire was dead, and every time he thought about the furnaces he thought about Joslire. Things were getting confused in Andrej's mind: between Joslire who had been sent on high in fire at the hospital, and prisoners whose bodies were destroyed by fire here; so that he found himself confounding Joslire with Nurail prisoners, imagining the horrors he had heard in evidence these past few days as happening to Joslire.

And it was bad enough that anyone should suffer through such fearful horrors, without the accusing ghost of a dead man coming into the picture.

Strolling with casual purposefulness with Belan through the halls of the Domitt Prison, Andrej concentrated his mind on where he was and what he was about. Why would Joslire's spirit be accusing? Never in his life had Joslire found fault with him, and yet it was the feeling that Andrej had.

There was no one in the corridors to see them, to report to Administrator Geltoi; Andrej had had Kaydence select the time very carefully, taking shift-change and assignment into account. No one to talk to. Andrej wanted to talk, because he was afraid. But if he let Belan know how reluctant he actually was to seek the furnaces, Belan might feel emboldened to resist, or try to run away.

He had to keep his fear within himself. He was in control here, after all. He was the Writ on site at the Domitt Prison.

And if atrocities were taking place under his Writ, and he did not end them, his ignorance of their existence might protect him from legal difficulties, but he would be damned just as deeply as if he had himself planned all of the crimes that he feared he suspected—

Downstairs into the basement levels, avoiding the lifts to minimize the chances of being noticed. Two levels down from the ground floor. It was murky and hot in these maintenance corridors, poorly lit, poorly ventilated, and a rumbling groan within the very walls of the maintenance fans venting the smoke and the stench of the fire into the damper-vent system and out through the roof. There at the corner of the basement, where the walls above turned, there was a wide chute from stories up; a wide chute, and a conveyer, silent and still for now.

Miss Samons was keeping an eye on Belan for him. Andrej stepped forward, past Kaydence and Toska, to peer up through the darkness above to try to see where the chute opened from and how far up it went. No luck; it was black, above, but there was a draft that made Andrej think the chute vented into the Domitt's courtyard. Outside, where it would be getting dark, where the temperature was falling even as the sun set. A rubbish-chute.

He leaned too far over the lip of the chute, looking up. Andrej lost his balance. Falling forward over the base of the chute, he put his hands out to steady himself; but slid down against the slippery surface of the chute to fall heavily against the conveyer, before Toska had pulled him safely to his feet again.

The conveyer started moving.

Weight-activated.

Once it had started, it didn't seem to notice that Andrej wasn't on it any longer. Standing there, watching it, Andrej stared stupidly at the conveyer for a long moment before he realized what it was saying to him.

Follow me.

Nodding his thanks to Toska for the welcome reassurance of Toska's protective strength, Andrej Koscuisko walked alongside the conveyer-track to see where it might lead.

It wasn't far.

The sound of cursing could be clearly heard as he went down the length of the conveyer to where it passed through the fabric-fringed maw of a thermal barrier, into the furnace room beyond

" . . . filthy piece of Nurail trash. Move it. Get that stack shifted, you, there's more trash coming, who's out there culling the cattle at this time of night?"

Cattle. Nurail prisoners, he meant, whoever it was who was swearing. There was a hand-secure on the entrance gate beside the conveyer belt; Andrej gestured with his head for Erish and Code to bring Belan forward.

"If you would be so kind." Andrej pointed. "Open, here."

At this point he could set himself to ride the conveyer belt through the thermal barrier, but there was no telling what was on the other side. It would be better not to risk it.

Belan palmed the secure.

Nothing happened.

With a look of sickened desperation, Belan pulled a white-square from a pocket in his sleeve and wiped his hand. Belan would rather almost anything than be here: so much was evident from his face. So Belan knew what was in the furnace-room. And Belan was dirty.

Dirty, but cooperating, because he put his hand to the secure once more, and this time the lock recognized his now-dry palm and bowed to his authority. Disengaged. Opened the door.

Quickly, without waiting for Security, Andrej stepped across the threshold and went in.

The furnace-room was brightly lit, two stories high, and three times as long as it was deep. Andrej could see a work-crew toiling at a pile of debris under the whip of a Pyana overseer, another overseer belaboring a man who knelt—trying to cover his head, to shield it from blows— near to one furnace-gate; another sitting at a table near the door, at the back wall, with the remains of a meal spread out before him and a jug of what was probably a beer of some sort that he was using even now to refresh his glass.

None of these things could distract him or diminish the visual impact of the furnaces themselves. Five furnace-gates, stretched along the back of the wall. Five great grim doors, and darkness behind two of them, but the other three gate-windows aglow either red or yellow or white.

They'd been noticed.

The overseer who'd been eating put down his jug, hastily, rising to his feet. "Assistant Administrator Belan!" He called the name out loudly enough to be heard from one end of the room to the other, even over the noise from the furnaces.

The overseer who'd been tormenting the lone Nurail coiled his whip into his hand hastily, hurrying forward. The other formed his work-party up between the furnaces and the door, where he could keep an eye on them while speaking to their superior.

"This is an unexpected pleasure, sir." The Pyana overseer had left his table to greet them more formally. All the same, the emphasis seemed to Andrej to be on the word *unexpected*, and the Pyana looked keenly into Belan's face with an unfriendly eye for all of Belan's superior rank. Belan was Nurail. Andrej hastened to claim the blame for himself.

"The visit is specifically to be unannounced," Andrej answered, in Belan's defense. The overseer should know who he was, even if the overseer had never met him. "For this reason I made quite sure that Administrator Belan could not be accused of having tipped you off in advance. In this manner there can be no question raised about whether the Administration has passed the audit honestly."

It was duplicitous of him to imply that the furnaces would pass audit. But Andrej wanted the truth of what went on down here; that meant getting the Pyana overseer's cooperation. "Now perhaps you would to me the operation show, furnace-master?"

It seemed to work.

"Well. If you say so, sir. Excellency, your Excellency?" the overseer corrected himself, hastily, glancing to Belan for verification. Pyana were precise where titles were concerned: every bit as concerned about correct categorization as Nurail, from whom they were—in the larger sense—culturally and linguistically indistinguishable. "No offense, your Excellency. Where to start. Well. Let's start here, then."

The conveyer. Where the debris to be burned was carried into the furnace-room. It had to be discrete chunks of debris, actually, rather than heaps of scraps and bits of things; because the conveyer's terminus was well short of the furnace-gates themselves.

"Waste comes in through here, bundled. The work-crew stacks it next to the furnace, depending on which furnace fires next."

Walking Andrej from the conveyer to the pile of debris that was being built next to the black mouth of one of the furnace-gates. The furnace-gates themselves were huge and heavy, by the looks of them, and got hot even past all of their thermal shielding; that was the reason for the club-like tool that leaned up against the hinges, Andrej supposed. To knock the bolt free when the furnace-gate was to be opened during use to accept a new pallet of fuel.

"Two kinds of debris to be disposed of, your Excellency. The office waste and such-like, that's no problem. It's these that take a bit more managing, if the officer please."

And "these" were the bodies of the dead.

Andrej had feared as much; it was not unexpected. And still the sight of the dead piled like kindling frightened him in some way that he could not quite explain to himself. It was not that it was indecent to burn the dead. He had burned Joslire, and it had been a comfort to protect the abandoned body by alchemical reduction to the ash; so it was not horror that bodies should be burned that frightened him.

There were too many bodies on that pile.

He'd done his research carefully, planning this inspection. He knew how many were on mortality report, day by day, over the past weeks. There should be no more than so many dead, waiting to be freed from the memory of their bodies in the fire. And there were more than there should be.

"In order to write the inspection report." His throat was dry. He wanted a swallow or two from the overseer's flask, but that was probably out of the question. "It will be necessary for me to examine these dead, and take a rough count. If you would provide for me the assistance of your work-crew, it would spare my gentlemen the unpleasantness."

Surely this was not unreasonable. The work-crews had to do this work day by day, surely they were in some part inured to it—unlike his gentlemen. Unlike himself, but he could not hope to be spared unpleasantness, it was for him to take responsibility for it.

The overseer shrugged and bowed and gestured, and his fellow hurried the work-crew over to where Andrej stood waiting for him. That one lone Nurail prisoner who had been beaten as Andrej came in was lying on the floor, apart, ignored. Andrej wanted to go see how bad it was. But he had to keep himself in character, aloof and professional, else he would not be able to observe everything that he needed to take in evidence.

The work-crew unpiled their careful heap of bodies, laying the dead out on the floor in rows. "It will be necessary for my report to identify this work-crew by their names," Andrej lied to the overseer, taking his little notebook out of the chest-plaquet of his over-blouse. "It's customary to provide this information for the prison's protection, so that anything I may say in my report may be challenged by witnesses. Your name?"

Not so much a lie, perhaps. But more important than the audit was his need to try to protect the work-crew from execution once he'd left. The prison might destroy the witnesses on instinct. If he knew them by name, perhaps the prison would have to think twice.

"Shan Morlaps. Good, yes, and your mother's people hold? The Ringing Rock." Oh, in that case, one of Shan Morlaps's family was dead, Andrej had murdered him not three weeks gone by. He had the weave. At least he had the words, and as much of the music as he'd been able to transcribe to his satisfaction.

As difficult as it could be to speak under torture, to sing melodiously was all but impossible; but the tune could be corrected from the threads in the woven-weave, if necessary, so that was not so much at issue as the words. "And your father's weave. Yes, I insist. You may whisper it to me in confidence, I know how prudish you Nurail are."

Better than that, if the overseers didn't know what name was given and written down it would decrease their confidence in being able to substitute. Andrej wanted these people alive.

The Nurail leaned closer, grabbing for Kaydence at Andrej's side to steady himself and keep his balance without giving offense by touching the officer's clean uniform with soiled hands. Whispering, he spoke, half-choked with grief or shame; or perhaps both.

"My father carried the Rose of Third-month, in his life. Write it all down and witness to it, officer. These men are murdered outside of the Law."

The Nurail had no reason to expect Andrej to keep his confidence, no reason to look to Andrej for hope or help at all. But had apparently made up his mind to take the chance that Andrej would listen and hear. Andrej kept his face clear of distress. "Thank you, very good. And next?"

Yes.

He knew that murder was being done.

Once he had evidence, he would see the murderers punished under Law, as they had punished and killed outside of it.

Justice would be done, or his name was not Koscuisko, and Joslire—and Robert, and Kaydence, and Toska, and the rest—had never trusted him.

And yet the strictest justice under Jurisdiction could never make this right, what had happened at the Domitt Prison . . .

Kneeling down next to the bodies, Andrej worked quickly. He didn't want to give the guards any cause to think twice, so it was important that he appear to be casual, even cursory, in his investigation. He was being watched, of course. But at least so far, the Pyana overseer didn't seem to have begun to worry.

And why should they?

Because they were the final damning link in the chain that was to bind Belan and the rest of the Administration over to the Bench for abuse of authority, and failure of Writ. That was why they should be worried.

Most of these dead seemed to have died of natural causes, not of trauma. Overwork and underfeeding, that was natural enough, wasn't it? Overwork, because hands were hardened and blistered beneath the calluses, torn even through skin toughened by hard physical labor. Underfed, because the muscle had wasted; and cardiac muscle would fail, under too great a strain, and leave the dead with just those expressions of surprise or startlement.

But there were also victims here of torture.

They were not people that Andrej knew, no names of weaves in his handbook. How could they be? He'd been taking evidence on speaksera alone, these three days past. The Darmon was long since burned. And it hadn't been Protocols that had killed the men he found, but brutal treatment of the less formal, less effective kind. Ingenious and abhorrent, but that wasn't what separated it from Andrej's Writ; only the fact that this torture had not been sanctioned under Jurisdiction.

It made no difference.

Or at least these men, these two tortured dead, were as dead as if they had been killed under the exercise of the Writ to Inquire; so what difference did it make?

It made a difference.

As indefensible as the tortures Andrej had to hand, they were still ruled by Jurisdiction, subject to the Bench. Lawful, if intolerably unjust.

And the torture that had killed these men was not even that.

All right, he had been wrong to think that the detention block had ceased to operate outside of the Law on his arrival. Darmon had told him that, if not in so many words. Andrej himself had all but realized that it had to be the explanation for the story of Shopes Ban; but he hadn't wanted to believe it. All of these months. Should he have kept a closer watch on things?

How many had been brutally tortured by Pyana for no reason and with less authority while he had kept to the comfort of his penthouse, and indulged himself in the long drawn-out agonies of the punishments available under Protocol, and ignored any questions that might have come to mind about where the referral information was coming from in the first place, or how it had been obtained?

He'd sat still in one place for too long, staring at the wounded face of one of the dead. The overseer had taken notice: would be wondering. "It is always satisfying, to see a thing thoroughly done." Rising to his feet, Andrej kept his voice as light and cheerful as possible. It was easier than he had expected: there was part of him that meant every word. "And now I have made more work for your crew, but I have seen all that is needful. What happens next, furnace-master?"

As if he didn't know. He didn't need to number every one; he had the information he'd wanted to gain, from the bodies that he had examined. Both in their number and the manner of their deaths, the Domitt was condemned.

"His Excellency will have noticed that three of the furnaces are on line. Two of them off." The overseer was a little more reserved; Andrej walked with him, smiling and attentive, to soothe what suspicion might have started to arise. "Two, here, was fired yesterday. It takes each of them six shifts to run a cycle, and then we do preventive maintenance once the oven has had time to cool, that takes another shift."

Raking the ashes. Recycling stubborn matter to the next firing. The body-mill at the hospital had been much more efficient, but had only been intended to take one body at a time. To burn as many so quickly would represent too great a cost in extra fuel and in heat-shielding: and there was no way in which the Domitt could have been designed from the start to burn so many dead so regularly.

Could there be?

"The fire feeds itself, furnace-master?" Andrej asked, to keep up his part of the conversation. To the far right of the furnace-room, the work-crew were piling the bodies back up on a low sort of a trolley. There were tracks, from the furnace gate out into the middle of the room. Andrej hadn't noticed them before: but now that the overseer opened one of the cold furnaces he could see that the whole floor of the furnace was on rollers.

Gridded.

A complicated apparatus, the furnace, with a false floor and a pit beneath as deep as his arm was long, nozzles and floor-vents and thermal gridding above. To capture the heat and inject oxygen, perhaps.

"Nothing wasted," the overseer agreed with a cheerful grin. "Any melt-off collected and added back. A beautiful piece of work if I say so myself, your Excellency, not that I had a hand in its design."

He couldn't grasp the implications of those words. He couldn't. He knew what the man was saying. His mind fled from the understanding. Andrej turned away, to walk back to the second cold furnace, before whose now-open door the work-crew were waiting with the loaded trolley.

"Such a conservation of resources can only be commended. Really, it takes one's breath away, furnace-master." If not in the sense it might be taken to mean. "They will fire this furnace for me now?"

The one prisoner who had been beaten had stumbled to his feet at last, and joined the others on work-crew. Pale and shaking, and bloodied on his face. The others tried to support him as best they could without being too obvious about it.

"Yes, your Excellency, we're going to put today's trash in the fire." The overseer had raised his voice so that it carried clearly; and his tone had become overtly threatening. Directed at the work-crew. "And if it wasn't for respect of his Excellency's presence, Mivish would go too. Right on top. Lazy. Filthy. Nurail."

That one prisoner, the beaten man. His whole body jerked, as if in a spasm of pure terror. The others restrained him from falling to his knees, holding his arms to prevent him from covering up his face in an agony of fear. The overseer smiled with savage pleasure.

"That's better. Professional bearing, Mivish. None of your malingering. Load the furnace, Mivish can stay out. For now."

It could be only a threat, cruel but never to be implemented.

And still it seemed too evident to Andrej that none of the work-crew took it for anything less than real, and near, and even commonplace.

It was getting harder by the moment for him to breathe, why was he stifling in this place?

The Nurail work-crew pushed the trolley from behind, guiding it forward with their hands against the bodies of their fellows. Fellow prisoners. Fellow Nurail. Family. Sons and brothers, fathers, nephews, cousins, brothers of mothers, husbands of daughters.

The trolley groaned beneath its burden of dead flesh, coming to rest within the furnace's oven with its rollers locking into place with a clearly audible report of metal against metal. The bodies had moved a little as the trolley tracked. The arms and legs were no longer as neatly stacked as they had been, although the work-crew had laid them down as decently as probably they dared.

Just this one final demonstration and he could be out of here, Andrej promised himself. He'd said he'd come down to inspect the furnaces. He couldn't really leave without standing to watch as the cycle was started with the day's debris. Only a few more moments and he could get out, get out and get away, and write the orders that would shut these furnaces down for good and all before a single Nurail the more could be so horribly threatened as Mivish had been—

But if the furnaces were on such a cycle, and if they had all the time they needed to cool down before they were opened up again for maintenance, why was a tool required to shoot the bolt?

And what was that club-like wooden instrument beside the furnace door if it was not needed to knock the furnace bolt back while the furnace was still hot?

Wondering, half-reluctantly, Andrej picked the wooden thing up from its resting place to examine it in the light.

Blood on the club-end of it.

Dried blood, and matted hair.

So now he knew, and was he any the better off, for knowing?

"There's sometimes sport to be had, your Excellency," the overseer called out. "Where's my friend Mivish? Come here, Mivish, I want you to see this, it will do you good."

Andrej put the club back down and went to join the overseer in front of the now-closed furnace door.

Secured and sealed, the furnace stood ready.

The overseer coded its initiate sequence.

There was nothing for a moment, except for a hissing sound— injection of oxygen, Andrej supposed, to fuel the fire.

Then the furnace seemed to blossom, inside, into a great strange flower made of red-gold petals quivering in profusion over the flowerbed of fuel that gave it life.

The furnace-window was wide, large and generous; there was room for more than one to stand and watch. The overseer had the hapless Mivish by his side, now, one arm around Mivish's neck; and talked to him.

"Take a good look, Mivish, how do you fancy being inside there? We have no use for boys who won't do as they're told, Mivish, but you're a good lad, I like you. So I'm going to give you one last chance to learn better."

And Mivish was no more a boy or lad than Andrej was. Andrej stared into the furnace, dazed with shock in the realization of how badly wrong it had all gone; how oblivious he had been to clues he should have pursued more aggressively, a long, long time ago. Blind and stupid with grief and lust. Blind with grief for Joslire, ever and always turning his face away from the furnaces, not willing to think about them. Taking pains not to think about them. Stupid with lust to make his prisoners suffer, and willfully unmindful of anything that might stand between him and the consummation of that destructive desire.

Something shifted, within the furnace.

Andrej sensed Mivish recoil in fear, but the overseer kept a good grip on the man. There was nothing to fear. Bodies moved in a fire.

Muscle warmed and relaxed or contracted, joints worked as heat grew intense enough to stiffen tendons; that was why poultry was trussed for the roasting, after all. Bodies moved, but slowly, and there was no sentient spirit that motivated them, it was only the heat.

Bodies moved, in the fire.

But not like this.

There was a man in the furnace, a living man, clawing his way out desperately from the middle of the pile of bodies. This was conscious movement, desperate beyond Andrej's will to understand it, a living man inside the furnace scrambling across the top of the pyre right toward him. Screaming. Reaching for the window as the skin of his palms blackened before Andrej's very eyes.

Scratching frantically at the window with blackening fingers, his mouth stretched impossibly wide in horror and in agony while the hair began to shrivel on his head for heat; and then his clothes caught fire—

The fire bloomed around him, all around him, flowing down his body like water as he screamed. Andrej knew that he could not be hearing the screams through the noise of the furnace. But he heard them regardless. The Nurail prisoner Mivish was retching now, in horror, and the Pyana overseer—chuckling indulgently—took Mivish's head by the hair, forcing Mivish to face forward and look.

"There, now. That's nice and cozy, isn't it? All of that could be yours, Mivish. And will be. The next time you give the least, I mean the very least, trouble."

He had not checked them all. Nor had he checked that they were all really dead. He had not thought. Darmon had told him; but he had not thought. It was his fault, that there was a living man inside the furnace.

"Can you not do something?" Andrej asked; and knew it was the strangled sound of his own voice that startled the overseer into releasing Mivish at last. "Shut it down. Make it stop. There is a man alive, in there."

But even as he asked it, he knew the answer.

"With respect, sir, can't be done." Once the man was burned like that there was nothing to do but to let him go. "It's too much heat inside to vent out all at once, your Excellency. The secures can't be forced."

Yes, and in such heat as that a man would not know how he was suffering. A man's brain was soft tissue, vulnerable to heat, and with the fire roaring within there would be nothing for the man to breathe. There was nothing to do. He had put a man living into the fire—

He was trembling, he couldn't help it. He couldn't speak; his words would not have made sense had he been able to. He could no longer see the furnace in front of him, and raised his hands toward his face to steady his head so that he could focus. He couldn't focus. It was too much. He coughed, to drain the fluid in his throat before it crept in the wrong direction to his lungs; and his cough came out a cry, instead. Horror and dread.

He had put a man still living into the furnace.

He couldn't stop the cries in his throat.

Security tried to restrain him, hold him, but they could not begin to understand. It was even worse that people were put into the fire. He had put a man into the fire. If he had only checked them all, but he had thought that they were dead. How could he have imagined they would dare show a living man inside the oven, in the presence of an inspecting officer? He'd fooled them all too well—but it didn't matter.

It was his fault.

He could have saved that man, had he but checked.

Crumpling slowly to the floor, supported and protected in the arms of his Security, Andrej Koscuisko collapsed against the furnace-gate and howled with guilt and all-consuming shame.

It was his fault.

It was all his fault.

He should have known that something was wrong, and much, much sooner.

How many had been burned since he'd been here?

How many of those burned had been alive?

And why should he not go into the fire, here and now, and pay the price for all that he had done?

"And so I came straightaway, Administrator," Belan concluded, in utter misery. Administrator Geltoi hadn't cared to be called back to the prison after dark. It interfered with the party his wife was hosting for their second daughter's birthday, but there was no help for it. "Koscuisko has been down to the furnaces, I think he may have been counting the bodies. What are we to do?"

He swallowed back his desperation. Geltoi would think of something. Geltoi was Pyana. Geltoi had everything under control.

Geltoi was angry with him, drumming his fingers against the desktop irately. "I don't know, Merig," Geltoi said flatly. "You've really done this one. I'm sorry to say it. Couldn't you have thought of any way to hold them off? Anything at all? Or were you only too happy just to do as you were told?"

That wasn't fair. He was supposed to do just as he was told. He was only Nurail. He didn't have Geltoi's brains. Geltoi would have come up with a way to avoid taking Koscuisko to the furnaces: but Geltoi hadn't been there.

Belan had no answer but to stand in silent agony, biting his lips.

After a moment Geltoi sighed.

"All right. I'll help you out of this one, Merig. It's our honor that's at stake." Geltoi toggled into the braid on his desk. "Administrator Geltoi. For the penthouse, please. And shut down all of the access routes first, the lifts, the emergency stairs, everything."

The penthouse?

Why the penthouse?

When the circuit cleared, it was the voice of Andrej Koscuisko. A little strained. Emphatically wary. Belan thought about the look he'd seen on Koscuisko's face when he'd been watching through the window into the furnace-gate, and shuddered.

"This is Andrej Koscuisko. And you are Administrator of a prison in which much fault is to be found. What is it, your word to me?"

It was a voice-link; Belan was just as glad. He could hardly bear the sound of furious contempt in Koscuisko's voice. To see it in Koscuisko's eyes would be difficult, and yet Geltoi seemed unmoved.

"And good-greeting to you as well, Koscuisko. It has come to my attention that you have declined to support your Judicial function over the past few days, preferring rather to construct specious arguments against this Administration. You are to be replaced as soon as orders come from Chilleau Judiciary."

Yes, well, but they hadn't heard from Chilleau Judiciary. They didn't know if Chilleau Judiciary was going to replace Koscuisko yet. Maybe it didn't matter. Maybe all that mattered was getting Koscuisko out of there, with enough time to clean out the furnaces and clean up the work-crews before the next inspection. If there was a next inspection.

"For the exercise of my Judicial function it is not my intent to even consider apologizing, Geltoi. What good do you imagine it will do, to send me to *Scylla* back? There is evidence to convict the Domitt of failure of Writ."

Geltoi smiled. Koscuisko had stepped foot into a Pyana trap, it seemed. "Which can only be cried by the Writ on site, Koscuisko. As of now I no longer consider you to be the Writ on site. You should be quite comfortable in the penthouse while you wait for orders. For your sake I hope it won't be long. Geltoi, away here."

Grinning broadly with evident self-satisfaction, Geltoi pulled the braid. Belan stared, confused and worried; Geltoi rose and stretched, signaling for his car.

"And that's—that. Security's shut down the penthouse, Belan, there was a reason why we wanted to be able to control access."

Shut Koscuisko up on the roof.

He could not cry for vengeance to the Bench if he could not gain access to the Bench.

And once Koscuisko's orders arrived from Chilleau Judiciary, he would have no standing to complain of the Domitt Prison; it would be only the new Writ assigned who could do that. By then they could be ready. This experience had been valuable, if too nerve-wracking for Belan's peace of mind. They knew better how to comport themselves in front of Inquisitors, now.

"Of course, Administrator." Belan didn't need to pretend to be impressed and humbled. Geltoi had it all in hand. Why had he ever worried? "My instructions, sir?"

Because he had been down to the furnace-room with Andrej Koscuisko. That was why he worried. He was the one who'd seen. Who'd heard. He was the one who'd been there.

"Take the furnaces offline as they complete cycle, Merig, clean them out and let them stand. We'll dump the leavings underneath the dike-wall when we're ready to pour the next course, and in the meantime we can just get ourselves so sweet and fresh and pretty that there'll be no proving we ever burned so much as a scrap of steak-bone in those furnaces."

"And in the penthouse, sir?" There were prisoners being held in the store-rooms by Koscuisko's office, prisoners secured under seals only Koscuisko could lift. There was water in the store-rooms, which had been built for cells. But who was to feed these people, if Koscuisko was to be prisoned in the penthouse?

"Oh, it won't be but a few days." Geltoi hadn't forgotten about the extra prisoners, surely. Geltoi had been too angry about them at the time Koscuisko had called for them because they diminished his work-crews, and he needed every available man on work-crew to make his ambitious construction schedule work. And because he couldn't figure out why Koscuisko had called for these people by name.

Belan knew.

Belan knew that the fog had told Koscuisko.

Belan also knew better than to even hint as much, to a Pyana like Geltoi.

And Geltoi was still talking, as he moved past Belan where he stood to go back to his gracious home in Rudistal once more and enjoy his middle daughter's birthday. "Won't do them any harm. Have a schedule ready for me in the morning, Merig, we can discuss the furnaces, all right? I'm sure you didn't have anything else planned."

No. He didn't have anything planned. And Geltoi knew quite well that Belan couldn't leave the Administration building if he was caught here after dark. The fog rose. And there were voices. "Of course not, Administrator. I'll get right on it. The least I could do, sir, after failing you so miserably in the first place."

He had to say it. He did feel utterly miserable though he wasn't quite sure it was because he'd failed Administrator Geltoi. How had he failed? What could Geltoi have done differently?

Why was it wrong to reveal the corruption at the heart of the Domitt Prison, rather than conceal it?

"Never mind that, Merig, we'll recover." Geltoi didn't think it was a problem. Geltoi only thought that other peoples' mistaken perception that it was a problem could create awkwardness. "We'll speak no more of it, but see you have that schedule in the morning."

There was work to do in his office, waiting for him.

And a bottle to drink himself stupefied as soon as he was finished with it.

Caleigh Samons rejoined the others in the officer's front room, shaking her head. "No luck, your Excellency. Locked down. Tighter than drunk-detention on an abstention ship."

Koscuisko sat on the couch, leaning well forward with his hands clasped across his splayed knees. He'd finally stopped shaking.

They were prisoners here.

Kaydence knelt down next to his officer with a cup of hot sweet rhyti, holding Koscuisko's hands around the cup as Koscuisko drank. All right, Koscuisko hadn't quite managed to stop shaking. As shocking as the impact of the furnace-room tour had been, she didn't think that was the entire explanation for Koscuisko's fit. This had to be something that had been creeping up on him, perhaps for weeks, possibly without his conscious notice.

"It is clear to me what must be done." Koscuisko's voice shook, even as his hands did. "Administrator Geltoi. I have given him too much time in which to understand. He means to keep us out of the way until he can get orders to relieve me."

The housekeepers had locked themselves into their rooms; Cook was in the kitchen, with nowhere else to go. The emergency exits were sealed shut: blast walls, solid across the floor of the stairwells. Solid as the lift-accesses were sealed, both of them.

This had been coordinated.

"What is happening? Sir." Ailynn was much more confused by this than anyone. She hadn't been down to the furnace-room.

"Thank you, Kaydence. Again, please." Koscuisko seemed to have recovered sufficiently to be able to drink his cup of rhyti on his own power. Kaydence hovered over him like an anxious parent, and it was always funny to see Security being protective of Koscuisko, when they could so easily have needed protection from Koscuisko instead. And not gotten it, being bond-involuntaries.

Beckoning for Ailynn to come and sit beside him, Koscuisko waited until Kaydence had come back with more rhyti, bringing the brewing-flask with him.

"Ailynn, I do not know what they say in service house about the Domitt Prison. I do not want to know," Koscuisko said quickly, to forestall a reply. "There will be time in which to provide testimony, later."

Chief Samons didn't think the penthouse was on monitor. They'd swept during the first few days, and periodically since. Koscuisko was being careful not to compromise Ailynn, just in case there were monitors that they didn't know about.

"We made an unannounced inspection of the furnace-room just

now, Ailynn. We have seen things that will be difficult for the prison administration to explain, and you heard Geltoi: they do not wish to be called to account for any of it. I hope they feed those men in second-holding." The thought seemed to distract Koscuisko for a moment. But he was surrounded by people waiting for his word; after a moment he returned to his main stream.

"The prison administration is fatally corrupt, and the people who have been responsible must be brought before the Bench to face extreme sanctions. It is called failure of Writ."

Koscuisko was speaking so calmly and carefully for the benefit of a woman who might not know the jargon that the critical phrase almost passed before Caleigh snagged on it.

Failure of Writ?

With the sanctions the Administration potentially faced, it was not out of the realm of imagination that the prison administration might try to arrange an accident—

"Administrator Geltoi must have me replaced before I can go on Record, if he hopes to evade his responsibility. Or face the possibility of a Tenth Level command termination."

Ailynn should have some idea. Surely. She had been the one to translate the narrative, after all. On the other hand, Koscuisko did not discuss the results of interrogation with anybody and Ailynn might easily have assumed that Koscuisko would take the torment of Nurail prisoners as inconsequential, the way the rest of the Judicial establishment seemed inclined to do.

"Sir, have you found—all true—" Ailynn's horror reached out and touched Caleigh's own feelings about the furnace-room; and Caleigh shuddered. She'd read the narrative, too.

Koscuisko nodded. "And the evidence I have taken in these last three days is damning. I have been blind to the enormity of this thing, Ailynn. And now that I understand what has been going on I must not fail in my duty. There are so many dead to cry for justice."

"If the officer, and his party. Should meet. With an unfortunate—accident—"

Erish had trouble getting the words out; Caleigh was surprised he spoke at all. It was a good sign, though. All of the things that had happened to them here. And her troops still knew that they could trust Koscuisko.

"It is an option."

Koscuisko's frank endorsement of what she'd been thinking was a little unnerving, in its calm acceptance of the possibilities. Calm? They had pulled Koscuisko away from the furnace-room in a fit. Maybe he was just in shock. He sounded perfectly lucid. But shock could do that.

"It would create more problems than it might solve, however, and upon this I must rely for now. There has been one threat against my life in Port Rudistal already, if one may be excused for interpreting Joslire's death in so selfish a fashion."

Well, that was all Fleet and the Bench made of it. Security's job was to die in the place of senior officers of assignment. Koscuisko simply wasn't very rational about the issue. But he did have a good grasp on the official interpretation of the incident.

"The Port Authority would be called upon to validate that any accident was not sabotage or terrorism, and if it could be covered up there would still be my family to deal with. The Combine would be sure to take an interest in how an accident could be permitted to damage the management resources of the Koscuisko familial corporation."

This seemed to comfort Koscuisko as he spoke; he even smiled. "In fact it would be almost certain to invoke the Malcontent, and no secret is safe from the slaves of Saint Andrej Malcontent, gentles. They are the Bench intelligence specialists of the holy Mother's church. No. I do not think a prudent murderer would try it, and we have no reason to suspect that Geltoi is a desperate or imprudent murderer. For now I think we are just prisoners."

There were pieces in Koscuisko's logic that Caleigh didn't quite follow. That was all right. She had no need to follow his meaning. She trusted his judgment. And it was true that Koscuisko was a political figure in his own right, even only in the Dolgorukij Combine, even only as an inheriting son.

Geltoi might not know that . . .

"For now we are safe. I must cry my claim to the Bench before orders of reassignment are received by the Domitt Prison. And I must do so before Geltoi has a chance to destroy the evidence of his crimes. Miss Samons. We will need to get to the Administration building tonight; please explain how we are to do so."

Desperate men did desperate things. Anybody with a potential

Tenth Level facing him could be excused for becoming desperate. Koscuisko was right, if for different reasons than Koscuisko might think.

Koscuisko was determined to declare failure of Writ while he still could.

Once Koscuisko was on-Record, killing him would no longer be of any earthly use to anyone.

Night, and the sky was black and clear and cold. The breeze that had blown from the river to the land in the hours around sunset had fallen still and calm, but the damned furnaces still sent their plumes of milky smoke into the sky. Andrej shuddered at the sight of the white feathers in the night. To think. No. He could not afford to think.

"Miss Samons, please forgive me, and I hope to ask you this question only this one time." He stood a little apart with his Chief of Security, watching Toska and Erish secure the cable around the anchors they had built in the garden. "It is a reflection of my ignorance, I do not mean to challenge your judgment. You are sure that this will work. It is a long way."

He was the one who had said they had to get to the Administration building.

That she should go over the wall on a cable braided of torn sheeting had not been something he could have anticipated.

"It'll hold, sir. And the distance parses out."

Two eights until daybreak, two hours until sunrise. The lights had been on in the Administration building all night. There would logically be someone in there on night-watch, if only for appearance's sake.

For the rest of it, during all the time they had been here there had been no surveillance or patrol of the space between the prison and the containment wall that anyone had noticed. Chief Samons was convinced that that was reasonable, given Kaydence's analysis of the other securities built into the installation. Andrej could only hope that she was right.

The Administration expected anyone who managed to escape from the prison to make straight for the containment wall, not break into Administrative offices. Andrej leaned cautiously over the low safety barrier that spanned the vista gap in the wall, looking down. Chief Samons pointed. "And the fog is on our side, look there."

She was right.

There was a filled-in construction pit to the south side of the Administration building. And from the pit, a mist he'd seen in the early morning hours, rising in frothy columns from the ground, tendrils of moisture curling in the absence of any breeze. Fog rose strangely when it rose. Andrej had never quite understood what it was that caused the mist to creep or rise; something to do with warm moist soil and cold air.

The fog from the construction pit had risen much more thickly than he had ever seen it; or perhaps it was just the difference in time? It was a solid blanket in the night; not even the lights from the Administration building could penetrate far into that fog. The fog would cover them for most of the descent down to the ground.

Would they be able to find each other in the dark?

There would be the lights from the Administration building.

And his gentlemen had their gear with them, and that meant one of them was carrying the night-scope.

Toska went back into the darkened penthouse to fetch something or another, and Erish came up to salute.

"We're ready, sir. Chief. Cousin Ailynn to go with Kaydence, sir?"

That had seemed best. Chief Samons had assured him that his Security were fit to make the descent safely, and that he himself was not to lose his grip and fall upon pain of her displeasure. Kaydence was the man they all agreed had the most strength in his upper body; he was to carry Ailynn on his back. Leaving her behind was out of the question, because of the evidence she had in her mind. Andrej had rather hoped they would suggest building a harness of some sort in which to lower her down; but he had not been so lucky.

Here was Toska back. Security formed up at the wall, the coils of braided cable glistening on the ground. It was a very great waste of sheeting, in a sense, and they'd been lucky that the linen stores had held clean linen for the ten souls that had been expected to sleep there. Good quality sheeting it had been, too, especially that intended for his bed and that of Chief Samons. Excellent for load-bearing.

So Security was kitted up and ready to go. The housekeepers had been barricaded into quarters, to ensure that there would be no interference. Cook locked into the pantry for prudence's sake, and very understanding Cook was about it all, too.

"You have the narrative?" Andrej asked Ailynn, who stood close to Kaydence in the line. She opened her front-wrap and showed him: tied on a cord, and hung around her neck. Yes.

All right.

"Chief Samons, your action."

She had briefed them.

They all knew what they were to do.

"Switch on your night-scope, Code." Code and Toska would go down first. There were two cables, and Kaydence and Erish were letting them down over the wall in preparation for the descent. "Two tugs, then three, when you're ready. Kaydence goes next with Ailynn, Code, on your side. The officer next on Toska's side. Erish and I come down last. Then we move."

Didn't he know they could do it?

Didn't he know they would be all right?

Code and Toska saluted briskly and stepped forward. The braided cables were stretched taut between the anchors and the wall, now, and Code and Toska each sat down on the low lip of the vista gap. Feet to either side of the knots they'd set in the cable at intervals. Leaning well back to slide slowly down the other side of the vista gap and start down.

Andrej made a prayer to the fog in his mind. *Hide these people. Protect these people. It is no disrespect we mean to the walls or the grounds of the Domitt Prison. It is only what has been done here on these grounds, within these walls. We come to remove the shame of those crimes from these grounds and walls. Protect these people, hide them from unfriendly eyes.*

They seemed to wait forever.

But the signal came up the cable strong and reassuring at last. Two long slow pulls at the now-slackened cable. Followed by three shorter pulls. Code and Toska were on the ground, and at least so far there was nothing they could see or hear that indicated the potential existence of a problem.

"Tuck up your skirts, cousin, and wrap your legs around my waist, now."

Kaydence's cheerful advice was carefully quiet, but the fun he had in his mildly suggestive comment was clear even so. It was too dark to see if Ailynn blushed. Kaydence took a moment, sitting on the lip of the vista gap with Ailynn pick-a-back, making sure of his grip, settling himself for the descent.

Andrej hated this.

Carefully, slowly, Kaydence edged himself over the wall, creeping down the rope in small controlled movements with Ailynn holding fast to his shoulders with her arms around his neck.

Kaydence could do it if anybody could.

Kaydence could do it.

The tension on the braided cable was terrible, and Andrej remembered the tests Chief Samons had insisted upon, unable to quiet his fear that it might fail regardless. He couldn't see them, when he looked; the fog was too thick. It had run well past the top of the Administration building; was it his imagination, or was it even thicker than it had been when Toska and Code had gone down?

Oh, clever fog, Andrej praised it, in his mind. *Gentle fog. Nobly born fog of a wealthy house begotten.*

The cable went slack.

Andrej stared at it in dread, willing his anxious gaze to travel down to the ground through the cable, desperate to be able to see what was happening.

Two tugs.

Three following.

Thanks be to all Saints.

Kaydence and Ailynn were down, and safe.

But now it was his turn.

Andrej sat down on the lip of the vista gap as he had seen the others do, and took the braided cable in his hands. Wondering what had possessed him to agree to this.

He had to get down from the roof, and his people with him.

"Find the rope between your feet, sir." Chief Samons had crouched down next to him, encouraging. "Let yourself slide the first few eighths. You don't want to knock your hands or your head against the wall. You'll be on the ground before you know it, all you have to do is hang on and control the speed of your descent. Let's go."

The braided cable was soft-edged and cool between his palms. Which were sweating. It was cold, and he was afraid of the drop.

He could feel the thickness of the cable caught securely between the edges of the soles of his boots.

He couldn't sit here and stare at the fog below him forever. He had people on the ground. The longer it took to get them all down, the more vulnerable they were.

Be soft for me if I should fall, you princess of fogs, you prince inheritor of fogs, you well-bred fog of regal parentage.

He let himself slip down the length of the cable.

It felt too much like falling, and Andrej clutched at the cable between his hands in a sudden fright. No. He was not falling. He was climbing down. He had only his own weight to manage, and Kaydence had just done this with Ailynn on his back, and he was Dolgorukij. He had more than enough strength in his hands and shoulders to hang on.

Hand over hand, the cable held close between his feet, sliding past his ankles. Hand over hand, Andrej descended into the fog.

Once the mist took him, his anxiety seemed to vanish, his apprehensions evaporated, his fear gone.

He felt secure.

He could do this.

His people could do this.

They would see justice done at the Domitt Prison.

He felt the ground brush against his feet, familiar hands reaching out to him to steady him as he stumbled away from the cable, stunned to find that he was already here.

It was colder on the ground. The fog was wet; the chill of it went through to the bone. But Andrej embraced the dank discomfort of it; sound did not carry, they were safely hidden in the fog. It was a shield in the night. It would conceal them until he could reach his goal.

Within moments Chief Samons and Erish came shimmying down out of the fog; and they were all together.

Fine.

Time to make a surprise attack on the Administration of the Domitt Prison.

CHAPTER THIRTEEN

Assistant Administrator Merig Belan had finished the furnace cleaning schedule at last. But it was still some time before the morning; and this was the worst time. The tide out in the Tannerbay was turning, down beyond the Iron Gate; and when conditions were right, the trouble of the waters echoed all the way up to Rudistal, eights and eights upriver. The chop on the water had always frightened Belan, for no particular reason.

Shuddering, Belan took another drink. He was safe here, far from the river, further yet from the Tannerbay. By himself, in his office, all alone. He didn't want to be alone: he could go and find the night-watchman, solicit a game of guesses or something. He outranked the night-watchman. He could insist.

And the night-watchman was Sentish, not Pyana, which would be all to the good; except that Sentish had been here when the Domitt Prison had come to Rudistal, and how was he to explain why he should be alive and here while the Nurail who had been part of Rudistal's life for all of this time were gone?

And no trace of them.

No trace except ash from the furnaces, laid down as drainage at the reclamation site and the roads leading from the prison to the work areas. No trace but for what might lie beneath the walls of the great dike that Geltoi was constructing to reclaim the land at the bend of the river from the water. Winter was coming; and after that, spring. How would it be if there was to be flooding when the snowmelt came?

The pontoon bridges across the river would be torn out, if they weren't moved in time. Rudistal might lose its land-bridge yet again. And if the reclamation site was flooded, if the river scoured beneath the foundations of the dike, if bone and hair and rotting flesh should surface in the black chop of the river as it fought its way through Rudistal toward the Iron Gate?

More liquor. Belan shook the bottle in his hand; empty, oh, this could not be allowed to happen. He was getting hysterical. Nothing was amiss. Nothing was wrong. Geltoi's request for relief of the Inquisitor had gone out on a standard receipt, normal priority. Business as usual.

No urgency, nothing wrong, simply a parting of the ways between a prison administration—whose documentation was perfectly in order, that had nothing to hide—and one over-young, arrogant Inquisitor with no respect for normal channels of authority or the common expectations of military courtesy. Nothing more.

So the recall orders would come soon. Administrator Geltoi would call a Fleet escort to see the Inquisitor out of the Domitt Prison. Whatever Koscuisko might say when he returned to *Scylla* would have to be referred through channels eight layers deep as a procedural complaint.

That process took weeks—sometimes even months—to reach the Bench level. There would be plenty of time to position themselves to answer any challenges from Koscuisko to the Bench's satisfaction. Geltoi was confident of his ability to smooth things over and explain any apparent anomalies for the simple misunderstandings that they were.

Perhaps they'd been a little careless, operating without any oversight for as long as they had done. Things would be different from now on.

Was Geltoi truly confident that he could survive anything Koscuisko said?

Or did he simply mean to put whatever blame on Merig Belan, and cry ignorance?

Geltoi had made him sign the kitchen audit—

No, Belan told himself firmly. He was not going to get paranoid.

And if Geltoi meant to do that, there wasn't anything Belan could do about it to protect himself anyway; Geltoi was Pyana, and Belan was no match for him. It was better to believe just what the Administrator said.

The orders would come, Koscuisko would leave. The woman would be returned to the service house, though they would have to question her about potentially compromising information she might have learned from the Inquisitor in bed. The cook would be questioned as well, if somewhat more carefully; they were not in too much danger from the cook, and the cook was to be paid, after all. It would all work out.

And once the sun but rose across the river he could leave, he could go to his little house and wash and eat and be away from here for a few hours at least. Administrator Geltoi would not be coming in before midmorning, surely, not after having been called back to the prison after supper. He could have five hours between sunup and return. But in order to survive till then he had to drink, because the trouble on the river raised the trouble in the fog, thick and white and murmurous on the south side of the building.

It had been Geltoi's idea of a joke to put Belan's office on the south side of the building. Belan was sure of it. That was just the sort of sense of humor Geltoi had. Belan turned on the lights, all of them, he shut the sun-shields to close out the night, but he knew that the fog was out there.

Waiting for him.

Wouldn't it be easier to take his life and go into the fog for once and all?

Wouldn't that be better than living in constant fear, fear of the fog, fear of Administrator Geltoi's ridicule, fear of the resentment the prison staff had for him, one lone Nurail in a nest of venomous Pyana?

Maybe if he got drunk enough he could find the nerve to do it, without having to think too hard about the irreversibility of the consequences.

To get drunk he needed liquor.

He'd finished what he'd had in his office hours ago.

He knew where he could get some more, though.

Administrator Geltoi kept several bottles of decent drinkable in his office. He wouldn't miss one of them. Belan could be sure it was replaced before that could happen. He could go quietly enough; the fog would not know that he was there, and it was nearly morning. The spirits would be losing their night-strength and retreating to their graves anyway. Unquiet; but impotent, or nearly so.

Right.

Rising from behind his desk-table, Assistant Administrator Belan went to open the closed door of his office, the door he had closed to shut out the voices in the fog. Someone had left a vent-shutter open, he was sure of it, he would have a search made in the morning; but once the sun had set he didn't dare get near any such vent that might let the fog in, and the spirits with it. With his door closed they wouldn't know where he was; there would be no reason for them to come in to look for him.

Quietly.

He almost thought he heard the whisper of the fog in the corridor outside, no sound of voices, but a sound of bodies. What bodies they had were rotted away by now, burned up by the poison of the accelerant even as the rest were burned in the furnace-fire. It was the night-watchman, surely. Only the night-watchman. He was drunk, Belan knew that. He was hearing things.

Taking care to make as little noise as possible, Belan eased the mechanical secures off the door-latch and turned the handle, opening up the door.

Only to fall back from the opening gap in horror and transcendent fear: because the dead were there.

Andrej Koscuisko, the demon Inquisitor, and who knew better than Merig Belan what Koscuisko could do with Nurail, when he chose?

Andrej Koscuisko, standing square in the doorway with the fog on his body and mist in his hair. People behind him, and oh, they might look like Koscuisko's Security, but Belan knew better. The fog gave them away. The fog surrounded them. They were ghastly and terrible with it, and the woman as well, the bondswoman from the service house, hadn't Belan guessed it would be a mistake to set her to serve a man who murdered Nurail?

"Assistant Administrator," Koscuisko said. Belan heard his voice echoing from a very great distance off, and far deeper than Koscuisko's voice had ever been. Because it wasn't Koscuisko's voice. It was the dead speaking, from beneath that weight of earth, their voices heavy and dark with death and rotting. "I'm glad to find you here, I need your help. Gentlemen, if you will."

The fog-policemen came into the room, came forward for him, took him by the arms to raise him up from the floor. The weight of the shackles they latched across his wrists was cold, but it would burn. He had seen the burning in the furnaces. He knew that Koscuisko had guessed, that it was not the first time.

And now he was just another Nurail prisoner, out of all the Nurail prisoners of the Domitt Prison. Merig Belan wept with hopeless despair as the Security brought him to stand before the Inquisitor.

"Very good," Koscuisko said, and he sounded mild-tempered and gentle, but Belan was not fooled. "We were told that you were in the building. I've a small chore for you, let's go upstairs, shall we?"

The fog-policemen moved him forward, out of his office, toward the lift. He didn't mind going upstairs, not so long as it was upstairs in the Administration building, not so long as it was only to Geltoi's office. Geltoi had created this, Geltoi had engineered the crimes that cried for vengeance, but it was Belan who would be punished for them. Poor Belan.

He had reviewed Koscuisko's interrogatories.

He knew what Koscuisko could do, with Nurail prisoners.

The dead men in the fog would have their vengeance . . .

Andrej put the dose through at Belan's throat, and the man relaxed at last. Not much. But enough. There was a look of madness to Belan's eyes, and a peculiar stink to his body that Andrej recognized. They were in the presence of a true psychosis. They would have to be very careful: there was information Belan had that Andrej needed, and he didn't care to lose it by inattention or accident.

That was one reason.

The other reason was that sentient creatures all responded to the near presence of great psychological disturbance by being disturbed themselves. And they were all stressed enough already. For everybody's sake Belan needed to be calmed and comforted, relaxed and reassured.

He needed much more than the emergency set of medications that a senior physician always carried with him, divided up amongst his Security. But Andrej would make do until he got access to Infirmary.

Belan needed help badly. Andrej meant for him to have it, but Andrej needed Belan's help first.

"Merig?" Andrej asked as gently as he could. Ailynn sat and held Belan's hand, stroking it soothingly. That was very good of her. Belan blinked; then looked up at Andrej, as though he was trying to focus.

"Koscuisko. Ah, your Excellency. Sorry, sir, how did you get?—Must have dozed off. What time?"

"Time to call the local Judiciary, I need a transmit. How do I find the direct, from here."

Administrator Geltoi's office was logically where access to the local Judiciary would be found, because only Administrator Geltoi—or his deputy—had business making direct contact with such exalted levels of authority.

Once Andrej but got to an appropriate transmit, he could cry his plaint, and be secure that it would be heard. He had to let Captain Vopalar know what was happening. But first he had to be sure he could get through to the Bench before anybody realized what was going on, to stop him.

"Oh, well, that." Belan struggled to his feet a little clumsily, staring at his shackled wrists in mild confusion. "Now, how did that happen? Oh, well. The Administrator's direct line here, your Excellency. Only be sure to engage the refer, or else Security won't get a listen-in. And, oh, the Administrator likes the recorder off, sensitive nature of the discussion. That kind of thing. Why, I remember, one day, I had to call to town for him about arranging for payment for the flour, and I forgot to set the recorder to null, and he was so angry."

Andrej nodded to Ailynn, and she drew Belan away with her to sit down on the low couch to one side of the room. Turn the Security refer off, so that nobody here would be on monitor, whether or not they happened to notice the communication going out. Turn the recorder on, to be sure he had evidence if necessary.

It took some moments for his transmit request to go through, since he was sending it as far as he was. He wanted to be sure to register his claim at the Bench level; there was too much at stake if he should complain only to Chilleau Judiciary. Too much of a temptation would exist to cover up, quiet things, hush it all over.

He couldn't risk that.

This had to be published, not to discountenance Chilleau

Judiciary—though it was perhaps unfortunately certain to, whether justly or not—but in order to surface the wider question. Chilleau Judiciary was not corrupt. How could this have been allowed to happen?

The counter-validation code showed in the communications screen.

Bench access.

Personal attention, na Roqua den Tensa, First Judge Presiding at Fontailloe Judiciary. Or her Court; it was all the same in Law for the purposes of crying his plaint. Receipt validation requested from Chilleau Judiciary.

Still Andrej hesitated.

He'd never so much as spoken to a Judge at such an exalted level before, and the prospect of standing before the First Judge at Fontailloe to speak his piece was a daunting one.

" . . . with sterile ash," Belan was saying. "Where was the harm in that?" Talking to Ailynn about whatever. Probably not about anything that anyone could even make sense of in his current state of mind, with the drugs Andrej had fed him taken into account.

The word "ash" caught in Andrej's mind, and gave him strength.

He was not standing alone in front of the Bench, to cry a claim like a private citizen.

He was a Bench officer, whose Fleet rank only betokened his Judicial function. And he was not alone. It was not his complaint. It was the cry of the murdered prisoners of the Domitt Prison that he made before the First Judge. It was the burned victims of the furnaces who put out their hands for justice, and not him.

"I am Andrej Ulexeievitch Koscuisko." It was to be spoken, because the Bench validated his identity on his voice as well as on the codes that had been assigned to him for his use when he had taken up his Writ. "I hold the Writ to Inquire at the Domitt Prison. Due to the existence of multiple and systematic improprieties having to do with prisoner processing and documentation it has become necessary to cry failure of Writ at the Domitt Prison."

He had no legal formula to declare failure of Writ. They hadn't really studied it at Fleet Orientation Station Medical, where he had received his training in jurisprudence and torture.

"The immediate assignment of a Bench audit team is respectfully solicited. I have made this Brief, and I will stand on the justice of the decision, and hazard what consequences may accrue should the Bench invalidate my finding."

He waited.

If the Bench reversed his finding, they would be clear to interpret his withdrawal of his Writ as an act of mutiny; and for mutiny even an Inquisitor was vulnerable to the most extreme penalty in the inventory.

There was no help for it.

He could not go quietly back to *Scylla* and let those furnaces continue to burn, not to save his life.

Was his cry to be intercepted, refused, declined by some Clerk of Court at Fontailloe Judiciary, too radical a plea to be admitted?

Failure of Writ.

It had not been cried against a Judicial institution that Andrej could remember in his life.

There was a clattering of sound in the com-access, and Andrej knew by the way in which the com-access fought to recalibrate itself that it was processing a clear-signal at the extreme limits of its tolerance.

Koscuisko. This is the duty. Officer, Fontailloe Judiciary. Stand by for the. First Judge.

But it was weeks and weeks between Rudistal and Fontailloe Judiciary . . .

Every booster station between here and the Gollipse vector had to be on maximum override.

Andrej sat down, frightened of his own temerity, awed by the immensity of what he had done; and the voice that sounded next— and it was a voice, garbled and indistinct though it was—chilled him through to bones he hadn't realized he even had.

"What do you claim to have. Been done, young man. Be sure of what you say to me."

The First Judge.

Na Roqua den Tensa, Fontailloe Judiciary.

The First Judge Presiding on the Jurisdiction's Bench.

She had maintained the Judicial order all of Andrej's life and her law was legend.

"Murder has been done, your Honor, to the great shame and disgrace of the Judicial order." He was so ashamed, to have come before her in such cause. This was the First Judge. And yet he knew that he was right. "Nurail are under Jurisdiction, they are not to be tortured and killed absent due and adequate process. The Writ has failed horribly at the Domitt Prison, your Honor, and we cannot in Law tolerate it."

How could he say such a thing to the First Judge?

He could hardly believe he was really speaking to her.

"What does Chilleau Judiciary say. Why take so drastic a step."

How could he challenge the First Judge, over a handful of Nurail lives?

Even if that handful should run to thousands, how could it compare to the greater good of all under Jurisdiction?

"I have cried direct, your Honor. I fear for loss of evidence."

Please.

He to whom so many useless pleas for mercy, pity, understanding had been addressed, he could not plead for mercy or understanding. He would stand or fail on the Judicial merit of his plaint.

"Do you know who I am, young Koscuisko?"

Was it his imagination, or was there amusement in that multiply transmitted and retransmitted voice?

"You are the First Judge." Before whom he could only bend his neck in humility. "Den Tensa, of good Precedent and grave ruling. Fontailloe Judiciary."

She was offended at him.

His cause was trivial, in the greater scheme of things.

He could not believe that the murder of guiltless parties was trivial, no matter how few. It was not an issue of relative importance. The rule of Law was absolute: or else it was not the rule of Law.

"Then be by me deputized, pending the arrival. Of an audit party. To you I grant authority in Port Rudistal, and any Fleet resources on call. Do your duty and uphold the rule of Law. Fontailloe Judiciary, away here."

The com-access cleared, the words resounding in his mind and heart.

Do your duty, and uphold the rule of Law.

Andrej wanted to weep, and guessed that he was still in a state of profound shock from what he had seen in the furnace-room, compounded by this unforeseen development.

He didn't have time to weep. There was no telling whether the destruction of evidence had already begun; whether the furnaces were already being sanitized. No asking Merig Belan either. Andrej mastered his emotion with a furious effort of will. He had work to do.

The receipt of the boosted signal would have alerted the Port Authority and the Dramissoi Relocation Fleet alike, though they would not have been able to read it. There was no time to lose. The prison might be on alert. Andrej studied the standard inquires on the com-access for a moment and made his selection.

"Andrej Ulexeievitch Koscuisko, at the Domitt Prison. For Bench Captain Sinjosi Vopalar, on emergency immediate."

He wanted a drink. Several.

But he needed troops, and Vopalar had them.

Oh, if it should give him second thoughts to assert his claim before the Bench, what was he to say to his father?

How could he ever excuse himself for challenging his lawful superiors?

He was already in disgrace for having so long resisted his father's will that he serve as Ship's Inquisitor.

He would never receive his father's blessing, now. Still less would his child gain acceptance.

"Skein in braid, your Excellency. Vopalar on thread, convert."

There was no help for it. He couldn't buy his father's blessing with the unavenged death of Nurail prisoners. He had no choice.

And utter despair was liberating, in a sense, because as long as there was no way in which he could be reconciled to his father—no matter how dutiful he strove to be—then there was no further use in duty; except to do justice. As he saw it. Not as his father would wish.

"Captain Vopalar?" he asked. "I beg your pardon, your Excellency. I have at the Domitt Prison a failure of Writ declared. And am in immediate need of your troops, in order to ensure that evidence be preserved."

The First Judge had spoken his name, and said that he was to do his duty.

For the first time in a long time, Andrej both understood his task and believed in it, completely.

⊕ ⊕ ⊕

Caleigh Samons stood in formation behind her officer of assignment, waiting for the gates to open.

It was sunrise in Port Rudistal; the fog was beginning to grow lighter, though as thick as it had come up from the river it would be hours before it actually burned off. And the fog had proved a valuable ally, during this past night.

It had concealed their descent from the penthouse from any stray observer's eye; it concealed the bulk of Vopalar's troops now. Three hundred troops, on either side of the containment wall. Belan had opened up the gate in the containment wall an hour ago. Now they were waiting for Belan to order the opening of the gates into the prison itself.

It was early yet.

The prison was still asleep.

Oh, the kitchen was awake, and the laundry, and the furnaces never stopped. The new shift had not come on since they had brought the officer up from the furnace-room. There was no way to be certain of what Administrator Geltoi might have told his staff; as far as they had been able to tell from what Belan had to say, Geltoi had left it all for the morning. They would be lucky, if it were so.

Almost unreasonably lucky.

Caleigh didn't like it.

It was more than the risk of destruction of evidence.

If Koscuisko could not find evidence, if Koscuisko's charges could not be proven out before the Bench—

The privilege of the Writ would not protect Koscuisko, if the Bench decided he had no cause to cry failure of Writ.

The knowledge that no other Inquisitor Caleigh had supported was capable of what Koscuisko could do with a Tenth Level command termination made the prospect of Koscuisko meeting his death that way no less horrible to her.

The fog dampened sound, as well as concealing troops. She heard nothing from behind them, though she knew that there were people waiting in formation, with Bench Lieutenant Goslin Plugrath to command them. Captain Vopalar they had left in the Administration building with Ailynn to coax Belan into what they needed from him; Caleigh wished they'd hurry up. She was cold. She didn't care to be frightened for Koscuisko's sake.

Had it been less than four shifts since this had started?

Was it really just yesterday they'd gone down to Infirmary, to audit?

Now she heard more activity up ahead; now she could sense movement, from the gates. Guards speaking to each other loud and careless, innocent of apprehension. So the Assistant Administrator wanted them to open the gates early. So what? Who knew what spooks that Nurail was seeing these days?

The gate began to track, heavy and ponderous.

A sudden lance of light shot out into the dark and lay across the graveled ground, widening moment by moment as the gate opened. Light from inside the prison. The great courtyard, empty now, and all the buildings dark except for the lights in the mess building reflected against the east interior wall of the prison.

"Gentles," Koscuisko said. They started forward.

Caleigh hated this, she hated it, it made her flesh creep. There was no reason to expect a problem. She knew that. And still she was letting Andrej Koscuisko walk into the prison courtyard, functionally alone, unarmed, the man who had cried failure of Writ down on the head of Administrator Geltoi and everyone on his staff—

They didn't know.

Yet.

That was the only thing that made it even possible.

Calm and collected, Koscuisko crossed the gate-track, stepped across the threshold with his Security, strolled toward the dispatch building to fetch the duty officer.

It was so quiet.

The fog seemed to follow them, pouring in through the gates. It could not penetrate. it was too warm inside the courtyard, with the lights. But still the fog came. Koscuisko waded through the fog up the steps of the dispatch building, and Caleigh followed in his wake. It was superstitious to imagine that the fog was following them. Fog had no volition.

The duty officer was sitting in the wide foyer of the dispatch building bent over a document on his desk. A narrative? Maybe he was working a puzzle; he seemed completely absorbed, one way or the other.

Koscuisko spoke.

"Good-greeting, duty officer."

It took a moment for the sound of an unfamiliar voice to register, apparently. Caleigh could sympathize. It was the end of the night-shift; and what could happen within a prison, really?

"We have to effect a change in duty rosters, duty officer. Your assistance will be required. Please come with me."

Comprehension came slowly; but the duty officer knew Koscuisko's rank by sight, if not the officer himself. "Your pardon, your Excellency, didn't—ah—didn't hear you come in, sir. What's needed? If the officer please."

No idea. No hint of discomfort or dissimulation. Caleigh knew a sigh of relief was bottled up inside of her, somewhere. If the duty officer was unconcerned, no one had warned him about anything, put him on notice, tipped him off. It could be all right.

"Thank you, duty officer, I wish for you to come with me to meet the Bench Lieutenant. His name is Goslin Plugrath, and he needs to examine the day's order of duty. It will be this way."

Back out of the building, onto the steps. The courtyard was full of Plugrath's troops, the gate-crew held in a small cluster now near the gatehouse. Plugrath was waiting for them, and not very patiently. The sun was coming up. The day-shift would be arriving soon. They had to be in control of the prison before that started happening. There weren't enough troops to relieve the current shift and turn the new shift back from the prison gates at the same time. Something would slip.

"Duty officer?"

Plugrath was too anxious about his task to think twice about protocol, but Koscuisko simply stood to one side to let him talk. The duty officer was pale now in the lights at the foot of the dispatch building. But he kept his voice low as he replied: no panic, no frantic attempts to give warning. Maybe the entire prison wasn't corrupt.

Or maybe there were people who were just as glad to be stopped, now that they were to be forced to stop.

"Bench Lieutenant Plugrath. The officer said you needed my assistance, sir."

Koscuisko was satisfied that Plugrath had things under control, one way or the other. Plugrath took the duty officer back into the building: he would get the location of all the night staff, who they were, where they were, and call them in one by one until Plugrath's people had replaced each and every one of them. Then they would be ready to receive the day-shift; but Koscuisko wasn't about to wait.

"Miss Samons, one of those squads belongs to me," Koscuisko said. True enough. Plugrath had agreed. Caleigh called out the appointed squad leader with a gesture of her hand.

"Section Leader Poris, your Excellency."

And would have a rough shift of it. But had been warned.

"Let us to the detention area go." Koscuisko was halfway down the stairs as he spoke, and his Bonds with him. "I fear trying work for you all, gentles, but soonest started is soonest sung, and this cannot be left for moment longer."

Punishment block.

People had been tortured, there.

With luck they would find evidence, but Caleigh couldn't help but hope there were no prisoners.

It stank.

Pausing on the threshold to the punishment block, Andrej Koscuisko gathered his courage into his two hands and found it pitifully inadequate to the challenge that faced him. More than anything he did not want to go into punishment block. And more than anything he knew that it had to be done.

He turned on the lights, and someone screamed in terror; and once one screamed, others joined in, frightened by the existence of such fear. Fear born of agony was communicable, especially to other souls who knew what it felt like.

How many cells were here, in punishment block?

And, oh, how long would it be before he had well cleared it?

Evidence, Andrej reminded himself, firmly. He had to preserve what evidence was here, and seal the cellblock for the forensic team that the Bench would send. If there were prisoners here who could be healed, he needed their evidence. If there were men here who could not be saved, he needed to enter that fact into evidence. And if there was suffering, it was outside the rule of Law, unlawfully inflicted, unlawfully invoked. It had to be stopped by any and all means at his disposal.

He took a step, two steps, and the night-guard opened up the cell for him. He could hear the sound of the cell's inmate breathing, as though blowing bubbles in the water; and knew without needing to look what had been done. But had to go in. Had to loose restraints, and press the doses through. Had to look, and see, and note, and take evidence.

There was nothing else that he could do, not for this man. "Let the Record show." He could hear the frantic horror in his voice, and choked it back into his belly. He was the officer in charge. He was responsible here. His report had to be complete and concise, too perfect to be challenged in evidence before the Bench.

"Nurail hominid, adult male. Unlawfully restrained, reference is made to the Eighth Level of Inquiry, partial suspension with restricted airway. Multiple lacerations, compound fracture at the left lower leg and upper right thigh, several days untreated to judge by necrosis of tissue. Administration of eleven units of midimic at jugular pulse, stabilization pending arrival of additional medical resources from Port Rudistal."

There, that was one.

And only one.

He could not stop and think. He had to go on. "Let the Record show."

And another. "Adult male hominid, Nurail or Sarcosmet."

Five.

"Burns of the third degree of severity, to the extent of approximately." Eight.

"No visible evidence, suspected use of psychoactive drugs. No intervention possible pending blood-panels. Patient to be restrained to await psychiatric evaluation."

Eleven.

"Consistent with employment of an instrument similar to a peony, dead for perhaps four eights at time of discovery."

Fourteen.

"With evident intent to mutilate. Partial recovery may be possible, cyborg augmentation to be implemented."

Seventeen.

The punishment block went on forever.

There were only twenty-three souls there.

And yet it seemed that there were three and twenty thousand of them, to Andrej.

And it was all his fault because he was the Writ on site at the Domitt Prison.

And he should have known.
And he had done nothing.

It was a beautiful day in Port Rudistal.

Administrator Geltoi had overslept, his fond indulgent wife letting him lie until mid-meal was on the table. He'd scolded her, very gently; his heart hadn't been in it, and besides a man didn't raise his voice to a woman. Let alone to his wife, who should be sacred to him.

Therefore he'd risen and washed, and dressed, and kissed his wife and the children who were at home; and now he was ready to face the scene that he was anticipating with Merig Belan. If he didn't hear from Chilleau Judiciary today, he would send a confirm message, and that would be enough. Chilleau Judiciary would send Andrej Koscuisko back to *Scylla* in disgrace. He would be rid of that concern.

There was a good deal to thank Koscuisko for: his impertinent curiosity had pointed out one or two areas in which potential for improvement existed in the documentation of prisoner processing. They would have time to recover from that. Koscuisko was going away.

Work on the land reclamation project would probably have to slow down, with the new atmosphere of accountability. Scrutiny. He had been free from any oversight till now, and Administrator Geltoi could find it in him to resent Chilleau Judiciary for the change in his status. He was accustomed to being an independent agent. He had earned autonomy. Hadn't he built the Domitt Prison from the ground up, on time, under budget?

What good were Nurail lives to Jurisdiction if not to toil in its service?

But the world changed, and a prudent man changed with it. He had his earnings either way. There was no fear of losing the fortune he'd made, and no sense complaining about his fate because the next would come more slowly.

He was looking forward to the arrival of Koscuisko's orders.

Should he have an interview with Koscuisko, their formal debriefing? Koscuisko would be confused and resentful. Geltoi would explain that he had no choice but to comply with direction. He would remind Koscuisko that it was he who was in command of the Domitt Prison, and not Andrej Koscuisko. He would dismiss Koscuisko to escort with the contempt Koscuisko's behavior had earned.

A beautiful day.

The sun was brilliant in an ice-blue sky. It was cold, but Geltoi insisted on leaving the roof of his new touring car open anyway, enjoying the brisk invigorating stream of cold air in his face. A good coat was proof against any chill, and he had one, with warm gloves besides; and he never tired of the view, approaching the containment wall of the Domitt Prison, the peaked roof of the Administration building rising above it, the great black wall of the prison proper above that. The penthouse, crowning the wall.

Geltoi looked up at the penthouse and smiled broadly. Koscuisko would not have had an easy night of it, wondering what was to become of him. And then the summons to Administrator Geltoi's office would come . . .

There was the penthouse on the roof.

But—oddly enough—

Geltoi frowned, searching the roofline.

The flue-vents of the furnaces.

No smoke.

No cheerful hygienic column of white cloud to reassure him that garbage was being disposed of properly. Burned beyond any hope of recognition or identification. Reduced to undifferentiated ash.

No smoke?

Belan had been a little premature, surely. It was true that they had to do a little emergency cleaning, just to be sure that nothing in the furnace-room could create an unfortunate impression. But Belan was to have presented a schedule first.

Maybe he needed to have a talk with Belan.

Standing on the earth that covered the crane-pit, perhaps, to provide a little background.

The Administration building seemed strangely quiet, at first glance; it was a little eerie. The courtyard in front of the Administration building was deserted. No sign of movement or activity within the building—except that, if he craned his neck, Administrator Geltoi could see that his office seemed to be occupied by someone.

His office.

He couldn't tell much more than that there was someone there, standing near the windows.

Belan took such liberties?

He'd soon see about that.

Geltoi strode into the building with confidence and fury alike animating his step. Where was the staff? Of course. It was time for the mid-meal break. There was a day-watchman on duty by the lift-nexus, and he should have been quick to come down the stairs and greet his Administrator with a polite bow. He hadn't come down at all. Geltoi ignored him with as much icy disdain as he could muster out of a cold fury.

The day-watchman could be dealt with later.

Right now he intended to find out what species of madness had overtaken Merig Belan and possessed him to make free with Geltoi's office in Geltoi's absence.

The lift opened onto the corridor, and his office was at the far end. The office doors wide open, both of them. There were Fleet Security posted at the lift, and again outside his office; they came to attention as he stepped out of the lift, snapping to with satisfying precision. Respect. What were they doing here? And outside his office, as well?

Administrator Geltoi hurried toward the office with all deliberate speed, pausing on the threshold to take stock of the situation.

His office was full of people.

There was someone in his chair, but Geltoi couldn't see who; the chair was turned to the window, with its back to the room.

Sitting on the couch to the left, a short blond man in a dark dusty uniform, slumped over on the edge of the seat with his shaggy head buried between the palms of his soiled hands.

Andrej Koscuisko?

There was that Security Chief of Koscuisko's, right enough, and Koscuisko's green-sleeved bond-involuntary troops as well.

Very good indeed.

Clearly orders had come in overnight, and Belan had wanted Koscuisko to be here waiting for his dismissal. Belan could be faulted on execution, but not on instinct. And it was enough of a relief to realize that Koscuisko's orders were in hand that Geltoi forgave Belan this misappropriation of his office in advance of Belan's explanation.

His role was to be that of the surprised senior administrator coming upon an unexpected occupation force: very close to exactly what he was, except that he knew what was going on, and was looking forward to playing it out.

"So. Doctor Koscuisko."

Koscuisko dropped his hands, raising his face to look at Geltoi as he strode confidently in. Koscuisko looked an absolute wreck. Perhaps the experience would teach him something: sober him, make him a better officer. As long as Koscuisko was a better officer far, far away from the Domitt Prison, Geltoi did not grudge him any good his brief imprisonment might have done him.

Geltoi stopped in front of the couch to put a point to the lesson. There were other Security in here as well as Koscuisko's: some Fleet security—but Geltoi ignored them.

"How unfortunate that it should have to end like this, Koscuisko. We acted in good faith, I remind you, and took great pains to see you lacked for nothing."

Koscuisko rose stiffly to his feet. His uniform was filthy and there was an unsubtle odor about it as well that Geltoi declined to identify. He had clearly been up all night; drinking, most likely. That would explain the blank hostile uncomprehending stare Koscuisko was giving him. It was a little uncanny. Stupid as Koscuisko looked, unkempt as he was, he almost did look Nurail to Geltoi.

The realization distracted Geltoi for a moment: what if Koscuisko had been found in the furnace-room, looking like that? Would it be so great a loss if his honest hard-working furnace-crew made a mistake, quite reasonable under the circumstances, and clubbed Koscuisko unconscious to feed the furnaces?

Calling his fantasies firmly to heel, Geltoi spoke on. "While you have done nothing but engage in obstructionary and insubordinate behavior since you got here. The rumors we'd heard were right about you all along. No respect for honest decent working folk. No respect for authority—"

Failure to know his place and keep to it, stubborn refusal to honor the natural order and respect his superiors. Nurail in more than one way. And Geltoi would have told Koscuisko, too, but for some unaccountable reason he found himself flat on his back on the floor. Koscuisko kneeling on his stomach. Koscuisko's hands, locked around his throat, and the thumbs pressed deep into the pulse on either side of his windpipe.

What—

Koscuisko's face was a blue-and-white mask of furious hatred and indescribable loathing, and all for being told a few home truths about himself?

He couldn't breathe.

"Murderer," Koscuisko hissed at him through teeth clenched tight and bared in savage contempt. "Impious. Unfilial. Outlaw. Vandal. Murderer—"

Then Koscuisko was pulled off, finally, though it took all four of his slave Security to do it. Fleet Security helped Geltoi to his feet, and Belan decided to turn around, finally.

It was about time.

Belan hadn't jumped out of the great desk chair at the sound of Geltoi's voice, which was annoying. Belan was turning slowly from the window with no evident intention of surrendering his place to its rightful occupant.

"Your Excellency. You must wait upon the judgment of the Bench for that, with respect, sir."

It wasn't Belan's voice.

The man in the chair was Bench Lieutenant Plugrath, swiveling to square himself to the desk-table's surface and toggle into braid. "Chanson, close the gates. Quarantine in effect for local staff. Good-greeting, Administrator Geltoi."

Koscuisko spoke, his struggle to master himself evident. "Yes, of course, Lieutenant. You are right." Security was not letting go of Koscuisko, holding him by his arms, standing close behind him. Oddly enough Security hadn't let go of Geltoi himself, either. "Geltoi, I never thought to believe it could be true. But I have learned. There is a crime under Jurisdiction that deserves Tenth Level command termination. And you have done it. I will have you, Geltoi."

Security appeared to relax as Koscuisko spoke. One of his green-sleeves bowed, presenting a white-square that Koscuisko declined; with a quick gesture of his head, by way of thanks.

Geltoi stared in shock at the officer in Geltoi's chair, seated behind Geltoi's desk-table, making himself perfectly at home in Geltoi's office. "Lieutenant. What is the meaning of this? Where is Assistant Administrator Belan?"

Belan had been here late last night working. Why hadn't Belan warned him that Plugrath had come to visit? What were these Fleet Security doing here, if not to escort Koscuisko out of the Domitt

Prison? Plugrath's escort, perhaps. Maybe the Dramissoi Relocation Fleet Commander had sent Plugrath with this escort in token of Koscuisko's rank. Yes. That could be. Geltoi felt a little better.

"Administrator Belan has been removed to a secure psychiatric facility in Port Rudistal, Administrator. On orders from the commander pro tem of the Domitt Prison, his Excellency, Andrej Koscuisko."

Koscuisko?

Commanding?

Impossible.

The carpeted flooring eroded like wet sand in a rising tide underneath Geltoi's feet. Shaking himself free from Security's grasp with an impatient twist, Geltoi staggered forward, catching at the fore-edge of the desk-table for balance. "Let me see if I take your meaning, Lieutenant. You have taken my poor Merig to the hospital. What wild claims has he been making?"

And what had Koscuisko said?

Security came up behind him, taking his arms once more. But not holding them this time. Security pulled his arms behind his back, and Geltoi felt the cold kiss of the manacles latching around his wrists without quite understanding what it was.

What was going on?

Were these actually chains? Was this how it felt to be made a prisoner? Interesting. But he was not a prisoner. He was the Administrator of the Domitt Prison. Something was not adding up.

"Quite an astonishing number," Plugrath admitted, almost cheerfully. "Not very coherent, any of it. His Excellency has sent for a Sarvaw forensics team to excavate. There will be physical evidence soon enough. And in the meantime—"

Sarvaw forensics? Whatever could that mean?

The construction pit.

The Nurail they had buried there.

Sarvaw forensics teams were top of the line for gathering physical evidence from mass burials. Koscuisko was Dolgorukij. He would know. It was Dolgorukij that had massacred all those Sarvaw for the forensics teams to practice on.

"I want him very carefully maintained," Koscuisko said to Lieutenant Plugrath. Koscuisko hardly deigned to notice he was there, any more. Koscuisko didn't have to. "There are reparations to be made, punishment owing too many times over to count. I do not mean to risk escape of any sort. I trust you take my meaning, Bench Lieutenant."

"Yes, sir. I understand." Plugrath's submission to Koscuisko's authority was too absolute. Geltoi could hardly bear to hear it. "I'll pledge his safety to you personally, your Excellency. You'll be wanting to move your people into town, I expect."

"Out of this place," Koscuisko agreed. "Thank you, Lieutenant."

The furnaces should have warned him. The furnaces had stopped. Koscuisko had people here to rake the furnaces out, and number up the unregistered dead to claim vengeance against him. Belan had whimpered to them about the dead in the construction pit, and Belan could tell a very great deal more to Geltoi's disadvantage. Belan was Nurail. He had no backbone, no courage, no strength of will to speak of.

Caught between a treacherous Nurail to one side and the prospect of being made to serve as Chilleau Judiciary's scapegoat on the other, Administrator Geltoi weighed his options as he weighed the stalloy cuffs that chained his wrists.

And decided.

"You're making a significant error, Lieutenant." He tried to sound sorrowful, while investing his words with as much aggrieved dignity as possible. "I don't know what allegations our poor Merig may have made, nor how much faith a prudent man should have in the ravings of a madman. I fear for your career; and you could profit by this instead, if you so chose."

He could brazen out the evidence somehow. He could see to it that Belan was silenced before evidence could be placed on-Record. But if he once allowed himself to be removed as a prisoner, he was as good as dead. He was not in a very good position here and now: he had been taken by surprise. He could still make it work, if only he could walk out of his office a free man.

"Not my mistake to make, Administrator Geltoi," Lieutenant Plugrath said, respectfully enough, but with no hint of regret or uncertainty in his voice. "His Excellency has cried failure of Writ against the Domitt Prison. The Bench will decide if there have been errors made. Not I."

Plugrath gave Koscuisko the nod as he said it. There was no love lost between the two officers, perhaps, but there seemed to be little hope of making a wedge between them, either. Administrator Geltoi sought for the right words, the right thing to say, something that would work to break this intolerable spell. This could not be happening. He'd walked into a nightmare.

Lieutenant Plugrath nodded at someone behind Geltoi. "Ready to transport, squad leader. Secure your prisoner and escort to custody as previously detailed, secured psychiatric."

No.

"You can't do this to me!" Geltoi shrieked. "You don't dare—do you know who I am—"

They picked him up and carried him away, kicking and screaming, his dignity lost to him now as finally as his position. As his future. As his life.

It didn't matter how much prisoners screamed.

The Bench would have its evidence.

Koscuisko was petty and vengeful, and Koscuisko was Nurail after all; but Koscuisko was an Inquisitor, with the ultimate penalty within his power to inflict if the Bench ruled—

Administrator Geltoi sank like a dead weight in the grasp of the Security who carried him, and wept like a man bereft.

His prison, his prisoners, his work-crews. His land reclamation project. His money.

All gone.

And nothing left—

Except that he could see to it that Chilleau Judiciary did not turn its back on him, he would give evidence.

Why couldn't they have listened to him, and called Andrej Koscuisko back to *Scylla* before any of this could have happened?

CHAPTER FOURTEEN

Andrej Koscuisko stood on the planking that protected the lip of the pit being excavated, watching the forensics team at their painstaking work below.

From where he stood he could see the careful grid marked off with chalked lines, and the bracing that supported a partially decayed body with too precise a correspondence to how it had been uncovered for anyone's peace of mind. Clawing its way frantically toward the surface, the head thrown back, the jaw carefully wired into the open-mouthed—dirt-filled—scream that had formed one last protest against atrocity.

There could be no possible hope of misinterpretation. Whoever it had been, it had been a living soul, buried alive, and fully awake to the horror of its cruel fate as it happened.

"Caustic losteppan, ground fine," the shift supervisor—Sarvaw, as was most of the team—noted, passing a closed vial of clear glass to Andrej for examination. "Broadcast into the pit before they started filling. Don't get it on your skin, sir, this stuff will start to dissolve flesh within moments."

Raising his eyes to the black wall that rose up in front of them on the other side of the pit, Andrej found he could not suppress a shudder. "What a fearful way to die." No one would challenge that, it was too obvious, but the horror he felt was too much to be held in. The excavation was too good. It was too clear. He could almost hear the screaming. "How many bodies in the pit? At a guess?"

651

But the shift supervisor shook her head. "No guessing yet, your Excellency. Imaging scans show too much confusion at the next level to be able to sort it out. Going by bone density it could be upwards of three hundred souls."

Andrej shuddered again, and it wasn't because of the cold or the smell of earth, heavy with decaying flesh. "Thank you, shift supervisor. You should receive every assistance, speak to the Administration if help should flag."

The woman bowed respectfully, but Andrej didn't think she cared what he said one way or the other. Why should she? She was Sarvaw, he was Dolgorukij. Worse than Dolgorukij, Aznir Dolgorukij, the twice-great-grandson of Chuvishka Kospodar. He could protest his outrage all he liked, in public or in private. No Sarvaw would believe him.

Or if they did, it would make no difference. This was still atrocity that the Sarvaw had learned to judge against the Kospodar rule.

Turning away from the grave pit, Andrej began to cross the planking toward the Administration building, and Security—Code and Erish—fell in to place behind him. There were people coming on foot from in front of the Administrative building toward them, a small group—six, and four of them Andrej thought he recognized.

He was not particularly farsighted. But Andrej knew his Bonds, and he had left Security 5.3 on *Scylla*, so what were they doing here?

Not only that.

It seemed to Andrej that Code knew more than just his fellow Bonds; and came as close as Andrej had ever known him to missing a step, near-stumbling.

Afraid.

As the party drew near, Andrej could get more of its members sorted one from the other. Cel Tonivish. Iyo Lorig. Hart Aicans. Specs Fiskka. Yes, Security 5.3. No Robert St. Clare, Andrej was grateful to see. It was hard enough for him to see all of these beaten punished prisoners who looked like Robert to him without Robert actually being here.

Two officers in Administrative grays, but Andrej wasn't familiar with the branch of service that the steel-gray piping on the uniform might indicate.

Erish was fearfully tense, all of a sudden.

Then Andrej knew.

These officers were dancing-masters.

And that could only mean—

"Your Excellency." The senior of the two dancing-masters brought up his detail and saluted, very solemnly. "News from the Bench, sir, perhaps you've been expecting us."

Dancing-masters were the people that the Bench put in charge of the difficult period of conditioning and training that a bond-involuntary underwent between the implantation of the governor and the first duty post. That was why bond-involuntaries were afraid of them. It was nothing personal. And very soon it would be over, at least for three of his Security; and it should have been four, but Joslire had claimed the Day.

Joslire.

"Indeed I hoped for you, in a sense." What was he to call them? He wasn't sure he was supposed to know that they were dancing-masters. He wasn't sure they knew what bond-involuntaries called them, come to that. "Where are the others? Because I think that they should be together."

He knew why they were here. Security 5.3 had clearly been briefed in advance as well, from the fiercely cloaked joy in their faces; and that had been kindly done. Code and Erish could not know and still gave him so much honor as to have relaxed once more within their bond-involuntary's discipline, secure that they were in no danger of bullying in his presence.

"His Excellency's Chief of Security has taken the other Security assigned up to the Administrator's office, sir. We were to tell his Excellency."

They would be waiting for him, then. And not know what it was that they were waiting for. Andrej wanted to hurry. "With dispatch, then, if you please. Code, lead the way."

Code would be staying. Andrej was conscious of the dancing-masters taking their subordinate positions behind him, as Security gathered into formation around them to move into the building. It annoyed him to realize that the dancing-masters were evaluating the performance of his gentlemen with every step they took. It annoyed him even more that he was anxious for their approval as though it meant anything at all to him.

They could not know.

There could be no bond-involuntary Security under Jurisdiction as perfect as his people; and yet Andrej knew too well that to a dancing-master they might seem half-ruined. A bond-involuntary might be said to lose the fine edge of his discipline when he lost his fear of punishment.

But not where Andrej could hear it.

Upstairs in the great gracious office that had belonged to Administrator Geltoi Andrej sat down behind the desk to see what the dancing-masters had brought him. Chief Samons formed 5.3 up in ranks outside of the office, in the hall; and held Code back with them. Security 5.4 stood in the office, with a blank space at the end of the line where Joslire should have been.

The senior officer set the flat tray that he'd been carrying down on the desk, and opened its secures. "His Excellency will wish to see to these himself," the dancing-master said. Safes. Three Safes, one for each of the surviving members of Security 5.4 that had been on board *Scylla* for that fateful event.

And each Safe on a necklace of fine chain to hang around a man's neck, and sit close to the governor, and transmit its carefully restricted signal to the governor to keep it lulled to sleep until such time as the governor could be surgically removed by someone with experience.

"Thank you." He still didn't know what to call them. "It is a very great privilege. And orders?"

He would have liked to do the surgery himself. But he wasn't sure he trusted the level of the technical sophistication at the local hospital to support so delicate a thing. The dancing-master smiled; a very warm and confiding smile, really. Andrej had not cared for the dancing-masters from the moment he realized that they frightened his people. The goodwill in the dancing-master's smile reconciled Andrej considerably.

"To be read aloud, your Excellency, before, during, or after. At his Excellency's discretion."

And it should be soon. At once. Immediately.

"Miss Samons, if you would close the door."

He would speak to Code and 5.3; but this was first. Rising to his feet, Andrej gathered the Safes up into his hand and approached the senior man on 5.4. Toska was as white in the face as Andrej had ever seen in his own mirror, mornings that followed an excess of drink. He could have smiled. But this was solemn business, more so than anything in these peoples' lives.

"Attention to orders," the senior dancing-master began. Andrej raised an eyebrow at Toska, who realized finally that he was to bow so that Andrej could slip the Safe over his head. "In the matter of the petition of Fleet Captain Irshah Parmin on behalf of Jurisdiction Fleet Ship *Scylla*. For meritorious service above and beyond the requirements of duty, Revocation of Bond is granted to the following Bench resources."

Toska, then Kaydence. The dancing-master read their names; they were different than the ones Andrej knew. Real names. Who had Joslire been?

Toska Simmanye. Kaydence Varrish. Finally Erish Tallis. They were all on Safe; free men, and soon to be free forever, once the governor in their brains that enforced their Bonds was removed. Free, but still and stiffly at attention. Andrej stepped back to stand with the dancing-master, who was finishing his speech.

"The before-named therefore to travel at Bench expense to the nearest Fleet rated facility for restoration of organic integrity." Surgery, he meant. "Cadre officers Attis and Fisemost to accompany and arrange for adequate debriefing prior to return to civilian life. Accrued pay and benefits to be awarded in addition to Fleet meritorious service pension for life. By the Bench instruction, na Roqua den Tensa, First Judge, Fontailloe Judiciary, Presiding."

Free.

Andrej stepped forward on impulse, not trusting himself to speak; and put his arms around Erish, who was nearest. Kissing him formally, with heartfelt emotion, first on one cheek and then on the other. Feeling his way, through the tears that blurred his vision, to the next man, to embrace him in like kind and be embraced. They were free. And to him it had been granted, through no merit of his own, to see at least these many of his gentlemen safe and away.

But there was one missing.

Andrej stared at the empty place for a long moment.

Joslire was free, too; and had known the time and the place of his emancipation. And had rejoiced in it.

"I must to the others go out and speak." They all knew but Code;

maybe Chief Samons was telling poor Code even now. "If you would stand by, gentles, it will be one moment."

Why should they?

He wasn't their officer any longer.

There was no reason they should listen to him.

But they would always have been his Security; and that reminded him, something of which he had only fantasized in years gone by. He could take care of them, as they had taken care of him.

"I will for you provide letters of introduction, you shall go to the familial corporation if you like." It could be that they would find themselves at loose ends, no matter how good the debriefing support to be provided. "That you are no longer bound to Fleet, I cannot but rejoice for you. And there is no claim I have to lay upon you for your service, but strong claim in your hands to make against my family, as it may please you."

He probably wasn't making sense. And they probably wouldn't get anywhere near anything that reminded them of him, not by choice, ever. Why should they? That they had shared an unequal partnership with him had been his privilege. But it had been their punishment. "For what has in the past been between us it is your right to claim honor and comfort, sustenance and maintenance and all due respect. For as long as you live, if you elect it."

And Joslire, Joslire was to be remembered in his turn . . .

"You're wrong, you know. Sir." Toska was clearly struggling with something, swallowing hard on his emotion. "To say you have no claim. After these three years, sir. You can't expect us to forget everything you've done for us. Just because we get—to go free."

Oh, he was going to miss them. But he'd know they were free, not under some other officer's direction, to be subject to potential reprimand. "You are right, Toska, and I am a sinner." Toska had taken better care of him than that. No governor under Jurisdiction could make a bond-involuntary extend his unspoken support by choice. "There is no use pretending that you have not been good to me over and above your Bond, all of this time. The bond that is between us cannot so easily be revoked, no matter the distance that should separate."

They would no longer be bond-involuntary troops, Security slaves. But they would always be bonded to him, and he to them.

There was no loss in them going after all.

Ailynn had seen the three reborn men on their way in the company of the dancing-masters. Code had introduced her to his fellows, the new team that had been sent to wait upon the officer, and gave her credence amongst them. Now it had been eight weeks since she had gone with Kaydence, who was no longer to be called Psimas, down the wall; and pleasant as her life had been, it could not last. She knew it.

Eight weeks.

First they had moved from the prison to a house in Port Rudistal, but the officer had not been satisfied with those lodgings; and had moved himself within days to a house he liked better. How he had come by it Ailynn didn't know, nor did she ask—she knew her place.

It was not so big a house, perhaps, but there was room enough for the officer and his Security and the house-staff besides. The officer had brought the cook from the penthouse at the prison to prepare their meals, but he would not have Pyana housekeepers, and had hired Nurail from the camps instead.

Left her to manage them.

Eight weeks, and she had ruled the officer's household as the keeper of his keys, and stirred neither foot nor finger to her own work except to see that the toweling was warmed for his bath and to warm the bed beside him while he slept. He'd mostly only slept in bed, these eight weeks past; busy at the prison and in the camps with the taking in of evidence and dispositions with speak-sera, and no torture.

It wore on him, regardless. He was deeper into drink than he had been before, and why should she take a second thought for it? Except that he had treated her decently.

Still, something that Ailynn didn't understand was happening.

The officer had received his orders; he was called back to his ship-duty and due to leave Port Rudistal within three weeks. The business of the Domitt was not concluded; it was hardly well begun, but Fleet would have its Inquisitor back, a good indication that the officer was half-vindicated already. The Bench had sent audit teams, and the officer had given his evidence, his personal evidence, even as she had. Now the Bench audit teams would take the matter in hand.

It was the Bench, and not Andrej Koscuisko, that would continue the work of excavating at the prison and the reclamation site for physical evidence. It was the Bench, and not the officer, that would sift through what records could be recovered and cross-reference them with those available at the relocation camp to try to quantify for good and all how many had died, and how.

The Bench, and not the officer, to pursue the horror of what had been the Domitt Prison, and how it had been allowed to come about, and what was to be done to ensure that it would not happen again. The officer would come back to Rudistal to execute what penalty the Bench adjudged against whichever parties were eventually found guilty of actual crimes: but had his duty to Fleet in the meantime, and could not be spared past three weeks the longer.

So why was he furnishing this house?

Why had he troubled to engage a gardener to tend the salad-plot, and had the compound wall repaired, the black slate roof inspected and re-proofed against the weather?

There had been workmen in the house all week with furnishings the like of which Ailynn had never seen before. Room by room, removing what had been there, replacing it all with strange rich alien forms that fascinated Ailynn.

It made her half-drunk just to look at such carpeting, as thick and wild and fanciful as its pattern was; drunker still to touch the roses that bloomed in well-oiled wood along the footboard of the small self-contained room that the moving crew had put into the officer's bedroom.

They were all Dolgorukij, the work-crew, the furnishings from the officer's home-world, and they treated her with a deference that Ailynn couldn't quite understand.

In the evening after the officer had washed and had his evening meal—a cold buffet, since Cook was struggling with an arcane toy in the kitchen, an intricate piece of machinery for the preparation and serving of rhyti—he drew her off with him to the side sitting-room, where an immense divan had been carefully placed to afford the best view of the garden. Or of the draperies, which were closed.

"Ailynn, please. A conversation. Something which I should have mentioned weeks ago, I do not know quite how to approach this."

He was wondering about her tip, perhaps. Such things were usually figured on the number of nights a patron had hired her; but he had merely slept in the same bed for three times as many nights as he had exercised himself with her for pleasure. Extra spending money was always nice, and she was allowed to keep her tips for her own use; but it didn't matter so much.

She'd had months now of liberty with him. Months of sleeping with only one man—how was she to go back to servicing multiple patrons, and every night?

"One hears stories about the things that go on in a service house. It may be indelicate to ask, but I am curious. If pressed hard to it I might even admit to having played some fantasy story or another in a service house, for amusement's sake."

Leaning well back into the cushions of the divan. Staring at the drapes. She had always thought his rest-dress made him look much younger than he did in duty uniform. "It's actually something to look forward to, most of the time. Breaks the monotony." He didn't care to be called "sir," and she couldn't quite bring herself to say "Andrej." She compromised by not calling him anything. "And usually light duty, if you follow. I don't mind it, dressing up."

He knew exactly what she was talking about. And grinned. She relaxed a bit into the cushions herself: they were very tempting. "The standard range of taboo violations, I would guess, Ailynn. Gender identification. Prohibited degrees of relationship. Unusual accommodations. Religion."

And more, yes. "Yes, but what religion? That can make all the difference. You can't begin to imagine. With respect." Why, when she thought of some of the scenes that she had helped to stage—

"Very true." The lights were not very bright in the sitting-room. Frowning, the officer fumbled at the base of the nearest table-lamp for a moment; it grew brighter, and he relaxed once more, his hands deep in his pockets now and his feet stretched stiffly out in front of him. "I suppose that if one's patron wished one to merely pray it need not be too strenuous."

"Pray how, to whom, how long, and in what manner?" she argued, half-serious. She enjoyed the conversations that she had with him, infrequent though they were. If it hadn't been that he was just a patron, she just a Service bond-involuntary, she would have had to seriously contemplate missing him, when he was gone. Rather than simply missing the privileged life that she had led with him.

"Oh. Let us say, on one's knees four days in a week, and with full prostrations on fifth-days. For example. To someone's Mother who is probably not listening, but never mind." Head leaned back against the edge of the divan, now, staring at the ceiling. She could interpret neither his expression nor his voice. He sounded as though he was just thinking out loud; and yet she somehow felt he had rehearsed this. "In two periods of prayer, morning and evening, and in a foreign language. For an hour each time. Sometimes two hours at a stretch. Every day."

It certainly sounded commonplace enough to Ailynn. "A foreign language? And what if one couldn't speak such a tongue? What sort of patron do we deal with, here, who takes gratification in such things?"

Turning his head to look at her now; she still couldn't decide about his face. "This would be much easier if you came to sit in my lap, here, Ailynn. It would be very good of you indeed to do so."

It would be only what she was paid to do. But never mind that. She was almost happy to oblige him for his own sake. It was comfortable, settling into his arms; she knew his warmth and his smell and the scent of the soap he used. He had taught her body to trust itself into his hands. Ailynn put her forehead to his cheek and pressed the issue.

"Now tell me why a man would spend good money just to have somebody pray twice a day. Even with prostrations, and a foreign tongue."

It was very nice to sit in the officer's lap. The strength of his arms was a comfort, when she knew it was just to hold her. "Well. We will say, let's suppose. First. That a man is too vain to wish to realize that he is to be compared with others, when he's gone. And to be found wanting."

Whatever that meant. He wasn't serious, she was sure. Ailynn rested herself in silence, content to listen while the officer mused aloud.

"Next it would have to be that a man had been killed, and deserved prayers. Hypothetically this would be Joslire, whom you have not met."

Not met, but had come to know by the echo of his absence. Even now Code suffered. It was getting better, but why did Koscuisko use the present tense?

"After that it would have to be a man with businesspeople to negotiate, and make a contract. But then here is a problem. We would have to suppose that such a man is also boneheaded enough to have simply decided, and made arrangements, without even once asking the lady. Because he was distracted, and could not decide how the issue to raise. It would seem that he had no respect for her, to arrange things behind her back in that manner."

The hesitation and regret in the officer's voice were too genuine. Ailynn sat up, to look him in the eye.

"What. Are you saying. Exactly. If you please. Sir."

"Angry with me," Koscuisko murmured as if to himself, raising his left hand to stroke her cheek gently with his fingertips. "And has a right to be. I will come out with it, all at once."

It took him a moment to collect his thoughts regardless. Then when he spoke, it was dead serious.

"Ailynn, I have seen the four of my gentlemen free, and three of them living. I cannot buy your Bond from the Bench, you know that." Only a member of her own family could redeem her. And her family were all dead; not as if they could have found the price of her Bond in any case.

"And Joslire's memory is to be served in a dedicated establishment, by the prayers of a nun. A religious professional. A woman who has been procured for that purpose. You need not go back to the service house, Ailynn, but if you do not you must say the prayers. Twice a day. Every day. For the next twenty-six years."

She couldn't believe him.

The words were so strange they seemed hardly in Standard.

Twenty-six years?

The term of her Bond ran for twenty-six more years.

Koscuisko knew that.

Had he done this for her?

"Oh, it must have cost you—no, too much money." She was horrified at the magnitude of it. "Do you mean it? I don't have to go back?"

Maybe he had done it; but not for her, for his man Joslire. It didn't matter. If she didn't have to go back to that place, she would learn whatever it was that they wanted, she'd learn how to pray, and she'd do it wholeheartedly, in thanks for deliverance.

"No one can make you." Cupping her face in the palm of his hand, now. "I have seen the contract, it says that I hire you for all day, every day, until the Day dawns for you. If you consent you will be Joslire's nun. This house will be for you, and people to run it; you will be mistress here. It need not be too hard for you, Ailynn, I promise. The life of a nun in the church of my blood is not at base difficult."

It didn't sound hard. It could be hard; she didn't care. He was willing to hire her out of the service house, and whatever it was to be a nun—or whatever else—to be clear of the service house was more than she'd dreamt of.

"You. Cannot know. You cannot imagine." Or maybe he could. Maybe that was why. "I would do anything. Learn Dolgorukij."

"Are not angry?" He was kissing her, now, kissing the tears from her cheeks one by one, supping her salt tears with tender care. "Very highhanded, and to have bought you. When you cannot be bought. Even though the Bench sold you."

It was too much.

She had to shut him up.

There was a way she had learned how to do it.

She had to be sure that he stayed shut up, so she did it again, and more thoroughly this time.

After a while it was quieter, between them, and the officer held her, stroking her hair. "There will be a tutor for you." As if he was thinking out loud, almost. Or as if he had kept the details to himself for so long that he needed to get them all out at once, since he'd finally told. "A Reconciler, of St. Andrej Malcontent I think. Uncle Radu would insist on a Filial Piety, but Joslire wasn't Dolgorukij, so I can get away with it. He will explain what it is all about, to be Joslire's nun. The word does not satisfy in the Standard phrase, does it not imply that one is celibate? Dolgorukij nuns are not celibate unless they like to be. I have told Kaydence. You will slap me, now, and I will deserve it."

She'd do no such thing. So she kissed him instead. "I'll be Joslire's nun for you," Ailynn promised. "I may even remember you to your, how do you say it, to your holy Mother. But only when I consider what this means to me. Every hour of every day, for the rest of my life."

"No, only for twenty-six—"

He started to protest. She kissed him again, to silence him. She knew what he was going to say. He wasn't paying attention. For an officer he could be very thickheaded.

Finally he yielded, and smiled and kissed back.

Oh Holy Mother, she thought to herself. Just to start practicing. *Holy Mother, I'm free.*

She could spend her life praying and never work off the debt that she owed to Andrej Koscuisko.

ANGEL OF DESTRUCTION
A Novel Under Jurisdiction

Bench Intelligence Specialist Garol Vogel is one of an elite few chartered by the Bench to uphold the rule of Law by any means he sees fit, to rewrite policy, assassinate corrupt officials, and topple planetary governments at his discretion.

His most treasured achievement was the amnesty he brokered for the Langsarik rebels. But someone is raiding depot stations in the Shawl of Rikavie around Port Charid, torturing and murdering with unprecedented savagery. Vogel knows the Langsariks are innocent, but who could be to blame, and how can he prevent a Judicial crime of horrific proportions?

Garol Vogel finds the answer on the wrong side of the Judicial order he's served faithfully all his life, and once he sets foot on a path of subversion and sabotage there will be no going back for him, forever.

Dedicated to Absent Friends

PROLOGUE

Garol Vogel stood in the wheelhouse of the flagship as the Langsarik fleet came off the exit vector and dropped to sub-tactical speed. The Langsarik commander stood beside him; together they watched the massed ships of the Jurisdiction's Second Fleet come to position, flanking the Langsariks as they progressed toward Port Charid and their new home.

Their prison.

The Langsarik commander—Flag Captain Walton Agenis—stared impassively, her expression so flatly neutral that Garol knew it was a struggle for her to contain her emotion. The Langsarik fleet surrendered under escort with full military honors, true enough, but surrender was surrender nonetheless, and now they were wards of Jurisdiction.

The terms of their probation were not punitively strict. Port Charid was a small tightly knit community dominated by the Dolgorukij Combine, people among whom the Langsariks would stand out by virtue of their accent and their non-Combine blood. The Bench was counting on Port Charid to deny the Langsariks access to space transport and to provide a certain basic level of population monitoring—roll call, head count, attendance reconciliation.

In return Port Charid received the Langsariks, a population of five thousand souls with sophisticated technical skills, proven adaptability, and nowhere for them to work but as cheap labor to fuel Port Charid's commercial expansion in cargo management and freight handling.

"Are we clear?" Agenis asked; and one of her lieutenants stood to answer. Hilton Shires was actually her nephew as well as her lieutenant, though Garol didn't think there was more than twelve years between them; and Agenis had yet to see forty years, Standard. She and Garol himself were almost the same age.

"Reports are complete, Captain, the fleet has cleared the vector. Standing by."

Walton Agenis had been a lieutenant herself when the Jurisdiction had annexed the Langsariks' home system. She had risen to command over the fifteen years of the Langsarik fleet's stubborn if futile resistance, forging what had been a local commerce patrol fleet into mercantile raiders whose continued evasion of Fleet's best efforts to locate and contain them had become a scandal from one end of the Bench to the other.

She'd seen her family either ostracized on her home-world—where it was no longer expedient to admit to having kin with the Langsarik fleet—or lost in battle; and now she stood witness to the final loss of the fleet itself.

Still, it was only the ships that they were losing.

The Langsariks themselves—people who had made the Langsarik fleet a challenge and a reproach to Jurisdiction—would live; and someday yet be free. Eight years of probation as Port Charid's labor pool was not so terrible a price to pay for reconciliation with the Bench; and once eight years had passed the Langsariks could go home.

"Specialist Vogel," Flag Captain Agenis said, not looking at him. Garol bowed in salute at her side.

"Ma'am."

"The fleet is assembled in good order and ready to surrender the controls as agreed. Your action, Bench specialist."

Langsariks didn't salute. It wasn't the Langsarik way. "Thank you, Flag Captain. Lieutenant Shires, if you would hail the *Margitov*, please."

Jils Ivers was on the Jurisdiction Fleet Flagship *Margitov*, waiting. She had worked as hard as Garol himself to see this happen: a peaceful solution to the Langsarik problem, one that avoided the crying waste that simple annihilation would have been. Lieutenant Shires made the call; and piped Jils Ivers's voice over the public address in the wheelhouse.

"Jurisdiction Fleet Flagship *Margitov*, standing by. Prepared to assume direction."

It was tactful of Jils to say "direction," and not "command" or "control." The reality of it was hard enough for those proud people to accept. They were under no illusions as to the impact of the change in status waiting for them. It was to their credit that they went forward into a sort of bondage as bravely as they ever had confronted the Bench in sortie.

"By direction from Flag Captain Walton Agenis," Garol said, choosing his words carefully. "Properly delegated by the Langsarik fleet to do so on its behalf. The Langsarik fleet surrenders the motivational controls to remote direction. Now."

Lieutenant Shires sat back at his post and folded his arms.

The images on the panoramic screens that lined the wheelhouse walls, the picture of space on monitor, faltered; then steadied again.

"The ship is on remote direction," Lieutenant Shires said, looking over his shoulder at Flag Captain Agenis. "They've got us, Captain."

I hope we're doing the right thing.

Shires didn't have to say it for the message to be clear, and Agenis didn't need to answer.

The Langsariks had made their decision.

They had agreed to accept amnesty and terms.

Not all of the Langsariks had agreed that it was their last best chance for survival under Jurisdiction, but the entire Langsarik fleet had sworn to be honor-bound by the majority vote, and Langsariks kept their promises. Sometimes all too well.

"Your ship, Bench specialist." Captain Agenis bowed her head and stepped back half a pace. "What are they going to do with it, may I ask?"

After the obvious, of course, repossession, disarmament, and evacuation of all Langsarik personnel on arrival at Port Charid. The Bench had hired transport from the mercantile resources in port to ferry the Langsariks from orbit to Port and from there to the nearby settlement that had been prepared for them.

Under the terms of the amnesty no Langsarik was to own, lease, direct, or appropriate space transport for the duration of the probationary period, unless under immediate and direct supervision by non-Langsarik employers. And these ships, the ships of the

Langsarik fleet, the ships whose computing systems had just been surrendered to remote control, these ships had been home to the Langsariks for more than fifteen years.

"I believe they're to be taken back to Palaam." The Langsarik system of origin had a technical claim on the ships. Once the planetary government—the puppet government—of Palaam had formally repudiated them, the Langsariks had become pirates in the eyes of the law, and the hulls they fought with and lived on belonged to Palaam. "I don't know what the Palaamese government will do with them."

Agenis made a sour face, but it was gone almost as quickly as it had appeared. In a sense it was no hardship for the Langsariks to be forbidden to return to Palaam for eight years, Garol knew. As far as the Langsariks were concerned they had been betrayed by their own government, their families, their communities all turning their backs under pressure from the Bench. Maybe after eight years the Langsariks would come to forgive their home-world for bowing to pressure. They were about to gain first-hand knowledge of how dispiriting life under Jurisdiction could be.

"Well. I hope they get some good maintenance people in. The condition of quarters, really, Bench specialist. It's shocking."

But her forced humor could not cover up her grief; and Garol could offer no help. He had already done everything he could for the Langsariks, not only to get the amnesty approved, but to structure the amnesty so that it would not become intolerable to the Langsariks. He felt responsible for them now; it was his doing that they were to accept probation here, his and Jils's. It had to work. Criminals by Bench definition, no question, but they were brave, smart, stubborn, strong-willed people, and the Bench could not afford to waste the resource they represented for the sake of mere vengeance, or ego-gratification on the part of Palaam's Bench-appointed puppet government.

Since he could not change the hard facts of the matter, Garol attempted to provide reassurance of another sort, instead.

"I've inspected the settlement, Flag Captain. All new construction." Put up in a hurry, and not the best quality. Fleet contracting, let to the lowest bidder, but Garol had been given the authority to demand some of the less satisfactory elements be upgraded and improved.

It wasn't luxury.

But it would keep weather out and heat in; and the Langsariks would be able to make changes themselves, as time went on. "Paint job all one color, more or less, but at least it's clean. Funny thing, though. Not a trace of rose gold to be seen in the entire settlement."

She smiled, as if despite herself, and glanced down at the front of the uniform that she wore. Rose gold. The colors of the Langsarik fleet. "Do we surrender our clothing as well, then, Garol?"

Negotiations had gone on for months, and they'd been intense. In all that time, she'd never used his personal name. Garol was pleased and honored by her grant of intimacy, formal though it was, and at the same time grieved by the depth of her personal distress.

"You'll remove all rank and insignia on the ferry shuttle between the ships in orbit and Port Charid. But no. You keep your clothing." The Langsariks didn't have any other clothing, not after fifteen years. For all Garol knew they slept in uniform. "There'll be a concession store to serve your needs at the settlement, but they haven't selected a vendor yet. Food service and clinic and utilities, yes."

There were five thousand people in the Langsarik fleet, men, women, and even children born to a people at war with the civilized worlds and the Bench that governed them.

There were many logistical details yet unresolved, but Chilleau Judiciary would do the best it could for the Langsariks.

Chilleau Judiciary had no choice.

The First Judge—the single most powerful individual under Jurisdiction, the woman who held the tiebreaking vote on the Bench—was old; the Second Judge at Chilleau Judiciary was ambitious, and well placed to mount a bid for the First Judge's position when it became vacant. But there were nine Judges in all, several with their own ambitions with respect to the ultimate position of influence under Jurisdiction, and the Second Judge had suffered a staggering humiliation within the past year.

Chilleau Judiciary's political rivals had made full use of the lurid details of torture, murder, and waste of lives and property that had been taken into evidence during the trial of the Domitt Prison's administration for failure to uphold the rule of Law.

If the Second Judge was to reclaim her honor from the blow it had received in the court of public opinion after the scandals at the Domitt Prison, the Langsarik settlement could not be allowed to fail.

CHAPTER ONE

"Okidan Yards, this is the freighter *Sevior*, requesting docking protocol. Please respond."

In the year since the Bench had settled the Langsariks at Port Charid, Port Charid itself had prospered, through its unequal partnership with its captive labor pool. Traffic was up more than thirty-five percent overall, and the arrival of a freighter at a warehouse yards excited much less notice these days than it might have done a year and a half gone by.

Fisner Feraltz stood in the dock-master's office on the asteroid warehouse complex of the Okidan Yards, watching the freighter's approach on monitor.

He could remember.

He'd been fifteen years old, interning on a Combine ship carrying a shipment of garments from the manufactory in Berin, in Givrodnye—where he'd been born—to the clearing-house at Corcorum, outside Combine space. They'd been attacked by Langsariks, ordered to stand by for boarding and prepare to surrender goods on demand. Someone—no one had ever claimed to know who it might have been—had fired the ship's signal guns, which weren't designed for offensive purposes.

So it hadn't even been Langsarik fire that had destroyed the ship. It had been an accident. The signal guns had never been used before, and somebody under the stress of the event hadn't unshipped the

677

barrel shunts. Or had used the wrong rounds. Or something; and it didn't really matter, in the end. The entire crew but one had been lost in the explosion.

The Langsariks had never hinted at suspecting him, and no one else who might have accused him had survived.

But he lived with shame that never ended.

The dock-master spoke from her post at her master-board. "We have you, freighter *Sevior*, Okidan Yards confirms. Stand by for transmission of docking protocol."

The Langsariks had boarded the crippled freighter and found him barricaded in the cargo holds, trembling in terror. They'd taken him with them, because the ship had been too badly damaged to hold its atmosphere for long enough for rescuers to reach him from any other source.

He had been the only survivor.

And how could he have gone home to his family, after that? How could he explain the fact that he was alive while his brothers, uncles, cousins were dead? How could he have hoped to tell the truth—that the Langsariks had offered threats, but no violence; and had cared for him with creditable charity until they could see him safely on neutral ground—without raising questions in people's minds that he could not bear to face?

No.

There was no hope of any such homecoming, not for him, not forever.

He had stayed with the Langsariks for almost a full year, Standard, until they found a way to smuggle him back into friendly hands. That had been at Markov, as it had happened, and Fisner had never gone home.

The freighter on-screen, *Sevior*, turned its great bulk slowly to sink down between the signal markers on Okidan's flat side and come to ground. The Shawl of Rikavie was full of asteroids like Okidan; large enough to site warehouses and docks, small enough to maneuver out of the way of other asteroids in orbit if need arose. There was plenty of room to maneuver in the Shawl—the asteroid belt halfway between the planet Rikavie and the Sillume vector, entry and exit, the space-lane terminals that gave Rikavie system its place in the web of transport under Jurisdiction.

The Jurisdiction had failed to take revenge for Fisner's family. After fruitless attempts to bring the pirates to account, the Bench had cravenly made peace with them instead, and left the crime unpunished to burn in Fisner's heart.

He had found work where he could, ending up at last within the Combine's mercantile authority, the oversight agency that coordinated trade on behalf of Combine interests within Jurisdiction as a whole.

It had been chance that had brought him to Port Charid, to work in the warehouses on-planet and oversee the Combine's yards on its own asteroid base in the Shawl.

But once the Jurisdiction had brought the Langsariks to settle at Port Charid and be its labor pool, Fisner Feraltz had understood the hand of the Holy Mother in his life, and known what he had to do.

If there had been no Langsariks, there would have been no accident.

It was their fault his family was dead, and he was exiled. No amount of self-serving charity on their part could wash away their guilt, or ease his suffering. Blood called for blood. Nor could he afford to forgive and forget in his heart, whatever the requirements of social discourse. The Holy Mother herself expected vengeance of him: the Angel had told him so.

On-screen, Fisner could see that the freighter *Sevior* had settled into its berth. Its umbilicus had completed its initial handshake, pressurized environment to pressurized environment. It was bright on the surface where the freighter lay, and the small sun of Rikavie shone like a beacon over the shoulder of the beast. The dock-master sat at her station, however, her fingers drumming the console absentmindedly.

"Funny," she said, and Fisner thought it was maybe only to herself—idle curiosity, but no alarm. "That doesn't look like the specs it sent. Didn't they say it was a dray? That looks like a distance carrier, to me."

"Hard to say," Fisner replied politely, just in case she was talking to him. "But it does seem a little other than one would expect. Maybe we could ask the captain about it. Get a tour. You never know what's coming out of shipyards these days."

He was lying, in a way, because he knew quite well that it was a heavy transport freighter. It hadn't come to deliver stores to Okidan. It was here to take the Okidan Yards for everything it could plunder.

The dock-master clearly didn't have a clue, not yet—just the germ of a suspicion. She pivoted slowly around in her seat and stood up, frowning slightly. "Good manners to go say something, either way. Coming?"

"No, thanks. I've got finishing up to do."

Inventory validation was a chore, but it had to be done. Since the Combine Yards were the largest in system, it had quite naturally fallen to the Combine Yards to oversee and facilitate, to manage all of the administrative details required to keep the flow of traffic moving, to provide insurers and contract holders alike with assurances as to the quality and condition of goods, to collect and remit fees and taxes, and generally to act as the Bench proxy in Port Charid.

The dock-master left Fisner to his task. He was alone; and after a moment he locked the office door, secure in the knowledge that the observation ports—which were proof against unplanned decompression—would not be easy to break in, should someone on staff try to find shelter in the office from what was to come.

On the station's master monitor screens Fisner could see the dock-master cross the load-in apron to where the freighter's cargo umbilicus debouched into the load-in docks. No one had appeared from the freighter yet. Abandoning his task for more pressing concerns, Fisner moved to the dock-master's master-board to cut the video feeds between the docks and the rest of the warehouse complex.

The dock-master's chair was still warm from her body heat. Fisner hefted it to test the weight, and smashed it down across the master communications nexus board. The auxiliary fail-safe panel was on a subsidiary board some paces removed, and he left that intact. He had no intention of dying here.

There were people coming out of the freighter's umbilicus now, the cheerful color of their Langsarik blouses clearly visible even at a distance. They had the dock-master, but she had yet to panic—at least to judge by appearances. Was it his imagination, or was she looking up into the monitor, up into the screens?

She knew he was in the office. She might be hoping for some quick-witted action on his part.

Fisner bore her no ill will. It wasn't her fault. It was the fault of the Bench, the Jurisdiction's fault for suffering Langsarik predation to go unpunished. Fisner set off the station alarms: standard emergency procedure, and it would bring everyone on station running to the load-in docks. The freighter's crew had had enough time to get themselves into position by now, and were lying in wait.

The Bench had said that he had no claim against Bench or Langsariks for damages, that the loss he had suffered had been through misadventure. An accident.

The Angel of Destruction said differently.

The Angel of Destruction said that it was an offense against the Holy Mother herself that an ungodly and alien hand had been permitted to steal from Dolgorukij, and with impunity; an amnesty was no punishment for such a crime. The Angel of Destruction had sought him out and recruited him, sounded him out and tested him, tried his mettle and his faith—but at the end of it all the Angel had opened its arms to him and welcomed him, granted him membership in its sacred fellowship and made him the agent of the vengeance of the Holy Mother against the Langsariks at Port Charid.

The warehouse staff were unarmed; the slaughter was quick and efficient, over almost as soon as it had begun. Fisner scanned the load-in docks outside the dock-master's office with the remote monitors, counting the bodies.

Everyone seemed to be accounted for.

The dock-master was to be shot over her boards, as if in the act of trying to call for help. She was still alive, standing under guard with two raiders in Langsarik dress as the plunder of the warehouse commenced. The hand of the Holy Mother was clearly discernible in the fortunate circumstance that had brought the Langsariks to Port Charid. They were a perfect cover for the Angel's fund-raising activities, and once they were shown guilty—too guilty for the Bench to overlook their faults and let them live free, this time—Port Charid would go begging for labor once more.

Labor that the Combine was in a position to provide, at a premium, of course.

Labor that would only solidify the hold the Holy Mother held over trade at Port Charid and access to the Sillume vector alike.

Meanwhile the Angel stood in need of goods to convert into funds, because the righteous were not welcome in the debased Church of the Autocrat's court. The Angel of Destruction had been outlawed through the malice of its enemies and the weak-spirited failings of the Autocrat himself octaves ago, when even Chuvishka Kospodar—the man who more than any other had nurtured their holy order, and welcomed it as the hand of the Holy Mother on Sarvaw—had been forced publicly to repudiate the Angel and its fearless defense of Her honor.

The money had to come from somewhere.

Just now it was coming out of the Okidan Yards, and the Langsariks would be blamed—two blessings in one devotion.

After a while the raiders in Langsarik dress came to the door of the dock-master's office, and Fisner opened the door. They had the dock-master with them, and her eyes brightened with sudden hope when she saw him.

Hadn't she figured it out yet?

No, for they had been coached very carefully, Langsarik phrases, Langsarik swear words, Langsarik songs. Langsariks were responsible for the slaughter here, not honest Dolgorukij.

"Here?" raid leader Dalmoss asked Fisner, gesturing toward the broken master console with a tilt of his chin. A shot could serve to disguise the previous damage that had been deliberately inflicted on the communications console; with enough blood, people would be discouraged from looking very closely. It wouldn't be a problem. There were good reasons for the Langsariks to have first smashed the console and then shot the dock-master, if anyone felt honor-bound to establish a precise sequence of events.

Fisner nodded.

Dalmoss bowed his head and glanced toward his people. They pulled the dock-master over to her console and turned her so that she faced Fisner and the raid leader alike; but the venom in her expression, the hatred in her eyes, the acid in her voice was all for Fisner.

"You. I should have known better."

It was as if she no longer even saw the others, staring at Fisner with baffled rage. "Sharing spit with Langsariks, you might as well have been one of them all along. Imagine you working for the Combine. I guess you must have grown to like the life, is that what happened?"

He could snatch Dalmoss's weapon and kill her himself.

But that would have been a gesture of anger, an act of violence done with a resentful heart. The Angel killed without mercy, but without malice. The Angel was only the humble tool of the Holy Mother, blessed by Her toward the furtherance of Her sacred plan; and therefore when the Angel killed it was without anger, without fear, without hatred or joy in cruelty.

It was for that reason that the Angel could kill, and not sin in doing so.

Therefore, Fisner simply nodded to Dalmoss. The raiders in Langsarik dress who had brought the dock-master to her console backed away; she was so focused on Fisner that there was no need to watch for any sudden moves on her part. She was paralyzed with hatred as surely as though it had been fear.

Dalmoss shot her in the middle of her body, and her shoulders and head fell backwards over the top edge of the communications console while her legs fell in opposite directions, to each side of her shattered pelvis, as her arms flew wide.

What a mess, Fisner thought. And Dalmoss had prudently used his sidearm. Had he used one of the other's more powerful weapons—it didn't bear thinking on.

Just as well that the false Langsarik colors didn't have to be particularly clean to be recognizable for what they were.

"And now you, firstborn and eldest brother," Dalmoss said respectfully.

This was the most challenging part of this raid; but Fisner almost welcomed it. He would put any lingering doubts about his courage to rest, he would bear witness to his devotion to the Holy Mother with his body. And not least of all, he would bear witness with his words as well, damning witness against the Langsariks—so long as he survived, and his testimony was properly handled.

"I'm going over here to the auxiliary call," Fisner explained, setting the scene, proud of himself for being able to speak so calmly. He was afraid. But he would not falter. "You shoot me down, I fall, you leave. Near miss, but there must be enough damage to make it convincing." They'd been over all that already. They'd carefully chosen the angle of the shot, and where Dalmoss should aim. "Here I go—to reach the auxiliary call, and give the alarm—"

He had his back turned, so he didn't have to see Dalmoss raise his weapon.

And when the blow came it was so huge and shocking that he completely lost track of what he was doing.

People were dragging him along the ground, why was that?

Lifting, pressing his hands against the console.

Something was wrong with him.

The right side of his body seemed to have disappeared, and yet he could see it well enough—arm, leg, foot, hand.

He was bleeding, and his clothing was torn. Something in his mind noticed that no blood gushed, though it seeped quickly, and took that for an encouraging sign.

He lay against the auxiliary communications console with his face to the panel. Someone moved his hand; and there was a light, there, very close to his eyes. Green. Communication. Sending.

"Help me," Fisner croaked. He was supposed to say something. What was he supposed to say? He needed help. Yes. Langsariks had attacked the Okidan Yards. "This is Okidan. Feraltz. We're raided. Dying. Help."

His hand dropped away from the toggle, then his body followed, sliding slowly to the floor.

He didn't feel the impact as he fell.

He lay on the floor and stared at the wall stupidly until the room went black on him.

Langsariks.

Langsariks had done this.

It was all the Langsariks' fault that this had happened.

Standing at the aide's station in the small Combine hospital, Garol Vogel scanned the status report. *Fisner Feraltz, Combine citizen, Givrodnye national. Injuries sustained at the hands of armed pirates at the Okidan Yards in the Shawl of Rikavie, Rikavie system.*

Rikavie system: port of departure, Charid—where the Langsariks had been settled by the Bench, just over a year ago, now. Checking the date on the status report Garol made a quick calculation. Twenty days. They'd brought Feraltz here as soon as he could be stabilized for distance transport; Port Charid had a small clinic of its own, and they could handle just about anything there, but Feraltz was Dolgorukij, and Dolgorukij suspected that nobody else really understood the intricacies of a Dolgorukij physique.

And perhaps they were right.

Injuries including but not limited to mass soft tissue laceration, especially of the right portion of the body. Knee joint requiring replacement, ankle may require fusing, biomedical netting wrap on long bones of thigh and lower leg, silica glazing therapy in effect over eighty-five percent of rightmost surface of hip.

"Lucky to be alive," Garol said to the patient's advocate who was serving as his guide and escort. The advocate nodded.

"That's what the staff says as well, Bench specialist. But since he is alive, the surgical board felt it best to postpone any interviews until he had regained at least some of his mobility. Since his basic evidence had already been read into the record at Port Charid."

Well, there wasn't a Record at Port Charid, not in the formal sense. For a Record to be official a Judicial officer qualified for custody was required, and Port Charid didn't rate any on-site staff, let alone a Record of its own. It was on circuit, yes, but that was it.

So far.

Once traffic started to pick up at Port Charid the Bench would site Chambers there—as well as a fleet detachment, to monitor attempts at unauthorized communication across the Sillume vector with Free Government insurrectionaries outside the pale of Jurisdiction, out in Gonebeyond space.

But first Port Charid had to grow its traffic. It took an on-site tax base to support Chambers and Fleet detachments, and so far Port Charid's tax base simply did not qualify.

"Langsariks, I heard." Garol frowned down at the closed medical record. "In fact I'm told there's been more than one disturbance at Port Charid recently."

The patient's advocate shrugged, looking almost bored. "If that's what they say, Bench specialist. Nothing to me one way or the other, except of course when they start shooting at honest Dolgorukij. No aspersion on the Bench umbrella, of course."

Of course not. Equal respect in theory for all hominid species under Jurisdiction was an important aspect of good Bench citizenship. And sensible acknowledgment of the fact that people would always favor their own was just common sense, and no offense to it.

"Very properly so, Advocate. Can we go in now?"

The patient's advocate looked to the medical aide who waited in the doorway; the medical aide nodded, and opened the door. It was a hinged door, here, in a hospital. Dolgorukij knew what was proper, at least what they believed to be proper. This little hospital smelled of money all the way out to the street. And Fisner Feraltz, the patient Garol had come to see, was here at his employer's expense, heroically wounded in a cowardly attack.

Garol had a notion that they'd made Feraltz very comfortable indeed, here.

The patient was in plain clothes, resting on an incline-board and doing a slow lift with his right leg. Physical therapy; Garol recognized the apparatus, and he could sympathize deeply with the look of carefully screened pain and concentration on Feraltz's face.

Even with the brace, it wasn't fun.

Feraltz wore bracing all over his right side, but Garol knew how little of the load the bracing really took off injured limbs and joints— not nearly enough. Feraltz would be wearing pieces of that body-bracing for months, if not years.

Personally Garol had always preferred to discard such aids as quickly as possible and pay the price of mobility in pain.

Garol stopped a pace or two from where Fisner Feraltz pursued his physical rehabilitation with grim determination and nodded a polite greeting.

"Thank you for seeing me, Feraltz. I'm Vogel, Bench specialist Garol Aphon Vogel. Doing your exercises I see."

Feraltz was middling tall but well made, to look at him, more bone than flesh but adequately muscled by his hands and shoulders, fair-skinned and blue-eyed and very nearly blond. It was a type more general than some Dolgorukij Garol had met, who could have never been mistaken for Dynad or Jekrab, Nurail, or any other similar ethnicity; still, it was a type. Garol was a mixed-category hominid himself, and his family generally tended toward a muddier complexion and less lithely limber a frame.

Feraltz lowered his eyes in acknowledgment. "Yes, thank you, Bench specialist.—Not at all, my pleasure, sir, as well as my duty." Well-spoken young man, and no trace of an accent that Garol could detect offhand. He noticed that. Dolgorukij generally had an accent, in part because of the basic conviction of the superiority of their blood and culture, in part because as a result of that conviction Dolgorukij who spoke Standard had very seldom learned to do so as children.

Nor had they taken it quite seriously as adults.

There almost wasn't any such thing as an unaccented Standard. The only people who spoke Standard as their native tongue were wards of the Bench raised at public expense; those, or the crèche-bred Command Branch officers the Bench was experimenting with, the orphaned children of the Bench's enemies raised by the Bench in strict indoctrination to serve the Bench and uphold the rule of Law.

"I'm concerned that the evidence I gave the Clerk of Court could be too liberally interpreted," Feraltz added, while Garol mused, distracted, on Feraltz's lack of an accent. "So I hope you haven't come on a misunderstanding, Bench specialist. But I'm glad to answer any questions you might have, sir."

Polite, as well as a well-spoken man. "How do you mean, 'liberally interpreted'?" It was an interesting thing to say, and could serve to ease in to the questions Garol had come to ask. "If you would care to elaborate."

The statements that had been forwarded to him said Langsariks. If there was going to be any trouble with the Langsarik settlement at Port Charid, Garol needed to cut it out quickly and quietly, before Chilleau Judiciary got any creative ideas about revising the amnesty.

Feraltz was very willing to elaborate, apparently. "If I can say so without reproach, Bench specialist, the Clerk of Court who came to see me seemed to be determined that she already knew exactly what had happened. She kept on helping me out, you know the kind of thing I mean, and I think she recorded things I didn't actually say. I really think she did. There's no real reason to blame the Langsariks for that raid, it's just circumstantial evidence, from start to finish."

Well, that was a start on what Garol wanted to hear; so it was that much more important to be careful about it, accordingly. "I've reviewed the evidence certified by the Clerk of Court who interviewed you, but it's been a few days since then. I do seem to recall a positive identification attributed to you. Langsariks, in the raiding party."

Difficult to tell whether Feraltz's pained expression resulted from psychological distress over a potentially serious misunderstanding, or just reflected physical pain. "I never made any such assertion, Bench specialist, I'd swear to it. I might not have been as coherent as I would have liked to be, though."

The statement had been taken only days after the Okidan Yards had been raided and its crew left for dead. Feraltz's statement had been taken at Port Charid while Feraltz had been waiting for transport to the private hospital here at Nisherre, and thus given while Feraltz had been surrounded by Langsariks—figuratively if not literally, the Langsarik labor force having relatively few technically proficient medical practitioners to spare from the clinic in the settlement for hire out to the port.

So in a sense Feraltz's continued survival argued against any Langsarik involvement in the Okidan raid; if Feraltz had been in a position to give credible evidence against Langsariks, to positively implicate Langsariks, the Langsariks in danger had had perfectly good opportunities to silence him before his evidence went anywhere.

And they hadn't.

So Feraltz wasn't and couldn't, and therefore hadn't needed to be silenced. Unless Feraltz's prior association with Langsariks, a detail Garol had found buried in the intelligence analysis, hinted at collusion; but if there was collusion, surely they would have managed a way to arrange Feraltz's survival without the risky cover of the physical injuries Feraltz had sustained?

"Without reference to your earlier testimony." Garol knew he could challenge that testimony, which had not been taken under appropriate controls, potential drug interactions compromising quality of evidence, and so forth. And he would, if he needed to; but first he needed to be sure of the facts. To the extent that there were facts. To the extent that objective truths even existed. "How about telling me what you remember that could be used to identify the raiders. Don't worry about anything you said before, for now. Just talk to me."

Feraltz let his leg rest, frowning. "That's probably the problem right there, Bench specialist. I don't have much to offer. I was in the dock-master's office doing inventory audit for the tax assessment, and I heard her talking to them on the comms, but I don't remember anything the least unusual about the conversation. I only barely remember hearing her talking to them at all."

He probably hadn't been paying attention. Dock-masters talked to inbound freighters all the time. A Langsarik accent was one of the more subtle ones—as if a Langsarik wouldn't have disguised his or her voice anyway. As if any pirate wouldn't have done that, out of baseline prudence.

As if Langsariks could have come up with a ship to mount a raid in the first place: unfortunately fifteen years of successful commerce raiding had created a belief in the public mind that the Langsariks could work miracles before breakfast, when it came to their ships.

"She went out, she shut the door; I remember thinking she might have some unrecorded transaction going with the freighter. And it's none of my business; I audit to the record, there are specialists who audit for unrecorded transactions. So I minded my own business."

It had just been bad luck for Feraltz that he'd even been there in the first place. But inventory audit was supposed to be unannounced, and the raiders wouldn't have expected him to be in the dock-master's office.

"I heard the door, it was pushed open with a crash. Startled me. There were three men, and the dock-master. She made a break for the master communications panel. They shot her. Into pieces."

The surprise of finding the dock-master's office occupied would explain it; otherwise, it would have been hard to understand the dock-master getting away from her escort, even for a short dash across the room. They'd probably meant to force her to open her safe room. If so, the death she'd won by resisting might well have been one infinitely to be preferred to the manner in which she might have died—except that Langsariks had never gone for torture in any big way. Nor massacre, come to that.

"And I think they were wearing that color, the yellow-pink. Langsarik colors. What is it called? Rose gold. It's a familiar color, Bench specialist, I should tell you that I spent some time as the guest of the Langsarik fleet, when I was younger." Garol made a mental note; Feraltz's candid confession simplified things a bit. "But that doesn't make them Langsariks. I could wear a Bench intelligence specialist's uniform if I wanted, but it wouldn't make me a Bench intelligence specialist."

No, it would make him a criminal. It was against the law to wear a uniform to which one was not legally entitled—or bound, in the case of the bond-involuntaries. The point was well taken, all the same.

"What do you remember about their appearance apart from the color of their clothing?" Garol prompted. "Anybody you may have thought you recognized, for instance. Cut of the garment. Hair color. Size and shape. Accent."

But Feraltz frowned, with apparent perplexity. "I'm sorry, Bench specialist. I didn't recognize anybody. They were all men, I think. I remember the color very vividly. But about the people themselves—not much."

Disappointing; but predictable. Feraltz had only seen them moments before he was shot, and then only under conditions of deep emotional shock and horror.

The Bench couldn't pin a Langsarik crime on the settlement on the basis of this evidence. Feraltz knew Langsariks, had lived with Langsariks, and refused to say that they were Langsariks; but the strength of the evidence went both ways. Maybe he was protecting someone.

And yet Garol couldn't discount the implications.

Maybe the raiders wore Langsarik colors in order to divert suspicion to a visible target in the event that they were seen. It would be a coup for Langsariks to manage a raid from quarantine; unfortunately, the Langsariks had proved—time and again—that they were capable of almost anything.

And therefore maybe the raiders wore Langsarik colors because they were Langsariks, and that was the only clothing they had.

That was the simplest—and therefore most obvious, if unlikely—explanation; and Garol did not look forward to taking this intelligence to Chilleau Judiciary.

It was his duty. He didn't have to like it.

The only way he was going to be able to determine whether or not there was a problem with the amnesty agreement was to go to Port Charid and see for himself. If nothing else, the public-relations angle had to be carefully managed, and he could best decide how to handle that on-site.

"Are you willing to do a pharmaceutical investigation?" Garol asked, because he had a duty to ask. Sometimes the right drugs could pull up a previously unretrieved detail from memory; but drugs were also frequently responsible for the spontaneous generation of false memories, or for complete misinterpretation of imperfectly understood information.

It took a real expert to hope to tell the difference, especially in circumstances where the subject witness might have ulterior motives that affected what and how much he remembered.

Garol wasn't particularly interested in risking the survival of the Langsarik settlement on a point of interpretation; so he was just as glad when Feraltz shook his head, rejecting the suggestion. Reluctantly. But absolutely.

"I'm sworn to Abstain, Bench specialist, and it's hard enough that I have to take all of this medicine, even though the priest insists on it. I'll do a drug inquiry if you come back with an Ecclesiastical Exception, of course I will. But I really don't want to. I'm sure I've already told you everything I remember."

The Dolgorukij church administration would make allowances for the requirements of Bench process, even for zealots like Abstainers. But zealots hated to compromise, on Ecclesiastical Exception or any other grounds. This young man had already suffered; Garol was quite willing to forgo a step that might only produce ambiguous or flawed evidence for which there was no pressing immediate need—at least for the time being.

If there were problems on Charid, he would find out about them his own way; too much potentially ambiguous information too soon would only seriously constrain his freedom of action.

"Let's not worry about that for now. Time enough later if we need corroborative evidence," Garol reassured Feraltz, who seemed to relax gratefully. "I'll be going, Feraltz. Thanks. for your time. And keep up with your therapy. It's the best thing for a complete recovery."

He should talk.

But maybe giving lip service to the acknowledged but disregarded truth would balance out his own personal and admittedly flamboyant disobedience of doctor's orders, and help even everything out in the end.

He was going to have to go to Chilleau Judiciary and talk to the Second Judge's First Secretary, Sindha Verlaine; that could be as unpleasant as rehabilitation therapy, so maybe that would count on the credit side of his personal register, too.

It was worth hoping for.

Garol set his mind firmly on that encouraging but unlikely idea and left Feraltz to exercise in peace.

Kazmer Daigule strolled casually through the narrow lanes of Port Charid's warehouse district with his hands deep in the worn pockets of his old coat, trying to guess how long it would take for the early-morning sun to warm the air at street level. It would be mid-morning before the shadows began to lift, as far as he could tell; these lanes were only wide enough to admit a small transport mover, and the warehouses themselves towered to the skies.

At least that was the impression from ground level, and the effect seemed to have a discouraging impact on the relatively few people Kazmer could see coming and going in the streets. Maybe they were all just minding their business; Kazmer could approve of that.

Then something caught his eye.

Didn't he know that man—

Kazmer had seen the familiar figure approach, but so far as he could tell he hadn't been remarked upon for his own part. This could be good. Looking around him quickly, Kazmer located the nearest doorway and ducked into the shallow alcove the doorway offered for concealment, then waited.

Moments passed.

Then the man crossed in front of him, and Kazmer knew him all right. Tall and thin, big-boned, almost gangly, with a fine sharp expression of quick intelligence and lively wit—and big ears that stood out from his head, though perhaps it took a friend to notice. Frowning, just now, and apparently sunk so deep in thought that he didn't so much as look up until Kazmer spoke.

"Hilton Shires, as I live and breathe. What brings you into Port Charid, Hilton?"

Kazmer stepped out of the alcove and extended his hand in greeting, but it seemed that the surprise he'd given Hilton was unpleasantly complete. It took Hilton a moment to respond.

"Kazmer. Hey. Long time, how've you been?"

Well, it hadn't been all that very long a time. Not really. He'd taken his leave of the Langsariks well ahead of their rendezvous with the Jurisdiction fleet, and he hadn't seen hide nor hair of a Langsarik since. Two years, maybe.

"I've got no complaints." Kazmer took a step or two down the street, to encourage Hilton to walk with him; but Hilton wasn't moving. Maybe Hilton was annoyed at Kazmer for getting the drop on him, which would be a little oversensitive on Hilton's part. It was Kazmer who owed his life to Hilton, and not the other way around. "You?"

"Life is changed." Hilton made the obvious point so blandly that it was almost as though the fact had just occurred to him. "Not like old times at all, Kazmer. What brings you to Port Charid?"

"I've been called in on a transport job." By Hilton's people, as a matter of fact. As if he didn't know, him with his Langsarik colors showing beneath the sober collar of a new if inexpensive work-shirt. But maybe he had gotten cautious, in his old age; or it could as easily be that Hilton felt they were too vulnerable to eavesdropping, out in the street like this. They'd be a lot less obvious if they were walking together, Kazmer told himself; but Hilton had a stubborn streak. "From what I've heard there's been more than one of that sort of thing through Port Charid lately."

But what could Langsariks need cargo transport for? The Langsariks' property had been impounded by the Bench, along with the Langsarik hulls—as a very practical means of assuring good behavior by removing the means of any independent behaviors at all.

The only transport a Langsarik could get would be illegal and surreptitious by definition. So the only need that Langsariks could have for a mercantile pilot to transport cargo was to move contraband, and Kazmer and Hilton both knew it.

Which only made Hilton's resolute play at oblivious ignorance all the more irritating. "Well, traffic is picking up. That's true. Plenty of work to go around." And Hilton actually leaned his back up against the external wall of the warehouse that fronted on the street, folding his arms across his chest as he did so. Those were his racing thermals that Hilton was wearing with his new work-shirt, Kazmer noted. Somewhat the worse for wear, too, but Hilton had always been hard on his racing thermals. A demon for speed, landborne, airborne, spaceborne. "Still. Isn't this a little out of the way?"

Yes, it was. "I'm a free agent, and I thought it sounded interesting." He wouldn't have come so far on a job offer for anyone but Hilton's people—let alone for a job offer that involved contraband. He was trying to get away from contraband. The least Hilton could do was acknowledge the debt, even if it was obliquely. "Are you on your way to anywhere in particular yourself?"

Of course he was. Hilton was there for the same reason Kazmer was; Kazmer was sure of it. Hilton, however, shook his head, and lied.

"Not really. There isn't much to do out in the settlement, though, and I got a pass. So I thought I'd come down to watch the shuttle traffic, kind of get away from it all for a bit."

Now Kazmer was annoyed, and beginning to think about being insulted. Prudence was one thing, but Hilton was taking this whole secrecy bit a little too far. And if that was the way Hilton was going to be, Kazmer would not keep him any longer.

"I see. Well, enjoy yourself, Hilton. Give my regards to your family, all right?"

Hilton's family.

There was a thought.

So long as Hilton was here in Port Charid maybe Kazmer would have a chance to get out to the settlement and see sweet little Cousin Modice.

Hilton had warned him—if only half-seriously—never to let him catch Kazmer in bed with his little girl-cousin ever again; and him knowing what the joke was, because it had been Hilton's idea. It hadn't taken Kazmer long to develop a crush on Modice, true, but he'd known from the start that there was no real future in it.

Modice's guardian—the Flag Captain of the Langsarik fleet herself—had let him know that Sarvaw mercantile pilots didn't figure into any Langsarik domestic equations that she was willing to consider for her niece. She'd done it gently and with humor, but the message had been clear enough.

Fine.

Hilton wouldn't catch him.

Modice was a grown girl, or close enough to it to make up her own mind. By now, anyway. It had been three years since the bed incident.

"Sure thing," said Hilton. "Maybe I'll see you around. Before you go. Where are you staying?"

Kazmer was tired of the game. "Just in, actually, I don't know yet. I'll be in touch. Nice to see you, Hilton."

He was on his way to meet with Hilton's people in a common meal-room two streets over, right now.

But if Hilton genuinely didn't know where he was, there was no danger of Hilton guessing that he had gone out afterward to see Modice.

That would pay Hilton out for being so excessively cagey with him in the street. Pleased with this thought, Kazmer went on to his meeting with his prospective employers in good humor once again.

Hilton Shires lingered on the pavement, leaning as casually as he could manage against the exterior wall of a featureless warehouse building, watching Kazmer Daigule's back as he lumbered out of sight.

Of all the bad luck, rotten luck, disgusting luck, unfair luck.

No, he had nothing against Sarvaw mercantile pilots, not in so many words. Kazmer was his friend; he'd saved Kazmer's life—or at least it had been his stratagem that had saved Kazmer's life—and there was little that endeared one man to another quite so strongly as the sense of being benefactor to a peer.

It was true that Kazmer had shown signs of getting sweet on Modice, but that was hardly Kazmer's fault; Modice had that sort of effect on a lot of people. And the provocation had been more extreme than usual, what with their first meeting being in such potentially compromising circumstances.

But mercantile pilot Kazmer Daigule was one of the last people Hilton had expected to see in Port Charid that morning, and the surprise rendered the awkwardness all the more unpleasant.

He'd made up his mind to take action. They were a displaced people on probation; and while the Bench provided well enough for them to evade public outrage and avoid creating discord from extremes of want, the Bench did not provide for them generously, in any sense.

Hilton's parents had grown old at war, serving with the Langsarik fleet. The cold season was coming on in the settlement, and the weary bones of retired warriors creaked in the chill wind that blew from the south-southwest. He was young and fit and could labor; and also he had destroyed the latest in a long line of speed machines, and needed the wherewithal to buy another.

But he wasn't about to admit to Kazmer, of all people, that Hilton Shires was looking for a job. Kazmer knew him as a lieutenant in the Langsarik fleet, a man of acknowledged capability, authority, daring. Kazmer still had space transport, and no Fleet directive to restrict him from using it. Hilton was grounded and flightless, emasculated, powerless.

He had swallowed a good deal of humiliation over the past two years, as the necessary price of purchasing their lives and eventual freedom from a vengeful Bench; but there were limits to how low he could tolerate forcing himself to bend, and confessing his sorry estate to Kazmer was right down there near rock bottom.

It was almost enough to put him off his enterprise altogether, but Kazmer was gone, and the weather was still slowly but surely on its way toward wintertime. The Combine Factor in Port Charid—a big, brash, bearded man named Shiron Madlev—had been a friend to the Langsarik settlement in too many quiet subtle ways to deserve rude behavior from Hilton. Accepting Madlev's offer of a job interview and then canceling at a moment's notice would be an entirely gratuitous slap in the face.

And without a speed machine to remind him, howsoever briefly, of the freedom of the stars, Hilton was not sure he could survive; so he took a deep breath and composed himself, and walked on.

It was easy enough to find the Factor's front office, even though Hilton hadn't been there before. There was a man behind a desk with a high counter, and another man sitting by the beverage server having a flask of the leaf-based beverage that Combine people drank by preference—rhyti, that was right. It smelled like flowers to Hilton, but his aunt liked the stuff.

"Good-greeting. My name is Hilton Shires." The man at the desk had watched him come in; clearly the doorkeeper, so Hilton spoke to him first. "I have an appointment for an interview."

Out of the corner of his eye Hilton saw the other man present put down his flask of rhyti and stand up. The doorkeeper nodded at the second man, but he was speaking to Hilton.

"Yes, Shires, you're expected. This is floor manager Dalmoss. Factor Madlev has asked the warehouse foreman to interview you, you're to go with Dalmoss to find him, if you please."

Well, Hilton had found the prospect of talking to Factor Madlev himself about a job a bit awkward. He was just as glad he would be talking to a foreman; the less overall power the foreman had in the organizational structure of the Combine Yards, the less keenly Hilton expected to feel the gap between what the foreman had the power to dole out and what he himself could expect or hope to be offered.

Something like that.

"Dalmoss Chzagul," the floor manager said, coming up to Hilton. Then, unexpectedly, Dalmoss offered his hand to clasp in the

Langsarik fashion. Hilton didn't particularly need to clasp hands with any non-Langsarik, but it was a nice gesture and would be rude of him to ignore it, so he took Dalmoss's hand and clasped it politely.

"Pleased. Hilton Shires. Thank you for seeing me."

Dalmoss seemed as willing as Hilton to call the gesture complete and break contact, but that was entirely fair as far as Hilton was concerned. "I'll be honest with you, Shires, it's not my idea." But the admission was merely frank, and not challenging; Hilton could find no cause to take offense. "Still, we need help. I can grant you that, without hesitation. Let's go find the foreman; he said he might be in the meal-room this time of the morning. We'll check there first."

It was a way of giving him a tour of the facility, maybe. Hilton looked around him with interest as Dalmoss led him through the administrative offices, across a load-in dock, past the great hulls of not one but three freighter tenders being off-loaded, and finally out into the street and down a half a block to a subsidized meal-room, where Dalmoss paused in the foyer to scan the crowded hall.

"Look at all these people," Dalmoss suggested. "You can see our problem. We keep on picking up freight. We're running out of capacity to handle it."

Hilton followed Dalmoss's lead in looking around him politely. It was very candid of Dalmoss to make such remarks when they both knew that the reason the Combine Yards were picking up freight was that the Okidan Yards and other yards before it had lost capacity, and the freight had to be handled somewhere. The Okidan Yards hadn't merely lost capacity, of course. The Okidan Yards had lost its staff and its plant, and there was a lot of gossip that blamed Langsariks. Hilton knew the gossip was baseless. It was still an awkward situation to be in.

Who was that over there by the far wall?

Kazmer Daigule, sitting at table with some people Hilton didn't recognize—discussing terms and conditions of hire, clearly enough, public meal-rooms being convenient meeting spaces for people without offices to call their own. Such as Sarvaw mercantile pilots.

So Kazmer was here to run a Combine cargo.

That would explain his refusal to come right out and say what he was doing here. Kazmer was Sarvaw. Hilton knew what Kazmer thought of the rest of the Dolgorukij Combine—or at least he knew what Kazmer had to say about other Dolgorukij.

"I don't see him here," Dalmoss said. "Something you need to know about the foreman, Shires. He was at the Okidan Yards when the— when it was hit. He's only been back at Charid for two days, still in med-assist; so it's hard for him to get around, or he'd have met you himself. You can thank him for your job. He saw your name on the resource list and grabbed for you."

Dalmoss had started to move again; Hilton had to keep up. "That's flattering. If confusing. What's one Langsarik among others? You know what I'm saying."

Dalmoss grinned. Hilton was beginning to think he liked the man. "I wondered myself. Feraltz insisted. Said you had the leadership skills we were going to need in the remote warehouse. You were an officer? If you don't mind me asking."

"'Was' being the pertinent word. Yes. Junior officer. But these days I'm just another unemployed Langsarik, like the rest of us."

That was unfair, maybe. There were plenty of jobs for Langsariks at Port Charid; that was one of the reasons the Bench had settled them there, after all, to be Port Charid's very own captive labor pool. There were all the nasty, difficult, soul-wearying, low-paying jobs anyone could want available.

"A cut above the rank and file, even so. We're expanding. Fisner will tell you all about it—he said to try Receiving if he wasn't having first-meal."

Fisner Feraltz.

The name seemed familiar, somehow.

Dalmoss moved quickly, and there was a lot of territory between the meal-room and the receiving floor. A man could clearly get his exercise, working here.

Hilton had heard about warehouse operations, and he had an idea of their size from living near Port Charid; but he'd never been so deep inside of a major mercantile complex before. The receiving floor was the size of an asteroid warehouse, it seemed, and there were more freighter tenders there, four of them.

Four.

Hilton let his eyes rest on the great beasts that Port Charid used to ferry cargo between the surface and the freighters in orbit, the ships that were too large to land and lift except from the yards in the Shawl of Rikavie, where the gravitational pull was minimal.

Four freighter tenders.

He'd seen passenger shuttles that would carry maybe a thousand souls, at least for two days or so, and these freighter tenders were even bigger than a mass passenger ferry. He slowed to a stop without noticing what he was doing and stared at the ships hungrily; then Dalmoss's voice called him back to where he was.

"There's the boss," Dalmoss said. "Over there. On the crate, by that mover. Come on."

Those freighter tenders might as well be crates themselves. He'd not be allowed to so much as move them into orbit, if he was allowed onto them at all. Hilton pushed his wild fantasies firmly into a comer of his mind and followed Dalmoss to where a man of Hilton's approximate age was sitting on a crate, waiting for them.

Fisner Feraltz only half-sat on the crate, his right leg stretched out straight and resting on the floor, covered in bracing. A little more to the fleshy side than Hilton himself was, perhaps, but then it wasn't as if the food in settlement encouraged overindulgence.

"Hilton Shires, Foreman," Dalmoss called. "We missed you in the meal-room, sorry."

Feraltz waved the apology off with his left hand. The right hand was braced stiff. "My fault, Dal, I didn't make it to first-meal. Too much effort. Hilton Shires? Fisner Feraltz. Excuse me if I don't offer my hand."

He was a lot more informal than Hilton had expected, which came as a relief. "Quite all right. When in Combine Yards do as Combine does, after all. Thanks for the opportunity to interview."

Feraltz beckoned him closer, so that he could speak more quietly Hilton supposed. "My pleasure, Shires. I owe a debt of gratitude to your family, but I'm keeping quiet about it. Sentiment isn't very supportive of Langsariks in Port Charid just now, I'm afraid."

Feraltz.

Of course.

Dalmoss wasn't looking surprised, so it apparently wasn't a particular secret; but Hilton could certainly understand why Feraltz might want to avoid calling attention to his personal history, just at the moment. To have spent a year with Langsariks was probably about the same as having been raised by wolves, as far as Feraltz's fellow Dolgorukij were concerned.

"So. Look at this, Shires." Feraltz's gesture took in the entire sweep of the receiving area, the tenders, the work crews, the load-in cranes. The crates. "The Combine Yards are picking up the slack for lost capacity elsewhere in system. We're going to have to make some pretty significant increases to accommodate the overflow. There's new facilities under construction—"

Hilton knew that. The Combine's new warehouse project had been one of the first things Port Charid had drawn on its new Langsarik labor pool to get started.

"—but we're not staffed for it, and I need someone with prior management experience to help us grow. I'll need to start you on the entry levels, of course, so you can familiarize yourself with the administration of this kind of an operation."

It sounded good.

"I don't have any prior management experience." It sounded a little too good. All right, Feraltz felt he owed something to Aunt Agenis's extended family for saving his life and getting him safely back to his own people, even though it had taken them a while. Hilton still wanted to be sure that Feraltz wasn't overestimating his ability, in his desire to be accommodating. "I was a lieutenant. It's people like my aunt who actually ran things."

He'd commanded raids, successful ones, but he wasn't about to make a point of that. Not here. Very poor taste.

Feraltz shook his head, rejecting Hilton's disclaimer. "I know what your position was, and I think the skills are transferable. I'd like you to accept an entry-level position in order to train for assistant floor manager, looking forward to the time when the new facility comes up to capacity. I can't promise anything, but I'm confident you'll demonstrate the qualities we need. Will you consider my offer?"

It really wasn't an option. He needed the job.

"I'll be happy to accept your offer, Foreman. I appreciate the opportunity to come work for the Combine Yards and learn about warehouse management. I see it as a long-term investment. And I'm not going anywhere."

Maybe he shouldn't have said that last bit. It sounded a little bitter, a little petty. He'd only make things worse if he made a fuss about it by qualifying or rephrasing, though, so he bit his tongue firmly to shut himself up, and waited.

Feraltz smiled sympathetically, while Dalmoss—his arms folded across his chest—looked at the floor, smiling as well, and scuffing his foot against some unseen object by way of making a show of going along with the joke.

"I understand perfectly," Feraltz said. "Dockman's wages to start, Shires; you'll report to Dalmoss here, you can discuss your shift with him once you've done your in-processing. Do we have a contract?"

Dockman's wages were better than the day laborer's rates usually offered to Langsariks. Maybe Feraltz was serious about his plans; one way or the other he was certainly making it much easier for Hilton to commit himself to regular employment than Hilton had expected.

"Contract," Hilton agreed. "Thank you, Foreman. Floor manager."

Dalmoss had waved someone over, and the man approached them with a look of genial curiosity on his face. "This is Ippolit," Dalmoss said. "Ippolit, Shires is coming on to join receiving and inventory. Would you take him out to personnel, please, they're expecting him."

Were they, indeed.

But the prospect of dockman's wages went a long way toward sweetening any residual difficulties Hilton might have experienced on that account; and he followed the man called Ippolit away to the personnel office, not so much happy as relieved enough to feel almost as though he were.

Fisner Feraltz watched Shires leave with Ippolit. Dalmoss was unhappy; Fisner knew it. He could tell.

"Was it prudent to remind him, firstborn and eldest?" Dalmoss asked, his voice pitched low enough to guard against anyone eavesdropping by accident. "He may speculate."

"He may." Fisner could afford to accept a portion of the rebuke from Dalmoss; it was no challenge to his authority. "But he's the Flag Captain's nephew. To not have at least mentioned it would look like ingratitude. He might have wondered why I'd not allowed the obligation."

Dalmoss thought about it for a moment, time Feraltz used to adjust his position on the crate. The bracing was awkward. He was having a hard time adjusting to it.

"I understand. Yes," Dalmoss said. Fisner knew that what Dalmoss understood about Fisner's history with Langsariks was not the whole truth, but that was the way it had to be. No one could know the true depths of his shame; that was between him, and the Angel of Destruction, and the Holy Mother. "Does the bracing trouble you, firstborn and eldest?"

Well, yes, it did. But Dalmoss's anxiety could be traced at least in part to the fact that it had been Dalmoss who had fired the round that had injured him.

"It's an annoyance, I admit." And there were drugs for annoyance, as there were drugs for pain. He'd told the Bench specialist that he was an Abstainer, but he'd had reason for that deception that did not extend so far as actually to abstain from medication required to heal flesh, knit bone, and ease one's way through life generally. "But a minor one. And it puts our purpose forward."

It was very convenient if others thought him to be Abstaining, of course.

It could only increase the effectiveness of his deception if people who saw him at all only ever saw him obviously crippled, dependent upon the medical brace to support a clearly only slowly healing frame.

Dalmoss nodded. "I'll go arrange for a team meeting, Foreman. To introduce our new employee. We start him on inventory, I believe."

Yes, so that it would be creditable to claim that Shires had learned to manipulate the inventory systems. Not only to learn the location of cargo to be appropriated, but also to hide stolen goods within the Combine Yards themselves, so that when the Bench finally sent troops to Port Charid to search, the evidence of Langsarik predation would be utterly damning. Unchallengeable.

"You have nothing with which to reproach yourself, Dalmoss." Since they both knew what they needed to do with Shires, Fisner decided to address the other issue instead. The one that had been there, unspoken but near palpable, hanging in the air between them since Fisner had returned from the hospital in Nisherre. "All went as expected, as hoped. As planned. Believe me, nextborn and second eldest. From my heart."

Dalmoss could not but accept his superior's assurances, whether or not he seemed fully convinced by them. "Just as you say, then, eldest and firstborn. I'll be going to call my crew meeting, with your permission."

Fisner was not concerned. Dalmoss would learn that Fisner spoke only plain truth.

Dalmoss had not done him any injury, even though Dalmoss's shot had injured him.

Dalmoss had made it possible for the plan to go forward and Fisner had nothing but gratitude to him, for that.

CHAPTER TWO

The rendezvous had been set for a public cafeteria deep in the warehouse district—a fine anonymous place for a plot, Kazmer told himself, pausing on the threshold to take in the scene. The morning meal line was beginning to slow down, and the room was neither so full that people could not sit apart without drawing attention to themselves nor so empty that individuals stood out against the general void. There was too much ambient noise to fear a directional sensor, but not so much that a man would need to raise his voice to make himself heard.

It was near perfect.

Kazmer paid for a breakfast tray and carried it over to one of the tables at the far wall. Third from the left, he'd been told. There were people there already; but none of them looked like Langsariks to Kazmer.

He sat down with his back to the wall, facing the entrance to the meal line. The woman who had moved over on the bench to make room for him eyed him with mild curiosity; then she spoke.

"It'd be Kazmer Daigule. Mercantile pilot. Didn't you carry some kennels of Clement's spotty dogs to Julerich, last year?"

Maybe he had, and maybe he hadn't. He took a drink of his morning brew and grimaced, reaching for the syrup packet on his tray. Sometimes the only thing to do was to syrup the stuff up and get it down somehow. A man needed his morning drink to help him get started on his day's work.

"What's your interest in spotty dogs?" he retorted, but mildly. "There are worse cargoes. And I know, because I've carried them."

There was an older man seated across from Kazmer; that would be the ship's master, Kazmer guessed. He had an accent that Kazmer couldn't place, but it wasn't any of his business.

"You can do better than spotty dogs, pilot. There's a chance of a cargo to leave from the Shawl soon, and a good market even for goods whose documentation might not be quite perfect."

So far, so good, but there was no sense letting down his guard before he was sure of his surroundings. "That's as may be. But it takes more than a pilot to move cargo."

The completely undistinguished person on the other side of the woman to Kazmer's left leaned forward, and looked directly at him. "Not too many more, if someone else does the load-out. There'll be resources on-site to transfer cargo, and I can get a ship packed and ready in three hours or less. Guaranteed."

"I can vouch for it," the man on the other side of that man said. "I've seen it happen." And Kazmer—looking down to the end of the table—got confirmatory, conspiratorial nods from the three other people at the foot of the table besides. All right.

"Navigator?" he asked, and the woman coughed discreetly.

"Ship's master," the man facing Kazmer said, the one who'd made the remark about goods and documentation. "So think of me as Engineer. To my right, your left, transmission specialist. To my left, your right, cargo disposition manager."

The fence, in so many words. The man who would be responsible for getting rid of stolen goods and paying them all off.

"And that's just cargo management," Fence emphasized, quietly, but with a solid sort of determination in his voice and his serious expression. "No wet goods. Or I'm not even playing. Anybody have any different ideas? There've been assurances given me, no squishy stuff."

Kazmer felt a little offended. "Come on. These people don't waste energy. It's not going to be a problem, I've seen them in action. I wouldn't touch a cargo with moisture on it."

That wasn't exactly true. He'd handled cargoes with blood on them before: just not life's-blood. He'd been prudish or he'd been lucky, or possibly both, but he'd stayed clear of blood-guilt since he'd taken his pilot's license, and he meant to keep it that way.

"You've been out of system, pilot," the woman—Navigator—said. Suggested, explained? "You haven't heard. The latest raid at Okidan, only one survivor."

She was right. He hadn't heard. Was there a problem? Kazmer tucked into his bowl of porridge, hoping to get most of it down before it congealed in the dish.

"I was promised different this time," Engineer said. "But I won't pretend it really matters. There's a job. I need one. Someone's going to do it, and I may as well collect the fee as any other man. Worth taking just to see how it's being managed, to my mind."

At least the engineer was honest. That didn't mean Kazmer had to respect the man's point of view. Still, he was curious about the logistics himself; and was there any sense in pretending to keep to high moral ground? Cargoes all came from someplace. People got in the way of live fire from time to time, without anyone meaning any harm. Accidents happened. Carrying contraband goods was against the law whether or not anyone had gotten hurt in the initial cargo-acquisition phase of the transaction.

But he'd never done more than economic harm to any man. He wasn't about to start now, not even to help Langsariks. Not even to help Hilton.

"I'm not getting paid to risk a capital charge," one of the crew said, her voice low enough to keep her words carefully within the limited area of the table without attracting attention by whispering. "They claimed you'd worked with this outfit before, pilot."

And so he had. "Where are they, by the way? Does anybody know?" He could tell them where one of the members of the group that had hired them was, or near to it, at least. Hilton had to be somewhere close.

The navigator shook her head. "The man who contacted me said that any direct contact would be too risky for all of us, especially so soon after Okidan. Said you could answer any questions we might have. We disperse, we get a call, we load and leave."

Oh, he'd disperse, all right. He'd disperse straight out to the Langsarik settlement to see Modice. The Langsariks were keeping a low profile? He'd be sure no one caught him on his way there or back. Hilton wouldn't be able to accuse him of any underhanded subterfuge; he would merely be taking prudent measures to avoid attracting any attention to himself.

"Well, it's true what they told you. About prior association," Kazmer added hastily. Hilton had a wickedly dry sense of humor; there was no telling what he might have said to these people. "I've always found them to be efficient. Conservative. No unnecessary effort." Meaning, by implication, no unnecessary violence. "I'd expect them to be especially careful to keep the noise level down. Frankly, I'm a little surprised they're risking any noise at all."

And maybe "they" weren't. Maybe this whole setup wasn't Langsariks at all, or at least not fully sanctioned. Maybe Hilton and some of his peers were just blowing off a little steam. It had to be hard on people like Hilton to settle down on dirt and look for mundane, lawful employment after having spent nearly sixteen years as a law unto themselves, answerable to none, taking what they needed when they needed it from wherever they could find it.

That could be.

The fence shrugged. "Who knows if what the authorities say about the other procurement is even true? Maybe there wasn't any broken furniture."

A good point, that, what with public propaganda being what it was. Maybe the events associated with this Okidan raid were being exaggerated for effect.

Just then something caught Kazmer's eye for the second time this morning, and it was the same something, too. Hilton, in the entryway that led to the meal line, standing in the entrance with someone, discussing something. Hilton looked across the room, looked right at him, but gave no sign of recognition; and moved on.

Kazmer decided.

Accidents happened and people changed, and Hilton was a Langsarik pirate; but Hilton would not involve himself with murder. If this was a Langsarik gig, and Hilton was in on it, it was a straightforward grab-and-run operation. And Hilton was in on it; there could be no question. There was no other reasonable explanation for his presence here, for his behavior earlier.

"I'm in." He'd had all the porridge he could stomach. Pushing the bowl away from him, he started to leave. "I'll see you all later."

The engineer nodded, and then the navigator. The fence stared at his hands, picking at the ragged cuticle of his left thumb, and finally nodded at the table in turn. "All right," the fence said. "I'll see you later, too."

The others had apparently already decided. So they were a crew. What had happened at Okidan?

It might call unwelcome attention to himself if he started asking questions. Maybe he'd hear some gossip in Port Charid. He could always get the details from the more well-informed members of this crew, once they were safely on their way to wherever it was they were going.

So there would be plenty of time to hear all of the news, public, private, rumored, and invented. At the moment Modice Agenis was waiting to see him, though she didn't know it yet.

Garol Vogel turned his shuttle over to the transport pool for maintenance and refueling. He never spent much time at Chilleau Judiciary's administrative center; he didn't intend to spend much time there now.

Chilleau Judiciary was within Garol's orb of assignment, so he had an office in Chambers—along with Jils Ivers, and whoever else was on rotation this cycle. It was nice to have someplace to come back to, even if it was at an administrative center. Nice to have a corner to himself, dark and cool and quiet, where he could be sure that things would be where he had left them and nobody would have tried to tidy up.

People might have been in to have a look at what he was doing, yes, that was something that happened from time to time; but sensitive information was always either secured or otherwise protected, and people who were after information they had no business being interested in could be relied upon to put things back carefully, as exactly as found as possible.

Garol walked through the great gates and into the administrative center of Chilleau Judiciary's Chambers in the middle of the night. Traffic on campus was relatively light, the corridors comparatively empty. He let himself into his office—three levels down from the senior administrative complex, fully five floors down from the Second Judge's personal quarters—and put his cloth pack down to one side of the door, pulling off the jacket he wore when he wasn't being official. Old campaign jacket, and from a really obscure planetary fleet; the cut and color offered few clues as to the identity of the wearer.

No clues whatever, in fact. Any branch-of-service markers that might once have decorated that old worn jacket had long since eroded with wear to the point of indecipherability, and Garol liked it that way.

He locked the door and turned on the desk lights, started some bean tea, sent the courtesy notifications to First Secretary Verlaine— the Second Judge's senior administrative official—and another message down to the media watch in Intelligence Analysis asking for the current situation report from Port Charid.

There were dockets on his desk he hadn't looked at, but he was in no hurry. He was here to brief the Second Judge about Port Charid and the Langsariks. Anything else Chilleau Judiciary got out of him this visit would be gravy for them, and since Jils had sent him a briefing packet on some of Verlaine's recent moves, Garol was not in a particularly gravy-ladling mood.

Putting his feet up on the dockets stacked on the desk, Garol meditated over a cup of hot bean tea, waiting for the runner from Intelligence Analysis.

He was halfway through the cup of tea when the signal came, and he had to get up and open the door. He could have left it unlocked, he supposed, but he didn't like being interrupted by well-wishers poking their heads in to attempt to cultivate his acquaintance.

Unlatching the door, Garol pulled it open. "Oh, hello. You've got the report I asked for? Thanks."

He knew the Clerk of Court who'd brought the report down, though.

Mergau Noycannir.

The rabid Inquisitor-without-portfolio that Verlaine had made as an experiment in shifting control of Inquiry from Fleet to the Bench— an experiment which had failed with Noycannir. The whole point of Inquiry was the use of judicial torture as an instrument of statecraft, and for torture to have the looked-for deterrent effect, it had to be perceived as something to be afraid of, something that could be used to obtain evidence against one's friends and family, something that could be used to render entire communities vulnerable to sanctions at the discretion of the Judge.

Noycannir just killed people.

That wasn't an enjoyable experience, at least not from any near-miss accounts that Garol had heard and fully acknowledging the lack of any real firsthand recitation from the dead concerning their feelings about the whole thing. But a threat that only endangered one's own self had nothing like the emotional impact of one that could be used to condemn one's near and dear based on one's own testimony.

Other Inquisitors could obtain incriminating evidence, and some of them actually found things out—Andrej Koscuisko, for one, the rash young Inquisitor who had cried Failure of Writ at the Domitt Prison, and set the wheels in motion of a scandal from which Chilleau Judiciary still reeled.

But not Noycannir.

Nor was she wearing the uniform of an Inquisitor, but the more plain and humble dress of a senior Clerk of Court; and she had come from Intelligence Analysis?

Garol took an almost involuntary step backward; he hadn't been prepared for this apparition at all, let alone its mind-boggling implications.

It was a mistake.

Noycannir lowered her head and followed him, as though she'd been invited in.

"I've been reviewing this information since word came you were in, Specialist Vogel," Noycannir said, and walked right past him to open the documents-case she'd brought and lay it out flat on the desk surface. "You'll find this interesting, I'm sure. Here. Have a look at these transport minutes."

Garol could only stand and stare in genuine admiration. She had nerve. No longer functioning as an Inquisitor, that much was obvious, but playacting the role of the peer of a Bench intelligence specialist when not even an Inquisitor was that, presuming responsibility and influence that were no longer hers—had never been hers.

She was a piece of work, was Noycannir.

But he wasn't interested in playing her game and declined her invitation to join her in review at his own desk. "I intend to do just that, but all in good time, Dame Noycannir."

If she was a senior Clerk of Court, she could still claim the courtesy title she had demanded as hers by right when she had held the Writ to Inquire. Garol wondered what the formal status of that Writ was. It was probably more than Verlaine's pride would allow actually to return the credentials to Fleet with an apology, or return them at all, though they could only be executed by Noycannir. No, he'd probably simply dispensed with Noycannir's services, started to send his witness interrogations to a qualified Fleet practitioner, and given her something else to do.

Noycannir didn't respond, standing at his desk with her back to him, leafing through the sections of the report he'd called for. "Taken together with the movement of goods through Sillume, I think you'll agree that a very interesting pattern emerges. I've been looking forward to sharing this with you."

But she wasn't sharing anything with him, when she had brought the report he'd requested.

She was running an errand.

Verlaine had apparently put her off to one side in Intelligence Analysis, a secure job, a comfortable placement, where he could keep an eye on her. Intelligence Analysis was strictly support. They had no authority, made no recommendations, controlled no data.

He'd never liked Noycannir.

He had reasons, too.

And now—though he could fully sympathize with the keen sense of lost status that had to be behind her pathetically desperate pretense—he was getting annoyed.

He didn't believe in gratuitous rudeness, but if she was going to ignore polite hints—

Garol opened his mouth to say something pointed, but a voice from the still-open doorway did the trick for him.

"Thank you, Mergau. Would you excuse us now, please."

That was the voice of the First Secretary, deep and powerful and utterly implacable. Noycannir stiffened when she heard it, and closed up the documents-case with almost fearful care.

"Of course, First Secretary. I'll be at my post should you wish to call for a tertiary analysis, good-greeting."

Bench intelligence specialists did their own tertiary analyses, and they all knew it.

Noycannir left the room with her head meekly lowered, her eyes carefully fixed on the floor. Verlaine stood aside to let her pass, watching her as she went with an expression that spoke volumes to Garol of the First Secretary's disappointment, disgust, and a guilty sort of forbearance. Well, the First Secretary had a reason to blame himself if Noycannir had failed. It had been his wish that she make the trial in the first place, and as much his failure as hers.

It couldn't be pleasant for Verlaine to be reminded of his responsibility for the unfortunate experience Noycannir had had with her Writ, rendering it almost admirable on Verlaine's part that he kept her close—protected her from the enemies she had made in plenty— and paid her salary, even if it was only that of a Clerk of Court.

Verlaine closed the door. "Excuse the intrusion, Bench specialist," Verlaine said. "Can I have a few moments?"

If Verlaine had called Garol to his office, Garol would have gone; it was a concession on Verlaine's part to come down to Garol instead— a concession, or a mark of the importance Verlaine put on the current health of the Langsarik settlement. Garol could respect that.

"Not at all, First Secretary. I've only just gotten in, though; I haven't had a chance to review the intelligence reports. Have a seat?"

Verlaine was staring at the documents-case that Noycannir had left on Garol's desk; Garol didn't think Verlaine was really listening. "But you've just come from Nisherre, talking to that survivor. The eyewitness. How bad is it? Can you tell me?"

Garol didn't have to. In point of law a Bench intelligence specialist was answerable to the Bench, not to any administrative officer. But Garol respected the working relationships Verlaine maintained with the Second Judge, and he wanted to keep Verlaine on his side, if possible. For protection against Mergau Noycannir's intrusions, among other things.

"Declines to state that Langsariks shot the crew. Declines to deny that they were Langsariks. My reasoned evaluation? They could have been Langsariks. Or at least Feraltz, that's the survivor, believes they could have been. There is circumstantial evidence as well."

Not what Verlaine wanted to hear, but that was all right—it wasn't what Garol wanted to tell him. Verlaine folded his arms across his chest and nodded, rolling his lower lip against his teeth. It gave him the appearance of an animal who was still deciding whether or not a physical attack would be required to assure his safety.

"I'm surprised at your acceptance, specialist. The amnesty agreement was in large part a personal accomplishment on your part. A very significant one, at that."

Garol sat down at his desk and tilted his chair back a bit. "I don't like it, but I'm not going to ignore the trends. There could be mitigating factors. I don't know. I came here to tell you that there appears to be a problem. You may wish to brief the Judge."

A real problem, that was to say, and not the product of idle rumor or frivolous gossip. Verlaine nodded again. "Your approach then, Bench specialist?"

"I'm going back to Port Charid. If Langsariks are up to something, I'd like to see how it's done, and the Flag Captain has a right to be given an opportunity to explain her perspective on things. I'll take it from there." He didn't know what his approach was going to be. He wouldn't know that until he got there. "Maybe it's still salvageable. I don't know."

Verlaine unfolded his arms, turning to go. "Well. I don't need to tell you how badly the Second Judge needs the Langsarik settlement to work. We're under fire on all sides, it seems. But we can't afford to shield any scofflaws either. The mercantile interests are very vocal. Anything else?"

Well, yes, as a matter of fact there was. "So long as you mention it. I heard about the assignment you arranged for Koscuisko. Can't say I understand your motivations there particularly well, First Secretary."

Jils had told him all about it. There was something about Koscuisko that interested her, the subtle tension between sanity and psychosis, perhaps. Verlaine blushed angrily, the red blossoming across his cheekbones visible even in the low light in Garol's office. But Verlaine was exceptionally fair-skinned, like many red-haired people in his class of hominid.

"Resource management is not in your brief, Bench specialist." But that was rude, as well as untrue, and Verlaine backed down fractionally from the claim as soon as he'd made it. "We filled the vacancy with the highest priority, no more, no less. The *Ragnarok* had been without a Ship's Surgeon for longer than any other ship in its own, or any equivalent, class."

The *Ragnarok* had no equivalent class. It was an experimental ship, black-hull technology, and commanded by a man who had become incapable of exercising battle command, by reason of a critical failure in the command relationship. "Because Captain Lowden goes through Ship's Surgeons at a pretty good clip. Uses them up, and not in trauma surgery; the *Ragnarok* is still in test status. Proving cruise. No live fire, no active engagements. It's a waste of medical resources to post Koscuisko to the *Ragnarok*."

Garol heard himself getting disgusted as he spoke. He hadn't realized he'd cared one way or the other, not really.

"Yes," Verlaine said; and his tone of voice was flat, unemotional, and completely implacable. "But we must look at the larger environment. The *Ragnarok* is on a proving cruise, so it tours, and the Judicial resources it carries are more frequently tapped than any other active-duty ship. What is the single most efficient use for a man like Koscuisko, Bench specialist?"

There were too many ways to answer that question, so Garol didn't try; and Verlaine had clearly not exhausted his thought.

"Ship's Surgeon, you impact the welfare of a ship's complement, a single ship's complement. Ship's Inquisitor, you materially reinforce the executive power of the Bench by expertly demonstrating the negative consequences of violating the rule of Law. You saw Koscuisko at Rudistal, Bench specialist, you were there—before and after. You tell me. Where does Koscuisko best serve the Judicial order?"

And Verlaine had a point. Koscuisko was a perfectly adequate surgeon, but a brilliant torturer; and after his highly publicized execution of the once-administrator of the Domitt Prison, Koscuisko was well known as someone to fear. Garol wasn't impressed, even so. It was all just rationalization on Verlaine's part. Andrej Koscuisko had embarrassed Chilleau Judiciary; Andrej Koscuisko was to be punished.

"You could serve the Judicial order even better by putting Lowden on ice." Because the *Ragnarok*'s notorious commander did no good at all for the public trust and confidence in the fairness and objectivity of the Bench and its officers. "And maybe Koscuisko would live to see forty, if you did. Not like the last Ship's Surgeon we sent to the *Ragnarok*."

Suicide was wasteful, and waste was offensive in principle. Ship's Surgeons were expensive, Ship's Inquisitors even more so.

"You have more urgent concerns than any Fleet officer's health and welfare, Bench specialist. If you don't mind my saying so." Verlaine had apparently decided to end a conversation whose subject was distasteful. "I'll hold the mercantile interests off Port Charid for as long as possible. Let me know how it goes and if I can help out in any way."

Garol took a deep breath, centering himself.

Verlaine had committed an act of petty revenge in Koscuisko's case, revenge that would be executed at the expense of whoever was unlucky enough to be in Bench custody when Captain Griers Verigson Lowden of the Jurisdiction Fleet Ship *Ragnarok* came looking for diversion and material with which to create an object lesson.

But it was Verlaine's call, and Verlaine's responsibility. Nobody had asked Garol's opinion. He'd said his bit, Verlaine had tolerated the impertinence; it was time to move on.

Garol stood up.

"Thank you for your support, First Secretary." He could say it without hypocrisy. First Secretary Verlaine had always been an honest player; it was just some of his game that Garol didn't like. Nothing personal. "I'll be leaving once I have a chance to review the intelligence reports. Specialist Ivers has agreed to accompany me. We'll keep you informed."

Verlaine closed the door behind him, firmly but quietly. Garol latched the door and settled in to work.

The sooner he got out of there the happier he'd be.

He had real problems waiting for him at Port Charid.

Walton Agenis sat bolt upright in her bed, her fingers tingling with adrenaline.

Something was wrong.

Stilling her breath with the self-discipline that had yet to desert her even in times of enforced placidity, she listened to the small sounds that the settlement house made in the night. The settlement housing had been built quickly and not over-carefully, and talked to itself as the outside temperature rose and fell and the wind shifted; she had learned to sleep through the creaks and moans and cracks and chirps of the structure that sheltered her family.

Why was she awake?

It was dead black outside; no light shone into the room through the chinks in the shutters. The local utility plant was obviously off-line for the night, and the predawn deliveries had apparently not started rounds; by that token, it was two to four hours before the little yellow sun of Rikavie rose to warm and wake the settlement.

The pounding of her own heart in her ears faded quickly as the energy surge that had jolted her awake subsided.

Walton began to hear things.

There was something clattering at the outside of the house, not loudly, but with too much deliberation for it to be the normal cooling of the plain metal-weave shutters, and it came with a scratching sound so faint she almost doubted she heard it at all.

Turning the bedclothes back, layer upon layer upon themselves, Walton stood up. The floor was cold beneath her bare and bony feet, rug or no rug.

But she knew she heard something.

There were sounds of movement from inside the house as well, the small noise muffled behind the closed door of one of the bedrooms. Walton slept with her door open. She could not bear not to hear what was happening in her own house.

She was beginning to think she might know what was going on. She picked up the truncheon she kept on the floor beside her bed for self-defense; she didn't like weapons that could be deployed at distance, not for protection of her own hearth. Accidents happened. Anyone close enough to hit with a truncheon was too close to be mistaken for an enemy rather than simply some imprudent young person who had made a mistake.

The shrill squeak of a shutter being raised on its track sounded clearly in the dark stillness; Walton grinned to herself.

Modice's room.

And there was conversation. The hissing sounds of whispered sibilants was clear enough; there was the pattern of language, but the sounds themselves could not be parsed into meaning.

Silent on bare feet, Walton crept down the hall to where her older sister's only daughter had her narrow bed. She heard no alarm in the drift of whispered words, no threat—no particular passion of any kind.

This sort of thing had happened more than once before. Was it Modice's fault? She was an utterly unspoiled beauty, and so sweet-spirited that she seemed to arouse as much fraternal as any other passion in the hearts of her admirers.

Here.

If Walton paused and listened very carefully, she could almost locate the source of the whispering as at the window; so maybe Modice hadn't let him in, whoever he was. Yet. This time.

The door was not quite latched. None of the doors hung true on their cheap hinges. Walton eased down on the lever carefully and pushed, wondering whether those very hinges would betray her before she could make a really dramatic entrance.

Who was at the window?

Walton could hear Modice, though she still couldn't quite make out the words. Modice's tone of voice was all surprise and perplexed joy; there was no alarm nor any uncertainty there. Whoever it was inspired no fear of any sort in Modice's nineteen-year-old heart. But Modice was fearless.

"—for a cargo. Of course I agreed. I haven't seen you in more than two years."

Walton frowned.

On the resource side of the status sheet, to judge by the sound of the voice the man who was explaining—excusing—his presence so blithely to Modice was at the window, yes, but on the other side of it yet. He was not in the room with her sister's daughter. Modice was in no danger of finding herself overcome by instinct, let alone violence, or at least not yet.

On the draw-down side was the fact that Walton thought she recognized that voice.

Modice said something, and stifled a giggle. Walton listened carefully to the man's reply, her suspicions mounting moment by moment.

"Forget you, never, Modice. There isn't anyone like you under Jurisdiction, and I've never been to Gonebeyond space. I'd have come to see you sooner if I'd had a decent chance."

That Sarvaw mercantile pilot.

What had his name been?

Kazmer. Kazmer Daigule.

The friend of her older brother's oldest son, Hilton, a big lumbering barge of a man with sufficient calm quiet charisma to have almost seriously disturbed Modice's psychological equilibrium, not too many years ago.

Modice was clearly not very disturbed right now; her voice had strengthened from a whisper to a murmur, and Walton could hear what she was saying even though Modice clearly had her back to the room, talking out the window.

"If you had the interest, you'd have come sooner. But it's nice to see you. And Hilton will be sorry he missed you. Hilton likes you, Kaz."

There was no venom to her scolding, but no childish uncertainty, either. Walton listened to her with pride and wonder: if only Modice's mother was alive, to hear how her daughter had grown. Modice seemed clearly confident of her ability to hold her own with a man several years her elder. She had learned well, during the years that the Langsariks had lived as a fleetborne community. She took after Walton herself a bit, maybe; or maybe it was just the result of having been beautiful all her life, Walton admitted to herself, reluctantly. Modice couldn't have learned that from her Aunt Walton.

"Oh, there are those in your family who don't like me at all, Modice." Daigule seemed to be teasing, but his tone of voice was ambiguous—was that genuine regret that she heard? "Your aunt doesn't care for me a bit. She told me so. Well, she told Hilton."

She would have to see his expression and his body language to decide for sure. For that she would have to be able to see into the room, to spy as well as eavesdrop.

"Aunt Walton is just a little overprotective. That's all."

Walton didn't know if she wanted to hear this. Raising Modice hadn't been her idea; she had neither expected nor been prepared to take responsibility for the child that Modice had been when her parents had been killed. She knew she hadn't done as good a job as a real mother could have, would have done. But if she withdrew—to avoid hearing scornful words from Modice—she would be leaving the situation unresolved; and she would not be able to close the door quietly enough to avoid alerting Modice to the fact that someone had been listening.

"She's no such thing." Given her suspicions about Daigule's designs on Modice, it certainly felt odd to hear him, of all people, come to her defense. "She just means to see you properly married to someone who shares your own culture. Sometimes I think she forgets that you and I have already been to bed together."

Walton tightened her grip on her truncheon. Been to bed together, was it? She'd give him "been to bed together" all over his foolish skull. *Been to bed together.* How dare he?

"Kazmer, no joking. That was serious. You know very well it was the only way to hide you. Shame on you."

That Sarvaw had been fully clothed at the time. At least from the waist down, a certain degree of bareness being necessary to carry the deception off. The soldiers had been too busy trying not to stare at the blinding perfection of Modice's flawless shoulders to think too deeply on the potential correspondences between the person of interest they were hunting for and the apparently naked young man in her niece's bed.

Or if they had made up their own minds about what was going on, their insufferable tyrant of a junior officer had arrived at no such conclusion, and nobody had bothered to disabuse him of a notion that he had clearly felt to be near sacred on account of having been his.

"Come on, Derchie, I'm only joking, it's just you and me. I didn't mean any harm by it, who else can I talk to? And I'm here to tell you that any man who got to share a bed with you, and didn't want to talk it up, would have to be crazy."

"No jokes!" Modice sounded exasperated; she had raised her voice, but quickly dropped it again. "We're in settlement now. We have to maintain appearances. If my aunt so much as caught you here, she'd call my cousins to beat you. And if you can't at least respect my feelings, I'll call for her, I'm warning you."

That was a good idea, too, Walton thought. The one about calling Modice's cousins to run Daigule off. How had he gotten past the perimeter watch? She'd have something to say to the night-security tomorrow morning at debriefing.

Still, Daigule hadn't done anything to deserve a beating—yet. And cousins could get overenthusiastic where they thought the honor of a girl-cousin was involved.

"I'm sorry, Derchie. I didn't come to quarrel." It seemed that Daigule finally realized that he'd overstepped the boundaries of Modice's maidenly modesty. It had been three years. Modice had been much younger, so much so that Walton doubted Daigule had fully realized the potential damage his lighthearted flirting might inflict. Modice had always looked older than she actually was; her beauty surrounded her with an aura of knowledge and power that was easy to mistake for that of an adult woman.

"It's all right, Kazmer, we're friends. But it hurts my feelings when you make fun of me. Nobody knows about that but family." No, they'd kept the secret of Kazmer's escape, to avoid compromise. And to spare

Modice the teasing. "Still. You should go now. Come in the daytime if you want to visit me. Bring a present for my aunt."

Walton held her breath.

Was Modice giving Daigule permission to court her?

Or was she just pointing out the awkwardness of coming to a young woman's window in the middle of the night?

"I did bring a present for you," Daigule said. "Don't worry, it's nothing that might embarrass you. Unless you have some bizarre objection to really tasteless patterns."

Modice almost succeeded in stifling an apparently involuntary shriek of thrilled horror, so that it came out a squeak. "Kazmer. It's awful. What is it?"

Walton listened eagerly for the answer.

"For your hair, Modice. Head scarf. Or a handkerchief. Rolled for a fabric belt, I don't know. Can be used to dust small and not easily breakable objects. Put this on first thing in the morning and nothing worse will happen to you for the rest of the day."

Well, it clearly wasn't an intimate garment, or something that would have been otherwise improper between friends. Walton relaxed a bit.

"Go away, Kazmer," Modice said, her voice soft with what sounded like affection. "And don't come back unless it's to the front door. In the daytime."

Where Walton could be waiting—with reinforcements, if necessary. Now that she knew that there was the possibility that Daigule would visit.

"By your command, beautiful Modice. Give my regards to your family. My respects to your aunt. No. Wait. Better hold off on that for a day or two. Give me time to get out of system. Good night."

Walton had to smile.

It was a shame Daigule was so unsuitable for a Langsarik household. He already knew them so well.

But he wasn't suitable for a Langsarik household—because he wasn't a Langsarik.

Walton heard the shutters click against one another as Modice closed her window. She pulled the bedroom door back shut, carefully matching her movements to the sounds Modice was making in order to mask anything that might draw attention to herself.

Modice had carried the mission on her own, and hadn't needed backup after all.

How long would it be before Modice told her about Daigule's visit? Would Modice tell her?

The only way to find that out was to wait and see; and that could be done just as well or better from the comfort of one's own bed as standing barefoot in a dark hall.

Her feet were cold.

Modice might decide to visit the bathroom before she went back to sleep. The hall had to be empty in case that happened.

Satisfied with Modice's handling of her midnight suitor, Walton Agenis went back to bed.

CHAPTER THREE

Kazmer Daigule stood close behind the Langsarik raid leader in the dock-master's office at the Tyrell Yards, keeping his head down and his eyes lowered. Between the visored cap pulled low over his brow and the artificial beard that covered most of the rest of his face there was little chance of anybody being able to recognize him later; but he was taking no chances.

"Sorry to make you wait," the Tyrell Yards' dock-master said to the raid leader, keying her transmit. "We just can't be too careful these days. Have you heard about what happened at Okidan?"

If Kazmer tilted his head just a bit and squinted hard he could see the message the dock-master sent scrolling across the capture unit. *Request confirmation, freighter on scheduled load-out from Port Charid to receiving office in Tweniva. Tyrell Yards. Please authenticate as follows.*

This was the tricky part.

There was a small courier shuttle in the vehicle transport bay of the freighter Kazmer had piloted from Port Charid to the Tyrell Yards, here in the Shawl of Rikavie. On board that shuttle was an illegal communications intercept board, and the woman working that board had to intercept the dock-master's signal and match it with precision and delicacy in order to ensure that it was fully damped—effectively canceled out—before it could reach Charid.

Then it was just a question of waiting for the right interval to pass before transmitting a false response with the right security characteristics to pass scrutiny.

"Okidan, yes." The raid leader had given his name as Noman, a transparent but perfectly acceptable label under the circumstances. "And everybody has their own theory of how it was managed, too. Which they'll tell you all about, if you don't get away in time."

Noman wasn't anyone that Kazmer recognized; not that he'd really expected to—Noman had taken prudent steps of his own to disguise his identity. A beard, a little transparent gum at the corners of his eyes to change their size and shape, all the tricks—and so well done that Kazmer had to really look closely to realize the deception.

Noman's voice was casual, even light; Kazmer envied his composure. Kazmer did his best to stay calm as the moments passed; finally, the dock-master's board chirped its receipt announcement. Kazmer already knew what this one was supposed to read, but he couldn't help being nervous about it.

We authenticate, Tyrell. Freighter Sansifer *en route to Tweniva with authorization to carry manifest as follows. You may proceed with assurance.*

Kazmer rubbed the back of his neck irritably as if scratching a sudden itch, just to cover the relief he felt.

The dock-master closed the transmission with a casual gesture; clearly, she hadn't been genuinely concerned—just prudent, in unsettled times. Nor was there any particular reason for her to be suspicious; there hadn't been a raid in weeks, and unannounced traffic was apparently not unusual.

"Right," the dock-master said. Turning around, she started toward the door to her office that would lead back out onto the load-in docks, beckoning for Noman and Kazmer to come with her. "Let's load cargo."

Time to get started, then.

Noman nodded to Kazmer, who acknowledged the unspoken command with a crisp nod of his own before breaking into a quick jog-trot, heading out toward the freighter, where it waited with its load-in ramp unshipped and ready. They had cargo to unload and cargo to load, and then just before they left they'd off-load the courier so that the raiding party could make a separate escape.

That way the freighter's cargo stayed clean, with no stray weapons or unexplained extra crew to cause suspicions in anyone's mind when they came to pass inspection by the Port Authority at Anglace. Kazmer was just as happy to be rid of the courier. The presence of the illegal communications equipment would be a dead giveaway to any inspector, and there was no sense in risk for risk's sake.

By the time the freighter's crew had the cargo crates ready to move, the dock-master had called up some station resources to help; the work went quickly. There were seven large cargo crates tagged for off-load at Tyrell, and once they were on the dock the engineer took charge of getting them lined up—at right angles to the back of the freighter—as Kazmer went to let Noman know that they were ready to start the load-in.

The freighter's crew all wore caps and gloves, but dockworkers frequently wore protective gear when load-in and unload-in cargo; it was nothing to remark upon. Meaning in turn very little danger of being recognized: final reassurance that there was to be no killing on this raid. The raid leader would hardly have gone to all the trouble he had to ensure their anonymity if he'd been planning on simply murdering any potential witnesses, after all.

The dock-master was reviewing the manifest with Noman. "This is an odd lot," she said; and there was a little hint of discomfort in her voice. Was she beginning to suspect something? "Here, Pettiche, take a look. This could take a while, there doesn't seem to be much coherence to the pull list."

If he looked behind him, Kazmer could see the engineer and the fence standing with the off-loaded crates, waiting for the next phase. Freighter to the left of them, the long wall of the dock-master's office to their right, they had a good view of the entire docking bay.

One of the people who had been helping them off-load joined Noman and the dock-master at the foot of the freighter's load-in ramp; Kazmer thought for a moment that he recognized the man.

"Er, well." Noman's voice was vibrant with slightly embarrassed apology. "The fact is, we're already late. My fault, not my crew's fault, so I owe them considerably. But we'll all lose our promptness bonus if we don't deliver in good time. Is there any way to hurry this along?"

The third person looked the manifest over, then handed it back to the dock-master. "We don't have to take all of that long." No, Kazmer realized, hearing the man speak. He didn't actually recognize the third person. He only recognized who the third person was, in a general sense. "If we called all available hands. They'll complain about losing their sleep-shifts, some of them, but I imagine the cargo-master here—" nodding at Noman— "could find some way to make it up to them, am I right?"

Kazmer was Sarvaw. He knew Dolgorukij when he saw one. The accent was as good as a star chart, and the face more so, familiar in the indefinable way that people of one's own blood were familiar. Veesliya Dolgorukij, or Kazmer missed his guess, and he didn't think he did. Sarvaw knew from Dolgorukij. A beaten dog never forgot the face of its tormentor.

"Oh, you can be sure of that," Noman replied with grateful enthusiasm. "If we can get our load-out done in time to meet the schedule, you won't be sorry. I know I've got something on board worth missing a sleep-shift for, I guarantee it'll be a memorable occasion."

The dock-master shrugged and smiled. An older woman, she had a professional smile, one of the kind that involved lips and teeth but no real feeling. It didn't seem to be anything personal, though; it seemed clearly to be her habit to be a little reticent. Because she sounded positive about the whole idea. "Well, all right. See it done, Pettiche. The sooner we get cargo off, the sooner we can all relax and enjoy a little well-earned treat."

Up into the freighter for the special crate, then. Kazmer and the navigator moved it down the ramp to the front of the load-in ramp, just to one side of Noman and the dock-master. By the time they got it into position cargo pallets were starting to arrive on the docks, and people with them.

Raising his head to get a good view, Kazmer scanned the busy scene quickly before adjusting his visor. There were a lot of people here, fifteen, twenty perhaps. A lot of cargo. Tyrell Yards was holding luxury fabrics and botanicals, and the freighter would carry a full load to Anglace.

With the station crew on hand to help, the load-in went as smoothly as anyone could wish. Kazmer watched the freighter's cargo bays fill with a mixture of satisfaction and anxiety. On the one hand a load-in was just a load-in, like any other; and load-in was unexciting drudgery by its very nature.

On the other hand, he'd never been so intimately involved in a raid before. He'd moved illegal cargo, and he'd participated in the illegal disposition of somebody else's goods, but this was the first time he'd ever participated in an actual raid. And yet what was there to worry about? These were Langsariks. They knew what they were doing.

When the load-in was finished Kazmer joined the freighter's crew gathered around the special crate at the side of the freighter while Noman and the dock-master reviewed the cargo manifest, checking for completeness.

The seven cargo crates they'd off-loaded first were big standard pre-pack units, each just less wide than a standard freighter corridor was wide, just less tall than a standard freighter's cargo bay overhead clearance.

The special crate was much smaller, table-top square, the sort of thing that usually held luxury goods. Specialty meats. Bulk confections and delicacies. Small containers of liquor or recreational drugs. The station crew had started to collect in the now-empty space between the freighter and the dock-master's office, clearly waiting for the promised reward that the special crate represented; endorsing the manifest with a satisfied chop of his personal hand-seal, Noman handed the documents board back to the dock-master, assessing the assembly with a measuring eye.

"This must be everybody on base," Noman said to the dock-master, but a little too loudly for just the casual remark that it seemed to be. "Can there be anyone at all who isn't here?"

Looking up from the completed manifest, the dock-master went from face to face, counting bodies against the backdrop of the seven cargo crates Kazmer had helped to unload earlier. One of the men Kazmer saw there was wearing the Langsarik colors, the uniform denuded of any identification markers but unmistakably Langsarik by its cut and shade. One of the people supposedly called in from sleep-shift, obviously, or he'd be wearing a station work suit instead of his personal clothing.

"That's everybody, all right," the Dolgorukij at the dock-master's side—Pettiche—answered.

Noman nodded.

"Very well, then. Ladies and gentlemen, I'm announcing a small change in plan."

It was the signal.

The fronts of the seven cargo crates exploded with sudden shocking violence, scattering chips of structural board across the load-in bay floor.

Startled and stunned like the rest of her crew, the dock-master took an involuntary step forward, trying to see what was going on. Raiders. The crates were full of raiders, two Langsariks to a crate, moving out quickly to form a tight-curved line with weapons trained on the station crew gathered in the load-in bay.

The engineer broke into the special crate and handed out the weapons that were there. Some of the station crew were starting to step back, looking to the belly of the freighter to take cover; but Kazmer and the other freighter crew had that escape route in their line of fire, now.

No escape.

The fence nudged the dock-master in the ribs with the muzzle of an assault weapon; and slowly—with visible reluctance, her face showing her confused shock and helpless rage—the dock-master raised her open hands away from her body, with her palms flat in a gesture of surrender.

"Let's everyone just sit down where you are," Noman suggested. "We don't want anybody getting hurt."

If anybody made a break for cover beneath the freighter, they could lose control of the situation. There would be shooting. Kazmer waited, holding his breath.

Nobody moved.

Then—slowly, and with evident reluctance—Pettiche the Dolgorukij bent his knees awkwardly and sank down slowly to sit cross-legged on the floor.

"Everybody sit down," Noman repeated. "Dock-master. We'd appreciate your cooperation. With a little luck and some common sense, nobody needs to be the worse for this. Except maybe the owners, and they're insured anyway, aren't they?"

Kazmer still didn't dare relax.

But the situation did seem unquestionably weighted in the Langsariks' favor; and nobody wanted trouble, after all.

The dock-master spoke, finally. "You heard the man." Her disgust was clear, but so was her evident realization that they were at the mercy of the raiders. "I'm making this an official direction, one you promised to obey when you endorsed your contract documentation. Everybody sits down. Slowly. No sudden moves. Two by two. We'll start with Gerig and Elsing, sit down on the floor and keep your hands where they can see them. Let's go, people. Move."

Kazmer could breathe again.

No bloodshed.

Once everyone was sitting down and under guard in the middle of the room, Noman spoke.

"Right, unship the courier and get out of here. Dock-master. New manifest. This will be easy to load. Everything's right through there, on the other side of the security door in your office. All we need are your security codes, and we can be out of your way in no time."

One of the Langsarik crate-raiders came around the outside of the perimeter to relieve Kazmer and his crew. Kazmer surrendered his weapon gratefully. As soon as the courier ship was unloaded they could leave.

Things were going as smoothly as any Langsarik raid should; but Kazmer didn't like what Noman had just said about the dock-master's secures.

And still, nothing bad had happened, at least not yet.

Why should anything bad happen at all?

It wasn't the most welcome experience for the staff here at the Tyrell Yards, perhaps, but it was just cargo. Not even their cargo. Someone else's cargo. And the Langsariks had been careful to leave them no choice in the matter, no choice at all.

With the courier on the floor and the freighter secured, Kazmer joined the navigator in the wheelhouse, and settled himself into the seat beside her. He was still tense; he couldn't shake a feeling of residual apprehension, and it apparently showed. The navigator took one look at him and grinned with what seemed to be sympathy, giving his shoulder a friendly shake.

"Almost ready to load-out," she said, reassuringly. "I just saw the boss Langsarik heading for Central Dispatch. He had another Langsarik with him. One from the Tyrell crew. There was an inside man."

Of course. There had to be.

Noman's talk about secures would be just talk, after all. They'd placed a man on-site; they already had the secures.

Kazmer was astonished at the depth of his relief.

The engineer came forward to give Kazmer the word, his face flushed with effort and his expression full of a grim sort of satisfaction.

"We're off," the engineer said. "Let's get out of here."

Kazmer toggled his comm. "Docking bay clear?" he asked the dock-master, or whoever was in Central Dispatch; but he wasn't too surprised when the voice that answered him had a distinctly Langsarik lilt to it.

"Docking bay clear and sealed for depressurization, all personnel safe and secure. Launch dome opening sequence."

The Langsarik crew he had brought with him in the decoy cargo stacks would secure the crews, destroy the station's communications to prevent a premature alarm, and ensure that nothing incriminating was left behind.

"Freighter initiating primary launch sequence. Issue warning order."

There were no Fleet patrols between him and the Sillume entry vector. Once they had reached the vector they would be safe, because there was no technology that could track a ship across a vector. The authorities would assume that they'd made for the sanctuary of Gonebeyond space.

The ship was fully pressurized; the docking-bay launch dome lay open. Kazmer fired his positioning jets, carefully maneuvering the freighter into the precise angle he wanted for the best—fastest—cleanest departure from Tyrell. They couldn't actually fire the main thrust until they were far enough from Tyrell to avoid perturbing its orbit, or risk someone at Port Charid noticing and sending up an alarm. That would be a dead giveaway. Whether or not there were any Fleet patrols in the neighborhood, it was idiocy to borrow trouble.

The freighter eased clear of the docking station and began to gain space between it and the Tyrell Yards.

Kazmer watched his power profiles as the freighter slowly picked up speed.

He'd learned that Langsarik raiding was something he simply wasn't comfortable doing. Not even with Langsariks. Not even with the best—most decent—people he knew, and Hilton Shires was way up toward the top of that list. It had been too tense. It could have gone wrong too easily.

He brought the fuel lines up to maximum feed carefully, gradually, slowly; and the freighter began to really move.

He was never going to get so close to a potential disaster ever again so long as he lived, if he had anything to say about it.

Raid leader Dalmoss Chzagul stood in the doorway of the dock-master's office within the sealed confines of Central Dispatch, rubbing the clear-gum from his face absentmindedly as he watched the freighter lifting away from the Tyrell Yards on monitor.

It was three days over the Sillume vector to the nearest Fleet detachment, so the freighter was in no danger from Fleet.

Port Charid had some police resources available, three swift cruisers with just enough firepower to stop the freighter short of the exit vector; but so long as no alarm reached Port Charid from Tyrell, the freighter was in no danger from Charid's own limited police either. No alarm would reach Port Charid until Dalmoss was finished here. He had complete confidence in the effectiveness of his communications intercepts, and for good reason—they had insider information, after all.

So the freighter was free and clear. They had plenty of time to finish up and make their escape.

"All quiet?" Dalmoss asked Pettiche, who sat outside the dock-master's office, monitoring the master communications board. Pettiche nodded.

"The freighter lifted away during a black slice on the sweeps, 'Noman.' Just as you planned. The most we have to watch for is a routine query if anyone at Port notices."

"Well done, Brother Charil." The alien name came strangely to his mouth, but they all used Langsarik names during a raid. Attention to detail was an important part of their success, even as it had been for the Langsariks themselves. "Thank you."

Now that the freighter was gone it was time to move to the next stage in the exercise, and Dalmoss stepped back into the relative privacy of the dock-master's office, calling to one of the men nearby. "Efons, take over on the panels, I need Charil's help. Brother Charil?"

The dock-master's office in Central Dispatch was glassed in along the side that fronted on the main room, so that the dock-master could keep an eye on her employees. Which was humorous, in a sense, because Dalmoss was using the dock-master's vantage point to keep an eye on the dock-master herself. She was sitting on the floor against the far wall of Central Dispatch with the rest of the station's crew, with her hands bound behind her back to encourage docility.

Pettiche stopped a respectful half a pace behind his superior, and bent his head in token of salute. A gesture small enough to avoid drawing attention to itself—Langsariks didn't salute—but Dalmoss knew that the respectful submission was genuine and heartfelt.

"Yes, Noman."

Dalmoss nodded in the direction of the station's crew, in turn. "This is everybody, Brother Charil? We need to be sure." That was Pettiche's job: to be sure. Pettiche had been placed here at Tyrell for months, just waiting for the time to come when he would be needed.

"I've cross-verified with Sumner, Noman. Everyone is here. No soul has been overlooked."

Good. "We'd best get on with it, then, Charil. Start with the dock-master. We had to get her security codes, after all."

It was therefore necessary that her corpse present clear evidence of the extraction process through which the station's security codes had been presumably obtained from her assumedly reluctant lips. Pettiche bent his head once more, a swift gesture of acknowledgment; but he didn't turn immediately to leave. What? Something was wrong? "Talk to me, Charil."

"Out of respect for hospitality, Noman. I have taken bread from her hands. I ask to be excused the letting of her blood."

Well, of course. Hospitality was Holy ordinance; it could not be set aside. The moment Pettiche said it Dalmoss realized the propriety of the objection, and was ashamed of himself for not taking it into account. "Truly I deserve rebuke, Charil. Tell Sumner, then. You take Parken and secure him on board the courier, yes?"

It was necessary for Tyrell's one Langsarik employee, Parken, to leave the station alive. There would be more than enough physical evidence to indict the Langsariks for this raid; but a bloodstain of the wrong type, if they were unfortunate enough to have it come to someone's attention, could conceivably raise questions in someone's mind. So the Langsarik would walk out. They'd dump his body somewhere it could be used to further incriminate the Langsariks. Later.

Pettiche's body wouldn't be found here either.

But they'd find a way to cover for that and negative evidence was always so much less obvious and persuasive than the positive evidence that they meant to provide.

Once Charil had left Central Dispatch, Silves—whom they called Efons when they were raiding—spoke from his station on monitor. "Noman. In the name."

Silves did not complete the formula, maintaining discipline as Pettiche had. Dalmoss watched Pettiche walk across the warehouse floor to give Sumner his orders.

"I'm listening."

The formula was the one they used when someone wanted to gain a deeper understanding of a senior's orders, and as such it was Dalmoss's duty to submit to questioning.

"It soils the soul, Noman. Is this really necessary?"

Silves's voice certainly held only respectful desire for understanding. There was no challenge there; and it was a reasonable question.

"The dock-master at least must suffer before she dies, Efons." They could expect an autopsy, to support Charges; the Bench made a clear distinction between the unlawful physical abuse of a living being and the much lesser crime of incidental mutilation of a corpse. "We can expect the most attention to be focused on her. The others—well. We'll see how the timing goes."

They might not have to torture more than three or four of the others to convince the Bench that an atrocity exceeding mere murder had taken place. But it was truly necessary to convince the Bench that murder had been wantonly committed in full knowledge of the crime as it was being done. The Angel would settle for nothing less than the destruction of the Langsariks as a people, for the insult they had given the Holy Mother in preying on Dolgorukij shipping and to take the blame for a systematic destruction of the physical assets of other trading interests at Port Charid.

Sumner came into Central Dispatch with the dock-master and two of Dalmoss's other men; Dalmoss pointed them through to the safe room, the place inside Central Dispatch where the small-heavies had been. Sumner closed the door. Sound would not carry far from inside the room.

He could start to compose his after action report—in his head, of course, it was never to be written or recorded.

They were very near their goal.

After just a few more Langsarik raids there would be no mercantile interests left in Port Charid with the resources to contest with the Dolgorukij Combine for primacy.

The Dolgorukij Combine could afford to rebuild infrastructure. The Dolgorukij Combine could afford to purchase and rebuild the damaged warehouses of its fellow mercantile interests, leasing them back at a reasonable premium to cover its expenses.

And the Holy Mother would grant Her blessings to Her faithful servitors forever, after they made Her Queen in Port Charid.

Chilleau Judiciary sat at the node of one of the most powerful vectors under Jurisdiction. The Chilleau vector gave access and egress to dozens of systems, but Port Charid wasn't one of them.

The easiest way from Chilleau Judiciary to Port Charid was through Renicks via Omot, but Garol was in a hurry, and the easy way took a good two days Standard more than the transit in through Garsite. Garsite was small and relatively out of the way, as vector nodes went, so there was a risk—if something went wrong in flight, the wait at Garsite for replacement parts could be tedious.

So nothing would go wrong in flight, and that was all there was to it.

The Chilleau vector was one that Garol traveled all the time. But if he'd ever jumped Garsite, it had been so long that he'd forgotten; and that meant taking advantage of Jils's presence to cross-check his setup stats, just for extra assurance. Once he was clear of the exit vector from Chilleau to Garsite and on arc toward the Garsite entry vector, Garol called back from the wheelhouse of the courier ship to the aft compartment for her.

"Hey, Jils." She was in the rear compartment of the courier, reviewing, he assumed, the intelligence reports they'd brought with them from Port Charid. She probably wouldn't mind a break. "Would you come give me your once-over on this?"

The angle of approach, rate of acceleration, and path of the courier had to be calculated to create a transit funnel that would drop them out of the figurative flume of the vector at the desired destination.

People made mistakes in vector calculations.

Some of those mistakes led to the discovery of new termini on a previously identified vector; but most of the time ships and crews simply vanished, leaving no sign of what might ultimately have happened to them.

Garol wasn't interested in finding out.

Garol wanted to go to Port Charid, not off into the unknown on an adventure.

Jils came forward slowly, rubbing her forehead. "Sure, Garol, let's have a look."

He hadn't been surprised when she'd expressed an interest in going to Rikavie with him; the Langsarik settlement was too important to the Second Judge's prestige and public opinion to take any chances. He didn't mind having her present, either, for moral support if for nothing else.

He angled the navigation calculation screen carefully toward her to minimize any glare, but Jils wasn't looking at his calculations, she was staring at the forward observation screens instead. Some things Garol didn't mind obtaining by virtue of rank. This courier had full-sweep screens. It was a new model out of the Arakcheyek shipyards—Dolgorukij Combine, absolutely state-of-the-art, and priced accordingly. All in support of the rule of Law.

"Hey," Jils said. "Space is pretty, out here."

Garsite space was pretty. She was right. The light bent softly around the flat almond-shaped boundaries of the vector, creating a subtle sort of back lighting. The vector had a halo.

"Yeah, and I'd like to be reasonably sure of seeing it again someday. So would you check the vector calculations please."

Jils shook herself slightly. "Oh. Right. Sorry, Garol. I'll do a scan on them. You go stow for vector transit, why don't you."

Undivided attention on vector calculations was a good thing. Garol was all in favor of enabling it on Jils's part, so he went off to lock things down. It wasn't that a ship risked losing its gravity during a vector transit, or at least not usually; but it was easier to recover from an accidental lapse in gravity if a person had taken measures to minimize the potential mess beforehand.

Jils had documents strewn from one end of the aft cabin to the other. Incident reports on raids at Sonder, Penyff, Tershid, Okidan, Tyrell. Forensic manifests, where available. Cause of death. Body counts.

Garol didn't like the picture that was forming. It didn't fit the Langsarik pattern; and how could the Langsariks have managed?

He'd have to get Jils's thoughts about it. Once they had the vector, maybe.

After the aft cabin was as thoroughly stowed as it could get, Garol went back forward. Jils was finishing a countercheck reconciliation, but everything looked pretty stable. He didn't see where she'd had to correct anything he'd done.

He waited until she'd completed the countercheck before speaking to her. "How's it look?"

Scanning the calculation set from start to finish one last time, Jils nodded. "You're solid, Garol, you can calculate vector transits for me anytime. Good to go. Let's do it."

And Jils was good. Methodical, precise, and much better at details of a certain sort than he was. If Jils said the calculation set was solid, it was solid.

"Strap yourself in, then, and let's go."

No time like the present.

He had set the ship's environmentals to low normal, so there were no artificially generated somatic signals that would indicate a change in their rate of speed; but the forward visual screens were in working order. Excellent working order. Really rather amazingly good working order, and worth almost the entire price the Bench had paid to get them from Combine shipyards.

Garol hit the sequence initiate instruction, and space on the forward visual screens started to spin, the status markers on the ship's vital signs creeping upward as the ship gained speed.

The courier ran for the vector like a child's playing sphere fired along the lip of a great funnel, gathering momentum as it got closer and closer to the funnel's mouth. Garol closed his eyes: looking at the forward screens was dizzying. He thought Jils looked a little green, as well, but he was in no shape to mention it.

With the ship's gravities set as low as they were, he could begin to feel the approach as pressure in his ears, like the sensation of spinning around in a chair until his head swam. He opened his eyes, swallowing back the sharp acid taste of bile that rose from his stomach as the nausea born of perturbations in the vestibular apparatus in his ears threatened to overwhelm him.

It was a clear, short approach to the vector transit for Rikavie. It was. Clean, sweet, easy, and nearly overdue, and Garol was anxious in spite of his faith in Jils's evaluation.

Any time now, Garol told the courier ship in his mind, trying not to focus on the unnatural whirling of light objects on the screens in front of him. *You can make the vector any time you'd like. In fact the sooner the better, for my money at least.*

The mad rotation of stars on-screen tightened and condensed to one bright spot of light that vibrated ever more quickly as the intensity of the light increased. They were close now. The glowing center of the visual display tightened and brightened and tightened moment by moment, gaining in intensity of brilliance as it shrank in size until it was almost too bright to bear; and then the screens blanked.

There would be nothing more to see until they reached Rikavie, and dropped out of the vector like a stone.

"We have the Garsite vector." Garol made the announcement with relief he didn't mind sharing with Jils. Vector transit was certain and secure enough to move ships by the hundreds of thousands from one end of Jurisdiction space to the other; and yet it was never completely, absolutely, entirely, eight-and-eighty-and-another-eight certain. "Next stop Rikavie. Port Charid. Warehouse asteroids; Langsariks."

"Spectacularly beautiful and very young women," Jils added, unfastening the secures of her harness. "Or at least one spectacularly beautiful and very young woman. Girl. How old would she be by now? Probably married, Garol, she *was* a looker."

What was she talking about?

Oh.

Modice Agenis.

Walton Agenis's niece.

All right, so he had noticed Modice—how could anyone have failed to? But it had been so long that Garol could laugh, without resentment. Without much resentment. "Old enough to know her own mind, Jils, now as then. You're on the wrong process branch about that. The girl was just a really sweet girl." A really sweet and astonishingly beautiful young girl, but there'd been no mistaking her for a serious prospect of any kind.

Not really.

It had been enough of a pleasure just to sit in her company and listen to her voice, and feel fellowship with all the other men who had noticed that she filled the world with her presence and validated their entire lives by just breathing.

"That's why you want me to go make the contacts with the Port Authority while you go straight out to the settlement. Right." But she was just teasing him. He knew it. Wasn't she?

"It's the Flag Captain I really want to see. Agenis the Deep-Minded. Before everybody in Port Charid knows we're there. She deserves to know right up front about the problem. And I want the straight story, direct from her."

He had made the treaty with the Langsariks, and Walton Agenis was their leader, then as now. They had come to terms of mutual understanding, founded on a necessarily qualified degree of trust. She had advised her people to accept the strict terms of the amnesty that the Bench offered through Garol in part on the basis of her evaluation of his personal integrity.

It had made him uncomfortable at the time, even while the personal if unspoken understanding between them had been what made the amnesty possible. If there was a problem, she would tell him. And if something had really gone wrong, he had to let her know that amnesty violation could mean an end to the amnesty, and slavery—death, and dispersal—for the Langsariks.

"Yeah, yeah." Jils's singsong rejection of his claims of disinterestedness was not entirely serious, if admittedly sharp. Not because she didn't believe him, but because if she admitted to understanding his motives, she'd have nothing to tease him about. "I'll take the first watch, Garol. You go catch up on your fantasy life."

He was a Bench intelligence specialist.

He didn't even have a fantasy life.

But if he had—

If he had a fantasy, it was that the Langsarik amnesty would work. That the Langsariks would prove their merit to the Bench in Port Charid and survive the test of years to be fully integrated as respected citizens of a benevolent Bench. That Modice Agenis would marry and be happy and secure . . . and that Walton Agenis would never have cause to decide that she'd been wrong when she'd trusted him with the future of the people who looked to her for leadership.

That was his fantasy. He could never admit it, though.

If he admitted that it was a fantasy, even to himself, he would have to acknowledge the fact that he was deeply worried about them all— the brave, proud, honorable people that he, himself, Garol Vogel, had essentially forced into settlement at Port Charid.

Kazmer Daigule stood in front of the receiving officer's desk at Anglace Port Authority, doing everything in his power to keep calm as she examined his forged cargo documentation. The contraband from the Tyrell Yards was fully accounted for, of course; the cargo manifest was one of the most beautiful works of art Kazmer could remember having seen.

It would have been much easier for him to feel confident about the validity of the counter-endorsements on his documentation if there hadn't been four fully armed representatives from Fleet's shore patrol with him in the office, along with the receiving officer; but there was no reason to fear that this unusually aggressive presence was in any way related to the potential weaknesses in his documentation.

No reason.

He had to stay calm.

"Grain, medicinal botanicals, and luxury fabrics from Shilling," the receiving officer read aloud. "Interesting mix, pilot."

Kazmer bowed. "Yes, ma'am. We had to piece a cargo together from odd lots to get a full load." Otherwise, grain and luxury textiles wouldn't normally be traveling together—the margins were all off. Without the grain they'd carried with them from Port Charid, however, it would have been too easy for a suspicious mind to match their cargo to a list of goods misappropriated in a raid on a warehouse at Rikavie.

There was obvious risk of arousing suspicion even with the camouflage the grain provided the cargo, but that was what they were being paid for—to run the risk of getting caught with stolen merchandise.

It went without saying that there was nothing in the documentation to indicate that the freighter had been anywhere near Rikavie recently.

"H'mm." She handed the documentation back to him, but she hadn't stopped to seal it for release. Maybe she'd just forgotten. Yes. Surely she'd just forgotten. It would be so embarrassing to be caught with irregular documentation. It had never happened to him. "Well, everything looks unobjectionable, pilot. But Fleet wants every freighter in your gross weight category off-loaded and searched. It'll be half a day, and Port Anglace apologizes for the inconvenience. Quarantine. These people will escort you."

It didn't have to be a problem. It didn't have to be. Ships were off-loaded from time to time as a check on blatant cargo fraud, but the ports resisted it, because it was a time-consuming inconvenience and discouraged traffic. Kazmer stalled, hoping for reassurance.

"Of course, receiving officer. I hadn't realized there was a new policy in place at Anglace, though. I have to admit I'd have gone to Isener, I'd have been able to pay the crew off that much sooner."

And since the chartering company he was claiming to represent was responsible for wages until the crew was released, and since Kazmer was representing himself as a joint owner of the small cargo-carrying venture, it was a direct hit to his very own personal profits.

The receiving officer's mouth twisted in a sour grimace. "So would everybody. But it wouldn't have done you any good."

Of course not, Kazmer thought. The fence's contact was here, and he was responsible for getting the goods to the drop site, and that meant Anglace. Not Isener. But the receiving officer didn't know that. What she apparently did know provided no particular comfort, unfortunately.

"This is system-wide, but only for ships of your weight class. There's been more trouble at Port Charid, and the mercantile corporations are screaming for Fleet support."

Bad. Very bad. "I heard some gossip at Shilling," Kazmer admitted, speaking slowly, hoping to encourage the receiving officer to talk. "A lot of inventory wastage going on at Port Charid. Some words about Langsariks, but that doesn't make sense—where would they even get ships?"

The shore patrol didn't seem to be in any particular hurry to rush him to quarantine, so it couldn't be an issue of any real urgency. He might have to pay off the Port Authority; that was going to be hard to manage with Fleet personnel on the premises. But he could still get through this all right.

The receiving officer shook her head with evident relish for her role as the source of sensational information. "It's not inventory wastage they're yelling about. There was a raid at Port Charid a few days ago; they tortured half the crew and merely murdered the rest.

Trashed the station's warehouse storage with high-energy impact rounds. Battle cannon. Where they've been hiding those all this time is anyone's guess."

Kazmer stood silent, stunned.

They'd only been on vector for a few days. Had someone mounted another raid after the Tyrell job?

Because she couldn't be talking about the Tyrell Yards. She couldn't be. There had been an inside man. Nobody had been tortured, that was why the Langsariks had planted an inside man, to get the information without resorting to uncertain and excessive means. They had all been alive when the freighter had left.

"That's, er, not common knowledge, pilot," one of the shore patrol troops said, a little apologetically. "We'd appreciate it if you didn't disclose any of the details to your people. Let's get you to quarantine; there's cots and food, and it'll only be half a day."

It couldn't have been the Tyrell raid.

And if they suspected him, what point would there be in asking for his cooperative silence?

Nodding politely to take leave of the receiving officer, Kazmer turned from her desk and went with two of the armed troops.

Were they actually covering him?

Or were they armed for show?

It made no real difference. He couldn't afford to try for a break. They'd have him within moments; and an attempt to flee was as good as a sworn admission of wrongdoing, whether it was theft or killing.

He'd done nothing wrong . . . or nothing so wrong as that.

He was innocent of any act of murder.

And it was entirely beyond belief that Hilton Shires could be responsible for the torture, let alone the murder, of disarmed and helpless warehouse staff.

Impossible.

But if Fleet started to ask questions . . . if they were implicated, howsoever unfairly, in murder, and the Bench authorized preliminary inquiry, and there was enough incriminating evidence to convince someone to implement the Question—

He couldn't protect Hilton under torture.

Kazmer had no illusions about the power of his own will in opposition to all of the tools and tricks that a Fleet Inquisitor had at command, and everyone had heard about the range of atrocity permitted an Inquisitor; there had been that Tenth Level Command Termination. Koscuisko. Kazmer had remembered the name of the Inquisitor, because a Sarvaw had good reason to be mindful of all of the descendants of Chuvishka Kospodar.

He had to do something.

But the first thing that he had, to do was wait, because this would all pass over. It had to. There was no connection between the freighter's cargo and any murders. Fleet would let them go.

There could be some penalty for the contraband they'd carried from Tyrell, but no more than that, and a good chance of getting off lightly even on that heading, since Fleet's interests were focused on the search for murderers. Not mere pirates.

Yes.

That was right.

Fleet had much more immediate concerns than one small-time operator from Port Charid, if there were murderers at large.

CHAPTER FOUR

Walton Agenis woke to the sounds of conversation in the house, an unfamiliar sensation—she was accustomed to quiet—and an unfamiliar voice. No, a familiar voice, but distantly so; coming from the kitchen, coupled with that of her niece.

What, had Kazmer Daigule come to the front door, as Modice had admonished him to do?

It wasn't Daigule's voice. It was deeper and lighter at the same time, lacking the reedy note of resigned weariness that gave everything the Sarvaw said its own characteristic wry humor. So Modice had another gentleman caller.

Walton sighed and rose, belting her robe around her, working her bare toes into her scuffs while she waited for her head to clear of sleep. She couldn't belt her robe around her waist, not really; because she'd never had much of a waist to belt anything around, being more or less all of one line from her shoulders to her hips with a miscellaneous diversion or two.

She secured the robe's ties around her middle instead and went out to find out who was courting Modice now, at this early hour of the morning.

The voices were coming from the kitchen, and Walton could smell the grain soup cooking—Langsarik breakfast, grain soup with shaved meat. Once it had been a fighting ration, easy to cook, easy to eat, easy to digest; now it was just daily fare. They'd lost so much, or they'd given it away, and they'd given it away on persuasion from the man who was sitting in the kitchen with Modice, peeling a dish of gourds for a porridge.

Garol Vogel.

Jurisdiction Bench intelligence specialist, and the negotiator who had secured the amnesty responsible for the Langsarik settlement at Port Charid.

Vogel rose hastily to his feet as Walton entered the room, snatching his old campaign hat off his knee to make a precise salute. Hat in hand. Well, of course, hat on head was impossibly incorrect, in a kitchen. For a moment Walton felt embarrassment on account of her rather worn robe; but Vogel's own jacket had seen better days, too, so she put it out of her mind.

"Flag Captain Agenis." It was oddly formal of him to call her that; she had no fleet to command, and she didn't know what the land-based equivalent of a space fleet commander might be. Militarization had come late to the Langsariks, their fleet originally nothing more than a well-ordered commercial enterprise with government oversight. She'd always thought that helped to explain their success as commerce raiders: their strong commercial foundation. "I'm sorry to come unannounced, Captain, and so early in the morning. It's important that I meet with you. Should I come back later?"

Her nightdress embarrassed him, robe and all. That was funny. If he was embarrassed by her nightdress, the sight of the kerchief that Daigule had given Modice would probably make him faint outright. It was worth a try.

"Be seated, Specialist, it's all right. Has Modice given you soup?"

Probably not, because the grain soup was still cooking. Vogel declined to sit down. "With respect, ma'am. I wouldn't have come this early at all if it hadn't been business. You might want to hear what I have to say before you extend your hospitality, and I don't want to share your meal under false pretenses."

He was a queer duck, was Vogel; she'd learned that much about him during the negotiation of the amnesty settlement. He slept on floors, ate when he remembered that he was hungry, and at one memorable meeting she had seen him rinse a drafting brush in his tea—and then drink his tea, having apparently forgotten that he'd rinsed his drafting brush in it.

And yet on certain forms and protocols he was absolutely formal and excruciatingly diffident.

"Vogel, we have a past relationship with you, and I accept that you speak for the Bench and not for yourself. Therefore, sit down and take grain soup on your behalf, and not that of the Bench. I grant hospitality to you, not to your Brief."

Now it would be rude of him to decline, so he accepted. He rolled his cap into a cylinder and thrust it deep into the left-hand pocket of his jacket before he sat back down to resume peeling gourds for Modice.

"Thank you, ma'am. Most gracious."

Modice set the morning tea on the table, with syrup and ground spice-bark to sprinkle on top. She could be a discreet little soul, Modice. Now that Walton was awake and on line Modice concentrated on breakfast, quiet, efficient, and as much in the background as she could manage.

Walton let her morning tea sharpen her consciousness, drinking in silence as Vogel peeled vegetables. She thought she could guess why he might have come. He'd wait for her to open the talks, though, his tact as much personal as professional; so once Walton felt a little more alert she fired the opening round.

"What business brings you out to the settlement, then? Periodic status check, maybe."

But probably not. Vogel shook his head. He seemed a little more bald on top than he had been the last time she'd seen him, but his moustache was still thick and iron gray and showed no signs of thinning.

"Special embassy, Flag Captain. Chilleau Judiciary sent me. Local area mercantile predation, concerns about the robustness of the amnesty."

Since this was what she'd suspected once she'd recovered from the surprise of seeing him, Walton had an answer at the ready. "As if Langsariks could raid warehouses in the Shawl from a settlement on Rikavie. We'd need transport, for a start. We haven't got any."

She was almost glad he'd come with the issue; she'd been pondering the news and dreading the inevitable questions. No one had come right out and accused her of breaking faith—yet. Probably because people who were the least bit familiar with the Langsarik settlement had to realize how improbable the logistics were.

Vogel tilted his head a bit to one side, presenting his case. "They're small raids, but well mounted. Transport was stolen for the Okidan raid at least, so it could come from anywhere but has been coming from Port Charid. Never been more than two ships involved. So the thinking tends to be that if anybody could manage it, it'd be Langsariks, quarantine or no."

Walton frowned, and Modice set a dish of grain soup down in front of her. Plenty of pepper. It smelled very appetizing; Modice was a good cook.

"I couldn't so much as lay hands on a single freighter, Specialist. Not without someone noticing." She'd only ever heard about single ships; where did "two ships" come from? "I could see a possibility that some of our young people might sneak into the occasional warehouse here at Port Charid. For creature comforts."

Vogel thanked Modice in a murmured aside for the dish she gave him. Modice smiled at him and took the dish of peeled vegetables and waste peelings away. Gazing at the surface of his dish of grain soup, Vogel replied to the food, with his eyes resolutely focused on the dish. Polite. Non-confrontational.

"Freighters. And battle cannon. The pattern doesn't exactly fit the Langsarik model, that's clear from intelligence sources. But the Bench is responsible for the protection of property and the maintenance of good order, and the rule of Law."

"Battle cannon? That's a good one." Walton ate grain soup, thinking. Vogel had information she hadn't heard yet, that much was now clear. "Where would I get battle cannon? Where would I hide battle cannon? If I had battle cannon, I certainly wouldn't blow my cover on any given raid; I'd keep them safe until I decided I really needed them."

Vogel seemed to remember, suddenly, that it would be rude to leave his meal uneaten, and attacked the problem with his spoon, with a strange sort of convulsive thoughtfulness. Walton didn't know whether Vogel's focus was a strictly personal characteristic or one common to Bench intelligence specialists; she was just glad he'd remembered his soup before it got cold.

If he'd come to court Modice, he would have tucked into it right away, in order to have the opportunity to compliment her cooking. So he had clearly gotten past the abstract sort of a crush he'd had on her.

"Um. Good soup. Thank you, Modice." But there was no particular weight to the phrase. Confirmed, then, Walton told herself: Vogel was polite as always, but he clearly had other things than her niece's beauty on his mind. "I can't answer that question, Flag Captain."

Question? Oh. About the battle cannon. Walton waited; Vogel spoke on.

"But I'm not sure it matters. We have three issues here. There's the apparent violation of amnesty."

He put a very careful weight on that word, *apparent*. Just enough to stress the hypothetical nature of the allegation without discounting the weight of the damning appearance.

"Then there's the Bench being pressured by the various big commercial interests with warehouses in the Shawl, along with other interests reluctant to invest, even at Chilleau Judiciary's very persuasively phrased invitation, so long as the area is not secure. The Bench wants the commercial investment. Finally, somebody is out there robbing warehouses. Killing people."

All three issues were intimately related. She didn't need Vogel to tell her that. "We may have been raiders, Bench Specialist. We may have been good at it. But we were never murderers."

Had people been killed during Langsarik raids? Yes. She wasn't going to deny it; she also didn't need to explain to Vogel. They carried blood guilt, because people had died as a result of Langsarik actions; but it was not guilt for murders either premeditated or accepted as any sort of an acceptable concomitant to raiding. It had always been an unfortunate accident when it happened. They'd always done what they could to minimize the chances that people would get hurt, because it had never been blood that they'd wanted, but freedom. And survival.

Now Vogel put the spoon down and met her gaze very directly. There was no accusation or deception in Vogel's sharp gray-green eyes. "That's as may be, Flag Captain. People are getting killed. There are capital crimes to account for. We don't have very much freeboard here."

Always set his documents on reader, Vogel had. Shared information, full disclosure, no hidden agenda. Asking her to engage with him in partnership for the accomplishment of mutually beneficial goals: pacification, survival.

Port Charid's administration treated her very much like the only marginally trustworthy representative of a defeated and criminal people. They were forced to rely on her for head-count reports and policing the settlement, but it was strictly for lack of any other resources.

Vogel was still negotiating with her as Flag Captain.

"What do you need from me, Garol?"

"Couple things. Thank you for asking."

Coming from almost anyone else, she would have sneered at the courtesy or simply ignored it. Anyone else, and it would have been meaningless; but Vogel meant it. Vogel was for real.

Vogel was talking; Modice was washing dishes, quietly, in the background. "Not to be insulting, Flag Captain. But are we clear on what happens if Langsariks are found to be violating the terms of the amnesty agreement?"

Yes. They were very clear. "Violation in substance of the amnesty agreement nullifies the Bench's suspension of prosecution. Execution for some of us. The Bond for any of our young people who test out." And Langsariks would test out well for enslavement under governor, Walton was uncomfortably sure of it.

It took a person with character, ability, and unusual psychological resilience to qualify for the Bench's most horrible punishment, the living death of enslavement as a Security bond-involuntary, conditioned to obey or suffer hugely disproportionate punishment from an internal governor, condemned to execute the orders of a Ship's Inquisitor as the hands of a torturer.

Langsariks could survive even that. Langsariks had what it took to make whatever sacrifices they had to make, in order to survive. "Penal colonies for everyone else. Dispersal and death. Dissolution as a people and disenfranchisement for next of kin still living on Palaam."

The Langsarik pirates per se were not a large community; there were only about five thousand of them in total.

But it was her community.

Vogel nodded grimly. "The stakes are too high to risk any stratagems on either of our parts, Flag Captain. Before I go any further with this issue I'd like permission to ask you up front, man to man. Just between us."

"Man to man," was it? Walton knew what was coming. "All right. Ask away."

"Are you personally aware of anything going on within the Langsarik community that we need to know about that might have a bearing on the recent warehouse invasions. And have you any unexplained anomalies with your head-count and reconciliation reports."

Incriminate her own?

Yes. If that was what it took to protect the community as a whole.

Luckily for her she didn't have to face sacrificing any of her people. "If I knew anything that would link any Langsarik to warehouse predation, I'd tell you, Vogel."

He would know that she was telling the truth; he'd as much as told her that her word was as good as her oath when he'd asked permission to ask the question. "But I don't. So far as I know there isn't anything going on. We've had the occasional anomaly—" the Sarvaw mercantile pilot who had slipped through the fire-watch perimeter, for instance—"but nothing that might enable any plots. And I have no idea where we could lay hands on a freighter, let alone a battle cannon, not with what we have to work with here."

Modice had left the kitchen as Walton spoke; now she came back again, standing beside Walton where she sat, with her hands folded underneath the apron she'd put on to do the dishes. Modice was very white in the face.

Vogel noticed.

"Are you all right, pretty lady?" Vogel asked, gently; and Modice drew her hands out from underneath her apron. She had something in one hand.

It was the scarf that Kazmer Daigule had given her, the night he'd turned up at Modice's window.

"The Bench specialist might want to talk to Hilton, Aunt Walton," Modice said, her voice a little quavery, but determined. "Hilton will know what his friends are up to, even if we don't. So the Bench specialist could give this to Hilton to give back to Kazmer. If you wouldn't mind, Specialist Vogel."

Thinking on her feet, was Modice. And clearly frightened.

Daigule had come to Port Charid, and probably not just to see her; it was logical to suppose that he had business, and—in the absence of any concrete knowledge of what that business was—not too far-fetched for Modice to wonder if there was something that Daigule had gotten himself tangled up with that he shouldn't have. Because Daigule was a man of immoderate enthusiasms and uncertain discretion.

Did Hilton know about Daigule's business?

Had Hilton been part of whatever had called Daigule to Port Charid in the first place?

Sending Daigule's scarf back through Hilton was as good as a warning to everybody, one way or the other. If Hilton didn't know that Daigule had been in Charid, sending the scarf to Daigule through Hilton would tip off her nephew and warn him of potential trouble.

If Hilton had called Daigule in on a raid, letting the Bench specialist return the scarf would put Hilton on notice that the authorities were close to him, and—since Modice had entrusted Vogel with the errand, with Walton's knowledge to be assumed—that he would not be protected if he endangered his people.

If Daigule was involved with something that Hilton didn't know about, getting the scarf returned to him by Hilton via Vogel would let Daigule know that the authorities were closing in on him, and that his activities were a danger to Modice as well as to himself.

And giving the scarf to Vogel was as much as telling Vogel that the Langsarik authorities were genuinely ignorant of the fact if it was a fact, with an entire sheaf of corollaries besides.

Walton couldn't believe that Hilton would be engaged in anything he knew could jeopardize his entire community.

If she thought about it, she couldn't really believe that Daigule was involved in murder, either.

She was still impressed with Modice for having the moral strength to admit the possibility and take action on the margin of the odds.

Vogel didn't know who Daigule was; obviously enough Vogel had no knowledge of Daigule's night visit. Modice had only told Walton herself about it within the past few days, and it had been twice that long since it had occurred. Vogel simply accepted the scarf at its face value and folded it into another pocket of his jacket. "To be returned by Modice Agenis to Kazmer Daigule through Hilton Shires. Glad to oblige. Where do I find the lieutenant these days, Flag Captain?"

Modice left the kitchen again, and Walton knew that she fled in her heart even while she walked with casual care in the flesh. If Modice liked Daigule, it would be torture to her to think that he might be involved.

If Modice liked Daigule, she would have to know whether he was involved or not, so that she could cut him out of her heart as soon as possible—should it be necessary.

There would be much to digest after this breakfast. "Hilton is in Port Charid. Doing orientation in the warehouses there." Vogel clearly remembered him from the negotiations; there was no need for anxious concern that the name and the relationship might be firm in Vogel's mind because Hilton was suspect. "He's gone to work for the Combine Yards. There's a new warehouse complex under construction."

Vogel nodded. "Well. I'll be going. I hope you won't hesitate to call on me if you think of anything or learn something. Is there anything I can send you from Port Charid?"

There was an unusual softness to his voice, and something in his expression that seemed almost tender. Caught by surprise, Walton felt a blush coming on like steam rising into her face from a cup of freshly boiled water for hot tea.

"Ah. No. Thank you. We're fine." Noodles. She wanted noodles. She liked noodles, especially with snap-spice broth, and poultry. They weren't expensive, but a person had to have a supplier, and the local concession hadn't stocked any as long as they'd been here. "Send me the news, Garol, when you can. I want to know what develops."

He stood in the middle of the kitchen with his cap in his hand for a moment, looking around the room as though he had forgotten something.

"And thanks for coming, Bench specialist. I'll let you know if I find out anything."

He seemed to give himself a mental shake. "Yes, of course. You're welcome, only due respect, and so forth. Good-greeting, Flag Captain, I'll show myself out."

Her grain soup had gotten cold, but she finished it anyway.

Modice, Daigule, Hilton. Vogel.

Battle cannon.

There could be no connection.

But if there was—

She was Flag Captain Walton Agenis; and it was up to her to protect the Langsariks.

Against her own family. If that was what it took.

Kazmer Daigule could hear the voice through the open doorway, clear and resonant and cold, like the penitence bell on the Day of Atonement. During the days he had been held in Fleet custody here at Anglace he had played this coming confrontation over and over and over in his mind, testing each link in the fearful chain, hoping in vain to find a weak spot somewhere. During hour after hour of restless solitude he had written and rewritten the story in his mind, the train of events, the best interpretation he could put on them; and hour after hour of restless solitude had led him ever and again to despair, in the bleak conviction that things could not possibly be worse for him.

And it was worse.

The Holy Mother loved her Sarvaw stepchildren: Kazmer had been catechized with care, during his short childhood. She cared for and nurtured the Sarvaw almost as tenderly as if they had been her own children, and not the offspring of bondservants. But the Holy Mother was a vicious bitch for all that.

This Inquisitor was Dolgorukij.

And of all the Inquisitors who could have been called off a routine cruise to take legal and binding testimony on Record, there was only one that Kazmer had ever heard of who was Dolgorukij; because after the Domitt Prison—and the execution of its master—everyone had heard of Andrej Koscuisko.

Someone came to the door of the interrogation room, someone in Fleet colors. Big. Very ugly. The officer's doorkeeper, perhaps; his narrow yellow eyes rested briefly on Kazmer's face without changing expression. Then he tilted his head with a decisive gesture.

"The officer is ready for you," the man said. His voice was as wrecked as his face was, so unlovely that Kazmer could almost pity him. Almost. "This is the pilot? Let's go."

They would question each of the crew members separately, and then check their stories against each other to decide who would go on to further interrogation. Kazmer had thought it all through. Contact with the Langsariks had been through anonymous drops, third-party relay, double-blind exchanges. None of the crew knew any more about who had hired them than the absolute minimum, unless, of course there was a Langsarik plant among them. He couldn't afford to postulate the presence of a Langsarik plant; it was too uncertain.

He had to proceed under the assumption that he was the only one among them who could point a finger and name a name.

His guards started him forward with a shove; he kept his balance, but not gracefully. He was tired, and he was hungry, and he'd been sleeping in his clothes for days. It demoralized a man. He knew very well that he stank; but was the subtle expression of disdain that crossed the Inquisitor's face a reflection of his all-too-powerful odor?

Or did Koscuisko recognize him as Sarvaw?

"Thank you, Mister Stildyne." Yes, it had been Koscuisko's voice he'd heard from outside the room. Tenor, and strangely feral. "Be seated, pilot, there is nothing to fear. For the moment. My name is Andrej Koscuisko, and I hold the Writ to which you must answer for questions that exist pertaining to the potential involvement of your ship and crew in murder and theft in the Shawl of Rikavie."

He'd heard some of the details by now, before the guards from the local port authority had realized that their gossip might contaminate his evidence. He still couldn't believe it. Either murder had not been done, or Hilton wasn't involved in it, but all the Bench would hear from him was the name, not his insistence on Hilton's innocence.

Kazmer had no confidence in his ability to withhold the name.

One of Koscuisko's people set a glass of water down on the table in front of Kazmer, where he could reach it with his hands chained at his waist. Kazmer stared at the man's sleeve as he placed the glass: a uniform-blouse with green piping at the cuff.

Green-sleeves.

Bond-involuntary.

That was what they would do to Hilton, to all of his family; plant a governor in his brain and set him to serve a torturer, or suffer torture himself. And Modice? Modice was so beautiful. They would prostitute her less horribly, perhaps, because it was more traditional a fate for a woman in the hands of her enemies; but they would put a meter on her body and vend the private secrets of her flesh to any bully who could come up with the price.

It made him sick just to think of it.

And he would be the cause of it, because he had seen Hilton in the street.

He took a drink of water to steady his resolve; and the Inquisitor—sitting across the table from him, with a tidy little rhyti-set at one elbow and a pair of black leather dress gloves laid casually to one side—nodded at him, as if approvingly. Kazmer could smell the perfume of hot sweet rhyti, and it made his mouth water with longing. He hadn't had a decent cup of rhyti since—

What did it matter?

He couldn't afford the quality of leaf that Koscuisko used anyway.

"Let us begin, then," the Inquisitor said. "State for me your name, pilot. And your cargo, your point of origin, and the identification of the ship on which you traveled here to Anglace."

Koscuisko knew his name.

The Inquisitor had the information there in front of him, the printed copy of the Port Authority's report in a neat and damning stack.

But there were rituals to all of one's interactions with the Bench and Kazmer could not afford to permit this one to go any further.

"I declare myself Sarvaw, your Excellency, Kazmer Daigule, from Peritrallneya near Sivan. I throw myself upon the mercy of the Malcontent, to answer to him or none. Sir."

The Inquisitor froze where he sat, staring, his pale eyes blank and unreadable. None of the others would know; it was lucky, in a way, that Koscuisko was here, because otherwise the declaration might not be read into Record until it was reviewed prior to logging at the end of the session. And there might have been unpleasantness, upcoming.

The ugly man spoke, from the post he'd taken at the officer's right hand. "Sir—"

Koscuisko silenced the ugly man with an upraised hand. "You will leave us, Mister Stildyne," Koscuisko said. "Robert may stay, and Lek. I place the Record in suspense, now excuse us please. Immediately."

The ugly man wasn't happy.

But the Inquisitor was senior, and rank apparently prevailed. Were they afraid he might assault the Inquisitor?

What physical damage could he do, with his hands chained and his feet shackled?

When the room held only the four of them—Kazmer, and the Inquisitor, and two bond-involuntary troops—the Inquisitor spoke.

"You have placed your election on record, Daigule, no one will defraud you of your choice. But consider. Is the penalty you face truly worth the sacrifice required to avoid it? You have spoken the name of the Malcontent, and your mother will wonder forever after how she failed you in your upbringing."

As if Koscuisko's own mother had no such doubts, and him a noble and upright pillar of the Judicial order.

"I have nothing further to say, your Excellency. To you or anybody." He had already said that he would answer to the Malcontent. But even the Malcontent would refrain from asking one question; that was the foundation of the contract. A man who elected the Malcontent gave over to the Saint his name, his freedom, his body, his mind and heart and soul; his all, in return for one thing: whatever it was that he wanted.

Would the Malcontent accept his contract?

The Malcontent turned no man away.

Koscuisko rose to his feet, with a decisive gesture of disgust. "Then you are guilty. You cannot be otherwise. It is the counsel of a coward, to seek the Saint to evade deserved punishment."

But Kazmer knew what he had to do. He had fought it out during those long hours of waiting and wondering what would happen. He could implicate Langsariks by name. So far as he knew he was the only one of the freighter's crew who could do that.

They gave him no option for any other escape; so the Malcontent was his only hope, and Hilton's only hope as well.

"I neither affirm nor deny your statements, your Excellency, but submit myself to the mercy of the Saint. In reverence. And silence."

Koscuisko wasn't looking at him.

Koscuisko was looking at one of the troops he'd kept with him in the room; and Kazmer remembered what the Inquisitor had said to the ugly man, as he sent the ugly man away. Robert and Lek, he'd said. Kazmer hadn't paid much attention to the bond-involuntaries, he'd been too wrapped up in his own issues to have energy to spare; but Lek was Sarvaw, too. Sarvaw with an Arakcheyek in his mother's nightmares, by his height; but Sarvaw nonetheless.

"Who am I to say?" Koscuisko asked Lek, with a little shrug that looked almost embarrassed. "It could be that there are worse things, whether guilty of greater or lesser crimes."

The bond-involuntary Sarvaw bowed his head in response, and Koscuisko nodded. Then shook his head, but apparently at some strictly personal regret or disappointment. Kazmer stared at the glass of water on the table in front of him. There were worse things than to elect the Malcontent. One of them was to be enslaved under Bond.

Let Koscuisko believe that that was what Kazmer feared.

Or let Koscuisko believe whatever he liked, just so long as Kazmer could protect the Langsariks from the fate that had been visited upon Lek, the fate worse even than the election of the Malcontent.

"Open the door, Robert," the Inquisitor said; then called out to the ugly man, who apparently stood waiting outside. "Mister Stildyne. It will be necessary to go and see the Consul, to obtain the representative of the Malcontent. Present my excuses to the Port Authority, and let us go directly."

The guards who had brought Kazmer in took Kazmer out, surprised enough by these developments that they forgot to shove, and let him walk at a normal pace. They went back to his cell. When he was alone again Kazmer put his face down between the palms of his chained hands, fighting to quiet his mind.

He had done it.

He had elected the Malcontent. Soon he would be damned as all Malcontents were damned, despised, disenfranchised, disdained, and disregarded.

He would be alive; and if an evil fortune should call Hilton's name up before that Dolgorukij Inquisitor, at least it would not be from Kazmer's mouth that it would go on Record. Or maybe not at all.

And Modice Agenis?

He could not even think of little Modice.

He would be Malcontent. He did not have the right.

Knowing that he had had no choice if he was to hope to protect his friend gave him no comfort, in the horrible certainty that even the hope of Modice was lost to him forever.

When he got back to Port Charid, Garol Vogel stopped at the yards where the courier was berthed, but Jils wasn't on board; there weren't any messages. There was news on the reader from Chilleau Judiciary, but Garol wasn't interested. He sat down at the scheduler instead, keying a line for Shiron Madlev, the Combine Factor at Port Charid.

He needed to pay a courtesy call.

The Bench recognized Factor Madlev as the spokesman for the local mercantile council, which made Madlev something close to the civilian authority here. The port's only secured communications with Chilleau Judiciary were held in Factor Madlev's office. It was politic to go and make appropriate noises expressive of profound concern on the part of the Bench, pledges of speedy resolution, promises of action—all of those things.

Therefore, Madlev was the obvious place to start, if Jils hadn't done the honors already. Madlev might well expect a call either way, after Garol's previous meeting with his foreman—what had the name been? Fisner Feraltz—at the hospital at Nisherre.

There was also an errand to run, for Walton Agenis.

When the access tone cleared, Garol identified himself, his voice a little strange in his own ears in the silence of the courier.

"Bench intelligence specialist Garol Vogel. I've been detailed by the Second Judge at Chilleau Judiciary to solve the piracy problem at Port Charid. Requesting an entrance interview with Factor Madlev, at his earliest convenience."

There were clicks and hushes on the line as the screener on the other end scrambled to take the message line. Garol could appreciate the humor in the situation. He was sitting in a quiet ship with his clothing in moderate disarray and what hair he had left in an emphatically uncombed condition from his journey to the Langsarik settlement and back on a speed machine; but a Bench intelligence specialist was a Bench intelligence specialist—and the line wasn't video. Just audio.

"Excuse me, Bench specialist." A live body, at the other end. "If you would care to nominate a time when Factor Madlev could look forward to receiving you."

The sooner he got his duty calls out of the way the better. Jils had already gone to tie in with local Judicial resources, such as they were in a mercantile port.

"I can be there inside of an hour, if that's convenient. And say, I heard there's someone I need to speak to, working in the Combine warehouses—somewhere in Charid. Maybe someone could show me where to find him, after I meet with Factor Madlev. Hilton Shires. Langsarik."

The voice at the other end sounded a little surprised, but seemed to be recovering. "He's a new man, Bench specialist, here this morning I believe. It shall be done. When may I tell the Factor to expect you, sir?"

Don't. It's better if he doesn't expect me. Garol resisted the temptation. He'd already lost the advantage of surprise anyway. As if he needed surprise when he was just giving an in-briefing, not probing for information.

Madlev would be expecting some questions.

Best to get them out of the way up front.

"Give me an hour. I'll be seeing you. Thanks for making the time."

When Garol Vogel walked into Factor Madlev's office—shaven and suited in uniform dress, and exact to the hour—he was not entirely surprised to find Jils Ivers waiting for him, with a documents-case in one hand and a face that spoke code. She had something interesting, then. She was a fast worker.

Garol was surprised to see Fisner Feraltz there as well—the sole survivor of the raid on the Okidan Yards, the man he'd interviewed in the private hospital at Nisherre. Feraltz didn't look much recovered to Garol; he was still braced from head to foot on his right side. Hadn't been doing his physical therapy, Garol concluded. Feraltz bowed a little stiffly in response to Garol's nod of greeting, but there was no other way to move in all that bracing but stiffly.

Factor Madlev was a big man whose face seemed fractionally too large for his head, even with his very full beard taken into account; but there was no faulting his enthusiasm, or his manners. Now that Garol had given Feraltz the nod, Madlev came forward to meet Garol with hearty goodwill, offering a greeting that seemed perfectly genuine.

"Bench specialist Vogel. An honor, sir. I'm Shiron Madlev, Factor Madlev, people call me Uncle. Or, er, Factor. You've met my foreman, I think? Welcome to Port Charid; we are very glad to see you."

"Pleasure to be here. Yes, in fact, I had a talk with Feraltz before he was released from hospital. Good to see you on the road to recovery, Feraltz."

Garol returned the Factor's eager embrace with one of moderate warmth, not entirely comfortable with Madlev's effusions of joy. "The Bench is deeply concerned about recent events in Rikavie, Factor Madlev, and we'll do our best to get to the bottom of the problem. I see my second has anticipated me, however."

No, she'd come because she knew he'd come here as soon as he got back from the settlement. The rental company's locator on the speed machine would have told her when that had happened. She wasn't supposed to be able to read the machine's locator, it was private information, after all. Proprietary to the rental company. But rank had its privileges; also its problems, inconveniences, headaches, warts, and the occasional lethal surprise.

"Yes, honored by two such visits, and on the same morning. Please. Be seated. Can I offer?"

Offer what? Offer anything. It was a subtle lure, equally receptive to requests for money or drugs as bean tea or cavene. Garol discarded the cynical reflection as uncalled-for, and settled himself. Feraltz simply leaned up against the Factor's desk, keeping to the background, resting his right leg; no sitting down in that medical web, or at least no sitting down in any chair with arms. No room.

"You're very kind." Garol had eaten breakfast already, a big bowl full of Modice Agenis's grain soup. Not that it was anyone's business. "Nothing for me, thanks. Just a moment or two of your time. The intelligence reports contain no anomalies in the head-count and reconciliation reports, yet rumor insists that Langsariks are responsible for recent raids in the Shawl of Rikavie."

Madlev shrugged with a smile, as impervious to Garol's lure as Garol to his. "Bench specialist. We have so few resources. What can I tell you? We have no choice but to rely on the Langsariks themselves, for self-policing."

Madlev was a little too big for his chair, which could barely contain the span of his broad thighs. Broad powerful, not broad fleshy, but the effect was a little ludicrous all the same; it reminded Garol of a grown man trying to make use of a child's seat, for want of anything more appropriately sized.

"Quite so. Very true." Madlev wasn't in a very expansive mood, it seemed; but it was hard to believe that Port security wouldn't have caught on by now, if something was going on. If. "But you do periodic spot checks, I understand. And there haven't been any problems there?"

The Bench had put the Langsariks here at Port Charid, but hadn't stationed any police resources to monitor them—that was up to the Port Authority. As far as the Bench was concerned the ban on transport was all that had been needed to ensure that Langsariks stayed here. Port Charid was responsible for overseeing that ban; how did Port Charid explain the apparent access of Langsarik raiders to hulls on which to raid?

Madlev nodded. "That's right, Specialist Vogel. We do unannounced spot checks three times a week, and we haven't found anyone missing yet." Madlev's response was ready and complete enough, but Garol thought there was a hint of defensiveness there all the same. "There have been one or two minor discrepancies, but all explained to my complete satisfaction. No transport gone missing from Port Charid either, and I think we'd notice, Bench specialist. They're good. If it's true what they say, of course, and there's no proof. Is there?"

No help there, in other words. Walton Agenis had claimed she didn't know where she'd find a freighter; Factor Madlev apparently had no insight on the question—none that he was willing to share, at least.

"The public word is very much Langsarik," Jils said, in a tone of mild—very mild—reproof. "It seems unnecessarily complicated to speculate on some unknown responsible party. They are Langsariks. And they are dangerous."

She was feeling Madlev out, Garol knew; repeating only what she'd heard said. Garol found her remarks a little distasteful, even so. Jils hadn't forgiven the Langsariks for having been as successful as they were. She seemed to have no room in her heart for admiration for the discipline and sacrifice of a worthy foe; or she felt it as keenly as he did, but would not acknowledge any foe worthy that challenged the rule of Law, let alone as profitably as the Langsarik fleet had done.

Madlev shrugged with his palms upturned in a gesture of conciliatory petition. "Of course everyone says Langsariks. They're a defenseless target. When were Langsariks ever stupid, though? And what would endangering the settlement be, if not sheer idiocy? No. I don't believe it."

It was interesting for Madlev to be so definite, with his foreman still visibly marked by injuries sustained in the Okidan raid. Feraltz didn't seem to find Madlev's insistence distasteful, even so. That was right: Feraltz's story had been that the raiders couldn't be proved to be Langsariks. Feraltz was on the Langsarik side, at least as far as sympathy went.

"We'll get it straightened out, Factor Madlev. That's what we're here for. Though I do have a personal request to make, as well."

"Yes, anything." Factor Madlev didn't really have much room to lean forward in his chair; his legs were too long for its height, so that leaning forward looked more awkward than sincere. He seemed to know that. "Office space. Local transport. Communications links; dinner. Anything."

All of which Garol could arrange just as well or better for himself, but there was no advantage to be gained by gratuitous rudeness. "You have a Langsarik in the warehouse. Hilton Shires." He had mentioned wanting to see Hilton when he'd made this appointment; had Madlev been told? "I have a message from his aunt; I promised I'd pass it on."

That, and he wanted access to Shires.

Garol was ready to believe that Agenis had told him the truth when she'd said that her hands were clean; she had more sense than to try to shield any guilty parties at the expense of the entire Langsarik settlement. That made the problem more complicated, but less stressful to Garol personally.

The scarf was a signal of some sort, and Agenis had chosen to let Garol deliver it. Agenis wanted Hilton to cooperate, in other words. Garol didn't need to know the ins and outs of it. All he needed to know was who was raiding, where they were, and how to stop them before they brought horror and destruction down on the heads of innocent people.

"Yes, of course. Immediately. Fisner?" Madlev pushed himself out of his too-small chair with evident relief; and Feraltz straightened up, clearly ready to receive instruction. Why didn't Madlev have all of his chairs done large enough to suit his size? Garol wondered. Was it because of the negotiating advantage Madlev gained, when people were foolish enough to read physical awkwardness for a relative dullness of wit and failed to shield their strategies or secrets accordingly?

Jils stood up, too.

Feraltz moved awkwardly toward the door, talking as he went. "I'm still at a bit of a disadvantage, Bench specialist, so I've taken the liberty of asking Dalmoss to come and escort you. He's one of our floor managers." There was a man waiting in the Factor's front room, newly arrived since Garol had gotten here; the man came forward at a signal from Feraltz.

"Dalmoss will take you to Shires's workstation, so you can talk privately if you like. Without publicity. And here's Dalmoss. Dalmoss, these are Bench intelligence specialists Vogel and Ivers, looking for Hilton Shires."

Perhaps not exactly "looking for," Garol thought. Wasn't there an implied accusation or assumption of guilt of some sort there? He'd asked to see Shires, he hadn't come looking for Shires to question him. And yet that could be what the foreman thought he was going to do; the foreman didn't seem to like the idea, either.

"If you'll come with me, gentles. I'll take it from here, sir. Shires? He'll be in receiving reconciliation this morning, we can run him to earth there. As it were."

Maybe he was being oversensitive, Garol decided. To consistently decline to identify the Langsariks as guilty, and then imply howsoever indirectly that Shires was a person of interest for a Bench investigation—it would mean that Feraltz was a hypocrite, or seriously ambivalent, or so secure in his conviction of Langsarik innocence that he hadn't given the phrase a second thought.

Overreacting.

Yes.

As an Abstainer, Feraltz was probably avoiding the drugs he needed to manage his pain. That would more than cover any apparent inconsistencies in his communications. He was probably exhausted, and almost certainly distracted by the trouble his still-healing injuries were undoubtedly giving him.

Yet something was ever so slightly off-kilter; and Garol didn't know what it was.

Oversensitive.

He'd talk it all out with Jils, as soon as he'd concluded his errand for Walton Agenis.

Hilton Shires set his mark to another line of audit code on the receiving report with a sense of accomplishment too thoroughly mixed with a sense of the ridiculous to be completely enjoyable.

He was learning to do receiving reconciliation and inventory management. The acquisition of new skills was an intrinsic good. There was no telling when it might turn up suddenly useful to be able to audit a cargo in record time and present a fair report on wastage and dilapidation.

But he was also Hilton Shires, a once-lieutenant in the Langsarik fleet that had exercised its own particular if not inimitable brand of wastage and dilapidations against cargoes permanently diverted from warehouses much like this one and absorbed directly against the bottom line of somebody else's books.

The contrast made for meditation that was not free from bitterness. It wasn't because he was ungrateful. The warehouse crew didn't go out of their way to be friendly, no, but he'd known Dolgorukij kept to themselves when he'd accepted the job. He'd been glad to accept the job. He'd wanted the money, and moldering in settlement without anything constructive to do could only lead to trouble.

He was glad to see the foreman coming toward him from the direction of the administrative offices; he could take a break from congratulating himself on learning how to count cargo crates. A little self-admiration went a long way. He had little enough he could admire in himself these days. Who was that with the foreman?

He watched them come.

Middling-sized man, square-shouldered and light on his feet, where had he seen that uniform before? Bench standard trousers, over-blouse, cap, footgear; but the color was a peculiar gray, and there was no rank that Hilton could see.

Bench intelligence specialist.

The woman, too, a little on the short side but as sturdy as a chisel. Once Hilton identified the uniform in his mind he remembered where he'd seen those people before, or at least the man. Garol Vogel. The man who had made it all possible, the settlement, the amnesty, Hilton's job, everything. He had a lot to thank Vogel for, but in his heart he knew that genuine thanks were owing.

So he would be polite.

His foreman waved to him, having obviously realized that Hilton had noticed them; so Hilton signed off on the counter—never leave a counter unsecured and open, he'd been told; otherwise, it was vulnerable to unauthorized emendation that would invalidate the count—to join the foreman and the people he had with him. He hadn't heard there were Bench intelligence specialists in Port Charid. Bench intelligence specialists were devious that way.

"Hilton Shires," the foreman said to Vogel, as Hilton approached. "This is the man you want? The Bench specialists are asking after you, Shires. Don't be too long, though, there's a lot to be done before we can load-out that shipment for storage, and our freighter's due to dock in less than two days."

Right.

The foreman walked on. Hilton stopped short and waited for Vogel to open the discussion.

"Garol Vogel," Vogel said, politely, in case Hilton hadn't recognized him, Hilton supposed. "I've just been out to see your aunt. There's a problem with raiding in the Shawl, I expect you've heard all about it."

As indeed he had. "Not since the hit on the Tyrell Yards." If there had been anything since then, it was news to Hilton. "Disgusting waste of time and energy. Not to mention the vandalism."

Vogel shook his head. "Nope, that's the last one. Till the next one. The Bench is worried, Shires; people are talking about Langsariks."

As if he didn't know, Hilton told himself, indignantly. The crew here in the warehouse were good about it—they seemed genuinely to admire the Langsarik fleet's history of successful, if ultimately futile, resistance to assimilation within the embrace of the Jurisdiction. The Combine itself hadn't been all that eager to make treaty, if he remembered his history correctly.

"Target of opportunity, Specialist Vogel. Specialist Ivers? Good to see you again. You were at the talks, weren't you?"

She wasn't giving him much of a reaction one way or the other, listening politely but without response. It didn't matter. He was just making his point. "You'll remember the terms, I expect. The Langsarik fleet to yield all transport and articles of war or aggression, including such weapons that might otherwise be granted for defensive purposes. The Bench to decline to exercise judgment on condition that behavioral guarantees are met. Yes, people talk, Specialist Vogel. But not even my aunt could manage to attack a warehouse in the Shawl from a shack on Rikavie. And if she had, she wouldn't have made such a sloppy botch of it."

People had been murdered. The authorities were keeping the details close in order to avoid compromising evidence; a person didn't need much imagination to guess at the general outlines of the crime. Langsariks had been commerce raiders. The Bench had called it piracy, but there was a world of difference between assisting the creative redistribution of material resources and killing people while one was at it.

"Even so." Vogel's voice was reasonable, even sympathetic. He had an open manner that invited confidence; it seemed to indicate an

honest heart—as far as that went. "The Bench isn't always as careful as
we'd like about politically volatile situations. Primary value is the rule
of Law and the maintenance of the Judicial order, which means that the
appearance of an issue can be an issue. The Flag Captain says she
doesn't know of anything going on in-house. Suggested that we see if
you had heard anything."

Hilton felt himself redden in the face with vexation. Aunt Walton
had said that? Sent Vogel here to get his assurances? Maybe she'd been
thinking about speed machines. It was true he'd succumbed to
temptation and borrowed one without having had the opportunity to
ask permission. He'd paid for the repairs, hadn't he? That machine had
been better than new once the work had been finished, too. He had even
been invited to wreck another of old Phiser's speed machines anytime.

"What Walton Agenis doesn't know about what's going on in
settlement isn't worth knowing. If she says there's nothing, then there's
nothing, Bench specialist. But since she told you to ask me. No. I
haven't heard any hints of raids or thievery from any Langsariks I
know. People are depressed, not stupid."

Vogel nodded. "Good enough for me, Shires. Your aunt is a woman
of her word. In fact, the Bench granted amnesty on the strength of that
word, pretty significant sign of respect there."

So don't embarrass her, Vogel was saying. What made Vogel think
he was involved in anything? Vogel was an intelligence specialist. He
surely knew exactly how much weight it was appropriate to give the
gossip of idle minds.

"And well placed, Bench specialist." His response sounded a little
stiff and offended to himself, but Vogel didn't seem to take offense. He
just reached into the front of his uniform blouse for a packet of some
kind.

"I agree. Well, we'll be going, Shires; if you hear anything that might
help us discover who's responsible for the Tyrell murders, I hope you'll
let us know. Here. The Flag Captain asked me to give this to you."

It was a scarf, and a hideous one, an incredibly garish length of
cloth patterned in great gouts of completely incompatible colors. Even
the color tones themselves were mismatched.

"I don't understand." It was beyond belief that his aunt would send
something so horrible as a gift. "Is there an explanation that goes with
this thing?"

Vogel folded his hands together in front of him, his fingers loosely interlaced. "Not much explanation, I'm afraid. Modice gave it to me to give to you, to be returned to someone named Kazmer Daigule, the next time you saw him. Does that mean anything to you?"

Ivers had been staring at the scarf in Hilton's grasp with horrified fascination. When Vogel said Kazmer's name she glanced up quickly at Vogel, though, as if she'd been taken by surprise.

Was this a setup, to see if they could get a guilty reaction out of him by surprising him with the name of a possible accomplice? It could be. But it wasn't.

If Vogel and Ivers had set a trap, Ivers would have watched his face, not looked at Vogel. So there was something going on that they hadn't worked out between themselves, yet.

"Kazmer Daigule is a friend of mine. He courts Modice to annoy me." What Kazmer had been doing in Port Charid the morning of Hilton's interview with Factor Madlev Hilton could only guess. He would rather Kazmer had not come into any conversation with Bench intelligence specialists, on principle; Kazmer had ferried the odd illegal cargo.

But Kazmer would never be party to murder.

Now that it was clear that the Bench specialists knew of Kazmer's visit, the best thing to do was make full disclosure and trust in truth. Hilton didn't like it, though.

"He was in port not long ago to move a cargo. I saw him, but we both had places to go. I guess he went out to the settlement. Aunt Walton doesn't approve of his suit for Modice's affections." Hilton refolded the scarf as he spoke, putting it away in the side pocket of his warehouseman's coveralls. "And with taste in scarves like this, I guess you can see why. Anything else?"

He was unhappy about the turn this talk had taken, and it showed—he could hear it in his own voice. Vogel shook his head.

"No, that about covers everything for now. Thank you for your time, Shires. Factor Madlev will know where to find us if you need to reach us about anything."

Good.

He could go back to receiving reconciliation, with the single worst pattern in known Space radiating great waves of sheer unadulterated tastelessness from his pocket. He probably glowed in the dark with it.

He hoped it wouldn't alter his genetic structure; he would probably be lucky if it merely scarred him for life.

He wished more than ever that he hadn't seen Kazmer in the street that day, but now it was more for Kazmer's sake than that of his self-pride.

He knew Kazmer wasn't a killer.

But he didn't trust the Bench to display equivalent perceptiveness; and not even Aunt Walton could wish the Bench on Kazmer Daigule, whether or not she thought he had any business courting Hilton's cousin Modice.

Walking in companionable silence out of the warehouse, Garol waited for Jils to make the first move. She had something on her mind; so much had been obvious by virtue of her presence at his interview with Factor Madlev. And he was interested in whatever it had been that caught her attention in his talk with Shires.

He found the speed machine where he had left it, parked outside of the warehouse's administrative offices. Jils stopped short of the machine while Garol straddled it with a certain degree of self-conscious bravado. He only had one safety helmet; but Jils liked to live dangerously.

At least any woman who voluntarily surrendered her body to the ministrations of bone-benders—dubious professionals at best, outright charlatans at worst—had nothing to say to anybody about merely riding a speed machine without a helmet. That would be his line, anyway.

"Hey, pretty lady, wanna ride? For you, no charge."

But she knew him too well to rise to the bait. She pulled a tab on one of the panniers behind the pillion seat, and there was a safety helmet. Damn. Perfectly good tease, shot to hell.

Fastening the helmet strap beneath her chin, Jils mounted the pillion seat behind him, passing him a piece of documentation as she settled herself. "Drive, you smooth-talking seducer of innocent young women," Jils suggested—in part because of the line he'd started to run, yes, but it would serve just as well to cover them from casual observation. "We have much to do, and time flies like youth itself."

What, had she been reading the Poetic Classics again?

The documentation was a receiving report from the Port Authority at Anglace, where the bulk cargo from the Tyrell raid had apparently turned up. Part of it, at least. There'd been an anonymous tip. Those were always interesting—anonymous tips almost never had anything to do with concern for law and order, and everything to do with personal malice of one sort or another.

But that wasn't the really interesting part.

The pilot of the impounded freighter was a Combine national named Kazmer Daigule.

Garol passed the documentation back to Jils and started his motor. "Say," he suggested, calling back to her over the sound of the speed machine's engine. "There isn't really a whole lot to do in Port Charid. Let's go find some action, shall we?"

Port Anglace.

Public opinion blamed the Langsariks for recent predation at Okidan, Tyrell, and several earlier targets.

Hilton Shires had been a lieutenant in the Langsarik fleet, and it couldn't be very easy for him—or any of his fellows—to adjust to their reduced expectations and meekly take direction from people who had been prey.

Kazmer Daigule had been in Port Charid recently, and was personally acquainted with both Hilton Shires and the lovely young Modice Agenis.

Walton Agenis said there was no Langsarik involvement that she knew of, but Modice had let Garol know that there was a connection between Daigule and Shires, so either the women were genuinely unaware of any deeper implications of Daigule's visitor—or they were giving Garol the keys he'd need—or they just didn't know, but felt that Shires and Garol should be equally warned.

It was enough to make a person think very hard about starting a melon patch and abandoning the whole Bench intelligence specialist thing for a quiet life of preserves, jams, jellies. Compost. Maybe a pond, with salamanders.

"Talked me into it," Jils responded, only Jils used the communications link built in to the safety helmet, rather than trying to make herself heard over the noise of the engine. The sound of her voice reminded Garol that he was the one who was supposed to be driving, instead of just sitting there brooding.

Garol nodded.

Slipping the neutral on the speed machine, Garol pulled away from the parking apron, heading back to the docks, where their courier was waiting.

This news from Anglace gave him the perfect excuse to depart Port Charid immediately and leave Hilton Shires alone with his thoughts.

If Shires was guilty, he had all the time he needed to make a run for it. Somewhere. Anywhere. Gonebeyond space, maybe, across the Sillume vector.

If Shires was innocent, he'd stay right where he was, oblivious to implications or standing on his integrity as a matter of principle, maintaining his honor in the face of adverse situational elements.

And if Shires were guilty, but didn't run, using his behavior to signal his innocence, intent on playing the game at its highest level—then Hilton Shires was Walton Agenis's own blood kin.

No help there.

Maybe they'd know more once they could talk with the Sarvaw pilot Kazmer Daigule, in Anglace.

CHAPTER FIVE

Three days of waiting after his interview with the Inquisitor had driven Kazmer almost to the point of distraction, torn between his relief in having found a way to protect Hilton, his sense of loss, and his shuddering horror of what he had done.

The Malcontent.

To elect the Malcontent meant to become one of them.

That meant doing anything they wanted him to do; and there were stories about what Malcontents were like behind the impenetrable walls of their safe houses.

He knew what his motives had been, but any casual acquaintance could only assume the most obvious explanation: that Kazmer had failed to reconcile his sexuality with the ordinance of the Holy Mother and the expectations of decency and morally upright behavior; that he had been forced to elect the Malcontent at last or face ostracism even more profound and absolute than simple criminality could ever have meant for him.

They'd think he wanted boys.

Modice would think that, if she ever heard. Maybe she wouldn't even hear. Maybe as far as Modice was concerned he would simply disappear and never be heard of or from again, ever. Aunt Agenis and Hilton himself would surely keep the truth of his fate to themselves, if they ever found out.

Boys.

It was almost more than Kazmer could bear, even knowing as he did what the Bench would do to Hilton—and Modice, and the rest of the Langsariks—if Kazmer had been referred to interrogation and implicated them all by virtue of simply knowing their names.

He'd visited Modice in Port Charid.

The Bench would be sure to see conspiracy there.

But boys?

To be a Malcontent could mean becoming the chartered agent of reconciliation for other Malcontents, people whose pain had forced them to take such drastic measures because they did like boys, or men; because their desire was not for the ocean within the sacred cradle of a woman's womb but for the succulent and inviting waters of an atoll, or even the narrow constrained channel of a dry wash.

Three days.

After three days, two guards came to the door of the holding cell to which the Inquisitor had returned Kazmer, calling him out to go back to the room in which he had had his fateful interview. There was someone waiting for him there, now as before.

For one confused moment Kazmer thought that the Inquisitor had come back—but why in plain clothes?

No, Koscuisko had pale eyes, and this man had not. The man who sat waiting for Kazmer was about Koscuisko's height, perhaps, and there were similarities in the face and in the expression. But this man had dark eyes, and hair that shaded several degrees further toward the tan side than Koscuisko's had done; and, most tellingly of all, this man was wearing a necklace made of bright red ribbon that showed clearly beneath his collar before disappearing beneath his shirt.

This man was Malcontent.

One of the slaves of the Saint, set apart by the halter he wore around his neck, collared with a necklace that marked him as a slave without any legal identity of his own.

Kazmer had sought that bondage of his own free will, because questions that one wished to ask of the Malcontent had to be addressed to the legal person of the Malcontent rather than to any mere slave; and the legal person of the Malcontent had been dead for octave upon octave—ever since the Malcontent's revolt against the autocrat's court, for excess tax impositions—rendering the entire issue a little problematic.

There was a legal entity to serve as the proxy of the Saint, of course—empowered to enter into contracts and to transact business on the Saint's behalf—but any particular question or demand could lawfully be referred to Saint Andrej Malcontent himself for a decision.

Some of the questions thus put before the Malcontent had been waiting for three or four lifetimes for a response, without notable success.

The Malcontent might or might not be actually and truly and traditionally dead, being a Saint. But it was certain that the Malcontent wasn't talking, at least not to answer claims that the Saint felt to be impertinent.

Kazmer sat down, not because he meant to presume the privilege without being asked, but because with every added notice of the reality of his election, the enormity of what he had done weighed more heavily upon him, so that he could not find the strength to stand.

"How fragrant are the little blue-and-yellow flowers that line the pathway to the kitchen-midden," the Malcontent said, his voice as deep as damnation for all the note of humor it might have contained.

He meant that Kazmer stank.

It had been more than a week, now, with no change of clothing or any chance to bathe—

The folkish homeliness of the old adage was too much for Kazmer. Sorrow and fear and grief overwhelmed him, and he was too deep in pain—even to care any longer when he began to cry.

Too much.

It was all too much.

The Malcontent let the storm pass without comment, waiting in compassionate silence for the moments it took for Kazmer to bring his emotions to heel once more.

Then the Malcontent pulled a white-square out of a pocket somewhere and passed it to Kazmer across the table. "Here. Wipe your face. The Bench expects you to suffer, Daigule, but you don't have anything to prove to me."

They were alone in the room. The Malcontent must have sent the guards away. Kazmer blew his nose, blotting his eyes with the residual clean portion of the white-square. His face was dirty; the white-square came away soiled. It was an offense against human dignity to deny a man the chance to wash. Kazmer supposed he was lucky enough that they'd fed him.

"Sorry." He handed the dirty white-square back, and the Malcontent accepted it without comment. Or recoiling, which was charity on his part. "This has all been a challenge. Maybe more than I'm really up to."

Yes, the Bench expected him to suffer. That was the only reason a Combine national was allowed to call for the Malcontent—to escape from the Judicial process—in the first place: because the Malcontent had successfully convinced the Bench that the life of a Malcontent was a comparable experience to whatever sanctions the Bench was likely to impose.

There were exceptions, of course; for certain classes of crimes— those against the Judicial order—not even the Malcontent could stay the hand of the Bench. That was what had happened to the Sarvaw bond-involuntary that Kazmer had seen with the Inquisitor, he supposed.

Kazmer was luckier.

The most his potential crime would have amounted to was an offense against private property and the lives of citizens under Jurisdiction, not a crime against the Judicial order itself.

There were so many gray areas, even so.

Kazmer knew he should count himself fortunate that the Inquisitor had not challenged the issue; or if the Inquisitor had, it had been after Kazmer had made the call, and if the Inquisitor had objected, the Inquisitor had obviously lost. Or the Malcontent would not be here.

"Well." The Malcontent leaned back in his chair, hooking one arm over the chair back and crossing his legs. "You called for the Malcontent, and I'm here. But before I lead you out of this place we need to talk. My name is Stanoczk, feel free to call me 'Cousin.'"

The Malcontent used a Dolgorukij word for the title that gave Kazmer a profound appreciation for the shakiness of the ground on which he stood. Religious professionals were all "Cousin," but Malcontents were usually addressed as the kind of cousin that was the barely legitimate offspring of the unfilial daughter of a younger son of a collateral branch of the family who had made an inappropriate liaison with a social inferior—possibly Sarvaw.

The "Cousin" that the Malcontent offered to permit Kazmer to call him was the older son of the older son of the direct lineage of a family to which one belonged only as the younger son of a younger son of a cadet line. There was no hope of truly expressing the nuances of such a thing in Standard; but Kazmer and the Malcontent would know.

"Thank you, Cousin Stanoczk." Kazmer used the Dolgorukij word back with humility in his voice and a determined submissiveness in his heart. "What do you need from me?"

Cousin Stanoczk nodded. "When a soul born of the Holy Mother's creation calls the name of my Patron, may he wander in bliss forever, they must do so in full knowledge of the price to be paid. And my Patron, he also must know what is required of him—in exchange for what he will exact from you."

The first part was easy. Kazmer knew the answer to the first part. "'Who calls the name of the Malcontent becomes no-soul with no name, no family, no feeling but the will of the Saint.' Yes, Cousin Stanoczk. I understand what duty I owe."

Straightening up in his chair, Cousin Stanoczk leaned forward over the table, so close that Kazmer could smell his breath. Stanoczk smoked lefrols. What was going on? "Then kiss me," Stanoczk said. "Convincingly, if you please. Demonstrate to me the depth of your commitment to the irreversible step that you propose to take."

Oh, Holy Mother.

Kazmer's stomach pitched at the very thought.

But he had said it. He needed the protection that he could only get from the Malcontent, protection not for himself, but for Hilton and Modice. For the Langsariks.

He reached forward slowly to put a hand to the side of Cousin Stanoczk's neck, sliding his fingers caressingly around to bend Stanoczk's head toward him. Maybe if he pretended. Maybe if he thought about Modice. But Stanoczk was not Modice, and could never be Modice; Stanoczk smelled of lefrols and musk, the scent of a man's sweat and a man's skin. Kazmer tilted his head to Cousin Stanoczk's mouth, shuddering in his heart, trembling like a man gripped deep in terror.

At the last possible moment Cousin Stanoczk spoke.

"Well, that'll do. For now." Kazmer opened his eyes, astonished, and found the Malcontent looking at him with a wry and moderately amused expression. "There is no need for you to turn your stomach inside out, it is a bad precedent for a first meeting."

Kazmer sat back down.

Had he passed the test?

Or failed it?

"I can do this thing, Cousin Stanoczk." He could take no chances with ambiguous signals. "I can do what I'm told. I will. No price is too great to pay for what only the Saint can grant me."

Cousin Stanoczk had settled back sidewise in his chair, and quirked his dark eyebrows at Kazmer skeptically. "It remains to be seen. The spirit is willing, but the flesh rebels, and to elect the Malcontent is to surrender body and soul. Yet there will be time to negotiate on some issues later."

It made no sense for the Malcontent to demand performance of a duty too strongly repugnant to him to be borne with a willing heart. The Malcontent was all about freedom from pain, even if it came at a high cost. Kazmer sat in his place, confused, feeling a little as though he was in shock.

"We move on. What is it that you of my Patron require?" Cousin Stanoczk asked. Did that mean that his failure to approach Stanoczk like a lover on demand was to be excused him, overlooked?

And exactly how was he to explain?

"Protect me from the Bench, Cousin Stanoczk. The Bench wants to ask me questions that I can't afford to answer. And I know I won't have any choice except to answer; I've heard the stories. Stand between me and the Inquisitor, and let me keep my answers to myself."

How much could he say without giving up the information he sought to protect?

If he told Stanoczk that he didn't want to give evidence, Stanoczk might guess that there was someone to be protected. From there it was a very short span to the obvious implication that the people Kazmer had to protect were Langsariks, so that electing the Malcontent was just another way of implicating Hilton, indirectly.

Implication was not evidence actionable under law.

Kazmer waited.

Langsarik predation was not an issue that could possibly interest the Malcontent—not unless and until Combine shipping became involved. By the time that happened Kazmer would not be in a position to implicate anybody, so maybe the Malcontent wouldn't care.

"That which the Malcontent directs, you must unfailingly perform," Stanoczk warned. "It may be that the information you wish to protect comes out through avenues other than a Bench claim against you. It may be that the mission upon which you will be sent will have as result exactly what you wish to avoid, revelation of information pertinent to whatever issue by another. Your duty to the Malcontent could require that you comply with your instructions, in such a case."

This helped. This clarified things. This gave Kazmer his mission, his pledge, the prize he was willing to trade his hope and future for. "Let me not incriminate people who may be guiltless by my testimony, Cousin Stanoczk, because testimony can be interpreted so wrongly. If there are guilty, let me find them. Only if a friend of mine is to face the Bench on Charges, let it be on evidence independent of any confidences between us."

Not as if there had been any.

Hilton had been very annoying about that, as Kazmer remembered.

Cousin Stanoczk stood up.

"Here's what we'll do, then."

Did that mean Kazmer had won? Or lost? Because to win was to lose, but to lose—would be to lose more than Kazmer could bear to contemplate . . .

"You are no longer Kazmer Daigule, and therefore you no longer have any information potentially of interest to the Bench. And yet the problem of the Langsariks may not be ignored, and if our holy patron deprives the Bench of information, it may be that we owe the Bench a decent story in return."

Kazmer hadn't said anything about Langsariks.

But Cousin Stanoczk had probably been fully briefed, as his next words proved.

"So we will go to Port Charid, where the Holy Mother cherishes many mercantile interests which are deserving of our Patron's protection accordingly. You will pledge your faith as one of the Saint's children to do your utmost to find who has been responsible for the raid on Tyrell Yards; and if the trail leads back to people you love—we will negotiate."

Kazmer thought about this.

The first and critically important thing was to ensure that Hilton Shires would not be named in evidence, that the Langsariks not face sanctions from the Bench for breach of amnesty on account of any testimony from Kazmer Daigule.

But the larger problem would not be solved thereby. Someone had raided Tyrell. Kazmer needed to know if the stories of torture and murder he'd heard were true. One way or the other the Langsariks had to be warned of the danger they were in.

If it had been Hilton Shires behind that raid, and people had been killed, then shielding Hilton further would no longer be the act of a friend, but that of an accomplice.

Slowly, Kazmer nodded his head. "Just give me the chance, Cousin Stanoczk, and I will find out what is at the bottom of all this. I know I can, if I have time, and the Saint's blessing on the enterprise."

It felt awkward using such language. "The Saint's blessing," indeed.

"Right. Put this on, then," Stanoczk said, tossing a small packet to him. Kazmer caught it by pure reflex, startled. A packet of ribbon: red ribbon, a band of ribbed silk ribbon as broad as the tip of his index finger was wide, and with a slip-noose in it. The halter of the Malcontent, the symbol of his self-elected slavery. "Only be sure of what you do, Daigule, because once I have led you on tether out from this place and into the street, there is no going back for you. Do you wish to take a moment to consider?"

Kazmer slipped the noose over his head and pulled it snug around his throat. "Get me out of here, Cousin Stanoczk," he said, holding the tag end of the ribbon-halter out in the open palm of his left hand. The hand for giving things away. "I will requite the Saint faithfully, in wholehearted fulfillment of my duty."

Cousin Stanoczk stood silent for a moment, as if making a final evaluation of Kazmer's sincerity.

Then he took the ribbon end from Kazmer's waiting hand. "Right. Let's go, then." Raising his voice, Stanoczk called out for the guards. "Security. Open the door, we're leaving."

The door to the interview room opened, and an orderly came in with a packet of documentation that she opened across the table.

Stanoczk pulled the ident-code that hung at the end of his own halter out from underneath his blouse and set his mark to the paperwork.

Kazmer felt his hope diminish with every emphatic strike of seal to document.

This was real.

It was official.

Stanoczk kept his hand low to obscure his grasp of the ribbon end, and Kazmer kept close behind to keep the halter slack so that it would draw as little attention to itself as possible; but he was being led out of the building at the end of the leash of the Malcontent, and once they reached the street—once he stepped clear of the Port Authority—it would be final.

Well, he had gotten what he'd needed.

The conflict between what he'd wanted out of his life, and what he had to accept as his life going forward, was no longer other than an empty issue for idle hypothetical debate.

Scowling, Garol tossed a data cube into the jumble of cubes on the table that formed the focus of the courier's small common room. "Okay. That's it for the interrogatories we have." They were good interrogatories, too, well developed, thorough, reasoned, and carrying the unmistakable stamp of a judicious mind. "But where is Kazmer Daigule in all this?"

Jils reached forward and tipped the data cube flat to the table's surface, marshaling the several records into a tidy array. "Well, he's the pilot," Jils said, but she didn't mean it. They both knew perfectly well that Daigule had been the pilot of the impounded freighter that Anglace had intercepted before the crew had had a chance to dump its incriminating cargo. She was just being provoking.

Garol suppressed a sigh. It wore on a man to be in transit, even when he could get information on transmit. The courier's address systems were robust, they could receive even priority transmission; but all they had seen during the past two days' time spent in vector transit were the files on other crew. All the other crew. Everybody who had been associated with that freighter, except Daigule.

"What in particular do you want from Daigule, anyway?" Jils asked, apparently by way of a conciliatory gesture. "These are all consistent. What can Daigule tell us that these people couldn't?"

Of course their stories were internally consistent. They'd had days in vector transit to themselves, time enough to practice a cover story. The freighter's crew had not apparently done so, however; the inquiring officer was on record with his assessment of that, and

Koscuisko knew his stuff. So much was obvious from the interrogatories he was producing.

But if the crew of Daigule's freighter had not coordinated a cover story amongst themselves, they were either stupid, arrogant, or truly unaware of the critical importance of a good explanation for their role in the murders at the Tyrell Yards. As though they had all been genuinely unaware of any such murders.

The inquiring officer was on record about that, too.

Koscuisko had logged a formal and judicial opinion that the crew members of the freighter that he had interrogated had been unaware of the carnage at Tyrell. That they were therefore liable to civil penalties for conspiracy to misappropriate private property, and for receiving stolen property with intent to intercept any proceeds for gain, but not liable for criminal penalties, as persons knowingly and willfully engaged in robbery by use of lethal force with intent to commit collateral murder—to the detriment of the rule of Law and the Judicial order.

"Daigule knows Shires. Shires is Flag Captain Agenis's nephew, and former Lieutenant. Daigule knows things about Langsariks that other people probably don't."

The interrogatories had established the pattern of recruitment, anonymous transmission of direction, care taken at every step to maintain a safe separation between the crew and the people who had chartered it. Maybe the crew should have guessed that such prudent people would not risk leaving any living witnesses.

But if whatever steps the raiders had taken to disguise themselves were good enough to protect them from incriminating testimony on the part of the crew, why had the raiders felt it necessary to murder those people at Tyrell?

"Well, it's got to be coming." Jils keyed the receiver on the table console, checking for any new information. "We have everybody but. Queue's still empty. Saving the best for last, maybe."

Maybe the interrogating officer had simply saved Daigule for the last of the series, waiting until a full picture of the pilot's exact role developed through the testimony of the other crew. Except that none of the other crew apparently believed that Daigule really knew any more about specific individuals than anybody else, even while reporting Daigule's apparent conviction that they'd been hired by

Langsariks. There was no reason for the interrogating officer to have known beforehand that Daigule was to be the key to the affair.

Koscuisko's intuition was apparently well developed, but he wasn't psychic, at least not from any evidence in the interrogatories Garol had reviewed.

Garol wanted Daigule's interrogatory.

He wanted it now.

He was going to have to talk to Chilleau Judiciary when he got to Anglace. He wanted a head start on analyzing what Daigule had to say.

"Go ahead, why don't you. Check." She was on line with the courier's link; she could just have a look. "At least find out how much longer we're going to have to wait. We're still a day out from Anglace. I've done all the word puzzles I can stand."

Jils frowned.

It wasn't an encouraging expression.

"There's nothing in the process queue at Anglace, Garol," Jils said. But she'd just said that. Hadn't she?

Garol waited. Jils addressed the courier's interface, and there was silence in the small cabin broken only by the shifting of a half-empty cup of bean tea atop a stack of pull-sheets. Garol caught it before it had a chance to tip. Jils was concentrating.

"Nothing in the queue. Nothing in holding." Leaning back in her chair, Jils ran one small square hand up across her flat forehead and through the thick black strands of her hair fringe. "He's not in the system, Garol; Anglace isn't holding any Kazmer Daigule. But he was there."

Garol had seen the receiving report she'd brought to Factor Madlev's office two days ago now. He knew Daigule had been there. "Incomplete inquiry?" Garol suggested, but even as he spoke he doubted the possibility that Daigule had died under interrogation. These interrogations weren't any more than drug-assist, not at this point; the Bench wanted information, not merely confession to a crime. They hadn't determined exactly what crime it was to be, yet. And Koscuisko didn't lose people in mid-inquiry, not from what Garol had seen of his work at Rudistal.

"There isn't even any session initiate on record. Nothing. Am I going out of my mind, or what?"

Garol had an idea, and it was an unpleasant one. "What," he agreed.

"It would be too frustrating. Jils. Daigule's the only one who might really be able to implicate the Langsariks, at least specifically enough to stand scrutiny on the Bench. And Kazmer sounds Dolgorukij to me, what do you think?"

She stared, but she caught on almost immediately, and her reaction was disgusted. "Damn. That's not fair. Are you sure? This is contrary to the maintenance of the common weal, we can protest."

Garol knew how she felt.

But there could be only one reason Garol could think of that would explain how a man who had been taken into custody could be suddenly no longer in custody, with no notation in the record about death or escape to cover the discrepancy.

Kazmer had got out somehow.

Dolgorukij could claim religious exception and go off to join the Dolgorukij church's secret service, penitents—or operatives—who identified themselves with an obscure parochial saint who had been dissatisfied with his life. No. Not dissatisfied.

Malcontent.

They couldn't afford to let Daigule escape so easily. Murder had been done at the Tyrell Yards, murder and torture. Langsariks were suspected. Daigule might be able to tell them, if not who had been the planning committee behind the raid, then perhaps at least for certain who had not.

Daigule's friend Hilton Shires, for instance.

"See if you can raise the local Combine consulate." There was nothing they could do until they reached Anglace, no physical action they could take. It was maddening, but there was no help for it. "Try to get an appointment. See if they'll admit to having a Malcontent on the premises."

Maybe it was just as well. They had a day to think about this, to decide what to do. How to approach the problem. What to say to gain cooperation from a government agency exempt by formal pact from many of the checks and balances otherwise imposed on organizations representing civil governments. How to get through to the Malcontent.

This unexpected setback only strengthened Garol's growing conviction—irrational though it was—that somehow Kazmer Daigule held a crucial piece of information that would lead him to the truth about what was going on at Port Charid.

He would get access to Kazmer Daigule, no matter what he had to do to get it.

Fisner Feraltz stood with his floor manager in the basket of a construction crane, surveying progress on the new warehouse complex west of Port Charid.

There were Langsarik work-crews busy across the entire span of the foundation clearing, from the dormitory buildings—still under construction, and meant to house the workers themselves now, the warehouse staff later—out to the old launch site that was being upgraded, hardened to withstand more frequent freighter-tender traffic than the six or seven a week that the port's main facility could handle.

A warehouse to store their loot, a dormitory to concentrate them, plenty of overlooked corners in which to hide illicit equipment, freighter tenders to be borrowed for illegal use—it was a brilliant trap.

He only hoped he would see it fully baited, before it was sprung.

"Another raid, eldest and firstborn?" There was a note of reluctant uncertainty in Dalmoss's voice. Dalmoss was frowning at the sun on the western horizon as it set. "It seems so soon. With humility I offer the words, eldest and firstborn—it seems precipitous."

It was unusual for Dalmoss to question direction from his superior at all. Fisner expected better of him. "We have been unfortunate in our intelligence, nextborn. There was no warning about the Bench intelligence specialist, and he was the one who won the settlement from the Bench for the Langsariks. It will take more to move him, if in fact he can be moved."

The evening breeze blew past the crane's basket, eights and eights above the ground. Dalmoss tightened his hold on the guardrail with a convulsive movement; Fisner noted that the knuckles of Dalmoss's hand had whitened, where Dalmoss gripped the rail. Maybe Dalmoss wasn't questioning his orders, Fisner realized. Maybe Dalmoss was simply afraid of heights.

It would be kindest not to notice, if it was nerves. If it was defiance, there would be time enough to raise the issue as a formal criticism once the Angel's work at Charid had been completed. One way or the other there was no profit to be gained from creating a confrontation now.

"So you force his hand, eldest and firstborn. As suits the agent of our divine Patron."

It would be almost vainglorious, foolhardy to mount a raid with Bench intelligence specialists actually at Port Charid. The Bench expected to receive its due respect, even if it was only to keep up appearances.

That Chilleau Judiciary would control public access to the news of raids and atrocities at Port Charid had been an accepted fact of the Angel's plan from its inception, but the personal involvement of one of the Bench's agents-outside-of-Bench-administration had the effect of flattening public outcry further than originally anticipated.

Bench resources at that level were more valuable than battlewagons and carried more of the Bench's prestige with them—there were three times as many cruiser-killer warships in Fleet than there were Bench intelligence specialists under Jurisdiction. So long as there were Bench intelligence specialists involved, no planetary government or mercantile interest could seriously accuse the Bench of failing to treat the problems at Port Charid with the appropriate degree of gravity.

Something needed to be done to increase the pressure on Chilleau Judiciary, so that the temper of the Second Judge could be reliably manipulated when the evidence that the Angel planned to reveal became public knowledge—or at least knowledge revealed to the Bench and related mercantile interests, which was as public as the disgraceful treachery of the Langsariks was likely ever to become.

"You have me precisely, second eldest and nextborn. What target would you guess I mean to take?" Fisner asked the question in a friendly tone. He had nearly decided that he was being oversensitive, in wondering if Dalmoss cherished defiance or resentment in his heart.

His own sense of cringing inadequacy could as easily be to blame. Just because he wondered if Dalmoss ever questioned the orders that had made Fisner his superior didn't mean that Dalmoss ever had any such thoughts. Fisner had come to the Angel later in life, in his twenties. Dalmoss had been the Angel's soldier in faith for longer than that.

Dalmoss didn't answer immediately; it was both polite and prudent of him to pretend that he'd had no thoughts of second-guessing his superior. Or maybe he was just thinking. "I would very much like to take Finiury, we know that there are armaments there. But the body count wouldn't make much of a splash. And the Bench couldn't afford publicity; we wouldn't get any noise out of it at all."

The Angel knew something about Finiury that wasn't in the public sphere: Finiury was managing illegal arms shipments for parties to civil unrest in Perk sector. Any publicity about a raid on the Finiury stores would have to gloss over the illegal armaments being stored there.

Nor could Maperna System—Finiury's sponsor—put much real pressure on Chilleau Judiciary for justice and revenge, once Finiury's illegal arms trade was uncovered; so all in all, Finiury was as safe as though it had been truly warehousing no more than industrial ceramics in quarantine. Dalmoss's reasoning was sound.

Fisner waited.

The sun was going down. They would have to return the crane's basket to ground level soon, and they would not be able to talk as openly on the surface. It was getting cold as well. The medical bracing Fisner continued to wear took the chill with annoying keenness.

"I can't pretend to have the same insight as you, eldest and firstborn." Meaning, Fisner supposed, to excuse his analysis if it turned out to conflict with Fisner's own. "But on the face of it. I would take Honan-gung. Some of its traffic is in cultural artifacts, which are therefore irreplaceable. And the casualty list will carry adequate weight."

The Combine Yards in the Shawl were out of the question, of course—at least for the immediate future. But Fisner had not thought seriously about Honan-gung. Baltovane had a much more tempting inventory.

Still, Baltovane's parent government would not make the noise that the planetary government of Yeshiwan system could be relied upon to make at the loss not only of innocent lives—that should be avenged by the Bench that had failed to protect them—but also of cultural artifacts. Historically priceless examples of Yeshivi art. Irreplaceable icons of the spirit of the Yeshivi people, destroyed with impunity by vandals the Bench itself had put in place and provided with opportunity.

Honan-gung was a much better choice, and there was an inside man there, as well as at Baltovane. Dalmoss need never know that he'd changed Fisner's mind.

"I could hardly have said it better." Fisner set the crane in motion to lower the basket. The floodlights were blooming to life on the field below; soon the second shift would come on. They were still months from bringing the new facility completely on line; but it could be ready well before then.

It only had to be far enough along to shelter the cargo pallets he had reserved for his purpose, and absorb three full shifts of Langsariks on-site. Once it was that far along it would be ready. They were already moving freighter tenders from its improved airfield.

Once they had reached that point, he would destroy the Langsariks.

Garol Vogel locked off the courier's communications systems and opened the maintenance codes to the Port Authority's computers. There were probably messages waiting for him, but he wasn't interested in any of them.

"Jils, come on. Let's go. There's things we need to do." He was in a hurry to leave the courier clear for maintenance and refueling, because he was heartily tired of it. It had been a long day span between finding out about Daigule and arriving at Anglace. Now he wanted to know whether it had done him any good to bother to come at all.

"No hurry." Jils was forward, doing some final something or another before she was ready to leave. "You're a Bench intelligence specialist, business will come to you. We have a visitor. Are you expecting anyone?"

What was she talking about? He didn't want to go forward to see. He was sick of going forward. He'd been doing nothing but going forward, then going back, then going forward again, for hours.

He went forward.

Jils had the docking bay on the forward screens. There was someone out on the load-in apron under the bright lights of the Port Authority's docks, someone in civilian dress who stood there with his hands clasped behind his back looking at the courier with what seemed to be genial curiosity. At least that was what it looked like from a distance.

Garol could guess who that was.

"Shut it down and let's go," he insisted, killing the display with an impatient gesture. "I'm telling you, the air in this courier is all used up. I've got to get out of here."

Jils had one of her tolerant faces on. She let his ill-tempered ranting wash over her without generating a similar impatience in her. He didn't know how she could be so calm.

Yes he did.

She didn't care.

The Langsarik settlement had been one successful negotiation among many, to Jils. If the Langsariks fell foul of the Bench after all the work they'd done to make a positive solution of howsoever imperfect a sort, she would feel regret, but mostly for the waste of time and energy.

It wasn't Jils that Walton Agenis had trusted to come to a fair agreement with the Bench.

"Coming, Garol. What are you waiting for? Let's go."

The man on the docks hadn't moved between the time Jils had pointed him out and the time Garol finally got her clear of the courier; he was still standing there, watching. He had to know they'd seen him, wasn't that the whole point of standing there out in the middle of a busy load-in apron doing nothing? Garol considered walking right past the man, just to be difficult. It would just put the progress of his investigation back if he did, though, so Garol made straight for the man, stopping when he was within speaking range.

Brown-eyed and blond, or maybe not quite blond; solid as a battering ram, and reminded Garol vaguely of Andrej Koscuisko. So he was Dolgorukij. It meant nothing. There were plenty of Dolgorukij.

From time to time Garol had found himself wondering whether there weren't perhaps possibly just one or two or several hundred thousand too many.

The man inclined his head politely.

"Cousin Stanoczk," he said in a voice as deep as an engine's sub-harmonics. Garol already knew that he wasn't anybody's Cousin Stanoczk and would have been surprised if Jils turned out to be somebody's Cousin Stanoczk. So he said nothing, and waited.

Cousin Stanoczk didn't seem to notice. "You have queried the Combine's administrative offices here at Anglace, looking for me—or for someone for whom I am responsible. I thought I would save you an unnecessary trip by meeting you, because I am certain there is not much to hold you in Anglace. You will wish to return to Port Charid immediately."

People generally didn't make assumptions about what Bench intelligence specialists did or didn't want, were or weren't going to do; or when they did they were usually wrong. Garol considered his options: *What makes you say that; who asked you; do you know something I don't know; who died and made you First Secretary?*

"I'm looking for Kazmer Daigule."

All of the other things that he could say would provide some emotional satisfaction, perhaps, but were unlikely to yield any real information. He could always fantasize about being gratuitously, flamboyantly, insanely rude at some other time. Personal feeling had no place where Bench business was concerned. "Am I correct in concluding that religious exception is to blame for the loss of his testimony?"

"Religious exception" was the formal legal term for it, when the Bench released a person of interest or an accused to the tender mercies of the Dolgorukij church. The interplay of concession and adjustment the Bench's relationships with all of its subject systems required in the interest of peace and good order created significant injustices, from time to time.

There was no telling whether Daigule's escape from questioning and prosecution was one such injustice. There would be no telling for Daigule at all, without the cooperation of the Malcontent.

Cousin Stanoczk nodded once more. "Religious exception is certainly the cause of his departure from incarceration at the Port Authority. It need not go so far as loss of testimony, Bench specialists. Excuse me, but which of you is Vogel and which Ivers? If I may ask."

Maybe Cousin Stanoczk didn't know, and maybe he was just being polite. "I'm Vogel." And Garol was frustrated. "What exactly do you want, Cousin Stanoczk. There are five thousand people at Port Charid whose lives may depend on my access to Kazmer Daigule. I need to talk to him."

"I want to take him back to the Tyrell Yards." Cousin Stanoczk's answer was straightforward, if confusing. "I don't care about five thousand Langsarik outlanders, Specialist Vogel, but I do care about one beloved son of the Holy Mother shot and left for dead at Okidan, and another as yet unidentified at the Tyrell Yards. I mean to go there with Daigule. You can grant access to the site."

Twenty-seven people dead at Tyrell, and Cousin Stanoczk only cared whether one of them might be Dolgorukij. Garol let go of his feeling of reflexive disgust; that *was* Cousin Stanoczk's job, he supposed. Look out for Combine interests, and only Combine interests, and never mind who else might suffer unjust death by violence. There was no sense in getting emotional about it. The Malcontent was a Combine operation, not a Bench resource.

"I clear you to Tyrell, you give me access to Daigule. Is that it?" Because it sounded too simple.

Sure enough, the Dolgorukij shook his head.

"Daigule kneels beneath the shield of my holy Patron, Specialist Vogel, I have no power to grant you access to him. But it may be that there is something he can tell us, about Tyrell. What he can tell us that I can share, I will share willingly. I am looking for one of the Holy Mother's children, you are looking for evidence. Perhaps we can help each other out."

Garol thought about it.

The forensics team was probably just getting started at Tyrell. The site had been secured, its atmosphere sealed to preserve evidence and inerted to avoid deterioration of the bodies prior to examination and autopsy. No identifications had been released, but any good intelligence agency would have been able to come up with the assignment list, so the Malcontent might have a valid interest in the site.

If Cousin Stanoczk wanted to take Daigule to Tyrell for whatever obscure purpose, it was possible that Daigule would say something under the stress of returning to the scene of his crime. Garol might be able to get somewhere with some incautiously blurted phrase or implication.

He had five thousand Langsariks to worry about, and no apparent chance of getting to talk to Daigule except through Cousin Stanoczk.

He was going to have to visit the Tyrell Yards sooner or later anyway. The only reason he'd not gone direct to Tyrell after checking in at Port Charid was that Jils had gotten news of the freighter impound here at Anglace. So now that Daigule was out of his official reach for purposes of formal interrogation, Tyrell was his next move anyway.

"I object in principle." In a perfect world he could violate religious exception if he had reasons of state for doing so. He was a Bench intelligence specialist. He had reasons of state by definition.

The Bench would not be well served by such an arbitrary action on his part, though, no matter how well justified Garol himself might feel it to be. A mere five thousand Langsarik lives—disposable, dispossessed, stateless, and criminal lives—were not as important as keeping the peace between the Dolgorukij Combine and the Bench.

There were potentially many more lives at stake than just five thousand if he violated the Combine's sense of entitlement. It had been luck and hard negotiating that had brought the Dolgorukij under Jurisdiction in the first place, one hundred and several years ago. The Combine was in a position to create major disruptions of the lawful conduct of trade to the detriment of the rule of Law if they were provoked to it.

So he would go along with Cousin Stanoczk's proposal and keep his hands off Kazmer Daigule.

He would also try every trick he could think of to work around Cousin Stanoczk and shake the truth out of the Malcontent's newest refugee, on the way from Anglace to Tyrell.

Garol inclined his head. "Still, you have me at a disadvantage. Very well, Cousin Stanoczk, I accept. Let's go to the Tyrell Yards. Let's go right now."

What questions Garol had to refer back to the other members of the freighter crew he could transmit en route.

What questions he could ask Kazmer Daigule—if he only once found a chance—he could consider as they returned to Rikavie.

"If you would care to accept the use of my courier. I have a suitable vehicle placed on alert status." Cousin Stanoczk neither paused to savor Garol's concession or even note it as such, sensitivity that Garol could appreciate. So the man was a diplomat. Well, the Malcontent had not become the secret service of the Dolgorukij church—and of the Autocrat herself, by extension—by mismanaging its relationships.

Still, Cousin Stanoczk's tact took much of the sting out of being on the wrong side of the balance of power for Garol as Stanoczk spoke on. "Secured transmission will be available, of course. So that you may report to the Bench, as you like. Or not."

If they turned around and went back to Rikavie on Cousin Stanoczk's offered transport, First Secretary Verlaine would not know where he was and could not query him for progress or status.

It was a tempting proposition.

He could always appropriate the vehicle on emergency loan if he had to. Knowing that was a portion of revenge in and of itself, but it was a real satisfaction for all its petty nature.

"Let's go."

He'd report back to Verlaine from Port Charid.

He wouldn't have anything real to report until he'd seen what had happened at Tyrell for himself anyway.

CHAPTER SIX

Without prior knowledge of what to listen for from which precise direction, with all of space to monitor the odds of any single short data-pulse being intercepted or observed was slim to the point of functional impossibility. It was the great distance between worlds that made transmission secure, not codes and ciphers per se. The Bench made use of every tool science had to offer to keep its sensitive information to itself; the Angel of Destruction put its faith in the Holy Mother and the huge background noise of random signals, and had never been betrayed in its trust.

The message was minute and modest.

Vogel leaves on arrival for Tyrell, with Malcontent. Daigule wears red.

Fisner Feraltz stared at the pulse on his screen, his gut gripped in the acid-sharp talons of a familiar anguish.

It would go wrong. He was worthless. He had failed in everything he had ever put his hand to; he had not even been raised by decent people, but was tainted beyond redemption by his life among the Langsariks.

Vogel leaves on arrival for Tyrell, with Malcontent. Daigule wears red.

It was a disaster.

After all that he had done, and all that he had planned, and all he had arranged so carefully and cleverly, Daigule had failed him. Daigule had not done as he was expected, intended, meant to do, had not told the Bench everything he knew about the Langsarik raid on the Tyrell Yards. Who would have guessed that a Sarvaw, of all people, would do so base a thing?

To protect his friend.

They had gone too far when they had made sure that Daigule would see Shires in the meal-room that morning. It had been a mistake. It had been his mistake. He was responsible for this disaster. But who would have thought it, of a Sarvaw?

Fisner toggled his transmit. "Send to me Dalmoss, Ippolit, if you please."

The Malcontent.

The greatest enemy that the Angel had, the bastard pervert among the Saints under canopy, not even a saint at all except by popular acclaim—he had no theological claim to the honorific. So what if there were healings, miraculous events, apparently divine interventions? It was all fraud and lies, like everything else about the Malcontent.

Perhaps the Saint himself had been Sarvaw, all along. There was a thought. No decent Dolgorukij could ever have tolerated such perversions as the Malcontent had during his life, and he had been near heretic as well—at least there were stories to that effect.

Health and happiness greater goods than loyalty and piety.

To feed the hungry more blessed than to rule them, schooling them to submission; alleviating suffering more pleasing in the eyes of the Holy Mother than teaching devout acceptance of all the lessons suffering had to offer—even that it was not blasphemy to think of the Holy Mother as a father, as well as mother, and that the Child of the Canopy might have an equal divinity with his Parent.

"You sent for me, Foreman?"

Dalmoss was at the door to the small office Fisner used while he was here at the new construction site. Fisner beckoned for Dalmoss to come in and close the door. It was tiresome to sit behind a desk, in bracing; but the illusion of bodily infirmity had to be maintained to minimize any chance that someone who might happen to see him late at night would make the connection between a dimly glimpsed, but able-bodied stranger going amongst the crates, and the still-disabled foreman Fisner Feraltz.

"The Sarvaw freighter pilot returns to Rikavie, nextborn and

second eldest. To Tyrell, and will almost certainly come back to Port
Charid." It was the clear implication of the message. The Malcontent
would go to Tyrell with the Bench intelligence specialist and had the
Sarvaw with him; from there they would quite naturally return to Port
Charid to make a report, think, discuss, strategize. Investigate. "We
can't risk him realizing that he has seen you before. This was not
planned."

He had no allowances for any such setback in any of his
contingency plans.

He had been sure of the Sarvaw.

Dalmoss stood humbly waiting for direction, saying only, "What
do you want me to do, firstborn and eldest?"

A test of his faith in Divine providence, perhaps, a gentle reminder
that it was through the will of the Holy Mother—and through Her will
alone—that the Angel triumphed over the enemies of the Church. A
mark of loving admonition.

If only he could be secure in that.

"Go tell Hilton Shires that you have been called to the factory at
Geraint for a few days. Tell him you have asked that he step up to
supervise the work-crews on construction in your absence. As a
temporary duty, and in light of his previous experience, Langsarik
supervising Langsariks."

Fisner spoke slowly, but gained confidence as he spoke. Yes.
Something was coming together. "We'll think of something to plant
the seed of Honan-gung in his mind. We'll let him think that he has
stumbled on information. Let him warn the Bench specialist."

The Honan-gung raid had been intended to force the Bench's hand,
to ensure that the momentum they were building up would not flag.
Shires could help. He could warn Vogel about a raid, send Vogel into
an ambush. If they took Vogel out, there would be no one for Chilleau
Judiciary to send as a troubleshooter, and no further question about
Langsarik involvement. The Bench would have no choice but to send
troops to arrest the Langsariks instead. No more hesitations,
qualifications, cautious investigation.

It could work.

The Holy Mother was merciful. She had sent this to show him the
way. He was not a failure. He was the Angel of Destruction in Port
Charid. She had as much as reached out Her hand to shadow his

forehead in benediction. Fisner's relief as he realized it was so immense that Dalmoss—looking at him with a quizzical if very small frown— would wonder about it, unless he distracted Dalmoss. Opening his heart to a subordinate was out of the question.

"Come up with a pretext, and speak to Shires. We will send Pettiche to Geraint in your place." He couldn't afford to let Dalmoss actually leave; Dalmoss was his raid leader. Dalmoss had to remain on-site, if hidden; and they needed to get Pettiche out of the way, as well. Though there was only a relatively small, if real, danger of the Sarvaw recognizing Dalmoss if he saw him, there was a much greater danger that the Sarvaw would realize that he had seen Pettiche before, at Tyrell. "You will have to stay out of sight, after that. It will be tedious. But it should not be for long."

Brilliant.

Dalmoss was right to salute him with undisguised admiration. "It shall be done, firstborn and eldest. I'll send you my formal request for Shires's temporary promotion within the day."

His mind had never worked so well, so quickly.

Surely the hand of the Holy Mother Herself was guiding him, to the complete fulfillment of Her purpose.

Kazmer Daigule stood at the side of Cousin Stanoczk in mute misery, his eyes fixed to the ground. The main docking bay at Tyrell Yards was splashed and stained with blood; he should have realized that it would still stink.

It had been nearly two weeks.

But the site had been secured and its atmosphere inerted, so that the bodies would be as fresh—their evidence as bald and horrible— when the autopsy specialists arrived as when they had been discovered, and they had been discovered a scant twelve hours after the killing had begun. Kazmer knew that, though he had not been told—the forensics people would fix the time well enough for Bench purposes.

Still, Kazmer knew. Twelve hours.

Three hours from Port Charid to the Shawl of Rikavie, traveling slowly in a freighter meant to present the appearance of being already almost fully loaded. Three hours on station. These people had all been alive when he had left, the alarm had been planned for ten hours after that, so the rescue party had arrived within two hours of the alarm and secured the site. He knew. Fourteen hours, at the absolute maximum.

"Complete jumble," one of the forensics people was saying to Cousin Stanoczk. "Here, have a look. At least five individuals, though we haven't really bothered with the detail, at least not yet. One percussion grenade. Result, meat paste, with bone and bits of clothing. Sorry, had you eaten?"

Forensics people saw horrors day to day, or at least they had too often in the Shawl of Rikavie. There had been Okidan, and one survivor. Kazmer thought he could remember hearing stories of at least two, possibly three raids, prior to that. He'd ignored the horror stories at the time, his mind full of Modice Agenis and his heart sure of Langsarik innocence—or had it been the other way around?

"But you can type for hominid at a gross level," Cousin Stanoczk insisted, after mastering an apparent wave of nausea. Of revulsion. "And I am responsible to the Church for it. Dolgorukij. Class two hominid. No?"

Kazmer could not stop himself.

He had to look around.

There was the dock-master's office, where torture had been done. Why? They'd had the security keys. There had been an inside man. Why had torture been done?

"No Dolgorukij." The forensics worker shook her head with emphatic conviction. "Nothing like anywhere near a Combine genotype, and the way the tissue got blended by that grenade we'd catch it if there had been any. Any at all. Maybe your Dolgorukij got away. There was a survivor at Okidan, wasn't there?"

She knew perfectly well that there had been no survivors here. She was just making conversation. Cousin Stanoczk shook his head in turn.

"I don't know what to say. Pilot. Let's go have a look at the others, he must be here. The rosters all confirm his presence."

Cousin Stanoczk had called him only "pilot" since the Bench intelligence specialists had come on board the courier Cousin Stanoczk had secured for this trip. Kazmer didn't think the Bench specialists were misled in the least, or that Cousin Stanoczk even cared if they were. Kazmer was grateful enough to be mere "pilot," even so.

As horrible as it was to be there, to see these brutalized and murdered bodies, and know that he had had a hand in it—howsoever indirectly—Kazmer could not imagine being able to stand if the others knew that he had been part of the raid. Part of the murders.

He hadn't really been able to believe it before. He hadn't wanted to believe it. The Bench's propaganda was as reliable as the word of a Dolgorukij; they could have been making it all up.

He knew better now.

These people had been done to death cruelly, atrociously, and for absolutely no good purpose. He shared the blame for it, because whether or not it had been his idea, he had been part of the raid. If he hadn't been so sure that it was a Langsarik raid when he'd met the others at Port Charid, he might not have convinced them to go along with it. So he was more to blame than they.

They'd believed him when he'd said it was Langsariks and that there would be no murder.

He, and not any of them, was to blame for their guilt by association. It was just and judicious that he become the slave of the Malcontent, fit and fair that he give up his life to the Saint in partial atonement for his crime.

He followed Cousin Stanoczk in silent anguish as his mentor, guide, master crossed the load-in dock around the corner behind the dock-master's office. There were bodies there that had been checked and cataloged, laid out and arrayed for transport as evidence once the on-site processing was done; Cousin Stanoczk paced the long row thoughtfully, looking at the faces.

Fourteen people.

None of them the man Cousin Stanoczk was looking for.

None of them Langsarik either, and Kazmer clearly remembered seeing a Langsarik on staff—the inside man. It had been part of why he hadn't minded leaving with the raiding party still there. There had been a Langsarik. Kazmer had seen him. That meant that there could have been no cause for any force to be used to get at secure codes—any inside man worth his wages would have that information at the ready.

No Langsarik.

No Dolgorukij.

Kazmer had seen the Dolgorukij, as well. Had recognized the man's ethnicity. He wasn't there.

There was only one more place to look.

Cousin Stanoczk looked up into Kazmer's face. His expression was sympathetic and supportive, but not sympathetic enough. Kazmer heard no "You stay here and wait for me," no "I'll just go have a look by myself" from Cousin Stanoczk. That meant that he was going with Cousin Stanoczk to look at the last of the dead.

It was part of his punishment, perhaps.

Kazmer hadn't elected the Malcontent to escape punishment—merely to escape becoming the instrument of unjust punishment of innocent parties. He couldn't quarrel with Cousin Stanoczk about that.

The Langsariks were innocent of any involvement in this raid, whether or not they'd found any Langsarik dead. These were brutalities possible only for hardened criminals to commit. The Langsariks had been pirates and commerce raiders and thieves, but never so criminal as to be capable of this. Whatever else Kazmer didn't understand, he knew that one thing to be the truth.

Kazmer followed Cousin Stanoczk into the dock-master's office, where the bodies of the people who had been slowly murdered were segregated. Where they could be hidden safely away from any chance glance or encounter.

The dock-master was there.

He could not tear his eyes away from her face for a long moment. She had been so unwary. She had been confident, comfortable with her crew, in control.

And had died so horribly—

"No," Cousin Stanoczk said, from the other side of the grim line of bodies. "I don't see any Dolgorukij. Do you, pilot? Do you recognize any of these people?"

He was to look at each and everyone. There was no particular note of gloating or sadistic pleasure in Cousin Stanoczk's voice, but Cousin Stanoczk clearly meant for Kazmer to see each element of this atrocity as individual and plumb the depths of his indirect guilt as part of the price for the protection that the Malcontent had granted to him. Cousin Stanoczk himself did not tarry; he had turned away to engage the Bench specialists in the outer office, with his back to the torture room with its plundered safe and mutilated corpses.

Fourteen people simply shot, five people tortured, at least five killed who knew how and then blown up with a percussion grenade—

Kazmer hoped they had been killed and then blown up, and not been killed by the grenade itself—

That brought the total up to twenty-four.

There had been twenty-seven people. He remembered counting them. Three were unaccounted for. One of those three Kazmer could understand not being there, at least if he didn't think too hard about it; if it had been a Langsarik raid the inside man—the Langsarik—would naturally have left, and not been murdered.

It hadn't been a Langsarik raid, so where was the Langsarik?

But he had thought it was a Langsarik raid. Everything he'd heard or seen had only supported that assumption. They'd worn Langsarik colors. They'd used Langsarik names. Langsarik habits. Someone had gone to a bit of trouble to make it look like a Langsarik raid: so the Langsarik was dead, even if he wasn't among the bodies.

Kazmer hadn't been mistaken.

He'd been set up.

Where was the Dolgorukij?

Kazmer stared helplessly at the bodies of tortured dead, half-blind with confusion. It simply didn't add up. It made no sense. And they could not find the body of their countryman. Or of Cousin Stanoczk's countryman, because Kazmer himself was Sarvaw, and no Dolgorukij would claim kinship with a Sarvaw except in opposition to other people of even more alien blood.

What kind of monster committed such crimes?

Killing could be clean, when done by luck against an armed opponent in active resistance. Murder could be swift and simple, a quick knifing, a shot to the head, the snap of a neck.

These killings had been done against people already disarmed, already helpless to protest against atrocity. Twisted rope. The slow cut. Blows from a club, a stick, a weighted baton. The mutilation of a living body, making grotesque sport with a man's own gizzard and guts—

Kazmer stared.

There was no earthly explanation for such horror.

And yet he knew where he'd seen it before, very exact, very precise.

There was no Dolgorukij body.

He opened his mouth to scream; but what came out was an animal sound, a wordless roar of outrage and blind fury.

⊕ ⊕ ⊕

"Naturally it is of concern, who is responsible," the Malcontent Cousin Stanoczk was saying. Garol and the Malcontent stood together with Jils Ivers in the dock-master's office; Stanoczk had left Kazmer Daigule to consider the tortured dead. "But first one must find one's countryman, and set his family's anxiety at rest. Who knows? If he cannot be found, perhaps he's still alive somewhere."

A slim enough chance, Garol thought, given what they were seeing. It was not merely grotesque. It was thorough. He never would have dreamed Langsariks could be capable of mass atrocity, but who was he to say?

Could something have gone this wrong, this quickly, in a population trapped and despairing? Was he ultimately to blame for having trapped the Langsariks into an amnesty settlement at Port Charid?

Then Kazmer Daigule, the Malcontent pilot who had brought them there, came roaring out of the inner chamber where the torture victims were; and flung himself headlong at Cousin Stanoczk, knocking him to the ground. Screaming.

Shock froze Garol in his place for just long enough to hear some of what Daigule was saying—he thought. His Dolgorukij was passable, but his Sarvaw was shaky. Though the Dolgorukij dialect he'd been taught had been High Aznir, the swear words were less dissimilar than some of the other elements of the dialects might be. Kazmer Daigule was howling about a bitch and a mad dog; then Cousin Stanoczk— who had struggled onto his back on the floor in the moments it took Garol to react—planted his boot in Daigule's belly and pushed, hard.

Garol stepped out of the way and Daigule went up and then back down again. Cousin Stanoczk was up and on the pilot in one swift predatory lunge, shaking Daigule ferociously with his hands gripping Daigule's shirt at the throat and shouting in turn. Cousin Stanoczk spoke High Aznir in his fury. Garol could tell exactly what Cousin Stanoczk was saying.

Profane as well as mad, shit-eating Sarvaw, no one protects the blasphemer. Shut your filthy mouth.

Daigule wasn't shutting up.

He had his hands up to Stanoczk's hands now, though he wasn't trying to get up. There was a wrenching note in his tone of voice that told Garol that Daigule wasn't raving, as Cousin Stanoczk's curse had seemed to imply; just insisting on something. There was the mad dog again, though Garol heard no more about bitches. Mad dogs, murderers, and a missal or devotional book of some sort. Maybe a counting string, it was hard to tell.

Cousin Stanoczk seemed to be in control of the situation.

Garol waited, to see what would happen.

Slowly the Malcontent straightened up, releasing his grip on Daigule's collar with what seemed to be a stern effort of will. It was hard to tell with Dolgorukij, but Garol thought that Stanoczk had paled. Turning his back on Daigule, Stanoczk raised his eyes to some point located halfway across the top of the doorway out into the load-in area; and when he spoke again, it was in plain Standard.

"You allow your imagination to run away with you, pilot. The mad dog of which you speak has been dead for more than one hundred years. You are grasping at smoke, to divert suspicion."

This was interesting. Garol sat down, deliberately drawing attention to himself with the action, just to be sure that they realized he was listening. He and Jils. He wanted to get through to Daigule very badly, but he wasn't about to steal access after having made a deal—howsoever unsatisfactory—with Cousin Stanoczk.

Daigule gathered himself to sit cross-legged, slumped at the floor and staring at the ground. "You say. But we know. They just went underground, Cousin Stanoczk, they've always been there. Waiting. Grant me at least the expert's eye in the matter."

The story was beginning to sort itself out to Garol's satisfaction. Whether or not he believed it was another matter.

"Nobody is going to take such a thing the least bit seriously." Oddly enough it seemed that Daigule had gotten through to Cousin Stanoczk, at least in some sense; Stanoczk sounded genuinely shaken. "You are afraid it was Langsariks, you wish to divert suspicion, you invent. What would the Angel be doing in Port Charid, what reason imaginable could there be? It's too forced, pilot, it won't do."

Daigule was shaking his head, though, rocking gently back and forth where he sat on the floor as if to give his insistence additional emphasis. "No Langsarik in the history of Langsariks ever did such a thing, but the mad dog was always accustomed to. For piety. This was not a Langsarik raid. This was a raid done by people wishing to be taken for Langsariks but betrayed by habit. Let me talk to the

Bench specialists, Cousin Stanoczk. I can tell them things they need
to know."

All of the time in transit between Anglace and Tyrell Yards the pilot
had kept strictly to himself, neither speaking nor responding when
spoken to by anyone but Cousin Stanoczk, but it had been perfectly
obvious to Garol that the pilot was Kazmer Daigule. He'd even felt a
little sorry for the man; it had to be an awkward position to be in.

"Out of the question," Cousin Stanoczk snapped, angrily. "You have
your oath taken on it already. I will not allow it. Still." He seemed to run
out of irate energy as he spoke, as if forced to entertain an alien and
unpleasant concept. "Still. It doesn't fit the Langsarik model. There is
the bracelet, I saw it. Why invoke the Angel, though, pilot?"

Bracelet, bracelet—what bracelet? Garol traded glances with Jils,
momentarily confused. He saw realization in her eyes even as he
grasped the meaning of the phrase himself. Torture victims,
mutilations, bodies cut open before the victim was dead. All right. He
could understand "bracelet."

"Because there was a Dolgorukij here, and we can't find him. There
was a Dolgorukij at Okidan, wasn't there? Who survived."

"If you mean to accuse—" Cousin Stanoczk started to say. He was
obviously angry again. Kazmer Daigule stood up and held his hands
out, petitioning.

"No accusations, Cousin Stanoczk. Just an observation. But
this—" Daigule spread both hands and opened his arms, to include all
of the carnage at the Tyrell Yards—"this is the very type and pattern of
the mad dog. Admit it. Why would Langsariks go crazy, in such
specific ways?"

"Not just one Dolgorukij is missing." Cousin Stanoczk seemed
determined to resist whatever conclusion it was that Daigule was
trying to communicate. "A Sarvaw also survived, pilot. I grant you that
no Sarvaw ever joined those ranks, that my holy Patron knows of."

The suggestion seemed to stagger Daigule, almost literally. It was a
moment before he could respond.

"If you were not my cousin," Daigule said, only he used one of the
dozens of words that Dolgorukij had for cousin, and Garol thought
this one was a particularly extreme form of the relationship from a
power standpoint. "And I didn't owe you. You'd take that back,
Stanoczk. And beg my mother's pardon, and her mother's pardon,

and the pardon of my mother's mother's mother, sincerely. I would see to it."

Mad dogs and bitches. Angels. Dolgorukij and Sarvaw.

Nobody said anything for a moment or two, as Daigule stared at Stanoczk, who stared back.

"We're being rude," Cousin Stanoczk said finally. "Bench specialists. We are finished here, Kazmer Daigule and I. Let's please leave this place. I will explain, but I warn you that I do not believe it."

It was an admirably restrained sort of thing to say after the fireworks Daigule had just set off. Garol could not bring himself to tarnish its perfection by elaborating or insisting on it.

"Your ship, Cousin Stanoczk." And therefore up to Cousin Stanoczk to decide when to leave, by implication. "Your pilot. Yes, we'd be happy to accept transportation to Port Charid, kind of you to offer."

Garol's own courier would be waiting there soon, freighter-ferried from Anglace. It had been relatively easy to arrange ferry transport; there seemed to be a surplus of available freight heading into Port Charid. Wholesalers weren't feeling very comfortable about the security of goods warehoused in the Shawl of Rikavie, it seemed; the business base at Charid was bound to be suffering. Chilleau Judiciary was going to want to talk to him about that.

Chilleau Judiciary was going to want to talk to him about a lot of things. An uneasy conviction that things just weren't adding up was not going to answer questions the Bench had a right to ask him about piracy and murder.

The floor manager, Dalmoss, was standing behind his desk as Hilton stepped into the open doorway. It looked as though he were packing. Hilton rapped sharply at the doorjamb with the curled knuckles of his left hand, to alert Dalmoss to his presence.

"You sent for me, floor manager?"

Dalmoss raised his head sharply, looking a little startled, then seemed to relax. "Shires. Don't creep up on a man like that. Come in, close the door."

The floor manager's office was just inside the small administrative area at one end of the new warehouse. Things were still unfinished. There was nobody else in the administrative complex—reception desk, foreman's office, storeroom and toilet all unoccupied; maybe it was just the draft Dalmoss wanted to shut out. Hilton shrugged mental shoulders and closed the door behind him.

"Are you leaving, floor manager?" Hilton started to ask the question, but it didn't quite come out the way he'd thought it might. The situation did seem obvious.

Nor did Dalmoss seem to take offense at any presumption on Hilton's part. "I have to go to Geraint for a few days, Shires, something's come up. I've asked the foreman to let you fill in on temporary assignment, and he's agreed. He's been very pleased at your progress so far."

That was a compliment, Hilton supposed, or at least it seemed that Dalmoss intended it as such. "Very kind. I'm sure." He wasn't sure, not really, what progress there was to impress anybody. He'd learned to tick boxes in array. That didn't take much progress.

Dalmoss grinned. "Not doing you any favors, really, Shires. You get to skip roll call because we expect you to be working early and late, but that's about it. Corporate practice. We'll work you for months under pretext of training before we get around to actually paying you for the job you're doing. Here, take this."

Dalmoss tossed something at Hilton, something small and light. Hilton caught it, curious: cylindrical, metallic, and the spider-brain that lived inside of it made its status lights sparkle. An identity chop.

"What's it for?"

It couldn't be Dalmoss's chop. Dalmoss was going to Geraint and would probably be needing his signature key. Even if he didn't, Dalmoss's chop was no good to anyone but Dalmoss; identity chops were tuned to the genetic markers in a person's sweat and skin, so that no one but Dalmoss could use his chop, not and get a seal. So it wasn't Dalmoss's chop.

"Backup release marker," Dalmoss explained. He'd dropped his voice, and was looking past Hilton to the door of his office—to make sure it was closed, Hilton supposed. "I don't like taking it off-site. Just hang on to it, Shires; you won't be asked to use it for anything, just make sure you keep track of where it is until I get back."

Backup release marker? "I don't want to be difficult," Hilton protested. "But I'm a little uncomfortable. My status, and all that. Are you sure it's a good idea to leave it with me? Why not the foreman?"

It wasn't an identity chop, it was a corporate marker, used to sign off on documents releasing ships and cargo. Authorizing movement of freighter tenders from surface to orbit. Clearing a pilot to take a ship and go.

Langsariks weren't to have access to such things.

Dalmoss came around from behind his desk to stand close to Hilton, speaking quietly and quickly. "We had to have the second one made when the foreman was injured at Okidan. But we got busy, I never got around to the documentation, you know how it's been around here. And the foreman doesn't want to know about it."

Oh, good.

Not only was it a violation of the amnesty for Hilton to be in possession of a backup release chop.

It was contraband in its own right, as well.

"Listen, floor manager, I appreciate the trust reposed and all that, but I really don't know if I can be comfortable holding on to this."

Undocumented backup release marker.

Black-market value, one full freighter load of dried confer wood, great thick fragrant bales of the stuff. A fortune for any man, let alone a disenfranchised Langsarik.

"It'll be all right." Dalmoss gave Hilton's shoulder a friendly reassuring shake and turned him toward the door. "The administrative stuff is in process, it's just a little behind, is all. I'll make it right with the foreman when I get back. And it's not a problem for you to have it, so long as you don't use it, that's all."

Feraltz didn't want to know about it, Dalmoss said.

Did that imply that Feraltz knew, and was politely ignoring the whole thing till the documentation was completed?

Maybe it was all right.

It wasn't as if there was any real danger of Hilton using the chop to lay hands on unauthorized transport, after all. And what did the terms of the amnesty say? Not that Langsariks were absolutely forbidden potential access; just that they were not to take advantage.

At least that was one way to interpret it.

"Well." If the foreman knew, Hilton felt it would be unnecessarily prudish of him to insist on the letter of the administrative regulations. "So long as the documentation is in work. I suppose." It couldn't be a real secret, then, not if the covering documentation was in process. A little irregular, maybe, but trade seldom ran precise to specification. "I'll hang on to it for you till you get back. What else, floor manager?"

The whole issue of the backup release marker was apparently so negligible to Dalmoss that Hilton's agreement was taken in stride, as only natural. Hilton felt himself relax a little bit more. Yes. It was all right. There was no cause for concern, it was just one of those administrative mismatches. That was all.

"I need you to take the floor meeting at second shift, the assignment matrix is posted to your reader, and I'm loading some notes. They'll be ready for you by the time you get back from the floor meeting, we can do final tie-in then. You'd better hurry."

It wouldn't do to be late for his first official acting-floor-manager assignment. No.

Tucking the little token into a shirt pocket absentmindedly, Hilton hurried out for his meeting, focusing his mind on the new challenges that had just been laid before him.

Once Cousin Stanoczk's sleek little courier had cleared the Tyrell Yards for Port Charid, Cousin Stanoczk sent his relief pilot forward and called for Kazmer Daigule. There were two to three hours of travel time between the Shawl of Rikavie and Port Charid from the Tyrell Yards, at this time of year. Garol supposed Stanoczk wanted to talk in a secure environment.

When they were all assembled in the courier's salon Cousin Stanoczk took a deep breath, and started to speak. "To your mother I apologize very humbly, Kazmer. And also to her mother, and her mother's mother; to the mother of your father, and her father's mother, as sincerely as I am able. I had no cause to suggest such a thing, but you made me angry, suggesting what you did. I tell you to explain, not to excuse the insult, for which I place myself in humility before your antecedents."

"Suggesting what? The Angel of Destruction?" Jils asked. She'd been quiet and self-contained since Daigule's outburst at Tyrell; Garol was surprised to hear her speak. Jils wasn't one to open her mouth unless she had something to say, though, and it sounded like she was ahead of him on this one. "I heard horror stories from the forensics team at the Domitt Prison in Port Rudistal. They were Sarvaw, too."

Now that she put it into context for him Garol began to make sense of it all. Sarvaw, terrorism, atrocity, the Angel of Destruction. Right,

"It is an outlaw, and has been for several lives."

Cousin Stanoczk was clearly not at all eager to talk about it. He could hardly refuse to discuss the issue once it was raised, however, not unless he wanted to focus their attention on the subject by so doing.

"Since the time of Chuvishka Kospodar, who was the grandfather of my grandfather's father. I have the family shame. Yet even at the time of its outlawry, there were questions, within privileged circles, about whether the monster were truly dead, or merely feigning."

"Start at the beginning," Garol suggested. It generally helped him make sense of things. "What's your angle in all of this, Stanoczk?"

Stanoczk had started to pace. The Malcontent's courier ship was considerably more commodious than Garol's usual transport. There was much more room in which to move.

"We were as skeptical of the Langsarik settlement as any, Garol Aphon." Stanoczk used two of his three names, Garol noted. Showing off that he knew them, perhaps? Stanoczk was obviously upset; maybe he was just reverting unconsciously to his natal syntax. Garol hoped Stanoczk regained control of his emotions soon. He'd never cared for his middle name.

"Therefore, someone was tagged to keep a watch on the progress of the experiment. The Langsariks were efficient predators, you may remember. We had no desire to see them continue to feed off Combine shipping."

Old news. Garol settled himself back in his chair, resigned to a long siege. Comfortable chair. The pilot didn't look very comfortable, though. Pity.

"Then there were problems, and it could have been youthful high spirits. Perhaps it was at first. The first of the raids where there was killing concerned us."

Hit-and-run raids were one thing, characteristic of Langsarik battle tactics. Warehouse invasion was not, nor had killing ever characterized a Langsarik operation. So far, so good.

"The Combine is in contention with other local interests for commercial ascendancy, here at Port Charid. Was it too convenient that the Combine's competition has been raided in series? And yet if there was a secret plot on the part of my government, I would know about it. I wouldn't tell you, of course. But I would know about it."

Interesting. Cousin Stanoczk might be a more highly placed player than Garol had realized; or he might be making this part up.

"Thus if there was no plan that we knew of, and yet events did seem to follow a plan to strengthen Combine interests at the expense of any others, who could be responsible? Raiding takes organization. And in this case murder."

"The Bench likes to consider itself responsible for that sort of problem," Jils noted, in a mild and dispassionate tone of voice. As if she was simply making an abstract and objective observation, not pointing out that the Bench saw no functional difference between lawbreaking and the unauthorized upholding of the Law, the upholding of the Law by persons not properly deputized to do so. "It has Bench intelligence specialists to work issues like raiding at Port Charid."

Cousin Stanoczk seemed to be trying to nod and shake his head at the same time, and ended up describing a sort of a figure eight with his chin. "But if this was Combine business, Bench specialist, it is our responsibility. We can't ask the Bench to intervene in family discipline."

Begging the question rather neatly. "Go on," Garol said. Maybe Jils had drawn her conclusions and filed her mental report, but he still wanted to hear Stanoczk's take. "Responsible."

"We are not so familiar as you with the Langsariks, Specialist Vogel. It could be that their styles had changed. What reason could Langsariks have to promote Combine interests, though, especially at the risk of their own lives and freedom? And then there were more raids. We began to see a pattern. One with potential historical precedent."

At that the pilot raised his head, staring at Cousin Stanoczk with black despair in his brown eyes.

"You knew all along it wasn't Langsariks." Daigule's claim was not so much an accusation as a flat statement. "And you let me give it all away. Knowing all along."

He seemed to hit a nerve with Cousin Stanoczk, even so. "We knew no such thing. I still don't know. There is potential evidence. Is it good enough for the Bench? Certainly not. What would have happened had I denied you, in violation of my sacred duty?"

Good question, Garol thought. "That's what I'd like to know." With Stanoczk here, it couldn't be said that he was going behind anyone's back. "If your evidence could divert suspicion, pilot, you logically would have wanted to give it." Which could presumably be exactly what Kazmer Daigule was doing even now, his utmost to divert attention from the Langsariks. "Apart from any personal vulnerability, your only likely reason for bolting has to be that your evidence would have indicted Langsariks."

"Because I thought it was Langsariks," Daigule said flatly.

Cousin Stanoczk started to raise his hand, as if to silence Daigule.

Lowering his head—so that he would be unable to see any such signal, Garol supposed—Daigule forged on. "I didn't know what to make of the rumors of killing; but I knew that if anyone got serious with questions, I was bound to mention Langsariks sooner or later. And I'd seen a friend of mine in the street the day I arrived to meet with the rest of the crew. If it really was a Langsarik raid, he almost had to be part of it, whether or not I ever saw him after that. If it wasn't a Langsarik raid, it was that much more vital to keep his name out of it. His, and that of any other Langsarik, including the name 'Langsarik.'"

Hilton Shires had known that Daigule had been in Port Charid, though he'd not wanted to say so. Garol understood. "And now you're sure it wasn't. Your evidence, please. If Cousin Stanoczk permits, of course."

Cousin Stanoczk had ceased his pacing to lean up against the bulkhead behind Daigule, folding his arms. Stanoczk said nothing, so Daigule answered, with evident eagerness.

"Everything points to Langsariks, don't you see? I was recruited anonymously, but there were hints. At every step, clues and indications. The raid party all wore pieces of Langsarik colors, nothing too obvious or overdone, just what you would expect. The Langsarik body is missing. But so is another body, and there's no sense in the murders. Especially not in torture."

Daigule's point presumably being that nobody could have so consistently given signs of being Langsarik and not been Langsarik unless they had been deliberately intent on presenting the impression that they were Langsariks.

First Secretary Verlaine was not likely to be convinced.

"It isn't evidence." Jils said the unpleasant truth for him, and Garol thanked her with a grateful glance. "As it stands it's just a coincidence. We can't even say if it's a real coincidence. The missing Dolgorukij may turn up somewhere alive and healthy. We need more to go on."

Garol didn't know exactly what would do it. But he agreed with Jils that what they had was not enough.

"If you blame Langsariks for these raids, the public may be appeased." Straightening, Cousin Stanoczk stood with his hands on his hips and a very determined expression on his face. "But it will neither effect the punishment of the guilty nor necessarily put a stop to the criminal activity if we do not correctly identify the criminals."

All right, they could all agree on that. "So what's your plan?" Garol asked. There had to be a plan. This Cousin Stanoczk was too devious not to have something already up his sleeve; so Garol wasn't surprised at Stanoczk's response.

"Work with me, Bench specialist, and every resource I command is at your disposal. It cannot be the Angel of Destruction. It must not be the Angel of Destruction. But if it is the Angel of Destruction, it must be stopped, and decisively."

Whether or not such action would place Cousin Stanoczk in violation of Bench direction.

Maybe the rule of Law could be stretched to cover an extrajudicial punitive transaction on neutral ground, in light of the fact that it was to be Combine against Combine . . . maybe.

"Can I get Daigule?"

Garol put his question to Cousin Stanoczk, careful to observe the appropriate protocol. "Bearing in mind that so far as I know this is still all just an elaborate ruse to protect Langsariks. Making no promises."

He had to be careful.

He wanted it not to be Langsariks.

He wanted it not to be Langsariks so badly that he could halfway convince himself that Cousin Stanoczk's wild talk about Dolgorukij terrorists made sense. It would comprise an explanation of sorts; but he'd have to review the elements with Jils in private before he could be sure that his own personal investment in the success of the Langsarik settlement wasn't adversely affecting his ability to weigh and judge.

Daigule started to speak, but Cousin Stanoczk spoke over him. Daigule shut up, looking surprised and a little sheepish.

"Daigule will offer you every cooperation at his command, so long as you respect his confidence. You may not ask him to name names. You must not use any part of his effort to incriminate the Langsariks. If the Langsariks are to be incriminated, you must find other means than Kazmer Daigule through which to do so. Kazmer, you will answer to these conditions, and say yes or no."

Who did Cousin Stanoczk think he was, to set limits on the rules of evidence?

A Malcontent.

It was galling to have to operate under such constraints, offensive in principle even if they made no functional difference.

Daigule nodded, looking first to Cousin Stanoczk and then to Garol. "If it's Langsariks, they know what they're risking," Daigule agreed, firmly. "But if it isn't, I'm not going to be the man who makes the case, just to cover the Bench. Yes, Cousin Stanoczk."

If they'd had this conversation at Anglace, they could have gotten Kazmer to do an interrogatory, saving themselves several awkward and unproductive days in transit.

But if they hadn't come to Tyrell Yards, he would still be struggling to gain access to Daigule, and Daigule's cooperation.

Maybe he didn't need an interrogatory.

Garol had a notion that he was going to want to stick close to Port Charid until he had an answer that he could be satisfied with.

"We'll start by retracing your steps in Port Charid, then." Now that Daigule had agreed, Garol didn't have to worry about going through Stanoczk, and addressed himself to Daigule directly. "Where you met with the rest of the crew, where you got transport, how you found your freighter. Be thinking about those things. Do your best to remember every detail."

They would be making planetfall at Port Charid very soon.

Hilton Shires had a scarf in his possession to be returned to Daigule; maybe a confrontation between the two men would shake something loose that would prove useful.

He was going to have to get back to Walton Agenis, to let her know the status of the threat to the settlement; and in the meantime he had damage control to conduct, with First Secretary Verlaine.

He wished more than anything that he had something more reassuring to transmit to the Flag Captain: but she trusted him, because he had been honest with her.

Whether or not the truth was something either of them wanted to face, he had to be honest with her.

Walton Agenis was weeding in her kitchen-garden when her nephew Hilton Shires peered over the short fence into the enclosure to hail her in the Standard fashion.

"Good-greeting, Aunt, how does the day find you?"

She'd been expecting to see Hilton. Sitting back on her heels, Walton wiped the sweat out of her eyes with the back of her hand, contemplating the tidy rows of tuber greens as she formulated her response.

"I'm well and doing tolerably, young Shires." It was a joke between them to emphasize the distance between nephew and aunt, though his father was her older brother. Her brother had gotten to be an old man, and could no longer weed tuber greens. It was a shame, because weeding in a garden had been one of the things she'd missed most, during the years of the Langsarik fleet's outlawry. "How's by you?"

Apparently encouraged, Hilton slipped the latch on the garden gate and let himself in. He had new clothes, she noticed; the collar of the undershirt that showed its crescent of fabric beneath his jacket was a generic white. Not rose gold. Going native. She wasn't exactly sure how she felt about that, though. Fitting in was good. Forgetting who you were and where you'd come from was not good.

"I've just come home with my wages for my folks. It's a decent job, Aunt Walton. They're talking about management."

He squatted down in the garden as he spoke, gathering the weeds into the wastebasket that lay at the head of the row. Hilton had always been good at making himself useful. "There'll be a lot of opportunity when the Combine's new warehouse complex opens. I heard Modice has gone to work for the administration out at the contractor site?"

His intelligence net was working. That was always a good thing. Walton smiled at the weeds, almost despite herself; she was as proud of Hilton—tall and whipcord-wiry and beautiful, intelligent and goodhearted—as though he had been her son, rather than her nephew.

"Shift scheduler, nights. They're keeping her busy."

Modice's new job had created some interesting byproducts as well. For one, there were fewer night prowlers and day callers. For another, some of the young people who had not quite nerved themselves up to go to work for outlanders had suddenly realized the dignity of honest toil—particularly at construction sites—shortly after Modice had gotten a job at the construction site. Modice had needed the distraction. Walton thought she was worrying about Kazmer Daigule.

"Um. I saw that Bench specialist in town the other day, by the way. What's his name. Garol Vogel."

Walton dug around the base of a sap-weed with her fingers. One needed to get as good a grip on the root as possible in order to pull it out. If you let the root break, the weed just came back, and seemed to be stronger than ever. Weed management was a near forgotten art among her fleet's crew, but the principle hadn't changed.

"Brought you a scarf, I expect. Were you able to return it? Because I'm absolutely not having that thing back. Not under my roof."

Reaching casually back toward a pocket on the back side of his work pants Hilton seemed to pause, hearing her warning, and think twice. Teasing her.

"Well. All right. I'm not sure it's safe for me to be carrying around, though. But seriously."

He'd picked up all the weeds that were there, so he joined her at the edge of the tuber bed to help her work. "Which ones? These? No. These. All right. I'm worried about Kaz, Aunt Walton."

He was worried, Modice was worried, why should Langsariks worry about any seventeen Sarvaw pilots? Daigule was a good-hearted man, and Hilton was fond of him. That was one thing. Modice being fond of him was something else altogether. "He was out here one night, courting your cousin. We haven't seen him since. You?"

Shaking his head, Hilton pulled a plant up out of the ground with a stern effort, only then seeming to notice that he'd pulled the wrong thing. Replanting it hastily, Hilton scowled at the dirt while Walton did what she could to avoid noticing the error.

"Once, in port. Days ago. Going on weeks. He had something on his mind, and I didn't want to talk to him. Pride. I was nervous about my job interview."

The tuber was back in the ground. It would survive. Now that

Hilton knew by experience which plant not to pull he would be that much more efficient, and that was all to the good.

"What do you mean, something on his mind. Worried?"

Hilton seemed to think about this, pulling weeds. The right ones. He had a good grip on things when it came to roots, Walton noticed.

"Not so much worried. He was dropping hints about his job. I didn't care, and he got irritated at me and left. Now I wish I knew more about what he was doing here."

Or, maybe not. Of course that was the whole problem, right there. "I can't see that man mixed up in the sort of trade they've been talking, about lately." Hilton would know what she meant. As hard as it was for her to say something nice about a brash young outlander, she had to be fair. "He's not a killer. Still less a murderer."

Brushing the dirt away from the roots of his latest conquest, Hilton held the weed up to the sky and squinted at it. "Here's my worry, though. Suppose he thought I was bald-facing him. Suppose he thought I'd hired him."

Yes, it was in fact a weed. Hilton tossed it over his left shoulder and rocked forward onto his hands and knees to seek out his next target. "Because if if if, we might have learned something. Something that might be important for a person to know."

Or, maybe not, as before. The dirt around one of her tubers had gotten kicked up as she pulled a weed; Walton patted the earth back down around its roots, thinking.

"What did you tell Vogel?"

Hilton shook his head. "I didn't have anything to tell Vogel. All right, I know about the problem Cheff's had with the bottling plant, but that's just hooliganism. There isn't anything to tell Vogel. You?"

His job had been keeping him very busy; he'd probably had to delegate some of the intelligence work. But he was a good intelligence officer, was her nephew. He would still have heard anything that might be important.

"About the same." So they both knew there was a problem. The Bench might lie to the public about raids on warehouses for obscure Bench purposes of its own. But Vogel would not come and ask her about it if it hadn't happened. "There's gossip, I expect."

Hilton nodded, grinning. "Oh, yes. We're much more dangerous people than we ever realized, Aunt Walton. But people do half-believe murder of us, and I don't care for that."

Nor did any of them.

Vogel would figure it out.

If Vogel didn't figure something out—they had more than just a problem; they had a potential crisis on their hands. That meant that she needed to think of some way, somehow, that they could protect themselves.

It was not going to be easy. The Bench had their transport, their weapons, their star charts, their communications equipment, their everything.

All they had was Langsariks.

It would have to do.

"There's this row left to finish, then you can start in on the next."

Walton dusted off her hands and stood up, thinking. "I'll send someone out with a drink of water in a bit. Come into the house when you're finished here, and I'll tell you what you can do next."

The muster net had been set up upon their arrival, and tested periodically since. It was time to make sure that the communications network was absolutely up-to-date. Just in case they needed to pass information in a hurry.

If they waited until they needed it, it would be too late.

"Aunt Walton, I'm on my day off. I was going to have a nap," Hilton protested. But it wasn't a serious complaint.

Leaving Hilton to the garden, Walton Agenis went into the house, to set the cultivation of the Langsarik self-defense communication network into order and get the weeding done while there was time.

CHAPTER SEVEN

Fisner Feraltz had gotten the word as soon as the Bench intelligence specialists docked in Port Charid. He'd hurried to Factor Madlev's office immediately. The priority transmit equipment the Bench specialists would be wanting was secured in Factor Madlev's office-safe within the jurisdiction of the Combine Yards, where Factor Madlev could provide oversight and regulation.

He barely had time to get settled and launch the report he'd brought to cover his errand when his quarry arrived: Bench intelligence specialist Garol Vogel, all right, coming into the room with a kind of focused determination that seemed to give him more momentum than mere mass and velocity could impart.

"Excuse me, Factor Madlev," Vogel said. "Feraltz. If you would be so kind. I'd like to engage priority transmit, I'll have to ask you to step outside for a moment or two."

Vogel hadn't called ahead; his visit was unannounced, and Factor Madlev was inclined to stand on his dignity a little. Fisner started to gather his documents up immediately, taking care to drop the odd document to the floor as he did so; nothing too obvious, of course, but Factor Madlev took the hint as though it had truly been his idea.

"I protest, Bench specialist," Factor Madlev said mildly—but he had not stood up when Vogel entered the room. "My foreman is my second-in-command, as it were, my proxy. I need hardly point out his very personal interest in your investigation; surely he can be trusted to keep a confidence?"

814

Fisner said nothing, continuing to collect himself. He didn't have to overact to make the point about how awkward it was for him to get around in the medical bracing. The awkwardness was genuine enough; the challenge was precisely how to avoid overplaying it.

"It's rather difficult for him to get out from the new warehouse to see me, I'd rather he were allowed to stay," Factor Madlev added, in a rather more ingratiating tone of voice. Vogel seemed to consider, watching Fisner packing, chewing on the left corner of his lower lip.

His decision when made was expressed abruptly and ungraciously, but Fisner didn't take it personally. Vogel was clearly absorbed in his own issues, and meant no particular offense. "Very well. Feraltz, this communication is Bench-restricted, not to be discussed. Factor Madlev, if you would do the honors, please?"

Bench-restricted. Fisner felt a little thrill go through him at the phrase. He wouldn't be hearing anything truly sensitive; if Vogel had had something important to say he would have summarily excused Factor Madlev as well as Fisner. But Fisner would get to hear the status of Vogel's investigation up front. It would save time and effort as he analyzed the movements of his antagonist.

Factor Madlev engaged the security web that shielded the walls and coded his secures into the priority-transmit apparatus. Then he gave Vogel the nod; and Vogel spoke clearly and carefully, so that the encoders could perform their voice confirms and clear his signal.

"Bench intelligence specialist Garol Vogel, for the First Secretary. Chilleau Judiciary. Priority transmit."

First Secretary Verlaine. Chilleau Judiciary would act as the Angel's weapon against the Langsariks. The Bench specialist would be the man to set the wave of destruction in motion.

"Stand by for Chilleau Judiciary, Specialist Vogel. Signal is clearing."

It was getting dark in Factor Madlev's office. The lights were still running on summer-cycle; though the sun was going down, the lights had not come on yet. The weather was turning as well. It was getting colder day by day, and the stiffness of his medical bracing was an increasing source of annoyance to him—one he welcomed for such use as he could make of that annoyance, as in this present instance.

"Signal is cleared. Specialist Vogel, I have the First Secretary, Chilleau Judiciary. Bench concern security in effect, go ahead please."

"First Secretary? Bench specialist Garol Vogel here. We've just come from the Tyrell Yards."

"Do you have a status report, Specialist Vogel?" That would be the voice of First Secretary Sindha Verlaine. Fisner felt a thrill go up his spine; this was his man, the one who would order the dissolution of the settlement and the dispersal—death, and slavery—of the surviving Langsarik pirates.

"Looks bad from Tyrell Yards, First Secretary." Specialist Vogel's tone of voice was mild and considering, almost neutral. Fisner was impressed at any man who could remain neutral after viewing the carnage at the Tyrell Yards. He hadn't seen it himself; but he'd heard Dalmoss's report. He could imagine.

"That tells me nothing, Vogel. I'm not exposing the Judge to public criticism on a 'looking bad.' What have you got that I can use?"

No, naturally the First Secretary would be sensitive about the Second Judge's position. There was the memory of the scandal at the Domitt Prison to take into account. Chilleau Judiciary would need persuasive evidence to show the media in order to justify the dissolution of the settlement; that was why those people at Tyrell had been tortured. Why those people at Honan-gung were going to be tortured.

One documented atrocity was as good as eight indications of unrest or possible infractions of amnesty. If the atrocity were grim enough, it didn't even have to be clearly Langsariks to be convincing. That was how mob psychology worked; Fisner was counting on it.

"What we haven't got is a body, First Secretary. The staff listing names a Langsarik warehouseman on staff and on duty at the Tyrell Yards, and there's no Langsarik corpse. The implications are obvious."

Fisner glanced quickly to the floor, in case any hint of an internal smile of satisfaction should show in his eye. Precisely so. No Langsarik body. Conclusion, Langsarik raid. Negative evidence would do in the absence of eyewitness testimony. There was eyewitness testimony to the Okidan raid after all—his. Carefully qualified, so as to avoid being so obvious that it might raise questions in someone's mind by its very clarity.

"But you'll find the body, Bench specialist. Dead or alive. I'm sure of it."

Fisner wondered whether the note of grim amusement he thought he heard in the First Secretary's voice was really there, or just his imagination. Vogel bowed slightly toward the priority-access channel's portal on Factor Madlev's desk as he replied.

"We'll mount a quiet search, of course, First Secretary. There appears to be more than one body missing, so we have good hope of finding something."

Vexing. They'd noticed that Pettiche wasn't there.

Should he have done that differently? After all—to die in the service of the Angel of Destruction was to go to heavenly glory and eternal overlordship beneath the canopy of Heaven—

It was too late now. Pettiche had gone to Geraint in Dalmoss's place, with Dalmoss's identity papers—since Fisner needed Dalmoss to remain behind for the raid on Honan-gung. Pettiche had been gone for two days now. No, there was no profit in second-guessing himself; best simply to concentrate on the piece of the puzzle that he still held and leave the rest for later.

He held the Langsarik they'd taken off Tyrell.

Vogel continued. "The principal problem is that for all the talk of Langsariks, there's no hints as to how the Langsariks are supposed to have pulled things off. No missing crews. No unexplained affluence in settlement. We can't make it stick without some explanation, First Secretary."

Verlaine wanted Vogel to find the body; very well, Vogel would find the body, and if he didn't, it would have to be the result of determined avoidance, as cleverly as Fisner meant to arrange things. Somehow. He didn't know exactly how it was going to be yet, but the Holy Mother would guide him, as She had before.

"The public believes that the Langsariks can do magic, Vogel, evidence or no evidence. This is five within the year, and blood makes a strong impression on the minds of governments with merchants to look out for and collect taxes from. Things are warming up uncomfortably for the Second Judge. I'm promising a resolution soon, and doing my best not to define 'soon.' Any assistance you can offer will be greatly appreciated."

Fisner had assistance to offer, though nobody here could even guess.

If the First Secretary is getting pressure now, Fisner told himself with satisfaction, *just wait till the raid at Honan-gung.* That would put First

Secretary Verlaine into a position such that he would have no choice but to revoke the Langsarik amnesty. He'd have all the evidence he needed to back him up. After that the Bench specialists could leave Port Charid and go on to bigger, better, more important issues than that of determining exactly who was actually responsible for commerce raiding in the Shawl of Rikavie.

"Understood, First Secretary. That's all I have. Bench specialist Garol Aphon Vogel, away, here."

He'd be away himself as soon as he could be.

Now that Vogel was back in Port Charid the Honan-gung raid could go forward, just as soon as Hilton Shires could be convinced that he had intercepted incriminating and important information.

"Chilleau Judiciary off transmit. Closing session, clear."

The Bench specialist terminated the transmit. "Thank you, Factor Madlev, I'll be going. We have some investigations to conduct, but I have no information I can share with you at the present time."

"Just keep me posted as you can, Bench specialist, and thank you. Don't forget. Anything we can do to put your efforts forward. Anything at all."

Vogel nodded and left; Fisner prepared to continue the presentation he'd used to cover his presence here for Vogel's visit. It wouldn't be long; he was nearly done.

Then he had things that he could do to put Vogel's efforts forward.

And Vogel would never even know whom he really had to thank.

It was well past the end of his scheduled shift, but Hilton Shires had things to do before he could be comfortable leaving the day's report for the foreman in the morning. Floor manager Dalmoss had apparently spent as much of his time in administrative tasks as in supervision, and while this new warehouse complex was still far from finished, the foreman had started to move crates into the roughed-out warehouse on overflow.

They simply didn't have anyplace else to put the cargoes that were coming clear through to Port Charid now that they could no longer be accommodated at Okidan, at Tyrell, at the Combine Yards within the Shawl of Rikavie that had been absorbing the orphaned cargoes for months.

There were three freighter tenders on the airfield just then, and one under cover in off-load; where were they going to put all of this merchandise?

It had to slow down.

It had to.

The Combine's cargo-handling facilities were already charging a significant premium for the service, in an attempt to bring demand into alignment with the increasingly limited supply of warehouse space and cargo-handling capability. Making money hand over fist, in Hilton's estimation, because he knew what the Factor was charging, and for amateur handlers in an unfinished warehouse—well.

The second shift on construction had gone off; third shift was at the far end of the facility trying to get the rest of the exterior walls up before the winter rains set in. Hilton was alone at his end of the warehouse, walking from cargo tower to cargo tower as he struggled to locate all of the lots his record showed as having been off-loaded on his shift.

It was quiet where he was.

The far end of the warehouse complex where third shift was at work was out of earshot; though Hilton could see movement down at the end of the facility, it was only in a vague and generalized fashion. Quiet, and he was tired; only three more columns of figures to locate and he'd be able to sign off on the receiving report and log his duty roster and go to bed.

The dormitory building was still under construction as well, but he could sleep there free of charge and be accounted for when the midnight tally report was done. He didn't relish the prospect of hiking all the way back out to the settlement at this hour. It was cold out there, and since the roads were not well lighted, it was a little difficult to navigate over the uneven terrain at the side of the transit track without mistaking a shadow for a rock or vice versa, with adverse consequences for one's flesh and clothing.

The dormitory would be warm and dry, and Factor Madlev made sure there was always hot soup in the communal kitchen for people coming off-shift. So that was dinner, as well, and his wages on top of it—it was a good bargain all around.

If it hadn't been for the uncertainty that hung over the entire Langsarik settlement, life would be good. Factor Madlev firmly discounted the gossip, coming out very strongly against any loose anti-

Langsarik talk on his work crews; but there would be no escaping it until the problem was solved somehow. Someone was raiding warehouses and murdering people. Langsariks had been very successful commerce raiders. Not all the public support Factor Madlev—and Foreman Feraltz, and floor manager Dalmoss, when he got back from Geraint—could give would change that fact.

Weaving his way through the towering stacks of off-loaded crates, Hilton checked crate markers against his list, filling out his tally sheet. Almost there. Less than two columns left to check, and he had hit a good grouping, the crates on this aisle seemed to have been stacked in order by accident. It didn't always turn out that way. Hilton had almost wondered if someone had jumbled the crates on him on purpose, earlier in the day, as part of a scheme of petty harassment or something—or maybe it was just a form of hazing, on the part of the crew.

Or maybe there was no intention to blame for the confusion at all, and that had just been the way the crates had stacked. It didn't matter. He was almost done. And he got paid for his overtime, so he had nothing to complain about.

He stopped at the end of one long row of crates to tilt his tally sheet to the light and check his figures; and then he heard something.

It was dead quiet in this part of the warehouse complex; there was no wind that night, and while the raw construction did creak and moan a bit while the temperature fell at sunset, what he thought he could hear was not the groaning of a growing building talking to itself but someone talking to himself.

Or at least someone talking.

Raising his head to cast about for the direction of the sound, Hilton thought quickly, his heart beating faster with involuntary excitement.

There was nobody there.

No one was on shift for cargo handling. He made up the shift roster himself in Dalmoss's absence. He knew. Not even he was scheduled to be there, but he was running late; on any normal day he would have left the area, hours ago.

Someone talking.

Hilton opened his mouth to give a hallo, then closed it again.

No one was supposed to be there; and the sound didn't quite seem like a normal conversation, somehow, it seemed to be near whispered. As though someone was telling secrets.

He couldn't see anything out of the ordinary down the long row of crates in either direction; but he thought he could get closer to the sound he heard. He had plenty of shadows to help him out. The lighting was still strictly minimal, and so far overhead that the cavernous deeps between rows of crates were almost as good as a shield against detection—so long as a man walked carefully, holding his tally board close so that any telltale glare off the document screen would remain hidden.

Whispering.

At the far end of the next row, at the back of the stacks, next to the rear wall that separated the warehouse from the back end of the administrative offices.

Hilton moved slowly and carefully through the shadows, keeping his breath quiet and his movement smooth.

He reached the far end of the back stacks, and when he bent his head—carefully, carefully—around the corner of the crates that ended the row, Hilton heard the voices quite distinctly.

Buyer at Kansin, especially the larger pieces. Guaranteed.

The speaker wasn't at the back of the row where Hilton was standing, but appeared to be at the back of the next row; so that only the width of the aisle and that of the row itself stood between them, and Hilton had the shadows in his favor.

Lost the better part of our last take. Boss isn't very happy about that. Not happen again.

He couldn't hear everything. Bits and pieces of the words were lost in the great hush of the warehouse, muffled by absorption by the bulk of the stacked crates. What he could hear electrified him.

Shut us down sooner or later. Honan-gung. While we can. The arrangements.

Hilton eased his body carefully around the corner of the stack of crates and peered into the darkness across the circle, hoping that the whites of his eyes would not catch the light. Two people. One of them talking. The outlines were indistinct, and the voice was oddly muted or muffled. He had to get closer to hear what they were talking about. To hear the details, because it was clear enough to Hilton what they were talking about.

He had to know who they were.

*While we can still blame Langsariks. Can't have very much longer.
One month, two months, tops.*

Measuring the distance carefully in his mind, Hilton crouched
down slowly to set the tally board on the ground. He could clear the
space between them in four paces. He would have the advantage of
surprise. He could get one of them, at least, and then they'd have a
good chance of finding out what had been going on all of these weeks
at Port Charid.

The tally board made no sound as he set it down.

But something alerted the whisperers regardless.

Hilton gathered up his energy to make his move, but one of them
pushed the other suddenly.

Run.

He sprinted after them furiously, but they had a head start on him.
They were both good runners. They had the darkness on their side.

Hilton followed the sound of footfalls as fast as he could run,
spurred on by desperate fear of losing this chance; but the rows and
rows of crates echoed the sound and confused the track, and Hilton
had to stop at last and admit it to himself.

He'd lost them.

He'd had them within his grasp, and he had lost them, but he could
go to the authorities and tell them . . .

Tell them what?

That he had heard someone plotting a raid, someone who took the
blame for previous raids and exonerated the Langsariks by
implication?

He couldn't even go to the authorities. Maybe they wouldn't laugh
in his face, but there was no hope that they would take him seriously.
He wouldn't take himself seriously, in their position.

He needed more information.

Slowly, Hilton worked his way back to where he'd been to find his
tally sheet. He would come back with a light and check the area, but he
didn't have much hope of finding anything.

He had the tally to complete.

If a raid was being plotted, and the conspirators had met among
the stacks of cargo to confer, some one or more people who worked in
the warehouse were in on it.

Not Langsariks. No Langsarik would have risked compromising the settlement by missing report in these troubled times.

There were other people on the various construction crews, and someone would give him a signal sooner or later. They didn't know how much he'd heard. They couldn't know. They'd think he'd just happened on them, and knew nothing.

He would be watching.

He wouldn't rest until he had information that would give the Bench specialist who had come to end the raids the hard facts he would need to find the damned pirates, and punish them for murderers.

Kazmer had no documentation to show; the Bench had everything that the freighter had been carrying when it had been impounded at Anglace.

He didn't need documentation.

"I was here not long before the raid on the Tyrell Yards," he explained to the man behind the counter. "I've shaved my beard since, but I was with my principal. Noman, his name was. We came for a freighter tender to move some grain out of atmosphere, do you remember? The freighter tender was just being released to service after maintenance."

The man behind the counter kept his face carefully expressionless. "I can't say that I do remember any such thing." No, of course he couldn't, especially not knowing exactly who Vogel—beside Kazmer, but ever so slightly in the background—might be. Vogel was not in uniform, but it wasn't a good time to trust strangers in Port Charid, especially not in seedy little third-rate freighter brokerages like this one.

"I'll tell you one thing, though," the man behind the counter said, turning and reaching behind him for a ledger portfolio. "All of our activity is fully documented. Correctly documented. Anything we do we get proper clearance for. See for yourself, maybe you can answer your own question."

Whatever that might be.

"I expect the records all got a pretty good going-over, after the last raid," Vogel said in a genial and conversational tone, stepping up to the counter. "More excitement than anyone really needs, if you ask me." Vogel had turned to the section in the portfolio where the hard-copy requisition documents were kept. The ones that showed original approvals for release of transport.

The man behind the counter was too suspicious to allow himself to be drawn into the complicity of complaint. "We have nothing to hide, and it's just what must be done. Our books are always open."

There it was—the release order Noman had brought to this broker to obtain the security keys to the freighter tender Kazmer had piloted through atmosphere to rendezvous with the freighter they'd taken to the Tyrell Yards.

Vogel pulled the document away from its secures and laid it on the counter, turning to the back of the portfolio where the receipts would be kept. "Nice release seal here," Vogel said, tapping the mark. "Combine Yards. Fisner Feraltz, that's his mark, isn't it? I suppose you've already had this run through authentication."

The man behind the counter was agitated, but still wary. "No, why should we? There's been no challenge. No question. What do you think you're doing?"

Vogel had completed the hand receipt and passed it across to the man behind the counter. "I'm taking this document. You'll initial, of course, as witnessing that all the information is correctly filled out? Thank you. Oh. Here. Have a look at this."

Kazmer couldn't tell exactly where Vogel got it, but Vogel was holding a little flat chop in his left hand. Could have been up his sleeve. On his chrono. Behind a button. Anything. "Bench special evidence sigil, there. This one's genuine." Vogel set chop to receipt, and the electronic traces of the micro-circuitry it embedded in the fibers of the document's matrix glittered unnervingly in the flat light of the little front office.

Vogel folded the freighter-tender release and tucked it into an inner pocket somewhere. "If you're lucky, you'll never see another one like it. Thank you for your time."

So they were leaving.

The man behind the counter was holding the receipt up to the light, staring at the seal Vogel had set upon it. Kazmer closed the office door behind him quietly, reluctant to interrupt the man's awestruck concentration.

Vogel was standing with his arms folded, looking at people in the street. "That little courier," Vogel said. That was right; he'd told Vogel about the Langsariks' escape craft, the one with the contraband communications equipment. "Was that on the freighter tender? Or on the freighter you joined?"

"We transferred it with the grain," Kazmer replied promptly. "And carrying battle cannon, they said? The freighter tender's fuel burn did seem a little odd, now that I think of it. But I was thinking about other things."

Vogel nodded. "It'd have to be a sweet little piece of machinery to carry battle cannon. I wonder whose it is."

Kazmer knew.

But he'd almost reconciled himself to the fact that nobody would believe him.

It didn't matter so much in the end if they believed him about the Angel. Most of the rest of the Combine had never believed Sarvaw about the Angel anyway; it was hard for people to face the fact that such atrocities occurred. What mattered first and foremost was only convincing the authorities that whatever was going on in Port Charid was not the doing of Langsariks breaching the terms of their amnesty agreement. If only that point got through, the Angel could go diddle itself blind, with Kazmer's heartfelt blessing.

"Well, let's go see whether Feraltz has any insight on this. It appears to be his chop. Let's go visit the foreman, Daigule. Come on. Maybe could learn something."

But Vogel didn't start back toward the business district of Port Charid.

Vogel signaled for an auto-rent vehicle instead, and told the navigation unit—once he and Kazmer had gotten in—that he wanted to go out to the new construction south of Port Charid, where the Combine interests were building a new cargo-handling facility.

"Heard Feraltz was out on-site by default when I ran into him yesterday at the Factor's office," Vogel explained, once the vehicle was under way. "Lots of activity out there. Probably best if we don't call him away from his job."

Probably best if they caught him off guard and by surprise, Kazmer decided. Vogel had no reason Kazmer could imagine for suspecting Fisner Feraltz of anything; it was probably just second nature for Vogel to plan to his advantage.

Kazmer had reasons to suspect Madlev's foreman, whether or not anyone would countenance them.

Madlev's foreman was Dolgorukij, and the Angel of Destruction was made up of Dolgorukij.

Madlev's foreman had been at the Okidan Yards and lived to tell the tale, as well; surely that could be suspicious in and of itself. The people who had done the murders Kazmer had seen at Tyrell Yards were not the kind to leave a man wounded but still alive to call for help.

In fact it was suspicious.

Wasn't it?

Or was his dread and horror of the Angel of Destruction poisoning his mind, so that he saw the enemy around every corner?

Fisner Feraltz struggled to his feet gamely as Garol was announced at his office door in the administrative area of the new warehouse facility. Garol could appreciate the effort it took; still, a man learned to work with his bracing. So he'd been told. Wanting to get as fresh a reaction as possible, Garol reached into his jacket's inner pocket as he entered the room, shaking the document free of its folds to set it down directly on the foreman's desk.

"Good-greeting, nice to see you," Garol said briskly, though he wasn't all that interested in being polite. Feraltz's maneuvers to be present at Garol's report to First Secretary Verlaine yesterday had annoyed him; they had also raised questions in his mind. "Have a look at this for me. Your mark, here?"

There was no reason to suppose that Feraltz had anything against Langsariks, and every reason to suppose the contrary. Feraltz had certainly given an excellent impression of a man wishing to avoid the appearance of implicating the Langsariks for the Okidan raid. Too good an impression was suspicious in and of itself. Wasn't it just that touch too convenient that Fisner Feraltz had been Okidan's sole survivor—the sole survivor of any of these raids to date?

Precisely how had Feraltz survived the Okidan raid?

"It looks like my mark," Feraltz agreed, readily enough. "But here. For the record." He sat back down, carefully. Garol watched him sit back down. He didn't think Feraltz moved like a man fully accustomed to his bracing; and there was no possible reason Garol could think of for so ungracious a thought but sheer contrariness on his part.

Feraltz pulled out the chop that he wore on a chain around his neck and keyed its confirm mode before he held it to the chop mark on the document.

The chop jumped in Feraltz's hand, its static charge registering rejection of the chop mark on the document.

Feraltz frowned.

Pulling a ledger board from a side-table, Feraltz leafed through the document originals until he found what he was looking for. Setting the open ledger board down on the desk beside the document Garol had brought, Feraltz keyed the confirm code on his chop again and held it to the chop mark on the document original in the ledger board.

The chop sang out its confirm code, shrill and self-confident. So Feraltz moved it over to the document Garol had brought once more, slowly, as if not to interrupt the micro-computer's concentration.

The chop shut up abruptly and bucked in Feraltz's hand.

"Interesting," Garol agreed, but he was not about to take Feraltz's word for it, and held out his hand for the chop. Feraltz passed it to him willingly, which told Garol all he needed to know; but he went through the motions anyway, comparing the chop to one or two other chop marks on document originals in the ledger board, then back to the one on the document he'd removed from the broker's office.

The chop mark on the document that had been on file in the broker's office was not genuine.

Forged.

"Any surrogate chops authorized?" Garol asked, passing Feraltz's chop back. He didn't have much hope of it, really, so it didn't disappoint him when Feraltz shook his head.

"None authorized, Bench specialist. I leave this one with Dalmoss whenever I leave Port Charid just so we don't get into that situation. Sorry. Is it important?"

Feraltz knew it was important.

Garol was increasingly convinced of that fact.

But he had nothing on which to base his suspicions.

"Maybe. Hard to tell. Where is Dalmoss, by the way."

Dalmoss had the chop while Feraltz was away from Port Charid, so Dalmoss had it when the Tyrell raid was being planned. Maybe. Had Feraltz been back to Port Charid by then? He could find out—but he didn't feel like simply asking, he was frustrated and starting to feel like somebody was leading him on a merry chase.

Some Dolgorukij.

Feraltz?

Or the Malcontent?

Garol had already marked out a block of time in his mental scheduler for when this was all over, in which to become deeply disturbed about the Malcontent. People like Cousin Stanoczk didn't come up out of nowhere. If there were more like him at home, there was trouble in store for the Jurisdiction's Bench when the day came that the Dolgorukij Combine decided to flex its economic muscle.

"Gone to Geraint on a special assignment," Feraltz answered, sounding apologetic. "Sorry. We could call him back if you needed him, Bench specialist."

No, he'd have someone speak to Dalmoss at Geraint.

And he needed to get an analysis of the forged chop on the freighter tender's release document. Folding the document carefully, Garol tucked it away once more. "Quite all right. Thank you for your time, Foreman, I'll see myself out."

What was the wilder claim?

That some ancient secret terrorist society was resurgent at Port Charid for no better reason than to destroy the Langsarik settlement?

Or that a man who owed his life to the Langsariks should be involved in planning a frame so massive and ornate that it staggered the imagination—and was willing to countenance the torture killing of sixteen upon sixteen of souls just to pin the blame on his once-benefactors?

Garol had seen irrational behavior before in his life. But there was something going on here that was beyond irrational.

It was going to be that much more difficult to make sense of it; and if he could not make sense of it, the Langsariks were doomed.

Hilton Shires came across the comer of the administrative complex at one end of the new warehouse facility with his checklist in his hand, intent on getting through the morning's receipts by the end of his shift. He was tired, but he was beginning to feel as though he understood what he was doing and why he was doing it the way he'd been taught. That was a good feeling. If it hadn't been for the problems that faced his family—his immediate family, along with all of the rest of the Langsariks—he would have enjoyed the learning in its own right.

As it was he could not relax and concentrate on inventory management.

It had been three days since he'd overheard someone plotting an attack, and he had nothing to show for his after-hours sleuthing but frustration and anxiety.

Halfway into the administrative area Hilton happened to look up from the tally screen in his hand to check on his exact location, so as to avoid knocking into people, to be avoided if possible even when he was in a hurry. But there was someone there.

Looked familiar.

A man standing outside the doorway into the administrative offices where Hilton kept a desk just inside. Not wearing a warehouseman's coveralls; leaning up against the inner wall with his arms folded and his head bent in evident study of the industrial flooring and the unfinished trim.

Looking for a job?

Waiting for someone.

And it looked a lot like Kazmer Daigule, but it couldn't be. Kazmer had been captured off an impounded freighter at Anglace, and stolen cargo taken from Tyrell with him. So clearly Kazmer could not possibly be here, free and whole, and waiting for someone outside the administrative offices of the warehouse facility.

"Can I help you."

Hilton raised his voice and hailed the waiting man, closing the distance between them as he spoke. He got more, and not less, confused as he came closer; because the man looked up at the sound of Hilton's voice, and it kept on looking so much like Kazmer Daigule that Hilton was beginning to really puzzle how it could possibly not be.

"The Bench specialist. Said you had something to give to me, Hilton."

Sounded like Kazmer, or like what Kazmer might sound like if his voice was being slowly strangled in the grip of some strong emotion or another. No, it made no sense. How did this person know Hilton's name? The reference to a Bench specialist was worrying—

"Sorry, help me out here."

It couldn't be Kazmer.

It was.

There couldn't be two people in the world with that exact same nose. Hilton stood and stared, stammering in his confusion. "Where did you come—how did you get—"

Kazmer looked awful: pale, worn, skinny. But it was Kazmer Daigule. "Long story," Kazmer said, his voice resonant with suppressed emotion. "Boring plot, though. I'm here with Specialist Vogel, you know him? He said."

Whatever it was that had happened to Kazmer it was terrible. The ferocious impact of Kazmer's fiercely contained grief was staggering.

Hilton thought fast.

Kazmer had been in Port Charid just before the Tyrell raid. Modice had been worried enough about what Kazmer might have been doing here that she'd used the Bench specialist to carry a message to Hilton, one that served as a warning. But something was wrong—if Kazmer actually had been compromised in the Tyrell raid, he would not be here now. But if he was free and clear of suspicion, what was the source of his evident anguish?

"Not on me, I'm afraid. The scarf. The sash. Whatever." He'd been afraid to carry it, for fear of genetic damage from corrosive radiation. A pattern like that was too perfectly awful to be truly harmless. "If you can tell me where you're lodging this time, I can bring it."

There had to be more at issue than the scarf. Kazmer seemed near tears; and while Kazmer was an emotional man, he'd never struck Hilton as maudlin. "Perhaps it's best if you just destroyed it, then, Hilton. A Malcontent has no personal possessions. And as much as I owe Cousin Stanoczk already, the additional burden of dealing with that scarf might be too much."

What was this, "Malcontent"?

Who was Cousin Stanoczk, and what did Kazmer owe him?

"Then what would happen?" He had too many questions, and Kazmer was clearly not going to answer any of them. It made Hilton a little angry, but in a sad way. He'd thought Kazmer was his friend. "You brought the thing for my innocent little cousin. If it's really so toxic as all that, what possessed you to give her the wretched cloth in the first place?"

"It was a joke," Kazmer said, and the depth of sorrow that the simple phrase carried into Hilton's heart hit him like a fist. "Just for fun. And if I try Cousin Stanoczk's patience, he might just cancel his protection, I suppose. Then it would be back to Anglace for me, and Ship's Inquisitor Andrej Koscuisko asking questions about the Tyrell raid, and who did I see at Port Charid, and could Langsariks have been involved. And what were their names. And murder done, Hilton; I didn't really believe it till I saw it for myself, but what difference does it make?"

The words came almost too relentlessly once they started coming. Concerned already, Hilton felt his face drain white with the shock of what Kazmer was telling him as Kazmer continued.

"I know Langsariks would never do that. I know that now. Langsariks were never involved from the beginning. It was all a setup. But it doesn't make any difference, I'm telling you. I thought it would help if I cried for the Malcontent, if I didn't give evidence. It hasn't helped. Stanoczk would rather it was Langsariks than who it is. The fix is too good. Nobody believes me, Hilton, nobody believes us; gather everyone you can and get out of here—get out of here now—"

Someone was coming out of the administrative area, and Kazmer mastered himself with an obvious effort. Bench specialist. Hilton recognized him.

"Good-greeting." Vogel nodded cheerfully to Hilton; if he'd heard any of Kazmer's mad spate, he gave no sign. "Well. No help there, unless that's help. Let's go out to the settlement, Shires, I'd like a word with your aunt. Care to join us?"

He couldn't possibly. He wasn't finished with what he wanted to get done today, and he didn't know how the foreman felt about floor managers absenting themselves on personal business in the middle of the day—regardless of whose suggestion it had been. Trying to put some polite words together, Hilton shook his head.

"I'd really like to, Bench specialist, but there's inventory yet to log, and—"

Vogel took Hilton by the arm and started toward the nearest exit door. "Good, good. Glad to hear it. The scheduled inventory will still be here, won't it? No freighter tenders for load-out tonight? Just work with me here, Shires, I'm not in a very good mood."

Oh.

Well.

If that was the way Vogel wanted it.

There was a hired vehicle on standby outside the warehouse; Vogel took the lever to guide the vehicle off the grounds, scowling in deep concentration. Or simply scowling. Once they'd cleared the construction site Hilton spoke; he knew how to defer to authority, he knew Vogel had authority, but Vogel's rather highhanded behavior had got Hilton's Langsarik up.

"I have a job." Maybe Vogel didn't understand how unusual that was—for Hilton to admit it, anyway. "I have responsibilities. There's no cost objective supported by home visits on duty hours. I expect a note for my foreman, at the very least."

Vogel didn't answer him directly.

He pulled off the roadway instead and turned around to face Daigule in the passenger compartment behind him.

"We have to figure out how to get it to make a difference."

What?

Kazmer just stared, and Hilton had no clue for his own part.

"I believe you, Daigule. I don't know about Cousin Stanoczk, but you convinced me. That means we have a serious problem, because the First Secretary can't take a hunch and a conviction to his Judge, and murder's been done. As you said."

Vogel had heard Kazmer, or at least enough of what Kazmer had been saying. Kazmer leaned forward and took the seat rail in his hands, as though to steady himself.

"They'll come for Hilton." What was Kazmer talking about? "They'll come for Modice. You know they will. We can't let it happen. We've got to do something."

As if Kazmer believed all the stories he'd ever heard about Bench specialists.

As if Kazmer believed that Vogel could set the Bench to rights by saying so.

"I don't know what we can do." It was too bad. Vogel didn't seem to have heard half the stories about Bench intelligence specialists that Kazmer seemed to have; he didn't sound the least bit confident.

Vogel being not confident was the worst thing Hilton could imagine there and then, with Kazmer Daigule in the car, once it was clear that Hilton understood what Kazmer was afraid of and how close they were to unimaginable disaster.

Kazmer was right.

They *would* come for Modice.

He would kill her first. Then at least it would be clean, and quick—

"Hilton's taking us home to visit with Agenis. I need you to go ask Cousin Stanoczk for a favor for me, so say what you need to say to Modice; she's worried you got mixed up in Tyrell, and you owe her an explanation. Hilton. Kazmer says it's Dolgorukij behind all this. I need to understand how it's managed, where they're hiding the communications equipment, what they're going to do next. We don't have much time."

Should he tell Vogel about what he'd heard?

"No help from the foreman?" Kazmer asked. It was as though there was so much to say, and so much to think about, that he could only deal with the most immediate issue. "You were hoping."

Vogel shook his head, steering the vehicle back out into the roadway. There wasn't much traffic going out to the settlement, mostly just the occasional delivery truck with stock for the small convenience store. "The chop was forged. Maybe Dalmoss knows about a duplicate, but Dalmoss has gone to Geraint, which is why I need Cousin Stanoczk to get to Dalmoss as soon as possible. Dead end. But I think he knows more than he's saying."

"Forged chop?" Hilton asked, startled out of conservative silence. "What chop is that?" He had the chop Dalmoss had left with him. He had it around his neck, as a matter of fact.

Vogel drummed his fingers against the steering lever thoughtfully. "Used to release the freighter tender to leave Port Charid with Daigule as pilot," Vogel said. "Right, Daigule? Claims to be Combine Yards. What, do you know something?"

Hilton felt sick to his stomach. It couldn't be the same one. Why would Dalmoss be connected with warehouse invasions? That was like parricide, in a way. Dalmoss was a floor manager. "Dalmoss gave it to me before he left, said it was his backup document-release marker, but he'd never gotten around to getting the authorizations all cleared. I didn't think the Bench expected Langsariks to be handling such things, but Dalmoss said it was all right so long as I didn't use it."

It had been a weak argument at the time, and it sounded weaker now. The outbuildings of the settlement were coming up fast; they were nearly there.

Slowing the vehicle to a crawl between residence buildings, Vogel frowned at the roadway, apparently considering what Hilton had to say.

"And we have only your word that you were given the chop." Vogel was thinking the grim equation through, from all appearances. "It's a set-up ripe and rectified. Give me the chop, Hilton, and don't say anything to anybody. I've got to brief your aunt, I'll let her know."

Hilton pulled the chop out from beneath his inner shirt, jerking at the chain impatiently. "What does it mean, Bench specialist?"

"Until we find more real evidence, it means nothing." Vogel tucked the wretched thing away in a trouser pocket. Hilton could only hope Vogel's pockets were in better repair than his own tended to be. "Daigule, keep it short, I need you back to Port Charid before too much longer. Let's go."

The midnight meeting he might have mentioned to Vogel had gone out of his mind, the warehouse whispers drowned beneath the crushing impact of this horrible realization.

Set up.

They were using him.

And all this time he'd thought that he'd actually been doing rather well.

He needed some private time to wrestle his emotions to the ground; and then he had to get back to work.

Part of the job was being able to do it without getting emotionally involved, but Garol had given up on that almost as soon as this Langsarik trouble had started. It wasn't getting any easier as he went along.

"I've been to Tyrell, and I brought Daigule back with me." Garol realized that he was skipping the normal courtesy of a greeting; Hilton's news had rattled him more deeply than he'd realized. Or else it was just that feeling that he got with Walton Agenis, of never actually ending a conversation, just picking up the threads after a longer than usual pause. "Daigule and I know where some of the transport may have come from, but it isn't enough."

Walton Agenis eyed Daigule a little sourly, but stood aside to let Modice through from the back of the house. "Come into the parlor," she suggested. "You can tell me all about it." It wasn't so much an offer as a demand, but she had a right. Garol followed her into the house without argument, leaving Daigule to speak to Modice at the front door—or not-speak to Modice. Whatever. Garol didn't care. He had other problems.

"All of the markers keep pointing back at Langsariks." Once the door was closed behind him he couldn't keep his anxiety to himself any longer, talking to Walton's back as he followed her through the cramped hall into the tiny front room with its three chairs and its one small incidental table. No lamp. There was a fixture overhead, but the dim light was almost worse than no light at all, to someone coming in from the bright sunlight outside. "But Daigule was there. He says fourteen, sixteen people at least, and the raid covered more than half a day's time. So if it was Langsariks, how'd they make muster?"

There were chairs, but Walton didn't sit down; nor did she invite Garol to be seated—not because he was unwelcome, Garol sensed, so much as that she was thinking too hard about his question. So he stood. Walton Agenis faced the blank wall at the south side of the small room, talking to the paint.

"We could find a way, Garol. But we haven't. We agreed to the amnesty, we mean to honor it." It was good of her to use the present tense, Garol felt; "mean," not "meant." The Langsariks hadn't given up on Jurisdiction. But he was almost ready to. "Is this the first time that any cargo has been intercepted?"

Garol nodded. "Right. There was an anonymous tip." Such things happened often enough; there was no reason to suspect it. Except that he was suspecting everything just now. "Jils has gone back to Anglace to run it down."

Someone had recruited Daigule, who knew Hilton. Maybe it had been a setup all along, and the cargo had been sacrificed to get Daigule's evidence of Langsarik involvement on Record—it wasn't the most valuable portion of the take that had been intercepted. Daigule's evidence was not on record; but Garol had the inside line on a forged seal, now, and Hilton had been holding it. The fix was so good.

"So, where's the other ship. They've got to be hiding those cannon somewhere. Probably illegal communications as well, for false positive identification." She'd spent a lot of time worrying that issue on her own, apparently. "But the traffic in and out of Port Charid is all freighter-driven. Very few craft as small as yours or that Dolgorukij's."

Few enough that Agenis had satisfied herself that the raider wasn't coming and going, apparently. "So the cannon are parked somewhere," Garol agreed. "We just need to find out where in the Shawl they are. Easy."

No, impossible. Locating something as small as a hardened courier with all of the space in the Shawl to cover would take a Fleet sweeps team a year or more, and Garol didn't have a year.

Walton shrugged, but it wasn't so much a gesture of dismissal as of frustrated despair. "Port Charid isn't staffed for long-term investigations, Garol. Everyone knows it's Langsariks. After a while that'll be all that matters. What are we going to do?"

She was not merely asking him to suggest a course of action. She was challenging him to make it right.

He'd promised her fair play, and she'd believed him; and based on his promise and her decision to trust his word, she had put the lives of five thousand Langsariks into the hands of the Bench here at Port Charid.

The Bench had other priorities than fair play.

The Bench could afford to sacrifice five thousand people to the rule of Law, especially if the public destruction of five thousand people would preserve civil order and prevent eventual disturbances that could easily cost far more lives over time.

The Langsariks were not very important lives when it came down to that. They had lived apart from their system of origin for more than fifteen years, they had become an embarrassment to the planetary government of Palaam. There would not even be much of an outcry.

Of course that was what the Bench had thought about the Nurail; and that had proved to be a miscalculation . . .

"We have another alternative."

It wasn't thinking of Nurail that gave Garol the idea. It was thinking of Langsariks.

Walton turned around to face him. "I'm listening."

Garol spoke slowly, feeling his way. "If we can find a way to force the enemy out into the open, we don't need to find the cannon—they'll bring the cannon to us."

It wasn't a very good strategy, but it was all he had. As he spoke, however, Walton's eyes sparked with a sudden understanding that heartened him.

"Entrapment," Walton said, with a cheerful bloodlust in her voice.

"I like it. It means holding out till frustration gets the better of the enemy, though, and he does something stupid. And if we can't straighten this out soon, the Bench will conclude that we've violated the amnesty, Garol."

He knew that.

"We'd better get it straightened out, then. I'll get a target analysis started. You get a list of places at Port Charid where I could hide a hardened sixteen-soul scout with the spine to deploy battle cannon. We don't have very much time."

He didn't know how much time there was. He only knew there couldn't be much more of it. The fiasco at the Domitt Prison would only increase Chilleau Judiciary's conviction that a satisfactory ending to the predation at Port Charid had to be demonstrated in a timely manner—whether or not it had any necessary resemblance to reality.

"Not good enough."

Walton Agenis rejected his facile response. Garol didn't respect her less for it; she was Flag Captain Walton Agenis, and she was responsible for her people. "Solving the problem is all very well and good, Specialist Vogel, but you've been working on it for ten days now and you haven't solved it yet. I need a contingency plan. What are we going to do if the problem does not get solved? Your suggestions, please."

He didn't have any.

If he couldn't convince First Secretary Verlaine that the Langsariks were not in flagrant and egregious violation of the amnesty agreement, the Bench would send the fleet to collect the entire population for processing: penal servitude at best—a death sentence, for those members of the Langsarik fleet who were no longer young—and the Bond at worst.

He had no contingency plans to offer.

He hated having to admit that.

"What was your contingency plan if the amnesty negotiations had fallen through, back when?"

Why couldn't he admit it to her, and leave her to factors more powerful than the will of one man to resist them? The rule of Law was the cause to which he had dedicated his life, and the rule of Law was not always fair or just.

But she had trusted him.

The confidence of a leader of the caliber of Flag Captain Walton Agenis was too precious to be allowed to slip away from him without a fight.

She made a show of thinking about it, and maybe she was calling some previously discarded alternative to mind. "Once the planetary government had denounced us we were running out of options fast. I'll grant you that."

That had been the death blow, though like many mortal blows its full impact had been felt only gradually.

In the beginning the Langsarik fleet had fought for recognition as a planetary defense fleet, in the face of the Bench's insistence that the existing fleet of Palaam's historical economic-competitor worlds be recognized as having lawful jurisdiction over Palaamese commerce. As long as the Langsarik fleet could hope for recognition they could look forward to the day when their cause would be won and they could return home as lawful citizens.

But once the newly installed puppet government of Palaam had formally repudiated the Langsarik resistance, they had no basis for a claim to armed resistance against an unfair and unacceptable imposition.

What else could the Langsarik fleet have done but seek an amnesty?

Walton Agenis politely declined to state the obvious, out of respect for Garol's position; but Garol knew the answer.

The Langsarik fleet could have continued to operate as an outlawed gang of thieves, facing capture and death on all sides and slowly dying of attrition until they grew too weak to run and could be captured, tried, sentenced.

Or the Langsarik fleet could have made a break for Gonebeyond space and tried to escape from Jurisdiction entirely. Now they could not do even that, desperate though it was.

The Langsariks no longer commanded the transport they would need to escape.

Had it been some subtle form of cruelty to place them at Port Charid, with the Sillume Vector so close—and yet so absolutely inaccessible?

"We'll find the raiders. We've got to. Let me know if someone comes up with a line on anything, anything at all. There are a Langsarik and a Dolgorukij still missing."

The longer he stood here casting about him for solutions, the more depressingly clear it became that there simply weren't any.

Walton Agenis nodded. "I will if you will, Specialist Vogel."

Bowing to take his leave, Garol turned around and left the room.

He had to get back to Port Charid.

If he couldn't solve this problem, more than just Walton Agenis would have just cause to regret that they had ever trusted in his word.

The Bench specialist went into the house with Flag Captain Walton; Hilton made himself scarce. Kazmer stood to one side of the front door with Modice in the doorway, wondering what there was that he could possibly say.

There was no question in his mind that anything he had done to protect her was the right thing, and only what he would do again and again and again if he had to. But the price—which had been difficult enough to accept when he had faced impending disaster at Anglace— was almost intolerable to contemplate now that he stood face-to-face with Modice Agenis, and her looking up into his face with faith and trust and anxious concern in her beautiful dark eyes.

"Hello, Modice, how are you?"

He'd expected never to see her again. He'd reconciled himself to never seeing her again. He could think of nothing intelligent to say. There was so much he had to tell her, and so much more that he dared not so much as hint at.

"I've been worried about you, Kazmer. There was the Tyrell raid, and you hadn't said anything about your cargo."

Direct and straight to the point. He could hardly bear it; his nerves were already raw with emotion. "But then you heard that there was killing, right? And you knew I'd never do such a thing."

He was lying to her. To Modice. What did he think he was doing? He was trying anything to escape connection with the raid in her eyes. Coward that he was. He couldn't lie to Modice. What difference did it make? He belonged to the Malcontent now. Malcontents couldn't marry, and some of them liked boys. The thought of some trifling liaison with Modice was unthinkable. She was too precious to be anything but a first, an only, a sacred wife.

Modice frowned, but her gaze didn't waver. "I was afraid you'd gotten mixed up in something that would get you into trouble. Why did you come back to Port Charid, Kazmer?"

Yes, what difference did it make? Her good opinion of him was immaterial now; so what could be the use of trying to maintain that good opinion, by lying to her? Better if he told her the truth, and let her despise him. Maybe that was it. Let Modice despise him; and then it would not make so much difference that he could never marry.

"It's a long story. But I'll summarize. I thought Langsariks were hiring me to pilot a freighter with stolen goods. Yes. It was Tyrell. Only one thing, Modice, if you ever loved me. If you ever thought that you could have loved me maybe if I wasn't so big and clumsy and stupid, and not Langsarik."

She slapped him.

Hard, and across the face, and there was a surprising amount of force behind the flat of Modice's beautiful white hand. Her once-white hand, tanned from working in the garden. He caught her hand as she raised it against him for a second time, and stared at it dumbly. Her fingernails were worn from physical labor, her knuckles roughened from work. Modice. Work.

"How dare you say such a thing to me." She was so angry with him that she almost wept; he heard the quivering in her voice. "How dare you."

He was at fault for his impertinence. She was right. He could claim some measure of affection from her, as due an acquaintance who adored her; it was improper to even hint at anything more.

"I'm sorry." His face stung where she'd struck him. "It's only this, Modice. They were all alive when I left them. I swear it, Modice, by everything I ever loved. Those people. They were alive."

"All right," Modice said. "But take that back. About being clumsy and stupid. No, you're not Langsarik, but that's not a crime. Take it back, Kazmer."

How could she even speak of two such disparate things in one breath? "It's true. It's important to me. Please. Say that you believe me, Modice. I'll never see you again. Maybe." Kazmer added the qualification hastily; he didn't want to extract her word with an appeal for charity, as a sort of parting gift.

"I believe you about the Tyrell raid." She seemed almost bitterly unwilling to admit it; or else she was still angry at him about something. "You're not a liar, Kazmer. You're just wrong about some things. What are you going to do now?"

Did she really believe him?

What was she talking about, wrong about some things?

"I'm probably going to Azanry. I guess. I don't know, it isn't up to me anymore, I've—taken holy orders. Hilton can just throw the scarf away, it's okay."

Holy orders. Well, he guessed that technically speaking the election of the Malcontent was just that. He wore the crimson cord around his neck; he stood outside the reach of Combine common law and Jurisdiction civil prosecution alike. Because he was answerable to a much stricter rule of obedience and submission.

"Is that the reason you haven't been back? I told you. To the front door. And to bring a gift for my aunt."

If he thought hard, Kazmer could almost remember her telling him that. It seemed so long ago that he'd seen her last that he could hardly believe it had been weeks, instead of years.

"I've been in custody. And then once I got out I had to do as Cousin Stanoczk said. So I guess that's the reason. Yes."

"And you say you'll never see me again. That's the reason for that, too."

Yes. "I was part of it, Modice, even though I didn't know they would kill those people. I was the one that promised the others that it wasn't going to be like Okidan, that the people we were dealing with were Langsariks, and Langsariks didn't do things like that. I've done wrong. I have to make it up."

As Kazmer said it something lifted in his heart, and opened his eyes.

He had done wrong.

He was obliged for reparations.

All of this time he had been so shocked at how wrong the raid had gone, so worried that he would implicate innocent Langsariks by default, so set on insisting that he had not done murder that he had not faced the truth that his heart knew.

His heart knew that whether or not he had meant it, whether or not he had been duped, whether or not he had been lied to, he shared the guilt for Tyrell Yards.

He had not been the one to cause the horror, but he had been part of making it happen. He owed the dead a contrite reckoning for his role—howsoever indirect—in their atrocious deaths.

He had not thrown his life away for nothing.

If he hadn't called for Cousin Stanoczk, if the Inquisitor had taken his testimony, his evidence would have been used against Hilton and the Langsariks. He would not have seen what he had seen of the carnage at the Tyrell Yards. He would not have understood that he was guilty of a crime for which atonement was necessary and required; he might well have died in willful denial of any guilt for the murders done at Tyrell.

Then the reckoning that was to come would have taken place in some other form, in some other mode of existence, when he would no longer have any understanding of why it was appropriate for him to suffer punishment.

"Well, tell Hilton," Modice said, and Kazmer remembered where he was. "He can bring the scarf back to me. If it's the last I'm to see of you. If you were part of it, you did wrong, maybe, but not murder. Oh. I'll miss you, Kazmer."

She wasn't angry at him, Kazmer realized.

She was fond of him. And grieved.

Clutching the front of Kazmer's blouse to her, Modice wept. Kazmer put his arms around the priceless treasure of her body and rocked her gently, too confused by conflicting emotions to have anything to say.

She had it exactly right.

He had not done murder, but he had done wrong.

She was a genius. As well as beautiful.

It was a good thing he'd brought that night-courting gift after all, because as garish as it was, she would have to smile in rueful disgust every time she thought of it or him.

There were worse ways to be remembered.

CHAPTER EIGHT

"There are security monitors in place at the Honan-gung Yards, firstborn and eldest," Dalmoss said respectfully. "The evidence of atrocity will be that much more persuasive. But we will have to be sure that our performance is flawless."

It was very early in the morning. The administrative offices in the new warehouse facility were still deserted; that was the only reason that Fisner could afford to speak to Dalmoss in his office. Dalmoss would be safely hidden away again in the courier ship concealed within an off-lined freighter tender well before the shift change brought any incidental traffic into this part of the warehouse.

There wasn't anyone on the day crews who was likely to recognize Dalmoss anyway—they were all of them new hires, by and large, Langsarik to a man—but vigilance demanded Dalmoss be gone before any chance meeting could betray his presence. The enforced inactivity was wearing on his second-in-command, Fisner knew; but the Angel tolerated no inefficiency and brooked no unwise gambles.

"Do we have a coverage map? With planning, the surveillance could be made to see only what we want on record." Dalmoss had plenty of time in which to choreograph his raid. Not that there was so very much time before the raid would occur; but Dalmoss had nothing else to do, and nobody to keep him company but the Langsarik they'd brought with them from the Tyrell Yards. The Langsarik was safely drugged senseless, though, and sealed in a life-litter. He would probably have had little by way of interesting conversation to offer under the best of circumstances.

"We have the security schematic, yes." So one of Fisner's men had left it for Dalmoss to pick up at the agreed-upon drop during the infrequent intervals when they could afford for Dalmoss to be out and about. "With respect, though, eldest and firstborn. It could be too great a chance to try to use the record. The more evidence there is on record, the more evidence there is for analysis, and perhaps discovery of the secret. We should rather have Jevan disable the entire system prior to our arrival, to be prudent."

Jevan was the Angel's man at Honan-gung, their on-site saboteur.

Dalmoss was letting his nerves get the better of him. "If there is analysis in the future, second-eldest and nextborn, what of it? It will be too late. The Langsariks will already have been dealt with, the raids will have ceased, and what better evidence of Langsarik guilt could there be than that once the Langsariks are gone the thieving stops?"

Nor would the Bench be able to tolerate the public scorn that would arise should they admit, even very quietly, that they had moved too quickly against the Langsariks, when they had evidence in hand to absolve them. So the Bench would not absolve them. There was nothing to worry about.

Dalmoss bowed his head in token of submission to Fisner's reasoning. After a moment he spoke.

"Your instructions for Honan-gung, then, eldest and firstborn."

Fisner had given it some thought. "How long has it been since Shires heard us talking, now? I have an idea for using our friend to put the play forward. You must stay well hidden, because he might recognize you, but I think the result will be well worth the effort."

Whether Shires had said anything to Vogel or not was not something Fisner knew. But he'd thought the situation through carefully.

The whole plan from the beginning was to let Shires incriminate himself by drawing Vogel into an ambush at Honan-gung. So if Shires told Vogel, they were on course with that plan; but if Shires kept the information to himself, it could only be in order to take some dramatic action on his own part—action that could be used to implicate Shires either directly or indirectly in the raid when it occurred.

Either way the game was well worth the effort of setting it up.

"I have the documents prepared, eldest and firstborn," Dalmoss said.

Good.

"Let's do the transfer tonight, then, second eldest and nextborn. That will leave a few days yet before Jevan will be ready for us at Honan-gung."

It would be good to be out of the bracing, even for just a little while. Dalmoss would be there to run interference in case Shires proved more fleet of foot than Fisner himself was, after spending so many hours of each day in self-imposed walking imprisonment.

It would not be long before the entire action would be completed. He could finally go back, then, back to his childhood home, and greet his surviving relatives, secure in the knowledge that the deaths of his family had been avenged.

Once he had accomplished the Angel's purpose in Port Charid he could go home an honorable and honored man, and be at peace at last.

He'd meant to get out early. Aunt Walton needed his help. It was frustrating to have to maintain the polite appearance of a normal day-to-day existence while others were working on exciting tasks. Maybe analyzing and cross-analyzing traffic patterns within and around the Shawl of Rikavie was not intrinsically exciting on the face of it; still, Aunt Walton believed that there was a murderer to be caught in just such a way.

Even his old folks were mobilized for the task.

So what was he doing here after dinnertime, yet again?

Running a cross-foot on some cargo on for the Okidan Yards, that was what, in response to the foreman's very distinctly expressed concern—a concern no less pressing for the fact that it had been transmitted to Hilton only third hand. Hilton had met Foreman Feraltz only the once; he knew what Feraltz looked like—bracing all over—but he hadn't really seen a very great deal of Feraltz since their first meeting.

Perhaps it was because of his junior and brevet status: all the more important that he not let the foreman down on recent cargo deliveries being held on behalf of the Okidan Yards. Okidan hadn't committed to rebuilding its warehouse facilities yet, but if trade was not to crash to a screeching halt for lack of a place to park the merchandise while it idled in search of a buyer, the inflated rates extorted by the Combine Yards had to be paid.

The least the Okidan Yards was entitled to in return for its payment of the premium on cargo handling in Port Charid these days was a careful and precise accounting for wastage and dwindling, as well as a reliable traffic report.

Hilton's stomach growled at him. He thought with longing of the hot soup that was waiting for him in the dormitory kitchen, but that only seemed to encourage his grumbling belly, so he put his hunger firmly to one side of his consciousness. Traffic report now; soup later.

It wasn't as though he was wasting his time there, not exactly. He was part of the vital playacting of normalcy, the critical window dressing in Aunt Walton's scheme to discover a raider while avoiding giving any advance warning before the troops arrived to make a spectacular raid. A legal raid. The raid that would provide evidence once and for all that the Langsariks were innocent of violating any part of the spirit of the amnesty settlement, and only very small and insignificant elements of the letter thereof.

Traffic report and reconciliation.

Yes.

But someone was singing outside the administrative offices. Hilton could hear the noise from his desk near the door—as far from the foreman's office as it was possible to get and still be in the administrative offices. Someone was out there in the warehouse singing a Langsarik love song too loudly and passionately for it to be a sober endeavor.

This was a problem on a number of levels. One, there was to be no liquor in the warehouse, and no coming into the warehouse under the influence of liquor—that was simple common sense. Whoever the singer was would lose his job if he was discovered, at least by anyone other than Hilton—quite apart from the potential curfew issues his presence there after hours presented.

Two, whoever it was could not carry a tune, and it was almost physically painful to hear such notes wrenched out of a perfectly harmless, basically innocuous, and certainly almost completely innocent tune. For the honor of the cultural heritage of the Langsarik fleet Hilton had to shut the drunkard up.

Then finally, whoever was out there singing was not inside trying to complete a traffic report and reconciliation. Was probably already fed and finished with the day's troubles. Had no business whatever being happy and relaxed and singing "Maid of the Forward Guns" while Hilton Shires was trying to get his work done so that he could get to bed.

Putting down his stylus and picking up a hand-beam, Hilton opened up the door between the administrative offices and the warehouse proper, careful to avoid making any unnecessary noise. The hand-beam was heavy and as long as his forearm and, apart from casting a bright focused beam of light, would serve as a satisfactory truncheon in case some drunk Langsarik wanted to fight. The longer Hilton had to listen to the murder of the song, the more he felt himself inclined to raise some welts on someone's head.

Where was that awful racket coming from?

The acoustics of the warehouse were unique; sound would either carry much farther than one would expect or not carry at all. That was why he'd lost those two men he'd heard talking in the warehouse the other night. He still hadn't quite made up his mind whether that incident had actually occurred, whether it meant what he'd thought at the time, and whether he should make an emergency trip to town to tell Garol Vogel all about it.

Setting off in a likely direction, Hilton stalked his prey, taking frequent stops to fix his direction in his mind. The topography of the warehouse changed on an almost daily basis as cargo moved in and out; that was why the traffic reconciliation was as complicated as it was, among other reasons. He didn't have any baseline mental grid to guide him.

But he was getting closer.

He could begin to make out words, and the occasional near miss of a melody.

Lovely maid that I adore. High-explosive rifled bore.

He'd learned the song as a child, well before he'd had much of any grasp of what the words actually meant. He had been just twelve or thirteen years old when the Langsarik fleet had taken its stand, and transformed itself by virtue of simple—and initially civil— disobedience from a commerce-administration fleet to a commerce raider. Pirates. Being raised on a pirate ship had disadvantages, but Hilton had had few complaints until now—when nothing in his personal history seemed quite so interesting and seductive as the idea of simply getting to bed before it was time to get up again.

Slinking down rows of cargo crates Hilton tracked his quarry. *Recoil knocks me off my feet, let me prime your mortar sweet.*

He was getting closer.

Because he was beginning to hear words between music. Whoever it was, was talking to someone. Two of them? At least only one of them was singing.

Let me help your expert gunnery, promise I'll max your trajectory. It was a very rude song really. And Hilton could see who was singing it.

There was someone sitting on the floor halfway down a long row of cargo crates, half in the cone of light from the shelf spot, half-concealed in the shadows. Langsarik leggings. Very worn boots. Waving a sheaf of papers clutched in one hand as though keeping time, but not keeping any sort of time at all. His companion was more centrally seated, well within the light cast by the shelf spot; but Hilton couldn't see his face. Passed-out drunk, to judge by the body language.

How should he approach this?

He could rush them. They had no business being there if they weren't part of a normal work shift, and if they were part of a normal work shift, he'd know. They had no business being there drunk, either, but since they were drunk he could rush the one unconscious man all he liked without any effect whatever, while the singer was so drunk that the effect of being startled would probably only leave them all with a mess to clear up off the flooring.

People frequently got confrontational when they were drunk.

No, it would be best to approach these people calmly and slowly, and get them out before anyone else noticed them. Recriminations and lectures could wait till they were sober. First things first. He was going to need the cooperation of the singer to move the unconscious companion; a friendly approach was clearly the more productive of his options.

Switching on his hand-beam, Hilton cleared his throat, sauntering slowly down the aisle as though he hadn't seen the two drunks in his warehouse. He could be the night watchman; except, of course, that they hadn't hired one yet. It didn't make much sense to pay for a guard in a warehouse that couldn't really be said to be secured anyway, especially as nobody really knew what was in which crate where.

"Haberdashery, convoy smashery, I'll show you some fancy danshery—"

Very drunk.

This called for more drastic measures. Hilton started to whistle as he walked, swinging his hand-beam from side to side to create as much visual noise as possible.

It finally seemed to work.

"Hsst." The singer finally shut up—singing, at least. "Makile. We've got to shift. Come on, come on."

No reaction from friend Makile. Too drunk, maybe.

Hilton closed the distance, swinging his hand-beam and whistling.

The singer continued to pound the inert body of his friend, his fistful of papers crumpling with every increasingly frantic blow. "Come on, Makile, let's get moving, now, you know we have curfew, mustn't violate the amnesty."

Nope.

No luck.

Hilton was close enough now to call out a friendly greeting. After all, who could really blame someone for taking shelter in the warehouse when he found himself at a temporary disadvantage? The man was right; there was a curfew. It was a pretty flexible curfew, but drunk and disorderly would emphatically violate it.

"All right! Company! Say. How about a sip of whatever it is you've been drinking? A man can get thirsty, walking night shift."

The singer pummeled his companion with one last desperate gesture, papers flying.

Then he took to his heels and fled, while Hilton watched him go with amused resignation.

Well, there was one down. One to go. It looked like he was going to handle the sleeper himself.

Hilton eased himself down to the ground next to the singer's silent partner, wondering what to do now. "So. What're you having."

No.

Something was wrong.

It was cold on the floor of the warehouse and no warmth came from the inert body beside him. Hilton felt the hairs on the back of his neck prickle with dread and horror and pushed himself away from the unbreathing body, hands to the floor.

Unbreathing?

He had to check.

Setting the hand-beam down on the floor where it could illuminate some of the shadows, Hilton approached the still body that lay propped up against the crates.

No life.

No breathing.

Legs stiff, because he was dead; with the light shining on his face, the unnatural paleness of a countenance from which the normal blush of circulation had departed was too clear and too horribly unambiguous. Hilton had seen dead people before. There was no mistaking the chalk white putty of light-colored Langsarik skin when blood had ceased to color and warm it because the heart had stopped pumping.

Dead.

But there was no smell of liquor on him.

Perplexed as well as shocked, Hilton sat back on his heels to look at the dead man's face. Did he know this person? Langsarik by the looks of him, but no one Hilton thought he recognized.

He cast about behind him with his hands, meaning to shift his rump from his heels to the floor so that he could contemplate this situation more in depth and needing to set his palms to the floor behind him for bracing as he moved his center of gravity.

He set his right hand flat on a piece of paper that slid under the pressure, destroying any chance Hilton might have had of keeping his balance. He fell over backwards and knocked his head against the hard warehouse floor with enough force to jar the curse he meant to speak on the slipping of his hand out of his mouth entirely, unspoken.

Lying on his back, staring up into the blackness of the warehouse's rafters high above, Hilton caught his breath and composed himself. He was holding something in his right hand—he'd tightened his fist around the piece of paper, clutching for a handhold as he slipped. He brought his hand up in front of his face and turned the piece of paper front to back in his fingers.

Just a scrap of paper, really.

Poor quality, waxy finish, no wonder it had slid so easily. Marked in a fine bold hand. Trajectory calculations for a vector transit.

Hilton sat up slowly, his head spinning. What would any Langsarik be doing with a trajectory calculation?

There were other pieces of paper, fragments apparently abraded or torn while the drunken singer had beaten his friend in his unsuccessful attempt to rouse him. Hilton could read what was there, though. It was unquestionably a vector calculation of some sort, but it was maddeningly incomplete: the angle of approach was not specified, nor the point of departure. The only thing Hilton could tell with confidence was that the calculation was for an approach that started no closer to Port Charid than the Shawl of Rikavie.

Exactly where, in the Shawl of Rikavie?

A dead man, a drunk companion with a handful of notes. Too much celebration, perhaps. Celebrating what? Finalization of plans for the next "Langsarik" raid on warehouses in the Shawl of Rikavie?

This was not evidence which reflected well on Langsarik claims of innocence.

Until he had consulted his elders, he could not call in the Port Authority. It was too risky.

Hilton gathered the scraps of paper up and folded them into his blouse. The dead man could wait. Hilton dragged the corpse into a dark and very narrow space between cargo crates and marked his position with the hand-beam so that he could be sure of finding it again.

His duty was clear: he needed to go see Aunt Walton and let her know about the overheard conversation that he had happened to interrupt. About this.

Then she and he could go together to put these findings before Bench specialist Garol Vogel, in Port Charid.

Garol Vogel woke up in the middle of the night because there was someone at the window coming in, and it was cold.

Startled awake, his physical twitch was enough only to shake his brain into consciousness—not enough to alert the intruder, apparently. The window was still on its way open. Garol sat immobile, listening, watching; he'd fallen asleep in the room's one armchair, rather than lying down on the bed, so he was ahead of the game.

He heard whispers.

This is not a good idea, he's a Bench intelligence specialist, he can probably shoot to kill in his sleep and not even wake up until morning.

Garol thought he recognized the voice. He couldn't be quite certain;

voices were different when a man was whispering. The window was open enough to admit a body, now, and the intruder angled himself through the gap awkwardly, a little too tall for a high-bay bandit—or just unschooled in his art.

Vogel. Hey. Wake up. Don't shoot me. I'm friendly. Are you here?

The intruder was silhouetted against the ambient light from the night sky outside the rooming house. It wasn't bright, in the street, but there were clouds, and the airfield outside of town ran around the clock, so there was plenty of light hitting the clouds from the working beams on the airfield. It was enough. Garol knew his visitor, once he could put body and voice together. Hilton Shires. Walton Agenis's nephew and once-lieutenant.

And behind him?

Walton Agenis.

For a moment the idea of Flag Captain Walton Agenis breaking into his bedroom in the middle of the night was almost too poignant for Garol to bear, but he put the irrelevant fantasy away immediately. For future reference.

Maybe he's not even here, the bed doesn't look particularly occupied to me. Damn. We'll have to wait.

Walton Agenis, all right. Garol stirred where he sat slumped in his chair so that they would not be startled when he spoke. "That's just a rumor, about me shooting in my sleep. Bad idea, keeping loaded weapons under the pillow." If for no other reason than that was the first place people looked. "What can I do for you, Flag Captain?"

Shires had been visibly startled at the first sound of Garol's voice, his body language evident even in the low light of the darkened room. Agenis took it all in stride, however.

"First you cannot turn on any lights; we'd rather stay secret till you've heard the news."

Fair enough. "No problem on this side. You might want to close the window. And the light-drape, while you're at it."

She kept to the wall, where the shadows were deepest. Shires shut the window and closed the light-drape carefully over it; Garol was happy to see that he used the drapes as his cover. Thinking every minute, that Shires. Agenis's nephew for a fact.

"Right," Walton said, once the room was safely shuttered against the night. "Have a seat, Shires. Talk to the Bench specialist. Tell him what we've been doing tonight."

Was this something he really wanted to hear? Garol wasn't sure.

But Walton hadn't asked him.

"You may remember that I've been filling in for my floor manager at the new warehouse, Specialist Vogel." Shires had sat down on Garol's bed; just as well it was still made up from the morning. Climbing up exterior walls in the middle of the night was frequently a messy business. "About five days ago I overheard an interesting conversation, or part of it. I hadn't told you because I hadn't told anybody."

He'd get to the details when the time came. Garol let him talk.

"Then tonight I heard a pair of drunks. Well, really only one drunk. There were two of them in the warehouse stacks, and one of them ran away. The other one was dead. There are incriminating but fragmentary documents. But the really interesting thing is that the body got up and walked off while I was briefing my Aunt Agenis."

Quite a lot of information. Succinctly presented.

"I don't suppose there's any chance he wasn't exactly dead when you left him?"

Movement in the shadows, vague and ill-defined. Garol turned his head away to let his peripheral vision work; Shires was shaking his head. "Body was cold, skin clammy to the touch, face and hands bloodless. Apart from that he wasn't breathing. And had no pulse. Nobody's gone missing tonight that we know of, Specialist Vogel, we checked."

Garol knew what he would think in Shires's place. At least approximately. "Your analysis, please, Lieutenant."

Shires took a moment to reply. Apparently he wasn't as sure of this next bit as he would have liked to be. "Well. You can call me paranoid, Specialist Vogel."

No, Garol had called him lieutenant.

"But I'm clearly meant to think that I'm picking up intelligence by lucky chance. There's that other thing to consider, I already know I'm being set up." The forged chop, he meant, Garol supposed. "But they don't necessarily know that I know that I'm being set up. If whoever the enemy is was usually so clumsy as to let either incident occur, they'd never have succeeded in staying unidentified for so long."

Garol had to agree. Shires's reasoning was sound; in retrospect, happening on the detail of the chop had put them ahead of the game—because Shires had trusted him enough to tell him about it, when Garol had mentioned the problem.

Suspicion was highly subjective. However, Hilton Shires could be expected to be highly motivated to believe that he was privy to evidence that might clear the Langsarik name and save the Langsarik settlement. He might be excused if he didn't examine the lucky chance that gave him such valuable information too closely.

"Let's hear some of the details of your experiences. It won't be sun-up for hours, take your time."

Nobody would wonder if they heard noises coming from his room in the middle of the night. This was a decent rooming house, but it was a rooming house, and not all of its transient guests were reliable sober people or never wanted company at night. That was a part of the reason Garol was here, instead of insulated from the life of the port either on the Malcontent's courier or in one of the few more expensive lodgings Port Charid had to offer; he liked to be in the middle of life.

He was also much more easily approachable, here, if anyone needed to come and tell him something and didn't particularly care to be observed.

"All right. First. Days ago. I was working late, doing cargo reconciliation."

Still, Port Charid did have a curfew; it was a common tactic for a port with limited police resources. A curfew, and the bars were all closed; so who was making that racket, on the stairs? The bars closed well before curfew, so that people had time to get off the street. But whoever it was who was just coming home was very drunk indeed, to go by the shouts and exaggerated hushes Garol could hear coming through from the stairwell down the hall.

"Checking in the stacks. I started to hear voices. Nobody should have been in that part of the warehouse."

Oh good, the drunk was on this floor. And had a friend with him. Annoying; but no more than a petty irritation—the drunk would pass out, his friend would do the same, and things would be quiet again soon.

"I wanted to know who it was and what they were talking about. I snuck up on them. Two men, or two people anyway, talking. I wrote down the exact words I heard as well as I could remember them. But it was about fencing a cargo. Someone may have mentioned Honan-gung, but I'm not sure anymore about that."

No, the drunk wasn't in another room on this floor, the drunk was at his door. Hammering on the wall and calling to be let in. "Oh, let me in, friend, comrade, cousin; come on, I know you're in there."

Drunks made mistakes like that all the time.

But this drunk had a Dolgorukij accent; and—drunk as he seemed to be—he still spoke a dialect of High Aznir that was pure and sweet and beautiful.

Garol stood up.

"Company," Garol said. "Cousin Stanoczk. Malcontent. And, logically, Kazmer Daigule with him. What do you want me to do, Flag Captain?"

Walton Agenis spoke from the shadows, and her voice was clear and calm and confident.

"I want you to stop calling me flag captain, Garol; after all we've been through together it's insulting. Let the Dolgorukij in. All right, let the Sarvaw in, too."

Well, if she was going to be that way about it.

He'd better get Cousin Stanoczk out of the hall before he woke the entire hostelry.

Garol turned on the overhead light. It didn't shed all that much light, but it would be a noticeable anomaly if he opened the door with the lights still out. Out in the hallway Cousin Stanoczk was singing a song so purely obscene that it made Garol blush to hear it.

"Can't you quiet him down?" Garol hissed, checking the securities, opening the door. "People are trying to sleep."

Cousin Stanoczk fell against the door as Garol opened it, toppling into the room to fall flat on his face. He was carrying a full flask of something; Garol was grateful that it didn't break as Stanoczk fell—even while he registered suspicion in his mind over the fact that it didn't seem to so much as spill.

"Come on, come on." Hurrying Daigule into the room, Garol checked the hallway with a quick scan. No heads poked out of the other rooms. At least one door was ajar, though, signaling the interest of someone within who was listening—but reluctant to be caught at it. "Sorry about the noise," Garol said. "I'll take care of things from here. Thank you for your concern, good night."

He waited.

The door that was ajar fluttered, wavered, and finally closed; but with a very adept air of having been on the way to closed anyway, no thanks to you, sir or madam.

Cousin Stanoczk was sitting on the floor at the far end of the room with his back leaned up against the bed, his knees splayed widely in front of him and an expression of utter stupidity on his face. Walton Agenis had taken the chair, with Shires behind her for protection. *Who was protecting whom?* Garol wondered. Perhaps the point was simply that they wouldn't be visible from the street or across the street in that position, should there be any gap in the light-drape across the window.

"To what do we owe the pleasure," Garol asked Stanoczk. Stanoczk waved the flask at him cheerfully.

"Little drink?" he asked. "Good clean stuff. Well. Stuff, anyway."

Speaking Standard. Garol raised an eyebrow at Kazmer Daigule, who had leaned his back up against the door after Garol had closed it. Daigule looked ready to collapse. "He sent me off on an errand to the Port Authority," Daigule said. "Some communications clearances he wanted. By the time I got back he was halfway into a bottle of wodac. That was hours ago. Now he decides it's time to come and see you, and I can't out-wrestle him, he's drunk. I could hurt him."

If anybody could out-wrestle a Combine hominid, it would be another. It would insult both men to suggest that Sarvaw and Aznir Dolgorukij were evenly matched, however. Daigule's point was perhaps simply that men who got too drunk didn't give the right cues when they were being pulled too far in the wrong direction; so a man could cause actual harm by accident. Stanoczk being too drunk to say "that hurts," for instance.

The truly interesting thing about Daigule's recitation, however, was that Stanoczk felt perfectly at ease sending him on errands without apparent concern that Daigule might not come back. Stanoczk had to be very sure of Daigule—one way or another. "Any idea what might have brought this on?"

Walton and Shires sat quietly, observing. Daigule shook his head, though.

"'Pologies."

It was Cousin Stanoczk speaking. He was enunciating very very carefully. "'Pologies all 'round. Especially you, Kazmer. I like you, you know? You'll make a lousy Malcontent. But I like you. Anyway."

Garol tried again. "Maybe there was a delivery while you were out. Maybe he wanted you out of the way for some reason. Where did he get the liquor, do we know?"

There were vague humming sounds from the Stanoczk direction of the room. Garol was beginning to worry. Stanoczk was speaking in plain Standard. If he started to sing that song in plain Standard, and in front of Walton Agenis—hell, in front of young Hilton Shires—

"Found your body," Stanoczk said.

He sounded very pleased with himself about it, too. The reference was too apposite to be coincidental, surely. How could Cousin Stanoczk possibly know anything about that? Had he been visited by informers? But surely Daigule had been with him all evening, and Shires had only just arrived.

"Were we missing a body, Cousin?" Garol asked. He selected an appropriately respectful version of the word "cousin," out of common courtesy; but child of unknown birth order born to the eldest daughter of the younger brother of a mutual grandparent was as far as he was willing to go. The man was drunk.

Stanoczk nodded emphatically, his brown hair falling into his face as he rocked his head. "Terrible thing. Nothing to tell the parents. Aged mother. Infirm father. Um. Except that his father's dead and his mother's gone to work for a stables, but who are we to judge. A man must ride."

It was very good. But Garol was getting suspicious. "You are not as drunk as you seem," he said. "So stop playing games. What's this all about?"

Stanoczk raised his eyebrows, both of them, and stared at Garol owlishly. Then took a drink. "But I wish to be drunk." As though he believed that was a genuine explanation. "I very sincerely wish to be drunk. We have found the body, and he is not dead, and that the Angel might walk is a horror that no outlander can truly fathom."

"From the Tyrell Yards." Daigule broke in, sounding as confident as he was surprised. "There's been no identification from the forensic team, though, he sent me for results yesterday."

"Not from the forensic team." Stanoczk looked at the flask in his hand, and set it aside. Garol marked its location carefully. If it should spill, there was no telling what it might do to the floor—let alone anyone who might be sleeping in the room beneath this. "From Geraint. Going by Dalmoss. But he's not Dalmoss, which is why we noticed, you'd asked us to see about Dalmoss."

Garol decided to sit down. There was only one chair, and Walton Agenis was in it, watching and waiting for sense to begin to surface. There was a perfectly good floor, however; so Garol sank down to sit cross-legged on the modestly nondescript carpeting in the middle of the room, where he could engage Stanoczk one to one, at eye level.

"Interesting." It was at least that. "Tell me more."

"It's perfectly clear," Stanoczk said, sounding irritated. Petulant. Garol revised his working assessment: while he still felt that Stanoczk was not as drunk as he'd wished to appear to be, he was clearly more drunk than Garol had suspected, at first.

"We couldn't find him at Tyrell. Maybe he wasn't there. You asked after Dalmoss, we sent a trace to Geraint. Pettiche from the Tyrell Yards at Geraint. Going by Dalmoss. The foreman at the Combine Yards, and you would have heard about Feraltz by now."

Heard what? Feraltz's previous association with Langsariks? Whether or not Garol had "heard about" Feraltz, he would have expected Stanoczk to have told him if there was something Stanoczk thought Garol might need to know. Maybe there were allowances to be made for whatever twisted procedures Malcontents observed when dealing with Dolgorukij malefactors and off-world law enforcement, but Garol wasn't interested in cultural niceties when they started to jeopardize other people's lives. If Cousin Stanoczk could break the case for him, of course, he'd be inclined to let it go this once—

"So when do we get an interrogatory from Geraint?" He could be patient. At least until he got his interrogatory. "And where is Dalmoss?"

He didn't like the way Cousin Stanoczk had dropped his head to stare at the floor, though. It looked too much like the prelude to a plea for understanding in the case of a monumental mismanagement of resources.

"*Found* the body," Cousin Stanoczk said. "Didn't say we *had* the body." Reaching for his flask, Stanoczk took a deep pull from the lip, tilting the flask toward the ceiling. Emptying it, then flinging the flask against the far wall with a furious grimace of disgust.

Garol had been half-expecting such a gesture. He caught the flask out of its path, setting it down quietly beside him. Couldn't have people breaking flasks against the walls of rooming houses in the middle of the night. Tended to wake people up. Again.

"I explain," Stanoczk said. Garol was all in favor. "We were looking for Pettiche, and if Pettiche, who was not found at the Tyrell Yards, was on unplanned leave, he would logically only have gone in sixteen or twenty-four directions. So the description was circulated. Also we like to oblige Bench intelligence specialists whenever possible, so when Geraint received Dalmoss we went to see how he was looking and faring directly, but he was not Dalmoss, he was Pettiche."

Stanoczk was disgusted at him, now, but basically simply disgusted, and ready to take it out on the world. "Pettiche at Geraint, but traveling as Dalmoss, against which there is no law either beneath the Canopy or before the Bench. But between the time of confirming the identity of the man who was not Dalmoss, and matching him to Pettiche, he has gone. We cannot find him. We only knew that he was there, at Geraint, days after the Tyrell raid, as Dalmoss."

Garol gathered his knees to his chest and stared at the worn carpeting, thinking hard.

His feelings of intense frustration over the loss of the interrogatory he could manage; since there was no way to tell whether Dalmoss would have provided useful information, there was no sense in worrying that bone.

He had thought that Cousin Stanoczk brought him hard evidence and a brief that would solve his problems at Port Charid, but Cousin Stanoczk had not brought him nothing, Cousin Stanoczk had brought him evidence that could be used—though it was indirect. Hearsay. It only meant that more steps would be required to transmute Cousin Stanoczk's information into salvation for the Langsariks.

"Found the body, lost the body, there is still no body, Cousin Stanoczk." Cousin Stanoczk knew that. The Malcontent was an irritation and had been nothing but an obstacle, but he was neither stupid nor willfully obstructionary. "So what's the point."

Cousin Stanoczk started to stand up. He didn't seem to be managing it very well; Daigule came forward to help him, and once Cousin Stanoczk was on his feet he faced Walton Agenis—of all people—and bowed very politely. But with apparent sincerity.

"It means that you are victimized by plots against you done by my countrymen, Flag Captain. Excuse me that I have not presented myself before now, my name is Stanoczk. I am a Malcontent, and responsible to the Saint my master for the good government of the children of the Holy Mother as they go out into the world. That you are wronged by Combine interests is no longer in dispute. We fear the worst. To Garol Vogel we ask: can we be of any help at all, to make atonement on behalf of the Holy Mother's Church for wrong done you by Her own wayward children?"

Long speech. Unusually coherent, for a drunk; so maybe Stanoczk meant it. Walton Agenis shifted a little to one side in the chair; looking at Garol.

Oh, bloody hell.

"He's got resources we're going to need." He was already unhappy about his role in having brought the Langsariks to Port Charid in the first place, worried and anxious about whether Walton Agenis's trust in him was ultimately to mean her destruction.

He didn't need to be reminded.

But he couldn't refuse Walton's implicit request either, just because it emphasized that she had not yet decided that it was time to begin to cease to trust him. "You're short access to computing power to run the traffic analysis. I've seen his comps. He can probably do things with them that I don't even want to know about." Because they were likely to be illegal, that was to say. "Send someone to the docks tomorrow as soon as you can. And assume that we're being watched at every moment."

Straightening up, Cousin Stanoczk spun drunkenly on his heel and staggered sideways, managing miraculously to land on his back on Garol's bed.

"One does assume so. Naturally," he said.

Daigule turned the light out, and Garol stood in the middle of his small room in the rooming house with Kazmer Daigule at the door, Cousin Stanoczk on the bed, Walton Agenis in his chair, and Hilton Shires standing calmly and quietly in a modified position of attention-rest behind her.

There was a way to get all of this sorted out, he knew it; but for a moment the insanity of the situation was almost too much.

"So, does anybody know any good jokes?" Hilton Shires asked. Garol shook his head vigorously, to clear it; he was losing his track.

"We'll probably have to wait for morning before we can disperse." They could take advantage of shift change, things got busy.

Agenis and Shires Garol trusted to have arrived unobserved, but getting away again was going to be a little different. Cousin Stanoczk's arrival had unfortunately probably focused the attention of the night watchman; if anyone was watching Stanoczk, they could be watching the window. "There are a few hours. Talk. Let's all get on the same vector transit. Shires. You first."

Maybe nobody was watching. It was probably a good idea to minimize any chance of their quarry noticing that they were getting closer . . . if they were getting closer.

"Funny that you should mention a vector transit, Bench specialist. I have these documents. And one of them may say 'Honan,' and another may say 'gung.'" Garol stooped to the floor to retrieve the empty flask he'd intercepted on its journey to the far wall.

He was almost regretful to find it truly empty.

It was going to be a long wait, till morning.

CHAPTER NINE

Fisner Feraltz had come to work in the Combine offices in Port Charid proper this morning for two or three reasons. One of them was the desirability of being close to Factor Madlev's office, so that if the Bench specialist arrived to call through to Chilleau Judiciary he could find an immediate pretext to be there by the time Vogel was announced— or at least be on-site to talk to Factor Madlev immediately afterward, to see if he could get some hints on what had been said.

Another was to be away from the warehouse construction site in order to minimize chance contacts with Hilton Shires—in case some subconscious connection should be made in Shires's mind between the drunk in the warehouse the previous night and his foreman. There was no accounting for the leaps of comprehension that could occur at the most inopportune times even in the brain of the outlander; so it was prudent for Fisner to keep his distance more carefully while the experience was still fresh in Shires's mind.

But mostly Fisner came to work in Combine offices at Port Charid that morning because he had been out late last night helping Dalmoss with the body, and was too tired to force himself into his medical bracing fast enough to get out to his branch office in time.

The trick with the documents and the body had gone off beautifully: they had passed the information about a planned raid on Honan-gung to Shires, and escaped without being exposed as anyone other than Langsariks.

But had it worked?

Shires had gone; Shires had come back, with some of his Langsarik fellows. By that time Fisner and Dalmoss had moved the body, because if someone recognized the Langsarik as Parken from the Tyrell Yards, it would queer the setup.

The presence of the corpse had served its purpose in representing a genuine Langsarik to Shires while startling him out of any potential analysis and suspicions up front. With the corpse missing it was only Shires's word that there had been a dead man there at all, and Shires might well be distracted enough by that issue to neglect to think too deeply on any other aspect of the incident.

It was early yet for gossip to have gotten out. He'd be hearing all about it soon enough, Fisner was sure. The people on his crew—including his agents, of course, but even the balance of his crew, the majority of whom were innocent of any involvement with the Angel of Destruction—were encouraged to come to him with rumors. It was a management-communications issue. Open-door policy. Free intelligence.

It was with pleasant expectations that Fisner looked up as someone knocked at his open office door. Rather than a report from one of his people or a bit of tasty gossip, however, it was his receptionist Hariv at the door with a frown on his face, and a man behind him that Fisner thought he'd seen in town before.

"Excuse me, Foreman, a Malcontent to see you. Cousin Stanoczk."

Oh, this was interesting.

The Malcontent had been the Angel's bitter enemy from the birth of their holy Order. The opposition that the Malcontent had offered to the Angel at every step had traditionally been requited by the heartfelt hatred of the loyal sons of the Holy Mother for the degenerate offspring of bastard Saints. The Angel rejoiced in the grace and blessing of the Holy Mother; the Malcontent had to content itself with the patronage of a drunk, a failure, an irreligious and impotent man whose every action during his lifetime had ultimately failed to achieve its purpose.

With the arrogance characteristic of a Malcontent's inflated opinion of himself and his mission, Cousin Stanoczk hadn't even had the common courtesy to present himself to Factor Madlev—the senior Combine official at Port Charid, and surely a man worthy of respect—upon his arrival. His appearance here now would have some purpose behind it. Fisner was curious to know what that might be.

"Thank you, Hariv. Cousin. Come in. A very great honor." Fisner rose slowly to his feet, careful neither to exaggerate the difficulties the medical bracing placed in his way nor seem too comfortable with it. One was in no way obliged to rise for a Malcontent.

He was deliberately showing greater respect than the bastard Saint had any right to expect; but Cousin Stanoczk, true to the mindless and deluded misapprehensions common to the Malcontent, merely accepted the courtesy as due to him by right, and bowed with gracious condescension.

"Too kind, Foreman. Is it permitted to call you Feraltz? Yes, thank you, Foreman Feraltz. If I may be seated, by your kind permission."

Which Fisner had neither volunteered nor agreed to extend; that was the Malcontent to the life. Fisner sat back down. "How may I put the purpose of your patron forward, Cousin Stanoczk?" he asked politely. The Malcontent had brought Kazmer Daigule back to Port Charid with him. It could well be that Cousin Stanoczk would reveal some interesting information if his ego was stroked agreeably enough.

Cousin Stanoczk smiled in what he apparently believed to be an ingratiating fashion, though it merely turned Fisner's stomach. He was glad he'd not had time for first-meal.

"You can do me very great service, in fact, Foreman. I have instructions to expedite handling of a freight cargo expected for Finiury, and we are particularly anxious that the freighter be processed as quickly as possible. It is awkward that I cannot say exactly when the freighter is expected, but our principal apparently has doubts about the security of the Finiury Yards in the Shawl and wishes us most particularly to shepherd the cargo ourselves through the Combine warehouses here at Port Charid."

Oh, this *was* interesting. Had the fish-eating Malcontent gone into trade in illegal armaments?

Did the Bench know?

"And in what way may we assist, Cousin Stanoczk," Fisner said, to remind the Malcontent that he had not answered the question.

The general outline of Cousin Stanoczk's request was clear enough: *I have an arms shipment coming in, it can't go to Finiury because there would be too much to explain to the Bench if Finiury were raided by*

Langsariks and the cargo discovered. I therefore need your help in getting the cargo hidden safely away as soon as possible at Port Charid.

Maximizing the off-load in order to minimize the time that the freighter with its ever-so-emphatically illegal cargo would be tied up in the process, to minimize the window in which a representative of what passed for the Port Authority in Port Charid might ask to have a look at the cargo for routine spot check.

And relying upon the extralegal position of the Malcontent within the Dolgorukij church to ensure that the Combine Yards would gladly accept its role as transfer-man, without questioning Cousin Stanoczk's motives or cargo.

"Procure for me freighter tenders on standby," Cousin Stanoczk replied. He apparently did not feel as confident as he would have liked to be; he seemed to be choosing his words carefully, as though feeling his way. "To be ready to off-load on two hours' advance notice. I will, of course, pay a reasonable holding charge, but eight freighter tenders empty and fueled are most sincerely desired, and as soon as possible."

Fisner pushed himself away from his desk in the chair and out at an arm's length from the near edge, staring at the desk furniture as he thought.

Eight freighter tenders.

It was not a small favor to ask, what with the increasing traffic that was coming through Port Charid these days rather than off-loading in the Shawl, where the freighters could dock directly.

Eight freighter tenders?

But, oh, if he could only pull it off. To suck an extra premium out of the pocket of the hated Malcontent to fund the Angel's own agendas, and gain the leverage that having the secret knowledge would grant— Cousin Stanoczk had made no incriminating statements, but Fisner knew things about Finiury that Cousin Stanoczk could not imagine he knew—

There would be troops in Port Charid once the Angel wrought its final raid. The new warehouse would be searched for contraband; some pretext to examine the Malcontent's crates from Finiury could easily be arranged while Fleet was on-site. It would be a scandal of monumental proportions. It would discredit the Malcontent in the eyes of the Autocrat's court at least, if not Combine-wide; not for trafficking in illegal arms, but for having done so clumsily, for having permitted themselves to be caught at it.

Beautiful.

"It will not be easy to arrange. Or to explain." Making his decision, Fisner gave his consent to Cousin Stanoczk's proposal in such a way as to assure that the premium to be offered would be adequate to account for the trouble the requirement would entail. "I only have five tenders idle even now, and the lull is only temporary. I could come up with some excuse for off-lining the tenders, but nothing I can think of will be good for very long, and we will lose money if we have to leave goods in orbit waiting for off-load."

Cousin Stanoczk was frowning, in a servile and overanxious sort of way. "It is very distressing, Foreman, but we cannot permit any traffic to be made to wait. It would draw attention to the priority off-load of our Finiury cargo. That is contrary to the modest and public-spirited desire of our client."

Good point. Fisner hadn't thought about it, but it was obvious once Cousin Stanoczk brought it up. If traffic was on hold while a Finiury cargo got priority handling, it would only draw attention. People would naturally be interested in what the Finiury cargo was and why someone was willing to pay the clearly implied premiums to get the cargo unshipped.

Then Fisner had an idea.

There were to be no Combine freighters within the next two weeks; Factor Madlev had rerouted some of the Combine shipping to maximize the extra revenue available from other firms wishing to use the Combine facilities.

"Very well, Cousin Stanoczk." He would call the reserve ships in for maintenance. There were two of those; he had five on the ground in the normal course of the day's traffic, that made seven; he would only have to reserve his raid ship itself on standby. The conduct of the raid could occupy the freighter tender for a day and a half, with everything taken into account, but he would so shuffle his freighter tenders that normal traffic would cover it. Brilliant.

"You shall have eight freighter tenders, all empty, all fueled, all ready at your word. We will direct your cargo to the new facility. There will be no excess and burdensome oversight; you may confidently rely upon our discretion."

It would leave them without any emergency capacity, but he could do it without attracting any particular attention. If he scheduled things cleverly enough, he need not declare any of Cousin Stanoczk's offered premium to Factor Madlev. It would be additional income to fund the Angel's work, on top of the generous proceeds from the raids themselves.

Cousin Stanoczk bowed politely, but the reality of his relief was unquestionable. "Thank you, Foreman, I am very much in your debt. May the Holy Mother prosper all lawful purposes."

"Thank you, Cousin Stanoczk. It is our pleasure to oblige."

The Angel of Destruction was above the law of men, be it the Autocrat's code or the Jurisdiction's Bench.

What more telling evidence of the Holy Mother's blessing, than that She turned even the Malcontent to serve the Angel's purpose?

Suppressing a yawn, Hilton marked off another hull on his list and reset the temperature sensor. He hadn't been getting his beauty sleep. He hadn't gotten any sleep at all since early yesterday morning, but who was counting? He wouldn't have traded the all-night staff meeting Aunt Walton had held in Garol Vogel's bedroom for money.

"Three more and we're out." Kazmer's voice came quietly over the earpiece. Hilton was on receive, not transmit, because if he had been hiding battle cannon in a warehouse, he certainly would have a monitor on communications transmissions in the area. "Next."

Kazmer didn't have to say much on his end. Kazmer was eights away in a little closet on his Cousin Stanoczk's courier at Port Charid, tapped into the warehouse's employee-location grid. As acting floor manager, Hilton carried a trace so that the foreman could find him at any time; Kazmer knew exactly where Hilton was. Also that Hilton hadn't found anything yet, because he meant to do his super-special secret version of the Hilton Happy Dance when he did, and there had been no dance activity on the warehouse floor so far that morning.

Someone had cannon hidden at Port Charid. If not cannon, at least a small courier hardened to take the deployment of battle cannon; when Kazmer had taken the freighter tender to rendezvous for the Tyrell raid, the courier had been on the freighter tender.

Hilton had a manifest list for each freighter tender at the warehouse, and the gross weights of each component part and total cargo were part of his records. Kazmer and Vogel had a rough estimate of weight for the courier Kazmer had helped to unload at Tyrell. Nothing on Hilton's docks would tip the scale at such a mass as that.

The warehouse floor was load-rated for freighter tenders with heavy ore cargoes. It flexed. There was a correlation between the thermal stress involved with flexing beneath the weight of the five freighter tenders currently parked at the new warehouse and the adjusted weight of the freighter tenders' cargoes, less fuel reserves. Hilton strolled casually down the line of parked freighter tenders with his tally screen and his thermal sensor, whistling to himself.

Let me help your expert gunnery, promise I'll max your trajectory.

The warehouse floor was warmer there than it had been beneath the prior freighter tender.

But was it because of the cargo load this freighter tender was carrying?

Or—Hilton asked himself with mounting excitement, strolling past the nose of the next freighter tender to scan the floor beneath the one after that from a distance—was it because there was something really, really heavy in the last freighter tender but one?

Frowning at his tally screen Hilton started down the pedestrian aisle between freighter tenders, his temperature probe casually aimed at the floor to his left.

Not the last in line, the first to be suspected, too easily moved in and out.

Not hidden in the middle of the line like a freighter tender cleared and locked down and waiting to take on cargo. The last but one, the next to last, swarming with Langsarik work crews—forward only, of course—and in the process of clearing its cargo.

Hilton checked his tally.

The cargo was under quarantine for release of goods. As good as locked away, secured, no better place to hide a courier, and the weight in the aft cargo compartment of the last freighter tender but one stressed the floor that supported it with a thermal trace that showed orange and yellow on Hilton's readout.

It was heavy enough to be holding the battle cannon.

Hilton walked slowly all the way around the great beast, taking his time to master his emotions. This was it. They had the courier. Now all they had to do was find its crew, and this would all be over.

They'd be safe.

"Very good." Kazmer's voice was calm, but resonant with the excitement Hilton knew Kazmer was sharing. "Trace. Off-line now."

Now that they knew which one it was, the Langsariks could set a watch. Kazmer closed his transmission, careful to minimize any chance of interception. Hilton checked the last freighter tender as he passed under pretext of doing something with his tally screen; light as a feather. As freighter tenders went.

He didn't dare lay a tag on record, for fear of discovery. But Kazmer had the fix on his position; and Hilton had Langsarik maintenance crews up on the bare beams of the warehouse ceiling, keeping watch.

Cold up there. Drafty. Thankless duty, Hilton knew; but they had the enemy now. That knowledge alone was enough to warm a man body and soul, even one on watch far far overhead.

It was the end of a long day, and Garol Vogel was walking Walton Agenis home. It was about an hour and a half on foot from Port Charid to the Langsarik settlement; Garol felt the need to get out under the sky, and Walton hadn't argued.

They'd been in bed together all day.

At least that was the story, if anyone asked.

Once they'd cleared the outskirts of Port Charid and were well on their way toward the new warehouse construction site, Garol spoke.

"So you managed to obtain a false chop," Garol said, just to get the story out in the open once and for all. "Somehow. It doesn't really matter, someone will think of a way. You used the chop to authorize moving freighter tenders into orbit."

Hilton's find out on the warehouse floor that morning had been the final evidence. There was no longer any question about where the battle cannon were being hidden; now it remained only to decide where the battle cannon would be deployed next, and Hilton was in Port Charid with Cousin Stanoczk and Kazmer Daigule running the last of the contingency exercises even now.

"You hid your raid ship and its battle cannon on a freighter tender out at the new warehouse that the Combine started to build as soon as the Langsariks got here. Perfect timing."

Walton walked slowly, shredding the long leaf of a late-flourishing plant in her strong slender fingers. She was clearly in no particular hurry to get back; and if they'd been in bed together all day—Garol thought, almost despite himself—she might be moving a little slowly anyway. Muscular soreness.

He was ashamed of himself for having such a thought about Walton Agenis. It was ungallant in the extreme to impose on a lady to such an extent. If he ever actually did go to bed with her—

"Too bad we can't figure out a way for that to have been part of the plot, all along." Walton's comment interrupted Garol's train of thought, and not a moment too soon. The late-afternoon breeze ruffled her short red hair; it was cool, when the breeze blew, and she was wearing Garol's old campaign jacket.

"Right." Garol set his mind resolutely to the issue at hand. "Hilton's got the chop, says he got it from Dalmoss, what Dalmoss will say is predictable. The courier could have been in the warehouse all this time, for all we know."

The Langsariks had been scrupulous about observing the letter and intent of the amnesty agreement. No one had gone poking around cargo holds of freighter tenders without leave and authorization. Who knew how long that raid ship had been there? And since the warehouse-construction crews were almost all Langsarik, the setup was compromising by definition. Physical evidence of Langsarik involvement could always be come by later.

She was listening, and he was getting it all straight in his mind by talking it out. "You get into orbit, you rendezvous with a freighter, you make a raid. Your hired crew escapes, you rejoin your freighter tender, and return to base at Port Charid with no one any the wiser. We have the crew from the Tyrell raid, we can demonstrate how you did it."

She tossed the shredded leaf away from her with a gesture of disgust. "Leaving us with only two questions. Who's behind it. What to do about it."

"Cousin Stanoczk says the Angel of Destruction," Garol reminded her. "He may have that part covered."

"He hasn't come out and said, though. I don't need any Cousin Stanoczk to tell me who's behind it, if there is a Dolgorukij plot. It's Feraltz. It's almost got to be."

Garol considered this in silence for a moment or two, watching the shadows change across the hills far to the south. "Why Feraltz?"

Granted that Garol himself had already decided that Feraltz was running a game; he still didn't understand why. "He's the one man in Port Charid with most owing."

That could be an answer of its own, of course, the ins and outs of gratitude and obligation being what they were.

Walton sighed. "Dalmoss is clearly part of it, if we believe Hilton about the chop—and I do, needless to say. Feraltz very specifically wanted Hilton as assistant floor manager at the new warehouse construction site, so Feraltz arranged to put Hilton in his very compromised position. But there's more to it than that. I'd normally not want to say anything about it, but—"

There was a vehicle approaching on the track from Port Charid. Walton glanced behind her; Garol put his arm around her shoulder to draw her with him well off the track. Just in case.

"More to it, you said?"

She shook her head. "Wait. This one's coming for us. I've seen my nephew drive before."

All right.

The vehicle pulled over ahead of them on the side to the track and skidded to a stop, raising a cloud of dust and gravel. The door on the driver's side was open before the vehicle stopped moving, and Hilton Shires fell out.

Did a very creditable tuck and roll, too, scrambling to his feet and starting toward them almost without a break. His momentum carried him flat into Garol where Garol stood waiting, and Garol steadied him with an effort.

"Results," Shires said. "Analysis complete. It's got to be Honan-gung. It's got to be."

Cousin Stanoczk's people had been working the analysis all day. The documents Shires had picked up in the warehouse after hours the evening before. The historical pattern, available cargo readily converted into untraceable cash, potential body count, everything.

Garol pushed Shires away, hard enough to stagger him. "I'll keep company with your aunt if I damn please," Garol said, loud-voiced and angry. "Who do you think you are?"

Shires was smart, he picked right up on things. He didn't try to close the distance, he put one hand on his hip and shook his finger accusingly. "We know the target," Shires said, low-voiced, as if angry in response. Scowling. Lips drawn thin, body tense and hunched slightly forward, as if about to attack. "What do we do now?"

Walton stepped between them, and put her hands out to either side in the classic gesture of forcing a separation. "We can't prove anything on what we have," she said soothingly. "All the circumstantial evidence and hearsay in the world won't help us. We need to catch the raiders in the act for a positive identification. You know we do."

Dropping her arms, she turned her back to both of them and stared out across the road into the middle distance. Garol folded his arms across his chest. *Enraged senior male, challenged by immature younger male stepping outside his boundaries.* "I know what you're suggesting. But I can't risk the lives of the crew at Honan-gung without a really solid backup. It's just not acceptable."

Shires had both hands on his hips, now, but he'd straightened up a bit. *Younger male, not ready to back down, but feeling obviously intimidated and looking for a face-saving escape route.* "But we have no direct incontrovertible evidence. We've got to give the enemy the opportunity to betray himself, in order to convince the Bench."

Shires and his aunt were right.

Yet Garol couldn't see a way around it. Garol unfolded his arms and reached for Walton, drawing her by the elbow to stand by his side. *Senior male making his position absolutely clear, but softening marginally on aggressive response to challenge from younger male.*

"Not an option, Shires; I'm not risking lives on an ego thing. If we had police. A dockworkers' association. Reservists. Anything. But we don't." He couldn't call on the Port Authority for support. The Port Authority was dependent on the local mercantile authority for its enforcers. That meant Factor Madlev's people, Combine people.

The enemy would be tipped off, or worse—the enemy would have advance intelligence and would be able to forestall them, or even subvert the very people Garol might need to back him up. No. Hopeless.

Now Walton Agenis tucked herself very confidentially against him and raised her head to look up into his face. *Female offers conciliatory gesture to reconcile senior male and younger male.*

"You've got Langsariks," she said.

What?

What was that supposed to mean, "you've got Langsariks"? He already knew that he had responsibility for the Langsariks here at Port

Charid, he'd brought them here, he'd negotiated the amnesty agreement, he'd promised them fair play. He hadn't told the truth. It wasn't for lack of goodwill on his part, but the Langsariks were not going to get fair play after all. The Langsariks were going to suffer for someone else's crime. There was nothing that Garol Vogel could see that he could do about it.

"It wasn't supposed to end this way, Flag Captain." He couldn't sidestep the issue. He owed it to Walton Agenis to tell her the truth, no matter how it would diminish him in her eyes. It was the only thing he had to offer by way of atonement for his role in the disaster that was almost upon the Langsariks. "Maybe we'll get a break. We could get lucky. But we've got to start preparing your people for the worst."

For all her submissive body language, Walton wasn't backing down a bit. "No, Bench specialist, we've got to start preparing for an ambush. They brought the raiders out as boxed cargo at Tyrell, Daigule said." The night before, during the marathon information-sharing session they'd held in Garol's bedroom, in fact. "We can use the same approach at Honan-gung."

All right, all right.

All right.

Garol caught her meaning, now. A seductive concept. But it would never work.

"I like it in theory," Garol said, and kissed the top of Walton's head on impulse—just to put the play forward, of course, for the benefit of whoever might be watching. "Don't get me wrong."

There was such a solid emotional satisfaction behind the proposal, and if the Langsariks couldn't pull it off, nobody could— or nobody within nine days' transit time of the Shawl of Rikavie, at any rate. But it wouldn't work. The Langsariks were prohibited any travel off Port Charid without strict supervision for a start, and forbidden to arm themselves without qualification—not even for self-defense.

Why wouldn't it work?

It was true what he'd just told himself: if the Langsariks couldn't do it, nobody could.

And Langsariks had pulled off more outrageous stunts still in their recent past, in their politely glossed-over but solidly successful careers as commerce raiders who had evaded the best efforts of the Fleet to pin them down and punish them for years.

"I've learned a lot about cargo-management systems, Specialist Vogel. I can make it work." Shires stepped forward with his shoulders rounded, his hands held out in front of him entreatingly. *Subordinate male yields, solicits forgiveness.* "Nobody needs to know that we've got troops on board. We can stay clear of the station monitors until we're needed."

Garol's head was spinning; he shook it several times, to try to clear his thoughts. *Senior male stands on his dignity, holds out for more abject apology in presence of female.*

"Lieutenant Shires. Hilton." It was so hard to reject, because it was so beautiful. He would enjoy it so much: to capture the raiders in the commission of a crime, to demonstrate the trustworthiness of the Langsariks, to keep the innocent civilians at Honan-gung safe from harm while giving him the data he needed to protect the Langsarik settlement.

He ached to embrace the idea.

He could not.

"It's been more than a year since any Langsarik has engaged in any action, at least that's the story I've heard. How are we going to keep someone in Port Charid from noticing? If you're discovered at Honan-gung before the raid, it will be the same as if you had been the raiders all along."

Shires was only smiling, his whole face full of such wolfish joy that Garol shuddered to see it. Pure. Brilliant. Savage in its certainty; and beautiful, as any perfect predator was beautiful. "That's one reason why we'll need you to come with us, Bench specialist. Legal authority. The apprehension won't be lawful without duly constituted Bench representation. You'll have to deputize us to cover for it. Besides, you'll want to be there."

Shires was right.

About both things.

"Puts the entire community at risk," Garol said, to Walton. *Senior male solicits option of female; should peace be made with subordinate male? Will his status suffer if he yields too easily?* "Are you sure about this, Flag Captain?"

She nodded with vigorous self-confidence. "It's my best alternative. And the other alternatives aren't worth considering."

It was not a brilliant idea, necessarily; merely a reasonable one—but the emotional payoff that it offered was almost irresistible.

"So let's get on with it. Hilton. Aren't you supposed to be on shift? Vogel and I will take the vehicle, you walk it off."

Female offers face saving extrication to both males, trading temporary inconvenience of walking to work for easy escape of young male from injudiciously invoked confrontation. Garol straightened his shirtfront with an exaggerated glare at Shires and followed Walton Agenis to the for-hire that Shires had brought from Port Charid.

Garol remembered what it was like to burn with the pure joy of approaching battle, hungry to starving for the chance to take action at last against a despised and cowardly opponent.

After all these years, did he have the moral courage to resist the temptation and deny Shires his chance to clear his name?

Or was he going to find himself agreeing to make use of the offered Langsarik resources, just because he'd never been able to forget what it had been like when he'd been twenty?

Midnight in Port Charid. The previous night had been absorbed in an ad-hoc strategy session in Garol's bedroom; Shires had located the battle cannon—or at least the freighter tender on which the battle cannon were presumed to be—that morning. Cousin Stanoczk and his people had completed the target analysis hours ago, and Garol had seen Walton Agenis safely returned to the Langsarik settlement himself.

He had everything he needed now, target, location of enemy resources, plan of attack.

He was almost ready to call it a plan and get going.

"I agree that the analysis factors all point to Honan-gung," Jils admitted, closing the portfolio containing the scraps of paper that Shires had picked up on the warehouse floor last night. "What is less obvious is whose target it is."

Garol Vogel sat in the small aft cabin of the courier he'd had sent from Anglace to Port Charid on freighter to meet him. Now that his own transport was there, he had less excuse for using that of Cousin Stanoczk, which was a shame in a sense—the Malcontent's courier was significantly more luxurious than his own, even if the technology standard was not all that different.

"It's Langsariks or it's not." He knew what she was getting at, but there was no reason to make it easy on her. "Let's assume for one moment that it's Langsariks. Why would they tip us off?"

"Because the Langsarik target isn't Honan-gung, Garol. Get you all excited about Honan-gung and you leave them time and opportunity to make one last hit somewhere else. Maybe Finiury. There are indications that arms shipments may be going through Finiury, Garol. The Bench is finalizing its case."

He knew that. He'd just been thinking about other things. He'd had other problems on his mind.

Jils continued. "But if there are arms at Finiury and the Langsariks raid, we could have a takeover situation on our hands. You've got to let Verlaine set Fleet on alert."

He hated it when Jils made too much good sense. Hated it. He pushed himself up out of his chair and covered his frustration with a quest for a cup of bean tea. You couldn't get bean tea on the Malcontent's courier, not unless you asked for it. Rhyti. Weak as water by comparison, even if rhyti's mix of naturally occurring and mood-altering chemical substances were seductive enough in its own right.

"We're saying it's Honan-gung if it's not Langsariks, and I'm dead on for Honan-gung because I believe it's not Langsariks," Garol said with his back to Jils, from the bean tea brewer. Basically, that was what she was telling him. "And there's still a chance that it is Langsariks, and my own emotional investment in the settlement has created a blind spot in my analysis."

"Our emotional investment," Jils said quietly, and Garol bowed his head in gratitude to her. "Yes. And if we've called it wrong, we've potentially endangered many more souls than just the warehouse crew at Finiury. If we're badly mistaken, it could be Tyrell all over again, but at Port Charid—with plenty of frustration on the Langsariks' part to work out. It's more than we can risk, and what's the harm of calling for Fleet for backup?"

But she knew the answer to that one already. "I don't know. That's the problem. You never know with Fleet. For all we know they'd send us the *Ragnarok*, and we all know that'd just mean a lot of unnecessary interrogations. I don't want Fleet involved if I can avoid it. I don't like the uncertainties."

Fleet was there for muscle, though. Fleet was the only enforcement muscle a Bench intelligence specialist had. Fleet was the police arm of the Bench. He was supposed to call for Fleet when he could no longer control the situation himself.

He wasn't willing to admit that the situation wasn't under control; and yet Jils was right. If he was wrong about the Langsariks . . .

"You're the man on the ground on this one, Garol." She'd given him her evaluation; she thought it was Honan-gung. She'd reminded him of the alternatives, too. Bench intelligence specialists didn't dice with the lives of innocent people. "It's your call."

It *was* his call.

He was responsible to the Bench for the success or failure of his solution to the problem Chilleau Judiciary faced at Port Charid, the apparent resurgence of Langsariks piracy, the contempt for the amnesty, the disruption of trade, the retardation of the economic development of the site.

He would put Port Charid on notice that a Fleet detachment was coming. That would force someone's hand; the only question remaining would be which someone, exactly, it would turn out to be.

If it was a raid on Honan-gung, he would be ready for them.

If it was a Langsarik raid on Finiury, there would be a bloodbath in Port Charid with Garol Aphon Vogel written all over it, and if that happened, he wanted to be the only one responsible.

"If that's the way you feel about it." On all levels. "I think you should leave, Jils."

She looked a little surprised, eyeing him sharply as if to judge whether he had taken offense or not. Her expression smoothed as he continued, however.

"Go back to Chilleau Judiciary and tell Verlaine all about it. Take me with you. I'll let them know we're coming."

Jils knew his mind. He didn't have to explain.

"We leave tomorrow, then. Good enough."

There were times when Garol wondered whether working with Jils was becoming dangerous. They knew each other almost too well. That could lead to a failure to detect a developing irregularity in the other's conduct, potentially injurious to the Judicial order and the maintenance of the rule of Law.

So long as justice was served, was that a problem? It was for Jils; and Garol knew that.

For Jils Ivers it was only justice if the rule of Law was served. If the Judicial order was violated, it could not be just or judicious, no matter what the surrounding circumstances might be. There was no point in exploring the issue with her, though, so Garol simply stood up, giving her a bow of formal thanks for her support and her acuity.

"I'll go make our call to Chilleau Judiciary."

If he was right about the Langsariks, it would work out.

If he was wrong?

Would he be able to live with himself if he unleashed the beast that had ravaged the Tyrell Yards on an undefended population at Port Charid?

There was only one way left to find out.

Time enough to ask himself that question once this was all over.

"There may be some irregularities in the cargo manifests at the development site," Fisner Feraltz admitted, generously. "But with Dalmoss away at Geraint, we're using a temporary floor manager. A man with experience and reliability, who was once an officer in the Langsarik fleet."

It was the morning of the second day after he and Dalmoss had played coy with the corpse of the murdered Langsarik from the Tyrell Yards. Fisner stood in Factor Madlev's office reviewing the morning reports, which were presenting some problems—some carefully constructed problems. Fisner had yet to see any real development from the seeds they had planted that night; so he had initiated further measures of his own, to be in place in case they should prove to be required.

Factor Madlev frowned. "But there are irregularities? Trusting to gain trust is all very well, Fisner, but we can't take chances with other people's cargo. It's our honor. As well as our duty."

Chewing on his lip, Fisner took a moment before he replied. As a matter of fact Shires was doing quite a good job at receiving reconciliation, by and large; but Fisner had reasons for planting the doubts in Factor Madlev's mind. "I'm sure it's just the learning curve, Factor. But I am concerned. I felt it should be laid before you, if only as an informational item."

Fisner heard footsteps approach the open doorway behind him; when he heard the Bench specialist's voice he closed his eyes, saying a silent prayer of submissive thanks.

"Good-greeting, Factor, thank you for seeing me. Foreman."

Bench Intelligence Specialist Garol Vogel.

Factor Madlev stood up politely, lowering his head in greeting. "At your disposal entirely, Specialist Vogel. Ah . . . Fisner, should you perhaps go?"

"Of course." Fisner could afford a prompt response. The Holy Mother would not have placed him here so fortuitously had She not arranged for him to remain.

"Not necessary, Factor, thank you for your concern." Vogel was but the tool of the Holy Mother's purpose. To that extent Fisner was Vogel's master; and Factor Madlev's, too. "I'm leaving Port Charid, and I'd like you both to be fully briefed. In strictest confidence, of course."

Fisner already knew part of what Vogel had to say. In general, if not in detail.

Vogel had apparently been expected, the link to Chilleau Judiciary set up in advance; Fisner stepped back to close the door to Factor Madlev's office—and efface himself, as well—as the communications link cleared.

First Secretary Verlaine came on over the line.

"This is Verlaine. Your status, Bench specialist?"

Was it his imagination—Fisner asked himself—or did Vogel actually hesitate? He certainly seemed to pause to take a breath before he spoke.

"Beg leave to inform you, leaving Port Charid for Chilleau Judiciary with evidence to lay before the Bench as to the precise identity of parties responsible for recent predation at Port Charid."

Very formal indeed. Factor Madlev had sat back down, staring at Vogel with wide-eyed wonder. Perhaps Vogel's certainty of phrase did seem like the result of some wonderful feat of Bench specialist ferret work, to Factor Madlev. Fisner knew exactly what Vogel thought he knew. Vogel was like warm dough in his hands; he had but to supply the yeast, and Vogel would puff the tale up to twice and three times its original size.

"Good news, Specialist Vogel. Here's mine."

The First Secretary's voice was so clear from the voice port on Factor Madlev's desk that Fisner almost believed he could see the skeptical expression on the First Secretary's face. He didn't even know what First Secretary Verlaine looked like. He had to be a big man, though, probably bearded, a Factor Madlev of a man; because his voice was of the depth and timbre that only resulted from great chests and substantial bulk.

"News, that is, not good," the First Secretary continued. "I have a Fleet Interrogations Group on alert." This news came as an obvious shock to Vogel; but not so much as Fisner might have thought. So perhaps Vogel was further along than even Fisner had hoped?

Verlaine was still talking. "We cannot justify an abeyance of sanctions for very much longer. As you know, the Second Judge's trust in your judgment is considerable, Specialist Vogel. She and I therefore both hope that you will be able to resolve the difficulties at Port Charid in an expeditious manner without resort to the expense of a Fleet Interrogations Group."

A Fleet Interrogations Group on alert?

What was its charter to be?

He could use this—it would be brilliant.

"I was going to suggest a Fleet detachment, First Secretary. There will be no need for a Fleet Interrogations Group, but I am asking that police resources be detailed immediately." Vogel sounded only reasonable and mild; but the First Secretary—Fisner was delighted to hear—was not having any of it.

"I have already made promises to representatives of the planetary governments concerned, Specialist Vogel. Pending a satisfactory resolution to the situation at Port Charid, the Third Fleet Interrogations Group at Dobe has been placed on standby alert to travel to Port Charid and investigate allegations of violation of the amnesty agreement on the part of the Langsarik settlement. If proved these violations will be construed as nullifying the amnesty, and the full range of Bench sanctions will be implemented immediately."

Beautiful.

Unleash a Fleet Interrogations Group with such a Brief, and they would find evidence of organized violation of the amnesty among the Langsariks. There was no question about it. That was what a Fleet Interrogations Group did. They would go through the Langsariks until they had collected enough by way of confessions to validate whatever measures the Bench could want to take. Given enough bodies to process, they would get what they were looking for, with certainty.

"I'm sorry to hear that, First Secretary," Vogel said; concerned, yes, but still confident. "Fleet Interrogations Groups so frequently generate their own momentum. I trust to satisfy the Second Judge as to the complete irrelevance of any such requirement. Leaving Port Charid today, expect arrival at Chilleau Judiciary in three days' time."

Yet until the Second Judge had reviewed Vogel's evidence, the Fleet Interrogations Group would logically remain on standby. Having been driven to the point of putting the Fleet Interrogations Group on standby in the first place, they would have to wait for dramatic news before they could issue a stand-down without losing credibility. Fisner knew exactly how he could get that Fleet Interrogations Group on its way to execute the vengeance of the Angel of Destruction against the Langsariks—before Vogel even got to Chilleau Judiciary.

By the time Vogel even knew what was happening it would be too late. The Fleet Interrogations Group would be on-site, at work, and Langsariks would confess to everything. Anything the Fleet Interrogations Group asked them.

"We'll wait." The First Secretary didn't sound convinced; the battle was half-won already. Soon it would be academic. "But not for very long. Priority call as soon as you arrive, Specialist Vogel. We're very anxious to review your findings."

Fisner had to stifle his grin of glee. It was an effort, but he managed.

Vogel bowed to the voice port on Factor Madlev's desk, saluting the Bench in the person of the Second Judge's principal administrator. "Leaving very soon, First Secretary. Vogel away, here."

"Looking forward to it. Chilleau Judiciary, away."

The First Secretary spoke for the Second Judge, and Vogel answered to the Bench. If the Bench decided not to wait any longer for Vogel's solution to its problem at Port Charid, that was the Bench's right and prerogative.

"So, we'll be having an end to all this, soon," Factor Madlev said. It was obviously as much as he dared say but so much less than he wanted to know.

Vogel nodded confidently. "That's right, Factor Madlev. The information I have for the Second Judge is conclusive. Once she but sees what I have to show her, it will be all over but the deliberations."

Vogel would never know; but the Angel of Destruction had bested even a Bench intelligence specialist and shaped Vogel to its will in the pursuit of its special mission.

Once the Fleet Interrogations Group arrived, with its Brief in full effect—

The Langsariks would die horribly, and he would be revenged.

Midmorning, the day after Hilton had located the battle cannon on the floor of the new warehouse, Kazmer Daigule sat before the console in the wheelhouse of the Malcontent's shuttle, watching as Garol Vogel's courier tracked for the Shawl of Rikavie and the Sillume vector.

"Good riddance," Cousin Stanoczk said, from behind him. "Nothing but trouble, Bench intelligence specialists. Now perhaps we can all get on about our business here, without the interference of persons impertinently trying to interest themselves in other people's affairs."

It was a pretty little thing, Vogel's courier. In his previous life Kazmer had dreamed of some year owning something like that. Now he owned nothing—but if he was to face a lifetime of service as pilot on craft such as the one Cousin Stanoczk had taken from Anglace, had he really lost? Since realistically speaking his chances of ever affording anything in either class were slim indeed—

"That's the idea, anyway," Garol Vogel said, from where he stood at Stanoczk's side. There was no hint of resentment in his voice, though Stanoczk could be unpleasantly sharp when it suited him. "Has the freighter tender we want moved yet, Daigule?"

No, it hadn't. In fact the freighter tender that Hilton had identified as the one to watch was the only one that Fisner Feraltz had not released to unload and stand by in response to Cousin Stanoczk's request, made a day ago, for eight freighter tenders to be made available.

Kazmer keyed his window on the warehouse's traffic monitors, just to be sure. "Stasis," Kazmer said, pointing to the screen with satisfaction. "Going nowhere. So we can be sure that it's the one."

Vogel nodded with grim satisfaction, then looked to Cousin Stanoczk. "How are we doing on the cargo for Honan-gung?"

Cousin Stanoczk bowed in polite response. "In final preparation even now, Specialist Vogel. The carpenters have been working without rest at the airfield, building a transfer case for the large refrigeration unit we hypothetically expect at Honan-gung. We can load for departure by evening."

Vogel nodded approvingly. "Fast workers, those Langsariks. I'm sorry, Daigule, but we can't take you with us."

Kazmer looked up over his shoulder at Cousin Stanoczk, surprised.

"Kazmer understands that he will be needed here," Cousin Stanoczk said firmly, but Kazmer imagined that his voice was not completely unsympathetic. "If for no other reason than to be seen. Were he to drop out of sight while I remained bustling about in Port Charid, the quarry might become suspicious. We do not love each other. We are always eager to expect the worst of each other."

The Malcontent, and the Angel of Destruction. Stanoczk was talking about the Angel. It was perhaps true that Kazmer and Cousin Stanoczk did not love each other; but love had nothing to do with the relationship. Kazmer was genuinely obliged to Cousin Stanoczk. And Cousin Stanoczk had treated him fairly enough, at least thus far.

"Also, Hilton Shires is leaving," Stanoczk said. "Kazmer will be waiting for opportunities to slip away, while I am not watching. So that he can go and make love to the cousin."

His role was to be that of the go-between, then, carrying messages between Cousin Stanoczk and Walton Agenis.

It was a good plan. But it meant talking to Modice. That was unkind of Stanoczk, to send him to talk to Modice, because it hurt.

He was resigned now to what he had done and what he had to do to make up for it. It was going to make him feel much better to see the murderers punished for their crimes, that was true enough. Still, the sooner he was away from Port Charid—the sooner he could start to pretend to forget Modice Agenis—the easier it would be for him to wear the red halter of the Malcontent.

"Well thought." Garol Vogel approved, but could hardly guess at what the arrangement was going to cost Kazmer in wear and tear on his emotions. Not that it mattered. As far as Garol Vogel was concerned, Kazmer was a criminal anyway, escaped from lawful punishment by stealth and worthily deserving any punishment that came his way by way of substitution. "I'll be seeing you, then, Cousin Stanoczk."

"Kazmer. I am going to go visit with Factor Madlev. Would this not be a good time for you to fetch a for-hire and go out to the airfield to see if Modice is there?"

He would be the package man, then. Vogel would hide in the

for-hire that Kazmer would take from the docks in Port Charid out to the airfield, and when Kazmer got to the airfield—to ask around for Modice—Vogel could slip away, unseen, undetected, to join the Langsarik ambush party load-in for transport to Honan-gung.

"You know Sarvaw, Cousin Stanoczk. We are completely untrustworthy. Ruled by our passions utterly."

He meant it to sound like an agreement, playful, entering into the spirit of the deception; but he had not fully mastered his bitterness. He could hear it in his own voice. Cousin Stanoczk surprised him; stepping forward, putting one hand on his shoulder, Cousin Stanoczk leaned over him and kissed his forehead with grave and absolute reverence.

"You are as good man as any and better than most, Kazmer Daigule. You will see vindication, it is my sacred duty to you.—Now I am leaving, I will see you later."

Kazmer didn't see what vindication had to do with Malcontents. But he was irrationally comforted by Cousin Stanoczk's gesture, nonetheless.

CHAPTER TEN

After his meeting that morning with Factor Madlev—with its bonus of seeing Specialist Vogel—Fisner had come back to his office in the new warehouse, taking Hariv with him to provide administrative support. He had some catching up to do, and plenty of work to keep Hariv busy; so it came as no surprise when Hariv knocked at the door to Fisner's office for instruction.

"Yes?"

Hariv looked a little unsure of himself.

"The floor manager to see you, Foreman. The Langsarik. Shires. Asks for a word."

Fisner thought fast. The office was well lighted; Shires had seen him in the warehouse only under conditions of low light and was less likely to make the connection accordingly. He had laid aside his over-blouse, sitting at his desk in his shirtsleeves; Shires had seen him in the warehouse only fully clothed and wearing warm clothing for going out at night, so there would not be any hinted connection there either.

Since he was seated Shires was likely not to notice that he had finally laid aside his medical bracing. So as far as Shires was concerned Fisner would still present the appearance of impaired physical performance—with the unconscious assumptions of limited mobility suggested by that.

He was probably as safe from exposure by Shires as it was possible for him to be. It would only attract unwelcome attention if he rejected a normal request during the normal course of the day's events without an obvious and self-evident excuse. Which he did not have.

"Thank you, Hariv, of course. Now?"

What would it matter if Shires did start to suspect something, at this advanced point in the campaign? To whom could Shires bring a half-formed suspicion? The Bench intelligence specialists had left. It was only a matter of hours before their courier would reach the Sillume entry vector. Once that happened they were as good as neutralized for three days, the time it took to travel on Sillume from Charid to Chilleau Judiciary via Garsite.

As Hariv opened the office door more widely to admit Shires, Fisner made another quick calculation. Shires had heard him whispering to Dalmoss in the warehouse. He would be sure to speak loudly and confidently.

"Foreman Feraltz. Thank you for seeing me, sir."

Shires came only part of the way across the room, stopping at a polite distance in the middle of the rug. Discomfort and uncertainty seemed to discourage him from seeking eye contact; Fisner relaxed a bit, but only internally, careful to maintain his formal posture.

"Something's come up, Foreman," Shires said. "This is awkward. I very much appreciate the trust you've reposed in me, opportunity to learn, and so forth. But it's a family matter."

Quitting?

"I'm afraid I don't understand, Shires, what's on your mind?"

Raising his eyes to Fisner's face for one quick glance, Shires seemed almost to blush, dropping his gaze again immediately. "There's a man working out in the Shawl at the Honan-gung Yards, not really my relative, but I am related to his sister. There's a situation. His family needs him, but there's the employment contract with Honan-gung. Hand for hand. I've got to get to Honan-gung so that Willet can get back to his family, I don't know how long I'm going to have to cover for him. I'm very sorry, Foreman."

Oh. Was that it? Or did Shires actually have something more subtle on his mind?

Disappointed understanding was clearly what was called for in this situation; Fisner frowned, to demonstrate concern. "I feel sure you wouldn't come asking if it weren't a real problem, Shires. But I have to note that this puts us in a very difficult situation, with Dalmoss not back from Geraint."

Now Shires took a deep breath and threw back his head, staring up at the ceiling for a moment—as though getting his thoughts together—before he met Fisner's gaze, very frankly. Utterly honest. "To be brutally explicit, Foreman, there's a certain sort of irregularity involved. Personal behavior. It can be put right if an intimate friend can be identified before much more time elapses, but timing is critical. For the family's sake."

That was a lot of inventing to do.

If it was inventing.

Maybe Shires had thought the clues through and arrived at Honan-gung; why not? There was the question of what exact evidence Bench specialist Vogel thought he had, to present to First Secretary Verlaine at Chilleau Judiciary.

It was at least possible that Shires actually had no other motive than to address a family problem. Somebody was pregnant, without benefit of prior family negotiation and agreement. It happened. It even happened to Dolgorukij.

Shires at Honan-gung . . .

Shires could not be hoping to rescue Honan-gung from a raid single-handedly; that would be insane. Perhaps Vogel had not believed him, and now he sought to put himself in a position to be an eyewitness for the Langsarik defense; but if that was what Shires had in mind, he was self-deluded. Who would take Shires's evidence on behalf of his people seriously?

There was more.

If Flag Captain Walton Agenis's own nephew and lieutenant should be at Honan-gung when it was raided, his presence—especially under such irregular circumstances as those represented by this sudden excuse to get out to the Shawl—would be powerful circumstantial evidence of Langsarik guilt.

"When must you go?" Fisner asked, careful to sound as reluctant as possible. Shires let his breath out in an audible sigh, as of relief.

"Willet can come back on an inbound that's scheduled to load at Honan-gung. I can get passage on outbound freighter, *Sarihelt* stopping at Honan-gung to take on cargo tonight. Thank you, Foreman."

He *was* in a hurry.

When his body was discovered at Honan-gung—a casualty of the firefight, overlooked by mischance—what would the Bench make of his eagerness to get to Honan-gung as soon as the Bench specialists had left, to be in place in time for the raid that was to come?

And Shires had Dalmoss's undocumented chop, the one they had used to obtain the freighter tender's release for the Tyrell raid; better and better.

"It can't be helped." Shires had apparently correctly guessed at Fisner's permission, so he wouldn't push that any further. "I can't promise that your place will be held for you. But you've done very well, Shires, I hope you'll give us a chance to employ you again once these domestic entanglements have been resolved. Good-greeting, then."

Fisner turned his attention back to the administrative details of his daily tasks, smiling.

It was a matter of hours from Port Charid to the Shawl of Rikavie. Once the freighter came up to speed, there was little for Hilton to do but brood about how the freedom that had been their natural right had been denied them as part of the terms of the amnesty agreement. Life at Port Charid had not been torture; it was knowing that he was trapped there that had shadowed his psyche, for more than a year now.

He didn't want to dock at Honan-gung.

He wanted to steal the freighter, hit the Sillume vector, and fly forever—or until his air ran out. It would be worth it, to die in space. It would be a good death. Satisfying. Fit. Appropriate.

He couldn't afford the distraction.

He had work to do.

The freighter docked at Honan-gung, but nobody came out of the dock-master's office to greet them. Hilton had his instructions. The freighter crew let down the load-in ramp, and Hilton stepped down out from the belly of the beast to the docking bay's load-in apron. Hilton walked by himself across the empty and unpeopled warehouse floor with his documents board in his hand to pay his respects to the dock-master, who was waiting for him in her office. He could see her standing at the office's observation port, watching him come, and someone behind her with a jelly-stick. Nasty.

What, didn't they trust him?

Just because he was Langsarik—

He was on camera, too. He knew it; Vogel had clipped into the communications braid as the freighter neared the Honan-gung Yards, checking to be sure they knew where the eyes were. Parking an access slip in the information stream, to be ready when the time came. Hilton stopped short of the dock-master's office and called out.

"Hilton Shires come from Charid to relieve Willet, Dock-master. We have your permission. May I come in?"

He had no intention of quarreling with a man with a jelly-stick. Get hit with a fist, and bruise your face; get hit with a jelly-stick and smash all the bones at the side of your face into a pulp. Hilton was not interested.

He did his best to look defenseless.

After a moment's consideration the man with the jelly-stick opened the door to the dock-master's office to let Hilton through. Hilton went, but only because he knew Vogel was watching. He hoped that someone would intervene if the dock-master decided that she didn't like his looks.

Marching up to the dock-master, Hilton bowed politely, holding his documents board in front of him so that she could read what was there. "Thank you for your confidence. My credentials, ma'am."

A personal request that she play along with the charade that was required to get the ambush in place without alerting the quarry; one signed by Garol Aphon Vogel, Bench intelligence specialist. Identity chops could be forged; the raiders who had vandalized Tyrell would hardly be deterred from attempted forgery of Jurisdiction chops by the relatively insignificant penalty of death for doing so.

But it was such a beautiful chop mark, crisp and sparkling and ornate and complicated, that it was convincing in and of itself. Hilton was sure the dock-master couldn't help but be impressed. He was impressed, but he already knew that the chop mark was the genuine article.

"Are they, really?"

The station's surveillance was focused in other directions than within the dock-master's office, but Hilton knew he couldn't afford anyone glimpsing any anomalous behavior. They'd start to wonder. The presence of the man with the jelly-stick was enough of a problem. If Jelly-stick turned out to be the enemy's inside man, they would have a piece of work to do to get him taken off line without alerting his principals either directly or indirectly. Jelly-stick didn't look Dolgorukij to Hilton, though, so maybe they were all right.

As though any seven people with jelly-sticks would present serious difficulties to people with Langsarik battle cannon tucked casually into their hip pockets, if Hilton actually had been a raider.

The Bench requests your cooperation in investigating a serious crime. Please take your cues from the bearer, Hilton Shires.

Signed and sealed.

The dock-master seemed undecided for a long and trepidatious moment.

Then she made up her mind, handing the documents board back to him with a nod of acquiescence.

"All right, Shires, what can I do for you?"

That was two.

One had been getting out of Port Charid with their cargo undetected. That left only three—getting set up here, while staying out of sight—and four.

Four.

Ambushing a raiding party, capturing the killers who had done their best to ruin the Langsarik settlement, and returning in vindicated triumph to Port Charid.

Maybe it was a little more than four, maybe that was actually four through eight, but there was no question about two, which meant four was coming.

"If you would care to accompany me, ma'am, to inspect the cargo seals in place prior to off-load. With your escort, of course."

Garol Vogel was waiting on the freighter, out of sight. In safe concealment. The man with the jelly-stick would have to be included, because though he might not have seen the text on the documents board with its impressive official chop mark, he certainly knew by now that something was going on.

There was a lot to do.

They had to locate the raiders' inside man, going on information from Kazmer Daigule and that Cousin Stanoczk of his. They had to get cargo into place. They had to find Willet and send him back to Port Charid. And then they had to wait.

"Lead on, then," the dock-master said, beckoning the man with the jelly-stick with a wave of her hand to let him know that he should come with them.

Soon, soon, soon he would have revenge for the dead and the honor of the Langsarik fleet; and he was eager for it.

From where she knelt in the garden pulling the weeds, Walton Agenis could see the dust on the vehicle track, someone approaching the settlement—in a transport van, rather than in a for-hire or on a speed machine. It was that size of a cloud. The vehicle track was graded and paved, but the autumn rains had yet to set in; the dust on the road was as good as an advance warning signal.

Who would it be?

Midweek. That explained it. Walton watched the dust cloud for a moment, evaluating its dimensions and its rate of travel; then bent her head to her weeding once again. Yes. Midweek. It would be the supply van from Port Charid coming out to stock the little concession store that the Fleet had put out here to serve the community's miscellaneous requirements for notions, sundries, small amounts of luxury foods. The supply van from Port Charid.

It was early for the concession truck to arrive, though, didn't that usually show up after midday? The morning was early yet. The first shift at the construction site down the road was no more than two hours old. Traveling a little quickly for the concession van, maybe. The driver of the concession van was usually in no particular hurry to get here, and in no particular hurry to leave.

She was not liking this.

She was not liking this more and more, moment by moment.

She sat back once again, watching the dust on the vehicle track. There were more than one of them approaching.

The settlement was as deserted as it ever got. Many of the Langsariks with physical labor left in them were at the construction site. Others were in Port Charid doing entry-level administrative or custodial jobs, oiling the machinery of commerce with their low-cost labor.

If someone was going to raid the settlement—

This was not the time to do it, not with most of the Langsariks population dispersed to one job or another.

Or was it?

Had someone decided to accept the added task of tracking down each and every one of her crew, as an acceptable price for avoiding any potential resistance in mass that might have threatened had they chosen another time? There were more Langsariks than police or Port Authority employees in Port Charid. There were almost more Langsariks than able-bodied others; where would the resources to take them all at once come from?

Pushing herself up off the ground, Walton stood up. She could see Modice at the side of the house, watching the road. The vehicles were turning off the main vehicle track, making for the settlement proper.

Three transport vans, not supply trucks; still, they were headed for the concession store.

What was going on?

Nobody pulled up to her door to require her presence, though she was one of the senior members on the municipal board of the settlement.

Modice was looking in her direction, now. Walton couldn't see the expression on Modice's face from where she stood, but Modice's body language was sufficiently eloquent to communicate concern and uncertainty.

All right, if they didn't come for her, she'd go to them. Tucking her gardening trowel into her belt loop, Walton stepped across the rows of ripening root vegetables to go see what this was all about.

Modice started moving, too.

Other people in the settlement had seen the transport vans arrive or heard them pass through the settlement on the way to the concession store, alerted by the unusual speed at which the vehicles were traveling. A small crowd had gathered by the time Walton arrived; but there didn't seem to be anybody near the store itself.

As Walton Agenis got closer she saw the reason why.

Troops.

There was a cordon of people between the small crowd and the concession store, drawn up in formal array. They weren't in uniform, and they weren't in very good position, but they were all carrying weapons; so troops it was.

What was this all about?

Walton pushed through to the front of the crowd of people, looking past the cordon now to see if there was anybody she recognized.

"Factor Madlev!"

He started when she called out to him, as though she'd frightened him. It *was* Factor Madlev, and someone she thought she vaguely recognized with him: her nephew's foreman from the new construction site, Fisner Feraltz.

That was why he was familiar, then.

She remembered Fisner Feraltz. He'd been much younger, but he hadn't changed so much; and nothing she had ever heard had hinted that he had yet dealt with the traumatic event that had made him an orphan.

Factor Madlev was a decent man, if unsure of the wisdom of placing Langsariks in positions of trust.

But Fisner Feraltz was the enemy.

Turning, Factor Madlev started toward her; Feraltz put out a hand to detain him, saying something in a low voice. There were people she didn't recognize in the store, going in and out with boxes, through the back. Whatever Feraltz said was apparently convincing, because Factor Madlev stopped; but then Madlev waved her forward to come and join him, so the armed men had to let her pass.

Feraltz stepped back and away from Factor Madlev, but Walton didn't care if he heard what she had to say or not. "Factor Madlev. A surprise. What's going on here? The store won't be opening for another hour or two yet."

Some kind of a search, that seemed obvious enough now that she was close enough to get an unobstructed view. What, did someone think you could hide Langsarik battle cannon in flour boxes? It was ludicrous on the face of it—but she couldn't deny her uneasiness.

Maybe it wasn't battle cannon they were looking for.

Maybe it was some other kind of contraband, and contraband could be planted.

The people who ran the supply transport between the concession store in the settlement and Port Charid were all Madlev's people, so at least some of them could be Fisner Feraltz's people. She didn't think the people who watched the store broke open every case when it came out, not until it was needed. It would be so easy . . .

Madlev was visibly uncomfortable. He nodded to her in greeting with a look of genuine concern on his face. "Good-greeting, Dame Agenis. My apologies for this unannounced visit, but. Well, frankly.

There was a tip. An anonymous tip. My clear duty, to see what might be at the heart of it."

Tension knotted in Walton's stomach like a muscle spasm; but she managed to keep her voice steady. "Tip. What was the nature of this tip, Factor Madlev?"

It was obvious, wasn't it?

Uncomfortable as he clearly was with his role, Factor Madlev was also determined not to shirk his duty as he saw it. "To be quite clear, a claim that evidence relating to raids within the Shawl of Rikavie could be recovered from the storage room here. We can't not test the claim."

Of course they couldn't.

Walton watched the searchers work with dread and with anticipation that was equal parts of apprehension and eagerness for the play to run out. They would search until they found what they were looking for. They would find something; the enemy would not have risked an anonymous tip unless they had their prize in place.

Vogel had gone to ground at Honan-gung to wait for the next raid, and was not available to help.

Did this development mean there wouldn't be a raid at Honan-gung? Had the complicated setup Hilton had witnessed been abandoned, for whatever reason, for this unexpected—unheralded—approach?

No, that didn't made sense.

Discovery of contraband was still strictly circumstantial, clearly ambiguous by virtue of its location. More than just Langsariks had access to the stores.

Two men came out through the back door to the concession store sideways, carrying a small crate between them. They set it down at Factor Madlev's feet, grim satisfaction clear in their determined expressions.

Walton didn't even need to look to know. If she didn't even look, though, it could be taken as evidence that she already knew quite well what was in the crate. So she stared with wide-eyed wonder at the contents of the crate: a nest of padding that surrounded a beautiful little clutch of crystal gems for energy arrays, the small-heavies that warehouses kept for emergencies.

The wrappings were all marked with the sigil that identified them to the Okidan Yards.

Small-heavies were the single most valuable commodity—in market price to mass ratio—in known Space: portable, untraceable, and very easily convertible into other forms of laundered cash besides.

"Your people broke the seals," Walton noted, pointing. "How are we going to be able to prove who hid these here?"

It didn't have to be a strong argument; all it had to be was strong enough.

Evidence recovered on an anonymous tip was purely circumstantial, suspect by its very nature. No matter how strongly implicated the Langsarik settlement was by this discovery, they could not be convicted on this evidence alone.

"It looks bad, though, Dame Agenis," Factor Madlev said. The regretful sorrow in his voice was genuine; Walton could respect his desire to put the best construction on things. "We'll have to make a report. To Chilleau Judiciary, with Garol Vogel gone."

More than that, Feraltz would have to carry out the raid on Honan-gung in order to put visual evidence of atrocities on the record.

She hoped that Feraltz's raid was at Honan-gung.

If it was anywhere but Honan-gung, they could be lost, despite the best efforts of Vogel and Hilton and Modice's Daigule combined.

He had coordinated the raid, arranged for an escort for Agenis afterward, and otherwise made himself so much a part of the day's work that Factor Madlev had no apparent questions in his mind about Fisner's right to be here for this one.

"Urgent news from Port Charid, First Secretary." Factor Madlev had been a silent witness during previous interviews between Specialist Vogel and the Second Judge's First Secretary; he seemed a little intimidated, now, but he knew his ground and field, growing more confident as he spoke. "I am of course not privy to what information the Bench specialist may have to present to you when he arrives. But I am fully familiar with the outrages we have suffered here at Port Charid over the past months."

Factor Madlev paused for a moment, glancing at Walton Agenis's impassive face. Madlev's misplaced sense of decency was to blame for her presence here. Fisner felt it unnecessary, but she could do no harm. Factor Madlev seemed finally to be convinced—so much was clear from his determined tone, as he continued.

"Now there is additional evidence linking terrorist acts to the Langsariks settled here at Port Charid. Dame Agenis herself will admit to what we all saw earlier today, plunder from Okidan, recovered from a hiding place within the Langsarik settlement."

Terrorist acts. It was a word choice that Fisner could appreciate; all the more so since Fisner had not had to take any hand in guiding Madlev to the right phrase.

"Recovered, yes," Walton Agenis said. She hadn't asked permission to speak; she was only here on sufferance—but her boldness won her the attention of the First Secretary, because Factor Madlev seemed too startled to rebuke her. "But on an anonymous tip, from an area to which other than Langsariks have had continuous and uncontrolled access since the very first days of the settlement. We have not violated the terms of our agreement with the Bench, First Secretary. I assert our complete innocence of any involvement with theft and violence in system."

Well, what else could she say?

And Factor Madlev, for once, insisted on his right as the acting governor and Bench proxy at Port Charid.

"Dame Agenis's position is reasonable and honorable, but there is cause to believe that she no longer speaks for the Langsariks. We have been patient, First Secretary. We have appealed to the Bench for help after the raid on Penyff. After the raid on Sonder. After the raid on Tershid. Okidan. Tyrell. You sent us Bench specialists. They have gone, and told us nothing."

Madlev warmed to his subject as he spoke. He was right. Absolutely right. Completely right. Unchallengeably right. "We are responsible citizens of the Bench, First Secretary. We have a right to security in the conduct of trade. Would the Bench tolerate these pirates if they were anyone else but Langsariks?"

There was silence from Chilleau Judiciary, as the First Secretary apparently took a moment to digest Factor Madlev's assertion.

"What do you want me to do, Madlev?"

Fisner caught his breath and held it, almost despite himself. This was crucial. If Madlev backed down now—

Madlev didn't back down. "I say it's time to admit that the Langsariks are our primary suspects, First Secretary, with respect. It may seem disrespectful to mention such a thing in this regard, but we have all heard a great deal about recent and regrettable failures within the Second Judge's administration to execute good governance and observe the rule of Law. At the Domitt Prison."

Far from backing down, Madlev pressed forward more strongly than Fisner would ever have imagined. He had not realized that Factor Madlev had such strong feelings about this—but perhaps Madlev took the Bench's inaction as a personal reflection. If not on him personally, than on the Bench's respect and consideration for his position here. Yes. Perhaps.

There was a sound from the communications link, as of clucking one's tongue. A sound of exasperation, or of warning. "You put your case very strongly, Factor Madlev."

Should he not?

Did Verlaine mean that Factor Madlev should comport himself with more submissive meekness in the presence of the First Secretary?

"I state only the facts as we see them, First Secretary. The firms who have invested in Port Charid did not expect to put lives as well as capital into the enterprise. Those lives deserve consideration. If Port Charid is truly important to the Bench for the development of trade routes across the Sillume vector, it is high time the Bench showed some evidence of its respect. Sending Vogel was a good first step. But Vogel's gone, we have heard nothing, the dead are unavenged, there is physical evidence here. I appeal to you."

No, Fisner realized, with satisfaction. Madlev did not appeal to Verlaine. Madlev demanded. "Send troops, if nothing else, to secure the Shawl. Do something."

There was no answer for several moments, but there were voices in the background. One of them Verlaine's.

When Verlaine came back at full volume he sounded both angry and resigned. "Very well, Factor Madlev," Verlaine said; and Fisner felt his heart leap in exultation. "I have spoken to Specialist Vogel. You are right, you deserve nourishment. Here's what I've decided to do."

Glancing at Agenis quickly, Fisner saw her face pale, dread evident in her eyes—no matter how resolute her expression. She was right to dread, Fisner told himself, guarding his fierce joy carefully to prevent any hint of his delight from escaping. This was the beginning of the end for the Langsariks.

"I will release the Third Fleet Interrogations Group to depart for Rikavie immediately, with a fully endorsed schedule of inquiry— pending final authorization, which I will issue or cancel once I have reviewed the evidence Garol Vogel promises. You have been asked to be patient for too long. There will be an end to it."

An end to the Langsariks.

A Fleet Interrogations Group would generate confessions, to be claimed as evidence; there would be more evidence on record after the Honan-gung raid. Walton Agenis's very own nephew was at Honan-gung. Hilton Shires would be easy to identify on Honan-gung's record scans; and there was reasonable hope that he had the forged chop with him. On his body.

There would be no claiming ignorance for the Langsariks after that; Verlaine would have to issue the final authorization. The Fleet Interrogations Group would already be on hand, ready and waiting. It would all be an accomplished fact before Vogel could hope to return to Port Charid, even if he turned around the moment he reached Chilleau Judiciary.

After that Vogel could raise concerns all he liked. Once the Bench had evidence on Record, the truth behind that evidence would be no longer relevant. The rule of Law and the upholding of the Judicial order would demand that the Bench proceed against a proven enemy, prosecuting the case against the Langsariks to the fullest extent of the Law.

"It can't come too soon, First Secretary. With respect." Factor Madlev had gained his point. He could step back, lower his head, bow politely to the communications port on the desk. "Thank you."

Agenis stood and stared at the far wall, and Chilleau Judiciary closed the communications link between them.

Madlev sighed deeply.

Then he walked over to his desk and sat down.

"Escort Dame Agenis back to the settlement," Madlev said, to Fisner. "No contact with other Langsariks. The household is under quarantine."

Fisner understood.

He knew there was nothing the Langsariks could do. But if they knew there was a Fleet Interrogations Group coming for them, they would unquestionably try something.

"Of course, Factor Madlev. Dame Agenis. If you'll come with me, ma'am, and please don't try to speak to anybody. We'll keep things as liberal as we can."

Everything was perfect. It had all added up, and now it was playing out beautifully.

Had Madlev published the coming of the Fleet Interrogations Group, Fisner might have had to reconsider the wisdom of the planned Honan-gung raid. It might be taken as anomalous behavior on the part of people expecting to be taken to task for their evil deeds in the near future. This way was much better. He could have his raid, his booty from Honan-gung, and his Fleet Interrogations Group, too.

Agenis looked at him, and for a moment Fisner imagined that there was something in her eyes that he did not like—wild contempt, and scorn, and challenging defiance.

It was only a flash, and only a moment.

"Very well, Foreman. Let's go. I don't need to make any trouble. We'll be vindicated by due legal process soon enough."

He had imagined it. Obviously.

Agenis turned toward the door in response to his gesture, and Fisner followed her out, to escort her back to the Langsarik settlement and place her under house arrest.

The Holy Mother smoothed the way of those who worked Her will in the world.

And the Angel of Destruction was invincible.

The Langsarik troops Garol had brought with him had been carefully dispersed quietly, surreptitiously, well out of the way of observation by either the station's monitors or any of the station's personnel—except for the dock-master herself, and the man who had met poor Shires with jelly-stick in hand and a threatening expression on his face. The maintenance chief. Garol's pod had been wheeled into the dock-master's safe room, where he had easy access to every incoming communication without the awkward complication of relays that could be noticed or misdirected.

The chime that went off to rouse him from his meditation was no signal incoming to Honan-gung, however.

It was Jils Ivers, in transit for Chilleau Judiciary.

Garol frowned, and toggled in.

"Vogel here." He spoke quietly. The pod was soundproof, but there was no sense in pushing his limits. "Go ahead."

She didn't sound happy, but there was no reason for her to call him unless there was a problem. "Verlaine. Trouble at Port Charid, a raid on the settlement, hot cargo. Stand by."

All right.

He was securely webbed into his station in the pod, so he didn't more than frown to prepare himself for a confrontation. He heard the signal tone that let him know Jils had braided into skein, and spoke. "First Secretary. Vogel here, sir."

Verlaine wasted no words, clearly under pressure. "I have Port Charid on my neck, Vogel. They raided the Langsarik settlement and found loot from Okidan. I need a convincing story if I'm going to hold action on this."

A raid. Garol thought fast. Such a ploy was a natural part of a conspiracy; maybe he should have expected it. But if it got the conspirators what they wanted—would the Honan-gung raid be abandoned?

"This is not totally unexpected, First Secretary." Not predicted, perhaps, but absolutely in character once it had happened. "I hold my point. My evidence will be definitive."

He just didn't have it yet; but he couldn't tell Verlaine that. Verlaine was on the line with Port Charid. Garol didn't know with certainty whether or not his quarry was listening in—one reason for the charade Jils put forward, the play that he was actually on the courier with her in transit to Chilleau Judiciary.

He could not afford to compromise his chances for the clear and undeniable proof of Langsarik innocence that he needed now more than ever.

"Reluctantly unable to accept as read, Vogel. I've got to think of the Second Judge's reputation. I don't like to override, it's your mission, but I'm running out of time. Give me something to hold Port Charid off. Please."

Garol had to respect the First Secretary's frustration.

But he couldn't say anything more, not and hope to complete the mission he had embarked upon. "I appreciate the delicacy of your situation, First Secretary. Anything you can do to suspend further decisions until I can show you the evidence will be very deeply appreciated."

Awkwardly phrased, but with luck his sincerity would come through. The only question was whether Verlaine felt he could afford to stand behind Garol, with mounting political pressure to take action.

There was a moment's silence; then Verlaine spoke.

"I'm sorry, Bench specialist. I have my Judge to think of. I accept as given your assertion that you can identify the guilty parties. However, I have perceptions to manage as well."

Lost.

"Understood, First Secretary."

Because, unfortunately, Garol did understand. Verlaine had been backed into a corner. The Second Judge had come under widespread criticism from political enemies for her failure to more aggressively detect and deter abuses of the Judicial order injurious to the rights of accused parties in detention at the Domitt Prison.

With publication of the incriminating results of a raid on the Langsarik settlement, Verlaine almost had to take action; it was either that or suffer a storm of criticism such that no responsible First Secretary could be asked to endure on behalf of the Judicial order.

Verlaine didn't even sign off.

The signal didn't drop; Garol listened in on Port Charid.

The Third Fleet Interrogations Group.

It was bad; but it was not over yet. He needed something to ensure that the Honan-gung raid would go off on schedule, whenever that was, and the Third Fleet Interrogations Group would have to do. They did not yet have lawful authority to make Port Charid their playground. If he got evidence before Verlaine released the Brief . . .

Now more than ever he needed the proof that only capture of the guilty during the active commission of a violent crime could provide him.

Jils came back on the line. "Garol. What do you want me to do?"

He didn't know yet. He needed to think things through. He had to have that raid; he didn't dare try to transmit from here to Chilleau Judiciary for fear of detection by the sophisticated communications equipment Daigule had indicated was at the enemy's disposal.

So long as the raid came quickly enough, he could still get his proof to Chilleau Judiciary in time to prevent the release of Brief to the Fleet

Interrogations Group. Once they had their Brief, they would not abort their mission for any Bench directive until they were finished—on their own terms.

Politics.

"Track that Fleet Interrogations Group for me, Jils. Let me know when they clear the exit vector at Sillume."

And thanks.

But she knew that.

Extra words were dangerous when communications were on redirect.

Jils was off; Chilleau Judiciary was off. He was alone with his thoughts.

If there was to be a raid at Honan-gung at all, it had to happen soon, before the Fleet Interrogations Group arrived.

Could he rely on the greed of this so-called "Angel of Destruction" of Cousin Stanoczk's to try for one last payout?

How long would the Angel keep him waiting—and how long could he afford to wait before he would be forced to admit defeat?

He was already defeated.

If he could not take prisoners in a raid at Honan-gung, there would be no proving to Chilleau Judiciary that the Langsariks were innocent victims of conspiracy.

He would hold where he was, and wait.

He had no acceptable alternatives to hope for.

Kazmer Daigule parked his for-hire well clear of the little house where Walton Agenis sat under house arrest. The lights that the guards had trained on the building cast shadows in sharp relief, so the scene took on an air of unreality, strange and oppressive in the darkness of the settlement. Was it some variety of harassment? Kazmer wondered. Or was it just unthinking cruelty, the sort of blind impersonal brutality that was that much the more difficult to bear for being so completely thoughtless?

The guards were warehousemen from the Combine Yards in Port Charid proper—Dolgorukij. Uncomfortable with their role as security, they gathered at the front of the house as Kazmer approached, frowning and doing their best to look stern, bulked up with cold-weather gear in the crisp night air.

When he was within easy hailing distance one of them spoke. "You, what's your business here? You can't go in, you know."

The awkwardness they clearly felt in their performance of their task was eased by their quick recognition of what, if not who, he was. Dolgorukij knew Sarvaw as Sarvaw knew Dolgorukij, and honest warehousemen were naturally put at ease by their inbred knowledge of their racial superiority.

It was a useful trick of the blood, something the Holy Mother had ordained to give Her Sarvaw children an edge even in adversity against their opponents. Kazmer knew how to deal with Dolgorukij bullies. It was nothing personal, not really.

"There should be no problem, cousin, surely." In the shadows cast by the bright lights against the greater darkness Kazmer could see eyes narrow in disdain and suspicion at his choice of words. But even a Sarvaw could lay claim to a privileged position, without blushing, when it was a Malcontent who spoke. "I'd just like to go and see Modice. She's at home? With her aunt?"

The guards were not receptive to his powers of persuasion, however. Kazmer fingered the neckline of his blouse nervously, pulling at the fabric next to his skin as though his collar were too tight—taking care that the red ribbon that he wore next to his skin showed clearly.

The guards relaxed.

"Sorry, cousin, no offense," the spokesman said. Kazmer was amused to note that he ranked greater kinship as a Malcontent than he could ever have been granted as a Sarvaw. "Don't bring us shame before the foreman, though. Go on in."

He was a Malcontent. He could go anywhere, do anything, and be bowed on his way by people who would never dream of granting such a privilege to anyone else. It *was* funny.

Crossing the brilliantly illuminated space between the cordon and the house, knocking softly at the door. "Is Modice home?"

They knew that he was there, of course. They'd seen him coming. It was almost as bright inside as if the lights had been on, and the lights weren't on, though the windows had been only partially screened over. Frugal. Saving of energy. Why turn on the lights when Port Charid provided such ample illumination at no charge?

Modice let him in and closed the door behind him.

Walton Agenis sat in the tiny living room watching him come.

The effect of the shadows on the wall from the lights outside was ghastly.

"You're looking well, Modice," Kazmer said. Modice had gone out to fetch the gel-sheets that she'd been preparing in the kitchen, but they wouldn't know that, outside. They could be listening. He had to assume that someone might be listening. But whoever might be listening could only guess at the potential meaning of whatever they might hear. "Are you getting enough rest?"

Modice was back with gel-sheets in a pan, paper—thin sheets of gelatin made opaque with starch. And a stylus. "Not very well, Kazmer, I'm afraid. These lights."

Kazmer wrote on the top gel-sheet and passed the pan to Walton Agenis. *FIG clears vector w/in 24 hrs. Must raid before pursuit possible.*

It was a form of freehand code; he couldn't afford to arouse suspicion by concentrating so long on what he needed to write that there was a break in the conversation. "Do you have something you could use as a compress, to cover your eyes? A scarf might do it. If the colors weren't too bright, of course."

Agenis lifted the gel-sheet from the pan and folded it up neatly. "Would you get me something to drink, girl." Writing on the next gel-sheet in the pan. "I don't want you coming around to court Modice, Daigule. I've told you before. You're not fit to husband a Langsarik."

Progress of organization. Contingency plan?

"Modice could do worse than take a Sarvaw sweetheart," Kazmer protested, mildly. Even a Malcontent lover would be a better fate than the Bond, after all. "I might be able to protect her. Things don't look very promising, you must know that."

Quiet, no alarm. Good progress. Vogel returns PC if raid delayed.

If the Angel cut the margin for its raid too fine, Vogel would be forced to abandon the ambush; Vogel was adamant on the subject. He would be at Port Charid before the Fleet Interrogations Group arrived, one way or the other.

Kazmer had his doubts about that.

Vogel was clearly all but desperate to prevent the Fleet Interrogations Group from settling in to do its work; but without the evidence that ambushing the raid would produce, how did Vogel hope to prevent it?

"Better pure and falsely accused than soiled and safe, Daigule," Agenis insisted, inflexibly. "Modice."

Modice had returned with a tray and a pitcher of water, three glasses.

"Modice, I don't want you seeing this person again. You are not to let him in, if he has the audacity to return to my house to insult me with his importunity. And in our hour of vulnerability, Daigule, you should be ashamed."

"Aunt Walton, please. You're just upsetting yourself. Here. I brought us all a nice glass of cold water." Three gel-sheets from the stack in the pan had been discarded; that was one for each glass. It would be a moment before the gel-sheet in his glass dissolved, however.

If anything goes wrong, Aunt Agenis wrote on the next gel-sheet in the pan. *Get Modice out of here.*

It was a firm hand, though written on a gel-sheet. The tension and the waiting, the uncertainty and the anxiety, were taking their toll on Walton Agenis; but she saw as clearly and as far as ever she had. Kazmer could only bow in her direction. It was not for nothing that she had been called the Deep-Minded.

"I'd better not, Modice, your aunt wants me out of the house. But if there's anything I can do, you send for me, all right? You don't have to toady to this harridan; she'd rather see you dead than with me. And I could make you happy."

He kept his tone very reasonable and calm, he thought. All things considered. Walton Agenis straightened up in her chair so abruptly that she spilled half the water in her glass, her face suddenly transfused with mirth despite it all, and mouthed the words back at him with a look of exaggerated outrage. *Harridan?*

"You can't talk about my aunt that way." Modice's voice trembled as she fought to keep her composure. "Perhaps you'd better leave, Kazmer."

The gel-sheet in his glass had dissolved; Modice would take the unused sheets back to the kitchen, to make cellophane dumplings. It took a steady hand to make Langsarik cellophane dumplings under the best of circumstances. That she could pretend to do so convincingly under these was a measure of her nerve.

"Well. I'm sorry you feel that way." He could express all the resentment he had a right to feel, without holding back. Modice made wonderful cellophane dumplings. He wouldn't be there to help eat them. "You'll be sorry. I wouldn't wait too long to change my mind if I were you, though. I've got my pride, you know."

And she could buy it for three dumplings and a smile. She had. Or rather she could have, in the past, because it was no good anymore, no matter how good a cook she was.

Take care of Modice, Walton Agenis had said.

Now that it was too late, she would trust him.

Kazmer paused on the threshold of Agenis's house to let the resentful anguish in his heart paint his countenance an appropriate shade of outrage and insulted fury; and left them there together in the surreal shadows of the floodlit house.

"The Third Fleet Interrogations Group is due off the Sillume exit vector in twenty hours." They would be able to stage from the new airfield at the construction site; Dalmoss was in no danger of an accidental meeting with any Malcontents, Sarvaw or otherwise, out here. Those people were in Port Charid proper, where they belonged.

No, they belonged in Hell, but it was not Fisner Feraltz's mission to see them escorted safely to their destination—he knew where his special duty lay. "You must be near enough to the entrance vector to make pursuit a clear waste of energy."

"How do I know that, eldest and firstborn?" Dalmoss asked, and there was just the slightest trace of insubordinate challenge in his voice. His long days of seclusion had worn upon him; the proximity of the Langsarik corpse had made him nervous. It would be all right. After this Dalmoss would be able to rest and recreate himself in the bosom of his family, at home, on Arakcheyek. "In order to time my raid. Must I have special knowledge?"

Good question. Fisner thought for a moment. "The Langsarik leader was present when we talked to Chilleau Judiciary. She passed on the information somehow. If you set your margin carefully enough, it will seem clear that you miscalculated, you didn't expect the Fleet Interrogations Group in system so soon, you flee in disarray—leaving the body of at least one of your people behind."

Hilton Shires.

How beautifully it all fit together, when the Holy Mother smiled upon the enterprise.

"Twenty hours. Ten hours from the exit vector to Port Charid." Dalmoss was talking it through, out loud. Fisner could bear the trivial details of it patiently; it would serve as a useful check on the soundness of Dalmoss's reasoning, tipping Fisner off if he needed to retire his raid leader. "Four hours from Port Charid to Honan-gung, at this time of year. So if we leave in panic and disarray as soon as the Fleet Interrogations Group clears the vector, there is no point in pursuing us."

Dalmoss would hit Honan-gung; there would be a raid in process as the Fleet Interrogations Group came off the Sillume exit vector. The raiders would escape, but they would not be able to save their families. The Bench's punishment would be stern and swift—though after the Fleet Interrogations Group had done its work, the Bench sanctions would be perhaps something of an afterthought.

"You must prepare," Fisner urged Dalmoss to energize him, get him going. "You must be away from Honan-gung inside of thirty-four hours. There is much to do. This is our finest moment, second eldest and next born."

Dalmoss bowed, his expression determined and joyful. "Sweet indeed is Holy ordinance, firstborn and eldest. With your blessing we triumph."

With the Holy Mother Herself on their side they were invincible.

Before two days had passed it would be over for the Langsariks at Port Charid.

CHAPTER ELEVEN

Hilton lay flat on his back on a scoot-plank on the floor beneath the crane's trolley with a probe in one hand and a gleam in the other. "What exactly am I looking for, Jevan?" he asked, trying to make sense of the bewildering array of nozzles and blind access bits on the underside of the crane's power box. "Hydraulic scan? Flux regulation coupling?"

Silence.

Hilton wondered if he'd lost his work partner. That was more serious than not knowing what to do with the problem at hand. Jevan was the only Dolgorukij on the crew here, the man the Malcontent had identified as a probable agent for the Angel of Destruction. Hilton needed Jevan where he could keep an eye on him, figuratively if not literally. If Jevan had some means of sending a covert signal to warn the raiders away, Hilton needed to know immediately.

So where had Jevan gone?

Footsteps approached the crane trolley where Hilton lay; Jevan. Maybe. "Sorry, Shires." Yes, that was Jevan. "Maybe we should hold off on this for now. I just heard, there's a freighter coming in. They might need help load-out."

Hilton thought for a moment. Jevan could have heard, yes, if he'd been chatting with someone in the dock-master's office when contact was made.

"Maybe we should all go get sticks," Hilton suggested, not moving. "Can't be too careful. Might be Langsariks."

Jevan laughed, crouching on his heels to stick his face into the gap between the bottom of the crane's trolley and the floor.

"You're a funny man."

Jevan could well laugh, Hilton told himself, excitement building within him. If Kazmer's Cousin Stanoczk was right, Jevan already knew that they weren't Langsarik raiders.

"Come out from there, Hilton, we'll be wanted."

Yes, he'd wager on it. Shutting off his gleam, arms straight to his sides, Hilton pushed himself out from underneath the crane's trolley on his scoot-plank, using his feet for propulsion. "No arguments from me, friend. I'd much rather load than muck around with this stuff."

He felt a tingling sensation, in the sole of his work boot.

Vibration from the movement of the scoot-plank?

No.

Vogel's signal.

Jevan was holding out a hand to help him up. Hilton took the welcome assistance in the spirit in which it was offered. It was nothing personal. Jevan was a perfectly amiable person; but he was in league with the enemy of the Langsariks, plotting the ruin of the Langsariks. There was blood to balance between them besides.

Maybe it was personal after all—at least on Hilton's part.

"Ready?" Jevan asked. "I should probably go and find the others. In case we're needed."

What made Jevan so sure that they would be?

Still, it might just be common practice on warehouse crews to minimize work effort. "I know," Hilton suggested, to enter into the spirit of the game. "I'll go help find people. I think Teller and Ames are on remote."

The hesitation in Jevan's eyes was very quickly masked. "Well. Sure. Why not? I'll get out to interim stores, then." But it was there; and Hilton could have smiled out loud to see it, except that he might be misinterpreted. Or tip Jevan off.

The signal buzzed twice more in his work boot and was still.

Hilton waited until Jevan was out of sight; then turned, heading toward the corridors that led to the maintenance tunnels for the remote sites where the solar arrays were generating the station's power.

Where he had a raiding party that needed to get to the docking bay.

They had been on alert for two days. They were ready for some action.

Garol Vogel stood behind the dock-master in her office with his back to the windows in the wall, watching as she engaged the incoming craft.

"All right, *Melrick*, your credentials clear. Permission to dock, transmit your manifest."

It claimed to be the freighter *Melrick* from the Bortic Yards, outbound from Charid for Lorton and scheduled to carry a consignment of cultural artifacts for the cultural institute there as well as licensed replicas for sale on the open market.

"Freighter *Melrick* here, thank you, Dock-master. Initiating transmit." Was it his imagination—Garol wondered—or did he recognize that voice? Had he heard it somewhere before? One thing was for certain—the accent was good. Garol knew it wasn't really Langsariks. He believed and hoped it wasn't Langsariks. But the freighter's captain sounded Langsarik to Garol.

The freighter claimed to have off-loaded at Port Charid and taken on cargo at the Combine Yards before paying a visit to Honan-gung as its next-to-last stop before it made the Sillume entry vector. The next-to-last part was a good touch, Garol felt. Subtle. These people were good.

Garol watched the freighter on approach as its manifest scrolled over the receiver. Shires was with the Dolgorukij, but not so close that the man had no opportunity to send the all clear for the raid to his headquarters. There had been no signal that Garol had intercepted: yet the freighter was here. Garol could only hope that meant that the signal would only have been sent if there had been a problem.

Kazmer Daigule had been tracking the freighter *Melrick* without pause since it had made rendezvous earlier today with a freighter tender from Port Charid—*that* freighter tender, the one whose weight indicated that it was carrying battle cannon or something equivalently and anomalously heavy.

This was what they had been waiting for.

The hardest part of this mission was about to start. He had to keep the raiders distracted while the Langsariks did their thing.

All he really wanted to do was to borrow someone's weapon and shoot them all, simply shoot them all, for the trouble they had caused and the people they had killed, for the hazard they'd created for a people trying to integrate peacefully into Jurisdiction, for the shockingly insolent disregard they showed toward civil society and the common right of common people to live free from fear in an ordered society.

And he couldn't.

He had a duty to the Bench to uphold the rule of Law. That meant not just doing the right thing, but doing it the right way.

"Pretty exhaustive," the dock-master said to the freighter on the communications line, as Garol tracked the progress of the docking sequence on the monitors. "This could take some putting together."

He had people in position, but if the freighter simply blew in, they would do him no good. He had to trust to the basic mercantile instinct of the Dolgorukij hominid. There was good loot to be had at Honan-gung. Even with its provenance destroyed or forged, the cargo that the freighter was requisitioning would generate a lot of free cash flow. Secret terrorist societies were almost always short of cash for funding.

"Yes, I know, Dock-master." The freighter captain's voice was regretful and a little diffident over the communications line. "Unfortunately for me, I'm already on deficit time. Any chance of putting a rush on? I've got ten casks of something here. I can't say it's drinking alcohol because it's on my manifest as syrup. We somehow didn't quite manage to obtain any tariff seals, either, so you know I have to get rid of it somehow before I reach the Port Authority in Lorton. Just in case."

So far it conformed to the pattern Daigule had described. There had to be a way to collect the crew all in one place, and it had to be something relatively unremarkable and ordinary, something that wouldn't arouse any suspicion. The raiders knew that Daigule was at Port Charid; but by the same token—if their intelligence was as good as their historical successes indicated—they also knew that Daigule's evidence had not been published. No one had been warned; at least not so far as the raiders knew.

"Well. In that case," the dock-master said, giving Garol a wink that went by too quickly for him to be sure he'd actually seen it. "I'll let the crew know. Pressurization sequence initiating. Stand by."

This was crucial.

The outer bay pressurized; the blast curtain rolled back, and the freighter tracked forward slowly into position with its cargo bays accessible.

The freighter captain's voice came back across the communications link. "We'll be doing some cargo shift while we're here," the captain said. "Won't be able to start load immediately. Should be ready by the time cargo's assembled, hope you understand."

Garol nodded to the dock-master. Perfect.

They didn't seem to be planning on moving troops onto the floor concealed in cargo cases this time. It was all to the good if the raiders stayed in the freighter until they thought it was time to make their move, though it complicated the task of Shires's commando. Garol wanted to minimize any potential shooting.

But there were no cameras, no motion detectors, no surveillance in the murky deeps of the docking bay on the other side of the freighter; there was no way to be sure that Shires and his team could pull it off.

"No problem," the dock-master said. "It'll give us a chance to get organized ourselves. We'll be ready when you are."

Garol hoped so.

It was all up to Shires now.

And Shires had even more to lose than he did.

Crouched behind the waist-tall roll of ground cloth at the far end of the docking bay, Hilton listened to the feed from the dock-master's office, scanning the freighter with an assessing eye. Late-model Corense shipyards, deep-space cruiser, fit for live and other perishable cargo; the perfect vehicle for transport of luxury goods, and if it carried cannon, what of it? A freighter had a right to self-defense. There were pirates to contend with.

"So. How's the weather in port?" the dock-master asked, her voice casual in Hilton's ear over the communications feed from the docking bay on the other side of the freighter. Making conversation. Keeping the freighter engaged.

People were starting to filter into the docking bay; the first cargo crates were arriving. He thought he could see Jevan among the workers.

Hilton looked down the line to his left. Leaning forward slightly,

Ousel met his eyes. Hilton looked to the flank of the freighter and back to Ousel; Ousel nodded.

Hilton slid to the right over the rough flooring to clear space for Ousel's people to exit. Four of them, keeping low but not crawling, careful to stay in the shadows that the freighter cast. There would be no sensor net that would pick up a hominid. Corense freighters carried damage control for space debris, but the ship's comps knew better than to irritate their master by sounding an alarm every time a maintenance crew came belly under in docks.

"Oh, about the same, Dock-master." The freighter captain didn't sound all that interested in the weather, though. "Say. We'll be ready to start load-in soon. We'd sure appreciate any help you can provide."

Jevan would be counting, probably, but there was no way Hilton could see that Jevan could communicate directly with the ship. Maybe the freighter captain was counting as well.

Filappe next.

The external accesses on Corense freighters were usually distributed evenly across three intervals aft, midship, and forward. Filappe had the spanners. There were no pressure alarms to fear, since the bay was pressurized. They had all studied the layout. If this wasn't the ship Kazmer had fingered, they were all in potential trouble—so Hilton wanted to find out as soon as possible.

"And we'll really appreciate your discards." The dock-master's voice was clear and carried well over the feed from the dock-master's office that Hilton was carrying. "Got one or two more people yet to notify, but cargo's coming together beautifully. You'll see."

He got the middle access.

Three of his team beside him, Hilton crept stealthily to the side of the freighter, anxious to identify his point of entry. He was off by some lengths, but it was all right, because Vogel had worked it with the dock-master. The lighting was on their side as much as possible. He could move down the flank of the freighter safe from observation.

But get in?

The bolts on the access port were clean and freshly coated. Hilton felt a moment's panic as he ran his hand around the outline of the access panel. It was too fresh. Had someone bolted it from inside?

Shilla had the wrench.

Torbe slid the cutting edge of a flexible knife around the edges of the bolts where they met the freighter's skin, then stepped back.

Shilla fit the tool to bolt and leaned on it, but nothing moved. Backing away, Shilla stared at the bolt with what looked like horror on her face, in the dim light. Then she leaned into the bolt again: it moved this time, it gave against her weight, and going by the grateful glance she flashed at Hilton—grateful for success, and sharing her emotion— it had been sheer anxiety, and not horror, that he'd seen before.

There were nine bolts.

Torbe and Vilner held the panel as Shilla pulled the last bolt, easing the panel away from the side of the freighter as it came down. Hilton gave Shilla a hand up into the freighter's outside maintenance passage. Once he and Shilla were both inside, Torbe and Vilner passed the outer panel through, so that they could lean it up against the wall of the passageway on the inside. No sense in putting it on the ground, where some ill chance might lead to premature discovery.

Holding up his hand for absolute stillness, Hilton listened for alarms that the ship might send if its hull was breached. There was a good reason to be confident that there would be none; most such alarms depended upon a sudden catastrophic loss of atmosphere, or some anomalous decline in the air pressure within the passageways closest to the hull.

He didn't hear any alarms.

He heard some sounds coming through the open hull, indistinct noises that bounced off the far wall of the docking bay from the opposite side of the ship. He heard—or thought he heard—the stealthy whisper of fabric against fabric from far down the corridors, on his right, on his left, as the other teams worked.

Satisfied, he gave his team the nod.

There were access portals between the maintenance passageways in the ship's hull and the ship's interior. Any such access portal was required by common practice and common sense to have an external override. People got trapped against the hull. It happened. They had to be able to get back into the ship whether or not the portal had been locked off from inside.

There would be a system alert this time, Hilton was sure of it. There were supposed to be system alerts any time a portal was opened between the maintenance hull and the ship's interior.

They had three things in their favor.

One was the possibility that no one on board would notice the visual alert; that was what the Corense lines used on hull access.

Then, since their commando attack had been carefully planned to come while the crew was busy, if anybody did notice the telltale alert they might just ignore it—assuming it to be some mechanical malfunction—until the excitement was over and there was slack time to investigate.

And, finally, they could hope that if anybody noticed, whoever on board went to check on the alert would come alone or in pairs, to be easily overpowered by Langsariks. Real ones.

Shilla cracked the seal on the access to the opening edge of the hatch to judge the potential air-pressure differential between the outer hull and the interior of the ship, to get an advance warning on whether or not the interior doors on the freighter were open or closed. Hilton didn't hear any hiss or sigh of air moving as she pushed the hatch open; so either the ship was open inside—or someone unsympathetic had opened the connecting door to whatever room this hatch led to and was waiting for them with a weapon at the ready.

They flattened themselves against the inner wall of the maintenance passageway, hiding themselves as best they could to be ready for an attack if one should come. Shilla pushed the hatch cover full open, with her body blocking anyone's view of the passage behind her. Hilton was impressed by her courage—it took nerve to expose yourself to enemy fire in order to win time for your team to respond.

Nobody shot Shilla.

Sticking her head through the open access port quickly, she checked left, then right, then left again; and then climbed through.

After a moment she was back. "All clear," she said, but quietly. A mere gesture might have been coerced at weapons point; this way they knew that she was her own woman and could follow her through with confidence.

Storeroom, and almost filled with crates except for the safety requirement of the clearway to the door.

The crates all carried Combine markings; but in the low light Hilton thought he could see the ghost of other seals, altered but not entirely obliterated.

So this was where at least some of the contraband was stored. On a freighter, in orbit. There would be little chance of the stores being discovered under Combine seal—and the foreman, Fisner Feraltz, had the chop. Ingenious. He would have to remember that. He had to complete his mission first and foremost, though, so Hilton went to the doorway, to listen.

All of the doorways would be open, if the evidence of this one could be taken as a measure. Freighters habitually opened all their doors when they were docked, to get the maximum benefit of free air circulation and replenishment. Trading old air for new.

He heard someone moving, but the sound was indistinct; he couldn't quite make it out. He was going to have to get closer. Hilton slipped out into the corridor, with his people behind him concealing themselves within open doorways and following as they could.

Somebody spoke.

"Well, that's done, then."

Hilton knew the voice.

"Come on, let's go tell the boss. Wonder if he's got all the cargo ready, yet."

It was Ippolit, from the warehouse construction site at Port Charid.

Hilton looked back over his shoulder at Vilner and Shilla, who were closest, and gave the sign. *At least two. Probably not more than three.* They had a small advantage of number if there were three. The advantage of surprise more than covered any potential difference.

Hilton straightened up and stepped across the threshold, a glad expression on his face.

"Hey! Ippolit! I didn't know you were here, friend, it's good to see you. What are you doing here?"

They could well know that he was at Honan-gung Yards, he'd gotten leave from Feraltz in person after all. He could almost see the calculation in Ippolit's face, the swift assessment of risk factors leading to a conclusion and a plan for action.

"Shires. Well. As I live and breathe. Have you met Berd, Shires?"

Reaching out for him to put a hand to Hilton's shoulder in friendly greeting, Ippolit advanced on Hilton. Hilton knew he couldn't let Ippolit lay hands on him, and retreated into the corridor. "I thought this was a Bortic ship. Second job, Ippolit?"

Ippolit followed; Hilton gave him no other choice. This was going to be tricky. Berd was still inside the storeroom, watching. Hilton needed to dislodge Berd from his defensive position in order to control the situation.

Ippolit helped.

"Well, it's a little more complicated than that, I'll tell you all about it. Berd! Berd, this is Hilton Shires from the warehouse. Langsarik. I've told you about him, come out and shake his hand."

The others on his team were nowhere in sight. Hilton didn't know which nearby open doorway might be sheltering whom. He certainly hoped that they were nearby.

"Oh. Yeah. Right, Shires, from the warehouse." Shifting himself out from behind the cargo crates that he'd been rearranging, Berd followed Ippolit out into the corridor. Hilton retreated from Ippolit's advance, hoping he wasn't too obvious, wondering where his people were.

"Say. Guys. What's this all about? You should be at Port Charid. Why were those crates marked Combine, if this is a Bortic ship?" Hilton asked nervously, backing down the corridor. Ippolit and Berd came on with steady confidence, as if secure that Hilton couldn't get away. He was backing up toward the front of the ship. There would be more of the raiding party waiting there, clearly.

"It's very simple, really," Ippolit assured him. "You see, Shires—"

Ippolit charged.

Right past an open doorway that let into a darkened storage room. Torbe was there.

Stepping out swiftly from his concealment, Torbe clubbed Ippolit as he went past. As soon as Torbe made his move, Vilner and Shilla made theirs; they had Berd restrained and silenced before Berd had time to react.

Maintenance tape, three times around the wrists behind the back, twice between, and the tag end pressed down firmly on the outside of the hand. The same thing again around the ankles, to control movement of the feet and prevent bolting or kicking.

Maintenance tape again in a broad patch over the lower part of the face, to cover the mouth. It could be worked loose over time, of course, with determination and enough spit. But it would do for as long as they needed to keep the two men from giving an alarm by calling out.

Two down.

How many to go?

They had to hurry.

Vogel would stall on the outside for as long as he could. They had to be ready to finish the act before the raid leader realized he was discovered and took some desperate measure to avoid capture.

Hilton wanted all of these people alive.

He would settle for nothing less than complete exoneration.

When the *Melrick's* captain finally deigned to make an appearance Garol retreated from the dock-master's office into her secured room and pulled a detail scan up on screen. The dock-master herself went out to talk to the freighter captain.

The freighter captain was not someone Garol recognized—he looked vaguely familiar in form, perhaps, but no more than that, and even that could just be his ethnicity—but there was no sense in making the false assumption that the freighter captain would not recognize him after he'd been in Port Charid for days.

Listening in on the conversation between the dock-master and the freighter captain, Garol waited.

"Ah, I'd hate to come across as ungrateful for your help," the freighter captain was saying. "Is it me, or is this taking a little longer than we'd hoped?"

Garol knew what the problem was: Shires hadn't shown up. They would particularly want Shires's presence on the record, as well as being sure to collect him for general purposes of leaving no survivors. The load-out was going as well as anyone could wish, the cargo manifest almost made up and ready to load. The raiders would want to quarantine the warehouse crew as soon as the work of fetching the booty had been completed.

"I think everybody's here," the dock-master replied, reassuringly. "You've got their full cooperation, no question about that."

Garol got the signal from Shires.

The freighter was secure.

It was time.

He pulsed the dock-master in turn; and she made a suggestion to the freighter captain, as if it was an afterthought.

"I'm not sure I see one of my people, though, you're quite right about that. Maybe Jevan knows, he and Shires were teaming on maintenance earlier. Hey! Jevan!"

Garol watched on the internal monitor, inside the dock-master's inner room. Jevan came into view on the screens, trotting across the floor to join the freighter captain and the dock-master. He wanted Jevan to be with the freighter captain, so that he would be able to take them together. The freighter captain would be relying on Jevan to know where everybody was.

"Jevan. Where's Shires? I don't see him."

Jevan looked from the dock-master to the freighter captain, but the picture was too small for Garol to decide on his exact expression. "He said he was going to go call up the people in the remote tunnels. Ames and Teller. They're here, he must have said something to them."

The dock-master nodded. "Well, I'll just go find out. No, you stay here, Jevan, entertain the captain, I'll be right back."

Garol had warned her to get clear of the freighter captain when the time came for him to make his move, to avoid any unpleasantness with hostage-taking. Turning around, the dock-master moved toward her work crew, calling for the people Jevan had identified. "Hey. You two. Over here, I need to ask you something."

That was his cue.

Garol left the dock-master's inner office, checking the transmits as he passed. He wanted this on record. He'd promised the First Secretary something to look at.

He opened the door of the dock-master's office and stepped out into the docking bay. The two people that the dock-master had called didn't pay much attention to him. As far as they were concerned he was probably someone from the freighter, which explained why they didn't know him.

The freighter captain stared, though, and Garol greeted him with a cheerful wave.

"Hello there," Garol called. "My name is Garol Vogel. Bench specialist. And you're under arrest."

The shock on the freighter captain's face was quickly replaced with an expression of satisfied vindication. The freighter captain clearly could hear the people leaving the freighter, behind him. He didn't have to look to know that they were his men and they were armed.

"I don't think so," the freighter captain—the raid leader—said.

"Specialist Vogel. The man we Langsariks have to thank for our vacation here at Port Charid, and all of this lovely loot. Really very much indebted to you, sir."

It was too bad for the raid leader that the people he heard coming out of the freighter were not his troops with weapons. They were Langsariks with weapons. Jevan was looking behind the freighter captain at the people coming out of the freighter, and there was horror clearly evident on Jevan's face. He probably recognized Shires right off. He might not recognize Shires's commando, but he wouldn't have to know them by name to realize who they were.

"You're not Langsariks, and it hasn't been a vacation, but I will accept responsibility for the arrest. You're Dalmoss, I expect."

The raid leader's confidence seemed to falter for the first time. None of the assembled warehouse workers was staring in shocked alarm at the armed men he clearly believed he had at his back. The dock-master had clued them in by now, and they were watching with keen interest, but no fear. The raid leader did not go so far as to look over his shoulder to see what was there: not yet. He glanced with almost perfectly concealed nervousness up toward one of the docking bay's security monitors, instead.

"My name is Noman," he said.

Well behind the raid leader, Shires had stepped clear of the captured crew of the freighter, unshipping a peculiar set of small stones or spheres that hung at the end of multiple strands of cord that looked to be about as long as he was tall.

"Just as well." It took Garol a moment to realize what Shires was doing. Once he grasped Shires's plan, Garol did what he could to put it forward. This was a dangerous and determined enemy, one they had been lucky to manage as well as they had done so far. They could not afford to risk any uncontrolled events so close to a complete triumph. "Dalmoss went to Geraint, after all. Funny thing, though. How do you suppose he turned from Pettiche into Dalmoss? And rose from the dead, because there were no survivors at the Tyrell Yards, were there? Especially not Dolgorukij ones."

Out behind the raid leader Shires had started his ropes spinning. All of the spheres were tethered to a common ring; he put them into motion one by one, over his head.

When he had them all moving together he started to walk forward.

Garol imagined he could hear the sound that the heavy spheres made whistling through the air, straining at the ends of the ropes. A rotor. A windmill. A wheel of a theoretical sort, but deployed hub to rim by wrist action rather than rim to hub by friction.

"I don't know anything about Dolgorukij." The raid-leader seemed determined to carry his course through. "But I am grateful to that fat old Madlev. His warehouse is a great hiding place. You could tell him I said so—if you weren't going to Hell—"

There it was, the telltale twitch of the hand toward the blouse, the reach into a pocket. For a bomb. Garol braced himself to spring, aiming low, knowing he had to cross the distance between them before the raid leader had a chance to arm his suicide device.

A whistling sound of thrown spheres sliced through the air like knives, the rope-wheel wrapping itself around the raid leader with a ferocious impact that pinned his arms and dropped him to the floor of the load-in bay in one swift movement. The raid leader shouted once in pain as the spheres took him, then once again as his head hit the ground; it happened too quickly for Garol to be able to reach him in time to break his fall.

Garol was with him in an instant, however, checking the pocket first before he dared check for breathing or a pulse. There would be a suicide device, and he'd seen evidence of an implosion grenade at Tyrell. Dying now would leave him with a definite sense of anticlimax. Garol expected to enjoy the denouement; for that he had to manage to live through to it.

The bomb was a tidy one, flat and innocuous in appearance. Garol sat back on his heels to examine it, turning it over and over in his hands and thanking the blind gods of fortunate happenstance for Dolgorukij arrogance. The suicide device had not been primed, or it would have been much easier to detonate. The raid leader—and Garol believed it probably *was* Dalmoss—had not been truly prepared to die, and Garol knew he might well owe his life, and those of everybody else nearby, to that one lapse in discipline.

Dalmoss stirred on the ground, coughing painfully as he regained consciousness. Shires came up to retrieve his spheres, grinning in enjoyment of his catch. "Don't move, floor manager," Shires warned, cheerfully. "Cracked ribs. Maybe fractured arms. You'll do yourself an injury, lie still. Hardly recognized you. New beard?"

The Dolgorukij, Jevan, had suffered himself to be bound by the dock-master herself, staring down at Dalmoss in a clear state of shock. "I don't understand," Jevan said. "I don't have the first idea who these people are. I've never seen them before in my life."

Which people?

The false Langsariks that Shires's people were marching out of the freighter under guard?

Or the Langsariks themselves?

"I'd like to believe you," Garol assured him. "Don't worry. Everything will be sorted out soon enough. All we need from you now is a little patience."

Some of the warehouse crew was bringing a stretcher for Dalmoss, one with stout straps to secure an unconscious patient. Another of the warehouse crew walked behind, towing the medical cart—the emergency medical technician, clearly enough. "Dock-master. We need help securing these people for transport. Can you hold them here for a few hours, while I arrange for an armed escort?"

He didn't want them under Langsarik guard. There were limits to the amount of temptation one could put before the best of people before they lost their sense of proportion in a rage for vengeance.

"We have a very nice transfer case for a refrigeration unit," the dock-master pointed out, agreeably. "You may remember having seen it. Easily modified for adequate segregation of belligerent parties. It'll be our pleasure."

Transfer case for a refrigeration unit?

Transfer case.

"Quite so. If you'd just be so kind as to secure these people, then, dock-master, being mindful of Shires's very useful warning in handling the raid leader. His name is Dalmoss. We hope he'll be in adequate condition to answer several questions of extreme interest."

He liked this dock-master; she stood for no nonsense, but she knew the value of a good joke. He had brought his Langsariks in a transfer case for a large refrigeration unit. What more poetic prison could there be?

"Oh, we'll be much more careful with them than they were with any of our warehouse people. My word on it, Specialist Vogel."

And he believed her.

Which was good, because he had to get to Port Charid as quickly as possible, now, to lay his evidence before First Secretary Verlaine and get that Fleet Interrogations Group turned around.

With this raid timed the way it had been, he hadn't a moment to waste. The Fleet Interrogations Group would be coming off the vector within four hours from now. And it was four hours from Honan-gung to Port Charid.

He could try for a contact with Chilleau Judiciary from here, from his station in the pod within the dock-master's inner room; but he needed Feraltz in hand before he published any bulletins. Try as he had, he hadn't quite convinced himself to trust that task to Cousin Stanoczk. Religious rivalry, the honor of the Dolgorukij Combine, saving face for the Autocrat—no. It was too risky. He had to do it himself.

"Thank you, ma'am, you're a gentlewoman and a scholar. Shires. Let's get out of here."

They would take the freighter back to Port Charid and park it off in orbit; Cousin Stanoczk would come aboard to ferry them down to Port Charid, as soon as they could get there.

Composing his message to the First Secretary in his mind, Garol followed the Langsariks up into the freighter for its preflight checks, happy to note a team doubling back to the opposite flank of the ship to close up the access portals in its side.

He was almost ready to relax and look forward to the confrontation with Feraltz yet to come.

Fisner Feraltz sat at his desk in the administration area of the warehouse construction site after the day-shift had gone to their dinners, reviewing the daily work sheets and smiling to himself.

All over but the shouting.

The Fleet Interrogations Group was due within nine scant hours. The freighter—with all the riches that the Holy Mother had bestowed upon Her faithful servants—would be leaving for the Sillume vector at any moment.

The distress call had been sent more than five hours ago now.

Not from Honan-gung itself, not really; from the freighter, but through the Honan-gung dispatch, so that there was no telling any difference. The port was even then preparing what relief ships it could muster, but it would be too little and too late.

Just like the Tyrell raid.

Just like Okidan, and the raids before; the earlier—less sophisticated—raids, when they had still been learning their role. It almost made one admire Langsariks. Learning to raid had been a useful measure of the caliber of the opponent that they faced; and the absolute requirement for the ruthless extirpation of any such challenge to Combine primacy at Port Charid.

All of the progress that the work crews had made, really, it was an admirable effort. These people had organization. Self-discipline. A good work ethic. How pleasant it was to know that he was not even going to have to pay for their work. He was free and clear of a good two weeks' wages for the entire construction effort.

Was there a way to paper that fact over and take the additional tithe for the Angel's use?

And his.

There was a good proportion of this wealth due him, not as a reward, but so that he could show what influence and luxury a man could earn in the service of the Holy Mother. Recruitment. As he had been recruited; and yet he had needed no such appeal to venal motives to gain his allegiance, but only this, position and authority and trust.

There was someone in the outer office but Fisner paid them no mind, absorbed in happy calculation. Until Hariv knocked almost in a panic at the door, opening it—before Fisner had a chance to agree to be seen or refuse to be bothered—to reveal the very unwelcome apparition of Bench Specialist Garol Aphon Vogel and Factor Madlev behind him.

Fisner sprang to his feet. He had an escape route, there was a washroom adjoining his office with an extra door that let on to an adjacent office whose exit was at the back of the administrative area. But why should he flee?

He bowed to Factor Madlev instead and remained on his feet to show deference to his superior. Factor Madlev would encourage him to be seated, he had been badly wounded scant months ago, after all.

Factor Madlev did not invite him to sit.

"Good to see you," Vogel said. "I was hoping we'd find you in. I've just come from Honan-gung, Feraltz, and it shouldn't surprise you to hear that the things I found out there make me very interested in your answers to some questions of Bench interest."

Behind Vogel, Madlev frowned, clearly unhappy. Factor Madlev had brought the Port Authority with him; none of the Angel's own people. All of the Angel's people were at Honan-gung, all except him. What did Vogel mean, he'd just come from Honan-gung? Vogel had gone to Chilleau Judiciary. Vogel was days away from Rikavie.

Unless it had been a ruse from the beginning . . .

Fisner sat down. If this was to be a confrontation, it would be on his own terms. "I can't imagine what you mean, Bench specialist." He could draw Vogel out, find out what Vogel knew. Then he'd know what Vogel didn't know. That would be a start on a strategy. "I had thought you were at Chilleau Judiciary."

It was true that Vogel hadn't been with the First Secretary when Factor Madlev had called just hours ago, though. After Factor Madlev had received the distress call from Honan-gung. The First Secretary had done the only thing he could have done; Fisner had taken care to leave him no choice. Did Vogel know that?

What did Vogel know?

Vogel wasn't saying. "As I have been, and expect to be in the future. These people will escort you to detention, Feraltz, to wait for the Fleet Interrogations Group arriving from Dobe. If you'd be so kind."

Factor Madlev's discomfort would permit him to endure in silence no longer. "But the Bench warrant was issued against Langsariks, Bench specialist," Madlev said, as Fisner watched Vogel's face avidly. "Not four hours gone past. When we told the First Secretary at Chilleau Judiciary about the distress call from Honan-gung."

Fascinating, Fisner thought. *Vogel had to be exhausted; there was no other possible explanation for the nakedness of the dismay in his face.*

"Honan-gung sent no distress calls, Factor Madlev," Vogel said, flatly. "I was there. I know."

Vogel's emphatic insistence seemed to put Madlev on the defensive. "Nevertheless, Specialist Vogel, Port Charid received a distress call from Honan-gung five hours ago. We were unable to get a response from Honan-gung on any frequency. We had to put it before the First Secretary."

Fisner closed his eyes and bowed his head as his heart sang.

It was so clear, so perfect, and so beautiful.

Vogel had set a trap at Honan-gung, but Vogel hadn't stopped the distress call—perhaps he hadn't realized that Dalmoss's freighter would be sending one.

Vogel had put Honan-gung on transmission silence while he returned from Honan-gung to Port Charid to make his crowning arrest, that of Fisner himself.

And even as Vogel had made his triumphant pilgrimage from Honan-gung to Port Charid, the Holy Mother had put out Her hand to turn his purpose to Her service. Factor Madlev had done what any decent honest man would do on receipt of such a distress call, he'd called for help, and Chilleau Judiciary had had no grounds to deny him—because the First Secretary was as much in the dark about Vogel's actual whereabouts and activities as Fisner himself had been.

Vogel had come from Honan-gung in triumph, to arrest him.

But the Angel of Destruction had triumphed over all.

"Well," Vogel said, and the word seemed all too inadequate for the worlds upon worlds of emotion that it bore. "We'll have to contact the First Secretary immediately, then. Nothing is changed, Feraltz, you are still under arrest, and there will be a reckoning in time. Factor Madlev. If you'll have your people take charge of the prisoner, I'd like to get back to Port Charid to contact the Bench at Chilleau Judiciary."

Vogel was wrong about that, too. There would be no reckoning. After all the Holy Mother had shown him of her power, how could he doubt for so much as a moment that she would bring him out of threatened captivity to honor and glory?

He would be looking forward to witnessing Vogel's discomfiture, on that day. It was uncharitable of him, yes, perhaps.

He owed Vogel no charity.

Vogel had done his utmost to thwart the sacred Will of the Holy Mother. Vogel deserved to suffer humiliation in return for his misguided meddling, if not worse.

"It's all right, Factor Madlev," Fisner declared firmly, as though Factor Madlev had hesitated to do as Vogel directed. Factor Madlev had not perhaps moved very quickly to put Fisner under arrest, but he seemed to cherish no reservations whatever beyond the reflection on his own pride to have his foreman accused, and looked a little puzzled, as Fisner continued.

"I have nothing to hide. Take me into custody, I'll be fully exonerated of whatever it is the Bench specialist means to accuse me—" which Vogel had neglected to divulge, which was a disappointment, he could have started to work on his story—"whatever that is. Shall we go? Guards?"

He would be out of custody again before daybreak. Perhaps before supper.

Vogel would realize that he was powerless against a far more formidable opponent than he could possibly imagine; and Fisner would go free, to watch the painful and appropriate conclusion to Vogel's misguided Langsarik experiment with amnesty at Port Charid.

CHAPTER TWELVE

Shutting the door behind him, Garol Vogel turned to pace in Factor Madlev's now-empty office, where the secured-communications portal was kept. He didn't want any witnesses. He had no confidence in his own discretion at this point, and he was not willing to berate the First Secretary in front of any local authorities that might lose respect for the Bench because of it.

Keying the transmit, Garol sat down at Factor Madlev's desk and engaged the privacy nets in the walls, mechanically, not really thinking about it. This was a disaster. He had worked so hard to prevent it. What was he going to do?

"Bench specialist Garol Vogel. For First Secretary Verlaine, priority transmit, urgency immediate."

He couldn't sit still.

He lunged to his feet from the chair in a convulsive movement, snatching his worn campaign hat off his head and crumpling it in his hands, stretching it and twisting it in a fury of agonized self-reproachful emotion before he jammed it back down at the back of his head, as though it were a personal enemy whose ultimate despite was to be worn on the head of a Bench specialist—all the while pacing, quartering the room in precise measure left to right, front to back, on the diagonal.

In the middle of the second or third such transit his signal cleared; Garol heard the concerned voice of the First Secretary. "Specialist Vogel. What news?"

What news. What news? How dare he ask what news? Garol couldn't stop moving. He would explode. He needed the physical stress of sustained if low-impact exertion to hone the wild edge off of his despair and free his mind for calculating evaluation. He was a Bench intelligence specialist. Calculating evaluation was what he was all about.

"I've just come from the Honan-gung Yards in the Shawl of Rikavie, where I and a properly deputized party of Langsarik commandos successfully interrupted a warehouse-invasion raid."

Striding without ceasing from wall to wall, from corner to corner, the placing of his feet somehow seemed to help him place his words with concise care.

"Returning to Port Charid under communications silence, I have just placed the ringleader under arrest. I can demonstrate with complete confidence that a group of Dolgorukij from the Combine Yards is responsible for staging the so-called Langsarik raids, including the torture and murder of warehouse crew."

Verlaine was listening, hearing him out. Maybe Verlaine was beginning to have a bad feeling about where Garol was going. Garol hoped so.

"It was never Langsariks, First Secretary, not since the real trouble began. Factor Madlev tells me that the Third Fleet Interrogations Group has received its charter activation orders. They'll be here inside of eight hours."

Then Verlaine spoke, since Garol's statement was as good as an accusation after all. "We were unable to make contact with you, and Ivers could share little by way of evidence, Specialist Vogel. I have been doing my best to win time for you to work, but even had I been aware of your plans—which I was not—"

It was mild enough, as an implicit criticism. It was also fair. Perhaps he could have approached this mission differently. Perhaps he could have laid it all out for the First Secretary, without risking compromise. But he'd had his reasons. He didn't know how sophisticated the abilities of his opponent might be. He still didn't know with certainty whether this secure line was actually secure.

"—I could no longer deny the right of the Port Authority to demand action and see sanctions levied. There was a distress call, Vogel, under the very nose of the Fleet Interrogations Group another raid. What would you have had me do?"

Anything but what he had done. Verlaine was not denying it. He had activated the mission of the Third Fleet Interrogations Group, and now it was functionally autonomous from the Bench until such time as it decided to declare its mission completed. Fleet was jealous of its Bench prerogatives. Politics had twisted the knife in the heart of the Langsarik settlement the final crucial fractions of a measure between a grave wound and a mortal one.

"The Langsariks are innocent." It was all Garol could think of to say. "I've had every cooperation from them. They've honored the terms of the amnesty, First Secretary. To see them destroyed by a Fleet Interrogations Group despite their best efforts to uphold the rule of Law is bitterly offensive."

"What difference does it make?"

Verlaine asked it with meditative gravity that weighted the flippant phrase, so that it came out a genuine request for a reply. "I'm not sure we're left with any other possible outcome, Bench specialist. The settlement has been too badly compromised. You may well have identified the true culprits, but can the Langsariks be said to have any real hope of a life at Port Charid yet before them?"

Three-eighths of the way from one corner of Factor Madlev's office to the other, Garol stopped and bowed his head. A genuine question deserved a genuine answer. It took him a moment to get one out, however.

"That's a true statement. As far as it goes."

The criminals, the Dolgorukij terrorists, this supposed "Angel of Destruction" had done too good a job of pretending to be Langsariks. Port Charid had learned over a period of months to blame the Langsariks, and not for mere piracy and theft but for murder and atrocity as well. He had failed in his mission. He could not salvage the amnesty agreement.

Nor could he accept that as a reason to abandon innocent people to a Fleet Interrogations Group. The Second Judge would be amply vindicated by the Fleet Interrogations Group's findings, that was almost certain—given the nature of its Brief.

And yet—if Fleet really wanted to play politics—

"But it doesn't mean we can sell the Langsariks out to the Fleet. And I see a potential problem."

There was no hope of simply canceling the activation order. It was one of the basic rules that governed the uneasy relationship between the Fleet and the Bench: the Fleet was subordinate to the civil authority, but once chartered was free to ignore the civil authority until the mission laid on it by the civil authority had been accomplished. And it was Fleet that decided when that was.

"I'm listening," the First Secretary said. But Garol thought that Verlaine was thinking, too.

"We can't afford another scandal along the lines of the recent unpleasantness at Port Rudistal." Where the Domitt Prison had stood. "And once Fleet realizes, as it must, that there is no true Brief at Port Charid—it could easily be used against Chilleau Judiciary, First Secretary."

Torture enough Langsariks to assure themselves that the confessions were all just the pain talking, something even the average Inquisitor could discern. Then torture another fifty or sixty more just for the sake of the argument.

Run a series of inquiries on drug-assist alone, and end up with proof of innocence.

Go public with the fact that an innocent and unarmed population had been foully betrayed by the Bench officers that had promised to protect them. It could get ugly.

It could even force the Second Judge into retirement—especially if Fleet chanced to discover that Garol had had the real criminals in custody before the Fleet Interrogations Group had even arrived at Port Charid.

Or the Fleet Interrogations Group might just do the job it had been sent to do and issue no challenge to the Second Judge's public image.

Was it worth the risk that Fleet would use its Brief to the discredit of the Second Judge?

Now that Verlaine knew that Garol had the truth, and that the Langsariks weren't to blame—

"I am at a loss to understand what you think the alternative might be." Garol thought he heard frustration there, in the First Secretary's voice. He hadn't been entirely fair to Verlaine, maybe. But Garol had no particular reason to trust anybody, First Secretaries emphatically included. "If you could keep the two of them apart, your Langsariks and the Fleet Interrogations Group. If you could wave the scepter of wonder, and transport the settlement intact to cloud-cuckoo land through lands of mist and magic. I might be able to work a nullification of Bench instruction, in a month or so. Maybe. If."

An impossible task.

But the First Secretary had suggested it.

With all other situational elements taken into consideration, Garol knew exactly what he had to do.

It went against nearly everything he had fought for during most of his adult life. But it was unquestionably the lesser of two evils.

"Yes. If the Langsarik settlement simply disappeared, there would in that case be no risk of negative public reaction consequent to a misplaced accusation of crimes against the Judicial order. I understand, First Secretary. I will do my utmost to protect the honor of the Second Judge and Chilleau Judiciary, in the service of the rule of Law. Vogel away, here."

He had only one escape route open to him now; and no time to lose if he was to hope to make it free and clear.

"Aunt Walton. Aunt Walton, please, wake up, something is wrong."

Walton Agenis struggled into consciousness, unable to parse Modice's frantic pleas into coherence but knowing by tone of voice that it was serious.

"Modice. I'm awake. You can stop shaking me now."

She was stiff and sore from sleeping in the chair in the front room; how did Vogel manage? She couldn't sleep at all in her bed, though, too unwilling to be caught at so much of a disadvantage when the soldiers came for her.

If she was going to die, she would do so with as much dignity as she could manage, for as long as the torturers of the Fleet Interrogations Group would permit.

"Unusual changes in pattern, Aunt Walton. There are transport trucks out there, and more coming, you can hear them from the roof." Where Modice had made an observation station for herself, in the unfinished attic space up beneath the eaves. "Something's coming."

And it didn't sound friendly.

"Do we have something to eat?" Walton asked, gathering her strength to stand up. "High-fat, we may need it. I'm going to go wash my face."

They'd be coming to the door soon enough.

She couldn't be looking very formidable, with her face dead pale and her hair in wild disarray, her clothing wrinkled from having been slept in. She was the Flag Captain, the representative of the Langsarik fleet before the world. She wanted to maintain appearances.

Modice brought breakfast as Walton tidied her person, combing her hair between bites of fried fat-meat and toast dripping with butter. There was a small ventilation window in the washroom; Walton could hear the roar of the trucks that Modice was worried about.

She could hear it when the noise of the engines stopped.

This was it, then.

She went to the door and stood behind it, waiting for the knock.

It was a knock that seemed somehow familiar, when it came. Walton waited for a suitable interval to pass to make it clear that her response was a considered action, not mere reaction to the demand for her attention—and nodded at Modice to open the door.

It was Garol Vogel, standing there.

"Ma'am," Vogel said, touching his fingertips to the brim of his dilapidated old campaign cap in some peculiar form of a salute. "I'm bringing an evacuation order. Langsariks to be removed from settlement at Port Charid immediately, by express direction from Chilleau Judiciary. If I could ask you to step outside."

He stepped back.

Walton could only stare.

There was her nephew, Hilton, behind Vogel; so they were back from Honan-gung—but if they were back from Honan-gung, why were the Langsariks evacuating?

Had they failed to acquire the evidence that they had hoped for?

Or was it even more simple than that?

Walton followed Vogel out of the house. There were transports lining the roadway into the settlement, dozens of transports, and at least some of the drivers were Langsariks by their body language. She didn't recognize anybody at the distance, her eyes were still half-asleep; but she knew her people. Those were Langsariks.

Factor Madlev stood several paces removed, with an armed escort; the people who had secured the perimeter around her house were formed up in a detachment to one side. It was not an impressive one, either, but these were not professional soldiers.

Once she was well clear of the doorway, Vogel stopped and stood with his back to her, assuming an approximation of a position of command attention that was too precise to result from imperfect learning—it was the gradual relaxation over time, rather, of a once-perfect discipline. Not for the first time Walton wondered about Vogel's past, but there was her own future to worry about, and she could not spare Vogel the energy.

"Factor Madlev," Vogel said, pitching his voice to carry to as many of the people who were there as possible, "as I have mentioned briefly to you on our way here, I have received instruction from First Secretary Verlaine at Chilleau Judiciary on behalf of the Second Judge. The amnesty agreement between the Langsariks and the Bench has been declared compromised, and I am to ensure that the Langsarik population at Port Charid vacates the settlement as quickly as possible. The Bench will pay commercial rates for every freighter and other appropriate transport that can be made available for this purpose."

She could hardly believe what she was hearing.

Nor did she seem to be alone.

"Specialist Vogel." Factor Madlev's reply was in a cautious tone of voice that only carried as far as Walton's doorstep. "Wouldn't it be just as efficient to leave these people here and let the Fleet Interrogations Group take over?"

Vogel shook his head. "I can't argue with you on the point, Factor Madlev. My instructions were to remove the Langsarik settlement from Port Charid as a failed enterprise. It is too much to expect the decent citizens of this port to tolerate the presence of persons suspected of crimes both mercantile and murderous for a moment longer. Do I have your support, Factor Madlev?"

Factor Madlev didn't really care. Walton could see it in the shrug of his shoulders, hear it in the tone of his voice.

"Of course we will fully support any Bench initiative, Specialist Vogel."

Madlev knew that Vogel meant to get them off-world before the Fleet Interrogations Group arrived. And Madlev was perfectly willing to go along with that.

It was too much to believe that Madlev would turn a blind eye to their escape, still believing that they were responsible for the raids—so Factor Madlev knew better, now.

That meant that Hilton and Vogel had succeeded at Honan-gung and brought back evidence that the Langsariks were innocent. What happened to the Langsariks now was not apparently an issue of keen concern to Factor Madlev, except that Factor Madlev would share a common understanding that vulnerability to a Fleet Interrogations Group was not something to be wished on innocent people.

Bowing crisply, Vogel turned away any lingering doubts or questions with a call for immediate action. "Thank you for your understanding, Factor Madlev. There are eight freighter tenders off-lined at the new airfield, you'll make them available? Very kind. Lieutenant Shires."

Hilton, looking very tired, looking very tense, but looking also absolutely energized by the activity to come. "Yes, Bench specialist."

"Lieutenant, you will go with Factor Madlev to identify and select suitable shipping, please. I want to begin to load within the hour."

Vogel didn't wait for acknowledgment; in the manner of a superior officer supremely confident of a subordinate's ability, he turned back to her directly. "Flag Captain."

Her turn now, to receive her orders. The idea appealed to her sense of the absurd, though her emotions were generally too stunned by what was happening and how fast it was happening to really enjoy the sensation. "Bench specialist?"

"If you would muster your command, ma'am, and be out at the new airfield absolutely as soon as possible. Because any Langsarik who is still at Port Charid when the Fleet gets here is as good as dead. But not quickly enough. If you know what I mean."

She understood him completely. The Langsarik fleet had lost people to interrogation before.

"Eight freighter tenders." She was impressed, and didn't mind him knowing. "I'd like to know how you managed that. But I don't see what good it does without transport, and it takes a few hours to bring freighters on line, once they've been parked out in geostationary orbit."

He knew that as well as she did. She was just making sure he knew that she knew. Did he mean to cram them all into a warehouse somewhere out in the Shawl of Rikavie? Because that was the maximum range of most freighter tenders, under ordinary conditions.

"Which is exactly why we're so lucky that Madlev got a distress call from Honan-gung. Even though it precipitated the danger from the

Fleet Interrogations Group." Vogel spoke softly, for her ears only. Well, hers and those of Modice, behind her. "There are seven freighters up there coming on line for a rescue mission. Some of them are even armed for pursuit. We brought an eighth back with us from Honangung. It's borderline workable. But it'll be enough."

She knew she'd been asleep. She knew she'd been under horrific stress, waiting to see her people condemned. She couldn't think. That had to be the reason that she thought what was happening, was happening. "You're taking a risk, Bench specialist. We could overpower the crew on the way into the Shawl. You'd never see your freighters again; think of the expense, not to mention the embarrassment."

Vogel had started to shift his weight, doing a species of dance on his feet. Impatient. "Nothing compared to the potential damage that another scandal like the Domitt Prison could create for the Second Judge. The First Judge is old. Verlaine wants his Judge to be in a good position when the post comes up vacant. We don't have much time, Flag Captain, let's get moving."

He meant for them to take the Sillume vector for Gonebeyond space. He really did.

"Modice," Walton said, and her niece stepped up smartly and nodded her head.

"Yes, Aunt Walton."

"You heard the Bench specialist, Modice, issue the assembly order, evacuation plan in effect, timing critical. Mark and move."

Modice had only been waiting for assurance that she was truly to send up the flags. As it were.

Vogel followed Modice into the house and came out again carrying a chair from the living room, setting it down in the pathway before the front door so that it faced the road.

Walton sat down, and Vogel posted himself behind her, doing his peculiar version of command wait.

Just as well.

She had too many things to ask and to tell and to say to him to be able to say a single word right now.

Standing in the dock's load-in bay behind Cousin Stanoczk, Kazmer Daigule ached to be going with the Langsariks.

"I'm afraid I cannot in good conscience offer the use of this courier,"

Cousin Stanoczk said with polite firmness to Hilton Shires. "It is not mine, and I am responsible for my husbandry of the Malcontent's resources. What I can do is release some stores to you. I have a list."

Kazmer had put it together himself. He hadn't understood why Stanoczk had wanted it, but it was complete: foodstuffs, clothing, and replacement parts, all held in Combine warehouses here at Port Charid. Kazmer was already serenely confident that the Langsariks had loaded all the contraband they'd been able to find out at the new warehouse construction site, where Feraltz had apparently been stashing it. Langsariks could move very quickly when they needed to.

"How about your comps, then?" Hilton suggested. "I could steal them at gunpoint. If it would help."

Cousin Stanoczk raised his hands in a gesture of mock horror; he was holding something in one hand. "Oh, the Saints forbid that such a thing should come to pass, Shires. You'll need the secure codes. Be gone when we get back, I've got an errand to run."

Stanoczk glanced back at Kazmer expectantly, glancing from him to whatever it was in his left hand. So Kazmer reached out and took it. The master code unit for the courier's communications equipment. Top-of-the-line. Beautiful stuff.

Stanoczk walked away toward the door at the back of the docking bay that would lead out to the receiving area and then out onto the street. Hilton stepped up to take the master code unit, but Kazmer could not quite bear to let go of it.

"So you're getting away?"

Hilton looked confused, but his small frown of concern gave way almost at once to one of sympathy. He let his hand drop back to his side. "Yeah, Kaz. We're out of here. Never thought it would end like this."

Kazmer had been part of the ending of it. But Hilton knew all about that; that wasn't the problem. The problem was that Kazmer wanted to go too.

"Probably for the best." He had caused so much trouble for the Langsariks, directly and indirectly, and it had all been because he had wanted to help. He could hardly stand the idea that they were leaving; and for Gonebeyond space. Kazmer had always wondered what was out there. Hilton would get to find out, but Kazmer had given his life away to the Malcontent, and there was no going back on the bargain.

"And we've got to hurry." Hilton's gentle reminder called Kazmer out of his self-pitying grief, his keen regret over the fact of Hilton's going away. He liked Hilton. He wanted the best for him. Cousin Stanoczk's comps were the best.

Kazmer pressed the master code unit into Hilton's waiting hand, and was almost ready to say good-bye with a willing heart; but he was interrupted before he could say anything more.

"Sometime this octave, Daigule, if you please."

Cousin Stanoczk called out to him in a firm voice, not needing to put any venom into the rebuke for Kazmer to recognize it for what it was. Kazmer was the slave of the Malcontent. Cousin Stanoczk was his master. Kazmer blushed in vexation to be publicly called to heel, and ducked his head—unwilling to let Hilton know how hard it was to see him go.

"You heard the boss. Don't scratch the furniture, Hilton, it's a nice ship."

He had to turn hastily and walk away, or he was going to say something he'd regret. Something stupid. Something like, *tell Modice I love her with all of my heart*, or *I would to all Saints I was going with you*.

He didn't look back. He didn't dare. Cousin Stanoczk was waiting for him impatiently, and he had no right to keep Cousin Stanoczk waiting. If it hadn't been for Cousin Stanoczk, none of this might have happened. The Inquisitor would have questioned him, it would have gotten ugly, he would have said Hilton's name. It would have been over, instead of just beginning, so how could he grieve just because he was not going to be allowed to be a part of it?

"I'm sorry, Cousin Stanoczk." *Forgive me.* "I didn't mean." *To keep you waiting.* Cousin Stanoczk didn't seem interested in Kazmer's incoherent attempts at an apology. Cousin Stanoczk took him firmly by the elbow and drew him out bodily into the receiving area.

"Enough talk, Kazmer. We have work to do, and not much time."

The other members of Stanoczk's crew were already waiting at the street entrance. They had a transport, and one of them was carrying a security hood. Kazmer wondered, dully, what Cousin Stanoczk had in mind. Over the past few hours, he hadn't been paying much attention to anything outside the problem of the Langsariks. Stanoczk had kept him busy.

They were six in all, with Kazmer himself and Cousin Stanoczk. The hired transport took them to the administrative headquarters of the Combine Yards in Port Charid and stopped outside one of the side entrances.

"We won't be long," Cousin Stanoczk said to the man he had driving. "Stay alert. I don't want any unnecessary complications."

Kazmer began to have an idea.

Into the building and through the corridors—Cousin Stanoczk had clearly been studying a schematic. Kazmer had to hurry to keep up with the others. It was the storage vaults Cousin Stanoczk wanted; when they got there, there was a guard posted, but Cousin Stanoczk did not seem to be surprised.

Kazmer stopped and stood waiting with the rest of them while Stanoczk went forward to speak to the guards.

"I've come for your prisoner," Cousin Stanoczk said. "Will you need a receipt? I have clearance."

They were just warehouse security, and they looked uncomfortable. By now every Dolgorukij in Port Charid knew who Cousin Stanoczk was. Dolgorukij noticed Malcontents, though they pretended to ignore their existence most of the time.

The guards—there were two of them—traded glances. "I'm not sure about that, Cousin," one of them said. Kazmer could tell by the degree of relationship that the guard was willing to grant to Stanoczk that he was feeling very uncertain indeed. "We weren't told. We'd better wait for the Bench specialist."

"Normally I would agree with you," Cousin Stanoczk assured the guards, speaker and silent alike. "But not this time. It is the honor of the Holy Mother herself that is at stake. The Malcontent requires the attendance of your prisoner at an inquest to be held in his honor. I take full responsibility."

An inquest, in the old and formal sense. An inquiry. A debriefing.

Interrogation, but under the control of the Malcontent, and no Fleet Inquisitor to share the shameful secrets of the Combine's sordid past—Kazmer could almost sympathize. The Bench would have Dalmoss and the other men being held even now at the Honan-gung Yards, for its interrogation. The Bench would naturally confine its questions to topics which interested the Bench; but the Malcontent would want the Angel of Destruction itself, and of all these prisoners only Fisner Feraltz—the apparent ringleader, chieftain, head—was likely to have any real information on the organization and operation of a terrorist society thought dead.

The one guard looked at the other, then shrugged. "I'm sure it's best for all of us," he said. "I can't imagine our Feraltz preferring to go to Fleet. But we have custody, Cousin. How can we in honor cede it to you?"

The guards clearly did not know the extent of the problem. Vogel had obviously said nothing about Angels, or else the guard would have known quite well that Feraltz would almost certainly rather anything than to fall into the hands of the Malcontent.

On the other hand—depending on what the guards themselves remembered of the horror stories of their youth—they might well be more, and not less, willing to see Feraltz in Stanoczk's hands if they did know. They might feel more guilty about it, though, if personal malice came into play, so it was best that Cousin Stanoczk made no such appeal.

"I can promise you absolutely that if you but tell the Bench specialist that I have assumed personal custody, he will understand." Kazmer had to agree. Vogel might not hold the guards blameless, but he would reserve his wrath for the man who really deserved it—Cousin Stanoczk.

The Malcontent was proof against the displeasure of even a Bench intelligence specialist, or his name wasn't Kazmer Daigule.

The guard shrugged again. "Very well, Cousin, but I will have a receipt. Yes. Thank you."

Cousin Stanoczk had one already prepared.

The guards opened the door to the storeroom they were using as a cell. Kazmer could see clear through to the back—it was a small room. Fisner Feraltz sat on a low cot with a strong-belt around his waist and his wrists shackled; when he saw Cousin Stanoczk standing in the doorway he stood up and took a step forward, his face full of alarm.

"What's he doing here, you can't—I won't—" Feraltz had not accounted for the hobbles he wore. He fell flat on his face, full-length on the floor, and two of Cousin Stanoczk's crew hurried forward with the security hood.

Feraltz was imprisoned in the walking cage of the security hood before he found his voice. The heavy fabric covered him from head to mid-thigh; as Kazmer watched in bemused wonder at the efficiency of the operation, Stanoczk's crew pulled Feraltz's shackled hands deftly through a panel to the outside of the hood, sealing the panel up again so that Feraltz's hands were isolated outside the hood.

There was a mesh panel in the thick and impermeable material of the hood where Feraltz's face would be, so that he could breathe; but Kazmer heard nothing but incoherent noises from beneath the hood.

So they'd brought the gag as well.

Kazmer thought of the bodies he'd seen at the Tyrell Yards, the look on the face of the dock-master; a woman who had been alive when he'd left her, a woman who had offered no threat to the raiders.

He found that his instinctive sympathy for any man in Feraltz's position—in the hood, and the gag—was absent.

"Thank you, gentlemen," Cousin Stanoczk said. "We'll be leaving. Should you be rebuked by the Factor or by the Bench specialist for transferring the prisoner just be in touch, and the Malcontent will see that all is made right for you."

The crewmen who had hooded Feraltz were already moving him down the hall and toward the exit as Stanoczk spoke. Feraltz couldn't walk very quickly with his ankles hobbled; but there were straps on the outside of the security hood, so the crewmen simply dragged Feraltz along with them. Kazmer hurried after them, while Cousin Stanoczk stayed behind for a moment to soothe any doubts that the two guards might have.

It took no time at all to reach the waiting transport. They loaded Feraltz into the passenger compartment, secured between two crewmen; but there was a problem.

It was a six-man transport, and Feraltz made seven.

Cousin Stanoczk stood beside the transport with Kazmer, scratching his head behind one ear as if in confusion.

"Well," Cousin Stanoczk said. "Kazmer, this won't do. I don't have room for you. You'd better see if you can get a berth with your Langsarik friends, and you'd better hurry, too, if you don't want to be left behind."

Kazmer frowned. What was Stanoczk saying? "Get a berth, Cousin Stanoczk, I don't understand. Oughtn't I be coming with you? I'll get a for-hire and meet you."

Stanoczk shook his head with impatient disgust. "I don't want you, Kazmer; I can't use you, and the Langsariks need you. You're a good pilot. You're none of mine, though, so give me your halter and get out to the airfield."

Give him his halter?

Was Stanoczk even speaking plain Standard?

Kazmer stood and stared. Stanoczk reached out for him with a short sharp obscenity, pulling Kazmer's collar open at the throat to snap off the red leash of the Malcontent in one quick and almost savage gesture.

"We made a contract so that you could protect your friends, Kazmer, and your friends have not been protected. There is no contract. What part of 'get out of my sight' did you not understand?"

This couldn't be happening.

It was too much to grasp.

Kazmer seized Cousin Stanoczk by the shoulders and kissed him passionately, first on one cheek and then on the other. Free. That was what Cousin Stanoczk was saying. He was free.

"Your for-hire is waiting," Stanoczk pointed out. "Stupid Sarvaw."

Free to court Modice like an honest man.

Kazmer fled from the street to the for-hire that Cousin Stanoczk had pointed out, the one Cousin Stanoczk had readied, waiting for him.

He had to get out to the airfield. Now.

Once he was away with the Langsarik fleet, he would see what the books said about how a man should honor the Malcontent, to give thanks for a miracle unsought but even so granted.

It was four hours till dawn, and the Fleet Interrogations Group had cleared the Sillume exit vector hours ago. It would reach Port Charid soon. Unless the Langsariks left local orbit at Port Charid within the hour, they would have no chance of outrunning a predictable attempt on the part of the Fleet Interrogations Group to stop them short of the entrance vector.

It was going to be complicated enough to move so many ships of so many sizes through the Sillume vector at something approaching one and the same time as it was.

Shires had mustered ten freighters in all, with the one they'd

Interrogations Group could intercept them, and the Fleet Interrogations Group had no Brief to try to do so—he intended to make that point very clear. As soon as the Langsarik fleet was safely away.

He'd given up too much to let any six Fleet Interrogations Groups stand in the way of a successful escape.

Standing in the traffic controller's map room at Combine headquarters, Garol Vogel watched the Third Fleet Interrogations Group on its way to Port Charid, and the ragtag Langsarik fleet nearing the Sillume entrance vector at the far end of the vector aisle.

It was going to be close.

The lead ships in the Fleet Interrogations Group convoy—three ships, out of twenty—were altering trajectory, but not on approach to Port Charid: on a course to bypass Rikavie entirely and head for some target as yet unidentified. In the Shawl of Rikavie, perhaps.

Garol knew better.

"Hail the Fleet convoy, please." The communications master was on his boards; by the swiftness of his reply he had anticipated Garol's request.

"Your channel is open, Bench specialist, skein in braid. Stand by for the commander, Third Fleet Interrogations Group, coming on-line. Now."

Garol meant to leave no doubt in the commander's mind as to who was in charge at Port Charid. So he spoke first. "This is Bench intelligence specialist Garol Vogel, on detail by instruction from Chilleau Judiciary. Why have your leaders changed course, please."

It annoyed Fleet when they were in the position of answering, rather than asking, the questions. That was all right. Garol didn't need them cooperative. He just needed them at Port Charid, rather than chasing out after ships on their way to the entrance of the Sillume vector.

The leading edges of the Langsarik fleet had begun their vector spins, their sensor traces distorting with the activity.

"Third Fleet Interrogations Group commander Minrodie, Bench specialist. We see a suspicious population movement in flight from Port Charid for the Sillume vector. The possibility exists that they are Langsariks. There is no response to lawful requests to stand down and return to Port Charid for interview. Pursuit is required to resolve questions about identity and motivation."

Yes, as he'd thought. Minrodie had done the analysis; Garol couldn't fault her reasoning. He was just going to have to be unreasonable. "Commander Minrodie. Does your Brief extend to conduct of search and seizure of commercial shipping? Abort your pursuit and make your scheduled orbitals at Port Charid. Acknowledge compliance."

No, her Brief did not authorize any such interference with trade. It was a formality, perhaps. But it was all Garol had to go on.

At the plotter scan to the right of the map wall Garol thought he saw the first of the Langsarik ships drop off the scope.

But the three ships from the Fleet convoy were making good progress and gaining on the tail end of the escaping Langsariks. A ship pursued by another of similar size accelerating in too-near pursuit could not make a vector transit; the perturbation in trajectory created by such pursuit made a correct calculation impossible. He had to call the Fleet convoy ships off.

"Request your confirmation that subject ships are civil transports engaged in the lawful conduct of Bench-sanctioned trade, Bench specialist."

Minrodie wasn't giving in. Garol didn't blame her for it, though he had to force her compliance any way he could.

"I affirm that to my personal knowledge subject ships are all commercial hulls en route to the Sillume vector, so directed by me in response to instruction received from First Secretary Verlaine, Chilleau Judiciary. Abort your pursuit. You are exceeding the terms of your Brief."

Not as if that ever stopped Fleet.

But Minrodie's conviction did seem to falter. The three pursuit ships had not swerved from their intercept course, but none of the other ships in the convoy showed any signs of joining the chase. Yet.

Three more of the Langsarik ships were gone, including the first of the freighters. Some Langsariks had escaped, then, but Garol needed them all to be out of there, because the Langsariks were going to need each other in order to survive. Not only that—but the last of the freighters, the last of the ships, the freighter that had been the last to clear Port Charid, that was the ship carrying Walton Agenis.

"Failure to respond to a lawful request to stand to is a violation of

Bench commercial procedure and within Fleet's Brief to enforce," Minrodie insisted.

Her three pursuit ships were gaining on the Langsarik fleet.

"And when a Fleet commerce-control group is posted at Port Charid it will duly enforce the commercial codes, that will be its charter. It is not your charter. You are not a Fleet commerce-control group, and you have been ordered to Port Charid. You will proceed to Port Charid. Any harassment on your part of commercial hulls can be expected to generate adverse notice at the highest level of authority."

He was beginning to sound desperate.

He was afraid it wasn't going to work after all. Agenis's freighter might be able to outrun the Fleet ships, but he couldn't risk finding out. If the Fleet ships got really annoyed, they could fire on the freighter. The Langsarik fleet needed its Flag Captain. Garol could not afford to contemplate what it would mean if Agenis were taken— Agenis, and her beautiful niece Modice, and her very capable nephew Shires, and even Kazmer Daigule, a basically decent man even if his grasp of Bench commercial codes was a little on the questionable side.

One of the ships among the fleeing Langsariks faltered.

It was a very small craft, the smallest on scan, so small in fact that it might well have escaped attention had it not started to transmit. A courier. A bomb ship? A decoy?

The acerbic tones of Cousin Stanoczk's strongly accented voice cracked over the comms, and Garol had to rub his chin briskly with his hand to cover a smile of relief and gratitude. Cousin Stanoczk. Intervening just as things were near critical, to hold the Fleet pursuit up just enough.

"This is a privately registered courier ship with diplomatic papers for the Dolgorukij Combine, what is the meaning of this outrage?"

Cousin Stanoczk, Garol noted, could do "outrage" with the best of them. There was a confused babble of circuit overrides and half-finished questions from the Fleet side of the communications; then Commander Minrodie was back.

"Transmit your clear codes, if you please. Confirmation of identity in progress."

The three pursuit ships slowed. The last Langsarik freighter was almost close enough to start its vector spin. Garol had to pay conscious attention to not holding his breath.

"Clear codes on transmit. You have not explained. The Combine will protest this arbitrary intervention in private business in the strongest possible terms unless we are permitted to continue on our way unmolested. Immediately."

Half the Langsarik fleet was away.

If Stanoczk could hold those three pursuit ships for just a while longer, it would be too late for them to ever catch up—and a pure waste of energy to even try. Not to mention the associated loss of face to go all-out in pursuit of a ship and not catch it. Fleet hated that. Bad for their image.

"We confirm identity and diplomatic immunity." Commander Minrodie sounded clearly reluctant to admit the fact, though. "On behalf of my command I apologize for the pursuit my ships executed on my direct orders. You are clear to go.—Abort pursuit."

It had to be difficult to see an enemy running away and not give chase; but Stanoczk had successfully interrupted the momentum of the pursuit, and Minrodie apparently knew when the balance of situational factors turned against her.

"Specialist Vogel," Commander Minrodie said, "I look forward to seeing you on our arrival. I'll want to hear all about the instructions of First Secretary Verlaine. I didn't know Combine diplomatic ships took direction from Chilleau Judiciary."

Or anywhere. She was quite right. She knew very well that something was wrong with the picture that she was seeing.

"At your convenience, Commander. Vogel away, here."

The communications line cut out, but the message on the scanning screens told him everything he needed to know.

Langsarik ships vanishing into the Sillume vector. The last of the ships just about ready to start vector spins; the Fleet convoy still steady for Port Charid, the three ships that had gone forward in pursuit turning back to rejoin their formation.

And then there was the tiny blip, the almost invisible trace, the surprising presence of Cousin Stanoczk in the train of the Langsarik fleet.

What was the Malcontent doing on his way to the Sillume vector?

Garol sat down.

Feraltz.

He'd been too busy worrying about Langsariks to check in on the ringleader of the false Langsariks. Stanoczk had to have left Port Charid in a hurry, in order to have gotten to where he was now. He'd sent Daigule to the freighter with the Langsariks. But had it been simply because of sympathy for Daigule's situation?

Or had there been something else going on as well?

"Son of a bitch," Garol said to himself. Half-infuriated; half-admiring.

If Stanoczk had taken Fisner Feraltz out from under the very nose of a Bench specialist—there would be merry Hell to pay at Chilleau Judiciary when the First Secretary found out that Garol had mislaid his most valuable prisoner.

It didn't matter.

Stanoczk had been where Garol needed him, when Garol had needed him there—to protect the rear guard of the Langsarik fleet and see Walton Agenis safe to the vector.

So long as the Langsarik fleet was safely away, he could face even Stanoczk's underhanded dealing with forbearance and equanimity.

They had done it.

The Langsariks were free.

He had actively aided and abetted the successful escape of the Langsariks from the custody of the Bench and the orderly conduct of the Judicial process. He had willfully and deliberately sent the Langsariks out from under Jurisdiction altogether, in flagrant violation of the rule of Law.

It was the first time he had ever acknowledged any higher priority than that to which he had dedicated his life since he had left his home system and sworn his oath of service to the Bench.

But if the rule of Law was not the greatest good, after all that he had done in his life to uphold it—

If he had not done right to have discarded a lifetime's devotion to the rule of Law, there was no future for him anywhere.

AFTERWORD

Garol Vogel sat quietly in the midmorning light of a street-side cafe in a small port halfway between one Judiciary's administrative center and another's, watching the steam rise from a cup of pressure-extracted bean tea.

Life was good, at least for a moment.

Nobody knew where he was or how to reach him; he was as close to off-duty as he could remember ever being. The air was crisp and cool; the spicy fragrance rising from his cup was a pleasure no less intense for being simple.

A dark shape passed across the face of the morning sun, a shape that brought with it a fragrance that Garol seemed to remember. The Malcontent Cousin Stanoczk had laundered his clothing with soap mixed with powdered piros resin, from the scent of it; at least that was the most likely explanation for it, in Garol's mind.

"You're blocking my light," Garol said.

Nobody was supposed to know where he was. But since his experiences at Port Charid, Garol knew better than to believe that this was a coincidence.

"Yes, thank you." Cousin Stanoczk pulled a wire chair clear of an adjacent table and sat down. "I don't mind if I *do* join you. What are you drinking?"

And wasn't Cousin Stanoczk in a good mood. Garol was still making up his mind whether he was going to yield to irritation or decline to give Stanoczk even so much honor as that.

"It's good." Tossing off his cup of bean tea—a little too hot, but pain helped him focus—Garol waved for the server, "You should try it. It'll put hair on your chest."

The server was prompt with two servings. Cousin Stanoczk recoiled with exaggerated timidity from the cup that the server set down in front of him. "I didn't know you cared. But you're not my type."

Garol had taken one hit of bean tea already; this would be his second. Three was his limit, when it was pressure-extracted. He had to give himself time to sneak up on this next one. "Shut up. You're disgusting."

Stanoczk laughed and took up his cup of bean tea with a gesture too absentminded to be that of a man who was unused to the beverage. "While you, on the other hand, are the man of the octave. Single-handedly clearing the vermin out of Port Charid. Elderly people safe to carry large sums of cash money, children frolic in the streets, grown men sleep more easily at night."

If only it had been that simple.

First Secretary Verlaine was still trying to decide whether he was more relieved than outraged, or the other way around.

As far as public relations went, it had come off. The Langsarik settlement had been removed from Port Charid, and it was really nobody's business where the Langsariks had actually gone. The raids had stopped, after all; that was all that people really cared about.

As far as the private man was concerned, though, Garol was resigned to waiting for a while before the First Secretary came around to Garol's way of looking at things.

"I've been meaning to speak to you about that." It hadn't been very high on his list of priorities, no. But it had unquestionably been in the back of Garol's mind. "You took something I wanted. I don't want it back. But I do want its evidence."

Stanoczk breathed deeply of his bean tea, his dark eyes hooded. Playing for time, obviously.

"Fisner has been badly damaged for a very long time."

Garol could take that in several ways. But Stanoczk seemed perfectly serious.

"It takes time to build trust, and he will be most useful to us when he grows willing to share the information he possesses. But there is something I am free to tell you."

It wasn't as if Garol had honestly expected any different.

He supposed it was petty of him to grudge Cousin Stanoczk his one source, when the Bench held ten. There was probably nothing he could really do about it anyway; unless he wanted to make an issue out of it—and Garol was fresh out of the energy required to take on ancient and entrenched secret services one-handed.

Maybe next year.

"Let's hear it."

Stanoczk had finished his bean tea and was running his ring finger around the rim to pick up the last traces of his drink. Disgusting. "Yes. I'm to invite you to a hand-fasting. It is not to be a traditional ceremony, because it is a mixed marriage. The bride is Langsarik, and her accepted suitor is Sarvaw."

Stanoczk had heard news?

"Where do we send our heartfelt expressions of goodwill?"

Stanoczk shook his head. "The happy couple haven't quite settled on a permanent address. But I'm to assure you that you'll always be welcome with the family."

Cousin Stanoczk had heard from Walton Agenis. Or at least from someone who had heard from Walton Agenis. Garol took a moment to observe the pain in his heart, mildly surprised at its intensity. He was usually better than this at losing people that he loved, but maybe that was the problem. She wasn't lost. She was waiting for him in Gonebeyond space . . . or if she wasn't waiting, she was there, and he could go.

But would not.

"Lost your new man, then." That'd be more than one of them with explaining to do. Not as if it was any of his business.

Stanoczk just shrugged. "Him? He'd never have worked out. No. I undervalue him. He could have been brilliant, but he would have been miserable. That's not the way we do business."

This was interesting. "Exactly how is it that you do, er, business, then?" Garol had been a little unclear on that, from the beginning.

"Simple exchange of absolutes." Stanoczk had waved for the server to come back and bring more bean tea. Two more. Both of which he gathered to himself; Garol hadn't touched his second cup yet. "You give me everything. I give you anything."

Well, that told Garol exactly nothing. "So what did you get?"

Stanoczk flashed him a quick look, and for a moment Garol wondered if he'd actually managed to take Cousin Stanoczk by surprise. It was hard to tell. Maybe Stanoczk was just offended.

"It is myself and the Saint between, Garol Aphon."

If not actually offended, emphatically standing on his dignity and his Dolgorukij syntax. So much for that.

"Thanks for stopping anyway," Garol said, as graciously as possible. "We'll do it again. Feel free to drop in any old time."

It was good to know that the Langsarik fleet had survived at least this long on the other side. They were resilient. They would make it work.

Kazmer Daigule and Modice Agenis. Like wedding a heavy mover to a racing shallop; but they had history between them, from what little Garol had ever been able to observe. Daigule had a good heart and strong will to carry it forward. Modice could do worse.

Garol couldn't imagine it could get any better for Daigule, marrying the spectacular beauty that he adored—smart and strong and brave, as well as beautiful. Almost too much for any one man.

Stanoczk slurped his bean tea hastily, one cup after the other, as he rose. "Right, Vogel. Same to you. Feel free to call on us if you need us. Any consular post or higher. Tell them that Cousin Stanoczk is looking for you, and they'll do the rest."

Shouldn't it be the other way around?

And surely there was more than one man named Stanoczk in service to the Malcontent. It was a relatively common name. At least among Dolgorukij.

"Thanks. I'll remember that."

Stanoczk left without paying.

But that was a signal, from someone like Cousin Stanoczk. He'd meant it when he'd said that Garol could call on him. And the price of a few cups of bean tea was as nothing compared to the value of the news that Cousin Stanoczk had brought him.

Langsariks safe, Modice to be married, and there was communication taking place between Gonebeyond space and worlds under Jurisdiction, however private and secretive.

Agenis had escaped.

The Bench had been saved from a shameful stain in its honor, a corrosive miscarriage of justice that could only have contributed to the increasing instability that bedeviled all of Jurisdiction space.

The First Secretary would come around, or he wouldn't.

It was only rarely that Garol had a chance to take pride in having made a decision, without it being tempered with regret for the consequences, the outcome of his actions.

Conflict and compromise, politics, propaganda—

Once in a great while he got a chance to act on his fundamental sense of fairness and equity, and have it come out right. Instead of just less wrong.

With that knowledge in his heart, and Cousin Stanoczk's message in his thoughts, Garol sat in the increasing warmth of the late morning; and for a small but sufficient space of time, he was happy.